W9-DHF-947

Murder in Triplicate

BY P. D. JAMES

Cover Her Face
A Mind to Murder
Unnatural Causes
Shroud for a Nightingale
An Unsuitable Job for a Woman
The Black Tower
Death of an Expert Witness
Innocent Blood

Murder in Triplicate

P. D. JAMES

THREE COMPLETE NOVELS
BY THE QUEEN OF CRIME

Unnatural Causes

An Unsuitable Job for a Woman

The Black Tower

CHARLES SCRIBNER'S SONS • NEW YORK

Introduction Copyright © 1980 P. D. James
UNNATURAL CAUSES, copyright © 1967 P. D. James
AN UNSUITABLE JOB FOR A WOMAN, copyright © 1972 P. D. James
THE BLACK TOWER, copyright © 1975 P. D. James

Library of Congress Cataloging in Publication Data

James, P. D.
Murder in triplicate.

CONTENTS: Unnatural causes.—An unsuitable job for a woman.—The black tower.
1. Detective and mystery story, English.
I. Title.
PZ4.J2847Mu [PR6060.A467] 823′.914 80-18493
ISBN 0-684-16748-4

This book published simultaneously in the United States of America and in Canada—
Copyright under the Berne Convention.

All rights reserved. No part of this book may be reproduced in any form without the permission of Charles Scribner's Sons.

1 3 5 7 9 11 13 15 17 19 V/C 20 18 16 14 12 10 8 6 4 2

Printed in the United States of America.

Foreword

The three stories in this my second omnibus volume differ widely in mood and plot but have one thing in common: in each of them, it was a place, rather than a character or a new or ingenious method of murder, which sparked my creative imagination and gave rise to the novel. Two of the stories are set by the sea on desolate, bleak, and sinister stretches of the English coastline: *The Black Tower* on the Purbeck coast of Dorset, where the high cliffs of black shale tumble into the English Channel; and *Unnatural Causes* in East Anglia, on the cold fringes of the North Sea. There, at Dunwich, a once prosperous medieval town has waged for centuries its losing battle against the encroaching sea, and now little remains but the ruins of the abbey, a few cottages, and crumbling tombstones at the cliff edge. I have a holiday cottage on this numinous coast, and when the wind is high it is easy to believe the old tradition that one can hear the bells of the nine drowned churches of Dunwich swinging under the tide.

Crime writers, by the necessity of their somewhat unpleasant craft, tend to invite dramatic and gruesome images, and it was while walking on the beach at Dunwich that I imagined the opening scene of *Unnatural Causes*—an oarless dinghy drifting ashore with its solitary burden, the body of a murdered man with the hands cleft off at the wrist. My detective hero, Adam Dalgliesh, has come to East Anglia on holiday, hoping by long walks and a little desultory bird-watching to rid himself of the deadening accumulation of crime and red tape that constitute his daily routine at Scotland Yard. But that mutilated body puts an end to peace and leisure, and, almost against his will, he is drawn into the investigation of a particularly ingenious murder.

The setting of *An Unsuitable Job for a Woman,* like its heroine, is gentler—the city of Cambridge, where I grew up and where my husband was at the university. In my eyes it is one of the loveliest in Europe, and I had always wanted to write about it. This novel is the "odd one out" among my detective stories in that Adam Dalgliesh appears only briefly, at the end of the book, although his personality, reputation, and methods pervade the action. *An Unsuitable Job for a Woman* introduces my amateur detective, Cordelia Gray, who is engaged by a brilliant Cambridge scientist to discover the reason for the suicide of his only son and finds herself investigating a heartless and horrible crime. If in creating Cordelia I wondered whether my readers, faithful to Dalgliesh, would resent her intrusion, I need not have worried. Cordelia has her own dedicated following of fans who occasionally attempt to reconcile their opposing loyalties by suggesting that I marry her to Dalgliesh, a solution that I feel holds as many potential hazards for the author as it does for the characters concerned.

After the sunlit Cambridge summer of *An Unsuitable*

Job for a Woman, some readers have found *The Black Tower* the most somber of my books in setting and plot. Certainly the scene of the action, a clifftop home for the permanently disabled, presents any novelist with themes of loss, regret, and despair, which are essentially tragic; and my twenty years of experience in the British National Health Service, where, among other duties, I was concerned with services for the chronically sick, gave me an insight into the needs and problems of this pathetic group of patients. But I have never felt that a crime novelist is barred from exploration of the realities of the human condition merely because, as in *The Black Tower,* she is working within the constraints of the classical English detective story. I have a particular fondness for *The Black Tower,* not only because it was the second of my novels to win the Silver Dagger of the British Crime Writers Association, but because I feel that it marks a significant step both in my development as a writer and in the character of my hero. Incidentally, I note that between *Unnatural Causes* and *The Black Tower* Dalgliesh gained his promotion from Detective Superintendent to Commander. Whether he has also gained in stature as a detective and a man is not, perhaps, for me to judge.

Unnatural Causes

P. D. JAMES

CHARLES SCRIBNER'S SONS • NEW YORK

COPYRIGHT © 1967 P. D. JAMES

All rights reserved. No part of this book
may be reproduced in any form without the
permission of Charles Scribner's Sons.

A - 8.67 [MC]

Printed in the United States of America
Library of Congress Catalog Card Number 67-24924

Book One

I

The corpse without hands lay in the bottom of a small sailing dinghy drifting just within sight of the Suffolk coast. It was the body of a middle-aged man, a dapper little cadaver, its shroud a dark pin-striped suit which fitted the narrow body as elegantly in death as it had in life. The hand-made shoes still gleamed except for some scruffing of the toe caps, the silk tie was knotted under the prominent Adam's apple. He had dressed with careful orthodoxy for the town, this hapless voyager; not for this lonely sea; nor for this death.

It was early afternoon in mid October and the glazed eyes were turned upwards to a sky of surprising blue across which the light south-west wind was dragging a few torn rags of cloud. The wooden shell, without mast or rowlocks, bounced gently on the surge of the North Sea so that the head shifted and rolled as if in restless sleep. It had been an unremarkable face even in life and death had given it nothing but a pitiful vacuity. The fair hair grew sparsely from a high bumpy forehead, the nose was so narrow that the white ridge of bone looked as if it were about to pierce the flesh; the mouth, small and thin-lipped, had dropped open to reveal two prominent front teeth which gave the whole face the supercilious look of a dead hare.

The legs, still clamped in rigor, were wedged one each side of the centre-board case and the forearms had been placed resting on the thwart. Both hands had been taken off at the wrists. There had been little bleeding. On each forearm a trickle of blood had spun a black web between the stiff fair hairs and the thwart was stained as if it had been used as a chopping block. But that was all; the rest of the body and the boards of the dinghy were free of blood.

The right hand had been taken cleanly off and the curved end of the radius glistened white; but the left had been bungled and the jagged splinters of bone, needle sharp, stuck out from the receding flesh. Both jacket sleeves and shirt cuffs had been pulled up for the butchery and a pair of gold initialled cuff links dangled free, glinting as they slowly turned and were caught by the autumn sun.

The dinghy, its paintwork faded and peeling, drifted like a discarded toy on an almost empty sea. On the horizon the divided silhouette of a coaster was making her way down the Yarmouth Lanes; nothing else was in sight. About two o'clock a black dot swooped across the sky towards the land trailing its feathered tail and the air was torn by the scream of engines. Then the roar faded and there was again no sound but the sucking of the water against the boat and the occasional cry of a gull.

Suddenly the dinghy rocked violently, then steadied itself and swung slowly round. As if sensing the strong tug of the on-shore current, it began to move more purposefully. A black-headed gull, which had dropped lightly on to the prow and had perched there, rigid as a figure-head, rose with wild cries to circle above the body. Slowly, inexorably, the water dancing at the prow, the little boat bore its dreadful cargo towards the shore.

2

Just before two o'clock on the afternoon of the same day Superintendent Adam Dalgliesh drove his Cooper Bristol gently on to the grass verge outside Blythburgh Church and, a minute later, passed through the north chantry-chapel door into the cold silvery whiteness of one of the loveliest church interiors in Suffolk. He was on his way to Monksmere Head just south of Dunwich to spend a ten-day autumn holiday with a spinster aunt, his only living relative, and this was his last stop on the way. He had started off from his City flat before London was stirring, and instead of taking the direct route to Monksmere through Ipswich, had struck north at Chelmsford to enter Suffolk at Sudbury. He had breakfasted at Long Melford and had then turned west through Lavenham to drive slowly and at will through the green and gold of this most unspoilt and unprettified of counties. His mood would have wholly matched the day if it weren't for one persistent nagging worry. He had been deliberately putting off a personal decision until this holiday. Before he went back to London he must finally decide whether to ask Deborah Riscoe to marry him.

Irrationally, the decision would have been easier if he hadn't known so certainly what her answer would be. This threw upon him the whole responsibility for deciding whether to change the present satisfactory status quo (well, satisfactory for him anyway, and it could be argued surely that Deborah was happier now than she had been a year ago?) for a commitment which both of them, he suspected, would regard as irrevocable no matter what the outcome. There are few couples as unhappy as those who are too proud to admit their unhappiness. Some of the hazards he knew. He knew that she disliked and resented his job. This wasn't surprising nor, in itself, important. The job was his choice and he had never required anyone's approval or encouragement. But it was a daunting prospect that every late duty, every emergency, might have to be preceded by an apologetic telephone call. As he walked to and fro under the marvellous cambered tie-beam roof and smelt the Anglican odour of wax polish, flowers and damp old hymn books, it came to him that he had got what he wanted at almost the precise moment of suspecting that he no longer wanted it. This experience is too common to cause an intelligent man lasting disappointment but it still has power to disconcert. It wasn't the loss of freedom that deterred him; the men who squealed most about that were usually the least free. Much more difficult to face was the loss of privacy. Even the loss of physical privacy was hard to accept. Running his fingers over the carved fifteenth century lectern he tried to picture life in the Queenhithe flat with Deborah always there, no longer the eagerly awaited visitor but part of his life, the legal, certificated next of kin.

It had been a bad time at the Yard to be faced with personal problems. There had recently been a major reorganization which had resulted in the inevitable disruption of loyalties and of routine, the expected crop of rumours and discontent. And there had been no relief from the pressure of work. Most of the senior officers were already working a fourteen-hour day. His last case, although successful, had been particularly tedious. A child had been murdered and the investigation had turned into a man hunt of the kind he most disliked and was temperamentally least suited for—a matter of dogged, persistent checking of facts carried on in a blaze of publicity and hindered by the fear and hysteria of the neighbourhood. The child's parents had fastened on him like drowning swimmers gulping for reassurance and hope and he could still feel the almost physical load of their sorrow and guilt. He had been required to be at once a comforter and father-confessor, avenger and judge. There was nothing new to him in this. He had felt no personal involvement in their grief, and this detachment had, as always, been his strength, as the anger and intense, outraged commitment of some of his colleagues, faced with the same crime, would have been theirs. But the strain of the case was still with him and it would take more than the winds of a Suffolk autumn to clean his mind of some images. No reasonable woman could have expected him to propose marriage in the middle of this investigation and Deborah had not done so. That he had found time and energy to finish his second book of verse a few days before the arrest was something which neither of them had mentioned. He had been appalled to recognize that even the exercise of a minor talent could be made the excuse for selfishness and inertia. He hadn't liked himself much recently, and it was perhaps sanguine to hope that this holiday could alter that.

Half an hour later he closed the church door quietly behind him and set off on the last few miles of the journey to Monksmere. He had written to his aunt to say that he would probably arrive at half-past two and, with luck, he would be there almost precisely on time. If, as was usual, his aunt came out of the cottage at two-thirty she should see the Cooper Bristol just breasting the headland. He thought of her tall, angular, waiting figure with affection. There was little unusual about her story and most of it he had guessed, picked up as a boy from snatches of his mother's unguarded talk or had simply known as one of the facts of his childhood. Her fiancé had been killed in 1918 just six months before the Armistice when she was a young girl. Her mother was a delicate, spoilt beauty, the worst possible wife for a scholarly country clergyman as she herself frequently admitted, apparently thinking that this candour both justified and excused in advance the next outbreak of selfishness or extravagance. She disliked the sight of other people's grief since it rendered them temporarily more interesting than herself and she decided to take young Captain Maskell's death very hard. Whatever her sensitive, uncommunicative and rather difficult daughter suffered it must be apparent that her mother suffered more; and three weeks after the telegram was received she died of influenza. It is doubtful whether she intended to go to such lengths but she would have been gratified by the result. Her distraught husband forgot in one night all the irritations and anxieties of his marriage and remembered only his wife's gaiety and beauty. It was, of course, unthinkable that he should marry again, and he never did. Jane Dalgliesh whose own bereavement hardly anyone now had the time to remember, took her mother's place as hostess at the vicarage and remained with her father until his retirement in 1945 and his death ten years later. She was a highly intelligent woman and if she found unsatisfying the annual routine of housekeeping and parochial activities, predictable and inescapable as the liturgical year, she never said so. Her father was so assured of the ultimate importance of his calling that it never occurred to him that anyone's gifts could be wasted in its service. Jane Dalgliesh, respected by the parishioners but never loved, did what had to be done and solaced herself with her study of birds. After her father's death the papers she published, records of meticulous observation, brought her some notice; and in time what the parish had patronizingly described as "Miss Dalgliesh's little hobby" made her one of the most respected of amateur ornithologists. Just over five years ago she had sold her house in Lincolnshire and bought Pentlands, a stone cottage on the edge of Monksmere Head. Here Dalgliesh visited her at least twice a year.

They were no mere duty visits, although he would have felt a responsibility for her if she were not so obviously self-sufficient that, at times, even to feel affection seemed a kind of insult. But the affection was there and both of them knew it. Already he was looking forward to the satisfaction of seeing her, to the assured pleasures of a holiday at Monksmere.

There would be a driftwood fire in the wide hearth scenting the whole cottage, and before it the high-backed armchair once part of his father's study in the vicarage where he was born, the leather smelling of childhood. There would be a sparsely furnished bedroom with a view of sea and sky, a comfortable if narrow bed with sheets smelling faintly of wood-smoke and lavender, plenty of hot water and a bath long enough for a six-foot-two man to stretch himself in comfort. His aunt was herself six foot tall and had a masculine appreciation of essential comforts. More immediately, there would be tea before the fire and hot buttered toast with home made potted meat. Best of all, there would be no corpses and no talk of them. He suspected that Jane Dalgliesh thought it odd that an intelligent man should choose to earn his living catching murderers and she was not a woman to feign polite interest where she felt none. She made no demands on him, not even the demands of affection, and because of this she was the only woman in the world with whom he was completely at peace. He knew exactly what the holiday offered. They would walk together, often in silence, on the damp strip of firm sand between the sea's foam and the pebbled rises of the beach. He would carry her sketching paraphanalia, she would stride a little ahead, hands dug in her jacket pockets, eyes searching out where wheatears, scarcely distinguishable from pebbles, had lighted on the shingle, or following the flight of tern or plover. It would be peaceful, restful, utterly undemanding; but at the end of ten days he would go back to London with a sense of relief.

He was driving now through Dunwich Forest where the Forestry Commission's plantations of dark firs flanked the road. He fancied that he could smell the sea now; the salt tang borne to him on the wind was sharper than the bitter smell of the trees. His heart lifted. He felt like a child coming home. And now the forest ended, the sombre dark green of the firs ruled off by a wire fence from the water-coloured fields and hedges. And now they too passed and he was driving through the gorse and heather of the heathlands on his way to Dunwich. As he reached the village and turned right up the hill which skirted the walled enclosure of the ruined Franciscan friory there was the blare of a car's horn and a Jaguar, driven very fast, shot past. He glimpsed a dark head, and a hand raised in salute before, with a valedictory hoot, the car was out of sight. So Oliver Latham, the dramatic critic, was at his cottage for the weekend. That was hardly likely to inconvenience Dalgliesh for Latham did not come to Suffolk for company. Like his near neighbour, Justin Bryce, he used his cottage as a retreat from London, and perhaps from people, although he was at Monksmere less frequently than Bryce. Dalgliesh had met him once or twice and had recognized in him a restlessness and tension which found an echo in his own character. He was known to like fast cars and fast driving, and Dalgliesh suspected that it was in the drive to and from Monksmere that he found his release. It was difficult to imagine why else he kept on his cottage. He came to it seldom, never brought his women there, took no interest in furnishing it, and used it chiefly as a base for wild drives around the district which were so violent and irrational that they seemed a kind of abreaction.

As Rosemary Cottage came into sight on the bend of the road Dalgliesh accelerated. He had little hope of driving past unobserved but at least he could drive at a speed which made it unreasonable to stop. As he shot past he just had time to see out of the corner of his eye a face at an upstairs window. Well it was to be expected. Celia Calthrop regarded herself as the doyen of the small community at Monksmere and had assigned herself certain duties and privileges. If her neighbours were so ill-advised as not to keep her informed of the comings and going of themselves and their visitors she was prepared to take some trouble to find out for herself. She had a quick ear for an approaching car and the situation of her cottage, just where the rough track across the headland joined the road from Dunwich, gave her every opportunity of keeping an eye on things.

Miss Calthrop had bought Brodie's Barn, re-named Rosemary Cottage, twelve years previously. She had got it cheap and by gentle but persistent bullying of local labour, had converted it equally cheaply from a pleasing if shabby stone house to the romanticised ideal of her readers. It frequently featured in womens' magazines as "Celia Calthrop's delightful Suffolk residence where, amid the peace of the countryside, she creates those delightful romances which so thrill our readers." Inside, Rosemary Cottage was very comfortable in its pretentious and tasteless way; outside, it had everything its owner considered appropriate to a country cottage, a thatched roof (deplorably expensive to insure and maintain), a herb garden (a sinister looking patch this; Miss Calthrop was not successful with herbs), a small artificial pond (malodorous in summer) and a dovecote (but doves obstinately refused to roost in it). There was also a sleek lawn on which the writers' community—Celia's phrase—was invited in summer to drink tea. At first Jane Dalgliesh had been excluded from the invitations, not because she didn't claim to be a writer but because she was a solitary, elderly spinster and therefore, in Miss Calthrop's scale of values, a social and sexual failure rating only a patronising kindness. Then Miss Calthrop discovered that her neighbour was regarded as a distinguished woman by people well qualified to judge and that the men who, in defiance of propriety, were entertained at Pentlands and who were to be met trudging along the shore in happy companionship with their hostess were frequently themselves distinguished. A further discovery was more surprising. Jane Dalgliesh dined with R. B. Sinclair at Priory House. Not all those who praised Sinclair's three great novels, the last written over thirty years ago, realized that he was still alive. Fewer still were invited to dine with him. Miss Calthrop was not a woman obstinately to persist in error and Miss Dalgliesh became "dear Jane" overnight. For her part she continued to call her neighbour "Miss Calthrop" and was as unaware of the rapprochement as she had been of the original disdain. Dalgliesh was never sure what she really thought of Celia. She seldom spoke about her neighbours and the women were too rarely in each other's company for him to judge.

The rough track which led across Monksmere Head to Pentlands was less than fifty yards from Rosemary Cottage. It was usually barred by a heavy farm gate but today this stood open, biting deep into the tall hedge of brambles and elders. The car bumped slowly over the potholes and between the stubble of hay which soon gave way to grass and then to bracken. It passed the twin stone cottages belonging to Latham and Justin Bryce but Dalgliesh saw no sign of either man although Latham's Jaguar was parked at his door and there was a thin curl of smoke from Bryce's chimney. Now the track wound uphill and suddenly the whole of the headland lay open before him, stretching purple and golden to the cliffs and shining sea. At the crest of the track Dalgliesh stopped the car to watch and to listen. Autumn had never been his favourite season, but in the moment which followed the stopping of the engine he wouldn't have changed this mellow peace for all the keener sensitivities of spring. The heather was beginning to fade now but the second flowering of the gorse was as thick and golden as the first richness of May. Beyond it lay the sea, streaked with purple, azure and brown, and to the south the mist-hung marshes of the bird reserve added their gentler greens and blues. The air smelt of heather and woodsmoke, the inevitable and evocative smells of autumn. It was hard to believe, thought Dalgliesh, that one was looking at a battlefield where for nearly nine centuries the land had waged its losing fight against the sea; hard to realize that under that deceptive calm of veined water lay the nine drowned churches of old Dunwich. There were few buildings standing on the headland now but not all were old. To the north Dalgliesh could just glimpse the low walls of Seton House, little more than an excresence on the edge of the cliff, which Maurice Seton, the detective novelist, had built to suit his odd and solitary life. Half a mile to the south the great square walls of Priory House stood like a last bastion against the sea and, on the very edge of the bird reserve, Pentlands Cottage seemed to hang on the brink of nothingness. As his eyes scanned the headland a horse and buggy came into sight on the far north track and bowled merrily over the gorse towards Priory House. Dalgliesh could see a stout little body hunchbacked in the driving seat and the whip, delicate as a wand, erect by her side. It must be R. B. Sinclair's housekeeper bringing home the provisions. There was a charming domestic touch about the gay little equipage and Dalgliesh watched it with pleasure until it disappeared behind the shield of trees which half hid Priory House. At that moment his aunt appeared at the side of her cottage and gazed up the headland. Dalgliesh glanced at his wrist. It was thirty three minutes past two. He let in the clutch and the Cooper Bristol bumped slowly down the track towards her.

3

Stepping back instinctively into the shadows of his upstairs room, Oliver Latham watched the car as it bounced gently up the headland and laughed aloud. Then he checked himself, silenced by the explosive sound of his laughter in the stillness of the cottage. But this was too much! Scotland Yard's wonder boy, still reeking from his latest blood sport, had come most promptly upon his cue. The car was stopping now on the crown of the headland. It would be pleasant if that damned Cooper Bristol had broken down at last. But no, it looked as if Dalgliesh was pausing simply to admire the view. The poor fool was probably relishing in advance the sweets of a fortnight's cossetting at Pentlands. Well, he was in for a surprise. The question was, would it be prudent for him, Latham, to stay around and watch the fun? Why not? He wasn't due back in town until the first night at the Court Theatre on Thursday week and it would look odd if he dashed back now so soon after his arrival. Besides, he was curious. He had driven to Monksmere on Wednesday expecting to be bored. But now, with luck, it was promising to be quite an exciting holiday.

4

Alice Kerrison drove the buggy behind the fringe of trees which shielded Priory House from the northern part of the headland, bounced down from her seat and led the mare through the wide crumbling archway to a row of sixteenth century stables. As she busied herself with the unharnessing, grunting a little with the effort, her practical mind complacently reviewed the morning's work and looked forward to the small domestic pleasures to come. First they would drink tea together, strong and over-sweet as Mr. Sinclair liked it, sitting one each side of the great fire in the hall. Even on a warm autumn day Mr. Sinclair liked his fire. And then before the light began to fade and the mists rose, they would take their daily walk together across the headland. And it wouldn't be a walk without a purpose. There was some burying to be done. Well, it was always satisfactory to have an object and for all Mr. Sinclair's clever talk, human remains however incomplete were still human remains and were entitled to respect. Besides, it was high time they were out of the house.

5

It was nearly half-past eight and Dalgliesh and his aunt, their dinner over, sat in companionable silence one each side of the living room fire. The room, which occupied almost the whole of the ground floor of Pentlands, was stone walled with a low roof buttressed by immense oak beams and a floor of red quarry tiles. In front of the open fireplace, where a wood fire crackled and spurted, a neat stack of driftwood was drying. The smell of wood smoke drifted through the cottage like incense; and the air vibrated endlessly with the thudding of the sea. Dalgliesh found it hard to keep awake in this rhythmic, somnambulant peace. He had always enjoyed contrast in art or nature and at Pentlands, once night had fallen, the pleasures of contrast were easily self-induced. Inside the cottage there was light and warmth, all the colours and comfort of civilized domesticity; outside under the low clouds there was darkness, solitude, mystery. He pictured the shore, one hundred feet below, where the sea was spreading its fringe of lace over the cold, firm beach; and the Monksmere bird reserve to the south, quiet under the night sky, its reeds hardly stirring in the still water.

Stretching his legs to the fire and wedging his head still more comfortably into the high back of the chair, he looked across at his aunt. She was sitting, as always, bolt upright and yet she looked perfectly comfortable. She was knitting a pair of woollen socks in bright red which Dalgliesh could only hope were not intended for him. He thought it unlikely. His aunt was not given to such domestic tokens of affection. The firelight threw gules on her long face, brown and carved as an Aztec's, the eyes hooded, the nose long and straight above a wide mobile mouth. Her hair was iron grey now, coiled into a huge bun in the nape of her neck. It was a face that he remembered from childhood. He had never seen any difference in her. Upstairs in her room, stuck casually into the edge of a looking glass, was the faded photograph of herself and her dead fiancé taken in 1916. Dalgliesh thought of it now; the boy, in the squashed peak cap and breeches which had once looked slightly ridiculous to him but now epitomised the romance and heartbreak of an age long dead; the girl half an inch taller, swaying towards him with the angular grace of adolescence, her hair dressed wide and ribbon bound, her feet in their pointed shoes just showing beneath the slim flowing skirt. Jane Dalgliesh had never talked to him of her youth and he had never asked. She was the most self-sufficient, the least sentimental woman that he knew. Dalgliesh wondered how Deborah would get on with her, what the two women would make of each other. It was difficult to picture Deborah in any setting other than London. Since her mother's death she hardly ever went home and, for reasons which they both understood only too well, he had never gone back to Martingale with her. He could only see her now against the background of his own City flat, of restaurants, theatre foyers and their favourite pubs. He was used to living his life on different levels. Deborah was not part of his job and as yet she had no place at Pentlands. But if he married her, she would necessarily have some share in both. Somehow, on this brief holiday he knew he had to decide if that was what he really wanted.

Jane Dalgliesh said:

"Would you like some music? I have the new Mahler recording."

Dalgliesh wasn't musical, but he knew that music meant a great deal to his aunt and listening to her records had become part of a Pentlands holiday. Her knowledge and pleasure were infectious; he was beginning to make discoveries. And, in his present mood, he was even ready to try Mahler.

It was then they heard the car.

"Oh, Lord," he said. "Who's this? Not Celia Calthrop, I hope." Miss Calthrop, if not firmly discouraged, was an inveterate dropper in, trying always to impose on the solitariness of Monksmere the cosy conventions of suburban social life. She was particularly apt to call when Dalgliesh was at the cottage. To her a personable and unattached male was natural prey. If she didn't want him herself there was always somebody who did; she disliked seeing anything go to waste. On one of his visits she had actually given a cocktail party in his honour. At the time he had enjoyed it, intrigued by the essential incongruity of the occasion. The little group of Monksmere residents, meeting as if for the first time, had munched canapes and sipped cheap sherry in Celia's pink and white drawing room and made inconsequent polite conversation while, outside, a gale screamed across the headland and the sou'westers and storm lanterns were stacked in the hall. Here had been contrast indeed. But it was not a habit to encourage.

Jane Dalgliesh said:

"It sounds like Miss Calthrop's Morris. She may be bringing her niece. Elizabeth is home from Cambridge convalescing from glandular fever. I think she arrived yesterday."

"Then she ought to be in bed. It sounds as if there are more than two of them. Isn't that Justin Bryce's bleat?"

It was. When Miss Dalgliesh opened the door they could see through the porch windows the twin lights of the car and a confusion of dark forms which gradually resolved themselves into familiar figures. It looked as if the whole of Monksmere was calling on his aunt. Even Sylvia Kedge, Maurice Seton's crippled secretary, was with them, creeping on her crutches towards the stream of light from the open door. Miss Calthrop walked slowly beside her as if in support. Behind them was Justin Bryce, still bleating inconsequently into the night. The tall figure of Oliver Latham loomed up beside him. Last of all, sulky and reluctant came Elizabeth Marley, shoulders hunched, hands dug into her jacket pockets. She was loitering on the path and peering from side to side into the darkness as if dissociating herself from the party. Bryce called:

"Good evening Miss Dalgliesh. Good evening Adam.

Don't blame me for this invasion. It's all Celia's idea. We've come for professional advice my dears. All except Oliver. We met him on the way and he's only come to borrow some coffee. Or so he says."

Latham said calmly:

"I forgot to buy coffee when I was driving from town yesterday. So I decided to call on my one neighbour who could be trusted to provide a decent blend without an accompanying lecture on my inefficient housekeeping. If I'd known you were having a party I might have waited until tomorrow."

But he showed no inclination to go.

They came in, blinking in the light and bringing with them a gust of cold air which billowed the white wood smoke across the room. Celia Calthrop went straight to Dalgliesh's chair and arranged herself as if to receive an evening's homage. Her elegant legs and feet, carefully displayed to advantage, were in marked contrast to her heavy, stoutly-corseted body with its high bosom, and her flabby mottled arms. Dalgliesh supposed that she must be in her late forties but she looked older. As always she was heavily but skilfully made up. The little vulpine mouth was carmine, the deep-set and downward sloping eyes which gave her face a look of spurious spirituality much emphasized in her publicity photographs were blue shadowed, the lashes weighted with mascara. She took off her chiffon headscarf to reveal her hairdresser's latest effort, the hair fine as a baby's through which the glimpses of pink, smooth scalp looked almost indecent.

Dalgliesh had only met her niece twice before and now, shaking hands, he thought that Cambridge had not changed her. She was still the sulky, heavy-featured girl that he remembered. It was not an unintelligent face and might even have been attractive if only it had held a spark of animation.

The room had lost its peace. Dalgliesh reflected that it was extraordinary how much noise seven people could make. There was the usual business of settling Sylvia Kedge into her chair which Miss Calthrop supervised imperiously, although she did nothing active to help. The girl would have been called unusual, perhaps even beautiful, if only one could have forgotten those twisted ugly legs, braced into calipers, the heavy shoulders, the masculine hands distorted by her crutches. Her face was long, brown as a gypsy's and framed by shoulder length black hair brushed straight from a centre parting. It was a face which could have held strength and character but she had imposed on it a look of piteous humility, an air of suffering, meekly and uncomplainingly borne, which sat incongruously on that high brow. The great black eyes were skilled in inviting compassion. She was now adding to the general fluster by asserting that she was perfectly comfortable when she obviously wasn't, suggesting with a deprecating gentleness which had all the force of a command that her crutches should be placed within reach even though this meant propping them insecurely against her knees, and by generally making all present uncomfortably aware of their own undeserved good health. Dalgliesh had watched this play-acting before, but tonight he sensed that her heart wasn't in it, that the routine was almost mechanical. For once the girl looked genuinely ill and in pain. Her eyes were as dull as stones and there were lines running deeply between her nostrils and the corners of her mouth. She looked as if she needed sleep, and when he gave her a glass of sherry he saw that her hand was trembling. Seized by a spasm of genuine compassion, he wrapped his fingers around hers and steadied the glass until she could drink. Smiling at her he asked gently:

"Well, what's the trouble? What can I do to help?"

But Celia Calthrop had appointed herself spokesman.

"It's too bad of us all to come worrying you and Jane on your first evening together. I do realize that. But we're very worried. At least, Sylvia and I are. Deeply concerned."

"While I," said Justin Bryce, "am not so much worried as intrigued, not to say hopeful. Maurice Seton's disappeared. I'm afraid it may only be a publicity stunt for his next thriller and that we shall see him among us again all too soon. But let us not look on the gloomy side."

He did, indeed, look very far from gloomy, squatting on a

stool before the fire like a malevolent turtle, twisting his long neck towards the blaze. His had been, in youth, a striking head with its high cheekbones, wide mobile lips and huge, luminous grey eyes under the heavy lids. But he was fifty now and becoming a caricature. Though they seemed even larger, his eyes were less bright, and watered perpetually as if he were always fighting against a high wind. The receding hair had faded and coarsened to dull straw. The bones jutted through his skin giving him the appearance of a death's head. Only his hands were unchanged. He held them out now to the fire, soft-skinned, white and delicate as those of a girl. He smiled at Dalgliesh:

"Lost, believed safe. One middle-aged detective writer. Nervous disposition. Slight build. Narrow nose. Buck teeth. Sparse hair. Prominent Adam's apple. Finder, please keep.... So we come to you for advice, dear boy. Fresh, as I understand it, from your latest triumph. Do we wait for Maurice to make his reappearance and then pretend we didn't notice that he got lost? Or do we play it his way and ask the police to help us find him? After all, if it is a publicity stunt, it would only be kind to co-operate. Poor Maurice needs all the help in that direction he can get."

"It's not a joking matter, Justin." Miss Calthrop was severe. "And I don't for one moment think that it's a publicity stunt. If I did, I wouldn't come worrying Adam at a time when he particularly needs a peaceful, quiet holiday to recover from the strain of that case. So clever of you, Adam, to catch him before he did it again. The whole case made me feel sick, physically sick! And now what will happen to him? Kept in prison for a few years at the State's expense, then let out to murder some other child? Are we all mad in this country? I can't think why we don't hang him mercifully and be done with it."

Dalgliesh was glad that his face was in shadow. He recalled again the moment of arrest. Pooley had been such a small man, small, ugly and stinking with fear. His wife had left him a year before and the inexpert patch which puckered the elbow of his cheap suit had obviously been his own work.

Dalgliesh had found his eyes held by that patch as if it had the power to assert that Pooley was still a human being. Well, the beast was caged now and the public and press were free to be loud in their praise of the police work in general and of Superintendent Dalgliesh in particular. A psychiatrist could explain, no doubt, why he felt himself contaminated with guilt. The feeling was not new to him and he would deal with it in his own way. After all, he reflected wryly, it had seldom inconvenienced him for long and never once had it made him want to change his job. But he was damned if he was going to discuss Pooley with Celia Calthrop.

Across the room his aunt's eyes met his. She said quietly:

"What exactly do you want my nephew to do, Miss Calthrop? If Mr. Seton has disappeared, isn't that a matter for the local police?"

"But is it? That's our problem!" Miss Calthrop drained her glass as if the Amontilado had been cooking sherry, and automatically held it out to be refilled.

"Maurice may have disappeared for some purpose of his own, perhaps to collect material for his next book. He's been hinting that this is to be something different—a departure from his usual classical detective novel. He's a most conscientious craftsman and doesn't like to deal with anything outside his personal experience. We all know that. Remember how he spent three months with a travelling circus before he wrote *Murder on the High Wire*. Of course, it does imply he's a little deficient in creative imagination. My novels are never restricted to my own experience."

Justine Bryce said:

"In view of what your last heroine went through, Celia darling, I'm relieved to hear it."

Dalgliesh asked when Seton had last been seen. Before Miss Calthrop could answer, Sylvia Kedge spoke. The sherry and the warmth of the fire had put some colour into her cheeks and she had herself well under control. She spoke directly to Dalgliesh and without interruption.

"Mr. Seton went to London last Monday morning to stay at his Club, that's the Cadaver Club in Tavistock Square. He always spends a week or two there in October. He prefers London in the autumn and he likes to do research for his books in the Club Library. He took a small suitcase with him and his portable typewriter. He went by the train from Halesworth. He told me that he was going to make a start on a new book, something different from his usual style, and I got the impression he was rather excited about it although he never discussed it with me. He said that everyone would be surprised by it. He arranged for me to work at the house for mornings only while he was away and said he would telephone me about 10 o'clock if he had any messages. That's the usual arrangement when he's working at the Club. He types the manuscript in double spacing and posts it to me in instalments and I make a fair copy. Then he revises the whole book and I type it ready for the publishers. Of course, the instalments don't always connect. When he's in London he likes to work on town scenes—I never know what's going to arrive next. Well, he telephoned on Tuesday morning to say that he hoped to post some manuscript by Wednesday evening and to ask me to do one or two small mending jobs. He sounded perfectly all right, perfectly normal then."

Miss Calthrop could contain herself no longer.

"It was really very naughty of Maurice to use you for jobs like darning his socks and polishing the silver. You're a qualified shorthand typist and it's a dreadful waste of skill. Goodness knows, I've enough stuff on tape waiting for you to type. However, that's another matter. Everyone knows my views."

Everyone did. There would have been more sympathy with them if people hadn't suspected that dear Celia's indignation was chiefly on her own account. If there was any exploiting to be done she expected priority.

The girl took no notice of the interruption. Her dark eyes were still fixed on Dalgliesh. He asked gently:

"When did you next hear from Mr. Seton?"

"I didn't, Mr. Dalgliesh. There was no call on Wednesday when I was working at Seton House but, of course, that didn't worry me. He might not telephone for days. I was there again early this morning to finish some ironing when Mr. Plant rang. He's the caretaker at the Cadaver Club and his wife does the cooking. He said they were very worried because Mr. Seton had gone out before dinner on Tuesday and hadn't yet returned to the Club. His bed hadn't been slept in and his clothes and typewriter were still there. Mr. Plant didn't like to make too much fuss at first. He thought that Mr. Seton might have stayed out for some purpose connected with his work—but he got worried when a second night went by and still no message. So he thought he'd better telephone the house. I didn't know what to do. I couldn't contact Mr. Seton's half-brother because he's recently moved to a new flat and we don't know the address. There aren't any other relations. You see, I wasn't sure whether Mr. Seton would want me to take any action. I suggested to Mr. Plant that we should wait a little longer and we agreed to phone each other the minute there was any news, and then just before lunch time, the post arrived and I got the manuscript."

"We have it here," proclaimed Miss Calthrop. "And the envelope." She produced them from her capacious handbag with a flourish and handed them to Dalgliesh. The envelope was the ordinary commercial, buff-coloured, four by nine inch size and was addressed, in typing, to Maurice Seton, Esq., Seton House, Monksmere, Suffolk. Inside were three quarto sheets of inexpert typescript, double spaced. Miss Kedge said dully:

"He always addressed the manuscript to himself. But that isn't his work, Mr. Dalgliesh. He didn't write it and he didn't type it."

"How can you be sure?"

It was hardly a necessary question. There are few things more difficult to disguise than typing and the girl had surely copied enough Maurice Seton manuscripts to recognize his style. But before she had a chance to reply, Miss Calthrop said:

"I think it would be best if I just read part of it."

They waited while she took from her handbag a pair of immense jewelled spectacles, settled them on her nose, and arranged herself more comfortably in the chair. Maurice Seton, thought Dalgliesh, was about to have his first public reading. He would have been gratified by the listeners' rapt attention and possibly, too, by Miss Calthrop's histrionics. Celia, faced with the work of a fellow craftsman and sure of the audience, was prepared to give of her best. She read:

"Carruthers pushed aside the bead curtain and entered the night club. For a moment he stood motionless in the doorway, his tall figure elegant as always in the well-cut dinner jacket, his cool ironic eyes surveying with a kind of disdain the close packed tables, the squalid pseudo-Spanish decor, the shabby clientèle. So this was the headquarters of perhaps the most dangerous gang in Europe! Behind this sordid but common-place night club, outwardly no different from a hundred others in Soho, was a master mind which could control some of the most powerful criminal gangs in the West. It seemed unlikely. But then, this whole fantastic adventure was unlikely. He sat down at the table nearest the door to watch and wait. When the waiter came he ordered fried scampi, green salad and a bottle of chianti. The man, a grubby little Cypriot, took his order without a word. Did they know he was here? Carruthers wondered. And, if they did, how long would it be before they showed themselves.

"There was a small stage at the end of the Club furnished only with a cane screen and a single red chair. Suddenly the lights were dimmed and the pianist began to play a slow sensuous tune. From behind the screen came a girl. She was blonde and beautiful, not young but mature and full bosomed, with a grace and arrogance which Carruthers thought might indicate White Russian blood. She moved forward sensuously to the single chair and with great deliberation began to unzip her evening dress. It fell about her knees to the ground. Underneath she wore nothing but a black brassiere and G string. Sitting now with her back to the audience she twisted her hands to unhook the brassiere. Immediately from the crowded tables there came a hoarse murmuring. 'Rosie! Rosie! Come on Rosie! Give! Give!' "

Miss Calthrop stopped reading. There was complete

silence. Most of her listeners seemed stunned. Then Bryce called out:

"Well, go on Celia! Don't stop now it's getting really exciting. Does Rosie fall on the Hon. Martin Carruthers and rape him? He's had it coming to him for years. Or is that too much to hope?"

Miss Calthrop said:

"There's no need to go on. The proof we need is there."

Sylvia Kedge turned again to Dalgliesh.

"Mr. Seton would never call a character Rosie, Mr. Dalgliesh. That was his mother's name. He told me once that he would never use it in any of his books. And he never did."

"Particularly not for a Soho prostitute," broke in Miss Calthrop. "He talked to me about his mother quite often. He adored her. Absolutely adored her. It nearly broke his heart when she died and his father married again."

Miss Calthrop's voice throbbed with all the yearning of frustrated motherhood. Suddenly Oliver Latham said:

"Let me see that."

Celia handed the manuscript to him and they all watched with anxious expectancy while he scanned it. Then he handed it back without a word.

"Well?" asked Miss Calthrop.

"Nothing. I just wanted to have a look at it. I know Seton's handwriting but not his typing. But you say that he didn't type this."

"I'm sure he didn't," said Miss Kedge. "Although I can't exactly say why. It just doesn't look like his work. But it was typed on his machine."

"What about the style?" asked Dalgliesh. The little group considered. At last Bryce said:

"One couldn't really call that typical Seton. After all, the man could write when he chose. It's almost artificial, isn't it? One gets the impression he was trying to write badly."

Elizabeth Marley had been silent until now, sitting alone in the corner like a discontented child who has been dragged unwillingly into the company of boring adults. Suddenly she said impatiently:

"If this is a fake it's obvious we were meant to discover it. Justin's right. The style's completely bogus. And it's too much of a coincidence that the person responsible should have hit on the one name which would arouse suspicion. Why choose Rosie? If you ask me, this is just Maurice Seton trying to be clever and you've all fallen for it. You'll read all about it in time when his new book comes out. You know how he loves experimenting."

"It's certainly the sort of childish scheme that Seton might think up," said Latham. "I'm not sure I want to be an involuntary participant in any of his damn silly experiments. I suggest we forget the whole thing. He'll turn up in his own time."

"Maurice was always very odd and secretive, of course," agreed Miss Calthrop. "Especially about his work. And there's another thing. I've been able to give him one or two useful little hints in the past. He's definitely used them. But never a word to me subsequently. Naturally I didn't expect a formal acknowledgement. If I can help a fellow writer I'm only too happy. But it's a little disconcerting when a book is published to find one or two of one's own ideas in the plot and never a thank you from Maurice."

"He's probably forgotten by then that he didn't think them out for himself," suggested Latham with a kind of tolerant contempt.

"He never forgot anything, Oliver. Maurice had a very clear mind. He worked methodically too. If I dropped a suggestion he'd pretend to be only half interested and mutter something about trying to work it in sometime or other. But I could see from the look in his eyes that he'd seized on it and was only waiting to get home to file it away on one of those little index cards. Not that I resented it really. It's just that I think he might have acknowledged the help occasionally. I gave him an idea a month or so ago and I bet you anything it will appear in the next book."

No one accepted the offer. Bryce said:

"You're absolutely right about him, Celia. One contributed one's own mite from time to time. God knows why except that one does get the occasional idea for a new method of murder and it seemed a shame to waste it when poor Seton was so obviously near the end of his resources. But, apart from that predatory gleam in his eye—not a sign of appreciation, my dears! Of course, for reasons you all appreciate, he gets no help from me now. Not after what he did to Arabella."

Miss Calthrop said:

"Oh, my idea wasn't for a new method of murder exactly. It was just a situation. I thought it might make rather an effective opening chapter. I kept telling Maurice that you must capture your readers from the very start. I pictured a body drifting out to sea in a dinghy with its hands chopped off at the wrists."

There was a silence, so complete, so sudden that the striking of the carriage clock drew all their eyes towards it as if it were chiming the hour of execution. Dalgliesh was looking at Latham. He had stiffened in his chair and was grasping the stem of his glass with such force that Dalgliesh half expected it to snap. It was impossible to guess what lay behind that pale, rigid, mask. Suddenly Bryce gave his high, nervous laugh and the tension broke. One could almost hear the little gasps of relief.

"What an extraordinarily morbid imagination you have Celia! One would never suspect. You must control these impulses, my dear, or the League of Romantic Novelists will hurl you out of the Club."

Latham spoke, his voice controlled, colourless. He said:

"All this doesn't help with the present problem. Do I take it that we're agreed to take no action about Seton's disappearance? Eliza is probably right and it's just some nonsense Maurice has thought up. If so the sooner we leave Mr. Dalgliesh to enjoy his holiday in peace the better."

He was rising to go as if suddenly wearied of the whole subject when there was a loud, authoritative knock on the cottage door. Jane Dalgliesh lifted an interrogative eyebrow at her nephew then got up quietly and went through the porch to open it. The party fell silent, listening unashamedly. A caller after dusk was rare in their isolated community.

Once night fell they were used to seeing only each other and knew by the instinct of long experience whose footstep was approaching their door. But this loud summons had been the knock of a stranger. There was the soft, broken mutter of voices from the porch. Then Miss Dalgliesh reappeared in the doorway, two raincoated men in the shadows behind her. She said:

"This is Detective Inspector Reckless and Sergeant Courtney from the County C.I.D. They are looking for Digby Seton. His sailing dinghy has come ashore at Cod Head."

Justin Bryce said:

"That's odd. It was beached as usual at the bottom of Tanner's Lane at five o'clock yesterday afternoon."

Everyone seemed to realize simultaneously how strange it was that a Detective Inspector and a Sergeant should be calling after dark about a missing dinghy but Latham spoke before the others had formed their questions:

"What's wrong Inspector?"

Jane Dalgiesh replied for him.

"Something very shocking, I'm afraid. Maurice Seton's body was in the boat."

"Maurice's body! Maurice? But that's ridiculous!" Miss Calthrop's sharp didactic voice cut across the room in futile protest.

"It can't be Maurice. He never takes the boat out. Maurice doesn't like sailing."

The Inspector moved forward into the light and spoke for the first time.

"He hadn't been sailing, Madam. Mr. Seton was lying dead in the bottom of the boat. Dead, and with both hands taken off at the wrists."

6

Celia Calthrop, as if relishing her own obstinacy, said for the tenth time.

"I keep telling you! I didn't say a word about the plot to anyone except Maurice. Why should I? And it's no good harping on about the date. It was about six months ago—perhaps longer. I can't remember just when. But we were walking along the beach to Walberswick and I suddenly thought that it would make a good start to a detective story if one described a handless corpse drifting out to sea in a boat. So I suggested it to Maurice. I certainly never mentioned it to anyone else until tonight. Maurice may have done so, of course."

Elizabeth Marley burst out irritably:

"Obviously he told someone! We can hardly suppose that he cut his own hands off in the cause of versimilitude. And it's stretching coincidence too far to suggest that you and the murderer happened to think of the same idea. But I don't see how you can be so certain that you didn't talk about it to anyone else. I believe you mentioned it to me once when we were discussing how slow Maurice was to get his plots under way."

No one looked as if they believed her. Justin Bryce said softly, but not so softly that the others couldn't hear:

"Dear Eliza! So loyal always." Oliver Latham laughed and there was a short, embarrassed silence broken by Sylvia Kedge's hoarse belligerent voice.

"He never mentioned it to me."

"No dear," replied Miss Calthrop sweetly. "But then, there were a great many things which Mr. Seton didn't discuss with you. One doesn't tell everything to one's maid. And that, my dear, was how he thought of you. You should have had more pride than to let him use you as a household drudge. Men prefer a little spirit, you know."

It was gratuitously spiteful and Dalgliesh could sense the general embarrassed surprise. But no one spoke. He was almost ashamed to look at the girl but she had bent her head as if meekly accepting a merited rebuke, and the two black swathes of hair had swung forward to curtain her face. In the sudden silence he could hear the rasping of her breath, and he wished he could feel sorry for her. Certainly Celia Calthrop was intolerable; but there was something about Sylvia Kedge which provoked unkindness. He wondered what lay behind that particular impulse to savagery.

It was nearly an hour since Inspector Reckless and his Sergeant had arrived, an hour in which the Inspector had said little and the rest of the company, except Dalgliesh and his aunt, had said a great deal. Not all of it had been wise. Reckless had settled himself on arrival in a high chair against the wall and sat there still, solid as a bailiff, his sombre eyes watchful in the light of the fire. Despite the warmth of the room he was wearing his raincoat, a grubby gaberdine which looked too fragile to sustain the weight of its armour of metal buttons, buckles and studs. On his lap he nursed with careful hands a pair of immense gauntlet gloves and a trilby hat as if fearful that someone was going to snatch them from him. He looked like an interloper; the minor official there on sufferance, the little man who dares not risk a drink on duty. And that, thought Dalgliesh, was exactly the effect he aimed to produce. Like all successful detectives, he was able to subdue his personality at will so that even his physical presence became as innocuous and commonplace as a piece of furniture. The man was helped by his appearance, of course. He was small—surely only just the regulation height for a policeman—and the sallow, anxious face was as neutral and unremarkable as any of a million faces seen crowding into a football ground on a Saturday afternoon. His voice, too, was flat, classless, giving no clue to the man. His eyes, wide spaced and deep set under jutting brows, had a trick of moving expressionlessly from face to face as people spoke which the present company might have found disconcerting if they had bothered to notice. By his side, Sergeant Courtney sat with the air of one who has been told to sit upright, keep his eyes and ears open and say nothing, and who is doing just that.

Dalgliesh glanced across the room to where his aunt sat in her usual chair, she had taken up her knitting and seemed serenely detached from the business in hand. She had been taught to knit by a German governess and held the needles upright in the Continental manner; Celia Calthrop seemed mesmerised by their flashing tips and sat glaring across at them as if both fascinated and affronted by her hostess's unusual expertise. She was less at ease, crossing and uncrossing her feet and jerking back her head from the fire as if she found its heat intolerable. It was certainly getting hot in the sitting room. All the other visitors, except Reckless, seemed to feel it too. Oliver Latham was pacing up and down, his brow wet with sweat, his restless energy seeming to raise the temperature still higher. Suddenly he swung round at Reckless:

"When did he die?" he demanded. "Come on, let's have some facts for a change! When did Seton die?"

"We shan't know that precisely until we get the P.M. report, Sir."

"In other words, you're not telling. Let me phrase it another way then. For what hours are we expected to provide alibis?"

Celia Calthrop gave a little squeak of protest but turned to Reckless as anxiously as the rest for his reply.

"I shall want a statement from all of you covering the time Mr. Seton was last seen, which was I understand, seven-thirty on Tuesday evening, until midnight on Wednesday."

Latham said:

"That's putting it a bit late surely? He must have been shoved out to sea long before midnight. Sunset and evening star and one clear call for me. . . . I'll begin, shall I? I was at the New Theatre Guild first night on Tuesday and afterwards went on to a party given by our dear theatrical knight.

I got back to my flat shortly after one and spent what remained of the night with a friend. I can't say who at present but I expect I'll be able to give you the name tomorrow. We got up late, lunched at the Ivy, and parted when I got out my car to drive down here. I arrived at my cottage shortly after seven-thirty yesterday evening and didn't go out again except to take a short walk along the beach before bed. Today I've spent driving around the country and getting in supplies. After dinner I discovered I hadn't bought any coffee and came to the one neighbour who could be relied upon to provide a drinkable blend without a coy accompanying lecture on men and their inefficient housekeeping. To make it easy for you, I would emphasis that I have, apparently, an alibi for the time of death—presuming him to have died on Tuesday—but not for the time he was sent off on his last journey, presuming that to have been yesterday night."

During the first part of this recital Miss Calthrop had assumed a quick variety of expressions—curiosity, disapproval, lubricity and a gentle sadness—as if trying to decide which suited her best. She settled for the gentle sadness, a good woman grieving once more over the frailty of men.

Inspector Reckless said quietly:

"I shall have to ask you for the lady's name Sir."

"Then you'll ask in vain, at least until I've had a chance to talk to her. Charming of you to assume that it was a woman, though. Look Inspector, be reasonable! If I had anything to do with Seton's death I should have fixed my alibi by now. And if I set out to concoct a false one it would hardly involve a woman. Apart from considerations of misplaced chivalry we could hardly fox you for long. No one remembers all the details. You would only have to ask what we talked about, who drew the curtains, on what side of the bed I slept, how many blankets, what we ate for breakfast. It amazes me that anyone tries to concoct an alibi. One would need a better head for detail than I lay claim to."

"Well, you seem to be in the clear, Oliver," proclaimed Celia severely. "It is a matter of murder after all. No reasonable woman could make difficulties."

Latham laughed.

"But she's not reasonable, my dear Celia. She's an actress. Not that I'm expecting trouble. My father gave me one piece of useful advice. Never go to bed with a woman if either of you would be embarrassed to admit the fact next morning. It's a little restricting to one's sex life but now you can see the practical advantages."

Dalgliesh doubted whether Latham found it in fact so very restricting. In his sophisticated circle few people minded a liaison becoming public provided it enhanced their standing, and Oliver Latham, wealthy, handsome, urbane and reputedly hard to get, stood high in the market. Bryce said peevishly:

"Well, you've nothing to worry about then if, as seems likely, Seton died on Tuesday night. Unless, of course, the Inspector is unkind enough to suggest that your sleeping partner would provide you with an alibi in any case."

"Oh, she would provide almost anything if asked nicely," said Latham lightly. "But it would be dangerous surely. It's a question of histrionics. As long as she was playing the gallant little liar, risking her reputation to save her lover from jail, I should be all right. But suppose she decided to change her role? It's probably as well that I shall be requiring her merely to tell the truth."

Celia Calthrop, obviously tired of the general interest in Latham's sex life, broke in impatiently:

"I hardly think I need to describe my movements. I was a very dear friend of poor Maurice, perhaps the only real friend he ever had. However, I haven't any objection to telling you, and I suppose it may help to clear some one else. Every piece of information is important, isn't it? I was at home for most of the time. On Tuesday afternoon however, I drove Sylvia to Norwich and we both had our hair washed and set. *Estelle's* near the Maddermarket. It makes a pleasant little treat for Sylvia and I do think it's important not to let oneself go just because one lives in the country. We had a late tea in Norwich and I took Sylvia home at about eight-thirty; then I drove back to my cottage. I spent yesterday morning working—I dictate on tape—and I drove to Ipswich yesterday afternoon to do some shopping and call on a friend, Lady Briggs of Well Walk. It was just a chance call. Actually she wasn't in, but the maid will remember me. I'm afraid I got a little lost coming home and wasn't back until nearly ten. By then my niece had arrived from Cambridge and she, of course, can vouch for me for the rest of the night. Just before lunch this morning Sylvia telephoned to tell me about the manuscript and Maurice being missing. I wasn't at all sure what to do for the best but when I saw Superintendent Dalgliesh driving past this evening I rang Mr. Bryce and suggested that we all come to consult him. By then I had a premonition that something was dreadfully wrong; and how right I am proved!"

Justin Bryce spoke next. Dalgliesh was intrigued by the readiness with which the suspects were volunteering information for which no one had yet officially asked. They were reciting their alibis with the glib assurance of converts at a revivalist meeting. Tomorrow, no doubt, they would pay for this indulgence with the usual emotional hangover. But it was hardly his job to warn them. He began to feel a considerably increased respect for Reckless; at least the man knew when to sit still and listen.

Bryce said:

"I was at my Bloomsbury flat in town until yesterday too but if Seton died late on Tuesday night I'm definitely out of the running my dears. I had to telephone the doctor twice that night. I was really dreadfully ill. One of my asthma attacks; you know how I suffer Celia. My doctor, Lionel Forbes-Denby can confirm it. I phoned him first just before midnight and begged him to visit at once. He wouldn't come, of course. Just told me to take two of my blue capsules and ring again if they hadn't acted in an hour. It was really naughty of him. I told him I thought I was dying. That's why my type of asthma is so dangerous. You can die with it if you think you're going to."

"But not if Forbes-Denby forbids it, surely?" said Latham.

"That's all very well, Oliver, but he can be wrong."

"He was Maurice's doctor, too, wasn't he?" asked Miss

Calthrop. "Maurice always swore by him. He had to be terribly careful of his heart and he always said that Forbes-Denby kept him alive."

"Well he should have visited me Tuesday night," said Bryce, aggrieved. "I rang again at three-thirty and he came at six but I was over the worst by then. Still, it's an alibi."

"Not really, Justin," said Latham. "We've no proof that you rang from your flat."

"Of course, I phoned from the flat! I told you. I was practically at death's door. Besides, if I sent a false message and was rushing around London murdering Seton what would I do when Forbes-Denby turned up at the flat? He'd never treat me again!" Latham laughed:

"My dear Justin! If Forbes-Denby says he isn't coming he isn't coming. And well you know it."

Bryce assented sadly; he seemed to take the destruction of his alibi remarkably philosophically. Dalgliesh had heard of Forbes-Denby. He was a fashionable West End practitioner who was also a good doctor. He and his patients shared a common belief in the medical infallability of Forbes-Denby and it was rumoured that few of them would eat, drink, marry, give birth, leave the country or die without his permission; they gloried in his eccentricities, recounted with gusto his latest rudeness and dined out on the recent Forbes-Denby outrage whether it were hurling their favourite patent medicine through the window or sacking the cook. Dalgliesh was glad that it would be Reckless or his minions who would have the task of asking this unamiable eccentric to provide medical information about the victim and an alibi for one of the suspects.

Suddenly Justin burst out with a violence that caused them all to turn and stare at him:

"I didn't kill him, but don't ask me to be sorry about it! Not after what he did to Arabella!"

Celia Calthrop gave Reckless the resigned, slightly apologetic look of a mother whose child is about to make a nuisance of himself but not altogether without excuse. She muttered confidentially:

"Arabella. His Siamese cat. Mr. Bryce thought that Maurice had killed the animal."

"One didn't think, Celia. One knew." He turned to Reckless.

"I ran over his dog about three months ago. It was the purest accident. I like animals. I like them, I tell you! Even Towser who, admit it Celia, was the most disagreeable, ill-bred and unattractive mongrel. It was the most horrible experience! He ran straight under my wheels. Seton was utterly devoted to him. He practically accused me of deliberately running the dog down. And then, four days later, he murdered Arabella. That's the kind of man he was! Do you wonder someone has put a stop to him?"

Miss Calthrop, Miss Dalgliesh and Latham all spoke at once thus effectively defeating their good intentions.

"Justin dear, there really wasn't a particle of proof. . . ."

"Mr. Bryce, no one is going to suppose that Arabella has anything to do with it."

"For God's sake Justin, why drag up. . . ."

Reckless broke in quietly:

"And when did you arrive at Monksmere, Sir?"

"Wednesday afternoon. Just before four. And I didn't have Seton's body in the car with me either. Luckily for me, I had trouble with the gear box all the way from Ipswich and had to leave it in Baines garage just outside Saxmundham. I came on by taxi. Young Baines brought me. So if you want to check the car for blood and fingerprints you'll find it with Baines. And good luck to you."

Latham said:

"Why the hell are we bothering, anyway? What about the next-of-kin? Dear Maurice's half-brother. Shouldn't the police be trying to trace him? After all, he's the heir. He's the one with the explaining to do."

Eliza Marley said quietly:

"Digby was at Seton House last night. I drove him there."

It was only the second time she had spoken since the Inspector's arrival and Dalgliesh sensed that she wasn't anxious to speak now. But no one hoping for a sensation could have wished for a more gratifying response. There was an astounded silence broken by Miss Calthrop's sharp, inquisitorial voice:

"What do you mean, drove him there?"

It was, thought Dalgliesh, a predictable question.

The girl shrugged:

"What I said. I drove Digby Seton home last night. He telephoned from Ipswich station before catching the connection and asked me to meet him off the eight-thirty train at Saxmundham. He knew Maurice wouldn't be at home and I suppose he wanted to save the cost of a taxi. Anyway, I went. I took the Mini."

"You never told me about this when I got home," said Miss Calthrop accusingly. The rest of the party shifted uneasily, apprehensive that they might be in for a family row. Only the dark figure sitting against the wall seemed utterly unconcerned:

"I didn't think you would be particularly interested. Anyway, you were pretty late back, weren't you?"

"But what about tonight? You didn't say anything earlier."

"Why should I? If Digby wanted to beetle off again somewhere it's no business of mine. Anyway, that was before we knew that Maurice Seton was dead."

"So you met Digby at his request off the eight-thirty?" asked Latham, as if anxious to get the record straight.

"That's right. And what's more, Oliver, he was on the train when it pulled in. He wasn't lurking in the waiting room or hanging about outside the station. I bought a platform ticket, saw him get off the train and was with him when he gave up his ticket. A London ticket, incidentally; he was complaining about the cost. The ticket collector will remember him, anyway. There were only about half-a-dozen other passengers."

"And presumably he hadn't a body with him?" asked Latham.

"Not unless he was carrying it in a hold-all measuring about three feet by two."

"And you drove him straight home?"

"Of course. That was the idea. Sax is hardly a haunt of gaiety after eight o'clock and Digby isn't my favourite drinking companion. I was just saving him the cost of a taxi. I told you."

"Well, go on, Eliza," encouraged Bryce. "You drove Digby to Seton House. And then?"

"Nothing. I left him at the front door. The house was quiet and there were no lights. Well, naturally. Everyone knows that Maurice stays in London during mid October. Digby asked me in for a drink but I said that I was tired and wanted to get home and that Aunt Celia would probably be home and waiting up for me. We said goodnight and Digby let himself in with his own key."

"He had a key, then?" interposed Reckless. "He and his brother were on those terms?"

"I don't know what terms they were on. I only know that Digby has a key."

Reckless turned to Sylvia Kedge.

"You knew about this? That Mr. Digby Seton had open access to the house?"

Sylvia Kedge replied:

"Mr. Maurice Seton gave his brother a key about two years ago. From time to time he did mention asking for it back but Mr. Digby used it so seldom when his brother wasn't at home that I suppose he thought it didn't matter letting him keep it."

"Why, as a matter of interest, did he want it back?" enquired Bryce. Miss Calthrop obviously considered this the kind of question that Sylvia should not be expected to answer. With an expression and voice clearly indicating "not in front of the servants", she replied:

"Maurice did mention the key to me on one occasion and said that he might ask for it to be returned. There was no question of not trusting Digby. He was merely a little worried in case it got lost or stolen at one of those night clubs Digby is so fond of."

"Well, apparently he didn't get it back," said Latham. "Digby used it to get into the house at about nine o'clock last night. And no one has seen him since. Are you sure the house was empty, Eliza?"

"How could I be? I didn't go in. But I heard no one and there were no lights."

"I was there at half past nine this morning," said Sylvia Kedge. "The front door was locked as usual and the house was empty. None of the beds had been slept in. Mr. Digby hadn't even poured himself a drink."

There was an unspoken comment that something sudden and drastic must indeed have occurred. There were surely few crises which Digby Seton would not suitably fortify himself to meet.

But Celia was speaking.

"That's nothing to go by. Digby always carries a hip flask. It was one of those little idiocyncracies of his that used to irritate Maurice so. But where on earth can he have gone?"

"He didn't say anything to you about going out again?" Latham turned to Eliza Marley. "How did he seem?"

"No, he didn't say anything; I'm not particularly perceptive of Digby's moods but he seemed much as usual."

"It's ridiculous!" proclaimed Miss Calthrop. "Digby surely wouldn't go out again when he'd only just arrived. And where is there for anyone to go? Are you sure he didn't mention his plans?"

Elizabeth Marley said:

"He may have been called out."

Her aunt's voice was sharp.

"Called out! Nobody knew he was there! Called out by whom?"

"I don't know. I only mention it as a possibility. As I was walking back to the car I heard the telephone ring."

"Are you sure?" asked Latham.

"Why do you keep on asking me if I'm sure? You know what it's like up there on the headland; the quietness; the loneliness and mystery of the place; the way sound travels at night. I tell you, I heard the phone ring!"

They fell silent. She was right, of course. They knew what it was like on the headland at night. And the same silence, the same loneliness and mystery waited for them outside. Despite the heat of the room Celia Calthrop shivered. But the heat was really getting intolerable.

Bryce had been crouching on a low stool in front of the fire feeding it compulsively from the wood basket like some demonic stoker. The great tongues of flame leapt and hissed around the drift wood; the stone walls of the sitting room looked as if they were sweating blood. Dalgliesh went over to one of the windows and wrestled with the shutters. As he pushed open the pane the waves of sweet cold air passed over him, lifting the rugs on the floor and bringing in like a clap of thunder the surge of the sea. As he turned again he heard Reckless' flat, unemphatic voice:

"I suggest someone takes Miss Kedge home. She looks ill. I shan't want to talk to her tonight."

The girl looked as if she were about to remonstrate but Elizabeth Marley said with brief finality:

"I'll take her. I want to get home myself. I'm supposed to be convalescent and this hasn't exactly been a restful evening, has it? Where's her coat?"

There was a little spurt of activity. Everyone seemed to feel relief in action and there was much fuss over Sylvia Kedge's coat, her crutches and her general comfort. Miss Calthrop handed over her car keys and said graciously that she would walk home escorted, of course, by Oliver and Justin. Sylvia Kedge, surrounded by a bodyguard of helpers, began to hobble her way to the door.

It was then that the telephone rang. Immediately the little party froze into a tableau of apprehension. The raucous sound, at once so ordinary and so ominous, petrified them into silence. Miss Dalgliesh had moved to the telephone and lifted the receiver when Reckless rose swiftly and without apology took it from her hand.

They could make little of the conversation, which on Reckless' part was conducted briefly and in monosyllables. He seemed to be speaking to a Police Station. For most of the time he listened in silence interspersed with grunts. He ended:

"Right. Thank you. I shall be seeing him at Seton House

first thing in the morning. Goodnight." He replaced the receiver and turned to face the waiting company who were making no effort to hide their anxiety. Dalgliesh half-expected him to disappoint them but instead he said:

"We've found Mr. Digby Seton. He has telephoned Lowestoft Police Station to say that he was admitted to hospital last night after driving his car into a ditch on the Lowestoft Road. They are discharging him first thing tomorrow morning."

Miss Calthrop's mouth had opened for the inevitable question when he added:

"His story is that someone telephoned him just after nine o'clock last night to ask him to go at once to Lowestoft Police Station to identify his brother's body. The caller told him that Mr. Maurice Seton's corpse had come ashore in a dinghy with both hands chopped off at the wrists."

Latham said incredulously:

"But that's impossible! I thought you said the body wasn't found until early this evening?"

"Nor was it, Sir. No one telephoned from the Lowestoft Police yesterday night. No one knew what had happened to Mr. Maurice Seton until his body came ashore this evening. Except one person, of course."

He looked round at them, the melancholy eyes moving speculatively from face to face. No one spoke or moved. It was as if they were all fixed in a moment of time waiting helplessly for some unavoidable cataclysm. It was a moment for which no words seemed adequate; it cried out for action, for drama. And Sylvia Kedge, as if obligingly doing her best, slid with a moan from Eliza's supporting arms and crumpled to the floor.

7

Reckless said:

"He died at midnight on Tuesday, give or take an hour. That's my guess based on the stage of rigor and the general look of him. I shall be surprised if the P.M. doesn't confirm it. The hands were taken off some time after death. There wasn't much bleeding but it looked as if the seat of the dinghy had been used as a chopping block. Assuming that Mr. Bryce was telling the truth and the dinghy was still beached here at five o'clock Wednesday afternoon, he was almost certainly pushed out to sea after the tide turned an hour later. The butchery must have been done after dusk. But he had been dead then for the best part of eighteen hours, maybe longer. I don't know where he died or how he died. But I shall find out."

The three policemen were together in the sitting room. Jane Dalgliesh had made an excuse to leave them alone by offering them coffee; from the kitchen Dalgliesh could hear the faint tinkling sounds of its preparation. It was over ten minutes since the rest of the company had left. It had required little time or effort to revive Sylvia Kedge and once she and Liz Marley were on their way, there had been a general tacit agreement that the excitements of the evening might now be drawn to a close. The visitors looked suddenly bedraggled with weariness. When Reckless, as if gaining energy and animation from their exhaustion, began to question them about a possible weapon, he was met by weary incomprehension. No one seemed able to remember whether he or she owned a chopper, a cleaver or an axe, where these implements were kept or when they had last been used. No one except Jane Dalgliesh. And even Miss Dalgliesh's calm admission that she had lost a chopper from her wood shed some months previously provoked no more than mild interest. The company had had enough of murder for one night. Like over-excited children at the end of the party, they wanted to go home.

It was not until Miss Dalgliesh had also left them that Reckless spoke of the case. This was to be expected but Dalgliesh was irritated to discover how much he resented the obvious implication. Reckless was presumably neither stupid nor crassly insensitive. He would utter no warnings. He wouldn't antagonize Dalgliesh by inviting a discretion and co-operation which both of them knew he had the right to take for granted. But this was his case. He was in charge. It was for him to decide at leisure which pieces of the puzzle he would lay out for Dalgliesh's inspection; how much he would confide and to whom. The situation was a novel one for Dalgliesh and he wasn't sure he was going to like it.

The room was still very close. The fire was dying now into a pyramid of white ash but the heat trapped between the stone walls beat on their faces as if from an oven and the air smelt heavy. The Inspector seemed unaffected by it. He said:

"These people who were here this evening, Mr. Dalgliesh. Tell me about them. Do they all call themselves writers?"

Dalgliesh replied:

"I imagine that Oliver Latham would call himself a dramatic critic. Miss Calthrop likes to be known as a romantic novelist, whatever that may mean. I don't know what Justin Bryce would call himself. He edits a monthly literary and political review which was founded by his grandfather."

Reckless said surprisingly:

"I know. *The Monthly Critical Review.* My father used to take it. That was in the days when sixpence meant something to a working man. And for sixpence the *Monthly Crit.* gave you the message, warm and strong. Nowadays it's about as pink as the *Financial Times;* advice on your investments, reviews of books which nobody wants to read; cosy competitions for the intelligentsia. He can't make a living out of that."

Dalgliesh replied that, so far from making a living, Bryce was known to subsidize the review from his private income.

Reckless said:

"He's apparently one of those men who don't mind people thinking he's a queer. Is he, Mr. Dalgliesh?"

It was not an irrelevant question. Nothing about a suspect's character is irrelevant in a murder investigation, and the case was being treated as one of murder. But, irrationally, Dalgliesh was irritated. He replied:

"I don't know. He may be a little ambivalent."

"Is he married?"

"Not as far as I know. But we surely haven't yet reached the point when every bachelor over forty is automatically suspect?"

Reckless did not reply. Miss Dalgliesh had returned with the tray of coffee and he accepted a cup with grave thanks but with no appearance of really wanting it. When she had again left them he began noisily sipping; his sombre eyes above the rim of the cup fixed on a water colour of avocets in flight by Jane Dalgliesh which hung on the opposite wall. He said:

"They're a spiteful lot, queers. Not violent on the whole. But spiteful. And there was a spiteful crime. That secretary girl, the cripple. Where does she come from, Mr. Dalgliesh?"

Dalgliesh, feeling like a candidate at a viva voce examination, said calmly:

"Sylvia Kedge is an orphan who lives alone in a cottage in Tanner's Lane. She is said to be a highly competent shorthand typist. She worked chiefly for Maurice Seton but she does quite a bit for Miss Calthrop and Bryce. I know very little about her, about any of them."

"You know enough for my needs at present, Mr. Dalgliesh. And Miss Marley?"

"Also an orphan. Her aunt brought her up. At present she's at Cambridge."

"And all these people are friends of your aunt?"

Dalgliesh hesitated. Friendship was not a word his aunt used easily and he thought it doubtful whether she would in fact speak of more than one person at Monksmere as a friend. But one does not willingly deny one's acquaintances when they are about to be suspected of murder. Resisting the temptation to reply that they knew each other intimately but not well, he said cautiously: "You had better ask my aunt. But they all know each other. After all, it's a small and isolated community. They manage to get on together."

Reckless said:

"When they're not killing each other's animals."

Dalgliesh didn't reply. Reckless added:

"They weren't particularly upset were they? Not a word of regret the whole evening. Being writers you'd think one of them might have managed a stylish little epitaph."

"Miss Kedge took it badly," suggested Dalgliesh.

"That wasn't grief. That was shock. Clinical shock. If she isn't better tomorrow someone should get a doctor to her."

He was right, of course, thought Dalgliesh. It had been shock. And that in itself was interesting. Certainly the evening's news had been shocking enough, but would it have been quite so shocking to someone to whom it wasn't news? There had been nothing faked about that final faint and it hardly suggested guilty knowledge.

Suddenly Reckless got up from his chair, looked at his empty cup as if uncertain how it came to be in his hand and replaced it with slow deliberation on the coffee tray. Sergeant Courtney, after a moment's hesitation, did the same with his. It looked as if they were at last preparing to go. But first there was something which Reckless had to be told. Since it was a perfectly straightforward piece of information which might or might not prove to be important, Dalgliesh was irritated at his reluctance to get it out. He told himself that the next few days were going to be difficult enough without letting Reckless inveigle him into a mood of morbid self-analysis. Firmly he said:

"There's something you ought to know about that fake manuscript. I may be wrong—there's not a lot to go on—but I think I recognize the description of the night club. It sounds like the Cortez Club in Soho, L. J. Luker's place. You probably remember the case. It was in 1959. Luker shot his partner, was sentenced to death, but was released when the verdict was quashed by the Court of Criminal Appeal."

Reckless said slowly:

"I remember Luker. Mr. Justice Brothwick's case wasn't it? The Cortez Club would be a useful place to know if you were hoping to pin a murder on someone. And Luker would be as good a man to pin it on as any."

He walked to the door, his Sergeant following him like a shadow. Then he turned for a last word.

"I can see that it's going to be a great advantage having you here, Mr. Dalgliesh."

He made it sound like an insult.

8

The contrast between the brightness of the sitting room and the cool darkness of the autumn night was absolute. It was like stepping into a pit. As the door of Pentlands closed behind them Celia Calthrop experienced a moment of blind panic. The night pressed around her. She breathed darkness like a physical weight. It was as if the air had thickened with night, had become a heaviness through which she had to fight her way. There was no longer direction nor distance. In this black and numinous void the sullen, melancholy thudding of the sea sounded on all sides, so that she felt menaced and rooted like a lost traveller on some desolate shore. When Latham shone his torch on the path the ground looked unreal and very far away like the surface of the moon. It was impossible that human feet could make contact with this remote and insubstantial soil. She stumbled and would have lost her balance if Latham hadn't gripped her arm with sudden and surprising force.

They started together on the inland path. Celia, who had not expected to walk home, was wearing light, high-heeled shoes which alternately skidded on the smooth sea pebbles which littered the path or sank into soft patches of sand so that she lurched forward in Latham's grip like a graceless and recalcitrant child. But her panic was over. Her eyes were getting accustomed to the night and with every stumble forward the roar of the sea grew fainter and less insistent. But it was a relief when Justin Bryce spoke, his voice unaltered, ordinary:

"Asthma is a peculiar complaint! This has been a traumatic evening—one's first contact with murder—and yet one feels quite well. Yet last Tuesday one had the most appalling attack with no apparent cause. One may get a reaction later of course."

"One certainly may," agreed Latham caustically. "Especially if Forbes-Denby doesn't confirm one's alibi for Tuesday night."

"Oh, but he will, Oliver! And one can't help thinking that his testimony will carry rather more weight than anything your sleeping partner may say."

Celia Calthrop, gaining confidence from their nearness, their normality, said quickly:

"It's such a comfort that Adam Dalgliesh happens to be here. After all, he does know us. Socially I mean. And being a writer himself I feel that he belongs at Monksmere."

Latham gave a shout of laughter.

"If you find Adam Dalgliesh a comfort I envy your capacity for self-deception. Do tell us how you see him, Celia! The gentleman sleuth, dabbling in detection for the fun of it, treating his suspects with studied courtesy? A kind of professional Carruthers, straight out of one of Seton's dreary sagas? My dear Celia, Dalgliesh would sell us all to Reckless if he thought it would enhance his reputation one iota. He's the most dangerous man I know."

He laughed again and she felt his grip tighten on her arm. Now he was really hurting her, hurrying her forward as if she were in custody. Yet she could not bring herself to shake free. Although the lane was wider here, the ground was still uneven. Stumbling and slipping, her feet bruised and her ankles aching, she had no chance of keeping up with them except in Latham's remorseless grip. And she could not bear to be left alone. Bryce's voice fluted in her ear.

"Oliver's right you know, Celia. Dalgliesh is a professional detective and probably one of the most intelligent in the country. I don't see that his two volumes of verse, much as I personally admire them, can alter that."

"Reckless is no fool though." Latham still seemed amused. "Did you notice how he said hardly a word but just encouraged us to babble on in our childish, egotistical way? He probably learned more from us in five minutes than other suspects would tell him in hours of orthodox questioning. When will we learn to keep our mouths shut?"

"As we've nothing to hide I don't see that it matters," said Celia Calthrop. Really Oliver was extraordinarily irritating tonight! One might almost imagine that he was a little drunk. Justin Bryce said:

"Oh, Celia! Everyone has something to hide from the police. That's why one is so ambivalent about them. Wait until Dalgliesh asks why you kept referring to Seton in the past tense, even before we heard that his body had been found. You did, you know. Even I noticed it so it must have struck Dalgliesh. I wonder whether he'll feel it his duty to mention the matter to Reckless."

But Celia was too tough to be intimidated by Bryce. She said irritably. "Don't be stupid Justin! I don't believe you. And, even if I did, it was probably because I was speaking of Maurice as a writer. And one does somehow feel that, as a writer, poor Maurice has been finished for quite a time."

"God yes!" said Latham. "Dead and done for. Finished. Written out. Maurice Seton only wrote one effective passage of prose in his life but that was straight from the heart all right. And from the brain. It produced exactly the effect he intended. Every word selected to wound and the whole—lethal."

"Do you mean his play?" asked Celia. "I thought you despised it. Maurice always said that it was your notice that killed it."

"Celia darling, if my notice could kill a play, half the little pieces now running in London would have folded after the first night." He jerked her forward with fresh impetus and for a minute Justin Bryce lagged behind them. Hurrying to catch them up he called breathlessly:

"Maurice must have been killed on Tuesday night. And his body was pushed out to sea late on Wednesday evening. So how did the murderer get it to Monksmere? You drove from London on Wednesday Oliver. It wasn't in the boot of your Jaguar, was it?"

"No dear," said Latham easily. "I'm very particular what I carry in the boot of my Jaguar."

Celia said complacently:

"Well, I'm in the clear. Sylvia can give me an alibi until late on Tuesday and that's obviously the crucial time. I admit that I was out alone on Wednesday night but Reckless will hardly suspect me of mutilating the body. And that reminds me. There's one person who doesn't even claim an alibi for Tuesday or Wednesday, Jane Dalgliesh. And what's more—it was her chopper!"

Latham said:

"Why in God's name should Miss Dalgliesh wish to kill Seton?"

"Why should any of us want to?" retorted Celia. "And I'm not saying she did. I'm merely pointing out that it was apparently her chopper."

Bryce said happily:

"I wanted to at one time. Murder Seton, I mean. After I found Arabella I could willingly have killed him. But I didn't. All the same, I can't feel sorry about it. I wonder if I ought to ask to view the body after the inquest. It might shock me out of this insensitivity which I can't feel is at all healthy."

But Latham was still meditating on the missing chopper. He said fiercely:

"Anyone could have taken it! Anyone! We all walk in and out of each other's houses at will. No one here locks up anything. There's never been the need. And we don't even know yet that it was the weapon."

"My dears," said Bryce. "Consider this and calm yourselves. Until we know the cause of death we can't even be sure that Maurice was murdered."

9

They left her at the door of Rosemary Cottage and she watched them disappear into the night. Justin's high voice and Latham's laugh came back to her long after their figures had merged with the darker shadows of hedgerow and tree. There were no lights in the cottage and the sitting room was empty. So Elizabeth was in bed. She must have driven home fast from Tanner's Cottage. Her aunt was uncertain whether to be glad or sorry. She had a sudden need of company but she couldn't face questions or arguments. There would be much to discuss, but not tonight. She was too tired. She switched on the table lamp and, kneeling on the hearthrug, poked ineffectually at the slates and ashes of the dead fire. Then she got unsteadily to her feet, grunting with the effort like an old woman, and let herself down into an armchair. Opposite her an identical chair loomed squat and solid, plump with cushions, empty and poignant. Here Maurice had sat on that October afternoon six years ago. It was the day of the Inquest; a day of cold and sudden squalls. There had been a good fire that evening. She had been expecting him and had taken care that both she and the room were ready. The firelight and the one discreet lamp had shed a nicely-calculated glow over the polished mahogany and cast soft shadows on the soft pinks and blues of cushions and carpet. The tray of drinks had been set ready to hand. Nothing had been left to chance. And she had waited for him as eagerly as a young girl before her first date. She had worn a dress of soft blue-grey wool. It had really made her look quite slim, quite young. It still hung in her wardrobe. She had never cared to wear it again. And he had sat opposite her, stiff and black in his formal mourning, an absurd little mannikin with his black tie and armband, his face rigid with grief. But she hadn't understood then that it was grief. How could she? It was impossible that he could be grieving for that shallow, egotistical, monstrous nymphomaniac. Of course, there had been the shock of hearing that Dorothy was dead, had killed herself, the horror of identifying the drowned body, the ordeal of the inquest, of facing the rows of white, accusing faces. He knew what they were saying all right, that he had driven his wife to suicide. No wonder he had looked shocked and ill. But grief? It had never occurred to her that he might grieve. Somehow she had taken it for granted that there must, in his heart, have been a spring of relief. Relief that the long years of torment and self-control were over at last, that he could begin to live again. And she would be there to help him, just as she had helped with her sympathy and advice when Dorothy was alive. He was a writer, an artist. He needed affection and understanding. From tonight he need never be alone ever again.

Had she loved him, she wondered. It was difficult to remember. Perhaps not. Perhaps it had never been love as she imagined love to be. But it had been as close as she would ever get to that longed-for, elusive, oft-imagined cataclysm. She had dealt with its counterfeit in nearly forty novels; but the coin itself had never come within her grasp.

Sitting in front of the dead fire she recalled the second when she had known the truth, and her cheeks burned at the memory. Suddenly he had begun to cry, awkwardly as a child. In that moment all artifice had been forgotten. Only pity remained. She had knelt beside him, cradling his head in her arms, murmuring her comfort and love. And then, it had happened. His whole body stiffened and withdrew. He looked at her, catching his breath, and she saw his face. It was all there. Pity, embarrassment, a trace of fear—and hardest of all to accept—physical repulsion. In one bitter moment of complete clarity she had seen herself with his eyes. He had been grieving for that slim, gay, beautiful creature; and an ugly middle-aged woman had chosen that moment to throw herself into his arms. He had recovered himself, of course. Nothing had been said. Even the dreadful sobbing had been cut off in mid-gasp like that of a child suddenly offered a sweet. She reflected bitterly that there was nothing like personal danger to take the edge off grief. Somehow, gracelessly, she had stumbled back to her own chair, her face burning. He had stayed for as long as politeness dictated and she had handed him his drinks, listened to his sentimental reminiscences about his wife—dear God, had the poor fool forgotten so soon?—and feigned interest in his plans for a long holiday abroad, "to try to forget". It was six months before he had thought it prudent to revisit Rosemary Cottage alone and even longer before he began tentatively to establish the understanding that she would be available whenever he wanted to escort a woman in public. Just before he left for his holiday he had written to tell her that she was named in his Will "in appreciation of your sympathy and understanding on the death of my dear wife". She had understood all right. It was the kind of crude, insensitive gesture which he would consider an adequate, appropriate apology. But her first reaction hadn't been anger or humiliation; she had merely wondered how much it would be. Since then she had wondered increasingly; and now the question had a fascinating immediacy. It might, of course, be a mere hundred or so. It might be thousands. It might even be a fortune. After all, Dorothy was reputed to have been a wealthy woman and Maurice hadn't anyone else to leave it to. He had never had much use for his half-brother and lately they had grown even further apart. Besides, didn't he owe it to her?

A slant of light from the hall fell across the carpet. Silently, Elizabeth Marley came into the room, her feet bare, her red dressing gown glowing in the half light. She stretched herself out stiffly in the chair opposite her aunt, her feet towards the dying fire, her face deep in the shadows. She said:

"I thought I heard you come in. Can I get you anything? Hot milk? Ovaltine?"

The tone was ungracious, embarrassed, but the offer was unexpected and Miss Calthrop was touched.

"No thank you dear. You go back to bed. You'll catch cold. I'll make the drink and bring yours up."

The girl did not move. Miss Calthrop made a fresh attack on the fire. This time a tongue of flame hissed round the coals and she felt the first welcome warmth on hands and face. She asked:

"You got Sylvia home all right? How did she seem?"

"Not too good. But then, she never does."

Her aunt said:

"I wondered afterwards whether we ought to have insisted that she stay here. She really looked very ill, not safe to be alone."

Elizabeth shrugged. "I did tell her that we had a spare bed until the new *au pair* girl comes and that she was welcome to it. She wouldn't consider it. When I pressed her she became overwrought, so I left it. After all, she's thirty, isn't she? She's not a child. I couldn't force her to stay."

"No, of course not." Celia Calthrop thought that her niece would hardly have welcomed Sylvia in the house. She had noticed that most women were less sympathetic to the girl than were men, and Elizabeth made no secret of her dislike. The voice from the armchair asked:

"What happened after we left?"

"Nothing very much. Jane Dalgliesh seems to think that he may have been killed with her chopper. Apparently she missed it about four weeks ago."

"Did Inspector Reckless tell you that he was killed that way?"

"No. But surely. . . ."

"Then we still don't know how he died. He could have been killed in a dozen different ways and his hands chopped off after death. I imagine that they were. It wouldn't be an easy thing to do if your victim were alive and conscious. Inspector Reckless must know if it happened that way. There wouldn't be very much bleeding for one thing. And I expect he knows the time of death to an hour or so even without the P.M. report."

Her aunt said:

"Surely he died on Tuesday night? Something must have happened to him on Tuesday. Maurice would never walk out of his Club like that and spend the night away without a word to anyone. He died on Tuesday night when Sylvia and I were at the pictures."

She spoke with stubborn confidence. She wished it to be so, therefore, it must be so. Maurice had died on Tuesday night and her alibi was assured. She added:

"It's unfortunate for Justin and Oliver that they happened to be in town that evening. They've got alibis of a sort, of course. But it's a pity all the same."

The girl said quietly:

"I was in London on Tuesday night too." Before her aunt could speak she went on quickly:

"All right, I know what you're going to say. I was supposed to be on a bed of sickness in Cambridge. Well, they let me up earlier than I told you. I took the first fast train to Liverpool Street on Tuesday morning. I was meeting someone there for lunch. No one you know. Someone from Cambridge. He's gone down now. Anyway he didn't turn up. There was a message of course, very polite, very regretful. It's a pity, though, that we arranged to meet where we were known. I didn't much enjoy seeing the head waiter look sorry for me. Not that I was surprised really. It isn't important. But I wasn't going to have Oliver and Justin gossiping over my affairs. I don't see why I should tell Reckless, either. Let him find out for himself."

Celia thought:

"But you told me!" She felt a surge of happiness so acute that she was glad that they sat in the shadows. This was the first real confidence she had ever received from the girl. And happiness made her wise. Resisting the first impulse to comfort or question she said:

"I'm not sure, dear, that it was sensible of you to spend the whole day in town. You're not really strong yet. Still, it doesn't seem to have done you any harm. What did you do after lunch?"

"Oh, worked for the afternoon in the London Library. Then I went to a news theatre. It was getting latish then so I thought I'd better stay the night. After all, you weren't expecting me at any particular time. I had a meal at the Coventry Street Lyons and then managed to get a room at the Walter Scott Hotel in Bloomsbury. Most of the evening I spent just walking in London. I suppose I collected my key and went to my room just before eleven."

Miss Calthrop broke in eagerly:

"Then the porter will be able to vouch for you. And perhaps someone will remember you at Lyons. But I think you were right to say nothing about it for the present. It's entirely your own concern. What we'll do is to wait until we know the time of death. We can reconsider the whole matter then."

It was difficult for her to keep the ring of happiness from her voice. This was what she had always wanted. They were talking together, planning together. She was being asked, however obliquely and unwillingly, for reassurance and advice. How odd that it should take Maurice's death to bring them together. She babbled on:

"I'm glad you're not upset about the luncheon date. Young men today have no manners. If he couldn't telephone you by the day before at the latest, he should have made it his business to turn up. But at least you know where you stand."

The girl got up from the chair and walked without speaking to the door. Her aunt called after her:

"I'll get the drinks and we'll have them together in your room. I won't be a moment. You go up and get into bed."

"I don't want anything, thank you."

"But you said you'd like a hot drink. You ought to have something. Let me make you some Ovaltine. Or just hot milk perhaps."

"I said I didn't want anything. And I'm going to bed. I want to be left in peace."

"But Eliza. . . ."

The door closed. She could hear nothing more, not even a soft footfall on the stairs. There was nothing but the hissing of the fire and, outside, the silence, the loneliness of the night.

10

Dalgliesh was woken next morning by the ring of the telephone. His aunt must have answered it quickly for the ringing stopped almost immediately and he dozed again into that happy trance between waking and sleeping which follows a good night. It must have been half an hour before the telephone rang again, and this time it seemed louder and more insistent. He opened his eyes wide and saw, framed by the window, a translucent oblong of blue light with only the faintest hairline separating the sea and the sky. It promised to be another wonderful autumn day. It was already another wonderful autumn day. He saw with surprise that his watch showed ten-fifteen. Putting on his dressng gown and slippers, he pattered downstairs in time to hear his aunt answering the telephone.

"I'll tell him, Inspector, as soon as he wakes. Is it urgent? No, except that this is supposed to be his holiday . . . I'm sure that he'll be glad to come as soon as he's finished breakfast. Goodbye."

Dalgliesh bent over and placed his cheek momentarily against hers. It felt, as always, as soft and tough as a chamois glove.

"Is that Reckless?"

"Yes. He says he is at Seton's house and would be glad if you would join him there this morning."

"He didn't say in what capacity I suppose? Am I supposed to work or merely to admire him working? Or am I, possibly, a suspect?"

"It is I who am the suspect, Adam. It was almost certainly my chopper."

"Oh, that's been taken notice of. Even so, you rate lower

than most of your neighbours, I imagine. And certainly lower than Digby Seton. We police are simple souls at heart. We like to see a motive before we actually make an arrest. And no motive so gladdens our heart as the prospect of gain. I take it that Digby is his half-brother's heir?"

"It's generally supposed so. Two eggs or one, Adam?"

"Two, please. But I'll see to them. You stay and talk. Didn't I hear two calls? Who telephoned earlier?"

His aunt explained that R. B. Sinclair had rung to invite them both to dinner on Sunday night. She had promised to ring back. Dalgliesh, paying loving attention to his frying eggs, was intrigued. But he said little beyond expressing his willingness to go. This was something new. His aunt, he guessed, was a fairly frequent visitor to Priory House but never when he was at Pentlands. It was after all well understood that R. B. Sinclair neither visited nor received visitors. His aunt was uniquely privileged. But it wasn't hard to guess the reason for this innovation. Sinclair wanted to talk about the murder with the one man who could be expected to give a professional opinion. It was reassuring, if a little disillusioning, to discover that the great man wasn't immune to common curiosity. Violent death held its macabre fascination even for this dedicated non-participant in the human charade. But, of course, Dalgliesh would go to dinner. The temptation was too great to resist. He had lived long enough to know that few experiences can be so disenchanting as meeting the famous. But, with R. B. Sinclair, any writer would be willing to take the risk.

Dalgliesh made an unhurried business of washing-up after his breakfast, put on a tweed jacket over his sweater, and hesitated at the cottage door where a jumbled collection of walking sticks, left by past guests as hostages against a happy return, tempted him to add a final touch to the part of an energetic holiday-maker. He selected a sturdy ash, balanced it in his hand, then replaced it. There was no point in overdoing the act. Calling "Goodbye" to his aunt he set off across the headland. The quickest way would have been by car, turning right at the road junction, driving about half a mile on the Southwold Road, then taking the narrow but reasonably smooth track which led across the headland to the house. Perversely, Dalgliesh decided to walk. He was, after all, supposed to be on holiday and the Inspector's summons had made no mention of any urgency. He was sorry for Reckless. Nothing is more irritating and frustrating to a detective than any uncertainty about the extent of his responsibility. In fact, there was none. Reckless was in sole charge of the investigation and both of them knew it. Even if the Chief Constable decided to ask for the help of the Yard it was highly improbable that Dalgliesh would be given the case. He was too personally involved. But Reckless would hardly relish conducting his investigation under the eyes of a C.I.D. Superintendent, particularly one with Dalgliesh's reputation. Well, it was hard luck on Reckless; but harder luck, thought Dalgliesh, on himself. This was the end of his hope of a solitary, uncomplicated holiday, that blessed week of undemanding peace which almost without effort on his part was to soothe his nerves and solve his personal problems. From the first this plan was probably an unsubstantial fabrication built on tiredness and his need to escape. But it was disconcerting to see it fall so early into ruin. He was as little inclined to interfere in the case as Reckless was to seek his help. There would have been tactful telephone calls to and from the Yard, of course. It would be understood by all concerned that Dalgliesh's familiarity with Monksmere and his knowledge of the people concerned would be at the Inspector's service. That was no more than any citizen owed the police. But if Reckless thought that Dalgliesh craved any more positive participation he must be speedily disillusioned.

It was impossible not to rejoice in the beauty of the day and as he walked much of Dalgliesh's irritation fell away. The whole headland was bathed in the yellow warmth of the autumn sun. The breeze was fresh but without chill. The sandy track was firm under his feet, sometimes passing straight between the gorse and heather, sometimes twisting among the thick brambles and stunted hawthorn trees which formed a succession of little caverns where the light was lost and the path dwindled to a thread of sand. For most of the walk Dalgliesh had a view of the sea except when he passed behind the grey walls of Priory House. It stood four square to the sea within a hundred yards of the cliff edge and was bounded on the south by a tall stone wall and on the north by a fringe of fir trees. At night there was something eerie and unwelcoming about the house which reinforced its natural privacy. Dalgliesh thought that Sinclair if he craved seclusion could hardly have found a more perfect site. He wondered how long it would be before Inspector Reckless violated that privacy with his questions. It would hardly take him long to learn that Sinclair had a private flight of steps leading to the beach from his land. Assuming that the body had been taken to the boat and not the boat rowed some considerable distance along the coast to the body, it must have been carried down to the beach by one of three paths. There was no other access. One way, and perhaps the most obvious, was Tanner's Lane which led past Sylvia Kedge's cottage. As the dinghy had been beached at the bottom of Tanner's Lane this would have been the most direct route. The second was the steep and sandy slope which led from Pentlands to the shore. It was difficult enough in daylight. At night it would be hazardous even to the experienced and unburdened. He could not see the murderer risking that route. Even if his aunt did not hear the distant car she would know that someone was passing the cottage. People who lived alone and in so remote a place were quick to sense the unfamiliar noises of the night. His aunt was the most detached, and incurious of women to whom the habits of birds had always appeared of greater interest than those of humans. But even she would hardly watch unconcerned while a dead body was carried past her door. There would, too, be the problem of carrying the corpse the half mile along the shore to where Sheldrake was beached. Unless, of course, the killer left it half buried in the sand while he collected the dinghy and rowed it to the corpse. But that would surely add unnecessarily to the risks and it would be impossible to remove all traces of sand from the body. More to the point, it would require oars and rowlocks. He wondered whether Reckless had checked on these.

The third way of access to the beach was by Sinclair's steps. These were only some fifty yards from the bottom of Tanner's Lane and they led to a small secluded cove where the cliffs, taller here than at any other point, had been crumbled and eroded by the sea into a gentle curve. This was the only part of the beach where the killer—if killer there were—could have worked on the corpse without fear of being watched either from the north or south. Only in the unlikely event of one of the local inhabitants deciding to take a late walk along the shore would there be danger of discovery; and in this place, once dusk had fallen, the countryman did not choose to walk alone on the shore.

Priory House was behind Dalgliesh now and he had come to the thin beech wood which fringed Tanner's Lane. Here the earth was brittle with fallen leaves and through the lattice of the bare boughs there was a haze of blue which could have been sky or sea. The wood ended suddenly and Dalgliesh clambered over a stile and dropped into the lane. Immediately before him was the squat, red-bricked cottage where Sylvia Kedge had lived alone since the death of her mother. It was an ugly building, as uncompromisingly square as a doll's house with its four small windows, each heavily curtained. The gate and the front door had been widened, presumably to take the girl's wheel chair, but the change had done nothing to improve the proportions of the house. No attempt had been made to prettify it. The diminutive front garden was a dark patch cut in two by a gravel path; the paint on doors and windows was a thick, institutional brown. Dalgliesh thought that there must have been a Tanner's Cottage here for generations, each built a little higher up the lane until it too crumbled or was swept away in the great storms. Now this square, red, twentieth-century box stood firm to take its chance against the sea. Obeying an impulse, Dalgliesh pushed open the garden gate and walked up the path. Suddenly his ears caught a sound. Someone else was exploring. Round the corner of the house came the figure of Elizabeth Marley. Unembarrassed, she gave him a cool glance and said: "Oh, it's you! I thought I heard someone snooping around. What do you want?"

"Nothing. I snoop by nature. Whereas you, presumably, were looking for Miss Kedge?"

"Sylvia's not here. I thought she might be in her little dark room at the back but she isn't. I've come with a message from my aunt. Ostensibly she wants to make sure that Sylvia's all right after the shock of last night. Really, she wants her to come and take dictation before Oliver Latham or Justin nab her. There's going to be great competition for La Kedge, and I've no doubt she'll make the most of it. They all like the idea of having a private secretary on call for two bob a thousand words, carbons supplied."

"Is that all Seton paid her? Why didn't she leave?"

"She was devoted to him, or pretended to be. She had her own reasons for staying, I suppose. After all, it wouldn't be easy for her to find a flat in town. It'll be interesting to know what she's been left in the Will. Anyway, she enjoyed posing as the loyal, overworked little help-meet who would be so happy to transfer to auntie if only it didn't mean letting poor Mr. Seton down. My aunt never saw through it, of course. But then, she's not particularly intelligent."

"Whereas you have us all neatly catalogued. But you're not suggesting that someone killed Maurice Seton to get his shorthand typist?"

She turned on him furiously, her heavy face blotched with anger.

"I don't care a damn who killed him or why! I only know that it wasn't Digby Seton. I met him off that train Wednesday night. And if you're wondering where he was on Tuesday night, I can tell you. He told me on the drive home. He was locked up in West Central Police Station from eleven o'clock onwards. They picked him up drunk and he came before the Magistrate on Wednesday morning. So, luckily for him, he was in police custody from eleven o'clock on Tuesday night until nearly midday on Wednesday. Break that alibi if you can Superintendent."

Dalgliesh pointed out mildly that the breaking of alibis was

Reckless's business, not his. The girl shrugged, dug her fists into her jacket pockets, and kicked shut the gate of Tanner's Cottage. She and Dalgliesh walked up the lane together in silence. Suddenly she said:

"I suppose the body was brought down this lane to the sea. It's the easiest way to where Sheldrake was beached. The killer would have to carry it for the last hundred yards, though. The lane's much too narrow for a car or even a motor cycle. He could have got it by car as far as Coles's meadow and parked the car on the grass verge. There were a couple of plain clothes men there when I came past, looking for tyre marks. They won't get much joy. Someone left the gate open last night and Coles's sheep were all over the lane this morning."

This, as Dalgliesh knew, was not unusual. Ben Coles, who farmed a couple of hundred unproductive acres on the east of the Dunwich Road did not keep his gates in the best of repair and his sheep, with the blind perversity of their kind, were as often in Tanner's Lane as in their own meadow. At tripper time the lane became a shambles when the bleating flock in full cry mingled with the herd of horn-happy motorists frantically trying to edge each other out of the only parking space in the lane. But that open gate might have been highly convenient for someone; Coles's sheep in their happy scamperings might have been following an old local tradition. It was well known that, in the smuggling days, the flocks were driven nightly along the sheep paths which crossed the Westleton marshes so that all traces of horses' hoofs were obliterated before the Excise Officers made their morning search.

They walked on together until they came to the stile which gave access to the northern half of Monksmere Head. Dalgliesh was pausing to say goodbye when the girl suddenly blurted:

"I suppose you think I'm an ungrateful bitch. She makes me an allowance, of course. £400 a year in addition to my grant. But I expect you know that. Most people here seem to."

There was no need to ask whom she meant. Dalgliesh could

have replied that Celia Calthrop was not the woman to let her generosities go unremarked. But he was surprised by the amount. Miss Calthrop made no secret of the fact that she had no private income—"Poor little me. I'm a working girl. I earn every penny I get"—but it was not therefore assumed that she lacked money. Her sales were large and she worked hard, incredibly hard by the standards of Latham or Bryce who were apt to assume that dear Celia had only to lean back in a comfortable armchair with her tape recorder on and her reprehensible fiction would gush forth in an effortless and highly rewarding stream. It was easy to be unkind about her books. But if one were buying affection, and the price of even a reluctant toleration was a Cambridge education and £400 a year, much might be necessary. A novel every six months; a weekly stint in *Home and Hearth*; appearances whenever her agent could get them on those interminably boring television panels; short stories written under one name or another for the women's weeklies; the gracious appearances at Church bazaars where the publicity was free even if the tea had to be paid for. He felt a spasm of pity for Celia. The vanities and ostentations which were such a source of amused contempt to Latham and Bryce suddenly appeared no more than the pathetic trappings of a life both lonely and insecure. He wondered whether she had really cared for Maurice Seton. And he wondered, too, whether she was mentioned in Seton's Will.

Elizabeth Marley seemed in no hurry to leave him and it was difficult to turn away from that resolutely persistent figure. He was used to being a confidante. That, after all, was part of his job. But he wasn't on duty now and he knew well that those who confided most were apt to regret it soonest. Besides, he had no real wish to discuss Celia Calthrop with her niece. He hoped the girl didn't intend to walk all the way to Seton House with him. Looking at her he could see where at least some of that £400 allowance went. Her fur lined jacket was real leather. The pleated skirt of thin tweed looked as if it had been tailored for her. Her shoes were sturdy but they were also elegant. He remembered something he had once heard Oliver Latham say; he couldn't remember when or why. "Elizabeth Marley has a passion for money. One finds it rather engaging in this age when we're all so busy pretending to have minds above mere cash."

She was leaning back against the stile now, effectively blocking his way.

"She got me to Cambridge, of course. You can't do that without either money or influence if you're only moderately intelligent like me. It's all right for the alpha people. Everyone's glad to get them. For the rest of us it's a matter of the right school, the right crammers, and the right names on your application form. Aunt could manage even that. She has a real talent for making use of people. She's never afraid of being a vulgar nuisance which makes it easier of course."

"Why do you dislike her so much?" enquired Dalgliesh.

"Oh, it's nothing personal. Although we haven't much in common, have we? It's her work. The novels are bad enough. Thank God we haven't the same name. People are pretty tolerant at Cambridge. If, like the waterman's wife, she was a receiver of stolen property under guise of keeping a brothel no one would care a damn. And nor would I. But that column she writes. It's utterly humiliating! Worse even than the books. You know the kind of muck." Her voice rose to a sickly falsetto. "Don't give in to him, dear. Men are only after one thing."

In Dalgliesh's view men, including himself, frequently were but he thought it prudent not to say so. Suddenly he felt middle-aged, bored and irritated. He had neither wanted nor expected company and if his solitude had to be disturbed he could have named more agreeable companions than this peevish and dissatisfied adolescent. He hardly heard the rest of her complaint. She had dropped her voice and the words were blown from him on the freshening breeze. But he caught the final mutterings. "It's so completely amoral in the real sense of the term. Virginity as a carefully preserved bait for eligible males. In this day and age!"

"I haven't much sympathy with that point of view myself," Dalgliesh said. "But then, as a man, your aunt would no doubt consider me prejudiced. But at least it's realistic. And you can hardly blame Miss Calthrop for dishing out the same advice week after week when she gets so many letters from the readers wishing they'd taken it in the first place."

The girl shrugged: "Naturally she has to adopt the orthodox line. The hag rag wouldn't employ her if she dared to be honest. Not that I think she knows how. And she needs that column. She hasn't any money except what she earns and the novels can't go on selling for ever." Dalgliesh caught the note of anxiety in her voice. He said brutally.

"I shouldn't worry. Her sales won't fall. She writes about sex. You may not like the packaging but the basic commodity will always be in demand. I should think your £400 is safe for the next three years."

For a moment he thought she was going to smack his face. Then surprisingly, she gave a shout of laughter and moved away from the stile.

"I deserved that! I've been taking myself too seriously. Sorry for boring you. You're on your way to Seton House, I suppose?" Dalgliesh said that he was and asked if he should give any message to Sylvia Kedge if she were there.

"Not to Sylvia. Why should you pimp for auntie? No, it's to Digby. Just to say that there will be meals for him at the cottage until he gets fixed up if he cares to come. It's only cold meat and salad today so he won't be missing much if he can't make it. But I don't suppose he'll want to depend on Sylvia. They hate each other. And don't get any wrong ideas, Superintendent. I may be willing to drive Digby home and feed with him for a day or two. But that's as far as it goes. I'm not interested in pansies."

"No," said Dalgliesh. "I wouldn't suppose that you were."

For some reason she blushed. She was turning away when, prompted by no more than mild curiosity, Dalgliesh said:

"One thing intrigues me. When Digby Seton telephoned to ask you to meet him at Saxmundham, how did he know you weren't at Cambridge?" She turned back and met his gaze without embarrassment or fear. She didn't even appear to resent the question. Instead, to his surprise, she laughed.

"I wondered how long it would be before someone asked that. I might have known it would be you. The answer's simple. I met Digby in London, quite by chance, on Tuesday morning. At Piccadilly Underground to be precise. I stayed in London that night and on my own. So I probably haven't an alibi. . . . Are you going to tell Inspector Reckless? But of course you are."

"No," replied Dalgliesh. "You are."

II

Maurice Seton had been fortunate in his architect and his house had that characteristic of all good domestic building: it seemed indigenous to its site. The grey stone walls curved from the heather to buttress the highest point of Monksmere Head, with a view north over Sole Bay and south over the marshes and the bird reserve as far as Sizewell Gap. It was an unpretentious and agreeable building, single-storied and L-shaped, and built only fifty yards from the cliff edge. Presumably, these elegant walls, like those of Sinclair's sturdy bastion, would one day crumble into the North Sea, but there seemed no immediate danger of it. The cliffs here had a strength and height which gave some hope of permanence. The long arm of the L faced south-east and was composed almost entirely of double-glazed windows which opened on to a terrace of paved stones. Here Seton had taken a hand in the planning. Dalgliesh thought it unlikely that the architect had chosen to set up the two ornate urns which marked the ends of the terrace and in which a couple of bushes, their boughs contorted by the cold winds of the Suffolk coast, were failing to thrive, nor the pretentious sign swinging between two low posts on which the words, "Seton House" were carved in Gothic lettering.

It didn't need the car parked at the terrace edge to tell Dalgliesh that Reckless was there. He could see no one, but he knew that his approach was being watched. The tall windows seemed full of eyes. One of them was ajar.Dalgliesh drew it open and stepped into the living room.

It was like walking on to a stage set. Every corner of the long narrow room was warm with light as if bathed in the glare of arc lamps. It was a modern set. From centre back an open staircase curved to the upper storey. Even the furniture contemporary, functional and expensive-looking added to the air of impermanence and unreality. Almost the whole of the window space was taken up with Seton's desk, an ingeniously designed fitment with a complex of drawers, cupboards and bookcases spreading each side of the central working surface. It had probably been made to the owner's specification, a functional status symbol in light polished oak. On the pale grey walls there were two popular Monet prints unimaginatively framed.

The four people who turned to watch unsmiling as Dalgliesh stepped over the window sill were as immobile and carefully disposed about the room as actors who have taken up their pose ready for the curtains to rise. Digby Seton was lying on a couch placed diagonally across the centre of the room. He was wearing a mauve dressing gown of artificial silk over red pyjamas and might have looked more the part of romantic lead had it not been for the cap of grey stockinette which fitted close to his head and came down level to his eyebrows. The modern method of bandaging is effective but scarcely becoming. Dalgliesh wondered whether Seton had a temperature. He would hardly have been discharged from hospital unfit and Reckless, who was neither inexperienced nor a fool, would have telephoned the doctor to make sure that the man was fit to be questioned. But his eyes were unnaturally bright and a red moon burnt high on each cheekbone so that he looked like a gaudy circus clown, a bizarre focus of interest against the grey couch. Inspector Reckless sat at the desk with Sergeant Courtney by his side. In this morning light Dalgliesh saw the boy clearly for the first time and was struck by his pleasant good looks. He had the type of honest, open face which looks out of advertisements extolling the advantages of a career in banking for the intelligent and ambitious young man. Well, Sergeant Courtney had chosen the police. In his present mood Dalgliesh thought it rather a pity.

The fourth player was hardly on stage. Through the open door which led to the drawing room Dalgliesh caught a glimpse of Sylvia Kedge. She was sitting at the table in her wheelchair. There was a tray of silver in front of her and she was engaged in polishing a fork with as little enthusiasm as a bit player who knows that the attention of the audience is elsewhere. She lifted her eyes momentarily to Dalgliesh and he was shocked by the misery in her drawn face. She looked very ill. Then she bent again to her task.

Digby Seton heaved his legs from the couch, walked deliberately to the dining room door and prodded it gently shut with his stockinged foot. None of the policemen spoke.

Seton said:

"Sorry and all that. Don't want to be rude, but she gives me the willies. Damn it all, I've said I'll pay her the £300 Maurice left her! Thank God you've come, Superintendent! Are you taking over the case?"

It could hardly have been a worse beginning. Dalgliesh said:

"No. It's nothing to do with the Yard. Surely Inspector Reckless has explained to you by now that he's the officer in charge?"

He felt that Reckless deserved that snide innuendo.

Seton protested:

"But I thought they always called in the Yard to tricky cases of murder?"

"What makes you think this is a case of murder?" asked Reckless. He was slowly sorting out papers from the desk and did not turn to Seton as he spoke. His voice was quiet, unemphatic, almost uninterested.

"Well, isn't it? You tell me. You're the experts. But I don't see how Maurice could have cut off his own hands. One perhaps, but hardly two. If that's not murder, then what is it? And damn it all, you've got a Scotland Yard chap on the spot."

"On holiday, remember," said Dalgliesh. "I'm in exactly the same position as you."

"Like hell you are!" Seton twisted himself into a sitting position and groped under the couch for his shoes.

"Brother Maurice hasn't left you £200,000. God, it's crazy!

It's unbelievable! Some sod pays off an old score and I get a fortune! Where the hell did Maurice get that kind of money, anyway?"

"Apparently partly from his mother and partly from the estate of his late wife," replied Reckless. He had finished with the papers and was now going through a small drawer of index cards with the methodical intentness of a scholar looking for a reference.

Seton gave a snort of laughter.

"Is that what Pettigrew told you? Pettigrew! I ask you, Dalgliesh! Trust Maurice to have a solicitor called Pettigrew. What else could the poor devil be with a name like that? Pettigrew! Doomed from birth to be a respectable provincial solicitor. Can't you picture him? Dry, precise, sixtyish, resplendent watch chain and pin stripes. God, I hope he knows how to draw up a valid Will."

"I don't think you need worry on that score," said Dalgliesh. Actually, he knew Charles Pettigrew who was his aunt's solicitor. It was an old firm but the present owner, who had inherited from his grandfather, was a capable and lively thirty year-old, reconciled to the tedium of a country practice by the nearness of the sea and a passion for sailing. He said:

"I gather you've found a copy of the Will?"

"It's here." Reckless passed over the single sheet of stiff paper, and Dalgliesh scanned it. The Will was short and soon read. Maurice Seton, after instructing that his body be used for medical research and afterwards cremated, left £2,000 to Celia Calthrop, "in appreciation of her sympathy and understanding on the death of my dear wife", and £300 to Sylvia Kedge, "provided she has been ten years in my service at the time of my death". The remainder of the estate was left to Digby Kenneth Seton, on trust until he married, and then to revert to him absolutely. If he died before his half-brother or died unmarried the estate went absolutely to Celia Calthrop. Seton said:

"Poor old Kedge! She's lost her £300 by two months. No wonder she looks sick! Honestly, I'd no idea about the Will. At least, I knew that I would very likely be Maurice's heir.

He more or less said so once. Anyway, he hadn't anyone else to leave it to. We've never been particularly close but we did have the same father and Maurice had a great respect for the old man. But £200,000! Dorothy must have left him a packet. Funny that, when you consider that their marriage was pretty well on the rocks when she died."

"Mrs. Maurice Seton had no other relatives then?" asked Reckless.

"Not that I know of. Lucky for me, isn't it? When she killed herself there was some talk of a sister who ought to be contacted. Or was it a brother? Honestly, I can't remember. Anyway, no one turned up and no one but Maurice was mentioned in the Will. Her father was a property speculator and Dorothy was left pretty well off. And it all came to Maurice. But £200,000!"

"Perhaps your half-brother did well with his books," suggested Reckless. He had finished with the card index but was still seated at the desk, making entries in a note book and seemingly only half-interested in Seton's reactions. But Dalgliesh, himself a professional, knew that the interview was going very much according to plan.

"Oh, I shouldn't think so! Maurice always said that writing wouldn't keep him in socks. He was rather bitter about it. He said that this was the age of 'Soap-powder fiction'. If a writer hadn't a gimmick no one was interested. Bestsellers were created by the advertisers, good writing was a positive disadvantage and the public libraries killed sales. I daresay he was right. If he had £200,000 I don't know why he bothered. Except, of course, that he liked being a writer. It did something for his ego, I suppose. I never understood why he took it so seriously, but then, he never understood why I wanted my own Club. And I'll be able to have it now. A whole chain of them if things go my way. You're both invited to the opening night. Bring the whole of West Central with you if you like. No sneaking in on expenses to check on the drinking and see that the floor show isn't too naughty. No women sergeants tarted up to look like provincial tourists on the spree. The best tables. Everything on the house. D'you know, Dalgliesh, I could have made a go of the Golden Pheasant if only I'd had the capital behind me. Well, I've got it now."

"Not unless you also get a wife," Dalgliesh reminded him unkindly. He had noted the names of the trustees in Seton's Will and couldn't see either of those cautious and conservative gentlemen parting with trust funds to finance a second Golden Pheasant. He asked why Maurice Seton had been so anxious for Digby to marry.

"Maurice was always hinting that I ought to settle down. He was a great one for the family name. He hadn't any children himself—none that I know of anyway—and I don't suppose he was keen to marry again after the Dorothy fiasco. Besides, he had a dicky heart. He was afraid, too, that I might set up house with a queer. He didn't want his money shared with a pansy boy friend. Poor old Maurice! I don't think he'd recognize a queen if he met one. He just had the idea that London, and West End Clubs in particular, are full of them."

"Extraordinary!" said Dalgliesh dryly. Seton seemed unaware of the irony. He said anxiously:

"Look, you do believe me about that phone call, don't you? The murderer phoned me as I arrived here Wednesday night and sent me off on a fool's errand to Lowestoft. The idea was to get me away from the house and make sure I hadn't an alibi for the time of death. At least, I suppose that was the idea. It doesn't make sense otherwise. It puts me in a spot all right. I wish to God that Liz had come in with me. I don't see how I can prove that Maurice wasn't in the house when I got here or that I didn't take a late night walk on the beach with him, conveniently armed with the kitchen knife. Have you found the weapon, by the way?"

The Inspector replied briefly that they hadn't. He said:

"It would help me, Mr. Seton, if you could remember more about this phone call."

"Well, I can't." Seton sounded suddenly peevish. He added sullenly: "You keep asking me about it and I keep telling you! I don't remember. Damn it, I've had a bloody great bang on the head since then! If you told me I'd imagined the whole thing I wouldn't be surprised except that it must have happened or I wouldn't have taken out the car. I was dog tired and I wouldn't have set off to Lowestoft just for the fun of it. Someone phoned. I'm sure of that. But I can't remember what the voice sounded like. I'm not even sure if it was a man or a woman."

"And the message?"

"I've told you, Inspector! The voice said it was speaking from Lowestoft Police Station, that Maurice's body had come ashore in my dinghy with the hands chopped off—"

"Chopped or cut?"

"Oh, I don't know! Chopped I think. Anyway, I was to go to Lowestoft at once and identify the body. So I set off. I knew where Maurice keeps the car keys and luckily the Vauxhall had plenty of juice in her. Or unluckily. I damn near killed myself. Oh, I know you're going to say it was my fault. I admit I had a pull or two from my hip flask on the way. Well, do you wonder! And I was bloody tired before I started. I had a lousy night on Tuesday—the West Central's hardly a hotel. And then that long train journey."

"And yet you set off for Lowestoft straight away without bothering to check?" asked Reckless.

"I did check! When I got to the road it occurred to me to see if Sheldrake had really gone. So I drove down Tanner's Lane as far as I could and walked to the beach. The boat wasn't there. That was good enough for me. I suppose you think that I ought to have rung back the police station but it never occurred to me that the message might be a hoax until I was on my way and then the easiest thing was to check on the boat. I say. . . ."

"Yes?" enquired Reckless calmly.

"Whoever phoned must have known that I was here. And it couldn't have been Liz Marley because she'd only just left when the phone rang. Now, how could anyone else have known?"

"You could have been seen arriving," suggested Reckless. "And I suppose you put the lights on when you got in. They could be seen for miles."

"I put them on all right. The whole bloody lot. This place gives me the creeps in the dark. Still, it's odd."

It was odd, thought Dalgliesh. But the Inspector's explanation was probably correct. The whole of Monksmere Head could have seen those blazing lights. And when they went out, someone would know that Digby Seton was on his way. But why send him? Was there something still to be done at Seton House? Something to be searched for? Some evidence to be destroyed. Was the body hidden in Seton House? But how was that possible if Digby was telling the truth about the missing boat?

Suddenly Digby said:

"What am I supposed to do about handing the body over for medical research? Maurice never said anything to me about being keen on medical research. Still, if that's what he wanted. . . ."

He looked from Dalgliesh to Reckless enquiringly. The Inspector said:

"I shouldn't worry about that now, Sir. Your brother left the necessary instructions and official forms among his papers. But it will have to wait."

Seton said: "Yes. I suppose so. But I wouldn't like . . . I mean, if that's what he wanted. . . ."

He broke off uncertainly. Much of the excitement had left him and he was looking suddenly very tired. Dalgliesh and Reckless glanced at each other, sharing the thought that there would be little more to be learnt from Maurice's body once Walter Sydenham had finished with it, the eminent and thorough Dr. Sydenham whose textbook on forensic pathology made it plain that he favoured an initial incision from the throat to the groin. Seton's limbs might be useful for raw medical students to practise on, which was probably not what he had had in mind. But his cadaver had already made its contribution to medical science.

Reckless was preparing to leave. He explained to Seton that he would be required at the inquest in five days' time, an invitation which was received without enthusiasm, and began putting his papers together with the satisfied efficiency of an insurance agent at the end of a good morning's work. Digby watched him with the puzzled and slightly apprehensive air of a small boy who has found the company of adults a strain but isn't sure that he actually wants them to leave. Strapping up his brief case, Reckless asked his last question with no appearance of really wanting to know the answer:

"Don't you find it rather strange, Mr. Seton, that your half-brother should have made you his heir? It isn't as if you were particularly friendly."

"But I told you!" Seton wailed his protest. "There wasn't anyone else. Besides, we were friendly enough. I mean, I made it my business to keep in with him. He wasn't difficult to get on with if you flattered him about his bloody awful books and took a bit of trouble with him. I like to get on with people if I can. I don't enjoy quarrelling and unpleasantness. I don't think I could have stood his company for long but then I wasn't here very often. I told you I haven't seen him since August Bank Holiday. Besides, he was lonely. I was the only family he had left and he liked to think that there was someone who belonged."

Reckless said:

"So you kept in with him because of his money. And he kept in with you because he was afraid of being completely alone?"

"Well, that's how things are." Seton was unabashed. "That's life. We all want something from each other. Is there anyone who loves you, Inspector, for yourself alone?"

Reckless got up and went out through the open window. Dalgliesh followed him and they stood together on the terrace in silence. The wind was freshening but the sun still shone, warm and golden. On the green-blue sea a couple of white sails moved fitfully like twists of paper blown in the wind. Reckless sat down on the steps which led from the terrace to the narrow strip of turf and the cliff edge. Dalgliesh, feeling unreasonably that he could hardly remain standing since it put Reckless at a disadvantage, dropped down beside him. The stones were unexpectedly cold to his hands and thighs, a reminder that the warmth of the autumn sun had little power. The Inspector said:

"There's no way down to the beach here. You'd have thought Seton would want his own way down. It's a fair walk to Tanner's Lane."

"The cliffs are pretty high here and there's little solid rock. It could be tricky to build a stairway," suggested Dalgliesh.

"Maybe. He must have been a strange sort of chap. Fussy. Methodical. That card index, for instance. He picked up ideas for his stories from newspapers, magazines, and from people. Or just thought of them for himself. But they're all neatly catalogued there, waiting to come in useful."

"And Miss Calthrop's contribution?"

"Not there. That doesn't mean very much though. Sylvia Kedge told me that the house was usually left unlocked when Seton was living here. They all seem to leave their houses unlocked. Anyone could have got in and taken the card. Anyone could have read it for that matter. They just seem to wander in and out of each other's places at will. It's the loneliness I suppose. That's assuming that Seton wrote out a card."

"Or that Miss Calthrop ever gave him the idea," said Dalgliesh. Reckless looked at him.

"That struck you too, did it? What did you think of Digby Seton?"

"The same as I've always thought. It requires an effort of will to understand a man whose passionate ambition is to run his own Club. But then, he probably finds it equally difficult to understand why we should want to be policemen. I don't think our Digby has either the nerve or the brains to plan this particular killing. Basically he's unintelligent."

"He was in the nick most of Tuesday night. I gave West Central a ring and it's true all right. What's more he was drunk. There was nothing feigned about it."

"Very convenient for him."

"It's always convenient to have an alibi, Mr. Dalgliesh. But there are some alibis I don't intend to waste time trying to break. And that's the kind he's got. What's more, unless he was acting just now, he doesn't know that the weapon wasn't a knife. And he thinks that Seton died on Wednesday night. Maurice couldn't have been in this house alive when Digby and Miss Marley arrived on Wednesday. That's not to say that his body wasn't here. But I can't see Digby acting the butcher and I can't see why he should. Even if he found the body here and panicked he's the sort to hit the bottle then belt off back to town, not to plan an elaborate charade. And he was on the Lowestoft not the London Road when he crashed. Besides, I don't see how he could have known about Miss Calthrop's pleasant little opening for a detective story."

"Unless Eliza Marley told him on the way here."

"Why should she tell Digby Seton? It's not a likely topic for conversation on the drive home. But all right. We'll assume that she did know and that she told Digby or that, somehow or other, he knew. He arrives here and finds his brother's body. So he immediately decides to provide a real life mystery by chopping off Maurice's hands and pushing the body out to sea. Why? And what did he use for weapon? I saw the body, remember, and I'd swear those hands were chopped off, not cut, nor sawed, chopped. So much for the kitchen knife! Seton's chopper is still in the pantry. And your aunt's—if that was the weapon—was stolen three months ago."

"So Digby Seton is out. What about the others?"

"We've only had time for a preliminary check. I'm taking their statements this afternoon. But it looks as if they've all got alibis of a sort for the time of death. All except Miss Dalgliesh. Living alone as she does, that's not surprising."

The flat monotonous voice did not change. The sombre eyes still looked out to sea. But Dalgliesh was not deceived. So this was the reason for the summons to Seton House, for the Inspector's unexpected burst of confidence. He knew how it must look to Reckless. Here was an elderly unmarried woman living a lonely and isolated life. She had no alibi for the time of death nor for Wednesday night when the body was launched out to sea. She had an almost private access to the beach. She knew where Sheldrake lay. She was nearly six foot tall, a strong, agile country woman, addicted to strenuous walking and accustomed to the night.

Admittedly she had no apparent motive. But what did that matter? Despite what he had said to his aunt that morning Dalgliesh knew perfectly well that motive was not the first concern. The detective who concentrated logically on the "where", "when", and "how", would inevitably have the "why", revealed to him in all its pitiful inadequacy. Dalgliesh's old chief used to say that the four L's—love, lust, loathing and lucre—comprised all motives for murder. Superficially that was true enough. But motive was as varied and complex as human personality. He had no doubt that the Inspector's horribly experienced mind was already busy recalling past cases where the weeds of suspicion, loneliness or irrational dislike had flowered into unexpected violence and death.

Suddenly Dalgliesh was seized with an anger so intense that for a few seconds it paralysed speech and even thought. It swept through his body like a wave of physical nausea leaving him white and shaken with self disgust. Choked with this anger he was luckily saved from the worst follies of speech, from sarcasm, indignation or the futile protest that his aunt would, of course, make no statement except in the presence of her solicitor. She needed no solicitor. She had him. But, God, what a holiday this was proving to be!

There was a creak of wheels and Sylvia Kedge spun her wheelchair through the french windows and manœuvred it up beside them. She didn't speak but gazed intently down the track towards the road. Their eyes followed hers. A post office van, brightly compact as a toy, was careering over the headland towards the house.

"It's the post," she said.

Dalgliesh saw that her hands were clamped to the chair sides, the knuckles white. As the van drew up before the terrace he watched her body half rise and stiffen as if seized with a sudden rigor. In the silence which followed the stopping of the engine, he could hear her heavy breathing.

The postman slammed the van door and came towards them, calling a cheerful greeting. There was no response from the girl and he glanced puzzled from her rigid face to the still figures of the two men. Then he handed Reckless the post. It was a single, foolscap envelope, buff coloured and with a typewritten address.

"It's the same kind as before, Sir," he said. "Like the one I gave her yesterday." He nodded towards Miss Kedge, then, still getting no response, backed awkwardly towards his van muttering "goodmorning."

Reckless spoke to Dalgliesh:

"Addressed to Maurice Seton, Esq. Posted either late on Wednesday or early on Thursday from Ipswich. Postmarked midday yesterday."

He held the envelope delicately by one corner as if anxious not to impose more finger prints. With his right thumb he edged it open. Inside there was a single sheet of foolscap paper covered with double spaced typescript. Reckless began to read aloud:

"The corpse without hands lay in the bottom of a small sailing dinghy drifting just within sight of the Suffolk coast. It was the body of a middle-aged man, a dapper little cadaver, its shroud a dark pin-striped suit which fitted the narrow body as elegantly in death as it had been tailored to in life. . ."

Suddenly Sylvia Kedge held out her hand.

"Let me see."

Reckless hesitated, then held the sheet before her eyes.

"He wrote it," she said hoarsely. "He wrote it. And that's his typewriting."

"Maybe," said Reckless. "But he couldn't have posted it. Even if this went into the box late on Wednesday night he couldn't have put it there. He was dead by then."

She cried out:

"He typed it! I know his work, I tell you. He typed it! And he hadn't any hands!"

She burst into peal upon peal of hysterical laughter. It rang over the headland like a wild echo, so startling a flock of gulls that shrieking their alarm they whirled from the cliff edge in a single white cloud.

Reckless looked at the rigid body, the screaming mouth,

with speculative unconcern, making no move to comfort or control her. Suddenly Digby Seton appeared in the french windows, his face white under the ridiculous bandage.

"What the hell. . . ?"

Reckless looked at him, expressionless, and said in his flat voice:

"We've just heard from your brother, Mr. Seton. Now isn't that nice?"

12

It took some little time to pacify Miss Kedge. Dalgliesh had no doubt that her hysteria was genuine; this was no play-acting. He was only surprised that she should be so upset. Of all the little community at Monksmere Sylvia Kedge alone seemed to be genuinely shocked and distressed at Seton's death. And, certainly, the shock was real enough. She had looked and behaved like a woman maintaining a precarious self-control which had snapped at last. But she made visible efforts to pull herself together and was at last well enough to be escorted back to Tanner's Cottage by Courtney who had succumbed entirely to the pathos of her drawn face and pleading eyes and who pushed her wheelchair down the lane like a new mother displaying her fragile newborn to the glares of a potentially hostile world. Dalgliesh was relieved to see her go. He had discovered that he did not like her and was the more ashamed of the emotion because he knew that its roots were unreasonable and ignoble. He found her physically repellant. Most of her neighbours used Sylvia Kedge to gratify, at small expense, an easy impulse to pity while ensuring that they got their money's worth. Like so many of the disabled she was at once patronized and exploited. Dalgliesh wondered what she thought of them all. He wished he could feel more sorry for her but it was difficult not to watch, with a kind of contempt, the way in which she made use of her disability. But then what other weapons had she? Despising the young constable for his easy capitulation and himself for lack of feeling, Dalgliesh set off back to Pentlands for lunch. He walked back by the road. It took longer and was less interesting but he had always disliked retracing his footsteps. The route took him past Bryce's cottage. As he reached it an upstairs window was opened and the owner shot his long neck out and called:

"Come in Adam, dear boy. I've been watching out for you. I know you've been spying for that dreary little friend of yours but I don't hold it against you. Just leave your rhino whip outside and help yourself to whatever drink you prefer. I'll be down in a jiffy." Dalgliesh hesitated then pushed open the cottage door. The little sitting room was as untidy as always, a repository of bric-à-brac which could not appropriately be housed in his London flat. Deciding to wait for his drink, Dalgliesh called up the stairs:

"He's not my dreary little friend. He's a highly competent police officer."

"Oh no doubt!" Bryce's voice was muffled. Apparently he was pulling clothes over his head. "Competent enough to nab me if I'm not cunning. I was stopped for speeding on the A 13 about six weeks ago and the officer concerned—a beefy brute with one of those metamorphic glares, was most uncivil. I wrote to the Chief Constable about it. It was a fatal thing to do, of course. I see that now. They've got it in for me all right. My name's on a little list somewhere, you may be sure."

He had padded into the room by now and Dalgliesh saw with surprise that he did indeed look concerned. Murmuring reassurance he accepted sherry—Bryce's drinks were always excellent—and settled himself in the latest acquisition, a charming Victorian high-backed chair.

"Well, Adam. Give, as they say. What has Reckless discovered? Such an inappropriate name!"

"I'm not altogether in his confidence. But another instalment of manuscript has arrived. It's rather better written this time. A description of a handless body in a boat and typed apparently by Seton himself."

Dalgliesh saw no reason why Bryce should be denied this bit of information. Sylvia Kedge was hardly likely to keep it to herself.

"Post when?"

"Before lunch yesterday. From Ipswich."

Bryce wailed his dismay.

"Oh no! Not Ipswich! One was in Ipswich on Thursday. One often is. Shopping you know. One hasn't an alibi."

"You're probably not the only one," Dalgliesh pointed out consolingly. "Miss Calthrop was out in her car. So was Latham. So was I, come to that. Even that woman from Priory House was out in the buggy. I saw her as I drove over the headland."

"That would be Alice Kerrison, Sinclair's housekeeper. I don't suppose she went any further than Southwold. Probably fetching the groceries."

"On Thursday afternoon. Isn't it early closing?"

"Oh Adam dear, what does it matter? I expect she was just out for a drive. She'd hardly drive the buggy as far as Ipswich just to post an incriminating document. She hated Seton, though. She was housekeeper at Seton House before his wife died. Sinclair took her on after Dorothy killed herself and she's been there ever since. It was a most extraordinary thing! Alice stayed with Seton until after the inquest, then, without a word to him, she packed her bags and walked up to Priory House to ask if Sinclair had a job for her. Apparently Sinclair had reached the point when the urge for self sufficiency didn't extend to the washing-up and he took her on. As far as I know neither has regretted it."

"Tell me about Dorothy Seton," invited Dalgliesh.

"Oh, she was lovely, Adam! I've got a photograph of her somewhere which I must show you. She was madly neurotic, of course, but really beautiful. Manic depressive is the correct jargon, I believe. Exhaustingly gay one minute and so down the next that one felt positively contaminated with gloom. It was very bad for me, of course. I have enough trouble living with my own neurosis without coping with other people's. She led Seton a terrible life, I believe. One could almost pity him if it weren't for poor Arabella."

"How did she die?" enquired Dalgiesh.

"It was the most appalling thing! Seton strung her up from that meat hook in the beam in my kitchen. I shall never forget the sight of that darling furry body hanging there elongated like a dead rabbit. She was still warm when we cut her down. Look, I'll show you."

Dalgliesh had been half dragged into the kitchen before he grasped that Bryce was talking about his cat. He successfully fought down the first impulse to nervous laughter and followed Bryce. The man was shaking with anger, grasping Dalgliesh's forearm in a surprisingly powerful grip and gesticulating at the hook in impotent fury as if it shared Seton's guilt. There seemed no immediate chance of getting any information about Dorothy Seton's death now that Arabella's end was so vividly recalled. Dalgliesh sympathized with Bryce. His own love of cats was as great if less vocal. If Seton had indeed wantonly destroyed a beautiful animal out of malice and revenge it was difficult to regret him. More to the point, such a man must have made his share of enemies.

Dalgliesh enquired who had found Arabella.

"Sylvia Kedge. She had come up to take some dictation for me and I was delayed arriving from London. I got here about five minutes later. She had phoned Celia to come and cut Arabella down. She couldn't reach the body herself. Naturally both of them were terribly upset. Sylvia was physically sick. We had to push the wheelchair to the kitchen sink and she threw up all over my washing up. I won't dwell on my own sufferings. But I thought you knew all the details. I asked Miss Dalgliesh to write. I hoped you might have come down to prove Seton did it. The local police were quite hopeless. Now, if it had been a human being, think of the fuss and nonsense! Just like Seton. It's so ridiculous. I'm not one of those sentimentalists who think that human beings are more important than any other form of life. There are too many of us anyway and most of us neither know how to be happy ourselves nor make any one else happy. And we're ugly. Ugly! You knew Arabella, Adam. Wasn't she the most beautiful creature? Didn't you feel it was a privilege to watch her? She was life-enhancing."

Dalgliesh, wincing at Bryce's choice of words, said the appropriate complimentary things about Arabella who had indeed been a beautiful cat with every appearance of knowing it. His aunt had told him of the incident in one of her fortnightly letters but not surprisingly had made no mention of Bryce's request that he should come down and take over the investigation. Dalgliesh forebore to point out that no actual evidence had been produced against Seton. There had been a great deal of anger, ill-feeling and suspicion but remarkably little rational thought applied to the problem. But he had no stomach for solving it now. He induced Bryce to return to the sitting room and asked again how Dorothy Seton had died.

"Dorothy? She had gone to Le Touquet for an autumn holiday with Alice Kerrison. Things were pretty bad between her and Seton by then. She had become terribly dependent on Alice and I suppose Seton thought it would be a good idea if there were someone to keep an eye on her. When they had been away a week Seton realized that he couldn't face living with her again and wrote to say he wanted a separation. No one knows what exactly was in the letter but Alice Kerrison was with Dorothy when she opened it and said at the inquest that it upset Mrs. Seton terribly and that she said they must go home at once. Seton had written from the Cadaver Club and the house here was empty when they got back. Alice said that Dorothy seemed all right, perfectly calm and really much more cheerful than usual. She began preparing supper for the two of them and Dorothy wrote at her desk for a short time. Then she said she would go for a walk along the beach to see the moon on the sea. She walked to the bottom of Tanner's Lane, stripped herself naked, put her clothes in a neat pile with a stone on top and walked out to sea. They recovered the body a week later. It was suicide all right. She left a little note under the stone to say that she realized now that she was no use to herself or to anyone else and had decided to kill herself. It was a very direct note, perfectly clear, perfectly lucid. I remember at the time thinking that most suicides talk about ending it all. Dorothy just wrote that she had decided to kill herself."

"What happened to the letter that Seton wrote her?"

"It was never found. It wasn't with Dorothy's belongings and Alice didn't see her destroy it. But Seton was quite open about it. He was sorry but he had acted for the best. It had become impossible to go on. I didn't realize exactly what living with Dorothy had done to him until I saw his play two years later. It was about marriage to a neurotic but in the play it's the husband who kills himself. Well, naturally. Seton wanted to cast himself in the major role. Not literally, of course. Still, he might just as well have played the part. He couldn't have been much worse than poor Barry. Not that one can blame the actors. Such a very bad play, Adam! And yet written with a kind of terrible honesty and pain."

"Were you there?" enquired Dalgliesh.

"Bang in the middle of the third row of the stalls my dear, and curling with embarrassment. Seton was in a box. He'd got Celia with him and one must say she did him proud. Hardly a stitch above the waist and tinkling away with imitation jewellery like a Christmas tree. Do you think Seton wanted people to think she was his mistress? I've a feeling our Maurice liked to be taken for a naughty boy. My dear, they looked like a couple of minor emigré royalties. Seton even wore a decoration. A Home Guard medal or something of the kind. I was with Paul Markham, such a sensitive boy. He was in tears by the end of the first act. So, admittedly, were a good third of the audience but in their case I suspect it was tears of laughter. We left in the first interval and spent the rest of the evening drinking at Moloneys. I can bear quite an amount of suffering provided it's not my own but I do draw the line at public executions. Celia, gallant girl, stuck it out to the last. They even had a party at the Ivy afterwards. When I think of that evening, oh Arabella, how thou art revenged!"

"Latham's notice was Latham at his most vicious wasn't it? Did you get the impression that he had a personal interest in killing the play?"

"Oh, I shouldn't think so." The large eyes bent on Dalgliesh were as innocent as a child's but Adam had a considerable respect for the intelligence behind them.

"Oliver can't tolerate bad writing nor bad acting and when they come together it tends to make him savage. Now if Oliver had been found dead with his hands hacked off one could have understood it. Half those illiterate little secondary-mods who swan around London calling themselves actresses could have done it happily given the wit."

"But Latham knew Dorothy Seton didn't he?"

"Oh Adam! How you do go on about a thing! Not very subtle, my dear. Yes, he knew her. We all did. She was a great dropper-in. Sometimes drunk and sometimes sober and equally tedious either way."

"Were she and Latham lovers?" enquired Dalgliesh bluntly. As he expected Bryce was neither disconcerted nor surprised by the question. Like all inveterate gossips he was fundamentally interested in people. This was one of the first questions he would ask himself about any man or woman in his circle who seemed to find each other's company agreeable.

"Celia always said so, but then she would. I mean the dear girl can't conceive of any other relationship between a heterosexual man and a pretty woman. And where Latham's concerned she's probably right. One could hardly blame Dorothy, stuck in that glass-house with Seton, so dull. She was entitled to find consolation anywhere so long as it wasn't with me."

"But you don't think Latham was particularly fond of her?"

"I don't know. I shouldn't have thought so. Poor Oliver suffers from self-disgust. He pursues a woman, then, when she falls in love with him, he despises her for lack of discrimination. The poor dears simply can't win. It must be so exhausting to dislike oneself so much. Now I'm lucky. I find myself fascinating."

The fascination was beginning to pall on Dalgliesh. He glanced at his watch, said firmly that it was 12.45 and his lunch would be ready and made to go.

"Oh, but you must see that snap of Dorothy. I've got it somewhere. It will give you some idea how lovely she was."

He opened the sliding lid of his writing desk and rummaged among the piles of paper. Dalgliesh thought that it looked a hopeless task. But there must have been some order in the chaos for, in less than a minute, Bryce had found what he wanted. He brought the photograph over to Dalgliesh.

"Sylvia Kedge took it when we were picnicking on the beach one July. She does quite a bit of amateur photography."

There was certainly nothing professional about the photograph. It showed the picnic party grouped around Sheldrake. They were all there, Maurice and Digby Seton; Celia Calthrop with a sulky looking child recognizable as Liz Marley; Oliver Latham and Bryce himself. Dorothy Seton, wearing a bathing costume, was leaning against the hull of the dinghy and laughing at the camera. The snap was clear enough but it told Dalgliesh nothing except that she had an agreeable figure and knew how best to show it off. The face was that of a pretty woman but no more. Bryce looked at the snap over his shoulder. As if struck by this fresh evidence of the perfidy of time and memory he said sadly. "Funny . . . It doesn't really give one any idea of her. . . I thought it was better than this. . ."

Bryce came to the cottage gate with him. As Dalgliesh was leaving an estate car came lurching up the lane and stopped with a bump at the gate. From it bounded a sturdy, black-haired women with legs like jambs above her white ankle socks and schoolgirl sandals, who was greeted by Bryce with squeaks of pleasure.

"Mrs. Bain-Porter! You haven't brought them! You have! How perfectly sweet of you."

Mrs. Bain-Porter had the deep, rich, upper-class female voice which is trained to intimidate the helots of empire or to carry across any hockey field in the teeth of a high gale. Her words boomed clearly in Dalgliesh's ears.

"When I got your letter yesterday I thought I'd take a chance. I've brought the three best from the litter. It's so much nicer to choose them in your own home I think. Nicer for them too."

The back of the car was opened now and Mrs. Bain-Porter, helped by Bryce, was carefully lifting out three cat baskets from which there rose at once an agitated squealing, treble descant to Mrs. Bain-Porter's bass and Bryce's joyful chirpings. The concert party disappeared through the cottage door. Dalgliesh trudged home to his lunch in contemplative mood. It was one of those little things which can mean everything or nothing. But if Mrs. Bain-Porter got a letter from Julian Bryce on Thursday it was posted on Wednesday at the latest. Which meant that on Wednesday Bryce had either decided to take a chance on Seton's cat-killing propensities, or had known that there was no longer anything to fear.

13

On Friday afternoon the suspects walked, drove or were driven to the small inn just outside Dunwich which Reckless had taken as his headquarters and there made their statements. They had always thought of the Green Man as their local pub—indeed they took it for granted that George Prike ran the place principally for their benefit—and the Inspector's choice was criticised as showing crass insensitivity and a general disregard for the comfort of others. Celia Calthrop was particularly bitter although she used the Green Man less than most and was scathing in her denunciation of George's folly in allowing himself to be inveigled into such an invidious position. She was not at all sure she would be happy to continue to buy her sherry from George if she were going to be reminded of Inspector Reckless every time she had a drink and a visit to the Saloon Bar would become intolerably traumatic. Latham and Bryce shared her view of the Inspector. Their first impression of him hadn't been favourable and thinking it over later they decided that they disliked him. Perhaps, as Bryce suggested, a too-close acquaintance with Seton's Inspector Briggs had spoilt them for the real thing. Briggs, who was occasionally called Briggsy by the Honourable Martin in an excess of spurious camaraderie, had a humility which they hadn't detected in Inspector Reckless. Despite his eminence at the Yard Briggsy was always happy to play second fiddle to Carruthers, and so far from resenting the Honourable Martin's interference with his cases, made a practice of calling him in when his special expertise was required. Since Carruthers was an expert on wine, women, heraldry, the landed gentry, esoteric poisons and the finer points of the minor Elizabethan poets, his opinion was frequently invaluable. As Bryce pointed out, Inspector Briggs did not turn people out of their favourite pub nor gaze at them fixedly from dark, morose eyes as if hearing only half they were saying and disbelieving that. Nor did he give the impression of regarding writers as no different from lesser men except in their capacity to invent more ingenious alibis. Inspector Briggs' suspects, if required to make statements—which was seldom—made them in the comfort of their own homes attended by obsequious policemen and with Carruthers present to ensure, in the nicest possible way, that Inspector Briggs kept his place.

They were careful not to arrive at the inn together; the artless confidences of Thursday night had been followed by a certain wariness. By Friday afternoon there had been time to think and Seton's death was seen less as a bizarre excursion of fiction into life than as a highly embarrassing fact. Certain unpalatable truths were recognized. Seton, admittedly, had last been seen alive in London, but his mutilated body had been floated out to sea from Monksmere Beach. It hardly needed any complicated calculations with charts, wind force or tide drift and race, to convince anyone of that. He might well have run into trouble in London in his naive search for copy, but the forged manuscript, the severed hands, the telephone call to Seton House, had a more local flavour. Celia Calthrop was the most voracious supporter of the London-gang-of-crooks theory, but even she could advance no convincing explanation of how the criminals knew where Sheldrake was beached or why they had chosen to bring the corpse back to Suffolk. "To throw suspicion on us, of course", was generally thought to beg more questions than it answered.

After the statements were made there was a certain amount of telephoning. Cautiously, as if half-believing that the lines were being tapped, the little community exchanged those scraps of information, rumour or guesswork which pieced together probably told as much as there was to know. They were reluctant at present to meet each other, afraid of what they might be told, or worse, inadvertently tell. But they were avid for information.

Telephone calls to Pentlands were invariably answered by Jane Dalgliesh, courteous, uncooperative and uncommunicative. No one liked to betray himself by asking to speak to Adam except Celia Calthrop and she met with such little success that she found it more convenient to believe that he had nothing to tell. But they spoke to each other, gradually abandoning caution in their need to confide and their hunger for news. The snippets of information, most of which changed subtly in the telling and some of which were founded on hope rather than fact, built up an incomplete and amphigoric picture. No one had changed his or her story and the various alibis for Tuesday night which had been put forward with such eager confidence had stood up to such investigation as there had been time for. It was understood that Latham's house guest had made no trouble in supporting his story, but as Reckless was completely uncommunicative and Latham was maintaining a gentlemanly reticence, the general curiosity about her name seemed likely to remain unsatisfied. The news that Eliza Marley had admitted to spending Tuesday night in London created a certain amount of pleasurable speculation, stimulated by Celia's frequent and unconvincing explanations of her niece's need to visit the London Library. As Bryce said to Latham, one could understand it if the poor girl had been at Redbrick but there had been quite a number of books in Cambridge when he was up. Both Bryce's and Latham's cars had been examined by the police but the owners had made so little protest over the proceedings that it was commonly agreed that they had nothing to fear. It was reported that Dr. Forbes-Denby had been gratifyingly offensive to Inspector Reckless on the telephone while Bryce was at the Green Man and had insisted on regarding Bryce's telephone call as a matter of sacred confidence between himself and his patient. Eventually, however, on Bryce's almost hysterical insistence he had agreed that it had been made. Celia's story that she had given Seton the idea for a floating corpse was supported by an old Walberswick fisherman who called at the Green Man to say that he remembered Mr. Seton enquiring some months previously where a body in a dinghy would come ashore if it were pushed out from Monksmere Beach. As no one had doubted Celia's statement this wasn't regarded as more than mildly interesting. In face of their united wish to find support for the London-gang-of-crooks theory it was depressing that no one except Bryce had seen any strangers at Monksmere on the Wednesday night. He had been outside bringing in wood from his shed shortly after seven when a motor cyclist had come roaring down the lane from the road and had reversed just outside his cottage. Justin abominated motor cycles and the noise had been quite unendurable. He had shouted his protest and the lad had retaliated by roaring up and down in front of the cottage for several minutes, making what Bryce described as obscene gestures. Eventually with a parting blast of his horn he had roared away. It wasn't known what Reckless made of this although he did ask Bryce for a full description of the cyclist, and would probably have noted it down if Bryce had been able to provide it. But the man had worn a black leather suit with helmet and goggles and Bryce could say no more than that he was obviously young and his manners were abominable. But Celia was sure he was a member of the gang. What else would he be doing at Monksmere?

By midday on Saturday the rumours had grown and multiplied. Digby had been left one hundred thousand, two hundred thousand, half a million; the post-mortem was held up because Dr. Sydenham couldn't discover the cause of death; the cause of death was drowning, strangulation, poison, suffocation, haemorrhage; Forbes-Denby had told Reckless that Seton was good for another twenty years; Seton's heart was liable to give out at any moment; Adam Dalgliesh and the Inspector were hardly on speaking terms; Reckless would have arrested Jane Dalgliesh if only he could have discovered a motive; Sylvia Kedge was being very difficult and wouldn't accept the legacy of £300 which Digby had offered to pay her; Reckless had called at Priory House late on Friday night and he and his men had been seen with torches on the cliff path; the inquest was to be held on Wednesday at two-thirty. Only on the last was there unanimity. The inquest was certainly arranged for the following Wednesday. Digby Seton and Sylvia Kedge had been summoned to attend. Those who had a choice in the matter were uncertain whether their presence would arouse curiosity, help allay suspicion or be prudent as showing a proper respect for the dead.

On Saturday morning it was made known that Inspector Reckless had left Monksmere for London by car late on Friday and wasn't expected back until Sunday morning. Presumably he had gone to check on the London alibis and investigate the Cadaver Club. There was no surprise that he was expected back so shortly. It was plain that he knew only too well where his business lay. But even this temporary absence was a relief. It was as if a cloud lifted from Monksmere Head. That gloomy, silently accusing presence had taken his preoccupations elsewhere and the air felt freer for his going. He left behind a restlessness which found relief in action. Everyone seemed anxious to get away from Monksmere. Even Jane Dalgliesh and her nephew who were the least affected by Reckless, were seen to set off early along the beach in the direction of Sizewell laden with painting paraphernalia, binoculars and knapsacks. It was obvious that they wouldn't be back until after dark. Latham drove off soon afterwards; the Jaguar was doing sixty-five when it passed Rosemary Cottage and Celia observed tartly that Oliver was off again on one of his attempts to break his neck. She and Eliza were to take Sylvia Kedge on a picnic to Aldeburgh but Eliza changed her mind just before they were due to start and set off on a solitary walk to Walberswick. No one knew what Digby Seton had planned, but a telephone call to Seton House by Miss Calthrop who hoped to persuade him to join the picnic, met with no reply. Bryce told everyone that he was driving to a country house sale just outside Saxmundham where he hoped to bid for some seventeenth-century porcelain. By half-past nine he too was far away and Monksmere was left to the half dozen autumn trippers who came in ones and twos throughout the day to park their cars in Tanner's Lane and to the occasional couple of walkers from Dunwich or Walberswick trudging along the sand dunes to the bird sanctuary.

Reckless must have driven back to Monksmere late on Saturday. When dawn broke his car was already outside the Green Man, and soon after nine o'clock Sergeant Courtney had rung most of the suspects to request their presence at the inn. The invitation was perfectly polite but no one was under the illusion that there was any choice in the matter. They took their time about arriving and, once again, there was a tacit understanding that they wouldn't arrive together. Sylvia Kedge was collected as usual in a police car by Sergeant Courtney. There was a feeling that Sylvia was, on the whole, quite enjoying herself.

Maurice Seton's portable typewriter was ready for them at the Inn, placed squat and shining on the edge of a small oak table in the saloon bar. The attentions of the finger print men and the typewriter experts seemed to have given it an added lustre. It looked at once ordinary and menacing, innocent and dangerous. It was, perhaps, the most intimate object that Seton had owned. Looking at the gleaming keyboard it was impossible not to think with repugnance of those bleeding stumps, to wonder what had happened to the severed hands. They knew at once why it was there. They were required to type two passages of prose; the description of Carruther's visit to the nightclub and of the handless corpse, drifting out to sea.

Sergeant Courtney, who was in charge of the exercise, was beginning to fancy himself as a student of human nature and the different reactions of his suspects provided gratifying material. Sylvia Kedge took some time to settle herself but once started the strong fingers, bony as a man's, danced above the keys to produce, in an incredibly short time, two accurate copies elegantly set out and perfectly typed. It is always satisfying to see a job performed perfectly and Sergeant Courtney received Miss Kedge's effort in respectful silence. Miss Dalgliesh, who arrived at the Inn twenty minutes later, was unexpectedly competent. She had been used to typing her father's sermons and the Church magazine and had taught herself with the aid of a manual. She used all five fingers correctly although her speed was only moderate and, unlike

Miss Kedge, she kept her eyes firmly on the keys. Miss Calthrop, staring at the machine as if she hadn't seen one before, protested shortly that she couldn't type—all her work was dictated on tape—and didn't see why she should waste her time trying. Eventually she was persuaded to make a start and after thirty minutes' effort, produced an appallingly typed two pages which she flourished at the Sergeant with the air of a vindicated martyr. Observing the length of Miss Calthrop's nails, Courtney was only surprised that she had managed to depress the keys. Bryce, when he could bring himself to touch the typewriter, was surprisingly quick and accurate although he found it necessary to keep up a scathing commentary on the style of the prose. Latham was almost as expert as Miss Kedge and rattled away in sullen silence. Miss Marley said briefly that she couldn't type but had no objection to trying. She refused Courtney's help, spent about five minutes examining the keyboard and the carriage and settled down to the laborious task of copying the passage, word by word. The result was quite creditable and Sergeant Courtney privately marked Miss Marley as an intelligent worker, in contrast to her aunt's assessment of "Could do better if she tried". Digby Seton was hopeless, but even Courtney couldn't believe that the man was faking. In the end, to everyone's relief he was allowed to give up. Predictably, none of the copies, including Digby's abortive effort, bore any resemblance to the originals. Sergeant Courtney, who believed that the second, and probably the first also, had been typed by Maurice Seton, would have been surprised if they had. But the final verdict would not be his. The copies would now be sent to an expert and examined for more subtle similarities. He didn't tell his suspects this; but then, he didn't need to. They hadn't read their Maurice Seton for nothing.

Before they left the inn their finger prints were taken. When her turn came, Miss Calthrop was outraged. She began for the first time to regret the desire to economize which had made her earlier decide not to seek the help of her solicitor. But she mentioned his name freely, together with that of her

Member of Parliament, and the Chief Constable. Sergeant Courtney, however, was so reassuring, so understanding of her feelings, so anxious for her help, so different in every way from that uncouth Inspector, that she was at last persuaded to cooperate. "Silly old bitch," thought the Sergeant as he directed the pudgy fingers. "If the rest of them make half this fuss I'll be lucky to be through before the old man gets back."

But the rest of them made no fuss at all. Digby Seton was tediously facetious about the whole proceedings, attempting to hide his nervousness by an exaggerated interest in the technique. Eliza Marley was sulkily aquiescent, and Jane Dalgliesh's thoughts appeared to be elsewhere. Bryce disliked it most. There was something portentous and irrevocable about parting with a symbol so uniquely peculiar to himself. He understood why primitive tribes were so careful that no scraps of their hair should fall into an enemy's hand. As he pressed his fingers on the pad with a moue of distaste he felt that virtue had gone out of him.

Oliver Latham jabbed his fingers into the pad as if it were Reckless's eye. When he looked up, he saw that the Inspector had come quietly in and was watching him. Sergeant Courtney got to his feet. Reckless said:

"Good evening, Sir. That's just a formality."

"Oh, I know all about that, thank you. The Sergeant has trotted out all the routine reassurance. I was wondering where you'd got to after your trip to town. I hope you enjoyed yourself questioning—as you would no doubt term her—'my lady friend'. And the porter at the flat? Duncombe was cooperative, I hope?"

"Everyone was very helpful, thank you, Sir."

"Oh, I'm sure they were! I've no doubt they enjoyed themselves immensely. Things are a bit quiet in town at present. I must be providing the best bit of gossip in weeks. And as we're all being so cooperative, what about a little cooperation from your end? I suppose there's no objection to my knowing how Seton died?"

"None at all, Sir—in due course. But we haven't got the P.M. report yet."

"Your chap's being a bit slow, isn't he?"

"On the contrary, Sir. Dr. Sydenham is very quick. But there are still a number of tests to be done. This isn't a straightforward case."

"I should rank that remark, Inspector, as the understatement of the year."

Taking his handkerchief from his pocket Latham carefully wiped his already clean fingers. Watching him the Inspector said quietly:

"If you're so impatient, Mr. Latham, why not ask some of your friends? You know as well as I do that someone at Monksmere could tell you precisely how Maurice Seton died."

14

Since his half-brother's death Digby Seton had taken to dropping in at Rosemary Cottage for meals, and his neighbours didn't fail to remark with wry amusement on just how often the Vauxhall was to be seen parked on the grass verge outside the cottage. They conceded that Celia was unlikely to discourage the company of a very rich young man but Digby's motives were less obvious. No one assumed that the charms of Eliza attracted him or that he saw in her sullen gracelessness a means of getting his hands on Maurice's capital. On the whole, people thought that he probably preferred Celia's food, uninteresting though it was, to the tedium of driving twice a day into Southwold or the effort of cooking for himself and that he was glad to get out of the way of Sylvia Kedge. Since the murder the girl had haunted Seton House with the persistence of a funeral mute waiting for her pay. The obsessional care which she had given to Maurice's work now seemed to be devoted to his house and she tidied, polished, cleaned, counted linen and dragged herself about on her crutches, duster in hand as if she expected the late owner to reappear any minute and run his finger over the window ledges. As Digby told Eliza Marley, it made him nervous. He had never liked Seton House which, despite its bright modernity, he found curiously sinister and depressing. Now, when those smouldering black eyes were liable to turn on him from every corner and cupboard, he felt he was living in one of the gloomier Greek dramas with the Eumenides lurking outside ready to make their entrance.

The remark had interested Eliza since it suggested that Digby might be more perceptive and sensitive than was commonly assumed. Without being in the least attracted to him physically she was beginning to find him interesting, even a little intriguing. It was surprising what the possession of £200,000 could do for a man. Already she could detect the subtle patina of success, the assurance and complacency which the possession of power or money invariably gives. The glandular fever had left her depressed and fatigued. In this mood, without the energy to work and fretted by boredom, almost any company was better than none. Despising the easy capitulation to self interest which had changed her aunt's opinion of him overnight from Maurice's problem brother to a perfectly charming young man, she nevertheless was beginning to admit that there might be more in Digby Seton than met the eye. But not much more.

He hadn't accepted Miss Calthrop's invitation to dinner on Sunday night but he turned up at Rosemary Cottage shortly after nine and having arrived was apparently in no hurry to leave. It was now nearly eleven but he was still there, swivelling himself to and fro on the piano stool and spasmodically playing snatches of his own or other people's tunes. Eliza, curled into her fireside chair, watched and listened and was in no hurry for him to go. He didn't play badly. There was no real talent there, of course, but when he was taking trouble, which was seldom, he was agreeably competent. She remembered that there had once been talk by Maurice of making a pianist out of Digby. Poor Maurice! That was when he was still desperately trying to persuade himself that his only living relative had some qualities to justify the relationship. Even when Digby was still at school his modest successes, the time he had won the boxing championship, for example, had been trumpeted by Maurice as major achievements. It was unthinkable that Maurice Seton's half-brother should be entirely without some talent. And nor was he. He had, single-handed, designed and built Sheldrake and had sailed her with competence even if his enthusiasm had only lasted a couple of seasons. But this hearty gamesmanship, in some way so untypical of Digby, was hardly likely to impress an intellectual snob like Maurice. In the end, of course, he had given up pretending just as Celia had given up hope that her niece was pretty, that she was going to have an orthodox success as a woman. Eliza glanced across at the large coloured photograph of herself that bore witness to Celia's humiliating and ludicrous ambitions. It had been taken when she was eleven, three years after the death of her parents. The thick dark hair was preposterously curled and ribboned, the white organdie dress with its pink sash looked vulgarly inappropriate to such a heavy featured and graceless child. No, it hadn't taken her aunt long to shed that particular delusion. But then, of course, it had been succeeded by another; dear Eliza, if she couldn't be pretty, had to be clever. Now the theme was: "My niece has a brilliant brain. She's at Cambridge, you know." Poor Aunt Celia! It was petty to grudge her this vicarious intellectual pleasure. After all she was paying hard cash for it. But Eliza felt some sympathy with Digby Seton. To an extent both of them had suffered from the pressure of another's personality, both had been accepted for qualities which they had no hope of ever possessing, both had been marked down as a bad buy.

On impulse she suddenly asked him:

"Which of us do you think killed your brother?"

He was syncopating a number from one of the recent London shows, inaccurately and rather too loudly for comfort. He had almost to shout above the noise of his own row:

"You tell me. You're the one who's supposed to be clever."

"Not as clever as Aunt makes out. But clever enough to wonder why it was I you phoned to meet you at Saxmundham. We've never been particularly friendly."

"Perhaps I thought it was time we were. Anyway, assuming I wanted a free lift to Monksmere, who else could I phone?"

"There is that. And, assuming you wanted an alibi for the time of the train journey."

"I had an alibi. The ticket collector recognized me; and I had an interesting chat with an old gentleman in the carriage about the naughtiness of the modern generation. I expect he would remember me. I can prove I was on that train, darling, without your help."

"But can you prove where you got on?"

"Liverpool Street. It was pretty crowded so I don't suppose anyone noticed me; but let Reckless try to prove that I didn't. Why are you so suspicious all of a sudden?"

"I'm not really. I don't see how you could have done it."

"Thank you for nothing. Nor do the police at West Central Station."

The girl shivered and said with sudden force: "Those hands—it was a horrible thing to do. Horrible! Don't you feel that? Particularly to a writer. Horrible and significant. I don't think you hated him that much."

He dropped his hands from the keys and swung round to face her.

"I didn't hate him at all. Damn it, Eliza! Do I look like a murderer?"

"How should I know? You're the one with the motive. £200,000 worth."

"Not until I get a wife. What about applying for the job?"

"No thank you. I like men to have an I.Q. at least approximate to mine. We wouldn't suit. What you want for the Club, surely, is a glamorous blonde with a forty-inch bust, a heart of low carat gold, and a mind like a calculating machine."

"Oh no!" he said seriously. "I know what I want for the Club. And now I've got the money I can pay for it. I want class."

The door into the study opened and Miss Calthrop poked her head through and gave them a vaguely puzzled look. She spoke to Eliza:

"I seem to have lost one of my new tapes. You haven't seen it, I suppose?"

Her niece's only response was a disinterested shrug but Digby sprang to his feet and peered hopefully around the room as if expecting the reel to materialize on top of the piano or pop out from under the cushions. Watching his ineffectual antics Eliza thought:

"Quite the little gentleman, aren't we? He's never bothered with Auntie before. What the hell is he playing at, anyway?"

The search was, of course, unsuccessful and Digby turned his charming deprecatory smile on Miss Calthrop.

"So sorry. It doesn't seem to be here."

Celia, who had been waiting with ill-concealed impatience, thanked him and went back to her work. As soon as the door closed behind her Digby said:

"She's taking it rather well, isn't she?"

"Taking what?"

"Maurice's Will. After all, if it weren't for me she'd be a very wealthy woman."

Did the fool really imagine that they didn't know it, that the arithmetic had somehow escaped them? She glanced across at him and caught his look of secret satisfaction, complacent, amused. It came to her suddenly that he must know something about Maurice's death, that the secret smile meant more than a momentary satisfaction at their disappointment and his own good luck. It was on the tip of her tongue to utter a warning. If he really had discovered something he would be in danger. He was typical of the fool who stumbles on part of the truth and hasn't the sense to keep his mouth shut. But she checked herself, irritated by that glimpse of secret satisfaction. Probably she was only being fanciful. Probably he had guessed nothing. And if he had? Well, Digby Seton would have to look after himself, would have to take his chance like the rest of them.

15

In the dining room at Priory House, dinner was nearly over. Dalgliesh had enjoyed his meal. He wasn't sure exactly what he had expected. It could have been a six course dinner served on Sèvres china or a nut cutlet eaten off wooden plates and followed by communal washing-up. Neither would have surprised him. They had, in fact, been given an agreeable chicken casserole cooked with herbs and followed by a salad and cheeses. The Bordeaux rouge had been cheap and a little rough but there had been plenty of it and Dalgliesh, no wine snob, had never subscribed to the view that the only proper alternative to good wine is no wine at all. He sat now, content, almost happy, in a gentle daze of well-being and let his eyes wander over the immense room, where the four of them sat, dwarfed as puppets, round the simple oak table.

It was easy to see that the house had once been part of a monastery. This room must have been the refectory. It was a huge version of the sitting room at Pentlands but here the oak hammer beams smoked with age, arched against the roof like great trees and merged into a black void nearly twenty feet above the faint sphere of the six tall candles which lit the dining table. The fireplace was the stone hearth of Pentlands but magnified into a small cavern in which the great logs burned steady as coal. The six vaulted windows to seawards were shuttered now but Dalgliesh could still hear the murmur of the sea and, from time to time, a soft moan which suggested the wind was rising.

Alice Kerrison sat opposite Sinclair, a plump, quiet, self-possessed woman, sure of her place and chiefly concerned, as far as Dalgliesh could see, to ensure that Sinclair over-ate. When they were first introduced he had the immediate sensation that he had met her before, that he had even known her well. Then almost instantly he realized why. Here, personified, was the Mrs. Noah of his childhood's Noah's ark. Here was the same straight hair, black and smooth as paint, drawn back from a centre parting into a tight little bun at the nape of the neck. Here was the same dumpy and compact figure with its tiny waist and the well recalled face, round, ruddy cheeked and beaded with two bright eyes. Even her clothes were familiar. She wore a plain black dress, long sleeved and bordered at neck and cuffs with narrow bands of lace. The whole was as evocative of the doldrums of childhood Sundays at his father's vicarage as the sound of Church bells or the morning smell of clean woollen underwear.

He glanced across at her as she poured the coffee and wondered what her relationship with Sinclair was. It was hard to guess. She didn't treat him as if he were a genius; he didn't treat her as a servant. Obviously she enjoyed looking after him but there was something matter-of-fact, almost irreverent in her calm acceptance of him. At times, bringing the food to the table together as was their obvious habit, conferring a little anxiously over the wine, they seemed as close and secret as conspirators. He wondered what had prompted her to pack her bags that morning, six years ago, and leave Maurice Seton for Sinclair. It struck him that Alice Kerrison probably knew more about Seton and his relationship with his wife than anyone else in the world. He wondered what else she knew.

He let his eyes slew round to where Sinclair sat with his back to the fire. The writer looked smaller than his photographs suggested but the broad shoulders, the long, almost simian arms, still gave an impression of great strength. His face was thickening with age so that the features were smudged and amorphous as an underexposed print. The heavy folds of skin hung about his face. The tired eyes were sunk so deep under the springing brows that they were almost invisible, but there was no mistaking the proud carriage of his head nor that great dome of white hair which shone now like a burning bush in the light of the fire, reinforcing the impression of some archaic Jehovah. How old was he, Dalgliesh wondered. The last of his three great novels had been published over thirty years ago and he had been middle-aged then. Three books were a slight foundation for such a solid reputation. Celia Calthrop, peeved by her failure to persuade Sinclair to participate in a Monksmere Literary Festival, accept the dedication of one of her novels, or even invite her to tea, was fond of saying that he was overrated, that it was quantity as well as quality that constituted greatness. Sometimes Dalgliesh thought that she had a point. But, always, one returned to the novels with a sense of wonder. They stood like great rocks on the foreshore where so many literary reputations had crumbled like sandcastles in the changing tide of fashion. Priory House would one day disappear beneath the sea but Sinclair's reputation would stand.

Dalgliesh was not so naive as to suppose that a great writer is necessarily a good talker nor presumptious enough to expect Sinclair to entertain him. But his host had not been silent during the meal. He had spoken knowledgeably and appreciatively of Dalgliesh's two volumes of verse but not, his guest felt, out of any desire to please. He had the directness and self absorption of a child. As soon as a topic ceased to interest him he changed the subject. Most of the talk was of books although he had no further interest it seemed in his own, and his favourite light reading was, it appeared, detective fiction. He was completely unconcerned with world affairs. "Men will either have to learn to love each other, my dear Dalgliesh, in the entirely practical and unsentimental use of the word or they will destroy themselves. I have no further influence either way." And yet, Dalgliesh felt that Sinclair was neither disillusioned nor cynical. He had detached himself from the world but neither out of disgust nor despair; it was merely that, in extreme old age, he had simply ceased to care.

He was talking now to Jane Dalgliesh, discussing apparently whether the avocet was likely to nest that year. Both of them were giving the subject the serious attention which other topics had failed to excite. Dalgliesh looked across the table at his aunt. She was wearing a cherry red blouse in fine wool, high necked and with the sleeves buttoned almost as high as the elbows. It was an appropriate dress for dining out on the cold eastern seaboard and she had worn it with little variation as long as he remembered. But now, inexplicably, it was in fashion and to her individual, dégagé elegance was added the hint of a contemporary smartness which Dalgliesh found alien to her. Her left hand was resting against her cheek. The long brown fingers were heavy with the family rings which she wore only in the evenings. In the candle light the rubies and diamonds struck fire. They were talking now of a skull which Sinclair had recently picked up on his stretch of the beach. It was usual for the drowned graveyards to yield up their bones and, after a storm, walkers on the shore could expect to find an occasional femur or scapular bleached by the sea and friable with age. But it was less usual to find a whole skull. Sinclair was discussing its probable age and with some expertise. But so far there had been no mention of that other, more recent body. Perhaps, thought Dalgliesh, he had been wrong about the motive for this dinner party. Perhaps Sinclair wasn't interested in Seton's murder after all. But it was difficult to believe that he had merely had a whim to meet Jane Dalgliesh's nephew. Suddenly his host turned to him and said in his slow, rumbling voice:

"I suppose a great many people ask you why you choose to be a detective?"

Dalgliesh answered evenly:

"Not many whom I care to answer . . . I like the job; it's one I can do reasonably well; it allows me to indulge a curiosity about people and, for most of the time, anyway, I'm not bored by it."

"Ah yes! Boredom. The intolerable state for any writer. But isn't there something else? Doesn't being a policeman protect your privacy? You have a professional excuse for remaining uninvolved. Policemen are separate from other men. We treat them, as we do parsons, with superficial fellowship but essential distrust. We are uneasy in their company. I think you are a man who values his privacy."

"Then we are alike," suggested Dalgliesh. "I have my job. you have Priory House." Sinclair said:

"It didn't protect me this afternoon. We had a visit from your colleague, Inspector Stanley Gerald Reckless. Tell Mr. Dalgliesh about it, Alice."

Dalgliesh was wearying of disclaiming any responsibility for Reckless but was curious to know how Sinclair had discovered the Inspector's full names. Probably by the simple expedient of asking.

Alice Kerrison said:

"Reckless. It isn't a Suffolk name. He looked ill to me. An ulcer most likely. Worry and overwork maybe. . . ."

She could be right about the ulcer, thought Dalgliesh, remembering the pallor, the pain-filled eyes, the deep clefts between nose and mouth. He heard the calm voice continue:

"He came to ask if we had killed Mr. Seton."

"But with more tact, surely?" suggested Dalgliesh.

Sinclair said:

"He was as tactful as he knew how to be. But that's what he came for, nevertheless. I explained to him that I didn't even know Seton although I had tried to read one of his books. But he never came here. Just because I can no longer write myself I'm under no obligation to spend my time with those who never could. Fortunately Alice and I can give each other an alibi for Tuesday and Wednesday nights which we understand are the significant times. I told the Inspector that neither of us had left the house. I am not sure that he altogether believed me. Incidentally, Jane, he asked whether we had borrowed your chopper. I deduced from that question that you had unwittingly supplied the weapon. We showed the Inspector our two choppers, both in excellent order I am glad to say, and he could see for himself that no one had used them to chop off poor Maurice Seton's hands."

Alice Kerrison said suddenly.

"He was a wicked man and he's better dead. But there's no excuse for murder."

"In what way was he wicked?" asked Dalgliesh.

The question was a formality. He was going to be told whether he wanted it or not. He could feel Sinclair's amused and interested eyes searching his face. So this was one reason for the dinner party. It wasn't just that Sinclair hoped to gain information. He had some to give. Alice Kerrison was sitting bolt upright, her face blotched with emotion, her hands clasped under the table. She gave Dalgliesh the truculent, half-pleading look of an embarrassed child and muttered:

"That letter he wrote to her. It was a wicked letter, Mr. Dalgliesh. He drove her to death as surely as if he'd forced her into the sea and held her head under the water."

"So you read the letter?"

"Not all of it. She handed it to me almost unthinking and then took it back again when she'd pulled herself together. It wasn't a letter any woman would want another woman to read. There were things in it I couldn't ever tell a soul. Things I'd rather forget. He meant her to die. That was murder." Dalgliesh asked:

"Can you be sure he wrote it?"

"It was in his handwriting, Mr. Dalgliesh. All five pages of it. He only typed her name at the top, nothing more. I couldn't mistake Mr. Seton's hand." Of course not, thought Dalgliesh. And Seton's wife would have been even less likely to mistake it. So Seton had deliberately driven his wife to suicide. If this were true it was an act of wanton cruelty greater in degree but of the same nature as the killing of Bryce's cat. But somehow this picture of a calculating sadist was subtly out of focus. Dalgliesh had only met Seton twice but the man had never struck him as a monster. Was it really possible that this pedantic, nervous and self-opinionated little man with his pathetically over-valued talent could have nourished so much hatred? Or was this scepticism merely the arrogance of a detective who was beginning to fancy himself as a diagnostician of evil? After all even if one gave little Crippen the benefit of the doubt, there were still plenty of nervous, ineffectual men on record who had proved far from ineffectual when it came to getting rid of their wives. How could he, after two brief meetings, know the essential Seton as well as Alice Kerrison must have known him? And there was the evidence of the letter, a letter which Seton, whose carefully filed correspondence at Seton House was all typewritten, had taken the trouble to write with his own hand.

He was about to ask what Dorothy Seton had done with it when the telephone rang. It was an incongruously strident noise in the silence of that immense, candle-lit room. Dalgliesh, startled, realized that he had unreasonably taken it for granted that there was no electricity at Priory House. He peered around for the instrument. The bell seemed to be ringing from a bookcase in the dark recess at the far end of the room. Neither Sinclair nor Alice Kerrison made any move to answer it. Sinclair said:

"That will be a wrong number. No one ever rings us. We only have the telephone in case of emergency but the number isn't in the book." He glanced across at the instrument complacently as if gratified to know that it was actually in working order. Dalgliesh got up: "Excuse me," he said. "But it may be for me." He groped for the instrument and laid hold of its smooth coldness among the impedimenta which littered the top of the bookcase. The irritating noise ceased. In the quiet he could almost believe that everyone present could hear Inspector Reckless speaking.

"Mr. Dalgliesh? I'm speaking from Pentlands. Something has happened which I think you should know about. Would it be convenient for you to come now?"

Then, as Dalgliesh hesitated, he added:

"I've got the P.M. report. I think it will interest you."

He made it sound like a bribe, thought Dalgliesh. But he would, of course, have to go. The formal, unemphatic tone of the request didn't deceive either of them. If they had been working on a case together Superintendent Dalgliesh would have summoned Inspector Reckless, not the other way round. But they weren't working on a case together. And if Reckless wanted to interview a suspect—or even the nephew of a suspect—he could choose his own time and place. All the same, it would be interesting to know what he was doing at Pentlands. Miss Dalgliesh hadn't locked the cottage when they left for Priory House. Few people at Monksmere bothered to lock up and the possible murder of a neighbour hadn't induced his aunt to change her habits. But it was unlike Reckless to make himself so at home.

He made his excuses to his host who accepted them with little sign of regret. Dalgliesh suspected that Sinclair, unused to company other than his aunt, was glad enough to see their party reduced to the familiar three. For some reason of his own he had wanted Dalgliesh to hear Alice Kerrison's story. Now it had been told and he could speed his guest with satisfaction and some relief. He merely reminded Dagliesh to pick up his torch on the way out and instructed him not to return for his aunt as he and Alice would escort her home. Jane Dalgliesh seemed happy enough with this arrangement. Dalgliesh suspected that she was being tactful. Reckless had only asked to see him and his aunt had no wish to be an unwelcome third even in her own house.

He saw himself out, stepping into darkness so impermeable that at first his eyes could distinguish nothing but the white blur of the path at his feet. Then the clouds moved from the face of the moon and the night became visible, a thing of forms and shadows heavy with mystery and pungent with the sea. Dalgliesh thought how in London one could rarely experience the night, riven as it was by the glare of lights and the restlessness of men. Here it was an almost palpable presence so that there moved along his veins the stirring of an atavistic fear of darkness and the unknown. Even the Suffolk countryman, no alien to the night, could hardly walk these cliff paths without a sense of mystery. It was easy to understand how the local legends had grown that sometimes, on an autumn night, one could hear the muffled beat of horses' hoofs as smugglers brought their kegs and bales from Sizewell Gap to hide them in the marshes or carry them inland across the desolate Westleton heathlands. Easy, too, on such a night to hear from the sea the faint bells of long drowned churches, St. Leonard's, St. John's, St. Peter's and All Saints clanging their dirges for the souls of dead men. And now there might be new legends to keep the countryman indoors on the autumn nights. The October legends. One of a naked woman, pale under the moon, walking through the waves to her death: one of a dead and handless man drifting out on the tide.

Dalgliesh perversely decided to walk home along the edge of the cliff. It would add fifteen minutes to his journey but it wouldn't hurt Reckless, comfortably ensconced at Pentlands, to wait another quarter of an hour. He found the path with his torch and followed the little pool of light which moved before him like a wraith. He looked back at the house. It was formless now, a black mass against the night sky with no sign of habitation except the thin shafts of light between the dining room shutters and one high round window which blazed out like a cyclops eye. While he watched, the light went out. Someone, probably Alice Kerrison, had gone upstairs.

He was nearing the edge of the cliff now. The waves thudded more clearly in his ears and somewhere, piercingly shrill, a sea bird called. He thought that the wind might be rising although it was still little more than a strong breeze. But here, on this exposed headland, it was as if sea, land and sky shared a perpetual and gentle turbulence. The path was becoming more overgrown. For the next twenty yards it was little more than a tortuous clearing through the brambles and gorse whose thorned branches caught at his legs. He was beginning to think that it would have been wiser to take the inland path. The gratification of making Reckless wait struck him now as irrational and childish and certaintly not worth the ruining of a pair of perfectly good trousers. If Seton's body had been carried from Priory House through this prickly jungle there should be some evidence of its passing. Reckless would certainly have gone over the ground with care; he wondered what, if anything, he had found. And it wasn't only the path. There would be the forty or so rackety wooden steps down to the beach to be negotiated. Sinclair was a strong man despite his age and Alice Kerrison was a healthy countrywoman; but Seton small as he was, would have been literally a dead weight. It would have been an exhausting, almost impossible journey.

Suddenly he saw a white shape to the left of the path. It was one of the few remaining tombstones on this part of the cliff.

Most of them had long since crumbled with age or been swept under the sea to yield in time their quota of bones to the human debris washed up by the tides. But this one stood and, on impulse, Dalgliesh went over to examine it. It was taller than he had expected and the lettering was cut clear and deep. Crouching low, he shone his torch on the inscription:

In Memory of
Henry Willm. Scrivener
Shot from his horse by a party of
smugglers while travelling in these
parts, 24th Sept. 1786.
The cruel balls have pierced me to the heart
No time have I to pray ere I depart.
Traveller pause, thou knowest not the Day
When thou must meet thy Maker on the Way

Poor Henry Scrivener! What ill chance, Dalgliesh wondered, had brought him travelling on the lonely road to Dunwich. He must have been a man of some substance. It was a fine stone. He wondered how many years it would be before Scrivener, his stone and its pious exhortation were in turn swept away and forgotten. He was scrambling to his feet when the torch jerked in his hand and shone full on the grave itself. He saw with surprise that someone had opened it. The turf had been replaced, the brambles twisted together again to form a dense and prickly panoply, but the grave had undoubtedly been disturbed. He knelt again and gently shifted the soil with his gloved hands. It was light and friable. Hands other other than his had been there before. Within a few seconds he unearthed a femur, then a broken scapular and, finally, a skull. Henry Scrivener had been given companions in death. Dalgliesh guessed at once what had happened. This was Sinclair or Alice Kerrison's way of disposing of the bones they found on the beach. All of them were very old, all bleached by the sea. Someone, and he thought it was probably Alice, had wanted to give them a reburial in consecrated ground.

He was musing over this fresh insight into the ways of that

odd couple at Priory House and turning the skull over in his hands when he caught the soft thud of approaching footsteps. There was a rustle of parted branches and suddenly a dark figure was standing over him, blotting out the night sky. He heard Oliver Latham's light, ironic voice:

"Still detecting, Superintendent? You look, if I may say so, like an under-rehearsed First Grave Digger. What a glutton for work you are! But surely you can let poor Henry Scrivener rest in peace? It's a little late, I should have thought, to start investigating that particular murder. Besides, aren't you trespassing?"

"Rather less than you are at the moment," said Dalgliesh evenly.

Latham laughed:

"So you've been dining with R. B. Sinclair. I hope you appreciated the honour. And what did our great apostle of universal love have to say about Seton's peculiarly unpleasant end?"

"Not much."

Dalgliesh scooped a hole in the soft earth and began covering up the skull. He smoothed soil over the pale forehead and trickled it into the eye sockets and the gaps between the teeth. Without looking up he said:

"I didn't know you were fond of nocturnal walks."

"It's a habit I've only recently taken up. It's most rewarding. One sees such interesting sights."

He watched Dalgliesh as the reburial was completed and the turfs replaced. Then, without speaking, he turned to go. Dalgliesh called quietly after him:

"Did Dorothy Seton send you a letter shortly before she died?"

The dark figure stood stock still, then slowly turned. Latham asked softly:

"Is that any concern of yours?" And, as Dalgliesh hesitated he added.

"Then why ask?"

Without another word he turned again and disappeared into the darkness.

16

The light was on over the cottage porch but the sitting room was almost in darkness. Inspector Reckless was sitting alone in front of the dying fire rather like a guest who, unsure of his welcome, is making a propitiatory gesture of economizing on the lights. He rose as Dalgliesh entered and switched on a small table lamp. The two men faced each other in its soft but inadequate glow.

"Alone Mr. Dalgliesh? You had some trouble perhaps in getting away?"

The Inspector's voice was expressionless. It was impossible to detect either criticism or enquiry in the flat statement.

"I got away all right. I decided to walk back along the cliff. How did you know where to find me?"

"When I found the cottage empty I supposed you and Miss Dalgliesh would be dining somewhere in the district. I tried the most likely house first. There are developments which I wanted to discuss with you tonight and I didn't want to talk on the phone."

"Well, talk away. But what about something to drink?"

Dalgliesh found it almost impossible to keep the note of cheerful encouragement from his voice. He felt uncomfortably like a housemaster jollying along a promising but nervous examination candidate. And yet Reckless was entirely at ease. The sombre eyes gazed at him with no trace of embarrassment or servility. "For God's sake, what's wrong with me?" thought Dalgliesh. "Why can't I feel at ease with the man?"

"I won't have anything now, thank you Mr. Dalgliesh. I thought you'd be interested in the pathologist's report, I got it early this evening. Dr. Sydenham must have been up all last night with him. Would you like to take a guess at the cause of death?"

"No," thought Dalgliesh, "I wouldn't. This is your case and I wish to God you'd get on with solving it. I'm not in the mood for guessing games." He said:

"Asphyxia?"

"It was natural causes, Mr. Dalgliesh. He died of a heart attack."

"What?"

"There's no doubt of it. He had a mild angina complicated by a defect of the left antrim. That adds up to a pretty poor heart and it gave out on him. No asphyxia, no poisoning, no marks of violence apart from the severed hands. He didn't bleed to death, and he didn't drown. He died three hours after his last meal. And he died of a heart attack."

"And the meal was? As if I need to ask!"

"Fried scampi with sauce tartare. Green salad with French dressing. Brown bread and butter, danish blue cheese and biscuits, washed down with Chianti."

"I shall be surprised if he ate that at Monksmere," said Dalgliesh. "It's a typical London restaurant meal. What about the hands, by the way?"

"Chopped off some hours after death. Dr. Sydenham thinks they may have been taken off on Wednesday night, and that would be logical enough, Mr. Dalgliesh. The seat of the dinghy was used as a chopping block. There wouldn't be much bleeding but if the man did get blood on him there was plenty of sea to wash it away. It's a nasty business, a spiteful business, and I shall find the man who did it, but that's not to say it was murder. He died naturally."

"A really bad shock would have killed him, I suppose?"

"But how bad? You know how it is with these heart cases. One of my boys has seen this Dr. Forbes-Denby and he says that Seton could have gone on for years with care. Well, he was careful. No undue strain, no air travel, a moderate diet, plenty of comfort. People with worse hearts than his go on to make old bones. I had an aunt with that trouble. She survived two bombing-outs. You could never count on killing a man by shocking him to death. Heart cases survive the most extraordinary shocks."

"And succumb to a mild attack of indigestion. I know. That last meal was hardly the most appropriate eating for a heart case, but we can't seriously suppose that someone took him out to dinner with the intention of provoking a fatal attack of indigestion."

"Nobody took him out to dinner, Mr. Dalgliesh. He dined where you thought he might have done. At the Cortez Club in Soho, Luker's place. He went there straight from the Cadaver Club and arrived alone."

"And left alone?"

"No. There's a hostess there, a blonde called Lily Coombs. A kind of right-hand woman to Luker. Keeps an eye on the girls and the booze and jollies along the nervous customers. You know her, I daresay, if she was with Luker in fifty-nine when he shot Martin. Her story is that Seton called her to his table and said that a friend had given him her name. He was looking for information about the drug racket and had been told that she could help." Dalgliesh said:

"Lil isn't exactly a Sunday school teacher but, as far as I know, she's never been mixed up in the dope business. Nor has Luker—yet. Seton didn't tell her the name of his friend, I suppose?"

"She says that she asked but he wouldn't tell. Anyway, she saw the chance of making a few quid and they left the Club together at nine-thirty. Seton told her that they couldn't go back to his Club to talk because women weren't admitted. That's true; they aren't. So they drove around Hyde Park and the West End in a taxi for about forty minutes, he paid her five quid for her information—I don't know what sort of a yarn she pitched him—and he got out at Paddington Underground Station leaving her to take the cab back to the Cortez. She arrived back at ten-thirty and remained there in view of about thirty customers until one in the morning."

"But why leave in the first place? Couldn't she have spun him the yarn at his table?"

"She said he seemed anxious to get out of the place. The

waiter confirmed that he looked nervy and on edge. And Luker doesn't like her to spend too much time with one customer."

"If I know Luker he'd take an even poorer view of her leaving the Club for forty minutes to take a trip round Hyde Park. But it all sounds very respectable. Lil must have changed since the old days. Did you think it a likely story?"

Reckless said:

"I'm a provincial police officer, Mr. Dalgliesh. I don't take the view that every Soho tart is necessarily a liar. I thought she was telling the truth, although not necessarily the whole truth. And then you see, we've traced the cab driver. He confirmed that he picked them up outside the Club at nine-thirty and dropped Seton outside the District Line entrance at Paddington about forty minutes later. He said they seemed to be talking together very seriously for the whole of the journey and that the gentleman made notes in a pocket book from time to time. If he did I should like to know what happened to it. There was no pocket book on him when I saw the body."

Dalgliesh said:

"You've worked quickly. So the time he was last seen alive is pushed forward to about ten-ten. And he died less than two hours later."

"Of natural causes, Mr. Dalgliesh."

"I think he was intended to die."

"Maybe. But I'm not arguing with facts. Seton died at midnight last Tuesday and he died because he had a weak heart and it stopped beating. That's what Dr. Sydenham tells me and I'm not going to waste public money trying to prove that he's wrong. Now you're telling me that someone induced that heart attack. I'm not saying it's impossible. I am saying that there's no evidence yet to support it. I'm keeping an open mind on this case. There's a lot we don't know yet."

That remark struck Dalgliesh as a considerable understatement. Most of the facts Reckless didn't yet know were surely almost as crucial as the cause of death. He could have catalogued the unanswered questions. Why had Seton asked to be dropped at Paddington? Who, if anyone, was he on the way to meet? Where had he died? Where was his body from midnight on Tuesday onwards? Who moved it to Monksmere and why? If the death had indeed been premeditated how did the murderer contrive so successfully to make it look like natural death? And this led on to a question which Dalgliesh found the most intriguing of all. Having done so, why didn't he leave the body in London, dumped perhaps at the side of the road to be later identified as that of a middle-aged, unimportant detective novelist, who had been walking in London on his own mysterious business and had been overcome by a heart attack. Why bring the body back to Monksmere and stage an elaborate charade which couldn't fail to arouse suspicion of foul play and which would inevitably bring the whole Suffolk C.I.D. buzzing around his ears?

As if he could read Dalgliesh's thoughts Reckless said:

"We've no evidence that Seton's death and the mutilation of his body are directly related. He died of natural causes. Sooner or later we shall find out where. Then we shall get a lead on the person responsible for all the subsequent nonsense; the mutilation; the false telephone call to Digby Seton—if it were made; the two manuscripts sent to Miss Kedge—if they were sent. There's a joker in this pack and I don't like his sense of humour; but I don't think he's a killer."

"So you think that it's all an elaborate hoax? With what purpose?"

"Malice, Mr. Dalgliesh. Malice against the dead, or the living. The hope of throwing suspicion on other people. The need to make trouble. For Miss Calthrop, maybe. She doesn't deny that the handless corpse in a dinghy was her idea. For Digby Seton. He stands to gain most by his half-brother's death. For Miss Dalgliesh, even. After all, it was her chopper."

Dalgliesh said:

"That's pure conjecture. The chopper's missing, that's all we know. There's no evidence whatsoever that it was the weapon."

"There's evidence now. You see, it's been returned. Switch on the lights, Mr. Dalgliesh, and you'll see."

The chopper had, indeed, been returned. At the far end of the room stood a small eighteenth-century sofa table, a delicate and charming thing which Dalgliesh remembered from his childhood as part of the furniture of his grandmother's sitting room. The chopper had been driven into the centre, the blade splitting the polished wood almost in two, the shaft curving upward. In the bright centre light which now flooded the room Dalgliesh could see clearly the brown stains of blood on the blade. It would be sent for analysis, of course. Nothing would be left to chance. But he had no doubt that it was Maurice Seton's blood.

Reckless said:

"I came to let you know the P.M. report. I thought you might be interested. The door was half open when I arrived so I came in, calling for you. I saw the chopper almost at once. In the circumstances I thought I'd take the liberty of staying around until you arrived."

If he were gratified by the success of his little charade, he made no sign. Dalgliesh hadn't credited him with a dramatic instinct. It had been quite cleverly stage managed; the soft conversation in the gloaming, the sudden blaze of light, the shock of seeing something beautiful and irreplaceable wantonly and maliciously destroyed. He would have liked to have asked whether Reckless would have broken his news with such spectacular éclat if Miss Dalgliesh had been present. Well, why not? Reckless knew perfectly well that Jane Dalgliesh could have driven that chopper into the table before she and Dalgliesh left for Priory House. A woman who could cleave off a dead man's hands to provide herself with a little private entertainment was hardly likely to jib at the sacrifice of a sofa table in the same cause. There had been method in the Inspector's excursion into drama. He had been hoping to watch his suspect's eyes for the absence of that first unmistakable flicker of surprise and shock. Well, he hadn't got much out of Dalgliesh's reaction. Suddenly, cold with anger, he made up his mind. As soon as he could control his voice he said:

"I shall be going to London tomorrow. I would be grateful

if you would keep an eye on this place. I don't expect to be any longer than one night."

Reckless said:

"I shall be keeping an eye on everyone at Monksmere, Mr. Dalgliesh. I shall have some questions for them. What time did you and your aunt leave the cottage?"

"At about six-forty-five."

"And you left together?"

"Yes. If you're asking whether my aunt popped back on her own to fetch a clean hankie the answer is no. And, just to get the record straight, the chopper was not where it is now when we left."

Unprovoked, Reckless said calmly:

"And I arrived here just before nine. He had nearly two hours. Did you tell anyone about the dinner engagement, Mr. Dalgliesh?"

"No. I didn't, and I'm sure my aunt wouldn't have talked about it. But that's not really significant. We can always tell at Monksmere whether people are at home by the absence of lights."

"And you always leave your doors conveniently unlocked. It's all made very easy. And if things run true to form on this case, either all of them will be able to produce alibis, or none of them will." He walked over to the sofa table, and pulling an immense white handkerchief from his pocket he wrapped it round the shaft of the chopper and jerked the blade out of the table. He carried it to the door, then turned to face Dalgliesh:

"He died at midnight, Mr. Dalgliesh. Midnight. When Digby Seton had been in police custody for over an hour; when Oliver Latham was enjoying himself at the theatrical party in full view of two Knights, three Dames of the British Empire and half the culture hangers-on in London; when Miss Marley was safely tucked up in her hotel bed as far as I or anyone else knows; and when Justin Bryce was battling with his first attack of asthma. At least two of them have foolproof alibis and the other two don't seem particularly worried. . . . I forgot to tell you, by the way. There was a telephone call for you while I was waiting. A Mr. Max Gurney. He wants you to ring back as soon as possible. He said that you knew the number."

Dalgliesh was surprised. Max Gurney was the last of his friends to ring him when he was on holiday. More to the point, Gurney was a senior partner in the firm which published Maurice Seton. He wondered whether Reckless knew this. Apparently not, since he made no comment. The Inspector had been working at tremendous pace and there were few people connected with Seton who hadn't been interviewed. But either he hadn't yet got round to seeing Seton's publisher, or he had decided that there was nothing to be gained.

Reckless finally turned to go:

"Goodnight, Mr. Dalgliesh. . . . Please tell your aunt that I'm sorry about the table. . . . If you're right about this being murder we know one thing about our killer, don't we? He reads too many detective stories."

He was gone. As soon as the departing roar of his car had died away, Dalgliesh telephoned Max Gurney. Max must have been waiting for he answered immediately.

"Adam? Good of you to telephone so promptly. The Yard were very naughty about letting me know where you were but I guessed it might be Suffolk. When are you coming back to town? Could I see you as soon as you do?"

Dalgliesh said that he would be in London next day. He could hear Max's voice lighten with relief.

"Then could we lunch together? Oh, lovely. At one o'clock say? Have you any preference about the place?"

"Max, weren't you once a member of the Cadaver Club?"

"I still am; would you like to lunch there? The Plants really do one very well. Shall we say one o'clock then at the Cadaver? Are you sure that's all right?"

Dalgliesh said that nothing would suit him better.

17

In the ground floor sitting room of the dolls' house in Tanner's Lane Sylvia Kedge heard the first sighs of the rising wind and was afraid. She had always hated a stormy night, hated the contrast between the violence around her and the deep calm of the cottage wedged damply into the shelter of the cliff. Even in a high wind the surrounding air was heavy and still as if the place bred a miasma of its own which no external force could disturb. Few storms shook the windows or set the doors and timbers of Tanner's Cottage creaking. Even in a high wind the branches of the elder bushes which clustered against the back windows only moved sluggishly as if they lacked strength to tap against the panes. Her mother, squatting in animal comfort in the fireside chair, used to say:

"I don't care what anyone says. We're very snug in here. I shouldn't like to be at Pentlands or Seton House on a night like this." It was her mother's favourite phrase. "I don't care what anyone says." Spoken always with the truculence of the widow with a grievance, permanently at odds with the world. Her mother had had an obsessional need of snugness, of smallness, of security. To her all nature was a subtle insult and in the peace of Tanner's Cottage she could shut from her thoughts more than the violence of the wind. But Sylvia would have welcomed the onslaught of cold, sea-heavy gusts against her door and windows. It would at least have reassured her that the external world existed and that she was part of it. It would have been infinitely less harrowing than this unnatural calm, this sense of isolation so complete that even nature seemed to pass her by as unworthy of notice.

But tonight her fear was sharper, more elemental than the unease of loneliness and isolation. She was afraid of being murdered. It had begun as a flirtation with fear, a nicely judged indulgence of that half pleasurable frisson which a sense of danger can bring. But suddenly and terrifyingly, her imagination was out of control. Imagined fear had become fear itself. She was alone in the cottage, and helpless. And she was horribly afraid. She pictured the lane outside, the path soft and moist with sand, the hedges rising black and high on either side. If the killer came for her tonight she would have no chance of hearing his approach. Inspector Reckless had asked her often enough and her answer had always been the same. It would be possible for a man treading warily to pass by Tanner's Cottage at night unseen and unheard. But a man burdened with a corpse? That had been more difficult to judge but she still thought it possible. When she slept she slept soundly with windows closed and curtains drawn. But tonight he wouldn't be carrying a body. He would be coming for her, and alone. Coming perhaps with a hatchet, or a knife, or twisting a length of rope in his hands. She tried to picture his face. It would be a face she knew; it had not needed the Inspector's insistent questions to convince her that someone living at Monksmere had killed Maurice Seton. But tonight the familiar features would be changed into a mask white and rigid with intent, the face of the predator stalking light footed towards his prey. Perhaps he was even now at the gate, pausing with his hand on the wood, wondering whether to risk the soft creak as it swung open. Because he would know that the gate creaked. Everyone at Monksmere must know. But why should he worry? If she screamed there would be no one near to hear. And he would know that she couldn't run away.

Desperately she looked round the sitting room at the dark and heavy furniture which her mother had brought with her when she married. Either the great ornate bookcase or the corner cupboard would have made an effective barrier to the door if only she could have moved them. But she was helpless. Heaving herself from the narrow bed she grasped her crutches and swung herself into the kitchen. In the glass of the kitchen cabinet she saw her face reflected, a pale moon with eyes like black pools, the hair heavy and dank like the hair of a drowned woman. A witch's face. She thought. "Three hundred years ago they would have burned me alive. Now they aren't even afraid of me." And she wondered whether it was worse to be feared or pitied. Jerking open the cabinet drawer she seized a fistful of spoons and forks. These she balanced in a row on the edge of the narrow window ledge. In the silence she could hear her own breath rasping against the pane. After a moment's thought she added a couple of glasses. If he tried to climb in through the kitchen window at least she would have some warning in the tinkle of falling silver and the smashing of glass. Now she looked round the kitchen for a weapon. The carving knife? Too cumbersome and not really sharp enough. The kitchen scissors perhaps? She opened the blades and tried to pull them apart but the rivet was too strong even for her tough hands. Then she remembered the broken knife which she used to peel vegetables. The tapering blade was only six inches long but it was keen and rigid, the handle short and easy to grasp. She whetted the blade against the stone edge of the kitchen sink and tested it with her finger. It was better than nothing. Armed with this weapon she felt better. She checked again that the bolts on the front door were secure and placed a row of small glass ornaments from the corner cupboard on the window ledge of the sitting room. Then, without taking the braces from her legs she propped herself upright on the bed, a heavy glass paper weight on the pillow beside her, the knife in her hand. And there she sat, waiting for fear to pass, her body shaken with her heart beats, her ears straining to hear through the far away sighing of the wind, the creak of the garden gate, the tinkle of falling glass.

Book Two

I

Dalgliesh set out next morning after an early and solitary breakfast, pausing only to telephone Reckless to ask for Digby Seton's London address and the name of the hotel at which Elizabeth Marley had stayed. He didn't explain why he wanted them and Reckless didn't ask but gave the information without comment except to wish Mr. Dalgliesh a pleasant and successful trip. Dalgliesh replied that he doubted whether it would be either but that he was grateful for the Inspector's cooperation. Neither troubled to disguise the irony in his voice. Their mutual dislike seemed to be crackling along the wire.

It was a little unkind to call on Justin Bryce so early but Dalgliesh wanted to borrow the photograph of the beach party. It was several years old but was a good enough likeness of the Setons, Oliver Latham and Bryce himself to help an identification.

Bryce came padding down in response to his knock. The earliness of the hour seemed to have bereft him of sense as well as speech and it was some time before he grasped what Dalgliesh wanted and produced the snap. Only then, apparently, was he struck with doubt about the wisdom of handing it over. As Dalgliesh was leaving he came scurrying down the path after him, bleating anxiously: "You won't tell Oliver that I let you have it, will you Adam? He'll be absolutely furious if he learns that one is collaborating with the police. Oliver is the teeniest bit distrustful of you, I'm afraid. One must implore secrecy."

Dalgliesh made reassuring noises and encouraged him back to bed, but he was too familiar with Justin's vagaries to take him at his face value. Once Bryce had breakfasted and gained strength for the day's mischief he would almost certainly be telephoning Celia Calthrop for a little cosy mutual speculation about what Adam Dalgliesh could be up to now. By noon all Monksmere including Oliver Latham would know that he had driven to London, taking the photograph with him.

It was a comparatively easy journey. He took the quickest route and, by half past eleven, he was approaching the city. He hadn't expected to be driving into London again so soon. It was like a premature ending to a holiday already spoilt. In a half propitiatory hope that this might not really be so, he resisted the temptation to call at his flat high above the Thames near Queenhithe and drove straight on to the West End. Just before noon he had garaged the Cooper Bristol in Lexington Street and was walking towards Bloomsbury and the Cadaver Club.

The Cadaver Club is a typically English establishment in that its function, though difficult to define with any precision, is perfectly understood by all concerned. It was founded by a barrister in 1892 as a meeting place for men with an interest in murder and, on his death, he bequeathed to the Club his pleasant house in Tavistock Square. The Club is exclusively masculine; women are neither admitted as members nor entertained. Among the members there is a solid core of detective novelists, elected on the prestige of their publishers rather than the size of their sales, one or two retired police officers, a dozen practising barristers, three retired judges, most of the better known amateur criminologists and crime reporters and a residue of members whose qualifiction consists in the ability to pay their dues on time and discuss intelligently the probable guilt of William Wallace or the finer points of the defence of Madeline Smith. The exclusion of women means that some of the best crime writers are unrepresented but this worries no one; the Committee take the view that their presence would hardly compensate for the expense of putting in a second set of lavatories. The plumbing at the Cadaver has, in fact, remained virtually unaltered since the Club moved to Tavistock Square in 1900 but it is a canard that the baths were originally purchased by George Joseph Smith. The Club is old-fashioned in more than its plumbing; even its exclusiveness is justified by the assumption that murder is hardly a fit subject for discussion in front of women. And murder at the Cadaver seems itself a civilized archaism, insulated from reality by time or the panoply of the law, having nothing in common with the sordid and pathetic crimes which took up most of Dalgliesh's working life. Murder here evokes the image of a Victorian maidservant, correct in cap and streamers, watching through a bedroom door as Adelaide Bartlett prepares her husband's medicine; of a slim hand stretched through an Edinburgh basement railing proffering a cup of cocoa and, perhaps, arsenic; of Dr. Lamson handing round Dundee cake at his wealthy brother-in-law's last tea party; or of Lizzie Borden, creeping, axe in hand, through the quiet house in Fall River in the heat of a Massachusetts summer.

Every club has its peculiar asset. The Cadaver Club has the Plants. The members are apt to say "What shall we do if we lose the Plants?" much as they might ask "What shall we do if they drop the Bomb?" Both questions have their relevance but only the morbid dwell on them. Mr. Plant has sired—one would almost believe for the benefit of the Club—five buxom and competent daughters. The three eldest, Rose, Marigold and Violet, are married and come in to lend a hand. The two youngest, Heather and Primrose, are employed in the dining room as waitresses. Plant himself is steward and general factotum and his wife is generally acknowledged one of the best cooks in London. It is the Plants who give the Club its atmosphere of a private town house where the family's comfort is in the hands of loyal, competent and discreet family servants. Those members who once enjoyed these benefits have the comfortable illusion that they are back in their youth, and the others begin to realize what they have missed. Even the eccentricities of the Plants are odd enough to make them interesting without detracting from their efficiency and there are few Club servants of whom this can be said.

Dalgliesh, although he was not a member of the Club, had

occasionally dined there and was known to Plant. Luckily, too, by that curious alchemy which operates in these matters, he was approved of. Plant made no difficulties about showing him round or answering his questions; nor was it necessary for Dalgliesh to emphasise his present amateur status. Very little was said but both men understood each other perfectly. Plant led the way to the small front bedroom on the first floor which Seton had always used and waited just inside the door while Dalgliesh examined the room. Dalgliesh was used to working under scrutiny or he might have been disconcerted by the man's stolid watchfulness. Plant was an arresting figure. He was six feet three inches tall, and broad shouldered, his face pale and pliable as putty with a thin scar sliced diagonally across his left cheekbone. This mark, the result of an undignified tumble from a bicycle on to iron railings in his youth looked so remarkably like a duelling scar that Plant had been unable to resist adding to its effect by wearing a pince-nez and cropping his hair en brosse, like a sinister Commander in an anti-Nazi film. His working uniform was appropriate, a dark blue serge with a miniature skull on each lapel; this vulgar conceit, introduced in 1896 by the Club's founder, had now, like Plant himself, been sanctified by time and custom. Indeed, members were always a little puzzled when their visitors commented on Plant's unusual appearance.

There was little to be seen in the bedroom. Thin terylene curtains were drawn against the grey light of the October afternoon. The drawers and wardrobe were empty. The small desk of light oak in front of the window held nothing but a clean blotter and a supply of club writing paper. The single bed, freshly made up, awaited its next occupant. Plant said:

"The officers from the Suffolk C.I.D. took away his typewriter and clothes, Sir. They looked for papers, too, but he hadn't any to speak of. There was a packet of buff envelopes and about fifty sheets of foolscap and a sheet or two of unused carbon paper but that's all. He was a very tidy gentleman, Sir."

"He stayed here regularly every October didn't he?"

"The last two weeks in the month, Sir. Every year. And he

always had this room. We've only got the one bedroom on this floor and he couldn't climb stairs because of his bad heart. Of course, he could have used the lift but he said he hadn't any confidence in lifts. So it had to be this room."

"Did he work in here?"

"Yes Sir. Most mornings from ten until half past twelve. That's when he lunched. And again from two-thirty until half past four. That's if he was typing. If it was a matter of reading or making notes he worked in the library. But there's no typing allowed in the library on account of disturbing other members."

"Did you hear him typing in here on Tuesday?"

"The wife and I heard someone typing, Sir, and naturally we thought it was Mr. Seton. There was a notice on the door saying not to disturb but we wouldn't have come in anyway. Not when a member's working. The Inspector seemed to think it might have been someone else in here."

"Did he now? What do you think?"

"Well, it could have been. The wife heard the typewriter going at about eleven o'clock in the morning and I heard it at about four. But we wouldn't either of us know whether it was Mr. Seton. It sounded pretty quick and expert like but what's that to go on? That Inspector asked whether anyone else could have got in. We didn't see any strangers about but we were both busy at lunch time and downstairs most of the afternoon. People walk in and out very freely, Sir, as you know. Mind you, a lady would have been noticed. One of the members would have mentioned it if there'd been a lady about the Club. But otherwise—well I couldn't pretend to the Inspector that the place is what he'd call well-supervised. He didn't seem to think much of our security arrangements. But, as I told him Sir, this is a Club not a police station."

"You waited two nights before you reported his disappearance?"

"More's the pity, Sir. And even then, I didn't call the police. I phoned his home and gave a message to his secretary, Miss Kedge. She said to do nothing for the moment and she would try to find Mr. Seton's half-brother. I've never met the gentleman myself but I think Mr. Maurice Seton did mention him to me once. But he's never been to the Club that I remember. That Inspector asked me particularly."

"I expect he asked about Mr. Oliver Latham and Mr. Justin Bryce too."

"He did, Sir. They're both members and so I told him. But I haven't seen either gentleman recently and I don't think they'd come and go without a word to me or the wife. You'll want to see this first floor bathroom and lavatory. Here we are. Mr. Seton used this little suite. That Inspector looked in the cistern."

"Did he indeed? I hope he found what he was looking for."

"He found the ballcock, Sir and I hope to God he hasn't put it out of action. Very temperamental this lavatory is. You'll want to see the library, I expect. That's where Mr. Seton used to sit when he wasn't typing. It's on the next floor as I think you know."

A visit to the library was obviously scheduled. Inspector Reckless had been thorough and Plant was not the man to let his protégé get away with less. As they crushed together into the tiny claustrophobic lift, Dalgliesh asked his last few questions. Plant replied that neither he nor any member of his staff had posted anything for Mr. Seton. No one had tidied his room or destroyed any papers. As far as Plant knew there had been none to destroy. Except for the typewriter and Seton's clothes, the room was still as he had left it on the evening he disappeared.

The library, which faced south over the square, was probably the most attractive room in the house. It had originally been the drawing room and, except for the provision of shelves along the whole of the west wall, looked much as it was when the Club took over the house. The curtains were copies of the originals, the wallpaper was a faded pre-Raphaelite design, the desks set between the four high windows were Victorian. The books made up a small but reasonably comprehensive library of crime. There were the notable British Trials and Famous Trials series, text books on medical jurisprudence, toxicology and forensic pathology, memoirs of judges, advocates, pathologists and police officers, a variety of books by amateur criminologists dealing with some of the more notable or controversial murders, text books on criminal law and police procedure, and even a few treatises on the sociological and psychological aspects of violent crime which showed few signs of having been opened. On the fiction shelves a small section held the Club's few first editions of Poe, Le Fanu and Conan Doyle; for the rest, most British and American crime writers were represented and it was apparent that those who were members presented copies of their books. Dalgliesh was interested to see that Maurice Seton had had his specially bound and embellished with his monogram in gold. He also noted that, although the Club excluded women from membership, the ban did not extend to their books, so that the library was fairly representative of crime writing during the last one hundred and fifty years.

At the opposite end of the room stood a couple of show cases containing what was, in effect, a small museum of murder. As the exhibits had been given or bequeathed by members over the years and accepted in the same spirit of uncritical benevolence they varied as greatly in interest as, Dalgliesh suspected, in authenticity. There had been no attempt at chronological classification and little at accurate labelling and the objects had been placed in the show cases with more apparent care for the general artistic effect than for logical arrangement. There was a flintlock duelling pistol, silver mounted and with gold-lined flashpans which was labelled as the weapon used by the Rev. James Hackman, executed at Tyburn in 1779 for the murder of Margaret Reay, mistress of the Earl of Sandwich. Dalgliesh thought it unlikely. He judged that the pistol was made some fifteen years later. But he could believe that the glittering and beautiful thing had an evil history. There was no need to doubt the authenticity of the next exhibit, a letter, brown and brittle with age from Mary Blandy to her lover thanking him for the gift of "powder to clean the Scotch pebbles"—the arsenic which was to kill her father and bring her to the scaffold. In the same case was a Bible with the signature "Constance Kent" on the flyleaf, a tattered rag of pyjama jacket said to have formed part of the wrapping around Mrs. Crippen's body, a small cotton glove labelled as belonging to Madeline Smith and a phial of white powder, "arsenic found in the possession of Major Herbert Armstrong." If the stuff were genuine there was enough there to cause havoc in the dining room and the show cases were unlocked. But when Dalgliesh voiced his concern Plant smiled:

"That's not arsenic, Sir. Sir Charles Winkworth said just the same as yourself about nine months ago. 'Plant', he said 'if that stuff's arsenic we must get rid of it or lock it up.' So we took a sample and sent it off to be analyzed on the quiet. It's bicarbonate of soda, Sir, that's what it is. I'm not saying it didn't come from Major Armstrong and I'm not denying it wasn't bicarb that killed his wife. But that stuff's harmless. We left it there and said nothing. After all, it's been arsenic for the last thirty years and it might as well go on being arsenic. As Sir Charles said, start looking at the exhibits too closely and we'll have no museum left. And now, Sir, if you'll excuse me I think I ought to be in the dining room. That is, unless there's anything else I can show you."

Dalgliesh thanked him and let him go. But he lingered himself for a few more minutes in the library. He had a tantalizing and irrational feeling that somewhere, and very recently, he had seen a clue to Seton's death, a fugitive hint which his sub-conscious mind had registered but which obstinately refused to come forward and be recognized. This experience was not new to him. Like every good detective, he had known it before. Occasionally it had led him to one of those seemingly intuitive successes on which his reputation partly rested. More often the transitory impression, remembered and analyzed, had been found irrelevant. But the subconscious could not be forced. The clue, if clue it were, for the moment eluded him. And now the clock above the fireplace was striking one. His host would be waiting for him.

There was a thin fire in the dining room, its flame hardly visible in the shaft of autumn sunlight which fell obliquely across tables and carpet. It was a plain, comfortable room, reserved for the serious purpose of eating, the solid tables well spaced, flowerless, the linen glistening white. There was a series of original "Phiz" drawings for the illustrations to Martin Chuzzlewit on the walls for no good reason except that a prominent member had recently given them. They were, Dalgliesh thought, an agreeable substitute for the series of scenes from old Tyburn which had previously adorned the room but which he suspected the Committee, tenacious of the past, had taken down with some regret.

Only one main dish is served at luncheon or dinner at the Cadaver Club, Mrs. Plant holding the view that, with a limited staff, perfection is incompatible with variety. There is always a salad and cold meats as alternative and those who fancy neither this nor the main dish are welcome to try if they can do better elsewhere. Today, as the menu on the library notice board had proclaimed, they were to have melon, steak and kidney pudding, and lemon soufflé. Already the first puddings, napkin swathed, were being borne in.

Max Gurney was waiting for him at a corner table, conferring with Plant about the wine. He raised a plump hand in episcopal salute which gave the impression both of greeting his guest and of bestowing a blessing on the lunches generally. Dalgliesh felt immediately glad to see him. This was the emotion which Max Gurney invariably provoked. He was a man whose company was seldom unwelcome. Urbane, civilized and generous he had an enjoyment of life and of people which was infectious and sustaining. He was a big man who yet gave an impression of lightness, bouncing along on small, high-arched feet, hands fluttering, eyes black and bright behind the immense horn-rimmed spectacles. He beamed at Dalgliesh.

"Adam! This is delightful. Plant and I have agreed that the Johannisberger Auslese 1959 would be very pleasant, unless you have a fancy for something lighter. Good. I do dislike discussing wine longer than I need. It makes me feel I'm behaving too like the Hon. Martin Carruthers."

This was a new light on Seton's detective. Dalgliesh said that he hadn't realized that Seton understood wine.

"Nor did he, poor Maurice. He didn't even care for it greatly. He had an idea that it was bad for his heart. No, he got all the details from books. Which meant, of course, that Carruther's taste was deplorably orthodox. You are looking very well, Adam. I was afraid that I might find you slightly derange under the strain of having to watch someone else's investigation."

Dalgliesh replied gravely that he had suffered more in pride than in health but that the strain was considerable. Luncheon with Max would, as always, be a solace.

Nothing more was said about Seton's death for twenty minutes. Both were engaged with the business of eating. But when the pudding had been served and the wine poured Max said:

"Now, Adam, this business of Maurice Seton. I may say I heard of his death with a sense of shock and" —he selected a succulent piece of beef, and speared it to a button mushroom and half a kidney— "outrage. And so, of course, have the rest of the firm. We do not expect to lose our authors in such a spectacular way."

"Good for sales, though?" suggested Dalgliesh mischievously.

"Oh no! Not really dear boy. That is a common misconception. Even if Seton's death were a publicity stunt, which, admit it, would suggest somewhat excessive zeal on poor Maurice's part, I doubt whether it would sell a single extra copy. A few dozen old ladies will add his last book to their library lists but that isn't quite the same thing. Have you read his latest, by the way? *One for the Pot,* an arsenic killing set in a pottery works. He spent three weeks last April learning to throw pots before he wrote it, so conscientious always. But no, I suppose you wouldn't read detective fiction."

"I'm not being superior," said Dalgliesh. "You can put it down to envy. I resent the way in which fictional detectives can arrest their man and get a full confession gratis on evidence which wouldn't justify me in applying for a warrant. I wish real life murderers panicked that easily. There's also the little matter that no fictional detective seems to have heard of Judges' Rules."

"Oh, the Honorable Martin is a perfect gentleman. You could learn a lot from him, I'm sure. Always ready with the apt quotation and a devil with the women. All perfectly respectable of course but you can see that the female suspects are panting to leap into bed with the Hon. if only Seton would let them. Poor Maurice! There was a certain amount of wish fulfilment there I think."

"What about his style?" asked Dalgliesh who was beginning to think that his reading had been unnecessarily restricted.

"Turgid but grammatical. And, in these days, when every illiterate debutante thinks she is a novelist, who am I to quarrel with that? Written I imagine with Fowler on his left hand and Roget on his right. Stale, flat and, alas, rapidly becoming unprofitable. I didn't want to take him on when he left Maxwell Dawson five years ago but I was outvoted. He was almost written out then. But we've always had one or two crime novelists on the list and we bought him. Both parties regretted it, I think, but we hadn't yet come to the parting of the ways."

"What was he like as a person?" asked Dalgliesh.

"Oh, difficult. Very difficult, poor fellow! I thought you knew him? A precise, self-opinionated, nervous little man perpetually fretting about his sales, his publicity or his book jackets. He overvalued his own talent and undervalued everyone else's, which didn't exactly make for popularity."

"A typical writer, in fact?" suggested Dalgliesh mischievously.

"Now Adam, that's naughty. Coming from a writer, it's treason. You know perfectly well that our people are as hard-working, agreeable and talented a bunch as you'll find outside any mental hospital. No, he wasn't typical. He was more unhappy and insecure than most. I felt sorry for him occasionally but that charitable impulse seldom survived ten minutes in his company."

Dalgliesh asked whether Seton had mentioned that he was changing his genre.

"Yes, he did. When I last saw him about ten weeks ago. I had to listen to the usual diatribe about the decline of standards and the exploitation of sex and sadism but then he told me that he was planning to write a thriller himself. In theory, of course, I should have welcomed the change, but, in fact, I couldn't quite see him pulling it off. He hadn't the jargon or the expertize. It's a highly professional game and Seton was lost when he went outside his own experience."

"Surely that was a grave handicap for a detective writer?"

"Oh, he didn't actually do murder as far as I know. At least, not in the service of his writing. But he kept to familiar characters and settings. You know the kind of thing. Cosy English village or small town scene. Local characters moving on the chess board strictly according to rank and station. The comforting illusion that violence is exceptional, that all policemen are honest, that the English class system hasn't changed in the last twenty years and that murderers aren't gentlemen. He was absolutely meticulous about detail though. He never described a murder by shooting, for example, because he couldn't understand firearms. But he was very sound on toxicology and his forensic medical knowledge was considerable. He took a great deal of trouble with rigor mortis and details like that. It peeved him when the reviewers didn't notice it and the readers didn't care."

Dalgliesh said:

"So you saw him about ten weeks ago. How was that?"

"He wrote and asked to see me. He came to London purposely and we met in my office just after 6.15 when most of the staff had left. Afterwards we came on here to dine. That's what I wanted to talk to you about Adam. He was going to alter his Will. This letter explains why." He took a folded sheet of writing paper from his wallet and handed it to Dalgliesh. The paper was headed "Seton House, Monksmere Head, Suffolk." The letter, dated 30th July, was typed and the typing, although accurate, was inexpert, with something about the spacing and the word division at the end of lines which marked it as the work of an amateur. Dalgliesh realized immediately that he had recently seen one other typescript by the same hand. He read:

Dear Gurney,

I have been thinking over our conversation of last Friday—and here I must digress to thank you again for a most enjoyable dinner—and I have come to the conclusion that my first instinct was right. There is absolutely no sense in doing things by half. If the Maurice Seton literary prize is to fulfil the great purpose which I plan for it the capital outlay must be adequate, not only to ensure that the monetary value of the award is commensurate with its importance, but also to finance the prize in perpetuity. I have no dependents with a legitimate claim on my estate. There are those people who may think they have a claim but that is a very different matter. My only living relative will be left a sum which hard work and prudence will enable him to augment should he choose to exercise these virtues. I am no longer prepared to do more. When this and other small bequests have been made there should be a capital sum of approximately £120,000 available to endow the prize. I tell you this so that you may have some idea of what I intend. As you know my health is not good and although there is no reason why I should not live for many years yet, I am anxious to get this affair under way. You know my views. The prize is to be awarded biennially for a major work of fiction. I am not interested particularly in encouraging the young. We have suffered enough in recent years from the self-pitying emotionalism of the adolescent writer. Nor do I favour social realism. A novel should be a work of imaginative craftsmanship not the dreary shibboleths of a social-worker's case book. Nor do I restrict the prize to detective fiction; what I understand by detective fiction is no longer being written.

Perhaps you will think over these few ideas and let me know what you suggest. We shall need trustees of course and I shall consult lawyers in regard to the terms of my new Will. At present, however, I am saying nothing about this plan to anyone and I rely on you to be equally discreet. There will inevitably be publicity when the details are known but I should much deplore any premature disclosures. I shall, as usual, be staying at the Cadaver Club for the last two weeks in October and I suggest that you get in touch with me there.

Yours sincerely,

MAURICE SETON.

Dalgliesh was conscious of Gurney's little black eyes on him as he read. When he had finished he handed back the letter, saying:

"He was expecting rather a lot of you, wasn't he? What was the firm getting out of it?"

"Oh, nothing, my dear Adam. Just a lot of hard work and worry and all of course for the greater glory of Maurice Seton. He didn't even restrict the prize to our list. Not that it would have been reasonable, I admit. He wanted to attract all the really big names. One of his chief worries was whether they would bother to apply. I told him to make the prize large enough and they'd apply all right. But £120,000! I never realized he was worth that."

"His wife had money. . . . Did he talk to anyone else about his plan do you know, Max?"

"Well, he said not. He was rather like a schoolboy about it. Tremendous swearings to secrecy and I had to promise I wouldn't even telephone him about it. But you see my problem. Do I, or do I not, hand this over to the police?"

"Of course. To Inspector Reckless of the Suffolk C.I.D., to be precise. I'll give you his address. And you'd better phone him to say it's on the way."

"I thought you'd say that. It's obvious, I suppose. But one has these irrational inhibitions. I know nothing of his present heir. But I imagine that this letter gives someone a whacking great motive."

"The best. But we've no evidence that his heir knew. And, if it's any comfort to you, the man with the strongest financial motive also has the strongest alibi. He was in police custody when Maurice Seton died."

"That was clever of him . . . I suppose I couldn't just hand this letter over to you, Adam?"

"I'm sorry, Max. I'd rather not."

Gurney sighed, replaced the letter in his wallet, and gave his attention to the meal. They did not talk again of Seton until lunch was over and Max was enveloping himself in the immense black cloak which he invariably wore between October and May, and which gave him the appearance of an amateur conjuror who has seen better days.

"I shall be late for our Board meeting if I don't hurry. We have become very formal, Adam, very efficient. Nothing is decided except by resolution of the whole Board. It's the effect of our new buildings. In the old days we sat closeted in our dusty cells and made our own decisions. It led to a certain ambiguity about the firm's policy but I'm not sure that was such a bad thing . . . Can I drop you anywhere? Who are you off to investigate next?"

"I'll walk, thank you Max. I'm going to Soho to have a chat with a murderer." Max paused, surprised.

"Not Seton's murderer? I thought you and the Suffolk C.I.D. were baffled. D'you mean I've been wrestling with my conscience for nothing?"

"No, this murderer didn't kill Seton although I don't suppose he would have had any moral objections. Certainly someone is hoping to persuade the police that he's implicated. It's L. J. Luker. Remember him?"

"Didn't he shoot his business partner in the middle of Piccadilly and get away with it? It was in 1959, wasn't it?"

"That's the man. The Court of Criminal Appeal quashed the verdict on grounds of misdirection. Mr. Justice Brothwick, through some extraordinary aberration, suggested to the jury that a man who made no reply when charged probably had something to hide. He must have realized the consequences as soon as the words were out of his mouth. But they were said. And Luker went free, just as he'd said he would."

"And how does he tie up with Maurice Seton? I can't imagine two men with less in common."

"That," said Dalgliesh, "is what I'm hoping to find out."

2

Dalgliesh walked through Soho to the Cortez Club. With his mind still freshened by the clean emptiness of Suffolk he found these canyoned streets, even in their afternoon doldrums, more than usually depressing. It was difficult to believe that he had once enjoyed walking through this shoddy gulch. Now even a month's absence made the return less tolerable. It was largely a matter of mood, no doubt, for the district is all things to all men, catering comprehensively for those needs which money can buy. You see it as you wish. An agreeable place to dine; a cosmopolitan village tucked away behind Piccadilly with its own mysterious village life, one of the best shopping centres for food in London, the nastiest and most sordid nursery of crime in Europe. Even the travel journalists, obsessed by its ambiguities, can't make up their minds. Passing the strip clubs, the grubby basement stairs, the silhouettes of bored girls against the upstairs window blinds, Dalgliesh thought that a daily walk through these ugly streets could drive any man into a monastery, less from sexual disgust than from an intolerable ennui with the sameness, the joylessness of lust.

The Cortez Club was no better and no worse than its neighbours. There were the usual photographs outside and the inevitable group of middle-aged, depressed-looking men eyeing them with a furtive lack of interest. The place wasn't yet open but the door yielded to his push. There was no one in the small reception kiosk. He went down the narrow stairs with their scruffy red carpet and drew aside the curtain of beads which divided the restaurant from the passage.

It was much as he remembered it. The Cortez Club, like its owner, had an inate capacity for survival. It looked a little smarter although the afternoon light showed up the tawdriness of the pseudo-Spanish decorations and the grubbiness of the walls. The floor was cluttered with tables, many only large enough for one and all too closely packed for comfort. But then, the customers did not come to the Cortez Club for family dinner parties, nor were they primarily interested in the food.

At the far end of the restaurant there was a small stage furnished only with a single chair and a large cane screen. To the left of the stage was an upright piano, its top littered with manuscript paper. A thin young man in slacks and sweater was curved against the instrument picking out a tune with his left hand and jotting it down with his right. Despite the sprawled attitude, the air of casual boredom, he was completely absorbed. He glanced up briefly as Dalgliesh came in but returned immediately to his monotonous stabbing at the keys.

The only other person present was a West African who was pushing a broom in leisurely fashion around the floor. He said in a low, soft voice:

"We're not open yet, Sir. Service doesn't begin until six-thirty."

"I don't want to be served, thank you. Is Mr. Luker in?"

"I'll have to enquire Sir."

"Please do so. And I'd like to see Miss Coombs too."

"I'll have to enquire, Sir. I'm not sure that she's here."

"Oh, I think you'll find that she's here. Tell her please that Adam Dalgliesh would like to speak to her."

The man disappeared. The pianist continued his improvisation without looking up, and Dalgliesh settled himself at the table just inside the door to pass the ten minutes which he judged Luker would feel it appropriate to keep him waiting. He spent the time thinking of the man upstairs.

Luker had said that he would kill his partner and he had killed. He had said that he wouldn't hang for it and he didn't hang. Since he could hardly have counted on Mr. Justice Brothwick's cooperation, the prediction had shown either uncommon prescience or remarkable confidence in his own luck. Some of the stories which had grown around him since his trial were no doubt apocryphal but he was not the man to repudiate them. He was known and accepted by the professional criminal classes without being one of them. They gave him the reverent half-superstitious respect of men who know exactly how much it is reasonable to risk, for one who in one irretrievable stride has stepped outside all the limits. There was an ambience of awe about any man who had come so close to that last dreadful walk. Dalgliesh was sometimes irritated to find that even the police weren't immune to it. They found it hard to believe that Luker, who had killed so casually to satisfy a private grudge, could content himself with running a string of second-class night clubs. Some more spectacular wickedness was expected of him than the manipulation of Licensing Laws or Income Tax returns and the selling of mildly erotic entertainment to his dreary expense account customers. But if he had other enterprises, nothing as yet was known of them. Perhaps there was nothing to know. Perhaps all he craved was this prosperous, semi-respectability, the spurious reputation, the freedom of this no-mans-land between two worlds.

It was exactly ten minutes before the coloured man returned to say that Luker would see him. Dalgliesh made his own way up the two flights to the large front room from which Luker chose to direct not only the Cortez but all his Clubs. It was warm and airless, over-furnished and under-ventilated. There was a desk in the middle of the room, a couple of filing cabinets against one wall, an immense safe to the left of the gas fire and a sofa and three easy chairs grouped around a television set. In the corner was a small washstand basin. The room was obviously designed to serve both as an office and a sitting room and succeeded in being neither. There were three people present; Luker himself, Sid Martelli, his general factotum at the Cortez, and Lily Coombs. Sid, in his shirt sleeves, was heating himself a small saucepan of milk on a gas ring at the side of the fire. He was wearing his usual expression of resigned misery. Miss Coombs, already in her evening black, was squatting on a pouffe in front of the gas fire varnishing her nails. She raised a hand in salute and gave Dalgliesh a wide, unworried smile. Dalgliesh thought that the manuscript description of her, whoever had written it, fitted her well enough. He couldn't personally detect the Russian aristocratic blood but this hardly surprised him since he knew perfectly well that Lil had been bred no further east than the Whitechapel Road. She was a large, healthy-looking blonde with strong teeth and the thick, rather pale skin which stands up well to ageing. She might be in her early forties. It was difficult to tell. She looked exactly as she had when Dalgliesh had first seen her five years earlier. Probably she would look much the same for another five years.

Luker had put on weight since their last meeting. The expensive suit was strained across his shoulders, his neck bulged over the immaculate collar. He had a strong, unpleasant face, the skin so clear and shining that it might have been polished. His eyes were extraordinary. The irises were set exactly in the centre of the whites like small grey pebbles, and were so lifeless that they gave the whole face a look of deformity. His hair, strong and black, came down low to a widow's peak imposing an incongruous touch of femininity to his face. It was cut short all over and shone like dog's hair, glossy and coarse. He looked what he was. But when he spoke his voice betrayed his origins. It was all there; the small town vicarage, the carefully fostered gentility, the minor public school. He had been able to change much. But he had not been able to alter his voice.

"Ah, Superintendent Dalgliesh. This is very pleasant. I'm afraid we're booked out this evening but Michael may be able to find you a table. You're interested in the floor show no doubt."

"Neither dinner nor the show, thank you. Your food seemed to disagree with the last of my acquaintances who dined here. And I like women to look like women, not nursing hippopotami. The photographs outside were enough. Where on earth do you pick them up?"

"We don't. The dear girls recognize that they have, shall we say, natural advantages, and come to us. And you mustn't be censorious, Superintendent. We all have our private sexual fantasies. Just because yours aren't catered for here it doesn't mean that you don't enjoy them. Isn't there a little saying about motes and beams? Remember, I'm a parson's son as well as you. It seems to have taken us rather differently, though." He paused as if for a moment interested in their separate reactions, then went on lightly:

"The Superintendent and I have a common misfortune, Sid. We both had a parson for dad. It's an unhappy start for a boy. If they're sincere you despise them as a fool: if they're not you write them off as a hypocrite. Either way, they can't win."

Sid, who had been sired by a Cypriot bartender on a mentally subnormal skivvy, nodded in passionate agreement.

Dalgliesh said:

"I wanted a word with you and Miss Coombs about Maurice Seton. It isn't my case so you don't have to talk if you don't want to. But you know that, of course."

"That's right. I don't have to say a damn word. But then I might be in a helpful accommodating mood. You can never tell. Try me."

"You know Digby Seton, don't you?"

Dalgliesh could have sworn that the question was unexpected. Luker's dead eyes flickered. He said:

"Digby worked here for a few months last year when I lost my pianist. That was after his Club failed. I lent him a bit to try and see him over but it was no go. Digby hasn't quite got what it takes. But he's not a bad pianist."

"When was he last here?"

Luker spread his hands and turned to his companions: "He did a week for us in May, didn't he, when Ricki Carlis took his overdose? We haven't seen him since."

Lil said:

"He's been in once or twice L.J. Not when you were here though." Luker's staff always called him by his initials. Dalgliesh wasn't sure whether the idea was to emphasise the general cosiness of their relationship with him or to make Luker feel like an American tycoon. Lil went on helpfully, "Wasn't he in with a party in the summer, Sid?"

Sid assumed an expression of lugubrious thought:

"Not summer, Lil. More like late spring. Didn't he come in with Mavis Manning and her crowd after her show folded up in May?"

"That was Ricki, Sid. You're thinking of Ricki. Digby Seton was never with Mavis."

They were as well-drilled, thought Dalgliesh, as a song and dance act. Luker said smoothly:

"Why pick on Digby? This isn't murder and, if it was, Digby's safe enough. Look at the facts. Digby had a rich brother. Nice for both of them. The brother had a dicky heart which might give out on him any minute. Hard luck on him but, again nice for Digby. And one day it does give out. That's natural causes, Superintendent, if the expression means anything at all. Admittedly someone drove the body down to Suffolk and pushed it out to sea. And did some rather messy and unpleasant things to it first, I hear. It looks to me as if poor Mr. Seton was rather unpopular with some of his literary neighbours. I'm surprised, Superintendent, that your aunt cares to live among these people, let alone leaving her chopper handy for the dead."

"You seem well informed," said Dalgliesh. He was remarkably quickly informed too. Dalgliesh wondered who had been keeping him so clearly in the picture.

Luker shrugged.

"There's nothing illegal in that. My friends tell me things. They know I'm interested in them."

"Particularly when they inherit £200,000 ?"

"Listen, Superintendent. If I want money I can make it, and make it legally. Any fool can make a fortune outside the law. It takes a clever man, these days, to make it legally. Digby Seton can pay me back the fifteen hundred I lent him when he was trying to save the Golden Pheasant if he likes. I'm not pressing him."

Sid turned his lemur-like eyes on his boss. The devotion in them was almost indecent.

Dalgliesh said:

"Maurice Seton dined here the night he died. Digby Seton

is connected with this place. And Digby stands to inherit £200,000. You can't blame people if they come asking questions, particularly as Miss Coombs was the last person to see Maurice alive."

Luker turned to Lil:

"You'd better keep your mouth shut, Lil. Or, better still, get yourself a lawyer. I'll phone Bernie."

"What the hell do I want Bernie for? I've told it all to him once when that C.I.D. chap was here. I'm telling the truth. Michael and the boys saw him call me over to his table and we sat there until nine-thirty when we left together. I was back here by ten-thirty. You saw me Sid, and so did the whole bloody Club."

"That's right. Superintendent. Lil was back by half past ten."

"Lil should never have left the Club," said Luker smoothly. "But that's my concern, not yours."

Miss Coombs appeared magnificently unconcerned at the thought of Luker's displeasure. Like all his employees she knew exactly how far she could go. The rules were few and simple and were well understood. Leaving the Club for an hour on a slack evening was venial. Murder, under certain well-understood circumstances, was probably venial too. But if someone at Monksmere hoped to pin this killing on Luker he was in for a disappointment. Luker was not the man to do murder for someone else's benefit nor did he trouble to cover up his tracks. When Luker killed he had no objection to leaving his prints on the crime.

Dalgliesh asked Lil what had happened. There was no more mention of lawyers and no difficulty in getting her story. Dalgliesh did not miss Lil's quick glance at her boss before she began her story. For some reason best known to himself Luker was willing to let her talk.

"Well, he came in at about eight o'clock and took the table nearest the door. I noticed him at once. He was a funny little man, small, very neat, nervous-looking. I thought he was probably a Civil Servant out for a spree. We get all types here. The regulars usually come with a party but we get the odd solitary chap. Mostly they're looking for a girl. Well, we don't cater for that kind of thing and it's my business to tell them so." Miss Coombs assumed an expression of pious severity which deceived no one and wasn't intended to. Dalgliesh enquired what had happened next.

"Michael took his order. He asked for fried scampi, green salad, bread and butter and a bottle of Ruffino. He seemed to know exactly what he wanted. No mucking about. When Michael served him he asked if he could speak to me. Well I went across and he asked me what I would drink. I had a gin and lime and drank it while he started picking at the scampi. Either he hadn't an appetite or he just wanted something to push around the plate while we were talking. He got quite a bit of the meal down eventually but he didn't look as if he was enjoying it. He drank the wine, though. Fairly put it away. Nearly the whole bottle."

Dalgliesh enquired what they had talked about.

"Dope," said Miss Coombs frankly. "That's what he was interested in. Dope. Not for himself, mind you. Well, it was plain enough he wasn't a junkie and he wouldn't have come to me if he was. Those boys know well enough where they can get the stuff. We don't see them in the Cortez. This chap told me that he was a writer, a very well known one, quite famous, and that he was writing a book about dope peddling. He didn't tell me his name and I never asked. Anyway, someone had told him that I might give him some useful information if he made it worth my while. Apparently this friend had said that if you want to know anything about Soho go to the Cortez and ask for Lil. Very nice, I must say. I've never seen myself as an authority on the dope racket. Still, it looked as if someone was trying to do me a good turn. There was money in it and the chap wasn't the sort to know whether he was getting genuine information. All he wanted was a bit of local colour for his book and I reckoned I could provide that. You can buy anything you want in London if you've got the cash and know where to go. You know that ducky, as well as I do. I daresay I could have given him the name of a pub or two where they say the stuff is passed. But what good would that be to him? He wanted a bit of glamour and excitement and there's no glamour about the dope racket, nor the junkies neither, poor devils. So I said that I might be able to give him a bit of information and what was it worth? He said ten quid and I said O.K. And don't you go talking about false pretences. He was getting value."

Dalgliesh said that he was sure Miss Coombs always gave value and Miss Coombs, after a brief struggle, decided prudently to let the remark pass. Dalgliesh asked:

"Did you believe this story of being a writer?"

"No dear. Not at first, anyway. I'd heard it too often before. You'd be surprised the number of chaps who want to meet a girl 'just to get authentic background for my new novel.' If it's not that then they're doing sociological research. I'll bet they are! He looked that type. You know, insignificant, nervous and eager at the same time. But when he suggested we should take a taxi and I could dictate the stuff to him and he type it straight away, I began to wonder. I said I couldn't leave the Club for more than an hour at most and I'd rather we went to my place. When you don't know who you're playing keep to the home ground, I always say. So I suggested we took a taxi to my flat. He said all right and we left just before nine-thirty. That right, Sid?"

"That's right Lil. Nine-thirty it was." Sid lifted sad eyes from his glass of milk. He had been contemplating, without enthusiasm, the puckered skin which had slowly formed on its surface. The smell of hot milk, sickly and fecund, seemed to permeate the claustrophobic office. Luker said:

"For God's sake drink the stuff or chuck it away, Sid. You make me nervous."

"Drink it up, darling," encouraged Miss Coombs. "Think of your ulcer. You don't want to go the way of poor Solly Goldstein."

"Solly died of a coronary and milk never helped that. The opposite I should think. Anyway, the stuff's practically radioactive. Full of strontium 90. It's dangerous, Sid."

Sid trotted to the washbasin and poured the milk away. Resisting the urge to throw open the window Dalgliesh asked:

"How did Mr. Seton appear while you were sitting together?"

"Nervy, dear. Excited but on edge at the same time. Michael wanted to move him to another table, it's a bit draughty near the door, but he wouldn't budge. He kept looking at the door while we were talking."

"As if he was expecting someone?"

"No dear. More as if he wanted to make sure it was still there. I half expected him to do a bunk. He was an odd fish and no mistake."

Dalgliesh asked what had happened when they left the Club.

"The same as I told that C.I.D. chap from Suffolk. We got a taxi at the corner of Greek Street and I was going to give the cabbie my address when Mr. Seton suddenly said that he'd rather just drive around for a bit and would I mind. If you ask me he'd suddenly got cold feet. Scared of what might happen to him, poor little twerp. Anyway, that suited me and we cruised around the West End a bit and then went into Hyde Park. I strung him a bit of a yarn about the dope racket and he made notes in a little book. If you ask me he was a bit drunk. Suddenly he got hold of me and tried to kiss me. Well, I was a bit fed up with him by then and didn't fancy being pawed about by that little twit. I got the impression that he only made a pass because he thought he ought to. So I said I ought to be back at the Club. He asked to be put down outside Paddington Underground and said he'd take a tube. No hard feelings. He gave me two fivers and an extra pound for the taxi fare."

"Did he say where he was going?"

"No. We came up Sussex Gardens—it's one way only down Praed Street now, as you know—and put him down outside the District Line. But he could have crossed the road to the Bakerloo I suppose. I didn't watch to see. I said goodbye to him at about quarter past ten outside Paddington Underground and that's the last I saw of him. And that's the truth."

Even if it weren't, thought Dalgliesh, it was difficult to see how the story could be disproved. There was too much corroborative evidence and Lil was the last woman in London to be panicked into changing a good story. It had been a waste of time coming to the Cortez. Luker had been unnaturally, almost suspiciously cooperative but Dalgliesh had learnt nothing which Reckless couldn't have told him in half the time.

Suddenly he felt again some of the uncertainties and the inadequacies which had tormented the young Detective Constable Dalgliesh nearly twenty years ago. When he took out Bryce's photograph of the beach party and handed it round it was with no hope of success. He felt like a doorstep salesman proferring his unwanted rubbish. They looked at it politely enough. Perhaps, like kindly householders, they were rather sorry for him. Doggedly persevering, he asked whether any of the people shown had been seen at the Cortez Club. Lil screwed up her eyes in an agony of effort while holding the snap at arm's length, thus effectively blurring her vision. Lil, Dalgliesh remembered, was like most women. She lied most effectively when she could convince herself that, essentially, she was telling the truth.

"No, dear, I can't say I recognize them. Except Maurice Seton and Digby, of course. That's not to say they haven't been here. Better ask them."

Luker and Sid, less inhibited, merely glanced at the photograph and averred that they hadn't seen the subjects in their lives.

Dalgliesh looked at the three of them. Sid had the pained, rather anxious look of an underfed little boy, hopelessly at sea in the world of wicked adults. Dalgliesh thought that Luker might be secretly laughing if the man had ever been known to laugh. Lil was looking at him with the encouraging, motherly, almost pitying look which, he thought bitterly, was usually reserved for her customers. There was nothing more to be learned from them. He thanked them for their help—he suspected that the note of cool irony wasn't lost on Luker—and let himself out.

3

When Dalgliesh had left Luker jerked his head at Sid. The little man left without a word or a backward glance. Luker waited until his footsteps had been heard going downstairs. Lil, alone with the boss, showed no particular anxiety but settled herself more comfortably in the shabby armchair on the left of the gas fire and watched him with eyes as bland and incurious as the eyes of a cat. Luker went to a wall safe. She watched his broad back as he stood there, motionless, turning the combination lock. When he turned round she saw that he held a small parcel, the size of a shoe box, covered with brown paper and loosely tied with thin white string. He laid it on his desk.

"Have you seen this before?" he asked.

Lil disdained to show curiousity.

"It came for you by this morning's post, didn't it? Sid took it in. What's wrong with it?"

"Nothing's wrong with it. On the contrary it is an admirable parcel. I've undone it once, as you can see, but it was a very neat little job when it arrived. You see the address? L.J. Luker, Esq., The Cortez Club, W.1. Neat capital letters, characterless, printed in Biro. Not very easy to identify that hand. I like the esquire. My family is not armigerous as it happens, so the writer is being a little pretentious but as he shares that failing with my Income Tax inspector and half the tradesmen in Soho, we can hardly consider it a clue. Then there's the paper. Perfectly ordinary brown paper; you can buy it in sheets from any stationer. And the string. Do you see anything remarkable about the string, Lil?"

Lil, watchful, admitted that there was nothing remarkable about the string. Luker went on:

"What is rather strange, though, is the amount of postage he—or she—paid. At least a shilling on the generous side by my estimate. So we take it that the parcel was stamped outside a post office and then pushed over the counter at a busy time. No waiting for it to be weighed. There would be less chance of the customer being noticed that way."

"Where was it posted?"

"In Ipswich on Saturday. Does that mean anything to you?"

"Only that it was posted a hell of a long way from here. Isn't Ipswich near that place where they found Maurice Seton?"

"The nearest large town to Monksmere. The nearest place where one could be certain of being unrecognized. You could hardly post this in Walberswick or Southwold and expect that no one would remember."

"For God's sake, L.J.! What's in it?"

"Open it and see for yourself."

Lil advanced cautiously but with an assumption of unconcern. There were more layers of the brown wrapping paper than she had expected. The box itself was revealed as an ordinary white shoe box but with the labels torn away. It looked very old, the kind of box that could be found tucked away in a drawer or cupboard in almost any house. Lil's hands hovered over the lid.

"If there's some bloody animal in here that jumps out at me I'll kill you L.J., God help me if I don't. I hate damn silly jokes. What's the stink, anyway?"

"Formaline. Go on, open it."

He was watching her closely, the cold grey eyes interested, almost amused. He had her worried now. For a second her eyes met his. Then she stepped back from the desk and, reaching forward, flipped off the lid with one jerk of her wrist.

The sweetly acrid smell rose like an anaesthetic. The severed hands were lying on their bed of damp cotton wool curved as if in a parody of prayer, palms touching briefly, finger tips pressed together. The puffy skin, what was left of it, was chalk white, and so crumpled that it looked as if the phalanges were loosely clothed with a pair of old gloves which would peel off at a touch. Already the flesh was shrinking from the butchered wrists and the nail of the right index finger had shifted from its bed.

The woman stared at the hands, fascinated and repelled. Then she seized the lid of the box and rammed it home. The cardboard buckled under her force.

"It wasn't murder, L.J. I swear it! Digby hadn't anything to do with it. He hasn't the nerve."

"That's what I would have said. You've told me the truth Lil?"

"Of course. Every word L.J. Look, he couldn't have done it. He was in the nick all Tuesday night."

"I know all about that. But if he didn't send these, who did? He stood to make £200,000 remember."

Lil said suddenly:

"He said that his brother would die. He told me that once."

She gazed at the box, fascinated and horrified.

Luker said:

"Of course he was going to die. Some time. He had a dicky heart, didn't he? That's not to say Digby put him away. It was natural causes."

Lil may have detected some tinge of uncertainty in his voice. She glanced at him and said quickly:

"He's always been keen to come in with you L.J. You know that. And he's got £200,000."

"Not yet. And he may never get his hands on it. I don't want a fool in with me, capital or no capital."

"If he put Maurice away and made it look like natural death, he's not all that of a fool, L.J."

"Maybe not. Let's wait and see if he gets away with it."

"And what about . . . those?" asked Lil jerking her head towards the innocuous looking box.

"Back in the safe. Tomorrow I'll get Sid to parcel them up and send them off to Digby. That should tell us something. It would be rather a nice touch to enclose my visiting card. It's time Digby Seton and I had a little talk."

4

Dalgliesh closed the door of the Cortez Club behind him and gulped in the Soho air as if it were as sweet as the sea wind on Monksmere Head. Luker had always had this effect of seeming to contaminate the atmosphere. He was glad to be out of that stuffy little office and free from the stare of those dead eyes. It must have rained briefly while he was in the Club for the cars were hissing over a wet road and the pavement was tacky under his feet. Soho was wakening now and the narrow street was swirling its gaudy flotsam from kerb to kerb. A stiff breeze was blowing, drying the road as he watched. He wondered if it were blowing on Monksmere Head. Perhaps even now his aunt would be closing the shutters against the night.

Walking slowly towards Shaftesbury Avenue he pondered his next move. So far this dash to London, prompted by angry impulse, had told him little that he couldn't have learnt in greater comfort by staying in Suffolk. Even Max Gurney could have told his news over the telephone although Max was, of course, notoriously cautious. Dalgliesh didn't altogether regret his journey; but it had been a long day and he wasn't disposed to make it longer. It was the more irritating, therefore, to find himself harrassed by the conviction that there was still something to be done.

It was difficult to decide what. None of the possibilities was attractive. He could visit the fashionable and expensive flats where Latham lived and attempt to get something out of the hall porter but, in his present unofficial capacity, he was unlikely to succeed. Besides, Reckless or his men would have been there before him and if Latham's alibi could be broken they would have broken it. He could try his luck at the eminently respectable Bloomsbury Hotel where Eliza Marley claimed to have spent last Tuesday night. There too his reception would hardly be cordial and, there too, Reckless would have been before him. He was getting a little tired of following in the Inspector's footsteps like a tame dog.

He could take a look at Justin Bryce's flat in the City; but there seemed little point in it. Since Bryce was still in Suffolk there could be no chance of seeing inside and he didn't imagine that there was much to be learned from an examination of the building itself. He already knew it well since it was one of the pleasanter architectural conceits in the City. Bryce lived over the offices of the *Monthly Critical Review* in a small eighteenth century courtyard off Fleet Street, so carefully preserved that it looked wholly artificial. Its only outlet to the street was through Pie Crust Passage, almost too narrow for a single man. Dalgliesh didn't know where Bryce garaged his car but it certainly wasn't in Pie Crust Court. He had a sudden fantastic vision of the little man staggering down Pie Crust Passage with Seton's body slung over his shoulder and stowing it in the back of his car under the interested gaze of the local traffic wardens and half the City police. He wished he could believe it.

There was, of course, another way to spend the evening. He could telephone Deborah Riscoe at her office—she would be almost due to leave—and ask her to join him at his flat. She would come, of course. Those days, sweet to the memory despite their occasional torments, when he could never be sure that she would come, were over now. Whatever else she might have planned for the evening, she would come. Then all the boredom, the irritation and the uncertainties would find at least a physical relief. And, tomorrow, the problem would still remain, casting its shadow between him and the first light.

Suddenly he made up his mind. He turned briskly towards Greek Street, hailed the first taxi that he saw, and asked to be put down outside Paddington Underground Station.

He decided to walk from Paddington Underground to Digby Seton's address. If Maurice Seton had come this way he might have taken a bus or even another taxi (had Reckless checked on that, Dalgliesh wondered) but the chances were that he had walked. Dalgliesh timed himself. It took exactly sixteen minutes of fast walking before he arrived at the archway of brickwork and crumbling stucco which led into Carrington Mews. Maurice Seton might have taken longer.

The cobbled entrance was uninviting, ill-lit and smelt strongly of urine. Dalgliesh, unobserved, since the place was obviously deserted, passed under the archway into a wide yard lit only by a solitary and unshaded bulb over one of a double row of garages. The premises had apparently once been the headquarters of a driving school and a few tattered notices still clung to the garage doors. But they were dedicated now to a nobler purpose, the improvement of London's chronic housing shortage. More accurately, they were being converted into dark, under-sized and over-priced cottages soon, no doubt, to be advertized as "bijou town residences" to tenants or owners prepared to tolerate any expense or inconvenience for the status of a London address and the taste for contemporary chi-chi. The existing double garages were being halved to provide a downstairs room while retaining space for one small car, and the lofts enlarged to form a couple of cells for bedroom and bath.

Digby Seton's cottage was the only one completed and the decor was depressingly orthodox. It had an orange door with a brass knocker in the shape of a mermaid, window boxes at the two minute square windows, and a lamp in a wrought iron holder above the lintel. The lamp wasn't alight but this was hardly surprising since, as far as Dalgliesh could see, it wasn't connected to the power. It struck him as being coy without being attractive and vulgar without being functional; in this it was symbolic of the whole house. The orange window boxes were sagging with their weight of caked earth. They had been planted with chrysanthemums and, when fresh, their gaiety had no doubt justified another two guineas on the rent. But the flowers, once golden, were now faded and brittle, the dead leaves stank of decay.

He prowled around the cobbled yard shining his pocket torch into the dark eyes of the windows. The two adjoining garages with the rooms above were now being modernized. The interiors had been completely stripped and the double garage doors taken off so that he could step inside the shell and note with interest that there was to be a connecting door between the sitting room and the garage. Everywhere there was a smell of new timber, paint and brickdust. The district had a long way to go, of course, before it became socially acceptable let alone fashionable, but it was on the way up. Digby had merely been the first to sniff the returning tide.

And that, of course, led to the intriguing question of why exactly he had come here. It wasn't an unlikely house for him to choose. In many ways this squalid little status symbol was entirely appropriate to Digby. But wasn't it altogether too much of a coincidence that he had chosen a house so convenient for murder? It was within twenty minutes walk of where Maurice Seton had been put down; it was in a dark inconspicuous yard which, once the workmen had left, would be uninhabited except for Digby; it had a garage with a direct door into the house itself. And there was another fact, perhaps the most significant of all. Digby Seton had only recently moved and he hadn't given his new address to anyone at Monksmere. When she had wanted to contact him after Maurice's death Sylvia Kedge hadn't known where to find him. And this meant that Maurice, if indeed he had been sent to Carrington Mews by Lily Coombs, wouldn't have known that it was Digby who was waiting for him. Certainly, Maurice had gone from the Cortez Club to his death. And Digby was the only suspect who was connected with the Club.

But all this was no more than suspicion. Nowhere was there any proof. There was no evidence that Lil had directed Maurice here; even if she had, Lil was capable of an obstinate adherence to a good story that would have been commendable in a better cause. It would need stronger measures than any English police force would tolerate to persuade Lil to talk. There was no proof that Maurice had been in the Mews. Dalgliesh couldn't get into the locked cottage but Reckless or his men would have been over it; if there had been anything to find they would have found it. There wasn't even any proof that Maurice had been murdered. Reckless didn't believe it, the Chief Constable didn't believe it and probably no one else did except Adam Dalgliesh, stupidly persistent, blindly following his hunch in the teeth of the evidence. And, if Maurice had been murdered, the biggest problem remained. He had died at midnight when Digby Seton and indeed most of the other suspects, had an unbreakable alibi. Until one could discover the "how" it was pointless to concentrate on the "who".

Dalgliesh shone his torch for the last time round the deserted yard, over the stacked timber under its tarpaulin cover, the piles of new bricks, the garage doors with their peeling notices. Then he passed under the arch as silently as he had entered and made his way to Lexington Street and his car.

It was just outside Ipswich that the tiredness hit him and he knew that it wouldn't be safe to drive much further. He needed food. It had been a long time since his substantial lunch with Max and he had eaten nothing since. He was perfectly happy to spend the night in a lay-by but not to wake in the early hours with a gnawing hunger and no chance of an early breakfast. But the problem was that it was too late for a pub and he had no intention of stopping at a country club or small hotel to do battle with the proprietor's fixed determination to serve meals only at regulated hours and at a price and quality to deter all but the starving. After a mile or two, however, he found an all night transport cafe, advertised by the black phalanx of lorries parked around its doors and the blaze of light from its low windows. The place was full, the air thick with smoke and jangling with talk and the cacophony of the juke box, but he sat undisturbed at a corner table, bare-topped but clean, and was served with a plate of eggs, sausage and crisply fried chips and a pint mug of hot, sweet tea.

Afterwards he went in search of the telephone, inconveniently placed in a narrow passage between the kitchen and the parking yard, and put through a call to Pentlands. There was no need to telephone. His aunt wasn't expecting him back at any particular time. But he was suddenly uneasy about her and determined if there were no reply to drive on. He told himself that it was an irrational anxiety. She might well be dining at Priory House or even be taking a solitary walk along the beach. He had discovered nothing to suggest that she was in any danger; but still there was this sense that all was not well. It was probably only the result of weariness and frustration, but he had to know.

It seemed an unusually long time before she answered and he heard the quiet, familiar voice. If she was surprised at his call she didn't say so. They spoke briefly against the clatter of washing-up and the roar of departing lorries. When he replaced the receiver he felt happier but still uneasy. She had promised him to bolt the cottage door tonight—thank God she wasn't the woman to argue, question or laugh over a simple request—and he could do no more. He was half irritated by this worry which he knew to be unreasonable; otherwise, whatever his tiredness, he must have driven on.

Before leaving the telephone booth a thought struck him and he searched in his pocket for a further supply of coins. It took longer to get through this time and the line wasn't clear. But eventually he heard Plant's voice and asked his question. Yes, Mr. Dalgliesh was quite right. Plant had telephoned Seton House on Wednesday night. He was sorry that he hadn't thought to mention it. Actually he had been phoning about every three hours that evening in the hope of getting Mr. Seton. About what time? Well, as far as he could remember at about six, nine and twelve o'clock. Not at all. Plant was only too glad to have been of help.

Was it any help? Dalgliesh wondered. It proved nothing except that Plant's unanswered call could have been the ringing telephone heard by Elizabeth Marley when she left Digby at Seton House. The time was about right and Reckless hadn't been able to trace the other call. But that didn't mean that no one had made it. He would need stronger evidence than this to prove Digby Seton a liar.

Ten minutes later Dalgliesh parked under the shelter of the hedge at the next lay-by and settled himself in the car as comfortably as was possible for a man of his height. Despite the pint of tea and the indigestible supper sleep came almost immediately and for a few hours it was deep and dreamless. He was awoken by a spatter of gravel against the car windows and the high keening of the wind. His watch showed three-fifteen. A gale was blowing and, even in the shelter of the hedge, the car was rocking gently. The clouds were scudding across the moon like black furies and the high branches of the hedge, dark against the sky, were groaning and curtseying like a chorus row of demented witches. He eased himself out of the car and took a short walk down the deserted road. Leaning against a gate he gazed out over the dark flat fields, taking the force of the wind full in his face so that it was difficult to breathe. He felt as he had as a boy on one of his solitary cycling trips when he would leave his small tent to walk in the night. It had been one of his greatest pleasures, this sense of complete loneliness, of being not only without a companion but with the knowledge that no one in the world knew exactly where he was. It was a solitude of the spirit as well as of the body. Shutting his eyes and smelling the rich dampness of grass and earth, he could imagine himself back in childhood, the smells were the same, the night was familiar, the pleasure was as keen.

Half an hour later he settled himself to sleep again. But before he dropped into the first layer of unconsciousness, something happened. He had been thinking drowsily and without effort of Seton's murder. It had been no more than the mind's slow recapitulation of the past day. And suddenly, inexplicably, he knew how it could have been done.

Book Three

I

It was just after nine o'clock when Dalgliesh got back to Pentlands. The cottage was empty, and for a moment, he felt again the foreboding of the night. Then he saw the note on the kitchen table. His aunt had breakfasted early and was walking along the shore towards Sizewell. There was a jug of coffee ready to be reheated and the breakfast table was laid for one. Dalgliesh smiled. This was typical of his aunt. It was her habit to take a morning walk along the beach and it would never occur to her to vary the routine merely because her nephew was flying backwards and forwards between London and Monksmere in chase of a murderer and might wish her to be immediately available to hear his news. Nor would she imagine that a healthy male was incapable of getting his own breakfast. But, as always at Pentlands, the essential comforts were there, the kitchen was warm and welcoming, the coffee strong, and there was a blue bowl of new laid eggs and a batch of home-baked rolls still warm from the oven. His aunt had obviously been up early. Dalgliesh breakfasted quickly, then decided to stretch his car cramped legs by walking along the shore to meet her.

He jumped his way down the uneven path of sand and rock which led from Pentlands to the beach. The leaping sea was white capped to the horizon, a brown-grey waste of heaving water, empty of sails and with only the sturdy silhouette of a coaster against the skyline. The tide was coming in fast. Lurching over the stones of the upper beach, he found the ridge of fine shingle which ran half-way between the sea's edge and the plateau of marram grass which fringed the marshes. Here walking was easier although, from time to time, he was forced to turn his back to the wind and fight for breath. Buffetted and foam-flecked, he squelched onward over the shingle finding the occasional and welcome stretch of firm serrated sand, and pausing from time to time to watch the smooth green underbelly of the waves as they rose in their last curve before crashing at his feet, in a tumult of flying shingle and stinging spray. It was a lonely shore, empty and desolate, like the last fringes of the world. It evoked no memories, cosily nostalgic, of the enchantments of childhood holidays by the sea. Here were no rockpools to explore, no exotic shells, no breakwaters festooned with sea weed, no long stretches of yellow sand sliced by innumerable spades. Here was nothing but sea, sky and marshland, an empty beach with little to mark the miles of outspate shingle but the occasional tangle of tar splotched drift wood and the rusting spikes of old fortifications. Dalgliesh loved this emptiness, this fusion of sea and sky. But today the place held no peace for him. He saw it suddenly with new eyes, a shore alien, eerie, utterly desolate. The unease of the night before took hold of him and he was glad to see, rising from the sand dunes, the familiar figure of his aunt braced like a flag staff against the wind, the edges of her red scarf flying.

She saw him almost immediately and came towards him. As they met and stood together, fighting for breath against a sudden gust of wind, there was a harsh "kraaank" and two heron flew low overhead, pounding the air with heavy, laborious wings. Dalgliesh watched their flight. Their long necks were drawn in, their delicate brown legs stretched straight behind them like a slipstream.

"Heron," he said with mock triumph.

Jane Dalgliesh laughed and handed him her field glasses.

"But what do you make of these?"

A small flock of grey-brown waders was twittering on the edge of the shingle. Before Dalgliesh had time to note more than their white rumps and blackish, down-turned beaks, the birds rose in one swift direct flight and faded into the wind like a wisp of thin white smoke.

"Dunlin?" he hazarded.

"I thought you might say dunlin. They're very similar. No, those were curlew-sandpipers."

"But the last time you showed me a curlew-sandpiper it had pink plumage," protested Dalgliesh.

"That was last summer. In the autumn they take on the buffish plumage of the young birds. That's why they look so like the dunlin. . . . Did you have a successful time in London?"

Dalgliesh said:

"Most of the day I spent following rather ineffectually in Reckless's footsteps. But during the course of a too-large lunch with Max Gurney at the Cadaver Club I learnt something new. Seton was proposing to use virtually all his capital to endow a literary prize. Having given up hope of personal fame he was proposing to buy a vicarious immortality. He wasn't skimping the price, either. Incidentally I have an idea now how Seton was killed but as it's going to be virtually impossible to prove, I don't think Reckless will thank me for it. I suppose I'd better phone him as soon as we get back."

He spoke without enthusiasm. Jane Dalgliesh cast a glance at him but asked no questions, and quickly turned her face away in case he should see, and be irritated by, her obvious concern.

"Did Digby know that he was likely to be done out of his inheritance?" she asked.

"Apparently no one knew except Max. The odd thing is that Seton wrote to him about it and typed the letter himself by the look of it. Yet Reckless didn't find the carbon at Seton House. He would certainly have mentioned it if he had. And he would certainly have questioned Sylvia Kedge and Digby to find out whether they knew."

"If Maurice wanted to keep his intention secret, wouldn't he have typed the letter without taking a carbon?" suggested Miss Dalgliesh.

"He took a carbon, all right. The bottom edge of the carbon got turned in when he put the paper into the machine and the last few words appear on the back of the letter. There's also a faint smear of carbon on the top edge. He might have decided later to destroy the copy but he was meticulous about his affairs and it doesn't seem likely. Incidentally, this isn't the only mystery about carbons. Seton is supposed to have typed that passage about his hero's visit to the Cortez Club while he was staying in London. But the servant at the Cadaver Club says that there were no carbon copies found in his room. So what happened to them?"

His aunt thought for a moment. This was the first time he had ever discussed a case with her and she was intrigued and a little flattered until she remembered that it wasn't, of course, his case. Reckless was the one responsible. It was Reckless who would have to decide the significance, if any, of those missing carbons at the Cadaver. But she was surprised at her own interest in the problem. She said:

"There are several possibilities, I suppose. Perhaps Seton didn't take carbons. In view of his meticulous habits I think that unlikely. Or perhaps he, or someone who had access to his room, destroyed them. Or perhaps the manuscript which Sylvia produced wasn't the one Seton actually sent her. I expect that Reckless has checked with the postman that a long, buff envelope was delivered to her but we've only her word that it contained the manuscript. And, if it did, presumably someone who knew that Seton was staying at the Club could have substituted one set of papers for another sometime between the sticking down of the envelope and its posting. Or could they? Do we know if Seton put the envelope out for posting where other people could see it? Or did he take it immediately to the post himself?"

"This was one of the things I asked Plant. No one at the Cadaver posted anything for Seton. But the envelope could have been left in his room long enough for someone to get at it. Or he could have handed it to someone else to post. But surely no one could have relied on that? And we know that this wasn't an unpremeditated killing. At least, I know it. I've yet to convince Reckless that it was a killing at all."

His aunt said: "Isn't there another possibility? We know that Seton couldn't have posted the second manuscript, the one describing the body drifting to shore. He was dead by then. And we've no reason to suppose that he even wrote it. We've only got Sylvia Kedge's word that it was his work."

"I think he wrote it," said Dalgliesh. "When Max Gurney showed me Seton's letter I recognized the typing. The same man typed the second manuscript."

As he spoke they were moving instinctively out of the bite of the wind into the shelter of the sunken lane which ran between the sand dunes and the bird sanctuary. Some twenty yards further on was the third in a series of small observation hides which overlooked the sanctuary. This particular hide made a natural turning point to their beach walks and Dalgliesh did not need to ask his aunt whether they should go in. To spend ten minutes scanning the reed beds through his aunt's binoculars and sheltering from the bitter east coast winds had become one of those rituals which were part of an autumn visit to Monksmere. The hide was typical of its kind, a rough wooden shelter, reed thatched, with a bench high enough to support tired thighs along the back wall and a slit at eye level giving a wide view over the marshes. In summer it smelt strongly of sun-baked wood, moist earth and lush grasses. Even in the cold months, this warmth lingered, as if all the heat and smells of summer were trapped within its wooden walls.

They had reached the hide and Miss Dalgliesh was about to step first through the narrow entrance when Dalgliesh suddenly said:

"No! Wait!" A minute earlier he had been strolling along almost in a dream. Now, suddenly, his brain awoke to the significance of the signs which his trained senses had subconsciously noted: the single line of male footprints leading from the sand dusted lane to the hide entrance, a trace on the wind of a sick stench which had nothing to do with the smell of earth or grasses. As his aunt paused he slipped in front of her and stood in the entrance of the hide.

His tall body blocked most of the light from the narrow entrance so that he smelt death before he saw it. The stench of sour vomit, blood and diarrhoea stung his nostrils as if the air of the little hut was saturated with corruption and evil. The smell was not unfamiliar to him but, as always, he had to fight against a momentary and intolerable urge to be sick. Then he bent down, the light streamed in behind him and he saw the body clearly for the first time.

Digby Seton had crawled like a dog into the corner of the hut to die and he had not died easily. The pathetic body, rigid and cold, was huddled along the far wall, the knees drawn up almost to the chin, the head twisted upwards as if the glazed eyes had made one last despairing effort to catch the light. In his agony he had bitten his bottom lip almost in two and a stream of blood, blackened now, had mixed with the vomit which encrusted his chin and the lapels of the once smart Melton overcoat. He had dug in the earth of the hut with torn and bleeding hands, smearing it over his face and hair and stuffing it even into his mouth as if in a last delirious craving for coolness and water. Six inches from his body lay his hip flask, the top unscrewed.

Dalgliesh heard his aunt's calm voice.

"Who is it, Adam?"

"Digby Seton. No, don't come in. There's nothing we can do for him. He's been dead for twelve hours at least; from some irritant poison by the look of it, poor devil."

He heard her sigh and she muttered something that he could not catch. Then she said:

"Shall I go for Inspector Reckless or would you rather I stayed here?"

"You go, if you will. I'll keep an eye on this place."

It was possible that he could have saved ten or fifteen minutes by going himself but there was nothing that anyone could do now to help Seton and he had no intention of leaving her alone in this stinking place of death. And she was a fast and strong walker; there would be little time wasted.

She set off at once and he watched her until a turn in the lane hid her from sight. Then he made his way to the top of the sand dunes and found a sheltered hollow in which to sit, his back wedged against a clump of marram grass. From this point of vantage he could keep the hide under observation and could see on his right the whole sweep of the beach and on his left the sunken lane. From time to time he caught a glimpse of his aunt's tall striding figure. She seemed to be making excellent time but it would be at least three quarters of an hour before Reckless and his men, laden with stretcher and their paraphernalia, came into view. There was no spot closer to the beach to bring an ambulance than Pentlands and no shorter way to the hide than by the lane. Burdened with their equipment, they would have a hard time of it against the wind.

Dalgliesh had spent only a few minutes in the hide but every detail was sharp and clear in his mind. He had no doubt that Digby Seton had been murdered. Although he had not searched the body—that was a job for Reckless—nor even touched it except to verify briefly that it was cold and that rigor mortis was well established, he had little doubt that no suicide note would be found. Digby Seton, that facile, uncomplicated, rather stupid young man, as pleased with his fortune as a child with a new toy and full of happy plans for bigger and brighter night clubs, was hardly a likely suicide risk. And even Digby had sense enough to know that there were easier ways of dying than to have one's stomach and guts burnt away with poison. There had been no bottle near the body except the hip flask. Almost certainly that had contained the stuff. The dose must have been very large. Dalgliesh's mind ranged over the possibilities. Arsenic? Antimony? Mercury? Lead? All could produce those signs. But this was mere speculation. In time the pathologists would have all the answers; the name of the poison, the dose, the time it had taken for Seton to die. And the rest would be for Reckless.

But assuming that the stuff had been put in the hip flask, who was a likely suspect? Someone who had access both to the poison and the flask. That was obvious. Someone who knew the victim well; knew that Digby, alone and bored, wouldn't be able to resist taking a pull at the flask before facing the bitter wind and the long walk home. And that implied someone who could persuade him to a rendezvous at the hide. Why else should he have gone there? No one at

Monksmere had ever known Digby Seton to be interested in bird watching or in walking. And he had not been dressed for either activity. Nor had he carried binoculars. This was murder all right. Even Reckless would hardly suggest that Digby Seton had died naturally or that someone with a perverted sense of humour had put his corpse in the hide with the object of inconveniencing Adam Dalgliesh and his aunt.

Dalgliesh had no doubt that the two murders were related but he was struck with their dissimilarity. It was as if two different minds were at work. The killing of Maurice Seton had been almost unnecessarily complicated. Although it might still be difficult to prove that the crime was indeed murder in face of the pathologist's report of death from natural causes, there was little else natural about it. The difficulty was not lack of clues. There were too many. It was as if the murderer had needed to demonstrate his cleverness as much as he had needed to kill Seton. But this new killing was simpler, more direct. There could be no possibility here of a verdict of death from natural causes. This murderer was not trying any double bluff. There hadn't even been an attempt to make it look like suicide, to suggest that Digby had killed himself in a fit of remorse over his brother's death. Admittedly it wouldn't have been easy to fake a suicide but Dalgliesh thought it significant that no attempt had been made. And he was beginning to understand why. He could think of one vital reason why this killer should want to avoid any suggestion that Digby had killed himself through remorse or had been in any way concerned in his brother's death.

Dalgliesh was surprisingly warm and comfortable in the shelter of the marram grass. He could hear the wind whistling in the dunes and the insistent thudding of the tide. But the tall clumps of grass shielded him so effectively that he had an odd sense of isolation as if the roar of wind and sea was coming from far away. Through the thin screen of grasses he could see the hide, a familiar, ordinary, primitive hut outwardly no different from half a dozen others which fringed the bird sanctuary. He could almost persuade himself that it was no different. Touched by this sense of isolation and unreality he had to resist an absurd impulse to see if Seton's body were really there.

Jane Dalgliesh must have made good time. It was less than forty-five minutes before he caught the first glimpse of approaching figures in the lane. The straggling group came briefly into view and then they were hidden again behind the dunes. The second time he glimpsed them they seemed no nearer. Then, unexpectedly, they turned the last bend in the lane and were with him. He saw a windblown, incongruous little group, burdened with equipment and having the air of a badly organized and slightly demoralized expedition. Reckless was there, of course, grim-faced and rigid with anger, the ubiquitous raincoat buttoned to his chin. He had with him his sergeant, the police surgeon, a photographer and two young detective constables, carrying a stretcher and a rolled canvas shield. Few words were exchanged. Dalgliesh bellowed his report in the Inspector's ear and then went back to his shelter in the dunes and left them to it. This wasn't his job. There was no sense in having an extra pair of feet churning up the moist sand around the hide. The men got to work. There was much shouting and gesticulating. The wind, as if in spite, had risen to a crescendo on their arrival and even in the comparative shelter of the lane, it was hard to make oneself heard. Reckless and the doctor disappeared into the hide. There at least, thought Dalgliesh, it would be sheltered enough. Sheltered, airless and stinking of death. They were welcome to it. After about five minutes they reappeared and the photographer, tallest of the group, bent nearly double and edged his equipment through the opening. Meanwhile the two constables were making ineffective efforts to get up a screen around the hide. The canvas leaped and whirled in their hands and whipped around their ankles with every gust of wind. Dalgliesh wondered why they bothered. There were hardly likely to be many sightseers on this lonely shore nor were the sandy approaches to the hide likely to yield further clues. There were only three sets of prints leading to the door; his own, those of his aunt, and the third set which were presumably Digby Seton's. They had already been measured and photographed and soon, no doubt, the flying sand would obliterate them completely.

It was half an hour before they got the corpse out of the hide and placed on the stretcher. As the constables struggled to hold down the mackintosh covers while the straps were applied, Reckless came over to Dalgliesh. He said:

"A friend of yours telephoned me yesterday afternoon. A Mister Max Gurney. It appears he's been keeping to himself some interesting information about Maurice Seton's Will."

It was an unexpected opening. Dalgliesh said:

"I lunched with him and he asked me whether he ought to get in touch with you."

"So he said. You'd imagine he would be capable of thinking it out for himself. Seton was found dead with marks of violence on the body. It stands to reason we'd be interested in the money side."

"Perhaps he shares your view that it was a natural death," suggested Dalgliesh.

"Maybe. But that's hardly his business. Anyway, he's told us now and it was news to me. There was no record of it at Seton House."

Dalgliesh said:

"Seton took a carbon of the letter. Gurney will be posting the original to you and you'll find the carbon markings on the back. Someone destroyed the copy, presumably."

Reckless said gloomily:

"Someone. Perhaps Seton himself. I haven't changed my mind yet about that killing, Mr. Dalgliesh. But you could be right. Especially in view of this." He jerked his head towards the stretcher which the two policemen squatting at the poles, were now bracing themselves to raise. "There's no doubt about this one. This is murder, all right. So we take our choice. One murderer and one unpleasant practical joker. Or one murderer and two crimes. Or two murderers."

Dalgliesh suggested that this last was unlikely in such a small community.

"But possible, Mr. Dalgliesh. After all, the two deaths haven't much in common. There's nothing particularly subtle or ingenious about this killing. Just a whacking great dose of poison in Seton's hip flask and the knowledge that, sooner or later, he'd take a swig at it. All the murderer had to do was ensure that he wasn't too close to medical help when it happened. Not that it would have done him much good by the look of it."

Dalgliesh wondered how the killer had succeeded in luring Seton to the hide. Had it been done by persuasion or by threats? Was Seton expecting to meet a friend or an enemy? If the latter, was he the sort of man to go alone and undefended? But suppose it were a different kind of assignation? For how many people at Monksmere would Digby Seton have been ready to walk two miles over rough ground on a cold autumn day and in the teeth of a rising gale?

The stretcher was moving forward now. One of the constables had apparently been instructed to stay on guard at the hide. The rest of the party fell into line behind the corpse like an escort of shabby and ill-assorted mourners. Dalgliesh and Reckless walked together and in silence. Ahead, the shrouded lump on the stretcher swayed gently from side to side as the bearers picked their way over the ridges in the lane. The edges of the canvas flapped rhythmically like a sail in the wind and overhead a sea bird hovered over the corpse, screaming like a soul in pain, before rising in a wide curve to disappear over the marshes.

2

It was early evening before Dalgliesh saw Reckless alone. The Inspector had spent the afternoon interviewing his suspects and checking on Digby Seton's movements during the past few days. He arrived at Pentlands just before six o'clock, ostensibly to ask Miss Dalgliesh again if she had seen anyone walking along the shore towards Sizewell on the previous day and whether she had any idea what could have induced Digby Seton to visit the hide. Both questions had been answered earlier when Dalgliesh and his aunt had met Reckless at the Green Man to give their formal account of the finding of the body. Jane Dalgliesh had stated that she had spent the whole of Monday evening at Pentlands and had seen no one. But then, as she had pointed out, it would be possible for Digby—or indeed, anyone else—to have walked to the hide by the sunken lane behind the sand dunes or by way of the beach, and this path for most of its length wasn't visible from Pentlands.

"All the same," said Reckless obstinately, "he must have come past your cottage to get into the lane. Would that really be possible without you seeing him?"

"Oh perfectly, provided he kept close in to the cliffs. There is a strip of about twenty yards between my access to the beach and the beginning of the lane when I might have glimpsed him. But I didn't. Perhaps he wanted to avoid notice and chose his moment to slip past."

Reckless muttered as if thinking aloud.

"And that suggests a secret assignation. Well, we suspect that. He wasn't the man to go bird watching on his own. Besides, it must have been dusk before he set off. Miss

Kedge said that he got his own tea at Seton House yesterday. She found the dirty tea things waiting for her to wash up this morning."

"But no supper?" enquired Miss Dalgliesh.

"No supper, Miss Dalgliesh. It looks as if he died before he had his evening meal. But the P.M. will tell us more, of course."

Jane Dalgliesh made her excuses and went into the kitchen to prepare dinner. Dalgliesh guessed that she thought it tactful to leave him alone with Reckless. As soon as the door closed behind her, he asked:

"Who saw him last?"

"Latham and Bryce. But nearly everyone admits to having spent some time yesterday with him. Miss Kedge saw him shortly after breakfast when she went up to the house to do her chores. He has kept her on as a kind of secretary-housemaid. Making use of her rather as his half-brother did, I imagine. Then he lunched with Miss Calthrop and her niece at Rosemary Cottage and left shortly after three. He called in on Bryce on his way home to Seton House to gossip about the return of your aunt's chopper and to try to find out what you were doing in London. That little trip seems to have aroused general interest. Latham was with Bryce at the time and the three of them were together until Seton left shortly after four."

"What was he wearing?"

"The clothes he was found in. He could have carried his flask in his jacket, trousers or overcoat pocket. He took the coat off, of course, at Rosemary Cottage and Miss Calthrop hung it in the hall cupboard. At Bryce's place he slung it over a chair. No one admits to seeing the flask. As I see it, any of them could have put in the poison, Kedge, Calthrop, Marley, Bryce or Latham. Any of them. And it needn't have been yesterday." He did not, Dalgliesh noted, add Miss Dalgliesh's name; but that didn't mean that she wasn't on the list. Reckless went on:

"I can't make much headway, of course, until I get the P.M. and know what the poison was. Then we shall get moving. It shouldn't be too difficult to prove possession. This wasn't the kind of stuff you get prescribed on E.C.10 or buy over the chemist's counter."

Dalgliesh thought he could guess what the poison was and where it had come from. But he said nothing. There had already been too much theorizing in advance of the facts and he judged it wiser to wait for the post-mortem. But if he were right, Reckless wasn't going to find it so easy to prove possession. Nearly everyone at Monksmere had access to this particular source. He began to feel rather sorry for the Inspector.

They sat together in silence for a minute. It wasn't a companionable silence. Dalgliesh could sense the stress between them. He couldn't guess what Reckless was feeling, he could only recognize with a kind of hopeless irritation his own awkwardness and dislike. He looked across at the Inspector's face with detached interest, building up the features in his mind as he might an identikit picture, observing the flatness of the wide cheekbones, the patch of white smooth-looking skin at each side of the mouth, the downward fold at the corners of the eyes and the little rhythmic twitch at the upper lid which was the only sign that the man had nerves. The face was uncompromising in its ordinariness, its anonymity. And yet, sitting there in that grubby raincoat, his face grey with tiredness, he still had force and personality. It might not be a personality which others found appealing. But it was there.

Suddenly Reckless, as if making up his mind to something, said harshly. "The Chief Constable wants to call in the Yard. He's sleeping on it. But I think he's already made up his mind. And there are those who will say it's none too soon."

Dalgliesh could find nothing appropriate to say to this. Reckless, still not looking at him, added:

"He seems to take your view, that the two crimes are connected."

Dalgliesh wondered whether he was being accused of trying to influence the Chief Constable. He couldn't recall expressing this view to Reckless but it seemed to him obvious. He said so and added:

"When I was in London yesterday it came to me how Maurice Seton could have been killed. It's little more than conjecture at present and God knows how you'll be able to prove it. But I think I know how it was done."

Briefly he outlined his theory, morbidly sensitive to every inflection in his own voice which the Inspector might interpret as criticism or self-congratulation. His story was received in silence. Then Reckless said:

"What put you on to that, Mr. Dalgliesh?"

"I'm not altogether sure. A number of small things I suppose. The terms of Seton's Will; the way he behaved at that basement table in the Cortez Club, his insistence on having one particular room whenever he stayed at the Cadaver Club; the architecture of his house even."

Reckless said:

"It's possible, I suppose. But without a confession I'll never prove it unless someone panics."

"You could look for the weapon."

"A funny kind of weapon, Mr. Dalgliesh."

"But a weapon and a lethal one."

Reckless drew an ordnance map from his pocket and spread it out on the table. Together they bent their heads over it, the Inspector's pencil hovering above the twenty mile radius around Monksmere.

"Here?" he asked.

"Or here. If I were the killer I'd look for deep water."

Reckless said:

"Not the sea, though. It might get washed up while we could still identify it. Not that I think it likely anyone would have connected it with the crime."

"But you might have. And the murderer couldn't risk that. Better get rid of it where there was every chance it wouldn't be found, or would be found too late. Failing an old mine shaft I'd have looked for a sluice or river."

The pencil came down and Reckless made three small crosses.

"We'll try here first Mr. Dalgliesh. And I hope to God you're right. Otherwise with this second death on our hands, it's all going to be a waste of time."

Without another word, he folded the map and was gone.

3

After dinner there was more company. Celia Calthrop, her niece, Latham and Bryce arrived within a short time of each other, driving or fighting their way through the rising storm to seek a spurious safety at Jane Dalgliesh's fireside. Perhaps, thought Dalgliesh, they could neither bear their own company nor feel at ease with each other. This at least was neutral ground, offering the comforting illusion of normality, the age-old protection of light and a warm fire against the darkness and enmity of the night. It certainly wasn't a time for the nervous or imaginative to be alone. The wind was alternately howling and moaning across the headland and a fast running tide was thundering up the beach driving the shingle in ridges before it. Even from the sitting room at Pentlands he could hear its long withdrawing sigh. From time to time a fitful moon cast its dead light over Monksmere so that the storm became visible and he could see, from the cottage windows, the stunted trees writhing and struggling as if in agony and the whole wilderness of sea lying white and turbulent under the sky.

The uninvited guests, their heads down, fought their way up the path to Miss Dalgliesh's door with the desperation of a fugitive band.

By half-past eight they had all arrived. No one had troubled to fetch Sylvia Kedge, but apart from her the little company of five nights earlier was met again. And Dalgliesh was struck by the difference in them. Analysing it, he realized that they looked ten years older. Five nights ago they had been only mildly concerned and a little intrigued by Seton's disappearance. Now they were anxious and shaken, possessed by images of blood and death from which they had little hope of shaking free. Behind the brave assumptions of ease, the rather desperate attempts at normality, he could smell fear.

Maurice Seton had died in London and it was still theoretically possible to believe that he had died naturally or that someone in London was responsible for his murder if not for the mutilation of his body. But Digby's death was on home ground and no one could pretend that there had been anything natural about it. But Celia Calthrop, apparently, was still prepared to try. She was squatting in the fireside chair, knees gracelessly splayed, her hands restless in the heavy lap.

"It's the most terrible tragedy. Poor boy! I don't suppose we shall ever know what drove him to it. And he had everything to live for: youth, money, talent, looks, charm."

This startlingly unrealistic assessment of Digby Seton was received in silence. Then Bryce said:

"I grant you he had money, Celia. Or the prospect of it anyway. Otherwise one did tend to think of poor Digby as a whey-faced, ineffectual, conceited, vulgar little twit. Not that one bore him the least ill-will. Nor, incidentally, does one believe that he killed himself."

Latham burst out impatiently:

"Of course he didn't! And Celia doesn't even believe it either! So why not be honest for a change, Celia? Why not admit that you're as scared as the rest of us?"

Celia said with dignity:

"I'm not in the least scared."

"Oh, but you ought to be!" Bryce's gnome-like face was creased with mischief, his eyes sparkled up at her. He looked suddenly less harassed, less like a tired old man.

"After all, you're the one who gains by his death. There should be a nice little sum left even after double death duties. And Digby's been a fairly regular visitor to you recently hasn't he? Didn't he lunch with you yesterday? You must have had plenty of opportunities to slip a little something into his flask. You were the one who told us that he always carried it. In this very room. Remember?"

"And where am I supposed to have got hold of arsenic?"

"Ah—but we don't know yet that it was arsenic Celia!

That's exactly the kind of remark that you shouldn't make. It doesn't matter in front of Oliver and me but the Inspector may get wrong ideas. I do hope you haven't been talking to him about arsenic."

"I haven't been talking to him about anything. I've merely answered his questions as fully and honestly as I can. I suggest you and Oliver do the same. And I don't know why you're so keen to prove Digby was murdered. It's this morbid love you both have for looking on the dark side."

Latham said dryly:

"Just a morbid love of looking facts in the face."

But Celia was undaunted:

"Well, if it were murder, all I can say is that Jane Dalgliesh was very lucky to have Adam with her when she found the body. Otherwise people might begin to think. But a C.I.D. Superintendent—well, naturally he knows how important it is not to disturb anything or tamper with the evidence."

Dalgliesh, too fascinated by the enormity of the remark and Celia's capacity for self-deception to make his protest, wondered whether she had forgotten that he was there. The others seemed to have forgotten too.

"What might people begin to think?" asked Latham quietly; Bryce laughed.

"You can't seriously suspect Miss Dalgliesh, Celia! If so you're shortly going to be faced with the delicate problem of etiquette. Your hostess is at this moment preparing coffee for you with her own hand. Do you drink it gracefully, or pour it surreptitously into the flower vase?"

Suddenly Eliza Marley swung round at them:

"For God's sake shut up, both of you! Digby Seton's dead and he died horribly. You may not have liked him but he was a human being. What's more he knew how to enjoy life in his own way. It may not have been your way but what of it? He was happy planning his horrible nightclubs and deciding how to spend his money. You may despise that but he wasn't doing you any harm. And now he's dead. And one of us murdered him. I don't happen to find that amusing."

"My dear, don't distress yourself." Celia's voice had taken

on the vibrant, emotional tone which she now almost unconsciously assumed when dictating the more highly-charged passages in her novels.

"We're all used to Justin by now. Neither he nor Oliver cared one whit for Maurice or Digby so it's no use expecting them to behave with ordinary decency, let alone respect. I'm afraid they care for no one but themselves. It's pure selfishness, of course. Selfishness and envy. Neither of them has ever forgiven Maurice for being a creative writer when all they're fit for is to criticise other people's work and batten on other men's talent. You see it every day; the envy of the literary parasite for the creative artist. Remember what happened to Maurice's play. Oliver killed it because he couldn't bear to see it succeed."

"Oh that!" Latham laughed. "My dear Celia, if Maurice wanted to indulge in emotional catharsis he should have consulted a psychiatrist, not inflicted it on the public in the guise of a play. There are three essentials for any play-wright, and Maurice Seton hadn't one of them. He must be able to write dialogue, he must understand what is meant by dramatic conflict, and he must know something about stage-craft."

This was no more than Latham's professional theme song and Celia was unimpressed.

"Please don't talk to me about craftsmanship, Oliver. When you have produced a work which shows the slightest sign of original creative talent there will be some point in discussing craftsmanship. And that goes for you too Justin."

"What about my novel?" demanded Bryce, affronted.

Celia cast him a long-suffering look and sighed deeply. She was obviously not prepared to comment on Bryce's novel. Dalgliesh recalled the work in question; a short exercise in sensitivity which had been well received but which Bryce had apparently never found the energy to repeat. He heard Eliza Marley's laugh.

"Isn't that the book the reviewers said had the intensity and the sensitivity of a short story? Hardly surprising when essentially that was all it was. Even I could keep the sensitivity going for a hundred and fifty pages."

Dalgliesh did not wait to hear more than Bryce's first protesting wail. Predictably the argument was degenerating into literary abuse. He wasn't surprised, having noticed this tendency before in his writing friends; but he had no wish to get involved. At any moment now they would be canvassing his opinion and his own verse no doubt would be subject to the devastating candour of the young. True, the argument appeared to be taking their minds from the subject of murder but there were more agreeable ways of getting through the evening.

Holding the door open for his aunt as she came in with the tray of coffee, he took the opportunity to slip away. It was perhaps a little unkind to abandon her just at this moment to the contentions of her guests but he didn't doubt her capacity to survive. He was less sure of his own.

His room was still and very quiet, insulated by sound building and oak boards from the jabber of the dissenting voices below. He unlatched the window on the seaward wall and forced it open with both hands against the blast of the gale. The wind rushed into the room swirling the bed cover into folds, sweeping the papers from his desk and rustling the pages of his bedside Jane Austen like a giant hand. It took his breath away so that he leaned gasping against the window ledge, welcoming the sting of spray on his face and tasting the salt drying on his lips. When he closed the window the silence seemed absolute. The thundering surf receded and faded like the far-away moaning on another shore.

The room was cold. He hitched his dressing gown around his shoulders and switched on one bar of the electric fire. Then he gathered up the scattered sheets of paper and replaced them with obsessive care, sheet on sheet, on the small writing table. The square white pages seemed to reproach him and he remembered that he hadn't written to Deborah. It wasn't that he had been too indolent, too busy or too preoccupied with the problem of Seton's murder. He knew perfectly well what had held him back. It was a cowardly reluctance to commit himself further by even one word until he had made up his mind about the future. And he was no nearer that tonight than he had been on the first day of the holiday. He had known when they said goodbye on his last evening that she understood and accepted that this break was in some way crucial for them, that he wasn't driving alone to Monksmere solely to escape from London or recover from the strain of his last case. There was no reason, otherwise, why she shouldn't have come with him. She wasn't as tied to her job as all that. But he hadn't suggested it and she had said nothing except that last "Remember me at Blythburgh." She had been at school near Southwold and knew and loved Suffolk. Well, he had remembered, and not only at Blythburgh. Suddenly he longed for her. The need was so intense that he no longer cared whether it were wise to write. In the face of this craving to see her again, to hear her voice, all his uncertainties and self-distrust seemed as unimportant and ludicrously unreal as the morbid legacy of a nightmare, fading in the light of day. He longed to talk to her, but with the sitting room filled with people there would be no chance of telephoning tonight. Switching on the desk lamp he sat at the table and unscrewed his pen. The words, as sometimes happened, came simply and easily. He wrote them down without pausing to think too much or even to wonder whether he was being sincere.

Remember me, you said, at Blythburgh,
As if you were not always in my mind
And there could be an art to bend more sure
A heart already wholly you inclined.
Of you, the you enchanted mind bereave
More clearly back your image to receive,
And in this unencumbered holy place
Recall again an unforgotten grace.
I you possessed must needs remember still
At Blythburgh my love, or where you will.

"This metaphysical conceit, like most minor verse, comes to you with an ulterior motive. I don't need to tell you what. I won't say that I wish you here. But I wish I were with you. This place is full of death and disagreeableness and I don't know which is worse. But God and the Suffolk C.I.D. willing I shall be back in London by Friday evening. It would be good to know that you might be at Queenhithe."

Writing this note must have taken longer than he thought for his aunt's knock on the door surprised him. She said:

"They're going, Adam. I don't know whether you feel the need to say goodnight."

He went down with her. They were, indeed, going and he was surprised to see that the clock said twenty past eleven. No one spoke to him and they seemed as unconcerned at his reappearance as they had been at his going. The fire had been let die and was now little more than a heap of white ash. Bryce was helping Celia Calthrop into her coat and Dalgliesh heard her say:

"It's naughty of us to be so late. And I've got to be up so early. Sylvia phoned me from Seton House late this afternoon and asked me to drive her to the Green Man first thing tomorrow. There's something urgent she has to tell Reckless."

Latham, already at the door, spun round.

"What does she mean—something urgent to tell him?"

Miss Calthrop shrugged.

"My dear Oliver, how can I know? She more or less hinted that she knew something about Digby but I imagine it's just Sylvia trying to make herself important. You know how she is. But one can hardly refuse to take her."

"But didn't she give you any idea what it's all about?"

Latham was sharply insistent.

"No she didn't. And I certainly wasn't going to give her the satisfaction of asking. And I'm not going to hurry myself. If this wind continues I shall be lucky to get much sleep tonight."

Latham looked as if he would like to have questioned further but Celia had already pushed past him. Murmuring a final and abstracted goodnight to his hostess, he followed the others into the storm. A few minutes later straining his ears against the howling of the wind, Dalgliesh heard the slamming of doors and the faint row of the departing cars.

4

The wind woke Dalgliesh just before three o'clock. As he drifted into consciousness he heard the three chimes of the sitting room clock and his first waking thought was a drowsy wonder that so sweet and uninsistent a sound could strike so clearly through the bedlam of the night. He lay awake and listened. Drowsiness gave way to pleasure, then to a faint excitement. He had always enjoyed a storm at Monksmere. The pleasure was familiar and predictable; the frisson of danger; the illusion of being poised on the very edge of chaos; the contrast between the familiar comfort of his bed and the violence of the night. He wasn't worried. Pentlands had stood for four hundred years against the Suffolk seas. It would stand tonight. The sounds he was hearing now hadn't changed with the years. For over four hundred years men had lain awake in this room and listened to the sea. One storm was very like another, all impossible to describe except in clichés. He lay still and listened to the familiar noises; the wind hurling itself against the walls like a demented animal; the perpetual background surge of the sea, the hiss of rain heard as the gusts abated; and, in the momentary calm, the trickle of falling shingle from roof and window sills. At about twenty to four the storm seemed to be dying away. There was one moment of complete peace in which Dalgliesh could hear his own breathing. Shortly afterwards he must have drifted again into sleep.

Suddenly he woke again to a gust so violent that the cottage seemed to rock, the sea roared as if it were about to break over the roof. He had never known anything like this before, even at Monksmere. It was impossible to sleep through such fury. He had an uncomfortable urge to be up and dressed.

He switched on his bedside lamp and, at that moment, his aunt appeared in the doorway, close buttoned into her old plaid dressing gown and with one heavy plait of hair hanging over her shoulder. She said:

"Justin is here. He thinks we ought to see if Sylvia Kedge is all right. We may have to get her out of that cottage. He says that the sea's coming in fast."

Dalgliesh reached for his clothes.

"How did he get here? I didn't hear him."

"Well, that isn't surprising, is it? You were probably asleep. He walked. He says we can't get the car to the road because of flooding. So it looks as if we'll have to go across the headland. He tried to telephone the coastguards but the line is down."

She disappeared and Dalgliesh hurriedly pulled on his clothes, cursing gently.

It was one thing to lie in warm security analysing the noises of the storm; it was another to fight one's way over the highest point of the headland on an adventure which could appeal only to the young, the energetic or the incurably romantic.

He felt unreasonably irritated with Sylvia Kedge as if she were somehow responsible for her own danger. Surely to God the girl knew whether the cottage was safe in a storm! It might, of course, be that Bryce was fussing unnecessarily. If Tanner's Cottage had stood through the 1953 flood disaster it would stand tonight. But the girl was a cripple. It was right to make sure. All the same it was hardly an enterprise to be welcomed. At best it would be uncomfortable, exhausting and embarrassing. At worst, especially with Bryce in tow, it had all the elements of farce.

His aunt was already in the sitting room when he went down. She was packing a thermos and mugs into a rucksack and was fully dressed. She must have been wearing most of her clothes under her dressing gown when she called him. It struck Dalgliesh that Bryce's call was not altogether unexpected and that Sylvia Kedge's danger might be more real than he knew. Bryce, wearing a heavy oilskin which reached to his ankles topped with an immense sou'wester, stood dripping and glistening in the middle of the room, like an animated advertisement for sardines. He was clutching a coil of heavy rope with every appearance of knowing what to do with it and had the air of a man dedicated to action.

He said:

"If there's any swimming to be done, my dear Adam, one must leave it to you. One has one's asthma, alas." He gave Dalgliesh a sly elliptical glance and added deprecatingly, "Also, one cannot swim."

"Of course," said Dalgliesh faintly. Did Bryce seriously believe that anyone could swim on a night like this? But there was no point in arguing. Dalgliesh felt like a man committed to an enterprise which he knows to be folly but which he can't summon up the energy to resist.

Bryce went on:

"I didn't call for Celia or Liz. No point in having a crowd. Besides, the lane is flooded so they wouldn't be able to get through. But I did try to get Latham. However, he wasn't at home. So we must just manage on our own." He was apparently unconcerned at Latham's absence. Dalgliesh bit back his questions. There was enough on hand without taking on fresh problems. But what on earth could Latham be doing on a night like this? Had the whole of Monksmere gone mad?

Once they had climbed out of the shelter of the lane and had mounted the headland there was energy for nothing but the effort of moving forward and Dalgliesh let the problem of Latham drop from his mind. It was impossible to walk upright and they clawed onwards like crouched beasts until aching thighs and stomach muscles forced them to kneel, palms pressed against the turf, to recover breath and energy. But the night was warmer than Dalgliesh had expected and the rain, less heavy now, dried softly on their faces. From time to time they gained the shelter of scrub and bushes and, released from the weight of the wind, trod lightly as disembodied spirits through the warm, green-smelling darkness.

Emerging from the last of these refuges they saw Priory House to sea-ward, the windows ablaze with light so that the house looked like a great ship riding the storm. Bryce drew them back into the shelter of the bushes and shouted:

"I suggest that Miss Dalgliesh calls Sinclair and his housekeeper to help. By the look of it they're up and about. And we shall need a long stout ladder. Our best plan is for you, Adam, to wade across Tanner's Lane if the water isn't too high and get to the house as soon as possible. The rest of us will move inland until we can cross the lane and approach the house from the north bank. We ought to be able to reach you with the ladder from that side."

Before he had finished expounding this unexpectedly lucid and positive plan Miss Dalgliesh without a word set off towards Priory House. Dalgliesh, cast without his consent in the role of hero, was intrigued by the change in Bryce. The little man obviously had a concealed passion for action. Even his affectations had fallen away. Dalgliesh had the novel and not disagreeable sensation of being under command. He was still unconvinced that there was any real danger. But if there were, Bryce's plan was as good as any.

But when they reached Tanner's Lane and stood sheltering in the slope of the south bank and looking down on Tanner's Cottage, the danger was apparent. Under a racing moon the lane shone white, a turbulent sheet of foam which had already covered the garden path and was sucking at the cottage door. The downstairs lights were on. From where they stood the squat, ugly doll's house looked strangely lonely and threatened. But Bryce apparently found the situation more hopeful than he had expected. He hissed in Dalgliesh's ear:

"It's not very high. You ought to be able to get across with the rope. Funny, I thought it would be well up by now. This may be as far as it will get. Not much danger really. Still, you'd better go in, I suppose." He sounded almost disappointed.

The water was incredibly cold. Dalgliesh was expecting it but the shock still took his breath away. He had stripped off his oilskin and jacket and was wearing only his slacks and jersey. One end of the rope was around his waist. The other, hitched around the trunk of a sapling, was being plied out inch by inch through Bryce's careful hands. The swift current was already armpit high and Dalgliesh had to fight hard to keep upright. Occasionally his feet stumbled into a rut in the lane's surface and he lost his footing. Then, for a desperate moment, it was a struggle to keep his head above water as he fought on the end of the rope like a hooked fish. It was hopeless to try to swim against this tide. The cottage lights were still on as he gained the door and braced his back against it. The sea was boiling around his ankles, each wave carrying it higher. Panting to get back his breath he signalled to Bryce to release the rope. In response the bulky little figure on the far bank flailed its arms enthusiastically but made no move to unhitch the rope from the tree. Probably his exuberant gestures were no more than a congratulatory acknowledgement that Dalgliesh had gained his objective. Dalgliesh cursed his folly in not having agreed with Bryce who should keep the rope before plunging to his task with such spectacular fervour. Any shouted communication between them was impossible. If he were not to remain tethered to the tree indefinitely—and his situation was already uncomfortably close to burlesque—he had better let Bryce have the rope. He released the bowline and the rope whipped free from his waist. Immediately Bryce began to coil it in with wide sweeps of his arms.

The wind had dropped a little but he could hear no sounds from inside the cottage and there was no answer to his shout. He pushed against the door but it was stuck. Something was wedged against it. He pushed harder and felt the obstruction shift as if a heavy sack were sliding across the floor. Then there was a gap wide enough for him to squeeze through and he saw that the sack was the body of Oliver Latham.

He had fallen across the narrow hall, his body blocking the sitting room doorway and his head resting face upward on the first stair. It looked as if he had struck the banister. There was a gash behind the left ear from which the blood was still oozing and another over the right eye. Dalgliesh knelt over him. He was alive and already regaining consciousness. At the feel of Dalgliesh's hand he groaned, twisted his head to one side and was neatly sick. The grey eyes opened, tried to focus, then closed again.

Dalgliesh looked across the brightly lit sitting room to the still figure sitting bolt upright on the divan bed. The face was an oval, deathly pale against the heavy swathes of hair. The black eyes were immense. They stared across at him, watchful, speculative. She seemed utterly unaware of the swirling water spreading now in waves across the floor.

"What happened?" Dalgliesh asked.

She said calmly:

"He came to kill me. I used the only weapon I had. I threw the paper weight at him. He must have caught his head when he fell. I think I've killed him."

Dalgliesh said briefly:

"He'll live. There's not much wrong with him. But I've got to get him upstairs. Stop where you are. Don't try to move. I'll come back for you."

She gave a little shrug of the shoulders and asked:

"Why can't we get across the lane? You came that way."

Dalgliesh answered brutally:

"Because the water's already up to my armpits and running in a torrent. I can't swim across burdened with a cripple and a semi-conscious man. We'll get upstairs. If necessary we'll have to get on the roof."

He edged his shoulder under Latham's body and braced himself for the lift. The staircase was steep, ill-lit and narrow but its very narrowness was an advantage. Once he had Latham balanced across his shoulders it was possible to pull himself up by both banisters. Luckily there were no corners. At the top he felt for the switch and the top landing was flooded with light. He paused for a moment recalling where the sky-light was. Then he pushed open the door to his left and groped round again for a light. It took him a few seconds to find. As he stood in the doorway grasping Latham's body with his left hand and running his right over the wall the smell of the room came out at him, musty, airless and sickly sweet like a faint stench of decay. Then his fingers found the switch and the room became visible, lit by a single unshaded bulb hanging from the centre of the ceiling. It had obviously been Mrs. Kedge's bedroom and looked he thought as it must have done when she last slept in it. The furniture was heavy and ugly. The great bed, still made up, occupied almost all the back of the room. It smelt of damp and decay. Dalgliesh dumped Latham gently on it and looked up at the slope of the roof. He had been right about the skylight. But there was only the one tiny square window and this faced the lane. If they were to get out of the cottage it would have to be by the roof.

He went back to the sitting room to fetch the girl. The water was waist high and she was standing on the divan bed and holding on to the mantelshelf for support. Dalgliesh noticed that she had a small plastic sponge bag hanging around her neck. Presumably it contained such valuables as she possessed. As he entered she gazed round the room as if to ensure that there was nothing else which she wished to take. He fought his way over to her, feeling the strength of the tide even in this tiny confined space and wondering how long the foundations of the cottage could stand against it. It was easy to comfort oneself with the thought that the cottage had survived earlier floods. But the tide and the wind were unpredictable. The water may have risen further in earlier years but it could hardly have burst in with greater force. Even as he struggled across to the waiting figure he thought he could hear the walls shake.

He came up to her and without a word, lifted her in his arms. She was surprisingly light. True, he could feel the downward drag of the heavy leg irons but the upper part of her body was so buoyant that it might have been boneless, sexless even. He was almost surprised to feel the rib cage under his hands and the firmness of her high breasts. She lay passively in his arms as he carried her sideways up the narrow stairs and into her mother's room. It was only then that he remembered her crutches. He felt a sudden embarrassment, a reluctance to speak of them. As if reading his thoughts she said:

"I'm sorry. I should have remembered. They're hitched on to the end of the mantelshelf."

That meant another trip downstairs but it was hardly

avoidable. It would have been difficult to manage both the girl and her crutches in one journey up those narrow stairs. He was about to carry her over to the bed when she looked at Latham's writhing body and said with sudden vehemence. "No! Not there! Leave me here." He slid her gently from his arms and she leaned back against the wall. For a moment their eyes were level and they gazed at each other, wordlessly. It seemed to Dalgliesh that in that moment some kind of communication passed but whether those black eyes held a warning or an appeal he was never afterwards able to decide.

He had no difficulty in retrieving the crutches. The water in the sitting room had now covered the mantelshelf and as Dalgliesh reached the bottom of the stairs they floated through the sitting room door. He grasped them by the rubber grips of the hand pieces and drew them over the banisters. As he retreated again up the stairs a great wave broke through the shattered front door and hurled him to his feet. The pedestal of the banisters broke free, spun as if in a whirlpool and was dashed into splinters against the wall. And this time there could be no doubt about it: he felt the cottage shake.

The skylight was about ten feet above the floor, impossible to reach without something to stand on. It was useless to try shifting the heavy bed, but there was a square substantial looking commode by the side of it and he dragged this across and positioned it under the skylight.

The girl said: "If you can push me through first I'll be able to help with . . . him."

She looked across at Latham who had now dragged himself upright and was sitting, head in hands, on the edge of the bed. He was groaning audibly.

She added: "I've got strong hands and shoulders."

And she held out the ugly hands towards him like a suppliant. This in fact had been Dalgliesh's plan. Getting Latham on to the roof was the trickiest part of the business. Without her help he doubted whether it would be possible.

The skylight, encrusted with dirt and festooned with grey cobwebs, looked as if it might be hard to shift. But when Dalgliesh punched at the frame he heard the splinter of rotting wood. The skylight jerked upwards and was immediately whirled away into the storm. Night came bursting into the close little room sweeping it with welcome gusts of cold, sweet air. At that moment the lights failed and they saw as from the bottom of a pit the small grey square of turbulent sky and the reeling moon.

Latham came lurching across the room towards them.

"What the hell . . . ? Someone's put out the bloody light."

Dalgliesh guided him back to the bed.

"Stay here and save your strength. You're going to need it. We've got to get out on the roof."

"You can. I'm staying here. Get me a doctor. I want a doctor. Oh God, my head!"

Dalgliesh left him rocking in lachrymose self-pity on the edge of the bed and went back to the girl.

Jumping from the chair he grasped the outer frame of the skylight and drew himself up. As he had recalled, the crown of the slated roof was only a few feet away. But the slope was steeper than he had expected and the chimney stack, which would afford them some shelter and support, was at least five feet to the left. He dropped again to the floor and said to the girl:

"See if you can get astride the roof and work your way back to the chimney. If you're in trouble, stay absolutely still and wait for me. I'll manage Latham once we're both out but I shall need you to help pull him up. But I won't shove him through until you're properly balanced. Give me a shout when you're ready. Do you want your crutches?"

"Yes," she said calmly. "I want my crutches. I can hook them on to the roof top and they may be useful."

He hoisted her through the skylight by the irons which braced both her legs from thigh to ankles. Their rigid strength made it easy for him to push her high on to the crown of the roof. She grasped it and swung one leg to the other side then crouched down low against the fury of the storm, her hair streaming in the wind. He saw her nod vigorously as a sign that she was ready. Then she leaned towards him and held out both her hands.

It was at that moment that he sensed a warning, the unmistakable instinct for danger. It was as much part of his detective's equipment as his knowledge of firearms, his nose for an unnatural death. It had saved him time and time again and he acted on it instinctively. There was no time now for argument or analysis. If the three of them were to survive they had to get out on that roof. But he knew that Latham and the girl mustn't be up there alone together.

It wasn't easy getting Latham through the skylight. He was only just conscious and even the swirls of water spreading now over the bedroom floor couldn't rouse him to a sense of danger. He craved only to be allowed to sink on to the pillows of the bed and fight his nausea in comfort. But at least he could cooperate to some extent. He wasn't yet a dead weight. Dalgliesh took off his own and Latham's shoes then urged him on to the chair and hoisted him through the skylight. Even when the girl's hands had caught Latham under his armpits he didn't let go but immediately swung himself through the hole bracing himself against the wind, his back to the flooded lane and his legs dangling into the room. Together they pulled and pushed the half-conscious man until his hands grasped the roof top and he pulled himself up and lay astride it, motionless. The girl released her hands and taking up her elbow crutches, edged herself backward until she was leaning against the chimney stack. Dalgliesh swung himself up to join Latham.

It was then that it happened. In the second when Dalgliesh weakened his hold on Latham she struck. It was so instantaneous that he hardly saw the vicious kick of the armoured legs. But the irons caught Latham's hands and, immediately, they loosed their hold of the roof and his body slipped. Dalgliesh shot out his hands and caught Latham's wrists. There was a sudden intolerable jerk and he took the full weight of Latham's body as it hung spread-eagled over the roof. Then she struck again and again. And now it was Dalgliesh's hands. They were too numb to feel the pain but he experienced the sudden scalding gush of blood and knew that it couldn't be long before the wrists were fractured and Latham slid out of his powerless hands. And then it would be his turn. She was braced securely against the chimney stack and armed with her crutches and those deadly irons. No one on the bank could see them. They were the wrong side of the roof and the night was dark. To those anxious watchers if indeed they were there they could be nothing more than crouched silhouettes against the sky. And when his and Latham's bodies were found there would be no injuries which couldn't be explained by the fury of the rocks and sea. There was only one chance for him and that was to let Latham go. Alone he could probably wrest the crutches from her. Alone he would have more than an even chance. But she knew of course that he wouldn't let Latham go. She had always known just how her adversary would act. He hung on doggedly; and still the blows fell.

They had both discounted Latham. Perhaps the girl thought he was unconscious. But suddenly a slate, dislodged by his fall, fell from the roof and his feet found a hold. Some desperate instinct for survival awoke in him. He lurched forward twisting his left hand from Dalgliesh's weakening hold and clutched with sudden force at her leg irons. Surprised she lost her balance and, at that moment, a gust of wind tore at the roof. Latham pulled again and she fell. Dalgliesh shot out his hand towards her and caught at the string of the little bag around her neck. The cord snapped and the body rolled past him. The clumsy surgical boots could find no hold and the rigid legs, powerless in their heavy irons rolled her over and over inexorably towards the edge. Then she hit the gutter and bounced into space, turning like a mechanical doll, her legs splayed against the sky. They heard the one wild cry and then nothing. Dalgliesh stuffed the little bag into his pocket and then lay motionless, his head resting on his bleeding hands. And it was then that he felt the ladder nudging his back.

Uninjured, the journey to the bank would have been relatively easy. But Dalgliesh's hands were now almost useless. The pain had started and he could hardly bear to flex the fingers. And there was no grip left. Latham's last effort seemed to have exhausted him. He seemed about to lapse again into unconsciousness. It took some minutes before Dalgliesh, shouting in his ear, could urge him on the ladder.

Dalgliesh went first, working his way backward and supporting Latham as best as he could with his hooked arms. Latham's face, beaded with sweat, was within inches of his own. Dalgliesh could smell his breath, the sweet-sour trace of too much drinking, too much high living. He wondered bitterly whether his last conscious discovery before they were hurled into the vortex was to be this realization that Latham had mild halitosis. There were more significant discoveries and there were pleasanter ways of dying. Surely Latham could make some effort! Why the hell couldn't the man keep himself in decent physical condition? Dalgliesh muttered alternate curses and encouragement under his breath and Latham, as if catching them, roused himself to a fresh effort, grasped the next rung with both hands and drew himself forward a few painful inches. Suddenly the rung bent, then snapped from the ladder. It spun from Latham's hand in a wide arch and disappeared, soundlessly, below the waves. For a sickening moment both their heads dropped through the gap and hung, wide-eyed above the boiling water only twenty feet below. Then Latham lifted his head to rest it on the edge of the ladder and grunted at Dalgliesh:

"You'd better get back. This ladder won't stand two. No sense in both of us getting wet."

"Save your breath," said Dalgliesh. "And keep moving."

He braced his elbows under Latham's armpit and lifted him forward a few rungs. The ladder creaked and bent. They lay immobile after the effort then tried again. This time Latham managed to grip a rung with his feet and lurched forward with such unexpected force that Dalgliesh was nearly thrown off his balance. The ladder, caught by a sudden gust, swung sideways. They could feel it shift on the roof. Neither dared move until the wild swing steadied. Then they inched forward again. They were nearing the bank now. Below they could see the dark shapes of tangled trees. Dalgliesh thought that they must be within earshot of the headland but there was no sound except the howling of the storm. He guessed that the little group was waiting in silence, terrified to break their fearful concentration even with shouts of encouragement. Suddenly it was all over. He felt a strong grip on his ankles. Someone was pulling him to safety.

He wasn't conscious of relief, only of intense weariness and self-disgust. There was no strength left in his body but his mind was clear enough and his thoughts were bitter. He had underestimated the difficulties, had allowed himself to be drawn by Bryce into the amateurish farce in a tolerant contempt of the danger, had behaved like an impulsive fool. They had set out like a couple of Boy Scouts to save the girl from drowning. And, as a result, the girl had drowned. All that had been necessary was to wait quietly in that upstairs bedroom until the water began to drop. The storm was already abating. By morning they could have been rescued in comfort, cold possibly, but unharmed.

And then, as if in answer to his thought, he heard the rumbling. It grew into a roar and the little group on the bank watched fascinated as the cottage with a kind of awkward grace curtseyed slowly into the sea. The roar reverberated around the headland and the waves, dashing against the dam of bricks, leaped and thundered. The spume rose dancing into the night sky, and floated into their eyes. And then the rumbling died away. The last Tanner's Cottage was under the sea.

The headland was peopled with black shapes. They crowded around him blotting out the storm. Their mouths opened and shut but he could hear nothing they said. He had one vivid picture of R. B. Sinclair's white hair streaming against the moon and he could hear Latham demanding a doctor with the querulous insistence of a child. Dalgliesh longed intolerably to sink down to the soft turf and lie there quietly until the pain had gone from his hands and this dreadful aching from his body. But someone was holding him up. He supposed it must be Reckless. The hands braced under his armpits were unexpectedly firm and he could smell the strong pungent smell of wet gaberdine and feel its harshness against his face. Then the mouths, opening and shutting like the jaws of puppets, began to make sounds. They were asking if he was all right and someone, he thought it was Alice Kerrison, was suggesting that they all go back to Priory House. Someone else mentioned the Landrover. It could probably get through the lane to Pentlands if Miss Dalgliesh would prefer to take Adam home. For the first time Dalgliesh noticed the Landrover, a dark shape on the outskirts of the group. It must be the one belonging to Bill Coles and that bulky figure in yellow oilskins must be Coles himself. How in the devil had he got here? The white blur of faces seemed to be expecting him to make up his mind to something. He said: "I want to go home."

He shook off their helping hands and hoisted himself by his elbows into the back of the Landrover. On the floor was a cluster of storm lanterns which cast their yellow light on the row of sitting figures. For the first time he saw his aunt. She had one arm round Latham's shoulders and he was leaning against her. He looked, thought Dalgliesh, like the romantic lead in a Victorian melodrama with his long pale face, his closed eyes, and the white handkerchief which someone had bound around his brow already showing a stain of blood. Reckless got in last and sat against Dalgliesh. As the Landrover lurched off across the headland Dalgliesh held out his torn hands like a surgeon waiting to be gloved. He said to Reckless:

"If you can get your hand into my pocket there's a plastic bag there which will interest you. I tore it from Sylvia Kedge's neck. I can't touch anything myself."

He shifted his body so that Reckless, bouncing violently with the shaking of the Landrover, could slide his hand into the pocket. He drew out the little bag, untied the cord and edging his thumb into the neck worked it open. Then he spilled the contents out on to his lap. There was a small faded photograph of a woman in an oval silver frame, a reel of recording tape, a folded wedding certificate and a plain gold ring.

5

Brightness was pressing painfully against Dalgliesh's eyeballs. He swam up through a kaleidoscope of whirling reds and blues and forced open his eyelids, gummed with sleep, to blink at the bright day. It must be long after his normal waking hour; already shafts of sunlight lay warm across his face. He lay for a moment, cautiously stretching his legs and feeling the ache return almost pleasurably to his sore muscles. His hands felt heavy. Drawing them from under the bedclothes he turned the two white cocoons slowly before his eyes, focussing on them with the strained intentness of a child. Presumably these professional looking bandages had been applied by his aunt but he had no clear recollection of her doing so. She must have used some ointment too. He could feel a disagreeable slipperiness inside the encasing gauze. He was becoming aware now that his hands still hurt but he could move the joints, and the tips of his three middle fingers, the only parts visible, looked normal enough. Apparently no bones were broken.

He wriggled his arms into his dressing gown and walked across to the window. Outside the morning was calm and bright, bringing an immediate memory of the first day of his holiday. For a moment the fury of the night seemed as remote and legendary as any of the great storms of the past. But the evidence was before him. The tip of headland visible from his eastward window was ravaged and raw as if an army had clumped across it littering its way with torn boughs and uprooted gorse. And, although the wind had died to a breeze so that the litter of the headland scarcely stirred, the sea was still turbulent, slopping in great sluggish waves to the horizon as if weighted with sand. It was the colour of mud, too turbid and violent to reflect the blue translucence of the sky.

Nature was at odds with itself, the sea in the last throes of a private war, the land lying exhausted under a benign sky.

He turned from the window and looked round the room as if seeing it for the first time. There was a folded blanket across the back of the easy chair by the window and a pillow resting on the arm. His aunt must have spent the night sleeping there. It could hardly have been because of concern for him. He remembered now. They had brought Latham back to Pentlands with them; his aunt must have given up her room. The realization irritated him and he wondered whether he was being petty enough to resent his aunt's concern for a man he had never liked. Well, what of it? The dislike was mutual if that were any justification and the day threatened to be traumatic enough without beginning it in a mood of morbid self-criticism. But he could have done without Latham. The events of the night were too raw in the memory to relish the prospect of exchanging small talk over breakfast with his partner in folly.

As he made his way downstairs he could hear a murmur of voices from the kitchen. There was the familiar morning smell of coffee and bacon but the sitting room was empty. His aunt and Latham must be breakfasting together in the kitchen. He could hear Latham's high arrogant voice more clearly now although his aunt's softer replies were inaudible. He found himself treading softly so that they might not hear him, tiptoeing across the sitting room like an intruder. Soon, inevitably, he would have to face Latham's excuses and explanations, even—horrible thought—his gratitude. Before long the whole of Monksmere would arrive to question, argue, discuss and exclaim. Little of the story would be news to him, and he had long outgrown the satisfaction of being proved right. He had known who for a long time now and since Monday night he had known how. But to the suspects the day would bring a gratifying vindication and they could be expected to make the most of it. They had been frightened, inconvenienced and humiliated. It would be churlish to grudge them their fun. But for the moment he trod warily, as if reluctant to waken the day.

There was a small fire burning in the sitting room, its thin flame flickering wanly in the brightness of the sun. He saw that it was after eleven o'clock and the post had already arrived. There was a letter for him propped on the mantelpiece. Even across the room he could recognize Deborah's large, sloping handwriting. He felt in his dressing gown pocket for his own unposted letter to her, and with difficulty propped it up beside that other envelope, his small and upright hand looking obsessionally neat beside her generous scrawl. Hers was a thin envelope. That meant one page at the most. Suddenly he knew just what Deborah could have written on no more than one quarto page and the letter became infected with the menace of the day, opening it a chore which could reasonably be postponed. As he stood there, angry at his own indecision and trying to force himself to that one simple action he heard the approaching car. So they were coming already, avid no doubt with curiosity and pleasurable anticipation. But when the car drew nearer he recognized the Ford which Reckless used and, moving to the window, could see that the Inspector was alone. A minute later the car door slammed and Reckless paused, as if bracing himself to approach the cottage. Under his arm he carried Celia Calthrop's tape recorder. The day had begun.

Five minutes later the four of them listened together to the murderer's confession. Reckless sat beside the tape recorder frowning at it constantly with the anxious, slightly peeved look of a man who expects it at any moment to break down. Jane Dalgliesh sat in her usual chair on the left of the fire, motionless, hands folded in her lap, listening as intently as if to music. Latham displayed himself against the wall, one arm drooping from the chimney piece, his bandaged head resting against the grey stones. He looked, thought Dalgliesh, like a slightly passé actor posing for a publicity photograph. He, himself, sat opposite his aunt balancing a tray on his knees, spearing with a fork the small cubes of buttered toast which she had prepared for him or cupping his hands, comfortably insulated, round a steaming beaker of coffee.

The voice of the dead girl spoke to them, not with the familiar irritating submissiveness, but clear, confident and controlled. Only from time to time was there a trace of excitement quickly restrained. This was her paean of triumph, yet she told her dreadful story with the assurance and detachment of a professional broadcaster reading a book at bedtime.

"This is the fourth time I've dictated my confession and it won't be the last. The tape can be used over and over again. One can always improve. Nothing need be final. Maurice Seton used to say that, working away at his pathetic books as if they were worth writing, as if anyone cared what word he used. And as likely as not it would be my word in the end, my suggestion, breathed oh so tentatively and quietly so that he wouldn't notice that it was a human being who spoke. I wasn't ever that to him. Just a machine who could take shorthand, type, mend his clothes, wash up, even do a little cooking. Not a really efficient machine, of course, I hadn't the use of my legs. But that made it easier for him in some ways. It meant that he didn't even have to think of me as female. He never saw me as a woman, of course. That was to be expected. But after a time I wasn't even female. I could be asked to work late, stay the night, share his bathroom. No one would talk. No one would care. There was never any scandal. Why should there be? Who would want to touch me? Oh, he was safe enough with me in the house. And, God knows, I was safe enough with him.

"He would have laughed if I had told him that I could make him a good wife. No, not laughed. He would have been disgusted. It would have seemed like mating with a half-wit, or an animal. Why should deformity be disgusting? Oh, he wasn't the only one. I've seen that look in other faces. Adam Dalgliesh. Why should I instance him? He can hardly bear to look at me. It's as if he's saying, 'I like women to be lovely. I like women to be graceful. I'm sorry for you but you offend me'. I offend myself Superintendent. I offend myself. But I mustn't waste tape on preliminaries. My first confessions were too long, imperfectly balanced. By the end they even bored me. But there will be time to get the story right, to tell it perfectly so that I can play the tape over and over for the rest of my life and yet feel the first keen pleasure. Then, perhaps, one day I shall clean it all away. But not yet. Perhaps never. It would be amusing to leave it for posterity. The only drawback to planning and carrying out a perfect murder is that no one else can appreciate it. I may as well have the satisfaction, however childish, of knowing that I shall make the headlines after my death.

"It was a complicated plot, of course, but that made it all the more satisfying. After all, there is nothing difficult about killing a man. Hundreds of people do it every year and have their brief moment of notoriety before they are as forgotten as yesterday's news. I could have killed Maurice Seton any day I chose, especially after I got my hands on those five grains of white arsenic. He took them from the Cadaver Club museum, substituting a bottle of baking powder, at the time he was writing *Death in the Pot*. Poor Maurice, he was obsessed by this urge for verisimilitude. He couldn't even write about an arsenical poisoning without handling the stuff, smelling it, seeing how quickly it would dissolve, enjoying the thrill of playing with death. This absorption in detail, this craving for vicarious experience, was central to my plot. It led him, the predestined victim, to Lily Coombs and the Cortez Club. It led him to his murderer. He was an expert in vicarious death. I should like to have been there to see how he enjoyed the real thing. He meant to put the stuff back, of course; it was only borrowed. But before he could do so I did some substituting of my own. The baking powder in the show case at the Club was replaced by Maurice with baking powder—again. I thought that the arsenic might come in handy. And it will. It will shortly come in very handy indeed. There will be no problem for me in putting it into that flask which Digby always carries. And then what? Wait for the inevitable moment when he is alone and can't face the next minute without a drink? Or tell him that Eliza Marley has discovered something about Maurice's death and wants to meet him secretly far along the beach? Any method will do. The end will be the same. And once he is dead, what can anyone prove? After a little time I shall ask to see Inspector Reckless and tell him that Digby has been complaining recently about indigestion and that I have seen him at Maurice's medicine chest. I shall explain how Maurice borrowed some arsenic once from the Cadaver Club but he assured me that he had replaced it. But suppose he didn't? Suppose he couldn't bring himself to part with it? That would be typical of Maurice. Everyone will say so. Everyone will know about *Death in the Pot*. The powder in the museum show case will be tested and found to be harmless. And Digby Seton will have died by a tragic accident but through his half-brother's fault. I find that very satisfying. It is a pity that Digby, who despite his stupidity, has been very appreciative of so many of my ideas, has to be kept ignorant of this final part of the plan.

"I could have used that arsenic for Maurice just as easily and seen him die in agony any day I chose. It would have been easy. Too easy. Easy and unintelligent. Death by poison wouldn't have satisfied any of the necessary conditions of Maurice's murder. It was those conditions which made the crime so interesting to plan and so satisfying to execute. Firstly, he had to die from natural causes. Digby, as his heir, would be the natural suspect and it was important to me that nothing should jeopardise Digby's inheritance. Then he had to die away from Monksmere; there must be no danger of anyone suspecting me. On the other hand I wanted the crime to be connected with the Monksmere community; the more they were harassed, suspected and frightened the better, I had plenty of old scores to be settled. Besides, I wanted to watch the investigation. It wouldn't have suited me to have it treated as a London crime. Apart from the fun of watching the reactions of the suspects I thought it important that the police work should be under my eye. I must be there to watch and, if necessary, to control. It didn't work out altogether as I had planned, but on the whole very little has happened which I haven't known about. Ironically, I have been less skilful at times than I hoped at controlling my own emotions, but everyone else has behaved strictly according to my plan.

"And then there was Digby's requirement to be met. He wanted the murder to be associated with L. J. Luker and the Cortez Club. His motive was different, of course. He didn't particularly want Luker to be suspected. He just wanted to show him that there were more ways than one of committing murder and getting away with it. What Digby wanted was a death which the police would have to accept as natural—because it would be natural—but which Luker would know had been murder. That's why he insisted on sending Luker the severed hands. I took most of the flesh off them first with acid—it was an advantage to have a dark room in the cottage and the acid available—but I still didn't like the idea. It was a stupid, an unnecessary risk. But I gave in to Digby's whim. A condemned man, by tradition, is pampered. One tries to gratify his more harmless requests.

"But before I describe how Maurice died there are two extraneous matters to get out of the way. Neither of them is important but I mention them because both had an indirect part in Maurice's murder and both were useful in throwing suspicion on Latham and Bryce. I can't take much credit for Dorothy Seton's death. I was responsible, of course, but I didn't intend to kill her. It would have seemed a waste of effort to plan to kill a woman so obviously bent on self destruction. It couldn't, after all, have been long. Whether she took an overdose of her drugs, fell over the cliff on one of her half-doped nocturnal wanderings, got killed with her lover on one of their wild drives around the country, or merely drank herself to death, it could only be a matter of time. I wasn't even particularly interested. And then, soon after she and Alice Kerrison had left for that last holiday at Le Touquet I found the manuscript. It was a remarkable piece of prose. It's a pity that people who say that Maurice Seton couldn't write will never have the chance to read it. When he cared, he could write phrases that scorched the paper. And he cared. It was all there; the pain, the sexual frustration, the jealousy, the spite, the urge to punish. Who better than I could know how he felt? It must have given him the greatest satisfaction to write it all down. There could be no typewriter, no mechanical keys between this pain and its expression. He needed to see the words forming themselves under his hand. He didn't mean to use it, of course. I did that; merely steaming open one of his weekly letters to her and including it with that. Looking back, I'm not even sure what I expected to happen. I suppose it was just that the sport was too good to miss. Even if she didn't destroy the letter and confronted him with it he could never be absolutely sure that he himself hadn't inadvertently posted it. I knew him so well, you see. He was always afraid of his own subconscious, persuaded that it would betray him in the end. Next day I enjoyed myself watching his panic, his desperate searching, his anxious glances at me to see whether I knew. When he asked whether I had thrown away any papers I answered calmly that I had only burnt a small quantity of scrap. I saw his face lighten. He chose to believe that I had thrown away the letter without reading it. Any other thought would have been intolerable to him so that was what he chose to believe until the day he died. The letter was never found. I have my own idea what happened to it. But the whole of Monksmere believes that Maurice Seton was largely responsible for his wife's suicide. And who could have a better motive for revenge in the eyes of the police than her lover, Oliver Latham?

"It is probably unnecessary to explain that it was I who killed Bryce's cat. That would have been obvious to Bryce at the time if he hadn't been so desperate to cut down the body that he failed to notice the slip knot. If he had been in any condition to examine the rope and the method he would have realized that I could have strung up Arabella without lifting myself more than an inch or two in my chair. But, as I had anticipated, he neither acted rationally nor thought coolly. It never occurred to him for a second that Maurice Seton might not be the culprit. It may seem strange that I waste time discussing the killing of a cat but Arabella's death had its place in my scheme. It ensured that the vague dislike between Maurice and Bryce hardened into active enmity so that Bryce, like Latham, had a motive for revenge. The death of a cat may be a poor motive for the death of a man and I thought it unlikely that the police would waste much time with Bryce. But the mutilation of the body was a different matter. Once the post-mortem showed that Maurice had died from natural causes the police would concentrate on the reasons for hacking off the hands. It was, of course, vital that they should never suspect why this mutilation was necessary and it was convenient that there should be at least two people at Monksmere, both spiteful, both aggrieved, both with an obvious motive. But there were two other reasons why I killed Arabella. Firstly I wanted to. She was a useless creature. Like Dorothy Seton she was kept and petted by a man who believed that beauty has a right to exist, however stupid, however worthless, because it is beauty. It took only two twitching seconds on the end of a clothes line to dispose of that nonsense. And then, her death was to some extent a dress rehearsal. I wanted to try out my acting ability, to test myself under strain. I won't waste time now describing what I discovered about myself. I shall never forget it; the sense of power, the outrage, the heady mixture of fear and excitement. I have felt that again many times since. I am feeling it now. Bryce gives a graphic account of my distress, my tiresomely uncontrolled behaviour after the body was cut down, and not all of it was acting.

"But to return to Maurice. It was by a lucky chance that I discovered the one fact about him that was crucial for my purpose—that he suffered badly from claustrophobia. Dorothy must have known of course. After all there were nights when she condescended to let him share her bedroom. He must have woken her sometimes with his recurring nightmare just as he woke me. I often wonder how much she knew and whether she told Oliver Latham before she died. That was a risk I had to take. But what if she did? No one can prove that I knew. Nothing can change the fact that Maurice Seton died from natural causes.

"I remember that night, over two years ago, very clearly. It was a wet, blustery day in mid-September and the evening grew wilder as darkness fell. We had been working together since ten o'clock that morning and it wasn't going well.

Maurice was trying to finish a series of short stories for an evening paper. It wasn't his métier and he knew it; he was working against time and he hated that. I had broken off only twice, to cook us a light lunch at one-thirty and again at eight o'clock when I prepared sandwiches and soup. By nine o'clock when we had finished our meal, the wind was howling around the house and I could hear a high tide pounding on the beach. Even Maurice could hardly expect me to get home in my wheelchair once darkness had fallen and he never offered to drive me home. That, after all, would put him to the trouble of fetching me again next day. So he suggested that I should stay the night. He didn't ask me if I were willing. It didn't occur to him that I might object or that I might perhaps prefer my own toothbrush or toilet things or even my own bed. The ordinary courtesies of life didn't apply to me. But he told me to put sheets on the bed in his wife's old room and he came himself to look for a nightdress for me. I don't know why. I think it may have been the first time since her death that he had brought himself to open her drawers and cupboards and that my presence was both an opportunity for breaking a taboo and a kind of support. Now that I can wear any of her underclothes or can rip them to shreds just as the fancy takes me, I can bring myself to smile at the memory of that night. Poor Maurice! He hadn't remembered that those wisps of chiffon, those bright transparencies in nylon and silk would be so pretty, so delicate, so very unsuitable for my twisted body. I saw the look on his face as his hands hovered over them. He couldn't bear to think of her clothes against my flesh. And then he found what he wanted. It was there at the bottom of the drawer, an old woollen nightdress which had belonged to Alice Kerrison. Dorothy had worn it once at Alice's insistance when she had been ill with influenza and was sweating with rigor. And it was this nightdress which Maurice handed to me. Would his fate have been any different, I wonder, if he had acted otherwise that night? Probably not. But it pleases me to think that his hands, hesitating over the layers of gaudy nonsense, were choosing between life and death.

"It was shortly after three o'clock when I was awoken by his scream. At first I thought it was a sea bird screeching. Then it came again and again. I fumbled for my crutches and went in to him. He was leaning, half dazed, against the bedroom window and had the last disorientated look of a man who has been sleep walking. I managed to coax him back into bed. It wasn't difficult. He took my hand like a child. As I drew the sheets up under his chin he suddenly seized my arm and said, 'Don't leave me! Don't go yet! It's my nightmare. It's always the same. I dream I'm being buried alive. Stay with me till I'm asleep.' So I stayed. I sat there with his hand in mine until my fingers were stiff with cold and my whole body ached. There were a great many things which he told me in the darkness about himself, about his great consuming fear, before his fingers relaxed, the muttering ceased and he dropped into peaceful sleep. His jaw had fallen open so that he looked stupid and ugly and vulnerable. I had never seen him asleep before. I was pleased to see his ugliness, his helplessness and I felt a sense of power which was so pleasurable that it almost frightened me. And, sitting there beside him, listening to that quiet breathing, I pondered how I might use this new knowledge to my advantage. I began to plan how I might kill him.

"He said nothing to me next morning about the events of the night. I was never sure whether he had completely forgotten his nightmare and my visit to his room. But I don't think so. I believe he remembered well enough but put it out of his thoughts. After all, he didn't have to apologize or explain to me. One doesn't need to justify one's weakness either to a servant or an animal. That's why it is so satisfying, so convenient to have a tame one in the house.

"There was no hurry over the planning, no time limit in which he had to die, and this in itself added to the interest and allowed me to develop a more complicated and sophisticated murder than would have been possible were I working against the clock. I share Maurice's view here. No one can do his best work in a hurry. Towards the end, of course, there was some urgency when I found, and destroyed, the carbon of the letter to Max Gurney announcing that Maurice was thinking of changing his Will. But, by then, my final plans had been ready for over a month.

"I knew from the beginning that I should need an accomplice and who that accomplice should be. The decision to use Digby Seton to destroy firstly his half-brother and then himself was so magnificent in its boldness that at times I was frightened at my own daring. But it wasn't as foolhardy as it appears. I knew Digby, I knew precisely his weaknesses and his strengths. He is less stupid and far greedier than people realize, more practical but less imaginative, not particularly brave but obstinate and persistent. Above all, he is fundamentally weak and vain. My plan made use of his abilities as well as his defects. I have made very few mistakes in my handling of him and if I underestimated him in some important respects this has proved less catastrophic than I might have feared. He is becoming a liability as well as a nuisance now, of course, but he won't be worrying me for long. If he had proved less irritating to me and more reliable I might have considered letting him live for a year or so. I should prefer to have avoided death duties on Maurice's estate. But I have no intention of letting greed trap me into folly.

"In the beginning I did nothing so crude as to present Digby with a plan for killing Maurice. What I suggested to him was no more than a complicated practical joke. He didn't, of course, believe this for long but then he wasn't required to. During all the preliminary planning, neither of us mentioned the word murder. He knew and I knew, but neither of us spoke. We conscientiously kept up the fiction that we were engaged in an experiment, not perhaps without some danger but completely without malice, to prove to Maurice that it was possible to transport a man from London to Monksmere secretly and without his knowledge or cooperation. That was to be our alibi. If the plot failed and we were discovered with the body on our hands our story was ready and no one would be able to disprove it. Mr. Seton had wagered us that we couldn't kidnap him and take him back to Monksmere without being discovered. He wanted to introduce such a scheme into his new book. There would be plenty of witnesses to testify that Maurice loved to experiment, that he was meticulous about detail. And if he should unexpectedly die of a heart attack during the journey, how could we be blamed? Manslaughter? Possibly. But murder, never.

"I think that Digby almost believed the fiction for a time. I did my best to keep it going. There are few men with the courage or the strength of mind to plan murder in cold blood and Digby certainly isn't one of them. He likes his unpleasant facts gift-wrapped. He prefers to shut his eyes to reality. He has always shut his eyes to the truth about me.

"Once he had convinced himself that it was all a cosy little game with easy rules, no personal risk and a prize of £200,000, he quite enjoyed planning the details. I gave him nothing to do which wasn't well within his peculiar capabilities and he wasn't pressed for time. Firstly, he had to find a second-hand motor cycle and long torpedo-shaped side car. He had to buy them separately and for cash in a part of London where he wasn't known. He had to rent or buy a flat with reasonable privacy and access to a garage, and keep his new address secret from Maurice. All this was relatively simple and I was pleased on the whole with the efficient way in which my creature coped. This was almost the most trying time for me. There was so little I personally could do to control events. Once the body had been brought to Monksmere I should be here to organize and direct. Now I had to rely on Digby to carry out instructions. It was Digby alone who must manage the business at the Cortez Club, and I had never been particularly happy about his plan to lure Maurice to the Mews Cottages. It seemed to me unnecessarily complicated and dangerous. I could think of safer and easier ways. But Digby insisted on bringing the Cortez Club into the plot. He had this need to involve and impress Luker. So I let him have his way—after all the plot couldn't incriminate me—and I admit that it worked admirably. Digby confided to Lily Coombs the fiction about the experiment to kidnap his half-brother and told her that Maurice had wagered a couple of thousand that it couldn't be done. Lily was paid a hundred in cash for her help. All she had to do was to watch out for Maurice, spin him a yarn about the dope traffic and direct him to Carrington Mews for any further information he wanted. If he didn't take the bait nothing would be lost. I had other plans for luring him to Carrington Mews and one of those could be used. But, of course, he took the bait. It was in the service of his art and he had to go. Digby had been carefully hinting about Lily Coombs and the Cortez Club on each of his visits and Maurice had typed out the inevitable little white reference card for future use. Once Maurice had arrived in London for his regular autumn visit it was as certain that he would show himself one night at the Cortez as it was that he would stay in his usual room at the Cadaver Club, the room which he could reach without having to use that small claustrophobic lift. Digby could even predict to Lily Coombe the night on which he would appear. Oh yes, Maurice took the bait all right! He would have walked into hell in the service of his writing. And that, of course, was what he did.

"Once Maurice appeared at the door of the Carrington Mews cottage Digby's part was relatively simple. The swift knock out blow, too slight to leave a mark but heavy enough to be effective, wasn't difficult for a man who had once been a boxing champion. The adaptations to the side car to convert it into a travelling coffin had been an easy matter for one who had built Sheldrake singlehanded. The side car was ready and waiting and there was access to the garage from the house. The slight body, unconscious and breathing stertorously—for Lily had done her part well and Maurice had drunk far more wine than was good for him—was slid into the side car and the top nailed in place. There were, of course, air holes in the sides. It was no part of my plan that he should suffocate. Then Digby drank his half bottle of whisky and set out to provide himself with his alibi. We couldn't know precisely when it would be required, of course, and this was a slight worry. It would be a pity if Maurice died too soon. That he would die, and die in torment, was certain. It was merely a question of how long that torment would last and when it would begin. But I instructed Digby to get himself arrested as soon as he was a safe distance from home.

"Later next morning, as soon as he was released, Digby set out with the motor cycle and side car for Monksmere. He didn't look at the body. I had instructed him not to open the side car but I doubt whether he was tempted. He was still living in the comfortable, imaginary world of the plot which I had created for him. I couldn't foresee how remarkably he would react when he could no longer pretend to believe in it. But when he set out secretly from Carrington Mews that morning I have no doubt that he felt as innocently excited as a schoolboy whose practical joke is going well. There was no trouble on the journey. The black plastic driving suit, the helmet and goggles were a perfect disguise as I had known they would be. He had a single ticket to Saxmundham from Liverpool Street in his pocket and before leaving the West End he posted to Seton House my description of the Cortez Club. It seems almost unnecessary to say that a typing style can easily be disguised but not the typewriter used. I had typed the passage some weeks earlier on Maurice's machine wearing a glove on my right hand and with bandaged left fingers. The passage about the mutilated body floating out to sea had been typed by Maurice and was taken by me from his papers. Using it was one of the small but agreeable refinements which I had incorporated into my plan when I learned about Miss Calthrop's idea for an effective opening for one of Maurice's books. It was in every sense a gift to me as well as to Maurice. To a large extent it determined the whole shape of the murder plot, and I made use of it brilliantly.

"But there was one vital part of my plot which I haven't yet mentioned. Strangely enough, although I expected it to be the most difficult, it was the easiest of all. I had to make Digby Seton marry me. I thought that bringing him to this might take weeks of skilful persuasion. And I didn't have those weeks. All the planning had to be done in those rare weekends when he was at Monksmere. I let him write to me because I could be sure that the letters would be burnt, but I never wrote to him and we never telephoned each other. But persuading him to this disagreeable and yet essential part of the plan wasn't the kind of thing I could do by post. I even wondered whether this would be the rock on which the whole scheme would be wrecked. But I misjudged him. He wasn't entirely stupid. If he had been I would never have risked making him a partner in his own destruction. He could recognize the inevitable. And after all, it was in his own interest. He had to marry to get his hands on the money. There was no one else he wanted. He certainly wasn't keen on a wife who would make demands on him or interfere in his life, a wife who might even want to sleep with him. And he knew that he had to marry me for one overriding reason. No one would be able to prove that we killed Maurice unless one of us talked. And a wife can't be made to give evidence against her own husband. It was arranged, of course, that we would divorce after a reasonable time and I was very generous about the marriage settlement. Not suspiciously generous. Just very very reasonable. I could afford to be. He had to marry me to keep me quiet and collect the cash. I had to marry him because I wanted the whole of his fortune. As his widow.

"We married by licence on 15th March at a London Registry Office. He hired a car and called for me early. No one saw us leaving the cottage. How could they? Celia Calthrop was away so there was no chance of her calling for me. Oliver Latham and Justin Bryce were in London. I neither knew nor cared whether Jane Dalgliesh was at home. I telephoned Maurice to say that I wasn't well enough to report for work. He was irritated but he wasn't concerned, and I had no fear that he might call at the cottage to see how I was. Maurice hated illness. He would care if his dog were sick. But then, he was fond of his dog. I find it very satisfying that he might be alive now if only he had cared enough to call at Tanner's Cottage that day, to wonder where I had gone—why I had lied.

"But time and this tape are running out. I have settled my account with Maurice Seton. This is my triumph not my justification and there is still much to be told.

"Digby, driving the motor cycle and side car, arrived at Tanner's Cottage just before six o'clock on Wednesday. It was dark by then and there was no one about. There never is once dusk has fallen on this coast. Maurice was dead, of course, Digby's face was very white under the helmet as he prised off the lid of the side car. I think he had expected to see his victim's face contorted into a grimace of horror, the dead eyes glaring accusingly. Unlike me he hadn't read Maurice's text-books on forensic medicine. He didn't know about the relaxing of muscles after death. The calm face, so ordinary, so vacuous, so completely without the power to be either frightening or pathetic seemed to reassure him. But I had forgotten to explain about rigor mortis. He hadn't expected that we should need to break the rigor in the knees so that the body could be fitted into my wheel chair and taken down to the shore. He didn't enjoy that necessary bit of business. I can still hear his high nervous giggle at the sight of Maurice's thin legs, clad in those ridiculous trousers and sticking straight out like the broomstick legs of a guy. Then Digby hit them and the rigor broke and they dangled and swung above the foot rest like the legs of a child. That small act of personal violence to the body did something to Digby. I was perfectly ready to take off the hands myself. I wanted to bring that chopper down. But Digby took it from me and waited without speaking while I laid out the hands ready for him on the thwart. I might have made a neater job of it. I doubt whether I would have enjoyed it any more than he. Afterwards I took the hands from him and put them in my mackintosh toilet bag. Digby had a use for them; he was determined to send them to Luker. But there were things I had to do to them first in the privacy of my dark room. In the meantime I slung the bag around my neck and enjoyed the feel of those dead hands, seeming to creep against my flesh.

"Last of all Digby pushed the dinghy out on the ebb tide, wading deep into the sea. I wasn't worried about bloodstains. The dead bleed slowly if they bleed at all. If there was spotting on the cycling suit the sea would wash it away. Digby waded back to me, glistening out of the darkness, hands clasped above his head, like someone who has been ritually cleansed. He did not speak as he wheeled me back to the cottage. As I have said, in some ways I under-estimated him, and it was only on that silent journey back through the narrow lane that it struck me he could be dangerous.

"The rest of the night's work should have been the simplest. The plan was for Digby to drive as fast as he could to Ipswich. On the way he would stop at a lonely place on the bank of the Sizewell Sluice, detach the side car and sink it into the deep water. Once in Ipswich he would take the number plates off the motor cycle and abandon it in a side street. It was an old machine and it was unlikely that anyone would bother to trace the owner. And, even if it were traced to Digby and the side car found, we still had our second line of defence: the story of the experiment to kidnap Maurice, the innocent wager that went so tragically wrong. And we should have Lily Coombs to corroborate our story.

"My instructions to Digby were very clear. After abandoning the cycle he would first post Maurice's manuscript describing the handless body drifting out at sea. Then he would go to the station, still wearing his overalls, and would take a platform ticket. I didn't want the ticket collector to note the passenger who was joining his train at Ipswich with a ticket issued in London. Digby would push through the barrier when there was a convenient crowd, join the Saxmundham train, change his overalls in the lavatory, put them in a small hold-all, and arrive at Saxmundham at eight-thirty. He would then take a cab to Seton House where I would be waiting for him in the darkness to check that all had gone according to plan and to give him any instructions for the future. As I have said, it was the easiest part of the night's work and I expected no trouble. But Digby was beginning to sense his power. He did two very stupid things. He couldn't resist the temptation to detach the side car and drive at top speed around the village, even showing himself to Bryce. And he invited Liz Marley to meet him at Saxmundham. The first was no more than childish exhibitionism; the second could have been fatal. I was physically very tired by now and emotionally unprepared to deal with this insubordination. As I heard Miss Marley's car drive up and was watching them both from the shadow of the curtains, the telephone rang. I know now that it was only Plant making a routine enquiry for Mr. Seton. At the time it shook me. Two unforeseen things were happening together and I was prepared for neither. If I had been given time to take myself in hand I should have coped with the situation better. As it was, I quarrelled violently with Digby. There is no point in wasting time with what either of us said, but it ended with Digby driving off furiously into the night with the intention, he said, of going back to London. I didn't believe him. He had too much at stake to throw in his hand now. This was no more than another childish gesture of independence provoked by the quarrel and intended simply to frighten me. But I waited until the early hours for the return of the Vauxhall, sitting there in the darkness since I dare not put on a light, wondering whether one moment of temper was to undo all my careful planning, and scheming how the situation might yet be retrieved. It was two in the morning before I made my way home. Next morning I was back at Seton House early. Still no sign of the car. It was not until Thursday night when the telephone call came through to Pentlands that I knew what had happened. By then I had no need to simulate shock. It is good to know that Digby Seton will soon be paying for what he did to me during those twenty-four hours. He was surprisingly resourceful about it all. His story about the false telephone call was very clever. It would explain any hints about Maurice's death which he may have let out during the periods of babbling semi-consciousness. It strengthened his alibi. It made things even more uncomfortable for the Monksmere community. I had to admire his ingenuity, his inventiveness. And I wondered how long it would be before he began thinking about ridding himself of me.

"There is little more to say. The return of the chopper to Jane Dalgliesh was no more difficult than stealing it had been. The plastic cycling suit was cut into shreds and floated out on the ebb tide. I took the flesh off the knuckles of Maurice's hands with acid from the dark room and Digby posted his parcel. It was all quite simple. All according to plan. And now there is only the last chapter. In a few days' time I shall be able to dictate this again. I feel no particular hatred for Digby. I shall be glad when he is dead but I am quite happy to picture his agony without wanting to see it. But I wish I could have been there when Maurice Seton died.

"And that reminds me of the last explanation of all. Why wasn't I content for his dead body to be left in London, a bundle of flesh and clothes in a Paddington gutter? The reason is simple. We had to take off his hands. Those tell-tale hands with the knuckles torn to the bone where he had battered them against his coffin lid."

The voice had finished. For a few seconds the tape ran on. Then Reckless leant across and it clicked to a stop. Without speaking he bent to pull out the cord. Jane Dalgliesh got up from her chair and with a murmured word to Latham went out to the kitchen. Almost at once Dalgliesh heard the splash of running water and the chink of a kettle lid. What was she doing, he wondered. Getting on with preparing the lunch? Making fresh coffee for her visitors? What was she thinking? Now that it was all over was she even interested in that tumult of hate which had destroyed and disrupted so many lives including her own? One thing was certain. If she did later talk about Sylvia Kedge she wouldn't indulge in sentimental regrets of "If only we had known! If only we could have helped her!" To Jane Dalgliesh people were as they were. It was as pointlessly presumptious to try to change them as it was impertinent to pity them. Never before had his aunt's uninvolvement struck him so forcibly; never before had it seemed so frightening.

Latham slowly released himself from his self-conscious pose in front of the fire and sank down into the empty chair. He laughed uncertainly. "Poor devil! Killed because of his choice of a nightdress. Or was it because of his choice of bedroom?"

Reckless didn't answer. Carefully he curled the flex of the

tape recorder then tucked the machine under his arm. Turning at the door he spoke to Dalgliesh.

"We've dredged up the side car. It was within twenty yards of the spot you marked. Another lucky guess, Mr. Dalgliesh."

Dalgliesh could picture the scene. It would be pleasant on the bank of the lonely sluice in the early morning sun, a green peace broken only by the distant rumble of traffic, the singing water, the deep voices of the men as they bent to the tackle, the squelch of mud as the waders sucked at the river bed. And then the thing they sought would break surface at last, shaped like a gigantic striped marrow, the black hull festooned with weeds and glistening as the gouts of mud slipped away. He had no doubt that it looked very small to the band of toiling policemen as they urged and steadied it towards the bank. But then, Maurice Seton had been a small man.

When Reckless had left, Latham said belligerently:

"I must thank you for saving my life."

"Must you? I should have thought it was the other way round. It was you who kicked her off the roof."

The reply was quick, defensive.

"That was an accident. I never meant her to fall."

Of course not, thought Dalgliesh. It had to be an accident. Latham was the last man to live with the thought that he had killed a woman, even in self defence. Well, if that was the way he had decided to remember it, he might as well begin now as later. And what the hell did it matter anyway? He wished that Latham would go. The thought of gratitude between them was ridiculous and embarrassing, and he was too sore in mind and body to relish a morning of small talk. But there was something he needed to know. He said:

"I've been wondering why you went to Tanner's Cottage last night. You saw them I suppose—Digby and Kedge?"

The two square envelopes propped side by side were starkly white against the grey stones of the chimney piece. He would have to open Deborah's letter soon. It was ridiculous and humiliating this urge to throw it into the fire unread, as if one could with a single assertive gesture burn away all the past. He heard Latham's voice:

"Of course. The first evening I arrived. I lied about the time, incidentally. I was here soon after six. Soon afterwards, I walked along the cliff and saw the two figures with the boat. I recognized Sylvia and I thought that the man was Seton although I couldn't be sure. It was too dark to see what they were up to but it was obvious that they were shoving the dinghy out to sea. I couldn't see what the bundle was in the bottom of it, but afterwards I could guess. It didn't worry me. Maurice had it coming to him as far as I was concerned. As you seem to have guessed, Dorothy Seton sent me that last letter he wrote to her. I suppose she expected me to avenge her. I'm afraid she mistook her man. I've seen too many second-rate actors make fools of themselves in that role to fancy playing it myself. I hadn't any objection to letting someone else do the job, but when Digby was murdered I thought it was time I found out what Kedge was playing at. Celia told us that Sylvia was planning to see Reckless this morning; it seemed prudent to get in first."

It would be futile, of course, to point out that Latham could have saved Digby's life by speaking sooner. And was it even true? The murderers had their story ready: the bet with Seton; the experiment that went horribly wrong; the panic when they discovered that Maurice was dead; the decision to take off the battered hands in an attempt to cover up. Would it really have been possible without a confession to prove that Maurice Seton hadn't died a natural death?

He gripped Deborah's letter between his left thumb and rigidly bandaged palm and tried to insinuate the tips of his right hand fingers under the flap; but the tough paper resisted him. Latham said impatiently:

"Here, let me do it!"

Under his long nicotine-stained fingers the envelope ripped open. He handed it to Dalgliesh:

"Don't mind me."

"It's all right," said Dalgliesh. "I know what's in it. It can wait." But he was unfolding the sheet as he spoke. There were only eight lines. Deborah had never been verbose even in her love letters but there was a brutal economy about these final staccato sentences. And why not? Theirs was a basic human dilemma. You could either spend a lifetime together laboriously exploring it, or you could dispose of it in eight lines. He found himself counting and recounting them, calculating the number of words, noticing with unnatural interest the spread of the lines, the details of the handwriting. She had decided to accept the job offered to her at the firm's American house. By the time he received this she would be in New York. She could no longer bear to loiter about on the periphery of his life waiting for him to make up his mind. She thought it unlikely that they would ever see each other again. It was better for them both that way. The sentences were conventional, almost trite. It was a goodbye without panache or originality, even without dignity. And if it had been written in pain there was no sign of it in that confident hand.

He could hear Latham's high arrogant voice running on in the background, saying something about an appointment at an Ipswich Hospital to have his head X-rayed, suggesting that Dalgliesh might go with him and have his hand examined, speculating spitefully on what Celia would have to pay in lawyer's fees before she could get her hands on the Seton fortune, attempting once more with the clumsiness of a schoolboy to justify himself for the death of Sylvia Kedge. Dalgliesh turned his back on him and taking his own letter from the mantelpiece, laid the twin envelopes together and tore at them impatiently. But they were too strong for him and, in the end, he had to throw them whole into the fire. They took a long time to burn, each separate sheet charring and curling as the ink faded so that, at last, his own verses shone up at him, silver on black, obstinately refusing to die, and he could not even grasp the poker to beat them into dust.

An Unsuitable Job for a Woman

P. D. JAMES

CHARLES SCRIBNER'S SONS • NEW YORK

For Jane and Peter
who kindly allowed two of
my characters to live at
57 Norwich Street.

Copyright © 1972 P. D. James

Copyright under the Berne Convention.
All rights reserved. No part of this book
may be reproduced in any form without the
permission of Charles Scribner's Sons.

3 5 7 9 11 13 15 17 19 C/C 20 18 16 14 12 10 8 6 4

Printed in the United States of America
Library of Congress Catalog Card Number 72-11140
SBN 684-13280-X (cloth)

Author's Note

A crime novelist, by virtue of his unpleasant craft, has the duty to create at least one highly reprehensible character in each book and it is perhaps inevitable that from time to time their sanguinary misdeeds should impinge upon the dwellings of the just. A writer whose characters have chosen to act out their tragicomedy in an ancient university city is in particular difficulty. He can, of course, call it Oxbridge, invent colleges named after improbable saints and send his characters boating on the Camsis, but this timid compromise merely confuses characters, readers and the author alike, with the result that no one knows precisely where he is and two communities are offered opportunities for offence instead of one.

The greater part of this story is unrepentantly set in Cambridge, a city in which, undeniably, there live and work policemen, coroners, doctors, students, college servants, flower sellers, Dons, scientists, and even, no doubt, retired Majors. None of them, to my knowledge, bears the slightest resemblance to his counterpart in this book. All the characters, even the most unpleasant, are imaginary; the city, happily for us all, is not.

P. D. J.

Chapter One

On the morning of Bernie Pryde's death—or it may have been the morning after, since Bernie died at his own convenience, nor did he think the estimated time of his departure worth recording—Cordelia was caught in a breakdown of the Bakerloo Line outside Lambeth North and was half an hour late at the office. She came up from Oxford Circus underground into the bright June sunshine, sped past the early morning shoppers scanning the windows of Dickins and Jones and plunged into the cacophony of Kingly Street threading her way between the blocked pavement and the shining mass of cars and vans which packed the narrow street. The hurry she knew was irrational, a symptom of her obsession with order and punctuality. There were no appointments booked; no clients to be interviewed; no case outstanding; not even a final report to be written. She and Miss Sparshott, the temporary typist, at Cordelia's suggestion were circulating information about the Agency to all the London solicitors in the hope of attracting custom; Miss Sparshott would probably be busy with it now, eyes straying to her watch, tapping out her staccato irritation at every minute of Cordelia's lateness. She was an unprepossessing woman with lips permanently taut as if to prevent the protruding teeth from springing from her mouth, a receding chin with one coarse hair which grew as quickly as it was plucked, and fair hair set in stiff corrugated waves. That chin and mouth seemed to Cordelia the living refutation that all men are born equal and she tried from time to time to like and sympathize with Miss Sparshott, with a life lived in bedsitting rooms, measured in the five-penny pieces fed to the gas stove and circumscribed by fell seams and hand hemming. For Miss Sparshott was a skilled dressmaker, an assiduous attender at the G.L.C. evening classes. Her clothes were beautifully made but so dateless that they were never actually in fashion; straight skirts in grey or black which were exercises in how to sew a pleat or insert a zip fastener; blouses with mannish collars and cuffs in insipid pastel shades on which she distributed without discretion her collection of costume jewellery; intricately cut dresses with hems at the precise length to emphasize her shapeless legs and thick ankles.

Cordelia had no premonition of tragedy as she pushed open the street door which was kept perpetually on the latch for the convenience of the secretive and mysterious tenants and their equally mysterious visitors. The new bronze plaque to the left of the door gleamed brightly in the sun in incongruous contrast to the faded and dirt-encrusted paint. Cordelia gave it a short glance of approval:

Pryde's Detective Agency
(*Props:* Bernard G. Pryde   Cordelia Gray)

It had taken Cordelia some weeks of patient and tactful persuasion to convince Bernie that it would be inappropriate to append the words "ex-C.I.D. Metropolitan Police" to his name or prefix "Miss" to hers. There had been no other problem over the plaque since Cordelia had brought no qualifications or relevant past experience to the partnership and indeed no capital, except her slight but tough twenty-two-year-old body, a considerable intelligence which Bernie, she suspected, had occasionally found more disconcerting than admirable, and a half exasperated, half pitying affection for Bernie himself. It was obvious very early to Cordelia that in some undramatic but positive way life had turned against him. She recognized the signs. Bernie never got the enviable front left hand seat in the bus; he couldn't admire the view from the train window without another train promptly obscuring it; the bread he dropped invariably fell buttered side downwards; the Mini, reliable enough when she drove it, stalled for Bernie at the busiest and most inconvenient intersections. She sometimes wondered whether, in accepting his offer of a partnership in a fit of depression or of perverse masochism, she was voluntarily embracing his ill-luck. She certainly never saw herself as powerful enough to change it.

The staircase smelt as always of stale sweat, furniture polish and disinfectant. The walls were dark green and were invariably damp whatever the season as if they secreted a miasma of desperate respectability and defeat. The stairs, with their ornate wrought-iron balustrade, were covered with split and stained linoleum patched by the landlord in various and contrasting colours only when a tenant complained. The Agency was on the third floor. There was no clatter of typewriter keys as Cordelia entered and she saw that Miss Sparshott was engaged in cleaning her machine, an ancient Imperial which was a constant cause of justified complaint. She looked up, her face blotched with resentment, her back as rigid as the space bar.

"I've been wondering when you would turn up, Miss Gray. I'm concerned about Mr. Pryde. I think he must be in the inner office but he's quiet, very quiet, and the door's locked."

Cordelia, chill at heart, wrenched at the door handle:

"Why didn't you do something?"

"Do what, Miss Gray? I knocked at the door and called out to him. It wasn't my place to do that, I'm only the temporary typist, I've no authority here. I should have been placed in a very embarrassing position if he had answered. After all, he's entitled to use his own office I suppose. Besides, I'm not even sure if he's there."

"He must be. The door's locked and his hat is here."

Bernie's trilby, the stained brim turned up all round, a comedian's hat, was hanging on the convoluted hatstand, a symbol of forlorn decrepitude. Cordelia was fumbling in her shoulder bag for her own key. As usual, the object most required had fallen to the bottom of the bag. Miss Sparshott began to clatter on the keys as if to disassociate herself from impending trauma. Above the noise she said defensively:

"There's a note on your desk."

Cordelia tore it open. It was short and explicit. Bernie had always been able to express himself succinctly when he had something to say:

"I'm sorry, partner, they've told me it's cancer and I'm taking the easy way out. I've seen what the treatment does to people and I'm not having any. I've made my will and it's with my solicitor. You'll find his name in the desk. I've left the business to you. Everything, including *all* the equipment. Good luck and thank you." Underneath with the inconsiderateness of the doomed he had scribbled a final unfair plea:

"If you find me alive, for God's sake wait before calling help. I rely on you for this, partner. Bernie."

She unlocked the door of the inner office and went inside, closing the door carefully behind her.

It was a relief to see that there was no need to wait. Bernie was dead. He lay slumped over the desk as if in an extremity of exhaustion. His right hand was half-clenched and an open cut-throat razor had slithered over the desk top leaving a thin trail of blood like a snail's track and had come to rest precariously poised on the extreme edge of the desk. His left wrist, scored with two parallel cuts, lay palm upwards in the enamel bowl which Cordelia used for the washing-up. Bernie had filled it with water but it was now brimfull with a pale pinky liquid smelling sickly sweet, through which the fingers, curved as if in supplication and looking as white and delicate as those of a child, gleamed as smooth as wax. The blood and water had overflowed on to the desk and floor soaking the oblong of garish rug which Bernie had recently bought in the hope of impressing visitors with his status but which Cordelia privately thought had only drawn attention to the shabbiness of the rest of the office. One of the cuts was tentative and superficial but the other had gone deep as the bone and the severed edges of the wound, drained of blood, gaped cleanly like an illustration in an anatomy text book. Cordelia remembered how Bernie had once described the finding of a prospective suicide when he was first on the beat as a young constable. It was an old man huddled into a warehouse doorway who had slashed his wrist with a broken bottle—but who had later been dragged back to reluctant half-life because an immense clot of blood had blocked the severed veins. Bernie, remembering, had taken precautions to ensure that his blood would not clot. He had, she noticed, taken another precaution; there was an empty tea cup, the one in which she served his afternoon tea, on the right of the desk with a grain or two of powder, aspirin perhaps or a barbiturate, staining the rim and side. A dried trickle of mucus, similarly stained, hung from the corner of his mouth. His lips were pursed and half open like those of a sleeping child, petulant and vulnerable. She put her head round the office door and said quietly:

"Mr. Pryde is dead; don't come in. I'll ring the police from here."

The telephone message was taken calmly, someone would come round. Sitting beside the body to wait and feeling that she needed to make some gesture of pity and comfort Cordelia laid her hand gently on Bernie's hair. Death had as yet no power to diminish these cold and nerveless cells and the hair felt roughly and unpleasantly alive like that of an animal. Quickly she took her hand away and tentatively touched the side of his forehead. The skin was clammy and very cold. This was death; this was how Daddy had felt. As with him, the gesture of pity was meaningless and irrelevant. There was no more communication in death than there had been in life.

She wondered when exactly Bernie had died. No one now would ever know. Perhaps Bernie himself had not known. There must, she supposed, have been one measurable second in time in which he had ceased to be Bernie and had become this unimportant but embarrassingly unwieldy weight of flesh and bone. How odd that a moment of time so important to him should pass without his knowledge. Her second foster mother, Mrs. Wilkes, would have said that Bernie did know, that there was a moment of indescribable glory, shining towers, limitless singing, skies of triumph. Poor Mrs. Wilkes! Widowed, her only son dead in the war, her small house perpetually noisy with the foster children who were her livelihood, she had needed her dreams. She had lived her life by comfortable maxims stored like nuggets of coal against the winter. Cordelia thought of her now for the first time in years and heard again the tired, determinedly cheerful voice "If the Lord doesn't call on his way out, He'll call on his way back." Well, going or coming, He hadn't called on Bernie.

It was odd but somehow typical of Bernie that he should have retained a dogged and invincible optimism about the business even when they had nothing in the cash box but a few coins for the gas meter and yet had given up hope of life without even a struggle. Was it perhaps that he had sub-consciously recognized that neither he nor the Agency had any real future and had decided that this way he could yield up both life and livelihood with some honour? He had done it effectively but messily, surprisingly so for an ex-policeman versed in the ways of death. And then she realized why he had chosen the razor and the drugs. The gun. He hadn't really taken the easy way out. He could have used the gun, but he had wanted her to have it; he had bequeathed it to her together with the rickety filing cabinets, the antique typewriter, the scene-of-crime kit, the Mini, his shock-proof and waterproof wrist watch, the blood-soaked rug, the embarrassingly large stock of writing paper with the ornate heading *Pryde's Detective Agency—We take a Pride in our Work. All* the equipment; he had underlined all. He must have meant to remind her about the gun.

She unlocked the small drawer at the base of Bernie's desk to which only she and he had a key and drew it out. It was still in the suede draw-string bag which she had made for it, with three rounds of ammunition packed separately. It was a pistol, a .38 semi-automatic; she had never known how Bernie had come by it but she was certain that he had no licence. She had never seen it as a lethal weapon, perhaps because Bernie's boyishly naive obsession with it had reduced it to the impotence of a child's toy. He had taught her to become—at any rate in theory—a creditable shot. They had driven for practice into the depths of Epping Forest and her memories of the gun were linked with dappled shade and the rich smell of decaying leaves. He had fixed a target to a convenient tree; the gun was loaded with blanks. She could still hear the excited staccato orders. "Bend your knees slightly. Feet apart. Arm full length. Now place the left hand against the barrel, cradling it. Keep your eyes on the target. Arm straight, partner, arm straight! Good! Not bad; not bad; not bad at all." "But, Bernie," she had said, "we can never fire it! We haven't a licence." He had smiled, the sly self-satisfied smile of superior knowledge. "If we ever fire in anger it will be to save our lives. In such an eventuality the question of a licence is irrelevant." He had been pleased with this rotund sentence and had repeated it, lifting his heavy face to the sun like a dog. What, she wondered, had he seen in imagination? The two of them crouching behind a boulder on some desolate moor, bullets pinging against the granite, the gun passed smoking from hand to hand?

He had said: "We'll have to go carefully with the ammunition. Not that I can't get it of course . . ." The smile had become grim, as if at the memory of those mysterious contacts, those ubiquitous and obliging acquaintances whom he had only to summon from their shadow world.

So he had left her the gun. It had been his most prized possession. She slipped it, still shrouded, into the depths of her shoulder bag. It was surely unlikely that the police would examine the drawers of the desk in a case of obvious suicide but it was as well to take no risk. Bernie had meant her to have the gun and she wasn't going to give it up easily. With her bag at her feet she sat down again by the body. She said a brief convent-taught prayer to the God she wasn't sure existed for the soul which Bernie had never believed he possessed and waited quietly for the police.

The first policeman to arrive was efficient but young, not yet experienced enough to hide his shock and distaste at the sight of violent death nor his disapproval that Cordelia should be so calm. He didn't spend long in the inner office. When he came out he meditated upon Bernie's note as if a careful scrutiny could extract some inner meaning from the bald sentence of death. Then he folded it away.

"I'll have to keep this note for the present, Miss. What did he get up to here?"

"He didn't get up to anything. This was his office. He was a private detective."

"And you worked for this Mr. Pryde? You were his secretary?"

"I was his partner. It says so in the note. I'm twenty-two. Bernie was the senior partner; he started the business. He used to work for the Metropolitan Police in the C.I.D. with Superintendent Dalgliesh."

As soon as the words were spoken, she regretted them. They were too propitiatory, too naive a defence of poor Bernie. And the name Dalgliesh, she saw meant nothing to him. Why should it? He was just one of the local uniformed branch. He couldn't be expected to know how often she had listened with politely concealed impatience to Bernie's nostalgic reminiscences of his time in the C.I.D. before he was invalided out, or to his eulogies on the virtues and wisdom of Adam Dalgliesh. "The Super—well, he was just an Inspector then—always taught us . . . The Super once described a case . . . If there was one thing the Super couldn't stand . . ."

Sometimes she had wondered whether this paragon had actually existed or whether he had sprung impeccable and omnipotent from Bernie's brain, a necessary hero and mentor. It was with a shock of suprise that she had later seen a newspaper picture of Chief Superintendent Dalgliesh, a dark, sardonic face which, on her closer scrutiny, disintegrated into an ambiguity of patterned micro dots, giving nothing away. Not all the wisdom Bernie so glibly recalled was the received gospel. Much, she suspected, was his own philosophy. She in turn had devised a private litany of disdain: supercilious, superior, sarcastic Super; what wisdom, she wondered, would he have to comfort Bernie now.

The policeman had made discreet telephone calls. He now prowled around the outer office, hardly bothering to hide his puzzled contempt at the shabby second-hand furniture, the battered filing cabinet with one drawer half-open to reveal teapot and mugs, the worn linoleum. Miss Sparshott, rigid at an ancient typewriter, gazed at him with fascinated distaste. At last he said:

"Well, suppose you make yourselves a nice cup of tea while I wait for the police surgeon. There is somewhere to make tea?"

"There's a small pantry down the corridor which we share with the other tenants on this floor. But surely you don't need a surgeon? Bernie's dead!"

"He's not officially dead until a qualified medical practitioner says so." He paused: "It's just a precaution."

Against what, Cordelia wondered—judgement, damnation, decay? The policeman went back into the inner office. She followed him and asked softly:

"Couldn't you let Miss Sparshott go? She's from a secretarial agency and we have to pay for her by the hour. She hasn't done any work since I arrived and I doubt whether she will now."

He was, she saw, a little shocked by the apparent callousness of concerning herself with so mercenary a detail while standing within touching distance of Bernie's body, but he said willingly enough:

"I'll just have a word with her, then she can go. It isn't a nice place for a woman."

His tone implied that it never had been.

Afterwards, waiting in the outer office, Cordelia answered the inevitable questions.

"No, I don't know whether he was married. I've a feeling that he was divorced; he never talked about a wife. He lived at 15, Cremona Road, S.E.2. He let me have a bed-sitting room there but we didn't see much of each other."

"I know Cremona Road; my aunt used to live there when I was a kid—one of those streets near the Imperial War Museum."

The fact that he knew the road seemed to reassure and humanize him. He ruminated happily for a moment.

"When did you last see Mr. Pryde alive?"

"Yesterday at about five o'clock when I left work early to do some shopping."

"Didn't he come home last night?"

"I heard him moving around but I didn't see him. I have a gas ring in my room and I usually cook there unless I know he's out. I didn't hear him this morning which is unusual, but I thought he might be lying in. He does that occasionally when it's his hospital morning."

"Was it his hospital morning to-day?"

"No, he had an appointment last Wednesday but I thought that they might have asked him to come back. He must have left the house very late last night or before I woke early this morning. I didn't hear him."

It was impossible to describe the almost obsessional delicacy with which they avoided each other, trying not to intrude, preserving the other's privacy, listening for the sound of flushing cisterns, tip-toeing to ascertain whether the kitchen or bathroom was empty. They had taken infinite trouble not to be a nuisance to each other. Living in the same small terraced house they had hardly seen each other outside the office. She wondered whether Bernie had decided to kill himself in his office so that the little house would be uncontaminated and undisturbed.

At last the office was empty and she was alone. The police surgeon had closed his bag and departed; Bernie's body had been manoeuvred down the narrow staircase watched by eyes from the half-opened doors of other offices; the last policeman had left. Miss Sparshott had gone for good, violent death being a worse insult than a typewriter which a trained typist ought not to be expected to use or lavatory accommodation which was not at all what she had been accustomed to. Alone in the emptiness and silence Cordelia felt the need of physical action. She began vigorously to clean the inner office, scrubbing the blood stains from desk and chair, mopping the soaked rug.

At one o'clock she walked briskly to their usual pub. It occurred to her that there was no longer any reason to patronize the Golden Pheasant but she walked on unable to bring herself to so early a disloyalty. She had never liked the pub or the landlady and had often wished that Bernie would find a nearer house, preferably one with a large bosomy barmaid with a heart of gold. It was, she suspected, a type commoner in fiction than in real life. The familiar lunch-time crowd was clustered around the bar and, as usual, Mavis presided behind it wearing her slightly minatory smile, her air of extreme respectability. Mavis changed her dress three times a day, her hair style once every year, her smile never. The two women had never liked each other although Bernie had galumphed between them like an affectionate old dog, finding it convenient to believe that they were great mates and unaware of or ignoring the almost physical crackle of antagonism. Mavis reminded Cordelia of a librarian known to her in childhood who had secreted the new books under the counter in case they should be taken out and soiled. Perhaps Mavis's barely suppressed chagrin was because she was forced to display her wares so prominently, compelled to measure out her bounty before watchful eyes. Pushing a half pint of shandy and a Scotch egg across the counter in response to Cordelia's order, she said:

"I hear you've had the police round."

Watching their avid faces, Cordelia thought, they know about it, of course; they want to hear the details; they may as well hear them. She said:

"Bernie cut his wrists twice. The first time he didn't get to the vein; the second time he did. He put his arm in water to help the bleeding. He had been told that he had cancer and couldn't face the treatment."

That, she saw, was different. The little group around Mavis glanced at each other, then quickly averted their eyes. Glasses were momentarily checked upon their upward way. Cutting one's wrist was something which other people did but the sinister little crab had his claws of fear into all their minds. Even Mavis looked as if she saw his bright claws lurking among her bottles. She said:

"You'll be looking for a new job, I suppose? After all, you can hardly keep the Agency going on your own. It isn't a suitable job for a woman."

"No different from working behind a bar; you meet all kinds of people."

The two women looked at each other and a snatch of unspoken dialogue passed between them clearly heard and understood by both.

"And don't think, now he's dead, that people can go on leaving messages for the Agency here."

"I wasn't going to ask."

Mavis began vigorously polishing a glass, her eyes still on Cordelia's face.

"I shouldn't think your mother would approve of you staying on alone."

"I only had a mother for the first hour of my life, so I don't have to worry about that."

Cordelia saw at once that the remark had deeply shocked them and wondered again at the capacity of older people to be outraged by simple facts when they seemed capable of accepting any amount of perverse or shocking opinion. But their silence, heavy with censure, at least left her in peace. She carried her shandy and the Scotch egg to a seat against the wall and thought without sentimentality about her mother. Gradually out of a childhood of deprivation she had evolved a philosophy of compensation. In her imagination she had enjoyed a lifetime of love in one hour with no disappointments and no regrets. Her father had never talked about her mother's death and Cordelia had avoided questioning him, fearful of learning that her mother had never held her in her arms, never regained consciousness, never perhaps even known that she had a daughter. This belief in her mother's love was the one fantasy which she could still not entirely risk losing although its indulgence had become less necessary and less real with each passing year. Now, in imagination, she consulted her mother. It was just as she expected: her mother thought it an entirely suitable job for a woman.

The little group at the bar had turned back to their drinks. Between their shoulders she could see her own reflection in the mirror above the bar. Today's face looked no different from yesterday's face; thick, light brown hair framing features which looked as if a giant had placed a hand on her head and the other under her chin and gently squeezed the face together; large eyes, browny-green under a deep fringe of hair; wide cheek bones; a gentle, childish mouth. A cat's face she thought, but calmly decorative among the reflection of coloured bottles and all the bright glitter of Mavis's bar. Despite its look of deceptive youth it could be a secret, uncommunicative face. Cordelia had early learnt stoicism. All her foster parents, kindly and well-meaning in their different ways, had demanded one thing of her—that she should be happy. She had quickly learned that to show unhappiness was to risk the loss of love. Compared with this early discipline of concealment, all subsequent deceits had been easy.

The Snout was edging his way towards her. He settled himself down on the bench, his thick rump in its appalling tweed pressed close to hers. She disliked the Snout although he had been Bernie's only friend. Bernie had explained that the Snout was a police informer and did rather well. And there were other sources of income. Sometimes his friends stole famous pictures or valuable jewellery. Then the Snout, suitably instructed, would hint to the police where the loot could be found. There was a reward for the Snout to be subsequently shared, of course, among the thieves, and a payoff, too, for the detective, who after all, had done most of the work. As Bernie had pointed out, the insurance company got off lightly, the owners got their property back intact, the thieves were in no danger from the police and the Snout and the detective got their payoff. It was the system. Cordelia, shocked, had not liked to protest too much. She suspected that Bernie too had done some snouting in his time, although never with such expertise or with such lucrative results.

The Snout's eyes were rheumy, his hand around the glass of whisky was shaking.

"Poor old Bernie, I could see he had it coming to him. He'd been losing weight for the last year and he had that grey look to him, the cancer complexion, my dad used to call it."

At least the Snout had noticed; she hadn't. Bernie had always seemed to her grey and sick-looking. A thick, hot thigh edged closer.

"Never had any luck, poor sod. They chucked him out of the C.I.D. Did he tell you? That was Superintendent Dalgliesh, Inspector at the time. Christ, he could be a proper bastard; no second chance from him, I can tell you."

"Yes, Bernie told me," Cordelia lied. She added: "He didn't seem particularly bitter about it."

"No use, is there, in being bitter? Take what comes, that's my motto. I suppose you'll be looking for another job?"

He said it wistfully as if her defection would leave the Agency open for his exploitation.

"Not just yet," said Cordelia. "I shan't look for a new job just yet."

She had made two resolutions: she would keep on Bernie's business until there was nothing left with which to pay the rent, and she would never come into the Golden Pheasant again as long as she lived.

This resolution to keep the business going survived the next four days—survived discovery of the rent book and agreement which revealed that Bernie hadn't, after all, owned the little house in Cremona Road and that her tenancy of the bedsitting room was illegal and certainly limited; survived learning from the Bank Manager that Bernie's credit balance would barely pay for his funeral and from the garage that the Mini was shortly due for an overhaul; survived the clearing up of the Cremona Road house. Everywhere was the sad detritus of a solitary and mismanaged life.

The tins of Irish stew and baked beans—had he never eaten anything else?—stacked in a carefully arranged pyramid as if in a grocer's window; large tins of floor and metal polish, half-used, with their contents dried or congealed; a drawer of old rags used as dusters but stiff with an amalgam of polish and dirt; a laundry basket unemptied; thick woollen combinations felted with machine washing and stained brown about the crotch—how could he have borne to leave those for discovery?

She went daily to the office, cleaning, tidying, rearranging the filing. There were no calls and no clients and yet she seemed always busy. There was the inquest to attend, depressing in its detached almost boring formality, in its inevitable verdict. There was a visit to Bernie's solicitor. He was a dispirited, elderly man with an office inconveniently situated near Mile End Station who took the news of his client's death with lugubrious resignation as if it were a personal affront, and after a brief search found Bernie's will and pored over it with puzzled suspicion, as if it were not the document he himself had recently drawn up. He succeeded in giving Cordelia the impression that he realized that she had been Bernie's mistress—why else should he have left her the business?—but that he was a man of the world and didn't hold the knowledge against her. He took no part in arranging the funeral except to supply Cordelia with the name of a firm of undertakers; she suspected that they probably gave him a commission. She was relieved after a week of depressing solemnity to find that the funeral director was both cheerful and competent. Once he discovered that Cordelia wasn't going to break down in tears or indulge in the more histrionic antics of the bereaved, he was happy to discuss the relative price and the merits of burial and cremation with conspiratorial candour.

"Cremation every time. There's no private insurance, you tell me? Then get it all over as quickly, easily and cheaply as possible. Take my word, that's what the deceased would want nine times out of ten. A grave's an expensive luxury these days—no use to him—no use to you. Dust to dust, ashes to ashes; but what about the process in between? Not nice to think about, is it? So why not get it over as quickly as possible by the most reliable modern methods? Mind you, Miss, I'm advising you against my own best interests."

Cordelia said:

"It's very kind of you. Do you think we ought to have a wreath?"

"Why not, it'll give it a bit of tone. Leave it to me."

So there had been a cremation and one wreath. The wreath had been a vulgarly inappropriate cushion of lilies and carnations, the flowers already dying and smelling of decay. The cremation service had been spoken by the priest with carefully controlled speed and with a suggestion of apology in his tone as if to assure his hearers that, although he enjoyed a special dispensation, he didn't expect them to believe the unbelievable. Bernie had passed to his burning to the sound of synthetic music and only just on time, to judge by the impatient rustlings of the cortège already waiting to enter the chapel.

Afterwards Cordelia was left standing in the bright sunlight, feeling the heat of the gravel through the soles of her shoes. The air was rich and heavy with the scent of flowers. Swept suddenly with desolation and a defensive anger on Bernie's behalf, she sought a scapegoat and found it in a certain Superintendent of the Yard. He had kicked Bernie out of the only job he had ever wanted to do; hadn't troubled to find out what happened to him later; and, most irrational indictment of all, he hadn't even bothered to come to the funeral. Bernie had needed to be a detective as other men needed to paint, write, drink or fornicate. Surely the C.I.D. was large enough to accommodate one man's enthusiasm and inefficiency? For the first time Cordelia wept for Bernie; hot tears blurred and multiplied the long line of waiting hearses with their bright coronets so that they seemed to stretch in an infinity of gleaming chrome and trembling flowers. Untying the black chiffon scarf from her head, her only concession to mourning, Cordelia set off to walk to the tube station.

She was thirsty when she got to Oxford Circus and decided to have tea in the restaurant at Dickins and Jones. This was unusual and an extravagance but it had been an unusual and extravagant day. She lingered long enough to get full value for her bill and it was after a quarter past four when she returned to the office.

She had a visitor. There was a woman waiting, shoulders against the door—a woman who looked cool and incongruous against the dirty paintwork and the greasy walls. Cordelia caught her breath in surprise, her upward rush checked. Her light shoes had made no sound on the stairway and for a few seconds she saw her visitor unobserved. She gained an impression, immediate and vivid, of competence and authority and an intimidating rightness of dress. The woman was wearing a grey suit with a small stand-away collar which showed a narrow band of white cotton at the throat. Her black patent shoes were obviously expensive; a large black bag with patch pockets was slung from her left shoulder. She was tall and her hair, prematurely white, was cut short and moulded to her head like a cap. Her face was pale and long. She was reading *The Times*, the paper folded so that she could hold it in her right hand. After a couple of seconds, she became aware of Cordelia and their eyes met. The woman looked at her wrist watch.

"If you are Cordelia Gray, then you're eighteen minutes late. This notice says that you would return at four o'clock."

"I know, I'm sorry." Cordelia hurried up the last few steps and fitted the Yale key into the lock. She opened the door.

"Won't you come in?"

The woman preceded her into the outer office and turned to face her without giving the room even a glance.

"I was hoping to see Mr. Pryde. Will he be long?"

"I'm sorry; I've just come back from his cremation. I mean . . . Bernie's dead."

"Obviously. Our information was that he was alive ten days ago. He must have died with remarkable speed and discretion."

"Not with discretion. Bernie killed himself."

"How extraordinary!" The visitor seemed to be struck by its extraordinariness. She pressed her hands together and for a few seconds walked restlessly about the room in a curious pantomime of distress.

"How extraordinary!" she said again. She gave a little snort of laughter. Cordelia didn't speak, but the two women regarded each other gravely. Then the visitor said:

"Well, I seem to have had a wasted journey."

Cordelia breathed an almost inaudible "Oh no!" and resisted an absurd impulse to fling her body against the door.

"Please don't go before talking to me. I was Mr. Pryde's partner and I own the business now. I'm sure I could help. Won't you please sit down?"

The visitor took no notice of the offered chair.

"No one can help, no one in the world. However, that is beside the point. There is something which my employer particularly wants to know—some information he requires—and he had decided that Mr. Pryde was the person to get it for him. I don't know if he would consider you an effective substitute. Is there a private telephone here?"

"In here, please."

The woman walked into the inner office, again with no sign that its shabbiness had made any impression on her. She turned to Cordelia.

"I'm sorry, I should have introduced myself. My name is Elizabeth Leaming and my employer is Sir Ronald Callender."

"The conservationist?"

"I shouldn't let him hear you call him that. He prefers to be called a micro-biologist, which is what he is. Please excuse me."

She shut the door firmly. Cordelia, feeling suddenly weak, sat down at the typewriter. They keys, oddly unfamiliar symbols encircled in black medallions, shifted their pattern before her tired eyes, then at a blink clicked back to normality. She grasped the sides of the machine, cold and clammy to the touch, and talked herself back to calmness. Her heart was thudding.

"I must be calm, must show her that I am tough. This silliness is only the strain of Bernie's funeral and too much standing in the hot sun."

But hope was traumatic; she was angry with herself for caring so much.

The telephone call took only a couple of minutes. The door of the inner office opened; Miss Leaming was drawing on her gloves.

"Sir Ronald has asked to see you. Can you come now?"

Come where, thought Cordelia, but she didn't ask.

"Yes, shall I need my gear?"

The gear was Bernie's carefully designed and fitted out scene-of-crime case with its tweezers, scissors, finger printing equipment, jars to collect specimens; Cordelia had never yet had occasion to use it.

"It depends upon what you mean by your gear, but I shouldn't think so. Sir Ronald wants to see you before deciding whether to offer you the job. It means a train journey to Cambridge but you should get back tonight. Is there anyone you ought to tell?"

"No, there's only me."

"Perhaps I ought to identify myself." She opened her handbag. "Here is an addressed envelope. I'm not a white slaver if they exist and in case you're frightened."

"I'm frightened of quite a number of things but not of white slavers and if I were, an addressed envelope would hardly reassure me. I'd insist on telephoning Sir Ronald Callender to check."

"Perhaps you would like to do so?" suggested Miss Leaming without rancour.

"No."

"Then shall we go?" Miss Leaming led the way to the door. As they went out to the landing and Cordelia turned to lock the office behind her, her visitor indicated the notepad and pencil hanging together from a nail on the wall.

"Hadn't you better change the notice?"

Cordelia tore off her previous message and after a moment's thought wrote:

I am called away to an urgent case. Any messages pushed through the door will receive my immediate and personal attention on return.

"That," pronounced Miss Leaming, "should reassure your clients." Cordelia wondered if the remark was sarcastic; it was impossible to tell from the detached tone. But she didn't feel that Miss Leaming was laughing at her and was surprised at her own lack of resentment at the way in which her visitor had taken charge of events. Meekly, she followed Miss Leaming down the stairs and into Kingly Street.

They travelled by the Central Line to Liverpool Street and caught the 17.36 train to Cambridge with plenty of time. Miss Leaming bought Cordelia's ticket, collected a portable typewriter and a briefcase of papers from the left luggage department and led the way to a first-class carriage. She said:

"I shall have to work in the train; have you anything to read?"

"That's all right. I don't like talking when I'm travelling either. I've got Hardy's *Trumpet Major*—I always have a paperback in my bag."

After Bishops Stortford they had the compartment to themselves but only once did Miss Leaming look up from her work to question Cordelia.

"How did you come to be working for Mr. Pryde?"

"After I left school I went to live with my father on the continent. We travelled around a good deal. He died in Rome last May after a heart attack and I came home. I had taught myself some shorthand and typing so I took a job with a secretarial agency. They sent me to Bernie and after a few weeks he let me help him with one or two of the cases. He decided to train me and I agreed to stay on permanently. Two months ago he made me his partner."

All that had meant was that Cordelia gave up a regular wage in return for the uncertain rewards of success in the form of an equal share of the profits together with a rent-free bedsitting room in Bernie's house. He hadn't meant to cheat. The offer of the partnership had been made in the genuine belief that she would recognize it for what it was; not a good conduct prize but an accolade of trust.

"What was your father?"

"He was an itinerant Marxist poet and an amateur revolutionary."

"You must have had an interesting childhood."

Remembering the succession of foster mothers, the unexplained incomprehensible moves from house to house, the changes of school, the concerned faces of Local Authority Welfare Officers and school teachers desperately wondering what to do with her in the holidays, Cordelia replied as she always did to this assertion, gravely and without irony.

"Yes, it was very interesting."

"And what was this training you received from Mr. Pryde?"

"Bernie taught me some of the things he learnt in the C.I.D.: how to search the scene of a crime properly, how to collect exhibits, some elementary self-defence, how to detect and lift finger prints—that kind of thing."

"Those are skills which I hardly feel you will find appropriate to this case."

Miss Leaming bent her head over her papers and did not speak again until the train reached Cambridge.

Outside the station Miss Leaming briefly surveyed the car park and led the way towards a small black van. Standing beside it rigidly as a uniformed chauffeur, was a stockily built young man dressed in an open-necked white shirt, dark breeches and tall boots who Miss Leaming introduced casually and without explanation as "Lunn." He nodded briefly in acknowledgement of the introduction but did not smile. Cordelia held out her hand. His grip was momentary but remarkably strong, crushing her fingers; suppressing a grimace of pain she saw a flicker in the large mud-brown eyes and wondered if he had hurt her deliberately. The eyes were certainly memorable and beautiful, moist calves' eyes heavily lashed and with the same look of troubled pain at the unpredictability of the world's terrors. But their beauty emphasized rather than redeemed the unattractiveness of the rest of him. He was, she thought, a sinister study in black and white with his thick, short neck and powerful shoulders straining the seams of his shirt. He had a helmet of strong black hair, a pudgy slightly pox-marked face and a moist petulant mouth; the face of a ribald cherub. He was a man who sweated profusely; the underarms of his shirt were stained and the cotton stuck to the flesh emphasizing the strong curve of the back and the obtrusive biceps.

Cordelia saw that the three of them were to sit squashed together in the front of the van. Lunn held open the door without apology except to state:

"The Rover's still in dock."

Miss Leaming hung back so that Cordelia was compelled to get in first and to sit beside him. She thought: "They don't like each other and he resents me."

She wondered about his position in Sir Ronald Callender's household. Miss Leaming's place she had already guessed; no ordinary secretary however long in service, however indispensable, had quite that air of authority or talked of "my employer" in that tone of possessive irony. But she wondered about Lunn. He didn't behave like a subordinate but nor did he strike her as a scientist. True, scientists were alien creatures to her. Sister Mary Magdalen was the only one she had known. Sister had taught what the syllabus dignified as general science, a hotch-potch of elementary physics, chemistry and biology unceremoniously lumped together. Science subjects were in general little regarded at the Convent of the Immaculate Conception, although the arts were well taught. Sister Mary Magdalen had been an elderly and timid nun, eyes puzzled behind her steel-rimmed spectacles, her clumsy fingers permanently stained with chemicals, who had apparently been as surprised as her pupils at the extraordinary explosions and fumes which her activities with test tube and flask had occasionally produced. She had been more concerned to demonstrate the incomprehensibility of the universe and the inscrutability of God's laws than to reveal scientific principles and in this she had certainly succeeded. Cordelia felt that Sister Mary Magdalen would be no help to her in dealing with Sir Ronald Callender; Sir Ronald who had campaigned in the cause of conservation long before his interest became a popular obsession, who had represented his country at International Conferences on Ecology and been knighted for his services to conservation. All this Cordelia, like the rest of the country, knew from his television appearances and the Sunday Colour Supplements. He was the establishment scientist, carefully uncommitted politically, who personified to everyone's reassurance the poor boy who had made good and stayed good. How, Cordelia wondered, had he come to think of employing Bernie Pryde?

Uncertain how far Lunn was in his employer's or Miss Leaming's confidence, she asked carefully:

"How did Sir Ronald hear about Bernie?"

"John Bellinger told him."

So the Bellinger bonus had arrived at last! Bernie had always expected it. The Bellinger case had been his most lucrative, perhaps his only, success. John Bellinger was the director of a small family firm which manufactured specialized scientific instruments. The previous year his office had been plagued by an outbreak of obscene letters and, unwilling to call in the police, he had telephoned Bernie. Bernie, taken on the staff at his own suggestion as a messenger, had quickly solved a not very difficult problem. The writer had been Bellinger's middle-aged and highly regarded personal secretary. Bellinger had been grateful. Bernie, after anxious thought and consultation with Cordelia, had sent in a bill the size of which had astounded them both and the bill had been promptly paid. It had kept the Agency going for a month. Bernie had said: "We'll get a bonus from the Bellinger case, see if we don't. Anything can happen in this job. He only chose us by picking our name from the telephone directory but now he'll recommend us to his friends. This case could be the beginning of something big."

And now, thought Cordelia, on the day of Bernie's funeral, the Bellinger bonus had arrived.

She asked no more questions and the drive, which took less than thirty minutes, passed in silence. The three of them sat thigh to thigh, but distanced. She saw nothing of the city. At the end of Station Road by the War Memorial the car turned to the left and soon they were in the country. There were wide fields of young corn, the occasional stretch of tree-lined dappled shade, straggling villages of thatched cottages and squat red villas strung along the road, low uplands from which Cordelia could see the towers and spires of the city, shining with deceptive nearness in the evening sun. Finally, there was another village, a thin belt of elms fringing the road, a long curving wall of red brick and the van turned in through open wrought iron gates. They had arrived.

The house was obviously Georgian, not perhaps the best Georgian but solidly built, agreeably proportioned and with the look of all good domestic architecture of having grown naturally out of its site. The mellow brick, festooned with wisteria, gleamed richly in the evening sun so that the green of the creeper glowed and the whole house looked suddenly as artificial and unsubstantial as a film set. It was essentially a family house, a welcoming house. But now a heavy silence lay over it and the rows of elegantly proportioned windows were empty eyes.

Lunn, who had driven fast but skilfully, braked in front of the porch. He stayed in his seat while the two women got out then drove the van round the side of the house. As she slid down from the high seat Cordelia could glimpse a range of low buildings, topped with small ornamental turrets, which she took to be stables or garages. Through the wide-arched gateway she could see that the grounds dropped slowly away to give a far vista of the flat Cambridgeshire countryside, patterned with the gentle greens and fawns of early summer. Miss Leaming said:

"The stable block has been converted into laboratories. Most of the east side is now glass. It was a skilful job by a Swedish architect, functional but attractive."

For the first time since they had met her voice sounded interested, almost enthusiastic.

The front door was open. Cordelia came into a wide, panelled hall with a staircase curving to the left, a carved stone fireplace to the right. She was aware of a smell of roses and lavender, of carpets gleaming richly against polished wood, of the subdued ticking of a clock.

Miss Leaming led the way to a door immediately across the hall. It led to a study, a room booklined and elegant, one with a view of wide lawns and a shield of trees. In front of the french windows was a Georgian desk and behind the desk sat a man.

Cordelia had seen his photographs in the press and knew what to expect. But he was at once smaller and more impressive than she had imagined. She knew that she was facing a man of authority and high intelligence; his strength came over like a physical force. But as he rose from his seat and waved her to a chair, she saw that he was slighter than his photographs suggested, the heavy shoulders and impressive head making the body look top-heavy. He had a lined, sensitive face with a high-bridged nose, deep-set eyes on which the lids weighed heavily and a mobile, sculptured mouth. His black hair, as yet unflecked with grey, lay heavily across his brow. His face was shadowed with weariness and, as Cordelia came closer, she could detect the twitch of a nerve in his left temple and the almost imperceptible staining of the veins in the irises of the deep-set eyes. But his compact body, taut with energy and latent vigour, made no concession to tiredness. The arrogant head was held high, the eyes were keen and wary under the heavy lids. Above all he looked successful. Cordelia had seen that look before, had recognized it from the back of crowds as, inscrutable, they had watched the famous and notorious pass on their way—that almost physical glow, akin to sexuality and undimmed by weariness or ill-health, of men who knew and enjoyed the realities of power.

Miss Leaming said:

"This is all that remains of Pryde's Detective Agency—Miss Cordelia Gray."

The keen eyes looked into Cordelia's.

"We take a Pride in our Work. Do you?"

Cordelia, tired after her journey at the end of a momentous day, was in no mood for jokes about poor Bernie's pathetic pun. She said:

"Sir Ronald, I have come here because your secretary said that you might want to employ me. If she's wrong, I would be glad to know so that I can get back to London."

"She isn't my secretary and she isn't wrong. You must forgive my discourtesy; it's a little disconcerting to expect a burly ex-policeman and to get you. I'm not complaining, Miss Gray; you might do very well. What are your fees?"

The question might have sounded offensive but it wasn't; he was completely matter-of-fact. Cordelia told him, a little too quickly, a little too eagerly.

"Five pounds a day and expenses, but we try to keep those as low as possible. For that, of course, you get my sole services. I mean I don't work for any other client until your case is finished."

"And is there another client?"

"Well, not just at present but there very well could be." She went on quickly:

"We have a fair-play clause. If I decide at any stage of the investigation that I'd rather not go on with it, you are entitled to any information I have gained up to that point. If I decide to withhold it from you, then I make no charge for the work already done."

That had been one of Bernie's principles. He had been a great man for principles. Even when there hadn't been a case for a week, he could happily discuss the extent to which they would be justified in telling a client less than the full truth, the point at which the police ought to be brought into an enquiry, the ethics of deception or lying in the service of truth. "But no bugging," Bernie would say "I set my face firmly against bugging. And we don't touch industrial sabotage."

The temptation to either wasn't great. They had no bugging equipment and wouldn't have known how to use it if they had, and at no time had Bernie been invited to touch industrial sabotage.

Sir Ronald said:

"That sounds reasonable but I don't think this case will

present you with any crisis of conscience. It is comparatively simple. Eighteen days ago my son hanged himself. I want you to find out why. Can you do that?"

"I should like to try, Sir Ronald."

"I realize that you need certain basic information about Mark. Miss Leaming will type it out for you, then you can read it through and let us know what else you require."

Cordelia said:

"I should like you to tell me yourself, please."

"Is that necessary?"

"It would be helpful to me."

He settled again into his chair and picked up a stub of pencil, twisting it in his hands. After a minute he slipped it absent-mindedly into his pocket. Without looking at her, he began to speak.

"My son Mark was twenty-one on the 25th April this year. He was at Cambridge reading history at my old college and was in his final year. Five weeks ago and without warning, he left the university and took a job as gardener with a Major Markland, who lives in a house called Summertrees outside Duxford. Mark gave me no explanation of this action either then or later. He lived alone in a cottage in Major Markland's grounds. Eighteen days later he was found by his employer's sister hanging by the neck from a strap knotted to a hook in the sitting-room ceiling. The verdict at the inquest was that he took his life while the balance of his mind was disturbed. I know little of my son's mind but I reject that comfortable euphemism. He was a rational person. He had a reason for his action. I want to know what it was."

Miss Leaming, who had been looking out of the french windows to the garden, turned and said with sudden vehemence:

"This lust always to know! It's only prying. If he'd wanted us to know, he'd have told us."

Sir Ronald said:

"I'm not prepared to go on in this uncertainty. My son is dead. *My* son. If I am in some way responsible, I prefer to know. If anyone else is responsible I want to know that too."

Cordelia looked from one to the other: She asked:

"Did he leave a note?"

"He left a note but not an explanation. It was found in his typewriter."

Quietly Miss Leaming began to speak:

> "Down the winding cavern we groped our tedious way, till a void boundless as the nether sky appeared beneath us, and we held by the roots of trees and hung over this immensity; but I said: if you please we will commit ourselves to this void, and see whether providence is here also."

The husky, curiously deep voice came to an end. They were silent. Then Sir Ronald said:

"You claim to be a detective, Miss Gray. What do you deduce from that?"

"That your son read William Blake. Isn't it a passage from *The Marriage of Heaven and Hell?*"

Sir Ronald and Miss Leaming glanced at each other. Sir Ronald said:

"So I am told."

Cordelia thought that Blake's gently unemphatic exhortation, devoid of violence or despair, was more appropriate to suicide by drowning or by poison—a ceremonious floating or sinking into oblivion—than to the trauma of hanging. And yet there was the analogy of falling, of launching oneself into the void. But this speculation was indulgent fantasy. He had chosen Blake: he had chosen hanging. Perhaps other and more gentle means were not to hand; perhaps he had acted upon impulse. What was it that the Super always said? "Never theorize in advance of your facts." She would have to look at the cottage.

Sir Ronald said, with a touch of impatience.

"Well, don't you want the job?"

Cordelia looked at Miss Leaming but the woman did not meet her eyes.

"I want it very much. I was wondering whether you really want me to take it."

"I'm offering it to you. Worry about your own responsibilities, Miss Gray, and I'll look after mine."

Cordelia said:

"Is there anything else that you can tell me? The ordinary things. Was your son in good health? Did he seem worried about his work or his love affairs? About money?"

"Mark would have inherited a considerable fortune from his maternal grandfather had he reached the age of twenty-five. In the meantime, he received an adequate allowance from me, but from the date of leaving college he transferred the balance back to my own account and instructed his Bank Manager to deal similarly with any future payments. Presumably he lived on his earnings for the last two weeks of his life. The postmortem revealed no illnesses and his tutor testified that his academic work was satisfactory. I, of course, know nothing of his subject. He didn't confide in me about his love affairs—what young man does to his father? If he had any, I would expect them to be heterosexual."

Miss Leaming turned from her contemplation at the garden. She held out her hands in a gesture which could have been resignation or despair:

"We knew nothing about him, nothing! So why wait until he's dead and then start finding out?"

"And his friends?" asked Cordelia quietly.

"They rarely visited here but there were two I recognized at the inquest and the funeral: Hugo Tilling from his own college and his sister who is a post-graduate student at New Hall, studying philology. Do you remember her name, Eliza?"

"Sophie. Sophia Tilling. Mark brought her here to dinner once or twice."

"Could you tell me something about your son's early life? Where was he educated?"

"He went to a pre-prep school when he was five and to a prep school subsequently. I couldn't have a child here running unsupervised in and out of the laboratory. Later, at his mother's wish—she died when Mark was nine months old—he went to a Woodard Foundation. My wife was what I believe is called a High Anglican and wanted the boy educated in that tradition. As far as I know, it had no deleterious effect on him."

"Was he happy at prep school?"

"I expect he was as happy as most eight-year-olds are, which means that he was miserable most of the time, interposed with periods of animal spirits. Is all this relevant?"

"Anything could be. I have to try to get to know him, you see."

What was it that the supercilious, sapient, superhuman Super had taught? "Get to know the dead person. Nothing about him is too trivial, too unimportant. Dead men can talk. They can lead you directly to their murderer." Only this time, of course, there wasn't a murderer. She said:

"It would be helpful if Miss Leaming could type out the information you have given to me and add the name of his college and his tutor. And please may I have a note signed by you to authorize me to make enquiries."

He reached down to a left-hand drawer in the desk, took out a sheet of writing paper and wrote on it; then he passed it to Cordelia. The printed heading read: From Sir Ronald Callender, F.R.S., Garforth House, Cambridgeshire. Underneath he had written:

The bearer, Miss Cordelia Gray, is authorized to make enquiries on my behalf into the death on 26th May of my son Mark Callender.

He had signed and dated it. He asked:

"Is there anything else?"

Cordelia said:

"You talked about the possibility of someone else being responsible for your son's death. Do you quarrel with the verdict?"

"The verdict was in accordance with the evidence which is all one can expect of a verdict. A court of law is not constituted to establish the truth. I'm employing you to make an attempt at that. Have you everything you need? I don't think we can help you with any more information."

"I should like a photograph." They looked at each other nonplussed. He said to Miss Leaming.

"A photograph. Have we a photograph, Eliza?"

"There is his passport somewhere but I'm not sure where. I have that photograph I took of him in the garden last summer. It shows him fairly clearly, I think. I'll get it." She went out of the room. Cordelia said:

"And I should like to see his room, if I may. I assume that he stayed here during his vacations?"

"Only occasionally, but of course he had a room here. I'll show it to you."

The room was on the second floor and at the back. Once inside, Sir Ronald ignored Cordelia. He walked over to the window and gazed out over the lawns as if neither she nor the room held any interest for him. It told Cordelia nothing about the adult Mark. It was simply furnished, a school boy's sanctum, and looked as if little had been changed in the last ten years. There was a low white cupboard against one wall with the usual row of discarded childhood toys; a teddy bear, his fur scuffed with much cuddling and one beady eye hanging loose; painted wooden trains and trucks; a Noah's Ark, its deck a-tumble with stiff-legged animals topped by a round-faced Noah and his wife; a boat with limp dejected sail; a miniature darts board. Above the toys were two rows of books. Cordelia went over to examine them. Here was the orthodox library of the middle-class child, the approved classics handed down from generation to generation, the traditional lore of Nanny and mother. Cordelia had come to them late as an adult; they had found no place in her Saturday comic and television-dominated childhood. She said:

"What about his present books?"

"They're in boxes in the cellar. He sent them here for storage when he left college and we haven't had time to unpack them yet. There hardly seems any point in it."

There was a small round table beside the bed and on it a lamp and a bright round stone intricately holed by the sea, a treasure picked up, perhaps, from some holiday beach. Sir Ronald touched it gently with long tentative fingers then began rolling it under his palm over the surface of the table. Then, apparently without thinking, he dropped it into his pocket. "Well," he said. "Shall we go down now?"

They were met at the foot of the stairs by Miss Leaming. She looked up at them as slowly they came down side by side. There was such controlled intensity in her regard that Cordelia waited almost with apprehension for her to speak. But she turned away, her shoulders drooping as if with sudden fatigue, and all she said was:

"I've found the photograph. I should like it back when you've finished with it, please. I've put it in the envelope with the note. There isn't a fast train back to London until nine thirty-seven, so perhaps you would care to stay for dinner?"

The dinner party which followed was an interesting but rather odd experience, the meal itself a blend of the formal and casual which Cordelia felt was the result of conscious effort rather than chance. Some effect, she felt, had been aimed at but whether of a dedicated band of co-workers meeting together at the end of a day for a corporate meal, or the ritual imposition of order and ceremony on a diverse company, she wasn't sure. The party numbered ten: Sir Ronald Callender, Miss Leaming, Chris Lunn, a visiting American Professor, whose unpronounceable name she forgot as soon as Sir Ronald introduced her, and five of the young scientists. All the men, including Lunn, were in dinner jackets, and Miss Leaming wore a long skirt of patchwork satin below a plain sleeveless top. The rich blues, greens and reds gleamed and changed in the candlelight as she moved, and emphasized the pale silver of her hair and the almost colourless skin. Cordelia had been rather nonplussed when her hostess left her in the drawing room and went upstairs to change. She wished that she had something more competitive than the fawn skirt and green top, being at an age to value elegance more highly than youth.

She had been shown to Miss Leaming's bedroom to wash and had been intrigued by the elegance and simplicity of the furniture and the contrasting opulence of the adjacent bathroom. Studying her tired face in the mirror and wielding her lipstick, she had wished she had some eye shadow with her. On impulse, and with a sense of guilt, she had pulled open a dressing-table drawer. It was filled with a variety of make-up; old lipsticks in colours long out-of-date; half used bottles of foundation cream; eye pencils; moisturizing creams; half-used bottles of scent. She had rummaged, and eventually found, a stick of eye shadow which, in view of the wasteful muddle of discarded items in the drawer, she had had little compunction in using. The effect had been bizarre but striking. She could not compete with Miss

Leaming but at least she looked five years older. The disorder in the drawer had surprised her and she had had to resist the temptation to see if the wardrobe and the other drawers were in a similar state of disarray. How inconsistent and how interesting human beings were! She thought it astonishing that such a fastidious and competent woman should be content to live with such a mess.

The dining room was at the front of the house. Miss Leaming placed Cordelia between herself and Lunn, a seating which held little prospect of pleasurable conversation. The rest of the party sat where they wished. The contrast between simplicity and elegance showed in the table arrangements. There was no artificial light and three silver branched candlesticks were placed at regular intervals down the table. Between them were set four wine carafes made of thick green glass with curved lips, such as Cordelia had often seen in cheap Italian restaurants. The place mats were of plain cork, but the forks and spoons were antique silver. The flowers were set in low bowls, not skilfully arranged but looking as if they were casualties of a garden storm, blooms which had snapped off in the wind and which someone had thought it kind to place in water.

The young men looked incongruous in their dinner jackets, not ill at ease since they enjoyed the essential self-esteem of the clever and successful, but as if they had picked up the suits second-hand or at a fancy dress costumier and were participating in a charade. Cordelia was surprised at their youth; she guessed that only one was over thirty. Three were untidy, fast talking, restless young men with loud emphatic voices who took no notice of Cordelia after the first introduction. The other two were quieter and one, a tall black-haired boy with strong irregular features, smiled at her across the table and looked as if he would like to have sat within speaking distance.

The meal was brought in by an Italian manservant and his wife who left the cooked dishes on hot plates on a side table. The food was plentiful and the smell almost intolerably appetizing to Cordelia, who hadn't realized until then just how hungry she was. There was a dish heaped high with glistening rice, a large casserole of veal in a rich mushroom sauce, a bowl of spinach.

Beside it on the cold table was a large ham, a sirloin of beef and an interesting assortment of salads and fruit. The company served themselves, carrying their plates back to the table with whatever combination of food, hot or cold, they fancied. The young scientists piled their plates high and Cordelia followed their example.

She took little interest in the conversation except to notice that it was predominantly about science and that Lunn, although he spoke less than the others, spoke as their equal. He should, she thought, have looked ridiculous in his rather tight dinner jacket but, surprisingly, he looked the most at ease, the second most powerful personality in the room. Cordelia tried to analyse why this was so, but was defeated. He ate slowly, with finicky attention to the arrangement of the food on his plate, and from time to time, smiled secretly into his wine.

At the other end of the table Sir Ronald was peeling an apple and talking to his guest, his head inclined. The green rind slid thinly over his long fingers and curved down towards his plate. Cordelia glanced at Miss Leaming. She was staring at Sir Ronald with such unwavering and speculative concern, that Cordelia uncomfortably felt that every eye present must be irresistibly drawn to that pale disdainful mask. Then, Miss Leaming seemed to become aware of her glance. She relaxed and turned to Cordelia:

"When we were travelling here together you were reading Hardy. Do you enjoy him?"

"Very much. But I enjoy Jane Austen more."

"Then you must try to find an opportunity of visiting the Fitzwilliam Museum in Cambridge. They have a letter written by Jane Austen. I think you'd find it interesting."

She spoke with the controlled, artificial brightness of a hostess trying to find a subject to interest a difficult guest. Cordelia, her mouth full of veal and mushrooms, wondered how she would manage to get through the rest of the meal. Luckily, however, the American professor had caught the word "Fitzwilliam" and now called down the table to enquire about the Museum's collection of majolica in which, apparently, he was interested. The conversation became general.

It was Miss Leaming who drove Cordelia to the station, Audley End this time instead of Cambridge; a change for which no reason was given. They didn't speak about the case during the drive. Cordelia was exhausted with tiredness, food and wine and allowed herself to be firmly taken in hand and placed in the train without attempting to gain any further information. She didn't really think she would have got it. As the train drew out, her tired fingers fumbled with the flap of the strong white envelope which Miss Leaming had handed to her and she drew out and read the enclosed note. It was expertly typed and set out, but told her little more than she had already learnt. With it was the photograph. She saw the picture of a laughing boy, his head half-turned towards the camera, one hand shielding his eyes from the sun. He was wearing jeans and a vest and was half lying on the lawn, a pile of books on the grass beside him. Perhaps he had been working there under the trees when she had come out of the french windows with her camera and called imperiously to him to smile. The photograph told Cordelia nothing except, that for one recorded second at least, he had known how to be happy. She placed it back in the envelope; her hands closed protectively over it. Cordelia slept.

Chapter Two

Next morning Cordelia left Cremona Road before seven o'clock. Despite her tiredness the night before, she had made her major preparations before she went to bed. They hadn't taken long. As Bernie had taught her, she checked systematically the scene-of-crime kit, an unnecessary routine since nothing had been touched since, in celebration of their partnership, he had first set it up for her. She put ready the polaroid camera; sorted into order the road maps from the jumble pushed into the back of his desk; shook out the sleeping bag and rolled it ready; filled a carrier bag with iron rations from Bernie's store of tinned soup and baked beans; considered, and finally decided to take, their copy of Professor Simpson's book on forensic medicine and her own Hacker portable radio; checked the first-aid kit. Finally, she found herself a fresh notebook, headed it *Case of Mark Callender* and ruled up the last few pages ready for her expense account. These preliminaries had always been the most satisfying part of a case, before boredom or distaste set in, before anticipation crumbled into disenchantment and failure. Bernie's planning had always been meticulous and successful; it was reality which had let him down.

Finally, she considered her clothes. If this hot weather continued her Jaeger suit, bought from her savings after much careful thought to see her through almost any interview, would be uncomfortably hot, but she might have to interview the head of a college and the dignified professionalism best exemplified by a suit would be the effect to aim at. She decided to travel in her fawn suede skirt with a short-sleeved jumper and pack jeans and warmer jumpers for any field work. Cordelia enjoyed clothes, enjoyed planning and buying them, a pleasure circumscribed less by poverty than by her obsessive need to be able to pack the whole of her wardrobe into one medium sized suitcase like a refugee perpetually ready for flight.

Once she had shaken free from the tentacles of north London, Cordelia enjoyed the drive. The Mini purred along and Cordelia thought that it had never run so sweetly. She liked the flat East Anglian countryside, the broad streets of the market towns, the way in which the fields grew unhedged to the edge of the road, the openness and freedom of the far horizons and wide skies. The country matched her mood. She had grieved for Bernie and would grieve for him again, missing his comradeship and his undemanding affection, but this, in a sense, was her first case and she was glad to be tackling it alone. It was one that she thought she could solve. It neither appalled nor disgusted her. Driving in happy anticipation through the sunbathed countryside, the boot of the car carefully packed with her gear, she was filled with the euphoria of hope.

When she finally reached Duxford village she had difficulty at first in finding Summertrees. Major Markland was apparently a man who thought that his importance warranted omitting the name of the road from his address. But the second person she stopped to ask was a villager who was able to point the way, taking infinite trouble over the simple directions as if fearing that a perfunctory answer might have seemed discourteous. Cordelia had to find a suitable place to turn and then drive back a couple of miles, for she had already passed Summertrees.

And this, at last, must be the house. It was a large Victorian edifice of red brick, set well back, with a wide turfed verge between the open wooden gate leading to the drive and the road. Cordelia wondered why anyone should have wanted to build such an intimidatingly ugly house or, having decided to do so, should have set down a suburban monstrosity in the middle of the countryside. Perhaps it had replaced an earlier more agreeable house. She drove the Mini onto the grass but at some distance from the gate and made her way up the drive. The garden suited the house; it was formal to the point of artificiality and too well kept. Even the rock plants burgeoned like morbid excrescences at carefully planned intervals between the terrace paving stones. There were two rectangular beds in the lawn, each planted with red rose trees and edged with alternate bands of lobelia and alyssum. They looked like a patriotic display in a public park. Cordelia felt the lack of a flag pole.

The front door was open, giving a view of a dark, brown-painted hall. Before Cordelia could ring, an elderly woman came round the corner of the house trundling a wheelbarrow full of plants. Despite the heat, she was wearing Wellington boots, a jumper and long tweed skirt and had a scarf tied round her head. When she saw Cordelia she dropped the handle of the wheelbarrow and said:

"Oh, good morning. You've come from the church about the jumble, I expect?"

Cordelia said:

"No, not the jumble. I'm from Sir Ronald Callender. It's about his son."

"Then I expect you've called for his things? We wondered when Sir Ronald was going to send for them. They're all still at the cottage. We haven't been down there since Mark died. We called him Mark, you know. Well, he never told us who he was which was rather naughty of him."

"It isn't about Mark's things. I want to talk about Mark himself. Sir Ronald has engaged me to try to find out why his son killed himself. My name is Cordelia Gray."

This news seemed to puzzle rather than disconcert Mrs. Markland. She blinked at Cordelia rapidly through troubled, rather stupid, eyes and clutched at the wheelbarrow handle as if for support.

"Cordelia Gray? Then we haven't met before, have we? I don't think I know a Cordelia Gray. Perhaps it would be better if you came into the drawing room and talked to my husband and sister-in-law."

She abandoned the barrow where it stood in the middle of the path and led the way into the house, pulling off her head scarf and making ineffective pats at her hair. Cordelia followed her through the sparsely furnished hall, smelling of floor polish, with its clutter of walking sticks, umbrellas and mackintoshes draping the heavy oak hat stand, and into a room at the back of the house.

It was a horrible room, ill-proportioned, bookless, furnished not in poor taste but in no taste at all. A huge sofa of repellent design and two armchairs surrounded the fireplace and a heavy mahogany table, ornately carved and lurching on its pedestal, occupied the centre of the room. There was little other furniture. The only pictures were framed groups, pale oblong faces too small to identify posed in straight innominate lines in front of the camera. One was a regimental photograph; the other had a pair of crossed oars above two rows of burly adolescents, all of whom were wearing low peaked caps and striped blazers. Cordelia supposed it to be a school boating club.

Despite the warmth of the day, the room was sunless and cold. The doors of the french windows were open. On the lawn outside were grouped a large swinging sofa with a fringed canopy, three cane chairs sumptuously cushioned in a garish blue cretonne, each with its footrest, and a wooden slatted table. They looked part of a setting for a play in which the designer had somehow failed to catch the mood. All the garden furniture looked new and unused. Cordelia wondered why the family should bother to sit indoors on a summer morning while the lawn was so much more comfortably furnished.

Mrs. Markland introduced Cordelia by sweeping her arm in a wide gesture of abandonment and saying feebly to the company in general:

"Miss Cordelia Gray. It isn't about the Church jumble."

Cordelia was struck by the resemblance that husband and wife and Miss Markland bore to each other. All three reminded her of horses. They had long, bony faces, narrow mouths above strong, square chins, eyes set unattractively close, and grey, coarse-looking hair which the two women wore in thick fringes almost to the eyes. Major Markland was drinking coffee from an immense white cup, much stained about the rim and sides, which had been set on a round tin tray. He held *The Times* in his hands. Miss Markland was knitting, an occupation which Cordelia vaguely felt was inappropriate to a hot summer morning.

The two faces, unwelcoming, only partly curious, regarded her with faint distaste. Miss Markland could knit without looking at the needles, an accomplishment which enabled her to fix Cordelia with sharp, inquisitive eyes. Invited by Major Markland to sit, Cordelia perched on the edge of the sofa, half expecting the smooth cushion to let out a rude noise as it subsided beneath her. She found it, however, unexpectedly hard. She composed her face into the appropriate expression—seriousness combined with efficiency and a touch of propitiatory humility seemed about right, but she wasn't sure that she managed to bring it off. As she sat there, knees demurely together, her shoulder bag at her feet, she was unhappily aware that she probably looked more like an eager seventeen-year-old facing her first interview than a mature business woman, sole proprietor of Pryde's Detective Agency.

She handed over Sir Ronald's note of authority and said:

"Sir Ronald was very distressed on your account, I mean it was awful for you that it should happen on your property when you'd been so kind in finding Mark a job he liked. His father hopes you won't mind talking about it; it's just that he wants to know what made his son kill himself."

"And he sent you?" Miss Markland's voice was a compound of disbelief, amusement and contempt. Cordelia didn't resent the rudeness. She felt Miss Markland had a point. She gave what she hoped was a credible explanation. It was probably true.

"Sir Ronald thinks that it must have been something to do with Mark's life at university. He left college suddenly, as you may know, and his father was never told why. Sir Ronald thought that I might be more successful in talking to Mark's friends than the more usual type of private detective. He didn't feel that he could trouble the police; after all, this sort of enquiry isn't really their kind of job."

Miss Markland said grimly:

"I should have thought it was precisely their job; that is, if Sir Ronald thinks there's something odd about his son's death . . ."

Cordelia broke in:

"Oh no, I don't think there's any suggestion of that! He's quite satisfied with the verdict. It's just that he badly wants to know what made him do it."

Miss Markland said with sudden fierceness:

"He was a drop-out. He dropped out of university, apparently he dropped out of his family obligations, finally he dropped out of life. Literally."

Her sister-in-law gave a little bleat of protest.

"Oh, Eleanor, is that quite fair? He worked really well here. I liked the boy. I don't think——"

"I don't deny that he earned his money. That doesn't alter the fact that he was neither bred nor educated to be a jobbing gardener. He was, therefore, a drop-out. I don't know the reason and I have no interest in discovering it."

"How did you come to employ him?" asked Cordelia.

It was Major Markland who answered.

"He saw my advertisement in the *Cambridge Evening News* for a gardener and turned up here one evening on his bicycle. I suppose he cycled all the way from Cambridge. It must have been about five weeks ago, a Tuesday I think."

Again Miss Markland broke in:

"It was Tuesday, May 9th."

The Major frowned at her as if irritated that he couldn't fault the information.

"Yes, well, Tuesday the 9th. He said that he had decided to leave university and take a job and that he'd seen my advertisement. He admitted that he didn't know much about gardening but said that he was strong and was willing to learn. His inexperience didn't worry me; we wanted him mostly for the lawns and for the vegetables. He never touched the flower garden; my wife and I see to that ourselves. Anyway, I quite liked the look of the boy and I thought I'd give him a chance."

Miss Markland said:

"You took him because he was the only applicant who was prepared to work for the miserable pittance you were offering." The Major, so far from showing offence at this frankness, smiled complacently.

"I paid him what he was worth. If more employers were prepared to do that, the country wouldn't be plagued with this inflation." He spoke as one to whom economics were an open book.

"Didn't you think it was odd, his turning up like that?" asked Cordelia.

"Of course I did, damned odd! I thought he had probably been sent down; drinks, drugs, revolution, you know the sort of things they get up to at Cambridge now. But I asked him for the name of his tutor as a referee and rang him, a fellow called Horsfall. He wasn't particularly forthcoming but he did assure me that the boy had left voluntarily and to use his own words, his conduct while in college had been almost boringly irreproachable. I need not fear that the shades of Summertrees would be polluted."

Miss Markland turned her knitting and broke into her sister-in-law's little cry of "What can he have meant by that?" with the dry comment:

"A little more boredom of that kind would be welcome from the city of the plains."

"Did Mr. Horsfall tell you why Mark had left college?" asked Cordelia.

"I didn't enquire. That wasn't my business. I asked a plain question and I got a more or less plain answer, as plain as you can expect from those academic types. We certainly had no complaint about the lad while he was here. I speak as I find."

"When did he move into the cottage?" asked Cordelia.

"Immediately. That wasn't our idea, of course. We never advertised the job as residential. However, he'd obviously seen the cottage and taken a fancy to the place and he asked if we'd mind if he camped out there. It wasn't practicable for him to cycle in from Cambridge each day, we could quite see that, and as far as we knew there was no one in the village who could put him up. I can't say I was keen on the idea; the cottage needs a lot doing to it. Actually we have it in mind to apply for a conversion grant and then get rid of the place. It wouldn't do for a family in its present state but the lad seemed keen on roughing it there, so we agreed."

Cordelia said:

"So he must have inspected the cottage before he came for the job?"

"Inspected? Oh, I don't know. He probably snooped around to see what the property was like before he actually came to the door. I don't know that I blame him, I'd have done the same myself."

Mrs. Markland broke in:

"He was very keen on the cottage, very keen. I pointed out that there was no gas or electricity but he said that that wouldn't worry him; he'd buy a primus stove and manage with lamps. There's water laid on, of course, and the main part of the roof is really quite sound. At least I think it is. We don't go there you know. He seemed to settle in very happily. We never actually visited him, there was no need, but as far as I could see he was looking after himself perfectly well. Of course as my husband said, he was very inexperienced; there were one or two things we had to teach him, like coming up to the kitchen early every morning for the orders. But I liked the boy; he was always working hard when I was in the garden."

Cordelia said:

"I wonder if I might have a look at the cottage?"

The request disconcerted them. Major Markland looked at hi swife. There was an embarrassed silence and for a moment Cordelia feared that the answer would be no. Then Miss Markland stabbed her needles into the ball of wool and got to her feet:

"I'll come with you now," she said.

The grounds of Summertrees were spacious. First there was the formal rose garden, the bushes closely planted and grouped according to variety and colour like a market garden, the name tags fixed at precisely the same height from the earth. Next was the kitchen garden cut in two by a gravel path with evidence of Mark Callender's work in the weeded rows of lettuce and cabbages, the patches of dug earth. Finally they passed through a gate into a small orchard of old and unpruned apple trees. The scythed grass, smelling richly of hay, lay in thick swathes round the gnarled trunks.

At the furthest end of the orchard was a thick hedge, so overgrown that the wicket gate into the rear garden of the cottage was at first difficult to see. But the grass around it had been trimmed and the gate opened easily to Miss Markland's hand. On the other side was a thick bramble hedge, dark and impenetrable and obviously allowed to grow wild for a generation. Someone had hacked a way through, but Miss Markland and Cordelia had to bend low to avoid catching their hair on its tangled tentacles of thorn.

Once free of this barrier, Cordelia lifted her head and blinked in the bright sunshine. She gave a little exclamation of pleasure. In the short time in which he had lived here Mark Callender had created a little oasis of order and beauty out of chaos and neglect. Old flower beds had been discovered and the surviving plants tended; the stone path had been scraped free of grass and moss; a minute square of lawn to the right of the cottage door had been cut and weeded. On the other side of the path a patch about twelve feet square had been partly dug. The fork was still in the earth, driven deep about two feet from the end of the row.

The cottage was a low, brick building under a slate roof. Bathed in the afternoon sunshine, and despite its bare, rain-scoured door, its rotted window frames and the glimpse of exposed beams in the roof, it had the gentle melancholy charm of age which hadn't yet degenerated into decay. Just outside the cottage door, dropped casually side by side, was a pair of heavy gardening shoes encrusted with earth.

"His?" asked Cordelia.

"Who else's?"

They stood together for a moment contemplating the dug earth. Neither spoke. Then they moved to the back door. Miss Markland fitted the key into the lock. It turned easily as if the lock had been recently oiled. Cordelia followed her into the sitting-room of the cottage.

The air was cool after the heat of the garden but unfresh, with a taint of contagion. Cordelia saw that the plan of the cottage was simple. There were three doors, one straight ahead obviously led to the front garden but was locked and barred, the joints hung with cobwebs as if it hadn't been opened for generations. One to the right led, as Cordelia guessed, to the kitchen. The third door was ajar and she could glimpse through it an uncarpeted wooden stairway leading to the first floor. In the middle of the room was a wooden-topped table, the surface scarred with much scrubbing, and with two kitchen chairs, one at each end. In the middle of the table a blue ribbed mug held a posy of dead flowers, black brittle stems bearing sad tatters of unidentifiable plants, their pollen staining the surface of the table like golden dust. Shafts of sunlight cut across the still air; in their beams a myriad of motes, specks of dust and infinitesimal life danced grotesquely.

To the right was a fireplace, an old-fashioned iron range with ovens each side of the open fire. Mark had been burning wood and papers; there was a mound of white ash in the grate and a pile of kindling wood and small logs placed ready for the next cool evening. On one side of the fire was a low wooden slatted chair with a faded cushion and on the other a wheel-backed chair with the legs sawn off, perhaps to make it low enough for nursing a child. Cordelia thought that it must have been a beautiful chair before its mutilation.

Two immense beams, blackened with age, ran across the ceiling. In the middle of one was fixed a steel hook, probably once used for hanging bacon. Cordelia and Miss Markland looked at it without speaking; there was no need for question and answer. After a moment they moved, as if by common consent, to the two fireside chairs and sat down. Miss Markland said:

"I was the one who found him. He didn't come up to the kitchen for the day's orders so after breakfast I walked down here to see if he had overslept. It was nine twenty-three exactly. The door was unlocked. I knocked, but there was no reply so I pushed it open. He was hanging from that hook with a leather belt round his neck. He was wearing his blue cotton trousers, the ones he usually worked in, and his feet were bare. That chair was lying on its side on the floor. I touched his chest. He was quite cold."

"Did you cut him down?"

"No. He was obviously dead and I thought it better to leave the body until the police arrived. But I did pick up the chair and place it so that it supported his feet. That was an irrational action, I know, but I couldn't bear to see him hanging there without releasing the pressure on his throat. It was, as I've said, irrational."

"I think it was very natural. Did you notice anything else about him, about the room?"

"There was a half-empty mug of what looked like coffee on the table and a great deal of ash in the grate. It looked as if he had been burning papers. His portable typewriter was where you see it now, on that side table; the suicide note was still in the machine. I read it, then I went back to the house, told my brother and sister-in-law what had happened and rang the police. After the police arrived I brought them to this cottage, and confirmed what I had seen. I never came in here again until this moment."

"Did you, or Major and Mrs. Markland, see Mark on the night he died?"

"None of us saw him after he stopped work at about six-thirty. He was a little later that evening because he wanted to finish mowing the front lawn. We all saw him putting the mower away, then walking across the garden towards the orchard. We never saw him alive again. No one was at home at Summertrees that night. We had a dinner party at Trumpington—an old army colleague of my brother. We didn't get home until after midnight. By then, according to the medical evidence, Mark must have been dead about four hours."

Cordelia said:

"Please tell me about him."

"What is there to tell? His official hours were eight-thirty to six o'clock, with an hour for lunch and half an hour for tea. In the evenings he would work in the garden here or round the cottage. Sometimes in his lunch hour he would cycle to the village store. I used to meet him there from time to time. He didn't buy much—a loaf of wholemeal bread, butter, the cheapest cut of bacon, tea, coffee—the usual things. I heard him ask about free-range eggs and Mrs. Morgan told him that Wilcox at Grange Farm would always sell him half a dozen. We didn't speak when we met, but he would smile. In the evenings once the light had faded, he used to read or type at that table. I could see his head against the lamplight."

"I thought Major Markland said that you didn't visit the cottage?"

"They don't; it holds certain embarrassing memories for them. I do." She paused and looked into the dead fire.

"My fiancé and I used to spend a great deal of time here before the war when he was at Cambridge. He was killed in 1937, fighting in Spain for the Republican cause."

"I'm sorry," said Cordelia. She felt the inadequacy, the insincerity of her response and yet, what else was there to say? It had all happened nearly forty years ago. She hadn't heard of him before. The spasm of grief, so brief that it was hardly felt, was no more than a transitory inconvenience, a sentimental regret for all lovers who died young, for the inevitability of human loss.

Miss Markland spoke with sudden passion as if the words were being forced out of her:

"I don't like your generation, Miss Gray. I don't like your arrogance, your selfishness, your violence, the curious selectivity of your compassion. You pay for nothing with your own coin, not even for your ideals. You denigrate and destroy and never build. You invite punishment like rebellious children, then scream when you are punished. The men I knew, the men I was brought up with, were not like that."

Cordelia said gently:

"I don't think Mark Callender was like that either."

"Perhaps not. At least the violence he practised was on himself." She looked up at Cordelia searchingly.

"No doubt you'll say I'm jealous of youth. It's a common enough syndrome of my generation."

"It ought not to be. I can never see why people should be jealous. After all, youth isn't a matter of privilege, we all get the same share of it. Some people may be born at an easier time or be richer or more privileged than others, but that hasn't anything to do with being young. And being young is terrible sometimes. Don't you remember how terrible it could be?"

"Yes, I remember. But I remember other things too."

Cordelia sat in silence, thinking that the conversation was strange but somehow inevitable and that, for some reason, she didn't resent it. Miss Markland looked up.

"His girl friend visited him once. At least, I suppose she was his girl friend or why should she have come? It was about three days after he started work."

"What was she like?"

"Beautiful. Very fair, with a face like a Botticelli angel—smooth, oval, unintelligent. She was foreign, French, I think. She was also rich."

"How could you tell that, Miss Markland?" Cordelia was intrigued.

"Because she spoke with a foreign accent; because she arrived driving a white Renault which I took to be her own car; because her clothes, although odd and unsuitable for the country, weren't cheap; because she walked up to the front door and announced that she wanted to see him with the confident arrogance that one associates with the rich."

"And did he see her?"

"He was working in the orchard at the time, scything the grass. I took her down to him. He greeted her calmly and without embarrassment and took her to sit in the cottage garden until it was time for him to stop work. He seemed pleased enough to see her but not, I thought, either delighted or surprised. He didn't introduce her. I left them together and returned to the house before he had the chance to. I didn't see her again."

Before Cordelia could speak she said suddenly:

"You're thinking of living here for a time, aren't you?"

"Will they mind? I didn't like to ask in case they said no."

"They won't know, and if they did, they wouldn't care."

"But do you mind?"

"No. I shan't worry you and I don't mind." They were talking in whispers as if in church. Then Miss Markland got up and moved to the door. She turned.

"You've taken on this job for the money, of course. Why not? But if I were you I'd keep it that way. It's unwise to become too personally involved with another human being. When that human being is dead, it can be dangerous as well as unwise."

Miss Markland stumped off down the garden path and disappeared through the wicket gate. Cordelia was glad to see her go. She was fidgeting with impatience to examine the cottage. This was where it had happened; this was where her job really began.

What was it that the Super had said? "When you're examining a building look at it as you would a country church. Walk round it first. Look at the whole scene inside and out; then make your deductions. Ask yourself what you saw, not what you expected to see or what you hoped to see, but what you saw."

He must be a man then who liked country churches and that at least was a point in his favour; for this, surely, was genuine Dalgliesh dogma. Bernie's reaction to churches, whether country or town, had been one of half-superstitious wariness. Cordelia decided to follow the advice.

She made her way first to the east side of the cottage. Here, discreetly set back and almost smothered by the hedge, was a wooden privy with its latched stable-like door. Cordelia peeped inside. The privy was very clean and looked as if it had been recently repainted. When she pulled the chain, to her relief, the bowl flushed. There was a roll of lavatory paper hanging by a string from the door and nailed beside it a small plastic bag containing a crumpled collection of orange papers and other soft wrappings. He had been an economical young man. Next to the privy was a large dilapidated shed containing a man's bicycle, old but well cared for, a large tin of white emulsion paint with the lid rammed down hard and a clean brush upended in a jam jar beside it, a tin bath, a few clean sacks, and a collection of gardening tools. All were shining clean and were neatly disposed against the wall or supported on nails.

She moved to the front of the cottage. This was in marked contrast to the southern aspect. Here Mark Callender had made no attempt to tackle the waist-high wilderness of nettles and grass which stifled the small front garden and almost obliterated the path. A thick climbing shrub sprinkled with small white flowers had thrust its black and thorned boughs to bar the two ground floor windows. The gate leading to the lane had stuck and would open only wide enough for a visitor to squeeze through. On each side a holly tree stood sentinel, its leaves grey with dust. The front hedge of privet was head-high. Cordelia could see that on either side of the path there had once been twin flower beds edged with large round stones which had been painted white. Now most of the stones had sunk out of sight among the encroaching weeds and nothing remained of the beds but a tangle of wild and straggling roses.

As she took a last look at the front garden, her eye caught a flash of colour half trodden among the weeds at the side of the path. It was a crumpled page of an illustrated magazine. She smoothed it open and saw that it was a colour photograph of a female nude. The woman had her back to the camera and was bending forward, gross buttocks splayed above booted thighs. She was smiling saucily over her shoulder in a blatant invitation made more grotesque by the long androgynous face which even tactful lighting couldn't make other than repellent. Cordelia noted the date at the top of the page; it was the May edition. So the magazine, or at least the picture, could have been brought to the cottage while he was there.

She stood with it in her hand trying to analyse the nature of her disgust which seemed to her excessive. The picture was vulgar and salacious but no more offensive or indecent than dozens on view in the side streets of London. But as she folded it away in her bag—for it was evidence of a kind—she felt contaminated and depressed. Had Miss Markland been more percipient than she knew? Was she, Cordelia, in danger of becoming sentimentally obsessed with the dead boy? The picture probably had nothing to do with Mark; it could easily have been dropped by some visitor to the cottage. But she wished that she hadn't seen it.

She passed round to the west of the cottage and made one more discovery. Hidden behind a clump of elder bushes was a small well about four feet in diameter. It had no superstructure but was closely fitted with a domed lid made of strong slatted wood and fitted at the top with an iron hoop. Cordelia saw that the cover was padlocked to the wooden rim of the well and the lock, although rusty with age, held firm at her tug. Someone had taken the trouble to see that there was no danger here to exploring children or visiting tramps.

And now it was time to explore the interior of the cottage.

First the kitchen. It was a small room with a window over the sink looking east. It had obviously been recently painted and the large table which took up most of the room had been covered with a red plastic cloth. There was a poky larder containing half a dozen tins of beer, a jar of marmalade, a crock of butter and the mouldy heel of a loaf. It was here in the kitchen that Cordelia found the explanation of the disagreeable smell which had struck her on entering the cottage. On the table was an open bottle of milk about half full, the silver top crumpled beside it. The milk was solid and furred with putrefaction; a bloated fly was sucking at the rim of the bottle and still stuck to its feast as, instinctively, she tried to flick it away. On the other side of the table was a twin-burner paraffin stove with a heavy pot on one burner. Cordelia tugged at the close-fitting lid and it came off suddenly, letting out a rich repulsive smell. She opened the table drawer and stirred the mess with a spoon. It looked like beef stew. Chunks of greenish meat, soapy looking potatoes and unidentifiable vegetables floated up through the scum like drowned and putrefying flesh. Beside the sink was an orange box placed on one side and used as a vegetable store. The potatoes were green, the onions had shrunk and sprouted, the carrots were wrinkled and limp. So nothing had been cleaned up, nothing had been removed. The police had taken away the body and any evidence they required but no one, neither the Marklands nor the boy's family or friends, had bothered to come back to clean up the pathetic leavings of his young life.

Cordelia went upstairs. A cramped landing led to two bedrooms, one obviously unused for years. Here the window frame had rotted, the ceiling plaster had crumbled and a faded paper patterned with roses was peeling away with the damp. The second and larger room was the one in which he had slept. There was a single iron bed with a hair mattress and on it a sleeping bag and a bolster folded in two to make a high pillow. Beside the bed was an old table with two candles, stuck with their own wax to a cracked plate, and a box of matches. His clothes were hung in the single cupboard; a pair of bright-green corduroy trousers, one or two shirts, pullovers and one formal suit. A few underclothes, clean but not ironed, were folded on the ledge above. Cordelia fingered the pullovers. They were hand knitted in thick wool and intricate patterns and there were four of them. Someone, then, had cared enough about him to take some trouble on his behalf. She wondered who.

She ran her hands over his meagre wardrobe, feeling for pockets. She found nothing except a slim, brown leather wallet in the bottom left-hand pocket of his suit. Excitedly she carried it over to the window hoping that it might contain a clue—a letter, perhaps, a list of names and addresses, a personal note. But the wallet was empty except for a couple of pound notes, his driving licence and a blood donor's card issued by the Cambridge blood transfusion service, which showed his group as B rhesus negative.

The uncurtained window gave a view of the garden. His books were arranged on the window shelf. There were only a few of them: several volumes of the *Cambridge Modern History*; some Trollope and Hardy; a complete William Blake; school text book volumes of Wordsworth, Browning and Donne; two paperbacks on gardening. At the end of the row was a white leather-bound book which Cordelia saw was the Book of Common Prayer. It was fitted with a finely wrought brass clasp and looked much used. She was disappointed in the books; they told her little beyond his superficial tastes. If he had come to this solitary life to study, to write or to philosophize he had come singularly ill-equipped.

The most interesting thing in the room was above the bed. It was a small oil painting about nine inches square. Cordelia studied it. It was certainly Italian and probably, she thought, late fifteenth century. It showed a very young tonsured monk reading at a table, his sensitive fingers enleafed between the pages of his book. The long, controlled face was taut with concentration, the heavy lidded eyes were fixed on the page. Behind him, a view from the open window was a miniature of delight. Cordelia thought that one would never tire of looking at it. It was a Tuscan scene showing a walled city with towers enclosed by cypresses, a river winding like a silver stream, a gaudily clad procession preceded by banners, yoked oxen working in the fields. She saw the picture as a contrast between the worlds of intellect and action and tried to remember where she had seen similar paintings. The comrades—as Cordelia always thought of that ubiquitous band of fellow-revolutionaries who attached themselves to her father—had been very fond of exchanging messages in art galleries and Cordelia had spent hours walking slowly from picture to picture, waiting for the casual visitor to pause beside her and whisper his few words of warning or information. The device had always struck her as a childish and unnecessarily histrionic way of communicating, but at least the galleries were warm and she had enjoyed looking at the pictures. She enjoyed this picture; he had obviously liked it too. Had he also liked that vulgar illustration which she had found in the front garden? Were they both an essential part of his nature?

The tour of inspection over, she made herself coffee using a packet from his store cupboard and boiling the water on the stove. She took a chair from the sitting-room and sat outside the back door with the mug of coffee in her lap, her head stretched back to feel the sun. She was filled with a gentle happiness as she sat there, contented and relaxed, listening to the silence, her half-closed lids impressed with the visage of the sun. But now it was the time to think. She had examined the cottage in accordance with the Super's instructions. What did she now know about the dead boy? What had she seen? What could she deduce?

He had been almost obsessively neat and tidy. His garden tools were wiped after use and carefully put away, his kitchen had been painted and was clean and ordered. Yet he had abandoned his digging less than two feet from the end of a row; had left the uncleaned fork in the earth; had dropped his gardening shoes casually at the back door. He had apparently burnt all his papers before killing himself, yet had left his coffee mug unwashed. He had made himself a stew for his supper which he hadn't touched. The preparation of the vegetables must have been done earlier in the same day, or perhaps the day before, but the stew was clearly intended for supper that night. The pot was still on the stove and was full to the brim. This wasn't a heated-up meal, one left from the evening before. This surely meant that he had only made the decision to kill himself after the stew had been prepared and had been put on the stove to cook. Why should he trouble to prepare a meal that he knew he wouldn't be alive to eat?

But was it likely, she wondered, that a healthy young man coming in from an hour or two of hard digging and with a hot meal waiting should be in that mood of boredom, accidie, anguish or despair which could lead to suicide? Cordelia could remember times of intense unhappiness, but she couldn't recall that they had followed purposeful outdoor exercise in the sun with a meal in prospect. And why the mug of coffee, the one which the police had taken away to analyse? There were tins of beer in the larder; if he had come in thirsty from his digging, why not open one of those? Beer would have been the quickest, the obvious way of quenching thirst. Surely no one, however thirsty, would brew and drink coffee just before a meal. Coffee came after the food.

But suppose someone had visited him that evening. It wasn't likely to have been someone calling with a casual message as he passed by; it was important enough for Mark to break off his digging even within two feet of the end of a row and invite the visitor into the cottage. It was probably a visitor who didn't like or drink beer—could that mean a woman? It was a visitor who wasn't expected to stay for supper but yet was at the cottage long enough to be offered some refreshment. Perhaps it was someone on his way to his own evening meal. Obviously, the visitor hadn't been invited to supper earlier or why would the two of them have begun the meal by drinking coffee and why would Mark have worked so late in the garden instead of coming in to change? So it was an unexpected visitor. But why was there only one mug of coffee? Surely Mark would have shared it with his guest or, if he preferred not to drink coffee, would have opened a tin of beer for himself. But there was no empty beer can in the kitchen and no second mug. Had it perhaps been washed and put away? But why should Mark wash one mug and not the other? Was it to conceal the fact that he'd had a visitor that evening?

The jug of coffee on the kitchen table was almost empty and

the bottle of milk only half full. Surely more than one person had taken milk and coffee. But perhaps that was a dangerous and unwarranted deduction; the visitor might well have had his mug refilled.

But suppose it wasn't Mark who had wished to conceal the fact that a visitor had called that night; suppose it wasn't Mark who had washed and put away the second mug; suppose it was the visitor who had wished to conceal the fact of his presence. But why should he bother to do that since he couldn't know that Mark was going to kill himself? Cordelia shook herself impatiently. This, of course, was nonsense. Obviously the visitor wouldn't have washed up the mug if Mark were still there and alive. He would only have obliterated the evidence of his visit if Mark were already dead. And if Mark had been dead, had been strung up on that hook before his visitor left the cottage, then could this really be suicide? A word dancing at the back of Cordelia's mind, an amorphous half-formed jangle of letters, came suddenly into focus and, for the first time, spelt out clearly the blood-stained word. Murder.

Cordelia sat on in the sun for another five minutes finishing her coffee, then she washed up the mug and hung it back on a hook in the larder. She walked down the lane to the road to where the Mini was still parked on the grass verge outside Summertrees, glad of the instinct that had led her to leave it out of sight of the house. Letting in the clutch gently, she drove it slowly down the lane looking carefully from side to side for a possible parking place; to leave it outside the cottage would only advertise her presence. It was a pity that Cambridge wasn't closer; she could then have used Mark's bicycle. The Mini was necessary to her task but would be inconveniently conspicuous wherever she left it.

But she was lucky. About fifty yards down the lane was the entrance to a field, a wide grass verge with a small copse at one side. The copse looked damp and sinister. It was impossible to believe that flowers could spring from this tainted earth or bloom among these scarred and mis-shapen trees. The ground was scattered with old pots and pans, the upended skeleton of a pram, a battered and rusty gas stove. Beside a stunted oak a matted heap of blankets were disintegrating into the earth. But there was space for her to drive the Mini off the road and under cover of a kind. If she locked it carefully it would be better here than outside the cottage and at night, she thought, it would be unobserved.

But now, she drove it back to the cottage and began to unpack. She moved Mark's few underclothes to one side of the shelf and set her own beside them. She laid her sleeping bag on the bed over his, thinking that she would be glad of the extra comfort. There was a red toothbrush and half-used tube of toothpaste in a jamjar on the kitchen window ledge; she placed her yellow brush and her own tube beside them. She hung her towel next to his across the cord which he had fixed between two nails under the kitchen sink. Then she made an inventory of the contents of the larder and a list of the things she would need. It would be better to buy them in Cambridge; she would only draw attention to her presence if she shopped locally. The saucepan of stew and the half bottle of milk were a worry. She couldn't leave them in the kitchen to sour the cottage with the stench of decay but she was reluctant to throw the contents away. She considered whether to photograph them but decided against it; tangible objects were better evidence. In the end she carried them out to the shed and shrouded them thickly with a piece of old sacking.

Last of all, she thought about the gun. It was a heavy object to carry with her all the time but she felt unhappy about parting with it, even temporarily. Although the back door of the cottage could be locked and Miss Markland had left her the key, an intruder would have no difficulty in breaking-in through a window. She decided that the best plan would be to secrete the ammunition among her underclothes in the bedroom cupboard but to hide the pistol itself separately in or near the cottage. The exact place cost her a little thought, but then she remembered the thick and twisting limbs of the elder bush by the well; by reaching high, she was able to feel for a convenient hollow near the fork of a branch and could slip the gun, still shrouded in its draw-string bag, among the concealing leaves.

At last she was ready to leave for Cambridge. She looked at her watch; it was half-past ten; she could be in Cambridge by eleven and there would still be two hours of the morning to go. She decided that her best plan would be to visit the newspaper office first and read the account of the inquest, then to see the police; after that she would go in search of Hugo and Sophia Tilling.

She drove away from the cottage with a feeling very like regret, as if she were leaving home. It was, she thought, a curious place, heavy with atmosphere and showing two distinct faces to the world like facets of a human personality; the north, with its dead thorn-barred windows, its encroaching weeds, and its forbidding hedge of privet, was a numinous stage for horror and tragedy. Yet the rear, where he had lived and worked, had cleared and dug the garden and tied up the few flowers, had weeded the path, and opened the windows to the sun, was as peaceful as a sanctuary. Sitting there at the door she had felt that nothing horrible could ever touch her; she was able to contemplate the night there alone without fear. Was it this atmosphere of healing tranquillity, she wondered, that had attracted Mark Callender? Had he sensed it before he took the job, or was it in some mysterious way the result of his transitory and doomed sojourn there? Major Markland had been right; obviously Mark had looked at the cottage before he went up to the house. Had it been the cottage he wanted or the job? Why were the Marklands so reluctant to come to the place, so reluctant that they obviously hadn't visited it even to clean up after his death? And why had Miss Markland spied on him, for surely such close observation was very close to spying? Had she only confided that story about her dead lover to justify her interest in the cottage, her obsessional preoccupation with what the new gardener was doing? And was the story even true? That ageing body heavy with latent strength, that equine expression of perpetual discontent, could she really once have been young, have lain perhaps with her lover on Mark's bed through the long, warm evenings of long-dead summers? How remote, how impossible and grotesque it all seemed.

Cordelia drove down Hills Road, past the vigorous memorial statue of a young 1914 soldier striding to death, past the Roman Catholic church and into the centre of the city. Again she wished that she could have abandoned the car in favour of Mark's bicycle. Everyone else seemed to be riding one and the air tinkled with bells like a festival. In these narrow and crowded streets even the compact Mini was a liability. She decided to park it as soon as she could find a place and set out on foot in search of a telephone. She had decided to vary her programme and see the police first.

But it didn't surprise her when at last she rang the police station to hear that Sergeant Maskell, who had dealt with the Callender case, was tied up all the morning. It was only in fiction that the people one wanted to interview were sitting ready at home or in their office, with time, energy and interest to spare. In real life, they were about their own business and one waited on their convenience, even if, untypically, they welcomed the attention of Pryde's Detective Agency. Usually they didn't. She hardly expected Sergeant Maskell to welcome it. She mentioned Sir Ronald's note of authority to impress her hearer with the authenticity of her business. The name was not without influence. He went away to enquire. After less than a minute he came back to say that Sergeant Maskell could see Miss Gray at two-thirty that afternoon.

So the newspaper office came first after all. Old files were at least accessible and could not object to being consulted. She quickly found what she wanted. The account of the inquest was brief, couched in the usual formal language of a court report. It told her little that was new, but she made a careful note of the main evidence. Sir Ronald Callender testified that he hadn't spoken to his son for over a fortnight before his death, when Mark had telephoned to tell his father of his decision to leave college and to take a job at Summertrees. He hadn't consulted Sir Ronald before making this decision nor had he explained his reasons. Sir Ronald had subsequently spoken to the Master, and the College authorities were prepared to take his son back for the next academic year if he changed his mind. His son had never spoken to him of suicide and had no health or money worries as far as he was aware. Sir Ronald's testimony was followed by a brief reference to other evidence. Miss Markland described how she had found the body; a forensic pathologist testified that the cause of death was asphyxia due to strangulation; Sergeant Maskell recounted the measures he had thought it proper to take and a report from the forensic science laboratory was submitted which stated that a mug of coffee found on the table had been analysed and found harmless. The verdict was that the deceased died by his own hand while the balance of his mind was disturbed. Closing the heavy file, Cordelia felt depressed. It looked as if the police work had been thorough. Was it really possible that these experienced professionals had overlooked the significance of the unfinished digging, the gardening shoes dropped casually at the back door, the untouched supper?

And now, at mid-day, she was free until half-past two. She could explore Cambridge. She bought the cheapest guide book she could find from Bowes and Bowes, resisting the temptation to browse among the books, since time was short and pleasure must be rationed. She stuffed her shoulder bag with a pork pie and fruit bought from a market stall and entered St. Mary's church to sit quietly and work out her itinerary. Then for an hour and a half she walked about the city and its colleges in a trance of happiness.

She was seeing Cambridge at its loveliest. The sky was an infinity of blue from whose pellucid depths the sun shone in unclouded but gentle radiance. The trees in the college gardens and the avenues leading to the Backs, as yet untouched by the heaviness of high summer, lifted their green tracery against stone and river and sky. Punts shot and curtsied under the bridges, scattering the gaudy water fowl, and by the rise of the new Garret Hostel bridge the willows trailed their pale, laden boughs in the darker green of the Cam.

She included all the special sights in her itinerary. She walked gravely down the length of Trinity Library, visited the Old Schools, sat quietly at the back of King's College Chapel marvelling at the upward surge of John Wastell's great vault spreading into curved fans of delicate white stone. The sunlight poured through the great windows staining the still air, blue, crimson and green. The finely carved Tudor roses, the heraldic beasts supporting the crown, stood out in arrogant pride from the panels. Despite what Milton and Wordsworth had written, surely this chapel had been built to the glory of an earthly sovereign, not to the service of God? But that didn't invalidate its purpose nor blemish its beauty. It was still a supremely religious building. Could a non-believer have planned and executed this superb interior? Was there an essential unity between motive and creation? This was the question which Carl alone among the comrades would have been interested to explore and she thought of him in his Greek prison, trying to shut her mind to what they might be doing to him and wishing his stocky figure at her side.

During her tour she indulged in small particular pleasures. She bought a linen tea cloth printed with a picture of the chapel from the stall near the west door; she lay on her face on the shorn grass above the river by Kings Bridge and let the cold green water eddy round her arms; she wandered among the book stalls in the market place and after careful reckoning bought a small edition of Keats printed on India paper and a cotton kaftan patterned in greens, blues and brown. If this hot weather continued it would be cooler than a shirt or jeans for wear in the evenings.

Finally, she returned to King's College. There was a seat set against the great stone wall which ran from the chapel down to the river bank and she sat there in the sun to eat her lunch. A privileged sparrow hopped across the immaculate lawn and cocked a bright insouciant eye. She threw him scraps from the crust of her pork pie and smiled at his agitated peckings. From the river floated the sound of voices calling across the water, the occasional scrunch of wood on wood, the harsh call of a duckling. Everything about her—the pebbles bright as jewels in the gravel path, the silver shafts of grass at the verge of the lawn, the sparrow's brittle legs—was seen with an extraordinarily and individual intensity as if happiness had cleared her eyes.

Then memory recalled the voices. First her father's:

"Our little fascist was educated by the papists. It accounts for a lot. How on earth did it happen, Delia?"

"You remember, Daddy. They muddled me up with another C. Gray who was a Roman Catholic. We both passed the eleven plus exam the same year. When they discovered the mistake they wrote to you to ask if you minded my staying on at the Convent because I'd settled there."

He hadn't in fact replied. Reverend Mother had tried tactfully to conceal that he hadn't bothered to answer and Cordelia had stayed on at the Convent for the six most settled and happy years of her life, insulated by order and ceremony from the mess and muddle of life outside, incorrigibly Protestant, uncoerced, gently pitied as one in invincible ignorance. For the first time she learned that she needn't conceal her intelligence, that cleverness which a succession of foster mothers had somehow seen as a threat. Sister Perpetua had said:

"There shouldn't be any difficulty over your 'A' Levels if you go on as you are at present. That means that we can plan for university entrance in two years' time from this October. Cambridge, I think. We might as well try for Cambridge, and I really don't see why you shouldn't stand a chance of a scholarship."

Sister Perpetua had herself been at Cambridge before she entered the Convent and she still spoke of the academic life, not with longing or regret, but as if it had been a sacrifice worthy of her vocation. Even the fifteen-year-old Cordelia had recognized that Sister Perpetua was a real scholar and had thought it rather unfair of God to bestow a vocation on one who was so happy and useful as she was. But for Cordelia herself, the future had, for the first time, seemed settled and full of promise. She would go to Cambridge and Sister would visit her there. She had a romantic vision of wide lawns under the sun and the two of them walking in Donne's paradise: "Rivers of knowledge are there, arts and sciences flow from thence; gardens that are walled in; bottomless depths of unsearchable councils are there." By the aid of her own brain and Sister's prayers she would win her scholarship. The prayers occasionally worried her. She had absolutely no doubt of their efficacy since God must necessarily listen to one who at such personal cost had listened to Him. And if Sister's influence gave her an unfair advantage over the other candidates—well, that couldn't be helped. In a matter of such importance neither Cordelia nor Sister Perpetua had been disposed to fret over theological niceties.

But this time Daddy had replied to the letter. He had discovered a need for his daughter. There were no "A" Levels and no scholarship and at sixteen Cordelia finished her formal education and began her wandering life as cook, nurse, messenger and general camp follower to Daddy and the comrades.

But now by what devious routes and for what a strange purpose she had come at last to Cambridge. The city didn't disappoint her. In her wanderings she had seen lovelier places, but none in which she had been happier or more at peace. How indeed, she thought, could the heart be indifferent to such a city where stone and stained glass, water and green lawns, trees and flowers were arranged in such ordered beauty for the service of learning. But as regretfully she rose at last to go, brushing the few crumbs from her skirt, a quotation, untraced and unsought, came into her mind. She heard it with such clarity that the words might have been spoken by a human voice—a young masculine voice, unrecognized and yet mysteriously familiar: "Then saw I that there was a way to hell even from the gates of heaven."

The police headquarters building was modern and functional. It represented authority tempered with discretion; the public were to be impressed but not intimidated. Sergeant Maskell's office and the Sergeant himself conformed to this philosophy. He was surprisingly young and elegantly dressed, with a square, tough face wary with experience and a long but skilfully cut hair style which, Cordelia thought, could only just have satisfied the Force requirements, even for a plain clothes detective. He was punctiliously polite without being gallant and this reassured her. It wasn't going to be an easy interview, but she had no wish to be treated with the indulgence shown to a pretty but importunate child. Sometimes it helped to play the part of a vulnerable and naive young girl eager for information—this was a role in which Bernie had frequently sought to cast her—but she sensed that Sergeant Maskell would respond better to an unflirtatious competence. She wanted to appear efficient, but not too efficient. And her secrets must remain her own; she was here to get information, not to give it.

She stated her business concisely and showed him her note of authority from Sir Ronald. He handed it back to her, remarking without rancour:

"Sir Ronald said nothing to me to suggest that he was not satisfied with the verdict."

"I don't think that's in question. He doesn't suspect foul play. If he did, he would have come to you. I think he has a scientist's curiosity to know what made his son kill himself and he couldn't very well indulge that at public expense. I mean, Mark's private miseries aren't really your problem, are they?"

"They could be if the reasons for his death disclosed a criminal offence—blackmail, intimidation—but there was never any suggestion of that."

"Are you personally satisfied that he killed himself?"

The Sergeant looked at her with the sudden keen intelligence of a hunting dog on the scent.

"Why should you ask that, Miss Gray?"

"I suppose because of the trouble you took. I've interviewed Miss Markland and read the newspaper report of the inquest. You called in a forensic pathologist; you had the body photographed before it was cut down; you analysed the coffee left in his drinking mug."

"I treated the case as a suspicious death. That's my usual practice. This time the precautions proved unnecessary, but they might not have been."

Cordelia said:

"But something worried you, something didn't seem right?"

He said, as if reminiscing:

"Oh, it was straightforward enough to all appearances. Almost the usual story. We get more than our share of suicides. Here is a young man who gave up his university course for no apparent reason and went to live on his own in some discomfort. You get the picture of an introspective, rather solitary student, one who doesn't confide in his family or friends. Within three weeks after leaving college he's found dead. There's no sign of a struggle; no disturbance in the cottage; he leaves a suicide note conveniently in the typewriter, much the kind of suicide note you would expect. Admittedly, he took the trouble to destroy all the papers in the cottage and yet left the garden fork uncleaned and his work half-completed, and bothered to cook himself a supper which he didn't eat. But all that proves nothing. People do behave irrationally, particularly suicides. No, it wasn't any of those things which gave me a bit of worry; it was the knot."

Suddenly he bent down and rummaged in the left-hand drawer of his desk.

"Here," he said. "How would you use this to hang yourself, Miss Gray?"

The strap was about five feet long. It was a little over an inch wide and was made of strong but supple brown leather, darkened in places with age. One end was tapered and pierced with a row of metal-bound eye holes, the other was fitted with a strong brass buckle. Cordelia took it in her hands; Sergeant Maskell said:

"That was what he used. Obviously it's meant as a strap, but Miss Leaming testified that he used to wear it wound two or three times round his waist as a belt. Well, Miss Gray, how would you hang yourself?"

Cordelia ran the strap through her hands.

"First of all, of course, I'd slip the tapered end through the buckle to make a noose. Then, with the noose round my neck, I'd stand on a chair underneath the hook in the ceiling and draw the other end of the strap over the hook. I'd pull it up fairly tight and then make two half-hitches to hold it firm. I'd pull hard on the strap to make sure that the knot didn't slip and that the hook would hold. Then I'd kick away the chair."

The Sergeant opened the file in front of him and pushed it across the desk.

"Look at that," he said. "That's a picture of the knot."

The police photograph, stark in black and white, showed the knot with admirable clarity. It was a bowline on the end of a low loop and it hung about a foot from the hook.

Sergeant Maskell said:

"I doubt whether he would be able to tie that knot with his hands above his head, no one could. So he must have made the noose first just as you did and then tied the bowline. But that can't be right either. There were only a few inches of strap between the buckle and the knot. If he'd done it that way, he wouldn't have had sufficient play on the strap to get his neck through the noose. There's only one way he could have done it. He made the noose first, pulled it until the strap fitted his neck like a collar and then tied the bowline. Then he got on the chair, placed the loop over the nail and kicked the chair away. Look, this will show you what I mean."

He turned over a new page of the file and suddenly thrust it towards her.

The photograph, uncompromising, unambiguous, a brutal surrealism in black and white, would have looked as artificial as a sick joke if the body were not so obviously dead. Cordelia felt her heart hammering against her chest. Beside this horror Bernie's death had been gentle. She bent her head low over the file so that her hair swung forward to shield her face and made herself study the pitiable thing in front of her.

The neck was elongated so that the bare feet, their toes pointed like a dancer's, hung less than a foot from the floor. The stomach muscles were taut. Above them the high rib cage looked as brittle as a bird's. The head lolled grotesquely on the right shoulder like a horrible caricature of a disjointed puppet. The eyes had rolled upwards under half-open lids. The swollen tongue had forced itself between the lips.

Cordelia said calmly:

"I see what you mean. There are barely four inches of strap between the neck and the knot. Where is the buckle?"

"At the back of the neck under the left ear. There's a phograph of the identation it made in the flesh later in the file."

Cordelia did not look. Why, she wondered, had he shown her the photograph? It wasn't necessary to prove his argument. Had he hoped to shock her into a realization of what she was meddling in; to punish her for trespassing on his patch; to contrast the brutal reality of his professionalism with her amateurish meddling; to warn her perhaps? But against what? The police had no real suspicion of foul play; the case was closed. Had it, perhaps, been the casual malice, the incipient sadism of a man who couldn't resist the impulse to hurt or shock? Was he even aware of his own motives?

She said:

"I agree he could only have done it in the way you described, if he did it. But suppose someone else pulled the noose tight about his neck, then strung him up. He'd be heavy, a dead weight. Wouldn't it have been easier to make the knot first and then hoist him on to the chair?"

"Having first asked him to hand over his belt?"

"Why use a belt? The murderer could have strangled him with a cord or a tie. Or would that have left a deeper and identifiable mark under the impression of the strap?"

"The pathologist looked for just such a mark. It wasn't there."

"There are other ways, though; a plastic bag, the thin kind they pack clothes in, dropped over his head and held tight against his face; a thin scarf; a woman's stocking."

"I can see you would be a resourceful murderess, Miss Gray. It's possible, but it would need a strong man and there would have to be an element of surprise. We found no sign of a struggle."

"But it could have been done that way?"

"Of course, but there was absolutely no evidence that it was."

"But if he were first drugged?"

"That possibility did occur to me; that's why I had the coffee analysed. But he wasn't drugged, the P.M. confirmed it."

"How much coffee had he drunk?"

"Only about half a mug, according to the P.M. report and he died immediately afterwards. Sometime between seven and nine p.m. was as close as the pathologist could estimate."

"Wasn't it odd that he drank coffee before his meal?"

"There's no law against it. We don't know when he intended to eat his supper. Anyway, you can't build a murder case on the order in which a man chooses to take his food and drink."

"What about the note he left? I suppose it isn't possible to raise prints from typewriter keys?"

"Not easily on that type of key. We tried but there was nothing identifiable."

"So in the end you accepted that it was suicide?"

"In the end I accepted that there was no possibility of proving otherwise."

"But you had a hunch? My partner's old colleague—he's a Superintendent of the C.I.D.—always backed his hunches."

"Ah, well, that's the Met, they can afford to indulge themselves. If I backed all my hunches I'd get no work done; it isn't what you suspect, it's what you can prove that counts."

"May I take the suicide note and the strap?"

"Why not, if you sign for them? No one else seems to want them."

"Could I see the note now, please?"

He extracted it from the file and handed it to her. Cordelia began to read to herself the first half-remembered words:

> *a void, boundless as the nether sky appeared*
> *beneath us . . .*

She was struck, not for the first time, by the importance of the written word, the magic of ordered symbols. Would poetry hold its theurgy if the lines were printed as prose, or prose be so compelling without the pattern and stress of punctuation? Miss Leaming had spoken Blake's passage as if she recognized its beauty yet here, spaced on the page, it exerted an even stronger power.

It was then that two things about the quotation caught at her breath. The first was not something which she intended to share with Sergeant Maskell but there was no reason why she should not comment on the second.

She said:

"Mark Callender must have been an experienced typist. This was done by an expert."

"I didn't think so. If you look carefully you'll see that one or two of the letters are fainter than the rest. That's always the sign of an amateur."

"But the faint letters aren't always the same ones. It's usually the keys on the edges of the keyboard which the inexperienced typist hits more lightly. And the spacing here is good until nearly the end of the passage. It looks as if the typist suddenly realized that he ought to disguise his competence but hadn't time to retype the whole passage. And it's strange that the punctuation is so accurate."

"It was probably copied direct from the printed page. There was a copy of Blake in the boy's bedroom. The quotation is from Blake, you know, the Tyger Tyger burning bright poet."

"I know. But if he typed it from the book, why bother to return the Blake to his bedroom?"

"He was a tidy lad."

"But not tidy enough to wash up his coffee mug or clean his garden fork."

"That proves nothing. As I said, people do behave oddly when they're planning to kill themselves. We know that the typewriter was his and that he'd had it for a year. But we couldn't compare the typing with his work. All his papers had been burnt."

He glanced at his watch and got to his feet. Cordelia saw that the interview was over. She signed a chit for the suicide note and the leather belt, then shook hands and thanked him formally for his help. As he opened the door for her he said, as if on impulse:

"There's one intriguing detail you may care to know. It looks as if he was with a woman some time during the day on which he died. The pathologist found the merest trace—a thin line only—of purple-red lipstick on his upper lip."

Chapter Three

New Hall, with its Byzantine air, its sunken court and its shining domed hall like a peeled orange, reminded Cordelia of a harem; admittedly one owned by a sultan with liberal views and an odd predilection for clever girls, but a harem nonetheless. The college was surely too distractingly pretty to be conducive to serious study. She wasn't sure, either, whether she approved of the obtrusive femininity of its white brick, the mannered prettiness of the shallow pools where the goldfish slipped like blood-red shadows between the water lilies, its artfully planted saplings. She concentrated on her criticism of the building; it helped to prevent her being intimidated.

She hadn't called at the Lodge to ask for Miss Tilling, afraid that she might be asked her business or refused admission; it seemed prudent just to walk in and chance to luck. Luck was with her. After two fruitless enquiries for Sophia Tilling's room, a hurrying student called back at her:

"She doesn't live in college but she's sitting on the grass over there with her brother."

Cordelia walked out of the shadow of the court into bright sunlight and over turf as soft as moss towards the little group. There were four of them, stretched out on the warm-smelling grass. The two Tillings were unmistakably brother and sister. Cordelia's first thought was that they reminded her of a couple of pre-Raphaelite portraits with their strong dark heads held high on unusually long necks, and their straight noses above curved, foreshortened upper lips. Beside their bony distinction, the second girl was all softness. If this were the girl who had visited Mark at the cottage, Miss Markland was right to call her beautiful. She had an oval face with a neat slender nose, a small but beautifully formed mouth, and slanted eyes of a strikingly deep blue which gave her whole face an oriental appearance intriguingly at variance with the fairness of her skin and her long blonde hair. She was wearing an ankle-length dress of fine mauve patterned cotton, buttoned high at the waist but with no other fastening. The gathered bodice cupped her full breasts and the skirt fell open to reveal a pair of tight fitting shorts in the same material. As far as Cordelia could see, she wore nothing else. Her feet were bare and her long, shapely legs were untanned by the sun. Cordelia reflected that those white voluptuous thighs must be more erotic than a whole city of sunburnt limbs and that the girl knew it. Sophia Tilling's dark good looks were only a foil to this gentler, more entrancing beauty.

At first sight the fourth member of the party was more ordinary. He was a stocky, bearded young man with russet curly hair and a spade-shaped face, and was lying on the grass by the side of Sophie Tilling.

All of them, except the blonde girl, were wearing old jeans and open-necked cotton shirts.

Cordelia had come up to the group and had stood over them for a few seconds before they took any notice of her. She said:

"I'm looking for Hugo and Sophia Tilling. My name is Cordelia Gray." Hugo Tilling looked up:

"What shall Cordelia do, love and be silent."

Cordelia said:

"People who feel the need to joke about my name usually enquire after my sisters. It gets very boring."

"It must do. I'm sorry. I'm Hugo Tilling, this is my sister, this is Isabelle de Lasterie and this is Davie Stevens.

Davie Stevens sat up like a jack-in-the-box and said an amiable "Hi."

He looked at Cordelia with a quizzical intentness. She wondered about Davie. Her first impression of the little group, influenced perhaps by the college architecture, had been of a young sultan taking his ease with two of his favourites and attended by the captain of the guard. But, meeting Davie Stevens's steady intelligent gaze, that impression faded. She suspected that, in this seraglio, it was the captain of the guard who was the dominant personality.

Sophia Tilling nodded and said "Hullo."

Isabelle did not speak but a smile beautiful and meaningless spread over her face. Hugo said:

"Won't you sit down, Cordelia Gray, and explain the nature of your necessities?"

Cordelia knelt gingerly, wary of grass stains on the soft suede of her skirt. It was an odd way to interview suspects—only, of course, these people weren't suspects—kneeling like a suppliant in front of them. She said:

"I'm a private detective. Sir Ronald Callender has employed me to find out why his son died."

The effect of her words was astonishing. The little group, which had been lolling at ease like exhausted warriors, stiffened with instantaneous shock into a rigid tableau as if struck to marble. Then, almost imperceptibly, they relaxed. Cordelia could hear the slow release of held breath. She watched their faces. Davie Stevens was the least concerned. He wore a half-rueful smile, interested but unworried, and gave a quick look at Sophie as if in complicity. The look was not returned; she and Hugo were staring rigidly ahead. Cordelia felt that the two Tillings were carefully avoiding each other's eyes. But it was Isabelle who was the most shaken. She gave a gasp and her hand flew to her face like a second-rate actress simulating shock. Her eyes widened into fathomless depths of violet blue and she turned them on Hugo in desperate appeal. She looked so pale that Cordelia half expected her to faint. She thought:

"If I'm in the middle of a conspiracy, then I know who is its weakest member."

Hugo Tilling said:

"You're telling us that Ronald Callender has employed you to find out why Mark died?"

"Is that so extraordinary?"

"I find it incredible. He took no particular interest in his son when he was alive, why begin now he's dead?"

"How do you know he took no particular interest?"

"It's just an idea I had."

Cordelia said:

"Well, he's interested now even if it's only the scientist's urge to discover truth."

"Then he'd better stick to his microbiology, discovering how to make plastic soluble in salt water, or whatever. Human beings aren't susceptible to his kind of experiment."

Davie Stevens said with casual unconcern:

"I wonder that you can stomach that arrogant fascist."

The gibe plucked at too many chords of memory. Wilfully obtuse, Cordelia said:

"I didn't enquire what political party Sir Ronald favours."

Hugo laughed.

"Davie doesn't mean that. By fascist Davie means that Ronald Callender holds certain untenable opinions. For example, that all men may not be created equal, that universal suffrage may not necessarily add to the general happiness of mankind, that the tyrannies of the left aren't noticeably more liberal or supportable than the tyrannies of the right, that black men killing black men is small improvement on white men killing black men in so far as the victims are concerned and that capitalism may not be responsible for all the ills that flesh is heir to from drug addiction to poor syntax. I don't suggest that Ronald Callender holds all or indeed any of these reprehensible opinions. But Davie thinks that he does."

Davie threw a book at Hugo and said without rancour:

"Shut up! You talk like the *Daily Telegraph*. And you're boring our visitor."

Sophie Tilling asked suddenly:

"Was it Sir Ronald who suggested that you should question us?"

"He said that you were Mark's friends; he saw you at the inquest and funeral."

Hugo laughed:

"For God's sake, is that his idea of friendship?"

Cordelia said:

"But you were there?"

"We went to the inquest—all of us except Isabelle, who, we thought, would have been decorative but unreliable. It was rather dull. There was a great deal of irrelevant medical evidence about the excellent state of Mark's heart, lungs and digestive system. As far as I can see, he would have gone on living for ever if he hadn't put a belt round his neck."

"And the funeral—were you there too?"

"We were, at the Cambridge Crematorium. A very subdued affair. There were only six of us present in addition to the undertaker's men; we three, Ronald Callender, that secretary/housekeeper of his and an old nanny type dressed in black. She cast rather a gloom over the proceedings, I thought. Actually she looked so exactly like an old family retainer that I suspect she was a policewoman in disguise."

"Why should she be? Did she look like one?"

"No, but then you don't look like a private eye."

"You've no idea who she was?"

"No, we weren't introduced; it wasn't a chummy kind of funeral. Now I recall it, not one of us spoke a single word to any of the others. Sir Ronald wore a mask of public grief, the King mourning the Crown Prince."

"And Miss Leaming?"

"The Queen Consort; she should have had a black veil over her face."

"I thought that her suffering was real enough," said Sophie.

"You can't tell. No one can. Define suffering. Define real."

Suddenly Davie Stevens spoke, rolling over onto his stomach like a playful dog.

"Miss Leaming looked pretty sick to me. Incidentally, the old lady was called Pilbeam; anyway, that was the name on the wreath."

Sophie laughed:

"That awful cross of roses with the black-edged card? I might have guessed it came from her; but how do you know?"

"I looked, honey. The undertaker's men took the wreath off the coffin and propped it against the wall so I took a quick butchers. The card read 'With sincere sympathy from Nanny Pilbeam'."

Sophie said:

"So you did, I remember now. How beautifully feudal! Poor old nanny, it must have cost her a packet."

"Did Mark ever talk about a Nanny Pilbeam?" Cordelia asked.

They glanced at each other quickly. Isabelle shook her head. Sophie said "not to me."

Hugo Tilling replied:

"He never talked about her, but I think I did see her once before the funeral. She called at college about six weeks ago—on Mark's twenty-first birthday actually, and asked to see him. I was in the Porter's Lodge at the time and Robbins asked me if Mark was in college. She went up to his room and they were there together for about an hour. I saw her leaving, but he never mentioned her to me either then or later."

And soon afterwards, thought Cordelia, he gave up university. Could there be a connection? It was only a tenuous lead, but she would have to follow it.

She asked out of a curiosity that seemed both perverse and irrelevant.

"Were there any other flowers?"

It was Sophie who replied:

"A simple bunch of unwired garden flowers on the coffin. No card. Miss Leaming, I suppose. It was hardly Sir Ronald's style."

Cordelia said:

"You were his friends. Please tell me about him."

They looked at each other as if deciding who should speak. Their embarrassment was almost palpable. Sophie Tilling was picking at small blades of grass and rolling them in her hands. Without looking up, she said:

"Mark was a very private person. I'm not sure how far any of us knew him. He was quiet, gentle, self-contained, unambitious. He was intelligent without being clever. He was very kind; he cared about people, but without inflicting them with his concern. He had little self-esteem but it never seemed to worry him. I don't think there is anything else we can say about him."

Suddenly Isabelle spoke in a voice so low that Cordelia could hardly catch it. She said:

"He was sweet."

Hugo said with a sudden angry impatience.

"He was sweet and he is dead. There you have it. We can't tell you any more about Mark Callender than that. We none of us saw him after he chucked college. He didn't consult us before he left, and he didn't consult us before he killed himself. He was, as my sister has told you, a very private person. I suggest that you leave him his privacy."

"Look," said Cordelia, "you went to the inquest, you went to the funeral. If you had stopped seeing him, if you were so unconcerned about him, why did you bother?"

"Sophie went out of affection. Davie went because Sophie did. I went out of curiosity and respect; you mustn't be seduced by my air of casual flippancy into thinking that I haven't a heart."

Cordelia said obstinately:

"Someone visited him at the cottage on the evening he died. Someone had coffee with him. I intend to find out who that person was."

Was it her fancy that this news surprised them? Sophie Tilling looked as if she were about to ask a question when her brother quickly broke in:

"It wasn't any of us. On the night Mark died we were all in the second row of the dress circle of the Arts Theatre watching Pinter. I don't know that I can prove it. I doubt whether the booking clerk has kept the chart for that particular night, but I booked the seats and she may remember me. If you insist on being tediously meticulous, I can probably introduce you to a friend who knew of my intention to take a party to the play; to another who saw some at least of us in the bar in the interval; and to another with whom I subsequently discussed the performance. None of this will prove anything; my friends are an accommodating bunch. It would be simpler for you to accept that I am telling the truth. Why should I lie? We were all four at the Arts Theatre on the night of 26th May."

Davie Stevens said gently:

"Why not tell that arrogant bastard Pa Callender to go to hell and leave his son in peace, then find yourself a nice simple case of larceny?"

"Or murder," said Hugo Tilling.

"Find yourself a nice simple case of murder."

As if in obedience to some secret code, they began getting up, piling their books together, brushing the grass cuttings from their clothes. Cordelia followed them through the courts and out of college. Still in a silent group they made their way to a white Renault parked in the forecourt.

Cordelia came up to them and spoke directly to Isabelle.

"Did you enjoy the Pinter? Weren't you frightened by that dreadful last scene when Wyatt Gillman is gunned down by the natives?"

It was so easy that Cordelia almost despised herself. The immense violet eyes grew puzzled.

"Oh, no! I did not care about it, I was not frightened. I was with Hugo and the others, you see."

Cordelia turned to Hugo Tilling.

"Your friend doesn't seem to know the difference between Pinter and Osborne."

Hugo was settling himself into the driving seat of the car. He twisted round to open the back door for Sophie and Davie. He said calmly:

"My friend, as you choose to call her, is living in Cambridge, inadequately chaperoned I'm happy to say, for the purpose of learning English. So far her progress has been erratic and in some respects disappointing. One can never be certain how much my friend has understood."

The engine purred into life. The car began to move. It was then that Sophie Tilling thrust her head out of the window and said impulsively:

"I don't mind talking about Mark if you think it will help. It won't, but you can come round to my house this afternoon if you like—57 Norwich Street. Don't be late; Davie and I are going on the river. You can come too if you feel like it."

The car accelerated. Cordelia watched it out of sight. Hugo raised his hand in ironic farewell but not one of them turned a head.

Cordelia muttered the address to herself until it was safely written down: 57, Norwich Street. Was that the address where Sophie lodged, a hostel perhaps, or did her family live in

Cambridge? Well, she would find out soon enough. When ought she to arrive? Too early would look over eager; too late and they might have set out for the river. Whatever motive had prompted Sophie Tilling to issue that belated invitation, she mustn't loose touch with them now.

They had some guilty knowledge; that had been obvious. Why else had they reacted so strongly to her arrival? They wanted the facts of Mark Callender's death to be left undisturbed. They would try to persuade, cajole, even to shame her into abandoning the case. Would they, she wondered, also threaten? But why? The most likely theory was that they were shielding someone. But again, why? Murder wasn't a matter of climbing late into college, a venial infringement of rules which a friend would automatically condone and conceal. Mark Callender had been their friend; to two of them he might have been more than a friend. Someone whom he knew and trusted had pulled a strap tight round his neck, had watched and listened to his agonized choking, had strung his body on a hook like the carcass of an animal. How could one reconcile that appalling knowledge with Davie Stevens' slightly amused and rueful glance at Sophie, with Hugo's cynical calm, with Sophie's friendly and interested eyes? If they were conspirators, then they were monsters. And Isabelle? If they were shielding anyone, it was most likely to be her. But Isabelle de Lasterie couldn't have murdered Mark. Cordelia remembered those frail sloping shoulders, those ineffective hands almost transparent in the sun, the long nails painted like elegant pink talons. If Isabelle were guilty, she hadn't acted alone. Only a tall and very strong woman could have heaved that inert body onto the chair and up to the hook.

Norwich Street was a one-way thoroughfare and, initially, Cordelia approached it from the wrong direction. It took her some time to find her way back to Hills Road, past the Roman Catholic church and down the fourth turning to the right. The street was terraced with small brick houses, obviously early Victorian. Equally obviously, the road was on its way up. Most of the houses looked well cared for; the paint on the identical front doors was fresh and bright; lined curtains had replaced the draped lace at the single ground-floor windows and the bases of the walls were scarred where a damp course had been installed. Number fifty-seven had a black front door with the house number painted in white behind the glass panel above. Cordelia was relieved to see that there was space to park the Mini. There was no sign of the Renault among the almost continuous row of old cars and battered bicycles which lined the edge of the pavement.

The front door was wide open. Cordelia pressed the bell and stepped tentatively into a narow white hall. The interior of the house was immediately familiar to her. From her sixth birthday she had lived for two years in just such a Victorian terraced cottage with Mrs. Gibson on the outskirts of Romford. She recognized the steep and narrow staircase immediately ahead, the door on the right leading to the front parlour, the second door set aslant which led to the back parlour and through it to the kitchen and yard. She knew that there would be cupboards and a curved alcove on each side of the fireplace; she knew where to find the door under the stairs. Memory was so sharp that it imposed on this clean, sun-scented interior the strong odour of unwashed napkins, cabbage and grease which had permeated the Romford house. She could almost hear the children's voices calling her outlandish name across the rookery of the primary school playground across the road, stamping the asphalt with the ubiquitous Wellington boots which they wore in all seasons, flailing their thin jersied arms: "Cor, Cor, Cor!"

The furthest door was ajar and she could glimpse a room painted bright yellow and spilling over with sunlight. Sophie's head appeared.

"Oh, it's you! Come in. Davie has gone to collect some books from college and to buy food for the picnic. Would you like tea now or shall we wait? I'm just finishing the ironing."

"I'd rather wait, thank you."

Cordelia sat down and watched while Sophie wound the flex around the iron and folded the cloth. She glanced around the room. It was welcoming and attractive, furnished in no particular style or period, a cosy hotch-potch of the cheap and the valuable, unpretentious and pleasing. There was a sturdy oak table against the wall; four rather ugly dining chairs; a Windsor chair with a plump yellow cushion; an elegant Victorian sofa covered with brown velvet and set under the window; three good Staffordshire figures on the mantel shelf above the hooded wrought-iron grate. One of the walls was almost covered with a notice board in dark cork which displayed posters, cards, *aides-mémoire*, and pictures cut from magazines. Two, Cordelia saw, were beautifully photographed and attractive nudes.

Outside the yellow-curtained window the small walled garden was a riot of greenery. An immense and multi-flowered holyhock burgeoned against a tatty looking trellis; there were roses planted in Ali Baba jars and a row of pots of bright-red geraniums lined the top of the wall.

Cordelia said:

"I like this house. Is it yours?"

"Yes, I own it. Our grandmother died two years ago and left Hugo and me a small legacy. I used mine for the down payment on this house and got a local authority grant towards the cost of conversion. Hugo spent all of his laying down wine. He was ensuring a happy middle age; I was ensuring a happy present. I suppose that's the difference between us."

She folded the ironing cloth on the end of the table and stowed it away in one of the cupboards. Sitting opposite to Cordelia, she asked abruptly:

"Do you like my brother?"

"Not very much. I thought he was rather rude to me."

"He didn't mean to be."

"I think that's rather worse. Rudeness should always be intentional, otherwise it's insensitivity."

"Hugo isn't at his most agreeable when he's with Isabelle. She has that affect on him."

"Was she in love with Mark Callender?"

"You'll have to ask her, Cordelia, but I shouldn't think so. They hardly knew each other. Mark was my lover, not hers. I thought I'd better get you here to tell you myself since someone's bound to sooner or later if you go around Cambridge ferreting out facts about him. He didn't live here with me, of course. He had rooms in college. But we were lovers for almost the whole of last year. It ended just after Christmas when I met Davie."

"Were you in love?"

"I'm not sure. All sex is a kind of exploitation, isn't it? If you mean, did we explore our own identities through the personality of the other, then I suppose we were in love or thought that we were. Mark needed to believe himself in love. I'm not sure I know what the word means."

Cordelia felt a surge of sympathy. She wasn't sure either. She thought of her own two lovers; Georges whom she had slept with because he was gentle and unhappy and called her Cordelia, a real name, her name, not Delia, Daddy's little fascist; and Carl who was young and angry and whom she had liked so much that it seemed churlish not to show it in the only way which seemed to him important. She had never thought of virginity as other than a temporary and inconvenient state, part of the general insecurity and vulnerability of being young. Before Georges and Carl she had been lonely and inexperienced. Afterwards she had been lonely and a little less inexperienced. Neither affair had given her the longed-for assurance in dealing with Daddy or the landladies, neither had inconveniently touched her heart. But for Carl she had felt tenderness. It was just as well that he had left Rome before his lovemaking had become too pleasurable and he too important to her. It was intolerable to think that those strange gymnastics might one day become necessary. Lovemaking, she had decided, was overrated, not painful but surprising. The alienation between thought and action was so complete. She said:

"I suppose I only meant were you fond of each other, and did you like going to bed together?"

"Both of those things."

"Why did it end? Did you quarrel?"

"Nothing so natural or uncivilized. One didn't quarrel with Mark. That was one of the troubles about him. I told him that I didn't want to go on with the affair and he accepted my decision as calmly as if I were just breaking a date for a play at the Arts. He didn't try to argue or dissuade me. And if you're wondering whether the break had anything to do with his death, well you're wrong. I wouldn't rank that high with anyone, particularly not Mark. I was probably fonder of him than he was of me."

"So why did it end?"

"I felt that I was under moral scrutiny. It wasn't true; Mark wasn't a prig. But that's how I felt, or pretended to myself that I felt. I couldn't live up to him and I didn't even want to. There was Gary Webber, for example. I'd better tell you about him; it explains a lot about Mark. He's an autistic child, one of the uncontrollable, violent ones. Mark met him with his parents and their other two children on Jesus Green about a year ago; the children were playing on the swings there. Mark spoke to Gary and the boy responded to him. Children always did. He took to visiting the family and looking after Gary one evening a week so that the Webbers could get out to the pictures. During his last two vacs he stayed in the house and looked after Gary completely while the whole family went off for a holiday. The Webbers couldn't bear the boy to go to hospital; they'd tried it once and he didn't settle. But they were perfectly happy to leave him with Mark. I used to call in some evenings and see them together. Mark would hold the boy on his lap and rock him backwards and forwards for hours at a time. It was the one way to quieten him. We disagreed about Gary. I thought he would be better dead and I said so. I still think it would be better if he died, better for his parents, better for the rest of the family, better for him. Mark didn't agree. I remember saying:

" 'Oh well, if you think it reasonable that children should suffer so that you can enjoy the emotional kick of relieving them——' After that the conversation became boringly metaphysical. Mark said:

" 'Neither you nor I would be willing to kill Gary. He exists. His family exists. They need help which we can give. It doesn't matter what we feel. Actions are important, feelings aren't.' "

Cordelia said:

"But actions arise out of feelings."

"Oh, Cordelia, don't you start! I've had this particular conversation too many times before. Of course they do!"

They were silent for a moment. Then Cordelia, reluctant to

shatter the tenuous confidence and friendship which she sensed was growing between them, made herself ask:

"Why did he kill himself—if he did kill himself?" Sophie's reply was as emphatic as a slammed door.

"He left a note."

"A note perhaps. But, as his father pointed out, not an explanation. It's a lovely passage of prose—at least I think so—but as a justification for suicide it just isn't convincing."

"It convinced the jury."

"It doesn't convince me. Think, Sophie! Surely there are only two reasons for killing oneself. One is either escaping from something or to something. The first is rational. If one is in intolerable pain, despair or mental anguish and there is no reasonable chance of a cure, then it's probably sensible to prefer oblivion. But it isn't sensible to kill oneself in the hope of gaining some better existence or to extend one's sensibilities to include the experience of death. It isn't possible to experience death. I'm not even sure it's possible to experience dying. One can only experience the preparations for death, and even that seems pointless since one can't make use of the experience afterwards. If there's any sort of existence after death we shall all know soon enough. If there isn't, we shan't exist to complain that we've been cheated. People who believe in an after life are perfectly reasonable. They're the only ones who are safe from ultimate disillusionment."

"You've thought it all out, haven't you. I'm not sure that suicides do. The act is probably both impulsive and irrational."

"Was Mark impulsive and irrational?"

"I didn't know Mark."

"But you were lovers! You slept with him!"

Sophie looked at her and cried out in angry pain.

"I didn't know him! I thought I did, but I didn't know the first thing about him!"

They sat without speaking for almost two minutes. Then Cordelia asked:

"You went to dinner at Garforth House didn't you? What was it like?"

"The food and the wine were surprisingly good, but I don't

suppose that's what you had in mind. The dinner party wasn't otherwise memorable. Sir Ronald was amiable enough when he noticed I was there. Miss Leaming, when she could tear her obsessive attention from the presiding genius, looked me over like a prospective mother-in-law. Mark was rather silent. I think he'd taken me there to prove something to me, or perhaps to himself; I'm not sure what. He never talked about the evening or asked me what I thought. A month later Hugo and I both went to dinner. It was then I met Davie. He was the guest of one of the research biologists and Ronald Callender was angling to get him. Davie did a vac job there in his final year. If you want the inside dope on Garforth House, you should ask him."

Five minutes later Hugo, Isabelle and Davie arrived. Cordelia had gone upstairs to the bathroom and heard the car stop and the jabber of voices in the hall. Footsteps passed beneath her towards the back parlour. She turned on the hot water. The gas boiler in the kitchen immediately gave forth a roar as if the little house were powered by a dynamo. Cordelia let the tap run, then stepped out of the bathroom, closing the door gently behind her. She stole to the top of the stairs. It was hard luck on Sophie to waste her hot water, she thought guiltily; but worse was the sense of treachery and shabby opportunism as she crept down the first three stairs and listened. The front door had been closed but the door to the back parlour was open. She heard Isabelle's high unemphatic voice:

"But if this man Sir Ronald is paying her to find out about Mark, why cannot I pay her to stop finding out?"

Then Hugo's voice, amused, a little contemptuous:

"Darling Isabelle, when will you learn that not everyone can be bought?"

"She can't, anyway. I like her."

It was Sophie speaking. Her brother replied:

"We all like her. The question is, how do we get rid of her?"

Then for a few minutes there was a murmur of voices, the words undistinguishable, broken by Isabelle.

"It is not, I think, a suitable job for a woman."

There was the sound of a chair scraping against the floor, a shuffle of feet. Cordelia darted guiltily back into the bathroom and turned off the tap. She recalled Bernie's complacent admonition when she had asked whether they needed accept a divorce case.

"You can't do our job, partner, and be a gentleman." She stood watching at the half-open door. Hugo and Isabelle were leaving. She waited until she heard the front door close and the car drive away. Then she went down to the parlour. Sophie and Davie were together, unpacking a large carrier bag of groceries. Sophie smiled and said:

"Isabelle has a party tonight. She has a house quite close to here in Panton Street. Mark's tutor, Edward Horsfall, will probably be there and we thought it might be useful for you to talk to him about Mark. The party's at eight o'clock but you can call for us here. Just now we're packing a picnic; we thought we'd take a punt on the river for an hour or so. Do come if you'd like to. It's really much the pleasantest way of seeing Cambridge."

Afterwards, Cordelia remembered the river picnic as a series of brief but intensely clear pictures, moments in which sight and sense fused and time seemed momentarily arrested while the sunlit image was impressed on her mind. Sunlight sparkling on the river and gilding the hairs of Davie's chest and forearms; the flesh of his strong upper arms speckled like an egg; Sophie lifting her arm to wipe the sweat from her brow as she rested between thrusts of the punt pole; green-black weeds dragged by the pole from mysterious depths to writhe sinuously below the surface; a bright duck cocking its white tail before disappearing in a flurry of green water. When they had rocked under Silver Street Bridge a friend of Sophie's swam alongside, sleek and snout-nosed like an otter, his black hair laying like blades across his cheeks. He rested his hands on the punt and opened his mouth to be fed chunks of sandwiches by a protesting Sophie. The punts and canoes scraped and jostled each other in the turbulence of white water racing under the bridge. The air rang with laughing voices and the green banks were peopled with half-naked bodies lying supine with their faces to the sun.

Davie punted until they reached the higher level of the river and Cordelia and Sophie stretched out on the cushions at opposite ends of the punt. Thus distanced it was impossible to carry on a private conversation; Cordelia guessed that this was precisely what Sophie had planned. From time to time, she would call out snatches of information as if to emphasize that the outing was strictly educational.

"That wedding cake is John's—we're just passing under Clare bridge, one of the prettiest, I think. Thomas Grumbald built it in 1639. They say he was only paid three shillings for the design. You know that view, of course; it's a good view of Queen's, though."

Cordelia's courage failed her at the thought of interrupting this desultory tourist's chat with the brutal demand:

"Did you and your brother kill your lover?"

Here, rocking gently on the sunlit river, the question seemed both indecent and absurd. She was in danger of being lulled into a gentle acceptance of defeat; viewing all her suspicions as a neurotic hankering after drama and notoriety, a need to justify her fee to Sir Ronald. She believed Mark Callender had been murdered because she wanted to believe it. She had identified with him, with his solitariness, his self-sufficiency, his alienation from his father, his lonely childhood. She had even—most dangerous presumption of all—come to see herself as his avenger. When Sophie took over the pole, just past the Garden House Hotel, and Davie edged his way along the gently rocking punt and stretched himself out beside her, she knew that she wouldn't be able to mention Mark's name. It was out of no more than a vague, unintrusive curiosity that she found herself asking:

"Is Sir Ronald Callender a good scientist?" Davie took up a short paddle and began lazily to stir the shining water.

"His science is perfectly respectable, as my dear colleagues would say. Rather more than respectable, in fact. At present the lab is working on ways of expanding the use of biological monitors to assess pollution of the sea and estuaries; that means routine surveys of plants and animals which might serve as indicators. And they did some very useful preliminary work last year on the degradation of plastics. R.C. isn't so hot himself, but then you can't expect much original science from the over fifties. But he's a great spotter of talent and he certainly knows how to run a team if you fancy that dedicated, one for all, band of brothers approach. I don't. They even publish their papers as the Callender Research Laboratory, not under individual names. That wouldn't do for me. When I publish, it's strictly for the glory of David Forbes Stevens and, incidentally, for the gratification of Sophie. The Tillings like success."

"Was that why you didn't want to stay on when he offered you a job?"

"That among other reasons. He pays too generously and he asks too much. I don't like being bought and I've a strong objection to dressing up every night in a dinner jacket like a performing monkey in a zoo. I'm a molecular biologist. I'm not looking for the holy grail. Dad and Mum brought me up as a Methodist and I don't see why I should chuck a perfectly good religion which served me very well for twelve years just to put the great scientific principle or Ronald Callender in its place. I distrust these sacerdotal scientists. It's a bloody wonder that little lot at Garforth House aren't genuflecting three times a day in the direction of the Cavendish."

"And what about Lunn? How does he fit in?"

"Oh, that boy's a bloody wonder! Ronald Callender found him in a children's home when he was fifteen—don't ask me how—and trained him to be a lab assistant. You couldn't find a better. There isn't an instrument made which Chris Lunn can't learn to understand and care for. He's developed one or two himself and Callender has had them patented. If anyone in that lab is indispensable it's probably Lunn. Certainly Ronald Callender cares a damn sight more for him than he did for his son. And Lunn, as you might guess, regards R.C. as God almighty, which is very gratifying for them both. It's extraordinary really, all that violence which used to be expressed in street fights and coshing old ladies, harnessed to the service of science. You've got to hand it to Callender. He certainly knows how to pick his slaves."

"And is Miss Leaming a slave?"

"Well, I wouldn't know just what Eliza Leaming is. She's responsible for the business management and, like Lunn, she's probably indispensable. Lunn and she seem to have a love-hate relationship, or, perhaps, a hate-hate relationship. I'm not very clever at detecting these psychological nuances."

"But how on earth does Sir Ronald pay for it all?"

"Well, that's the thousand-dollar question, isn't it? It's rumoured that most of the money came from his wife and that he and Elizabeth Leaming between them invested it rather cleverly. They certainly needed to. And then he gets a certain amount from contract work. Even so, it's an expensive hobby. While I was there they were saying that the Wolvington Trust were getting interested. If they come up with something big—and I gather it's below their dignity to come up with anything small—then most of Ronald Callender's troubles should be over. Mark's death must have hit him. Mark was due to come into a pretty substantial fortune in four years' time and he told Sophie that he intended to hand most of it over to Dad."

"Why on earth should he do that?"

"God knows. Conscience money, perhaps. Anyway, he obviously thought it was something that Sophie ought to know."

Conscience money for what, Cordelia wondered sleepily. For not loving his father enough? For rejecting his enthusiasms? For being less than the son he had hoped for? And what would happen to Mark's fortune now? Who stood to gain by Mark's death? She supposed that she ought to consult his grandfather's will and find out. But that would mean a trip to London. Was it really worth it?

She stretched back her face to the sun and trailed one hand in the river. A splash of water from the punt pole stung her eyes. She opened them and saw that the punt was gliding close to the bank and under the shade of overhanging trees. Immediately in front of her a torn branch, cleft at the end and thick as a man's body, hung by a thread of bark and turned gently as the punt passed beneath it. She was aware of Davie's voice; he must have been talking for a long time. How odd that she couldn't remember what he'd been saying!

"You don't need reasons for killing yourself; you need reasons for not killing yourself. It was suicide, Cordelia. I should let it go at that."

Cordelia thought that she must have briefly slept, since he seemed to be answering a question she couldn't remember having asked. But now there were other voices, louder and more insistent. Sir Ronald Callender's: "My son is dead. *My* son. If I am in some way responsible, I'd prefer to know. If anyone else is responsible, I want to know that too." Sergeant Maskell's: "How would you use this to hang yourself, Miss Gray?" The feel of the belt, smooth and sinuous, slipping like a live thing through her fingers.

She sat bolt upright, hands clasped around her knees, with such suddenness that the punt rocked violently and Sophie had to clutch at an overhanging branch to keep her balance. Her dark face, intriguingly fore-shortened and patterned with the shadow of leaves, looked down at Cordelia from what seemed an immense height. Their eyes met. In that moment Cordelia knew how close she had come to giving up the case. She had been suborned by the beauty of the day, by sunshine, indolence, the promise of comradeship, even friendship, into forgetting why she was here. The realization horrified her. Davie had said that Sir Ronald was a good picker. Well, he had picked her. This was her first case and nothing and no one was going to hinder her from solving it.

She said formally:

"It was good of you to let me join you, but I don't want to miss the party tonight. I ought to talk to Mark's tutor and there may be other people there who could tell me something. Isn't it time that we thought about turning back?"

Sophie turned her glance on Davie. He gave an almost imperceptible shrug. Without speaking, Sophie drove the pole hard against the bank. The punt began slowly to turn.

Isabelle's party was due to begin at eight o'clock but it was nearly nine when Sophie, Davie and Cordelia arrived. They walked to the house which was only five minutes from Norwich Street; Cordelia never discovered the exact address. She liked the look of the house and wondered how much it was costing

Isabelle's father in rent. It was a long, white, two-storey villa with tall curved windows and green shutters, set well back from the street, with a semi-basement and a flight of steps to the front door. A similar flight led down from the sitting-room to the long garden.

The sitting-room was already fairly full. Looking at her fellow guests, Cordelia was glad that she had bought the kaftan. Most people seemed to have changed although not necessarily, she thought, into something more attractive. What was aimed at was originality; it was preferable to look spectacular, even bizarre, than to appear nondescript.

The sitting-room was elegantly but unsubstantially furnished and Isabelle had impressed on it her own untidy, impractical and iconoclastic femininity. Cordelia doubted whether the owners had provided the ornate crystal chandelier, far too heavy and large for the room, which hung like a sunburst from the middle of the ceiling, or the many silken cushions and curtains which gave the room's austere proportions something of the ostentatious opulence of a courtesan's boudoir. The pictures, too, must surely be Isabelle's. No house owner letting his property would leave pictures of this quality on the walls. One, hanging above the fireplace, was of a young girl hugging a puppy. Cordelia gazed at it in excited pleasure. Surely she couldn't mistake that individual blue of the girl's dress, that marvellous painting of the cheeks and plump young arms, skin which simultaneously absorbed and reflected light—lovely, tangible flesh. She cried out involuntarily so that people turned to look at her:

"But that's a Renoir!"

Hugo was at her elbow. He laughed.

"Yes; but don't sound so shocked, Cordelia. It's only a small Renoir! Isabelle asked Papa for a picture for her sitting-room. You didn't expect him to provide a print of the Haywain or one of those cheap reproductions of Van Gogh's boring old chair."

"Would Isabelle have known the difference?"

"Oh, yes. Isabelle knows an expensive object when she sees one."

Cordelia wondered whether the bitterness, the hard edge of contempt in his voice, was for Isabelle or for himself. They looked across the room to where she stood, smiling at them. Hugo moved towards her like a man in a dream and took her hand. Cordelia watched. Isabelle had dressed her hair in a high cluster of curls, Grecian style. She was wearing an anke-length dress of cream matt silk, with a very low square neckline and small intricately tucked sleeves. It was obviously a model and should, Cordelia felt, have looked out of place at an informal party. But it didn't. It merely made every other woman's dress look like an improvization and reduced her own, whose colours had seemed muted and subtle when she bought it, to the status of a gaudy rag.

Cordelia was determined to get Isabelle alone some time during the evening but could see that it wasn't going to be easy. Hugo stuck tenaciously to her side, steering her among her guests with one proprietorial hand on her waist. He seemed to be drinking steadily and Isabelle's glass was always filled. Perhaps as the evening wore on they would get careless and there would be a chance to separate them. In the meantime, Cordelia decided to explore the house, and a more practical matter, to find out before she needed it where the lavatory was. It was the kind of party where guests were left to find out these things for themselves.

She went up to the first floor and making her way down the passage pushed gently open the door of the far room. The smell of whisky met her immediately; it was overpowering and Cordelia instinctively slipped into the room and closed the door behind her, afraid that it might permeate the house. The room, which was in an indescribable state of disarray, wasn't empty. On the bed and half covered by the counterpane a woman was lying; a woman with bright ginger hair splayed over the pillow and wearing a pink silk dressing-gown. Cordelia walked up to the bed and looked down at her. She was insensible with drink. She lay there emitting puffs of foul, whisky-laden breath which rose like invisible balls of smoke from the half-open mouth. Her lower lip and jaw were tense and creased, giving the face a look of stern censoriousness as if she disapproved strongly of her own condition. Her thin lips were thickly painted, the strong purple stain had seeped into the cracks around the mouth so that the body looked parched in an extremity of cold. Her hands, the gnarled fingers brown with nictotine and laden with rings, lay quietly on the counterpane. Two of the talon-like nails were broken and the brick-red varnish on the others was cracked or peeled away.

The window was obstructed by a heavy dressing-table. Averting her eyes from the mess of crumpled tissues, open bottles of face cream, spilt powder and half drunk cups of what looked like black coffee, Cordelia squeezed behind it and pushed open the window. She gulped in lungfulls of fresh, cleansing air. Below her in the garden pale shapes moved silently over the grass and between the trees like the ghosts of long dead revellers. She left the window open and went back to the bed. There was nothing here that she could do but she placed the cold hands under the counterpane and, taking a second and warmer gown from the hook on the door, tucked it around the woman's body. That, at least, would compensate for the fresh air blowing across the bed.

That done, Cordelia slipped back into the passage, just in time to see Isabelle coming out of the room next door. She shot out an arm and half dragged the girl back into the bedroom. Isabelle gave a little cry, but Cordelia planted her back firmly against the door and said in a low, urgent whisper:

"Tell me what you know about Mark Callender."

The violet eyes slewed from door to window as if desperate for escape.

"I wasn't there when he did it."

"When who did what?"

Isabelle retreated towards the bed as if the inert figure, who was now groaning stertorously, could offer support. Suddenly the woman turned on her side and gave a long snort like an animal in pain. Both girls glanced at her in startled alarm. Cordelia reiterated:

"When who did what?"

"When Mark killed himself; I wasn't there."

The woman on the bed gave a little sigh. Cordelia lowered her voice:

"But you were there some days earlier, weren't you? You called at the house and enquired for him. Miss Markland saw you. Afterwards you sat in the garden and waited until he'd finished work."

Was it Cordelia's imagination that the girl suddenly seemed more relaxed, that she was relieved at the innocuousness of the question?

"I just called to see Mark. They gave me his address at the college Lodge. I went to visit him."

"Why?" The harsh question seemed to puzzle her. She replied simply:

"I wanted to be with him. He was my friend."

"Was he your lover too?" asked Cordelia. This brutal frankness was surely better than asking whether they had slept together, or gone to bed together—stupid euphemisms which Isabelle might not even understand: it was hard to tell from those beautiful but frightened eyes just how much she did understand.

"No, Mark was never my lover. He was working in the garden and I had to wait for him at the cottage. He gave me a chair in the sun and a book until he was free."

"What book?"

"I don't remember, it was very dull. I was dull too until Mark came. Then we had tea with funny mugs that had a blue band, and after tea we went for a walk and then we had supper. Mark made a salad."

"And then?"

"I drove home."

She was perfectly calm now. Cordelia pressed on, aware of the sound of footsteps passing up and down the stairs, of the ring of voices.

"And the time before that? When did you see him before that tea party?"

"It was a few days before Mark left college. We went for a picnic in my car to the seaside. But first we stopped at a town—St. Edmunds town, is it?—and Mark saw a doctor."

"Why? Was he ill?"

"Oh no, he was not ill, and he did not stay long enough for what you call it—an examination. He was in the house a few minutes only. It was a very poor house. I waited for him in the car, but not just ouside the house you understand."

"Did he say why he went there?"

"No, but I do not think he got what he wanted. Afterwards he was sad for a little time, but then we went to the sea and he was happy again."

She, too, seemed happy now. She smiled at Cordelia, her sweet, unmeaning smile. Cordelia thought: it's just the cottage that terrifies her. She doesn't mind talking about the living Mark, it's his death she can't bear to think about. And yet, this repugnance wasn't born of personal grief. He had been her friend; he was sweet; she liked him. But she was getting on very well without him.

There was a knock at the door. Cordelia stood aside and Hugo came in. He lifted an eyebrow at Isabelle and, ignoring Cordelia, said:

"It's your party, ducky; coming down?"

"Cordelia wanted to talk to me about Mark."

"No doubt. You told her, I hope, that you spent one day with him motoring to the sea and one afternoon and evening at Summertrees and that you haven't seen him since."

"She told me," said Cordelia. "She was practically word perfect. I think she's safe to be let out on her own now."

He said easily:

"You shouldn't be sarcastic, Cordelia, it doesn't suit you. Sarcasm is all right for some women, but not for women who are beautiful in the way that you are beautiful."

They were passing down the stairs together to meet the hubbub in the hall. The compliment irritated Cordelia. She said:

"I suppose that woman on the bed is Isabelle's chaperone. Is she often drunk?"

"Mademoiselle de Congé? Not often as drunk as that, but I admit that she is seldom absolutely sober."

"Then oughtn't you to do something about it?"

"What should I do? Hand her over to the twentieth-century Inquisition—a psychiatrist like my father? What has she done to us to deserve that? Besides, she is tediously conscientious on the few occasions when she's sober. It happens that her compulsions and my interest coincide."

Cordelia said severely:

"That may be expedient but I don't think it's very responsible and it isn't kind."

He stopped in his tracks and turned towards her, smiling directly into her eyes.

"Oh, Cordelia, you talk like the child of progressive parents who has been reared by a nonconformist nanny and educated at a convent school. I do like you!"

He was still smiling as Cordelia slipped away from them and infiltrated into the party. She reflected that his diagnosis hadn't been so very wrong.

She helped herself to a glass of wine, then moved slowly round the room listening unashamedly to scraps of conversation, hoping to hear Mark's name mentioned. She heard it only once. Two girls and a very fair, rather insipid young man were standing behind her. One of the girls said:

"Sophie Tilling seems to have recovered remarkably quickly from Mark Callender's suicide. She and Davie went to the cremation, did you know? Typical of Sophie to take her current lover to see the previous one incinerated. I suppose it gave her some kind of a kick."

Her companion laughed.

"And little brother takes over Mark's girl. If you can't get beauty, money and brains, settle for the first two. Poor Hugo! He suffers from a sense of inferiority. Not quite handsome enough; not quite clever enough—Sophie's First must have shaken him—not quite rich enough. No wonder he has to rely on sex to give him confidence."

"And, even there, not quite . . ."

"Darling, you should know."

They laughed and moved away. Cordelia felt her face burning. Her hand shook almost spilling her wine. She was surprised to find how much she cared, how much she had come to like Sophie. But that, of course, was part of the plan, that was Tilling strategy. If you can't shame her into giving up the case, suborn her; take her on the river; be nice to her; get her on our side. And it was true, she was on their side, at least against malicious detractors. She comforted herself with the censorious reflection that they were as bitchy as guests at a suburban cocktail party. She had never in her life attended one of those innocuous if boring gatherings for the routine consumption of gossip, gin and canapés but, like her father who had never attended one either, she found no difficulty in believing that they were hot beds of snobbery, spite and sexual innuendo.

A warm body was pressing against her. She turned and saw Davie. He was carrying three bottles of wine. He had obviously heard at least part of the conversation, as the girls had no doubt intended, but he grinned amiably.

"Funny how Hugo's discarded women always hate him so much. It's quite different with Sophie. Her ex-lovers clutter up Norwich Street with their beastly bicycles and broken-down cars. I'm always finding them in the sitting-room drinking my beer and confiding to her the awful trouble they're having with their present girls."

"Do you mind?"

"Not if they don't get any further than the sitting-room. Are you enjoying yourself?"

"Not very much."

"Come and meet a friend of mine. He's been asking who you are."

"No thank you, Davie. I must keep myself free for Mr. Horsfall. I don't want to miss him."

He smiled at her, rather pityingly she thought, and seemed about to speak. But he changed his mind and moved away, clutching his bottles to his chest and shouting a cheerful warning as he edged himself through the throng.

Cordelia worked her way around the room, watching and listening. She was intrigued by the overt sexuality; she had thought that intellectuals breathed too rarified air to be much interested in the flesh. Obviously this was a misapprehension. Come to think of it, the comrades, who might have been supposed to live in randy promiscuity, had been remarkably staid. She had sometimes felt that their sexual activities were prompted more by duty than instinct, more a weapon of revolution or a gesture against the bourgeois mores they despised than a response to human need. Their basic energies were all devoted to politics.

It was not difficult to see where most of the energies of those present were directed.

She needn't have worried about the success of the kaftan. A number of men showed themselves willing or even eager to detach themselves from their partners for the pleasure of talking to her. With one particularly, a decorative and ironically amusing young historian, Cordelia felt that she could have spent an entertaining evening. To enjoy the sole attention of one agreeable man and no attention at all from anyone else was all she ever hoped from a party. She wasn't naturally gregarious and, alienated by the last six years from her own generation, found herself intimidated by the noise, the underlying ruthlessness and the half-understood conventions of these tribal matings. And she told herself firmly that she wasn't here to enjoy herself at Sir Ronald's expense. None of her prospective partners knew Mark Callender or showed any interest in him, dead or alive. She mustn't get herself tied for the evening to people who had no information to give. When this seemed a danger and the talk became too beguiling, she would murmur her excuses and slip away to the bathroom or into the shadows of the garden where little groups were sitting on the grass smoking pot. Cordelia couldn't be mistaken in that evocative smell. They showed no disposition to chat and here, at least, she could stroll in privacy gaining courage for the next foray, for the next artfully casual question, the next inevitable response.

"Mark Callender? Sorry—we never met. Didn't he go off to sample the simple life and end by hanging himself or something?"

Once she took refuge in Mademoiselle de Congé's room, but she saw that the inert figure had been unceremoniously dumped on a cushion of pillows on the carpet and that the bed was being occupied for quite another purpose.

She wondered when Edward Horsfall would arrive or whether he would arrive at all. And if he did, would Hugo remember or bother to introduce her? She couldn't see either of the Tillings in the hot crush of gesticulating bodies which by now had crammed the sitting-room and spilled into the hall and half-way up the stairs. She was beginning to feel that this would be a wasted evening when Hugo's hand fell on her arm. He said:

"Come and meet Edward Horsfall. Edward, this is Cordelia Gray; she wants to talk about Mark Callender."

Edward Horsfall was another surprise. Cordelia had subconsciously conjured up the picture of an elderly don, a little distrait with the weight of his learning, a benevolent if detached mentor of the young. Horsfall could not have been much over thirty. He was very tall, his hair falling long over one eye, his lean body curved as a melon rind, a comparison reinforced by the pleated yellow shirt front under a jutting bow tie.

Any half acknowledged, half shameful hope which Cordelia may have nourished that he would immediately take to her and be happily ungrudging of his time so long as they were together was quickly dispersed. His eyes were restless, flicking obsessively back to the door. She suspected that he was alone by choice, deliberately keeping himself free from encumbrances until the hoped-for companion arrived. He was so fidgety that it was difficult not to be fretted by his anxiety. She said:

"You don't have to stay with me all the evening you know, I only want some information."

Her voice recalled him to an awareness of her and to some attempt at civility.

"That wouldn't exactly be a penance. I'm sorry. What do you want to know?"

"Anything you can tell me about Mark. You taught him history didn't you? Was he good at it?"

It wasn't a particularly relevant question but one which she felt all teachers might respond to as a start.

"He was more rewarding to teach than some students I'm afflicted with. I don't know why he chose history. He could very well have read one of the sciences. He had a lively curiosity about physical phenomenon. But he decided to read history."

"Do you think that was to disoblige his father?"

"To disoblige Sir Ronald?" He turned and stretched out an arm for a bottle. "What are you drinking? There's one thing about Isabelle de Lasterie's parties, the drink is excellent, presumably because Hugo orders it. There's an admirable absence of beer."

"Doesn't Hugo drink beer then?" asked Cordelia.

"He claims not to. What were we talking about? Oh, yes, disobliging Sir Ronald. Mark said that he chose history because we have no chance of understanding the present without understanding the past. That's the sort of irritating cliché people come out with at interviews, but he may have believed it. Actually, of course, the reverse is true; we interpret the past through our knowledge of the present."

"Was he any good?" asked Cordelia. "I mean, would he have got a First?"

A First, she naively believed, was the ultimate in scholastic achievement, the certificate of pronounced intelligence that the recipient carried unchallenged through life. She wanted to hear that Mark was safe for a First.

"Those are two separate and distinct questions. You seem to be confusing merit with achievement. Impossible to predict his class, hardly a First. Mark was capable of extraordinarily good and original work but he limited his material to the number of his original ideas. The result tended to be rather thin. Examiners like originality but you've got to spew up the accepted facts and orthodox opinions first if only to show that you've learnt them. An exceptional memory and fast legible handwriting; that's the secret of a First. Where are you, incidentally?" He noticed Cordelia's brief look of incomprehension.

"At what college?"

"None; I work. I'm a private detective."

He took this information in his stride.

"My uncle employed one of those once to find out if my aunt was being screwed by their dentist. She was, but he could have found out more easily by the simple expedient of asking them. His way, he lost the services of a wife and of a dentist simultaneously and paid through the nose for information he could have got for nothing. It made quite a stir in the family at the time. I should have thought that the job was——"

Cordelia finished the sentence for him.

"An unsuitable job for a woman?"

"Not at all. Entirely suitable I should have thought, requiring, I imagine, infinite curiosity, infinite pains and a penchant for interfering with other people." His attention was wandering again. A group near to them were talking and snatches of the conversation came to them.

"——typical of the worst kind of academic writing. Contempt for logic; a generous sprinkling of vogue names; spurious profundity and bloody awful grammar."

The tutor gave the speakers a second's attention, dismissed their academic chat as beneath his notice and condescended to transfer his attention but not his regard back to Cordelia.

"Why are you so interested in Mark Callender?"

"His father has employed me to find out why he died. I was hoping that you might be able to help. I mean, did he ever give you a hint that he might be unhappy, unhappy enough to kill himself? Did he explain why he gave up college?"

"Not to me. I never felt that I got near him. He made a formal goodbye, thanked me for what he chose to describe was my help, and left. I made the usual noises of regret. We shook hands. I was embarrassed, but not Mark. He wasn't I think, a young man susceptible to embarrassment."

There was a small commotion at the door and a group of new arrivals pushed themselves noisily into the throng. Among them was a tall, dark girl in a flame-coloured frock, open almost to the waist. Cordelia felt the tutor stiffen, saw his eyes fixed on the new arrival with an intense, half anxious, half supplicating look, which she had seen before. Her heart sank. She would be lucky now to get any more information. Desperately trying to recapture his attention, she said:

"I'm not sure that Mark did kill himself. I think it could have been murder."

He spoke inattentively, his eyes on the newcomers.

"Unlikely, surely. By whom? For what reason? He was a negligible personality. He didn't even provoke a vague dislike except possibly from his father. But Ronald Callender couldn't have done it if that's what you're hoping. He was dining in Hall at High Table on the night Mark died. It was a College Feast night. I sat next to him. His son telephoned him."

Cordelia said eagerly, almost tugging at his sleeve.

"At what time?"

"Soon after the meal started, I suppose. Benskin, he's one of the College servants, came in and gave him the message. It must have been between eight and eight-fifteen. Callender disappeared for about ten minutes then returned and got on with his soup. The rest of us still hadn't reached the second course."

"Did he say what Mark wanted? Did he seem disturbed?"

"Neither. We hardly spoke through the meal. Sir Ronald doesn't waste his conversational gifts on non-scientists. Excuse me, will you?"

He was gone, threading his way through the throng towards his prey. Cordelia put down her glass and went in search of Hugo.

"Look," she said, "I want to talk to Benskin, a servant at your college. Would he be there tonight?"

Hugo put down the bottle he was holding.

"He may be. He's one of the few who live in college. But I doubt whether you would winkle him out of his lair on your own. If it's all that urgent, I'd better come with you."

The college porter ascertained without curiosity that Benskin was in the college and Benskin was summoned. He arrived after a wait of five minutes during which Hugo chatted to the porter and Cordelia walked outside the Lodge to amuse herself reading the college notices. Benskin arrived, unhurrying, imperturbable. He was a silver-haired, formally dressed old man, his face creased and thick skinned as an anaemic blood orange, and would, Cordelia thought, have looked like an advertisement for the ideal butler, were it not for an expression of lugubrious and sly disdain.

Cordelia gave him sight of Sir Ronald's note of authority and plunged straight into her questions. There was nothing to be gained by subtlety and since she had enlisted Hugo's help, she had little hope of shaking him off. She said:

"Sir Ronald has asked me to enquire into the circumstances of his son's death."

"So I see, Miss."

"I am told that Mr. Mark Callender telephoned his father

while Sir Ronald was dining at High Table on the night his son died and that you passed the message to Sir Ronald shortly after dinner began?"

"I was under the impression at the time that it was Mr. Callender who was ringing, Miss, but I was mistaken."

"How can you be sure of that, Mr. Benskin?"

"Sir Ronald himself told me, Miss, when I saw him in college some few days after his son's death. I've known Sir Ronald since he was an undergraduate and I made bold to express my condolences. During our brief conversation I made reference to the telephone call of 26th May and Sir Ronald told me that I was mistaken, that it was not Mr. Callender who had called."

"Did he say who it was?"

"Sir Ronald informed me that it was his laboratory assistant, Mr. Chris Lunn."

"Did that surprise you—that you were wrong, I mean?"

"I confess that I was somewhat surprised, Miss, but the mistake was perhaps excusable. My subsequent reference to the incident was fortuitous and in the circumstances regrettable."

"But do you really believe that you mis-heard the name?"

The obstinate old face did not relax.

"Sir Ronald could have been in no doubt about the person who telephoned him."

"Was it usual for Mr. Callender to ring his father while he was dining in College?"

"I had never previously taken a call from him, but then answering the telephone is not part of my normal duties. It is possible that some of the other college servants may be able to help but I hardly think that an enquiry would be productive or that the news that college servants had been questioned would be gratifying to Sir Ronald."

"Any enquiry which can help ascertain the truth is likely to be gratifying to Sir Ronald," said Cordelia. Really, she thought, Benskin's prose style is becoming infectious. She added more naturally:

"Sir Ronald is very anxious to find out everything possible about his son's death. Is there anything that you can tell me, any help that you can give me, Mr. Benskin?"

This was perilously close to an appeal but it met with no response.

"Nothing, Miss. Mr. Callender was a quiet and pleasant young gentleman who seemed, as far as I was able to observe him, to be in good health and spirits up to the time he left us. His death has been very much felt in the college. Is there anything else, Miss?"

He stood patiently waiting to be dismissed and Cordelia let him go. As she and Hugo left college together and walked back into Trumpington Street she said bitterly:

"He doesn't care, does he?"

"Why should he? Benskin's an old phoney but he's been at college for seventy years and he's seen it all before. A thousand ages in his sight are but an evening gone. I've only known Benskin distressed once over the suicide of an undergraduate and that was a Duke's son. Benskin thought that there were some things that the college shouldn't permit to happen."

"But he wasn't mistaken about Mark's call. You could tell that from his whole manner, at least I could. He knows what he heard. He isn't going to admit it, of course, but he knows in his heart he wasn't mistaken."

Hugo said lightly:

"He was being the old college servant, very correct, very proper; that's Benskin all over. 'The young gentlemen aren't what they were when I first came to college.' I should bloody well hope not! They wore side whiskers then and noblemen sported fancy gowns to distinguish them from the plebs. Benskin would bring all that back if he could. He's an anachronism, pottering through the court hand in hand with a statelier past."

"But he isn't deaf. I deliberately spoke in a soft voice and he heard me perfectly. Do you really believe that he was mistaken?"

"Chris Lunn and his son are very similar sounds."

"But Lunn doesn't announce himself that way. All the time I was with Sir Ronald and Miss Leaming they just called him Lunn."

"Look, Cordelia, you can't possibly suspect Ronald Callender of having a hand in his son's death! Be logical. You accept, I suppose, that a rational murderer hopes not to be found out. You admit, no doubt, that Ronald Callender, although a disagreeable bastard, is a rational being. Mark is dead and his body cremated. No one except you has mentioned murder. Then Sir Ronald employs you to stir things up. Why should he if he's got something to hide? He doesn't even need to divert suspicion; there has been no suspicion, there is no suspicion."

"Of course I don't suspect him of killing his son. He doesn't know how Mark died and he desperately needs to know. That's why he's taken me on. I could tell that at our interview; I couldn't be wrong about that. But I don't understand why he should have lied about the telephone call."

"If he is lying there could be half a dozen innocent explanations. If Mark did ring the college it must have been something pretty urgent, perhaps something which his father didn't particularly want to make public, something which gives a clue to his son's suicide."

"Then why employ me to find out why he killed himself?"

"True, wise Cordelia; I'll try again. Mark asked him for help, perhaps an urgent visit which Dad refused. You can imagine his reaction. 'Don't be ridiculous, Mark, I'm dining at High Table with the Master. Obviously I can't leave the cutlets and claret just because you telephone in this hysterical way and demand to see me. Pull yourself together.' That sort of thing wouldn't sound so good in open court; coroners are notoriously censorious." Hugo's voice took on a deep magisterial tone. " 'It is not for me to add to Sir Ronald's distress, but it is, perhaps, unfortunate that he chose to ignore what was obviously a cry for help. Had he left his meal immediately and gone to his son's side this brilliant young student might have been saved.' Cambridge suicides, so I've noticed, are always brilliant; I'm still waiting to read the report of an inquest where the college authorities testify that the student only just killed himself in time before they kicked him out."

"But Mark died between seven and nine p.m. That telephone call is Sir Ronald's alibi!"

"He wouldn't see it like that. He doesn't need an alibi. If you know you're not involved and the question of foul play never arises, you don't think in terms of alibis. It's only the guilty who do that."

"But how did Mark know where to find his father? In his evidence Sir Ronald said that he hadn't spoken to his son for over three weeks."

"I can see you have a point there. Ask Miss Leaming. Better still, ask Lunn if it was, in fact, he who rang the college. If you're looking for a villain Lunn should suit admirably. I find him absolutely sinister."

"I didn't know that you knew him."

"Oh, he's pretty well known in Cambridge. He drives that horrid little closed van around with ferocious dedication as if he were transporting recalcitrant students to the gas chambers. Everyone knows Lunn. Seldom he smiles and smiles in such a way as if he mocked himself and scorned his spirit that could be moved to smile at anything. I should concentrate on Lunn."

They walked on in silence through the warm scented night while the waters sang in the runnels of Trumpington Street. Lights were shining now in college doorways and in porters' lodges and the far gardens and inter-connecting courts, glimpsed as they passed, looked remote and ethereal as in a dream. Cordelia was suddenly oppressed with loneliness and melancholy. If Bernie were alive they would be discussing the case, cosily ensconced in the furthest corner of some Cambridge pub, insulated by noise and smoke and anonymity from the curiosity of their neighbours; talking low voiced in their own particular jargon. They would be speculating on the personality of a young man who slept under that gentle and intellectual painting, yet who had bought a vulgar magazine of salacious nudes. Or had he? And if not, how had it come to be in the cottage garden? They would be discussing a father who lied about his son's last telephone call; speculating in happy complicity about an uncleaned spade, a row of earth half dug, an unwashed coffee mug, a quotation from Blake meticulously typed. They would be talking about Isabelle who was terrified and Sophie who was surely honest and Hugo who certainly knew something about Mark's death and who was clever but not as clever as he needed to be. For the first time since the case began Cordelia doubted her ability to solve it alone. If only there were someone reliable in whom she could confide, someone who would reinforce her confidence. She thought again of Sophie, but Sophie had been Mark's mistress and was Hugo's sister. They were both involved. She was on her own and that, when she came to think about it, was no different from how essentially it had always been. Ironically, the realization brought her comfort and a return of hope.

At the corner of Panton Street they paused and he said:

"You're coming back to the party?"

"No, thank you, Hugo; I've got work to do."

"Are you staying in Cambridge?"

Cordelia wondered whether the question was prompted by more than polite interest. Suddenly cautious, she said:

"Only for the next day or two. I've found a very dull but cheap bed and breakfast place near the station."

He accepted the lie without comment and they said good-night. She made her way back to Norwich Street. The little car was still outside number fifty-seven, but the house was dark and quiet as if to emphasize her exclusion and the three windows were as blank as dead rejecting eyes.

She was tired by the time she got back to the cottage and had parked the Mini on the edge of the copse. The garden gate creaked at her hand. The night was dark and she felt in her bag for her torch and followed its bright pool round the side of the cottage and to the back door. By its light she fitted the key into the lock. She turned it and, dazed with tiredness, stepped into the sitting-room. The torch, still switched on, hung loosely from her hand, making erratic patterns of light on the tiled floor. Then in one involuntary movement it jerked upwards and shone full on the thing that hung from the centre hook of the ceiling. Cordelia gave a cry and clutched at the table. It was the bolster from her bed, the bolster with a cord drawn tight about one end making a grotesque and bulbous head, and the other end stuffed into a pair of Mark's trousers. The legs hung pathetically flat and empty, one lower than the other. As she stared at it in fascinated horror, her heart hammering, a slight breeze wafted in from the open door and it swung slowly round as if twisted by a living hand.

She must have stood there rooted with fear and staring wild-eyed at the bolster for seconds only, yet it seemed minutes before she found the strength to pull out a chair from the table and take the thing down. Even in the moment of repulsion and terror she remembered to look closely at the knot. The cord was attached to the hook by a simple loop and two half-hitches. So, either her secret visitor had chosen not to repeat his former tactics, or he hadn't known how the first knot had been tied. She laid the bolster on the chair and went outside for the gun. In her tiredness she had forgotten it, but now she longed for the reassurance of the hard cold metal in her hand. She stood at the back door and listened. The garden seemed suddenly full of noises, mysterious rustlings, leaves moving in the slight breeze like human sighs, furtive scurryings in the undergrowth, the bat-like squeak of an animal disconcertingly close at hand. The night seemed to be holding its breath as she crept out towards the elder bush. She waited, listening to her own heart, before she found courage to turn her back and stretch up her hand to feel for the gun. It was still there. She sighed audibly with relief and immediately felt better. The gun wasn't loaded but that hardly seemed to matter. She hurried back to the cottage, her terror assuaged.

It was nearly an hour before she finally went to bed. She lit the lamp and, gun in hand, made a search of the whole cottage. Next she examined the window. It was obvious enough how he had got in. The window had no catch and was easy to push open from outside. Cordelia fetched a roll of Scotch tape from her scene-of-crime kit and, as Bernie had shown her, cut two very narrow strips and pasted them across the base of the pane and the wooden frame. She doubted whether the front windows could be opened but she took no chances and sealed them in the same way. It wouldn't stop an intruder but at least she would know next morning that he had gained access. Finally, having washed in the kitchen, she went upstairs to bed. There was no lock on her door but she wedged it slightly open and balanced a saucepan lid on the top of the frame. If anyone did succeed in getting in, he wouldn't take her by surprise. She loaded the gun and placed it on her bedside table, remembering that she was dealing with a killer. She examined the cord. It was a four-foot length of ordinary strong string, obviously not new and frayed at one end. Her heart sank at the hopelessness of trying to identify it. But she labelled it carefully, as Bernie had taught her, and packed it in her scene-of-crime kit. She did the same with the curled strap and the typed passage of Blake, transferring them from the bottom of her shoulder bag to plastic exhibit envelopes. She was so weary that even this routine chore cost her an effort of will. Then she placed the bolster back on the bed, resisting an impulse to sling it on the floor and sleep without it. But, by then, nothing—neither fear nor discomfort—could have kept her awake. She lay for only a few minutes listening to the ticking of her watch before tiredness overcame her and bore her unresisting down the dark tide of sleep.

Chapter Four

Cordelia was awakened early next morning by the discordant chattering of the birds and the strong clear light of another fine day. She lay for several minutes stretching herself within her sleeping-bag, savouring the smell of a country morning, that subtle and evocative fusion of earth, sweet wet grass and stronger farmyard smell. She washed in the kitchen as Mark had obviously done, standing in the tin bath from the shed and gasping as she poured saucepans of cold tap water over her naked body. There was something about the simple life which disposed one to these austerities. Cordelia thought it unlikely that, in any circumstances, she would willingly have bathed in cold water in London or so much relished the smell of the paraffin stove superimposed on the appetizing sizzle of frying bacon, or the flavour of her first strong mug of tea.

The cottage was filled with sunlight, a warm friendly sanctum from which she could safely venture out to whatever the day held. In the calm peace of a summer morning the little sitting-room seemed untouched by the tragedy of Mark Callender's death. The hook in the ceiling looked as innocuous as if it had never served its dreadful purpose. The horror of that moment when her torch had first picked out the dark swollen shadow of the bolster moving in the night breeze now had the unreality of a dream. Even the memory of the precautions of the night before were embarrassing viewed in the unambiguous light of day. She felt rather foolish as she unloaded the gun, secreted the ammunition among her underclothes, and hid the pistol in the elder bush, watching carefully to see that she wasn't observed. When the washing-up was done and the one teacloth washed through and hung out to dry, she picked a small posy of pansies, cowslips and meadow-sweet from the far end of the garden and set them on the table in one of the ribbed mugs.

She had decided that her first task must be to try to trace Nanny Pilbeam. Even if the woman had nothing to tell her about Mark's death or his reason for leaving college, she would be able to speak about his childhood and boyhood; she, probably better than anyone, would know what his essential nature had been. She had cared enough about him to attend the funeral and to send an expensive wreath. She had called on him in college on his 21st birthday. He had probably kept in touch with her, might even have confided in her. He had no mother and Nanny Pilbeam could have been, in some sense, a substitute.

As she drove into Cambridge Cordelia considered tactics. The probability was that Miss Pilbeam lived somewhere in the district. It was unlikely that she actually lived in the city since Hugo Tilling had only seen her once. From his brief account of her, it sounded as if she were old and probably poor. It was unlikely, therefore, that she would travel far to attend the funeral. It was apparent that she hadn't been one of the official mourners from Garforth House, hadn't been invited by Sir Ronald. According to Hugo, none of the party had even spoken to each other. This hardly suggested that Miss Pilbeam was the elderly and valued retainer of tradition, almost one of the family. Sir Ronald's neglect of her on such an occasion intrigued Cordelia. She wondered just what Miss Pilbeam's position in the family had been.

If the old lady lived near Cambridge, she had probably ordered the wreath at one of the city florists. Villages were very unlikely to provide this kind of service. It had been an ostentatious wreath, which suggested that Miss Pilbeam had been prepared to spend lavishly and had probably gone to one of the larger florists. The likelihood was that she had ordered it personally. Elderly ladies, apart from the fact that they were seldom on the telephone, like to attend to these matters direct, having, Cordelia suspected, a well-founded suspicion that only face-to-face confrontation and the meticulous recital of one's precise requirements extracted the best service. If Miss Pilbeam had come in from her village by train or by bus, she had probably selected a shop somewhere near the centre of the city. Cordelia decided to begin her search by enquiring of passers-by if they could recommend the name of a good florist.

She had already learned that Cambridge was not a city for the cruising motorist. She drew up and consulted the folding map at the back of her guide book and decided to leave the Mini on the car park next to Parker's Piece. Her search might take some time and would be best done on foot. She daren't risk a parking fine nor the impounding of the car. She checked her watch. It was still only a few minutes after nine o'clock. She had made a good start to the day.

The first hour was disappointing. The people of whom she enquired were anxious to be helpful but their ideas of what constituted a reliable florist somewhere near the centre of the city were peculiar. Cordelia was directed to small greengrocers selling a few bunches of cut flowers as a side line, to the supplier of gardening equipment who dealt in plants but not in wreaths, and once to a funeral director. The two florists' shops which at first sight seemed possible had never heard of Miss Pilbeam and had provided no wreaths for the Mark Callender funeral. A little weary with much walking and beginning to feel despondent, Cordelia decided that the whole quest had been unreasonably sanguine. Probably Miss Pilbeam had come in from Bury St. Edmunds or Newmarket and had bought the wreath in her own town.

But the visit to the undertakers was not wasted. In reply to her enquiry, they recommended the name of a firm which provided "a very nice class of wreath, Miss, really very nice indeed." The shop was further from the centre of the city than Cordelia had expected. Even from the pavement it smelt of weddings or funerals, as one's mood dictated, and as she pushed open the door Cordelia was welcomed by a gush of sweet warm air which caught at the throat. There were flowers everywhere. Large green buckets lined the walls holding clumps of lilies, irises and lupins; smaller containers were packed tight with wall flowers and marigolds and stocks; there were frigid bundles of tight budded roses on thornless stems, each flower identical in size and colour and looking as if it had been cultivated in a test tube. Pots of indoor plants, decorated with variegated ribbon, lined the path to the counter like a floral guard of honour.

There was a room at the back of the shop where two assistants were working. Through the open door Cordelia watched them. The younger, a languid blonde with a spotted skin, was assistant executioner, laying out roses and freesias, predestined victims, graded according to type and colour. Her senior, whose status was denoted by a better fitting overall and an air of authority, was twisting off the flower heads, piercing each mutilated bloom with wire and threading them closely on to a huge bed of moss in the shape of a heart. Cordelia averted her eyes from this horror.

A buxom lady in a pink smock appeared behind the counter apparently from nowhere. She was as pungently scented as the shop, but had obviously decided that no ordinary floral perfume could compete and that she had better rely on the exotic. She smelt of curry powder and pine so strongly that the effect was practically anaesthetizing.

Cordelia said her prepared speech:

"I'm from Sir Ronald Callender of Garforth House. I wonder whether you can help us? His son was cremated on 3rd of June and their old nurse very kindly sent a wreath, a cross of red roses. Sir Ronald has lost her address and very much wants to write to thank her. The name is Pilbeam."

"Oh, I don't think we executed any orders of that type for 3rd June."

"If you would be kind enough to just look in the book——"

Suddenly the young blonde looked up from her work and called out:

"It's Goddard."

"I beg your pardon, Shirley"? said the buxom lady repressively.

"The name's Goddard. The card on the wreath said Nanny Pilbeam, but the customer was a Mrs. Goddard. Another lady came to enquire from Sir Ronald Callender and that was the name she gave. I looked it up for her. Mrs. Goddard, Lavender Cottage, Ickleton. One cross, four foot long in red roses. Six pounds. It's there in the book."

"Thank you very much," said Cordelia fervently. She smiled

her thanks impartially at the three of them and left quickly in case she got embroiled in an argument about the other enquirer from Garforth House. It must have looked odd, she knew, but the three of them would no doubt enjoy themselves discussing it after she had left. Lavender Cottage, Ickleton. She kept repeating the address to herself until she was at a safe distance from the shop and could pause to write it down.

Her tiredness seemed miraculously to have left her as she sped back to the car park. She consulted her map. Ickleton was a village near the Essex border about ten miles from Cambridge. It wasn't far from Duxford so that she would be retracing her steps. She could be there in less than half an hour.

But it took longer than she had expected to thread her way through the Cambridge traffic and it wasn't until thirty-five minutes later, that she came to Ickleton's fine flint and pebble church with its broach spire, and drove the Mini close to the church gate. It was a temptation to take a brief look inside, but she resisted it. Mrs. Goddard might even now be preparing to catch the Cambridge bus. She went in search of Lavender Cottage.

It wasn't, in fact, a cottage at all but a small semi-detached house of hideous red brick at the end of the High Street. There was only a narrow strip of grass between the front door and the road and neither smell nor sight of lavender. The iron knocker, in the form of a lion's head, fell heavily, shaking the door. The response came, not from Lavender Cottage, but from the next house. An elderly woman appeared, thin, almost toothless and swathed in an immense apron patterned with roses. She had carpet slippers on her feet, a woollen cap decorated with a bobble on her head and an air of lively interest in the world in general.

"You'll be wanting Mrs. Goddard, I daresay?"

"Yes. Could you tell me where I could find her?"

"She'll be over at the graveyard, I don't doubt. She usually is this time of a fine morning."

"I've just come from the church. I didn't see anyone."

"Bless you, Miss, she's not at the church! They haven't been burying us there for many a year now. Her old man is where they'll be putting her in time, in the cemetery on Hinxton Road. You can't miss it. Just keep straight on."

"I'll have to go back to the church for my car," said Cordelia. It was obvious that she was going to be watched out of sight and it seemed necessary to explain why she was departing in the opposite direction to the one indicated. The old woman smiled and nodded and came out to lean on her gate for a better view of Cordelia's progress down the High Street, nodding her head like a marionette so that the bright bobble danced in the sun.

The cemetery was easily found. Cordelia parked the Mini on a convenient patch of grass where a signpost pointed the footpath to Duxford and walked the few yards back to the iron gates. There was a small flint chapel of rest with an apse at the east end and beside it an ancient wooden seat green with lichen and spattered with bird lime which gave a view of the whole burial ground. A wide swathe of turf ran straight down the middle and on each side were the graves, variously marked with white marble crosses, grey headstones, small rusted circles of iron heeling over towards the smooth turf and bright splashes of flowers patchworked over the newly dug earth. It was very peaceful. The burial ground was surrounded by trees, their leaves scarcely stirring in the calm, hot air. There was little sound except the chirruping of crickets in the grass and from time to time the nearby ringing of a railway level-crossing bell and the swooping horn of a diesel train.

There was only one other person in the graveyard, an elderly woman bending over one of the far graves. Cordelia sat quietly on the seat, arms folded in her lap, before making her way silently down the grass path towards her. She knew with certainty that this interview was going to be crucial yet paradoxically she was in no hurry to begin. She came up to the woman and stood, still unnoticed, at the foot of the grave.

She was a small woman dressed in black whose old-fashioned straw hat, its brim wreathed with faded net, was screwed to her hair with an immense black bobbed hat pin. She knelt with her back to Cordelia showing the soles of a pair of mis-shapen shoes from which her thin legs stuck out like sticks. She was weeding the grave; her fingers, darting like a reptile's tongue over the grass, plucked at small, almost undetectable weeds. At her side was a punnet holding a folded newspaper and a gardening trowel. From time to time, she dropped into the punnet her little mush of weeds.

After a couple of minutes, during which Cordelia watched her in silence, she paused satisfied and began smoothing the surface of the grass as if comforting the bones beneath. Cordelia read the inscription carved deep on the headstone. "Sacred to the memory of Charles Albert Goddard beloved husband of Annie who departed this life 27th August 1962, aged 70 years. At rest." At rest; the commonest epitaph of a generation to whom rest must have seemed the ultimate luxury, the supreme benediction.

The woman rested back for a second on her heels and contemplated the grave with satisfaction. It was then that she became aware of Cordelia. She turned a bright much wrinkled face towards her and said without curiosity or resentment at her presence:

"It's a nice stone, isn't it?"

"Yes, it is. I was admiring the lettering."

"Cut deep that is. It cost a mint of money but it was worth it. That'll last, you see. Half the lettering here won't, it's that shallow. It takes the pleasure out of a cemetery. I like to read the grave stones, like to know who people were and when they died and how long the women lived after they buried their men. It sets you wondering how they managed and whether they were lonely. There's no use in a stone if you can't read the lettering. Of course, this stone looks a bit top-heavy at present. That's because I asked them to leave space for me: 'Also to Annie his wife, departed this life, . . .' and then the date: That'll even it up nicely. I've left the money to pay for it."

"What text were you thinking of having?" enquired Cordelia.

"Oh, no text! At rest will be good enough for the both of us. We shan't be asking more of the good Lord than that."

Cordelia said:

"That cross of roses you sent to Mark Callender's funeral was beautiful."

"Oh, did you see it? You weren't at the funeral were you? Yes, I was pleased with it. They made a nice job of it, I thought. Poor boy, he hadn't much else, had he?"

She looked at Cordelia with benign interest:

"So you knew Mr. Mark? Would you be his young lady perhaps?"

"No, not that, but I care about him. It's odd that he never talked about you, his old nurse."

"But I wasn't his nurse, my dear, or at least, only for a month or two. He was a baby then, it meant nothing to him. No, I was nurse to his dear mother."

"But you visited Mark on his twenty-first birthday?"

"So he told you that, did he? I was glad to see him again after all those years, but I wouldn't have pushed myself on him. It wouldn't have been right, his father feeling as he did. No, I went to give him something from his mother, to do something she had asked me to do when she was dying. Do you know, I hadn't seen Mr. Mark for over twenty years—odd, really, considering that we didn't live that far apart—but I knew him at once. He had a great look of his mother about him, poor boy."

"Could you tell me about it? It's not just curiosity; it's important for me to know."

Leaning for support on the handle of her basket, Mrs. Goddard got laboriously to her feet. She picked at a few short blades of grass adhering to her skirt, felt in her pocket for a pair of grey cotton gloves and put them on. Together they made their way slowly down the path.

"Important, is it? I don't know why it should be. It's all in the past now. She's dead, poor lady, and so is he. All that hope and promise come to nothing. I haven't spoken to anyone else about it, but then who would care to know?"

"Perhaps we could sit on this bench and talk together for a time?"

"I don't see why we shouldn't. There's nothing to hurry home for now. Do you know, my dear, I didn't marry my husband until I was fifty-three and yet I miss him as if we had been childhood sweethearts. People said I was a fool to take on a man at that age but you see I had known his wife for thirty years, we were at school together, and I knew him. If a man's good to one woman, he'll be good to another. That's what I reckoned and I was right."

They sat side by side on the bench gazing over the green swathe towards the grave. Cordelia said:

"Tell me about Mark's mother."

"She was a Miss Bottley, Evelyn Bottley. I went to her mother as under-nursemaid before she was born. There was only little Harry then. He was killed in the war on his first raid over Germany. His Dad took it very hard; there was never anyone to match Harry, the sun shone out of his eyes. The master never really cared for Miss Evie, it was all the boy with him. Mrs. Bottley died when Evie was born and that may have made a difference. People say that it does, but I've never believed it. I've known fathers who loved a baby even more—poor innocent things, how can they be blamed? If you ask me, it was just an excuse for not taking to the child, that she killed her mother."

"Yes, I know a father who made it an excuse too. But it isn't their fault. We can't make ourselves love someone just because we want to."

"More's the pity, my dear, or the world would be an easier place. But his own child, that's not natural!"

"Did she love him?"

"How could she? You won't get love from a child if you don't give love. But she never had the trick of pleasing him, of humouring him—he was a big man, fierce, loud talking, frightening to a child. He would have done better with a pretty, pert little thing, who wouldn't have been afraid of him."

"What happened to her? How did she meet Sir Ronald Callender?"

"He wasn't Sir Ronald then, my dear. Oh, dear no! He was Ronny Callender the gardener's son. They lived at Harrogate you see. Oh, such a lovely house they had! When I first went into service there they had three gardeners. That was before the war, of course. Mr. Bottley worked in Bradford; he was in the wool trade. Well, you were asking about Ronny Callender.

I remember him well, a pugnacious, good-looking lad but one who kept his thoughts to himself. He was clever that one, oh he was clever! He got a scholarship to the grammar school and did very well."

"And Evelyn Bottley fell in love?"

"She may have done, my dear. What there was between them when they were young, who can tell. But then the war came and he went away. She was wild to do something useful and they took her on as a V.A.D., though how she passed the medical I'll never know. And then they met again in London as people did in the war and the next thing we knew they were married."

"And came to live here outside Cambridge?"

"Not until after the war. At first she kept on with her nursing and he was sent overseas. He had what the men call a good war; we'd call it a bad war I daresay, a lot of killing and fighting, imprisonment and escaping. It ought to have made Mr. Bottley proud of him and reconciled to the marriage but it didn't. I think he thought that Ronny had his eye on the money, because there was money to come, no doubt about that. He may have been right, but who's to blame the boy? My mother used to say, 'Don't marry for money, but marry where money is!' There's no harm in looking for money as long as there's kindness as well."

"And do you think there was kindness?"

"There was never unkindness that I could see, and she was mad about him. After the war he went up to Cambridge. He'd always wanted to be a scientist and he got a grant because he was ex-service. She had some money from her father and they bought the house he lives in now so that he could live at home when he was studying. It didn't look the same then, of course. He's done a lot to it since. They were quite poor then and Miss Evie managed with practically no one to help, only me. Mr. Bottley used to come and stay from time to time. She used to dread his visits, poor darling. He was looking for a grandchild, you see, and one didn't come. And then Mr. Callender finished at the university and got a job teaching. He wanted to stay on at college to be a don or something like that, but they wouldn't have him. He used to say it was because he hadn't influence, but I think he may not have been quite clever enough. In

Harrogate we thought he was the cleverest boy in the grammar school. But then, Cambridge is full of clever men."

"And then Mark was born?"

"Yes, on the 25th April 1951, nine years after they were married. He was born in Italy. Mr. Bottley was that pleased when she became pregnant that he increased the allowance and they used to spend a lot of holidays in Tuscany. My lady loved Italy, always had, and I think she wanted the child to be born there. Otherwise she wouldn't have gone on holiday in the last month of her pregnancy. I went to visit her about a month after she came home with the baby and I've never seen a woman so happy. Oh, he was a lovely little boy!"

"But why did you visit her; weren't you living and working there?"

"No, my dear. Not for some months. She wasn't well in the early days of her pregnancy. I could see that she was strained and unhappy and then one day Mr. Callender sent for me and told me that she had taken against me and that I'd have to leave. I wouldn't have believed it, but when I went to her she just put out her hand and said: 'I'm sorry, Nanny, I think it would be better if you went.'

"Pregnant women have strange fancies, I know, and the baby was so important to them both. I thought she might have asked me to come back afterwards and so she did, but not living in. I took a bedsitting room in the village with the postmistress and used to give four mornings a week to my lady and the rest to other ladies in the village. It worked very well, really, but I missed the baby when I wasn't with him. I hadn't seen her often during her pregnancy but once we met in Cambridge. She must have been near the end of her time. She was very heavy, poor dear, dragging herself along. At first she pretended that she hadn't noticed me and then she thought better of it and came across the road. 'We're off to Italy next week, Nanny,' she said. 'Isn't it lovely?' I said: 'If you're not careful, my dear, that baby will be a little Italian,' and she laughed. It seemed as though she couldn't wait to get back to the sun."

"And what happened after she came home?"

"She died after nine months, my dear. She was never strong,

as I said, and she caught influenza. I helped look after her and I'd have done more but Mr. Callender took over the nursing himself. He couldn't bear anyone else to be near her. We only had a few minutes together just before she died and it was then that she asked me to give her prayer book to Mark on his twenty-first birthday. I can hear her now: 'Give it to Mark when he's twenty-one, Nanny. Wrap it up carefully and take it to him when he comes of age. You won't forget will you?' I said: 'I'll not forget, my darling, you know that.' Then she said a strange thing. 'If you do, or if you die before then, or if he doesn't understand, it won't really matter. It will mean that God wants it that way.' "

"What do you think she meant?"

"Who's to say, my dear? She was very religious was Miss Evie, too religious for her own good, I sometimes thought. I believe we should accept our own responsibilities, solve our own problems, not leave it all to God as if He hadn't enough to be thinking about with the world in the state it is. But that's what she said not three hours before she died and that's what I promised. So when Mr. Mark was twenty-one, I found out what college he was at and went to see him."

"What happened?"

"Oh, we had a very happy time together. Do you know, his father had never spoken about his mother. That sometimes happens when a wife dies but I think a son ought to know about his mother. He was full of questions, things that I thought his father would have told him.

"He was glad to get the prayer book. It was a few days later that he came to see me. He asked the name of the doctor who had treated his mother. I told him that it was old Dr. Gladwin. Mr. Callender and she had never had any other doctor. I used to think it a pity sometimes, Miss Evie being so frail. Dr. Gladwin must have been seventy then, and although there were people who wouldn't say a word against him, I never thought much of him myself. Drink, you know, my dear; he was never really reliable. But I expect he's gone to his rest long since, poor man. Anyway, I told Mr. Mark the name and he wrote it down. Then we had tea and a little chat and he left. I never saw him again."

"And no one else knows about the prayer book?"

"No one in the world, my dear. Miss Leaming saw the florist's name on my card and asked them for my address. She came here the day after the funeral to thank me for attending but I could see it was only curiosity. If she and Sir Ronald were so pleased to see me, what was to stop them from coming over and shaking hands? She as good as suggested that I was there without an invitation. An invitation to a funeral! Who ever heard of such a thing?"

"So you told her nothing?" asked Cordelia.

"I've told no one but you, my dear, and I'm not sure why I've told you. But no, I didn't tell her. I never liked her, to tell you the truth. I'm not saying there was anything between her and Sir Ronald, not while Miss Evie was alive anyway. There was never any gossip and she lived in a flat in Cambridge and kept herself to herself, I'll give her that. Mr. Callender met her when he was teaching science at one of the village schools. She was the English mistress. It wasn't until after Miss Evie died that he set up his own laboratory."

"Do you mean that Miss Leaming has a degree in English?"

"Oh, yes, my dear! She wasn't trained as a secretary. Of course she gave up the teaching when she started working for Mr. Callender."

"So you left Garforth House after Mrs. Callender died? You didn't stay on to care for the baby?"

"I wasn't wanted. Mr. Callender employed one of those new college-trained girls and then, when Mark was still only a baby, he was sent away to school. His father made it plain that he didn't like me to see the child and after all, a father has his rights. I wouldn't have gone on seeing Mr. Mark knowing that his father didn't approve. It would have only put the boy in a false position. But now he's dead and we've all lost him. The coroner said that he killed himself, and he may have been right."

Cordelia said.

"I don't think he killed himself."

"Don't you, my dear? That's kind of you. But he's dead, isn't he, so what does it matter now? I think it's time for me to go home. If you don't mind, I won't ask you to tea, my dear, I'm a little tired today. But you know where to find me, and if ever you want to see me again, you'll always be welcome."

They made their way out of the burial ground together. At the gates, they parted. Mrs. Goddard patted Cordelia on the shoulder with the clumsy affection she might have shown to an animal, then walked off slowly towards the village.

As Cordelia drove round the curve of the road, the level-crossing came into sight. A train had just passed and the barriers were being raised. Three vehicles had been caught at the crossing and the last in line was quickest away, accelerating past the first two cars as they bumped slowly over the rails. Cordelia saw that it was a small black van.

Later Cordelia remembered little of the journey back to the cottage. She drove fast, concentrating on the road ahead, trying to control her rising excitement by meticulous attention to gears and brakes. She drove the Mini hard against the front hedge, careless of whether it were seen. The cottage looked and smelt just as she had left it. She had almost expected to find it ransacked and the prayer book gone. Sighing with relief, she saw that the white spine was still there among the taller and darker covers. Cordelia opened it. She hardly knew what she expected to find; an inscription perhaps, or a message, cryptic or plain, a letter folded between the leaves. But the only inscription could have no possible relevance to the case. It was written in a shaky, old-fashioned hand; the steel nib had crawled spider-like over the page. "To Evelyn Mary on the occasion of her confirmation, with love from her Godmother, 5th August 1934."

Cordelia shook the book. No slip of paper fluttered out. She skimmed through the pages. Nothing.

She sat on the bed drooping with disappointment. Had it been unreasonable to imagine that there was something significant in the bequest of the prayer book; had she fabricated a promising edifice of conjecture and mystery on an old woman's confused recollections of a perfectly ordinary and understandable action—a devout and dying mother leaving a prayer book to her son? And even if she hadn't been wrong, why should the message still be there? If Mark had found a note from his mother, placed between the leaves, he might well have destroyed it after reading. And if he hadn't destroyed it, someone else might have done so. The note, if it ever existed, was now probably part of the shifting heap of white ash and charred debris in the cottage grate.

She shook herself out of her despondency. There was still a line of enquiry to pursue; she would try to trace Dr. Gladwin. After a second's thought she put the prayer book in her bag. Looking at her watch, she saw that it was nearly one o'clock. She decided to have a picnic lunch of cheese and fruit in the garden and then set off again for Cambridge to visit the central library and consult a medical directory.

Less than an hour later she found the information she wanted. There was only one Dr. Gladwin still on the register who could have attended Mrs. Callender as an old man of over seventy, twenty years ago. He was Emlyn Thomas Gladwin who had qualified at St. Thomas's Hospital in 1904. She wrote down the address in her note book: 4 Pratts Way, Ixworth Road, Bury St. Edmunds. Edmunds town! The town which Isabelle had said that she and Mark had visited on their way to the sea.

So the day hadn't been wasted after all—she was following in Mark Callender's footsteps. Impatient to consult a map she went over to the atlas section of the library. It was now two-fifteen. If she took the A45 road direct through Newmarket she could be in Bury St. Edmunds in about an hour. Allow an hour for the visit to the doctor and another for the return journey. She could be home at the cottage before half past five.

She was driving through the gentle unemphatic countryside just outside Newmarket when she noticed the black van following her. It was too far away to see who was driving but she thought it was Lunn and that he was alone. She accelerated, trying to keep the distance between them, but the van drew a little nearer. There was no reason, of course, why Lunn shouldn't be driving to Newmarket on Sir Ronald Callender's business, but the sight of the squat little van perpetually in her driving mirror was disconcerting. Cordelia decided to throw him off. There were few side turns on the road she was travelling and the country was unfamiliar to her. She decided to wait until she reached Newmarket and seize what opportunity offered.

The main through street of the town was a tangle of traffic and every turn seemed to be blocked. It was only at the second set of traffic lights that Cordelia saw her chance. The black van was caught at the intersection about fifty yards behind. As the light turned green, she accelerated quickly and swung round to the left. There was another turn to the left and she took it, then one to the right. She drove on through unfamiliar streets, then after about five minutes, stopped at an intersection and waited. The black van did not appear. It looked as if she had succeeded in shaking him off. She waited for another five minutes, then made her way slowly back to the main road and joined in the flow of eastward traffic. Half an hour later she had passed through Bury St. Edmunds and was driving very slowly down the Ixworth Road, watching for Pratts Way. Fifty yards farther on she came to it, a row of six small stucco houses standing back from a lay-by. She stopped the car outside number four remembering Isabelle, biddable and docile, who had obviously been told to drive further on and wait in the car. Was that because Mark thought the white Renault too conspicuous? Even the arrival of the Mini had provoked interest. There were faces at upper windows and a small group of children had mysteriously appeared, clustered around a neighbouring gate and watching her with wide and expressionless eyes.

Number four was a depressing house; the front garden was unweeded and the fence had gaps where the planks had rotted or had been wrenched apart. The external paint had flaked away to the bare wood and the brown front door had peeled and blistered in the sun. But Cordelia saw that the bottom windows were shining and that the white net curtains were clean. Mrs. Gladwin was probably a careful housewife, struggling to keep up her standards but too old for the heavy work and too poor to afford help. Cordelia felt benevolently towards her. But the woman who, after some minutes, finally opened to her knock —the bell was out of order—was a disconcering antidote to her sentimental pity. Compassion died before those hard distrustful eyes, that mouth tight as a trap, the thin arms clasped in a bony barrier across her chest as if to repell human contact. It was difficult to guess her age. Her hair, screwed back into a small tight bun, was still black but her face was deeply lined and the sinews and veins stood out in the thin neck like cords. She was wearing carpet slippers and a gaudy cotton overall. Cordelia said:

"My name is Cordelia Gray. I wondered if I could talk to Dr. Gladwin, if he's in. It's about an old patient."

"He's in, where else would he be? He's in the garden. You'd better go through."

The house smelt horrible, an amalgam of extreme old age, the sour taint of excreta and stale food, with an overlay of strong disinfectant. Cordelia went through to the garden, carefully avoiding looking at the hall or kitchen since curiosity might seem impertinent.

Dr. Gladwin was sitting in a high Windsor chair placed in the sun. Cordelia had never seen a man so old. He seemed to be wearing a woollen track suit, his swollen legs were encased in immense felt slippers and there was a knitted patchwork shawl across his knees. His two hands hung over the arms of the chair as if too heavy for the frail wrists, hands stained and brittle as autumn leaves which trembled with a gentle insistence. The high-domed skull, spiked with a few grey bristles, looked as small and vulnerable as a child's. The eyes were pale yokes swimming in their glutinous blue-veined whites.

Cordelia went to him and called him gently by his name. There was no response. She knelt on the grass at his feet and looked up into his face.

"Dr. Gladwin, I wanted to talk to you about a patient. It was a long time ago. Mrs. Callender. Do you remember Mrs. Callender of Garforth House?"

There was no reply. Cordelia knew that there wouldn't be. Even to ask again seemed an outrage. Mrs. Gladwin was standing beside him as if displaying him to a wondering world.

"Go on, ask him! It's all in his head you know. That's what he used to tell me. 'I'm not one for records and notes. It's all in my head.' "

Cordelia said:

"What happened to his medical records when he gave up practice? Did any one take them over?"

"That's what I've just told you. There never were any records. And it's no use asking me. I told the boy that too. The doctor was glad enough to marry me when he wanted a nurse, but he didn't discuss his patients. Oh, dear no! He was drinking all the practice profits away, but he could still talk about medical ethics."

The bitterness in her voice was horrible. Cordelia could not meet her eyes. Just then she thought she saw the old man's lips move. She bent down her head and caught the one word. "Cold."

"I think he's trying to say that he's cold. Is there another shawl perhaps that he could have round his shoulders?"

"Cold! In this sun! He's always cold."

"But perhaps another blanket would help. Shall I fetch it for you?"

"You let him be, Miss. If you want to look after him, then look after him. See how you enjoy keeping him clean like a baby, washing his nappies, changing the bed every morning. I'll get him another shawl, but in two minutes he'll be pushing it off. He doesn't know what he wants."

"I'm sorry," said Cordelia helplessly. She wondered whether Mrs. Gladwin was getting all the help available, whether the District Nurse called, whether she had asked her doctor to try to find a hospital bed. But these were useless questions. Even she could recognize the hopeless rejection of help, the despair which no longer had energy even to look for relief. She said:

"I'm sorry; I won't trouble either of you any further."

They walked back together through the house. But there was one question Cordelia had to ask. When they reached the front gate she said:

"You talked about a boy who visited. Was his name Mark?"

"Mark Callender. He was asking about his mother. And then about ten days later we get the other one calling."

"What other one?"

"He was a gentleman all right. Walked in as if he owned the place. He wouldn't give a name but I've seen his face somewhere.

He asked to see Dr. Gladwin and I showed him in. We were sitting in the back parlour that day as there was a breeze. He went up to the doctor and said 'Good afternoon, Gladwin' loudly as if talking to a servant. Then he bent down and looked at him. Eye to eye they were. Then he straightened up, wished me good day and left. Oh, we're getting popular, we are! Any more of you and I'll have to charge for the show."

They stood together at the gate. Cordelia wondered whether to hold out her hand but sensed that Mrs. Gladwin was willing her not to go. Suddenly the woman spoke in a loud and gruff voice, looking straight ahead.

"That friend of yours, the boy who came here. He left his address. He said he wouldn't mind sitting with the doctor on a Sunday if I wanted a break; he said he could get them both a bit of dinner. I have a fancy to see my sister over at Haverhill this Sunday. Tell him he can come if he wants to."

The capitulation was ungracious, the invitation grudging, but Cordelia could guess what it had cost her to give it. She said impulsively:

"I could come on Sunday instead. I've got a car, I could get here sooner."

It would be a day lost to Sir Ronald Callender, but she wouldn't charge him. And even a private eye was surely entitled to a day off on Sundays.

"He won't want a slip of a girl. There's things to do for him that need a man. He took to that boy. I could see that. Tell him he can come."

Cordelia turned to her.

"He would have come, I know he would. But he can't. He's dead."

Mrs. Gladwin did not speak. Cordelia put out a tentative hand and touched her sleeve. There was no response. She whispered:

"I'm sorry. I'll go now." She nearly added: "If there's nothing I can do for you," but stopped herself in time. There was nothing she or anyone could do.

She looked back once as the road bent towards Bury and saw the rigid figure still at the gate.

Cordelia wasn't sure what made her decide to stop at Bury and walk for ten minutes in the Abbey gardens. But she felt she couldn't face the drive back to Cambridge without calming her spirits and the glimpse of grass and flowers through the great Norman doorway was irresistible. She parked the Mini on Angel Hill, then walked through the gardens to the river bank. There she sat for five minutes in the sun. She remembered that there was money spent on petrol to be recorded in her notebook and felt for it in her bag. Her hand brought out the white prayer book. She sat quietly thinking. Suppose she had been Mrs. Callender and had wanted to leave a message, a message which Mark would find and other searchers might miss. Where would she place it? The answer now seemed childishly simple. Surely somewhere on the page with the collect, gospel and epistle for St. Mark's Day. He had been born on April 25th. He had been named after the Saint. Quickly she found the place. In the bright sunlight reflected from the water she saw what a quick rustle through the pages had missed. There against Cranmer's gentle petition for grace to withstand the blasts of false doctrine was a small pattern of hieroglyphics so faint that the mark on the paper was little more than a smudge. She saw that it was a group of letters and figures.

E M C
A A
14.1.52

The first three letters, of course, were his mother's initials. The date must be that on which she wrote the message. Hadn't Mrs. Goddard said that Mrs. Callender had died when her son was about nine months old? But the double A? Cordelia's mind chased after motoring associations before she remembered the card in Mark's wallet. Surely these two letters under an initial could only show one thing, the blood group. Mark had been B. His mother was AA. There was only one reason why she should have wanted him to have that information. The next step was to discover Sir Ronald Callender's group.

She almost cried out with triumph as she ran through the gardens and turned the Mini again towards Cambridge. She hadn't thought out the implications of this discovery, or even whether her arguments were valid. But at least she had something to do, at least she had a lead. She drove fast, desperate to get to the city before the post office closed. There, she seemed to remember, it was possible to get a copy of the Executive Council's list of local doctors. It was handed over. And now for a telephone. She knew only one house in Cambridge where there was a chance of being left in peace to telephone for up to an hour. She drove to 57, Norwich Street.

Sophie and Davie were at home playing chess in the sitting-room, fair head and dark almost touching over the board. They showed no surprise at Cordelia's plea to use the telephone for a series of calls.

"I'll pay, of course. I'll make a note of how many."

"You'll want the room to yourself, I expect?" said Sophie. "We'll finish the game in the garden, Davie."

Blessedly incurious they carried the chess board with care through the kitchen and set it up on the garden table. Cordelia drew a chair to the table and settled down with her list. It was formidably long. There was no clue about where to begin but perhaps those doctors with group practices and addresses near the centre of the city would be the best bet. She would start with them, ticking off their names after each call. She remembered another reported pearl of the Superintendent's wisdom: "Detection requires a patient persistence which amounts to obstinacy." She thought of him as she dialled the first number. What an intolerably demanding and irritating boss he must have been! But he was almost certainly old now—forty-five at least. He had probably eased up a bit by now.

But an hour's obstinacy was unfruitful. Her calls were invariably answered; one advantage of ringing a doctor's surgery was that the telephone was at least manned. But the replies, given politely, curtly or in tones of harassed haste by a variety of respondents from the doctors themselves to obliging daily women prepared to convey a message, were the same. Sir Ronald Callender was not a patient of this practice. Cordelia repeated her formula. "I'm so sorry to have troubled you. I must have misheard the name."

But after nearly seventy minutes of patient dialling she struck lucky. The doctor's wife answered.

"I'm afraid you've got the wrong practice. Dr. Venables looks after Sir Ronald Callender's household."

This was luck indeed! Dr. Venables wasn't on her preliminary list and she wouldn't have reached the V's for at least another hour. She ran her finger quickly down the names and dialled for the last time.

It was Dr. Venables' nurse who answered. Cordelia spoke her prepared piece:

"I'm ringing for Miss Leaming from Garforth House. I'm sorry to trouble you but could you please remind us of Sir Ronald Callender's blood group? He wants to know it before the Helsinki Conference next month."

"Just a minute, please." There was a brief wait; the sound of footsteps returning.

"Sir Ronald is Group A. I should make a careful note of it if I were you. His son had to ring a month or so ago with the same enquiry."

"Thank you! Thank you! I'll be careful to make a note." Cordelia decided to take a risk.

"I'm new here, assisting Miss Leaming, and she did tell me to note it down last time but stupidly I forgot. If she should happen to call, please don't tell her that I had to trouble you again."

The voice laughed, indulgent to the inefficiency of the young. After all, it wasn't likely to inconvenience her much.

"Don't worry—, I shan't tell her. I'm glad she's got herself some help at last. Everyone's well, I hope?"

"Oh, yes! Everyone's fine."

Cordelia put down the receiver. She looked out of the window and saw that Sophie and Davie were just finishing their game and were putting the pieces back in the box. She had just finished in time. She knew the answer to her query but she still had to verify it. The information was too important to leave to her own vague recollection of the Mendelian rules of inheritance gleaned from the chapter on blood and identity in Bernie's book on forensic medicine. Davie would know, of course. The quickest way would be to ask him now. But she couldn't ask Davie. It would mean going back to the public library, and she would have to hurry if she were to be there before it closed.

But she got there just in time. The librarian, who by now had got used to seeing her, was as helpful as ever. The necessary reference book was quickly produced. Cordelia verified what she had already known. A man and wife both of whose bloods were A could not produce a B group child.

Cordelia was very tired by the time she got back to the cottage. So much had happened during one day; so much had been discovered. It seemed impossible that less than twelve hours previously she had started out on her search for Nanny Pilbeam with only a vague hope that the woman, if she could be found, might provide a clue to Mark Callender's personality, might tell her something about his formative years. She was exhilarated by the success of the day, restless with excitement, but too mentally exhausted to tease out the tangle of conjecture which lay knotted at the back of her mind. At present the facts were disordered; there was no clear pattern, no theory which would at once explain the mystery of Mark's birth, Isabelle's terror, Hugo and Sophie's secret knowledge, Miss Markland's obsessive interest in the cottage, Sergeant Maskell's almost reluctant suspicions, the oddities and unexplained inconsistencies which surrounded Mark's death.

She busied herself about the cottage with the energy of mental overtiredness. She washed the kitchen floor, laid a fire on top of the heap of ash in case the next evening should be chilly, weeded the back flower patch, then made herself a mushroom omelette and ate it sitting, as he must have done, at the simple table. Last of all, she fetched the gun from its hiding place and set it on the table beside the bed. She locked the back door carefully and drew the curtains across the window, checking once more that the seals were intact. But she didn't balance a saucepan on the top of her door. Tonight that particular precaution seemed childish and unnecessary. She lit her bedside candle then went to the window to choose a book. The night was balmy and windless; the flame of the candle burned steadily in the still air. Outside, darkness had not yet fallen but the garden was very quiet, the peace broken only by the distant crescendo of a car on the main road or the cry of a night bird. And then, seen dimly through the gloaming, she glimpsed a figure at the gate. It was Miss Markland. The woman hesitated, hand on the latch, as if wondering whether to enter the garden. Cordelia slipped to one side, back pressed against the wall. The shadowy figure was so still that it seemed as if she sensed a watching presence and had frozen like an animal surprised. Then, after two minutes, she moved away and was lost among the trees of the orchard. Cordelia relaxed, took a copy of *The Warden* from Mark's row of books, and wriggled into her sleeping-bag. Half an hour later, she blew out the candle and stretched her body comfortably for the slow acquiescent descent into sleep.

She stirred in the early hours and was instantly awake, eyes wide open in the half darkness. Time lay suspended; the still air was expectant as if the day had been taken by surprise. She could hear the ticking of her wrist watch on the bedside table and could see beside it the crooked, comforting outline of the pistol, the black cylinder of her torch. She lay and listened to the night. One lived so seldom in these still hours, the time most often slept or dreamt away, that one came to them tentative and unpractised like a creature newly born. She wasn't aware of fear, only of an all-embracing peace, a gentle lassitude. Her breathing filled the quiet room, and the still, uncontaminated air seemed to be breathing in unity with her.

Suddenly, she realized what had woken her. Visitors were coming to the cottage. She must subconsciously in some brief phase of uneasy sleep have recognized the sound of a car. Now there was the whine of the gate, the rustle of feet, furtive as an animal in undergrowth, a faint, broken murmur of voices. She wriggled out of her sleeping-bag and stole to the window. Mark hadn't attempted to clean the glass of the front windows; perhaps he hadn't had time, perhaps he welcomed their occluding dirt. Cordelia rubbed her fingers with desperate haste against the gritty accretion of years. But, at last, she felt the cold smooth glass. It squeaked with the friction of her fingers, high and thin like an animal's squeal so that she thought the noise must betray her. She peered through the narrow strip of clear pane into the garden below.

The Renault was almost hidden by the high hedge but she could see the front of the bonnet gleaming by the gate and the two pools of light from the side lamps shining like twin moons on the lane. Isabelle was wearing something long and clinging; her pale figure trembled like a wave against the dark of the hedge. Hugo was only a black shadow at her side. But then he turned and Cordelia saw the flash of a white shirt-front. They were both in evening dress. They came together quietly up the path and conferred briefly at the front door, then moved towards the corner of the cottage.

Snatching up her torch, Cordelia rushed on silent, naked feet down the stairs and threw herself across the sitting-room to unlock the back door. The key turned easily and silently. Hardly daring to breath she retreated back into the shadows at the foot of the stairs. She was just in time. The door opened, letting in a shaft of paler light. She heard Hugo's voice:

"Just a minute, I'll strike a match."

The match flared, illuminating in a gentle, momentary light the two grave anticipatory faces, Isabelle's immense and terrified eyes. Then it went out. She heard Hugo's muttered curse followed by the scratch of the second match striking against the box. This time he held it high. It shone on the table, on the mute accusing hook; on the silent watcher at the foot of the stairs. Hugo gasped; his hand jerked and the match went out. Immediately, Isabelle began to scream.

Hugo's voice was sharp.

"What the hell——"

Cordelia switched on her torch and came forward.

"It's only me; Cordelia."

But Isabelle was beyond hearing. The screams rang out with such piercing intensity that Cordelia half feared that the Marklands must hear. The sound was inhuman, the shriek of animal terror. It was cut short by the swing of Hugo's arm; the sound of a slap; a gasp. It was succeeded by a second of absolute silence, then Isabelle collapsed against Hugo sobbing quietly.

He turned harshly on Cordelia:

"What the hell did you do that for?"

"Do what?"

"You terrified her, lurking there. What are you doing here anyway?"

"I could ask you that."

"We came to collect the Antonello which Isabelle lent to Mark when she came to supper with him, and to cure her of a certain morbid obsession with this place. We've been to the Pitt Club Ball. It seemed a good idea to call here on our way home. Obviously, it was a bloody stupid idea. Is there any drink in the cottage?"

"Only beer."

"Oh God, Cordelia, there would be! She needs something stronger."

"There isn't anything stronger, but I'll make coffee. You set a light to the fire. It's laid."

She stood the torch upright on the table and lit the table lamp, turning the wick low, then helped Isabelle into one of the fireside chairs.

The girl was trembling. Cordelia fetched one of Mark's heavy sweaters and placed it round her shoulders. The kindling began to flame under Hugo's careful hands. Cordelia went into the kitchen to make coffee, laying her torch on its side at the edge of the window sill so that it shone on the oil stove. She lit the stronger of the two burners and took from the shelf a brown earthenware jug, the two blue-rimmed mugs and a cup for herself. A second and chipped cup held the sugar. It took only a couple of minutes to boil half a kettle of water and to pour it over the coffee grains. She could hear Hugo's voice from the sitting-room, low, urgent, consolatory, interposed with Isabelle's monosyllabic replies. Without waiting for the coffee to brew she placed it on the only tray, a bent tin one patterned with a chipped picture of Edinburgh castle, and carried it into the sitting room, setting it down in the hearth. The faggots spluttered and blazed, shooting out a falling shower of bright sparks which patterned

Isabelle's dress with stars. Then a stouter brand caught flame and the fire glowed with a stronger, more mellow, heart.

As she bent forward to stir the coffee Cordelia saw a small beetle scurrying in desperate haste along the ridges of one of the small logs. She picked up a twig from the kindling still in the hearth and held it out as a way of escape. But it confused the beetle still more. It turned in panic and raced back towards the flame, then doubled in its tracks and fell finally into a split in the wood. Cordelia pictured its fall into black burning darkness and wondered whether it briefly comprehended its dreadful end. Putting a match to a fire was such a trivial act to cause such agony, such terror.

She handed Isabelle and Hugo their mugs and took her own. The comforting smell of fresh coffee mingled with the resinous tang of the burning wood. The fire threw long shadows over the tiled floor and the oil lamp cast its gentle glow over their faces. Surely, thought Cordelia, no murder suspects could have been interrogated in a cosier setting. Even Isabelle had lost her fears. Whether it was the reassurance of Hugo's arm across her shoulders, the stimulus of the coffee or the homely warmth and crackle of the fire, she seemed almost at ease.

Cordelia said to Hugo:

"You said that Isabelle was morbidly obsessed by this place. Why should she be?"

"Isabelle's very sensitive; she isn't tough like you."

Cordelia privately thought that all beautiful women were tough—how else could they survive?—and that Isabelle's fibres could compare well for resilience with her own. But nothing would be gained by challenging Hugo's illusions. Beauty was fragile, transitory, vulnerable. Isabelle's sensitivities must be protected. The toughies could look after themselves. She said:

"According to you, she's only been here once before. I know that Mark Callender died in this room, but you hardly expect me to believe that she's grieving over Mark. There's something that both of you know and it would be better if you told me now. If you don't I shall have to report to Sir Ronald Callender that Isabelle, your sister and you are somehow concerned in his son's death and it will be up to him to decide whether to call in the police. I can't see Isabelle standing up to even the mildest police questioning, can you?"

Even to Cordelia it sounded a stilted, sententious little speech, an unsubstantiated accusation backed up by an empty threat. She half expected Hugo to counter it with amused contempt. But he looked at her for a minute as if assessing more than the reality of the danger. Then he said quietly:

"Can't you accept my word that Mark died by his own hand and that if you do call in the police it will cause unhappiness and distress to his father, to his friends and be absolutely no help to anyone?"

"No, Hugo, I can't."

"Then if we do tell you what we know, will you promise that it won't go any further?"

"How can I, any more than I can promise to believe you?"

Suddenly Isabelle cried:

"Oh, tell her, Hugo! What does it matter?"

Cordelia said:

"I think that you must. I don't think you've any choice."

"So it seems. All right." He put his coffee mug down in the hearth and looked into the fire.

"I told you that we went—Sophie, Isabelle, Davie and I—to the Arts Theatre on the night Mark died but that, as you've probably guessed, was only three-quarters true. They had only three seats left when I booked so we allocated them to the three people mostly likely to enjoy the play. Isabelle goes to the theatre to be seen rather than to see and is bored by any show with a cast of less than fifty, so she was the one left out. Thus neglected by her current lover, she very reasonably decided to seek consolation with the next."

Isabelle said with a secret, anticipatory smile:

"Mark was not my lover, Hugo."

She spoke without rancour or resentment. It was a matter of putting the record straight.

"I know. Mark was a romantic. He never took a girl to bed—or anywhere else that I could see—until he judged that there was an adequate depth of inter-personal communication, or whatever jargon he used, between them. Actually, that's unfair.

It's my father who uses bloody awful meaningless phrases like that. But Mark agreed with the general idea. I doubt whether he could enjoy sex until he'd convinced himself that he and the girl were in love. It was a necessary preliminary—like undressing. I gather that with Isabelle the relationship hadn't reached the necessary depths, hadn't achieved the essential emotional rapport. It was only a matter of time, of course. Where Isabelle was concerned, Mark was as capable of self-deception as the rest of us."

The high, slightly hesitant voice was edged with jealousy.

Isabelle said, slowly and patiently, like a mother explaining to a wilfully obtuse child:

"Mark never made love to me, Hugo."

"That's what I'm saying. Poor Mark! He exchanged the substance for the shadow and now he has neither."

"But what happened that night?"

Cordelia spoke to Isabelle, but it was Hugo who replied.

"Isabelle drove here and arrived shortly after half past seven. The curtains were drawn across the back window, the front one is inpenetrable anyway, but the door was open. She came in. Mark was already dead. His body was hanging by the strap from that hook. But he didn't look as he did when Miss Markland found him next morning."

He turned to Isabelle:

"You tell her." She hesitated. Hugo bent forward and kissed her lightly on the lips.

"Go on, tell. There are some unpleasantnesses which all Papa's money can't entirely shield from you and this, darling, is one."

Isabelle turned her head and looked intently into the four corners of the room as if satisfying herself that the three of them were really alone. The irises of her remarkable eyes were purple in the firelight. She leaned towards Cordelia with something of the confiding relish of a village gossip about to relate the latest scandal. Cordelia saw that her panic had left her. Isabelle's agonies were elemental, violent but short lived, easily comforted. She would have kept her secret while Hugo instructed her to keep it, but she was glad of his order of release. Probably her instinct told her that the story, once told, would lose the sting of terror. She said:

"I thought I would call to see Mark and, perhaps, that we would have supper together. Mademoiselle de Congé was not well and Hugo and Sophie were at the theatre and I was bored. I came to the back door because Mark had told me that the front door would not open. I thought that I might see him in the garden, but he was not there, only the garden fork in the ground and his shoes at the door. So I pushed open the door. I did not knock because I thought that I would be a surprise for Mark."

She hesitated and looked down into the mug of coffee, twisting it between her hands.

"And then?" prompted Cordelia.

"And then I saw him. He was hanging there by the belt from that hook in the ceiling and I knew he was dead. Cordelia, it was horrible! He was dressed like a woman in a black bra and black lace panties. Nothing else. And his face! He had painted his lips, all over his lips Cordelia, like a clown! It was terrible but it was funny too. I wanted to laugh and scream at the same time. He didn't look like Mark. He didn't look like a human being at all. And on the table there were three pictures. Not nice pictures Cordelia. Pictures of naked women."

Her wide eyes stared into Cordelia's, dismayed, uncomprehending. Hugo said:

"Don't look like that, Cordelia. It was horrible for Isabelle at the time and disagreeable to think about now. But it isn't so very uncommon. It does happen. It's probably one of the more innocuous of sexual deviations. He wasn't involving anyone but himself. And he didn't mean to kill himself; that was just bad luck. I imagine that the buckle of the belt slipped and he never had a chance." Cordelia said:

"I don't believe it."

"I thought you might not. But it's true, Cordelia. Why not come with us now and ring Sophie? She'll confirm it."

"I don't need confirmation of Isabelle's story. I already have that. I mean I still don't believe that Mark killed himself."

As soon as she spoke she knew that it had been a mistake. She shouldn't have revealed her suspicions. But it was too late now and there were questions she had to ask. She saw Hugo's face, his quick impatient frown at her obtuseness, her obstinacy. And then she detected a subtle change of mood; was it irritation, fear, disappointment? She spoke directly to Isabelle.

"You said that the door was open. Did you notice the key?"

"It was in this side of the door. I saw it when I went out."

"What about the curtains?"

"They were like now, across the window."

"And where was the lipstick?"

"What lipstick, Cordelia?"

"The one used to paint Mark's lips. It wasn't in the pockets of his jeans or the police would have found it, so where was it? Did you see it on the table?"

"There was nothing on the table except the pictures."

"What colour was the lipstick?"

"Purple. An old lady's colour. No one would choose such a colour I think."

"And the underclothes, could you describe them?"

"Oh, yes! They were from M & S. I recognized them."

"You mean that you recognized those particular ones, that they were yours?"

"Oh, no Cordelia! They were not mine. I never wear black underclothes. I only like white next to my skin. But they were the kind I usually buy. I always get my underclothes from M & S."

Cordelia reflected that Isabelle was hardly one of the store's best customers, but that no other witness would have been as reliable when it came to details, particularly of clothes. Even in that moment of absolute terror and revulsion, Isabelle had noticed the type of underclothes. And if she said that she hadn't seen the lipstick, then it was because the lipstick hadn't been there to see.

Cordelia went on inexorably:

"Did you touch anything, Mark's body perhaps, to see if he was dead?"

Isabelle was shocked. The facts of life she could take in her stride, but not the facts of death.

"I couldn't touch Mark! I touched nothing. And I knew that he was dead."

Hugo said: "A respectable, sensible, law-abiding citizen would have found the nearest telephone and rung the police. Luckily Isabelle is none of these things. Her instinct was to come to me. She waited until the play ended, and then met us outside the theatre. When we came out she was pacing up and down the pavement on the other side of the road. Davie, Sophie and I came back here with her in the Renault. We only stopped briefly at Norwich Street to collect Davie's camera and flash."

"Why?"

"That was my idea. Obviously, we had no intention of letting the fuzz and Ronald Callender know how Mark had died. Our idea was to fake a suicide. We planned to dress him in his own clothes, clean his face and then leave him for someone else to find. We hadn't it in mind to fake a suicide note; that was a refinement somewhat outside our powers. We collected the camera so that we could photograph him as he was. We didn't know what particular law we were breaking in faking a suicide, but there must have been one. You can't do the simplest service for your friends these days without it being liable to misconstruction by the fuzz. If there were trouble we wanted some evidence of the truth. We were all fond of Mark in our different ways, but not fond enough to risk a murder charge. However, our good intentions were frustrated. Someone else had got here first."

"Tell me about it."

"There's nothing to tell. We told the two girls to wait in the car, Isabelle because she had already seen enough and Sophie because Isabelle was too frightened to be left alone. Besides, it seemed only fair to Mark to keep Sophie out of it, to prevent her from seeing him. Don't you find it odd, Cordelia, this concern one has for the susceptibilities of the dead?"

Thinking of her father and Bernie, Cordelia said:

"Perhaps it's only when people are dead that we can safely show how much we cared about them. We know that it's too late then for them to do anything about it."

"Cynical but true. Anyway, there was nothing for us to do here.

We found Mark's body and this room as Miss Markland described them at the inquest. The door was open, the curtains drawn across. Mark was naked except for his blue jeans. There were no magazine pictures on the table and no lipstick on his face. But there was a suicide note in the typewriter and a mound of ash in the grate. It looked as if the visitor had made a thorough job of it. We didn't linger. Someone else—perhaps someone from the house—might have turned up at any minute. Admittedly, it was very late by then but it seemed an evening for people to pop in. Mark must have had more visitors that night than during his whole time at the cottage; first Isabelle; then the unknown samaritan; then us."

Cordelia thought that there had been someone before Isabelle. Mark's murderer had been there first. She asked suddenly:

"Someone played a stupid trick on me last night. When I got back here from the party there was a bolster slung from that hook. Did you do that?"

If his surprise were not genuine, then Hugo was a better actor than Cordelia thought possible.

"Of course I didn't! I thought you were living in Cambridge not here. And why on earth should I?"

"To warn me off."

"But that would be crazy! It wouldn't warn you off, would it? It might scare some women, but not you. We wanted to convince you that there was nothing to investigate about Mark's death. That sort of trick would only convince you that there was. Someone else was trying to scare you. The most likely person is the one who came here after us."

"I know. Someone took a risk for Mark. He—or she—won't want me ferreting around. But he would have got rid of me more sensibly by telling me the truth."

"How could he know whether to trust you? What will you do now, Cordelia? Go back to town?"

He was trying to keep his voice casual but she thought she detected the underlying anxiety. She replied.

"I expect so. I'll have to see Sir Ronald first."

"What will you tell him?"

"I'll think of something. Don't worry."

Dawn was staining the eastern sky and the first chorus of birds was noisily contradicting the new day before Hugo and Isabelle left. They took the Antonello with them. Cordelia saw it taken down with a pang of regret as if something of Mark were leaving the cottage. Isabelle examined the picture closely with a grave professional eye before tucking it under her arm. Cordelia thought that she was probably generous enough with her possessions, both people and pictures, provided they were on loan only, to be returned promptly on demand and in the same condition as when she parted with them. Cordelia watched from the front gate as the Renault, with Hugo driving, moved out of the shadow of the hedge. She lifted her hand in a formal gesture of farewell like a weary hostess speeding her final guests, then turned back to the cottage.

The sitting room seemed empty and cold without them. The fire was dying and she hastily pushed in the few remaining sticks from the hearth and blew on them to kindle the flame. She moved restlessly about the little room. She was too lively to go back to bed, but her short and disturbed night had left her edgy with tiredness. But her mind was tormented by something more fundamental than lack of sleep. For the first time she knew that she was afraid. Evil existed—it hadn't needed a convent education to convince her of that reality—and it had been present in this room. Something here had been stronger than wickedness, ruthlessness, cruelty or expedience. Evil. She had no doubt that Mark had been murdered, but with what diabolical cleverness it had been done! If Isabelle told her story, who now would ever believe that he hadn't died accidentally, but by his own hand? Cordelia had no need to refer to her book on forensic medicine to know how it would appear to the police. As Hugo had said, these cases weren't so very uncommon. He, as a psychiatrist's son, would have heard or read of them. Who else would know? Probably any reasonably sophisticated person. But it couldn't have been Hugo. Hugo had an alibi. Her mind revolted at the thought that Davie or Sophie could have participated in such a horror. But how typical that they should have collected the camera. Even their compassion had been overlaid with self concern. Would Hugo and Davie have stood here, under Mark's grotesque body, calmly discussing distance and exposure before taking the photograph which would, if necessary, exonerate them at his expense?

She went into the kitchen to make tea, glad to be free of the malignant fascination of that hook in the ceiling. Previously it had hardly worried her, now it was as obtrusive as a fetish. It seemed to have grown since the previous night, to be growing still as it drew her eyes compulsively upwards. And the sitting room itself had surely shrunk; no longer a sanctum but a claustrophobic cell, tawdry and shameful as an execution shed. Even the bright morning air was redolent with evil.

Waiting for the kettle to boil she made herself contemplate the day's activities. It was still too early to theorize; her mind was too preoccupied with horror to deal rationally with its new knowledge. Isabelle's story had complicated, not illumined the case. But there were still relevant facts to be discovered. She would go on with the programme she had already planned. Today she would go to London to examine Mark's grandfather's will.

But there were still two hours to get through before it was time to start out. She had decided to travel to London by train and to leave the car at Cambridge station since this would be both quicker and easier. It was irritating to have to spend a day in town when the heart of the mystery so obviously lay in Cambridgeshire, but for once she wasn't sorry at the prospect of leaving the cottage. Shocked and restless, she wandered aimlessly from room to room and prowled around the garden, fretting to be away. Finally in desperation she took hold of the garden fork and completed the digging of Mark's unfinished row. She wasn't sure that this was wise; Mark's interrupted work was part of the evidence for his murder. But other people, including Sergeant Maskell, had seen it and could testify if necessary, and the sight of the partly-completed job, of the fork still askew in the soil, was unbearably irritating. When the row was completed she felt calmer and she dug on without pausing for another hour before carefully cleaning the fork and placing it with the other tools in the garden shed.

At last it was time to go. The seven o'clock weather forecast had prophesied thundery storms in the south-east so she put on her suit, the heaviest protection she had brought with her. She hadn't worn it since Bernie's death and she discovered that the waist band was uncomfortably loose. She had lost some weight. After a moment's thought, she took Mark's belt from the scene-of-crime kit and wound it twice round her waist. She felt no repugnance as the leather tightened against her. It was impossible to believe that anything he had ever touched or owned could frighten or distress her. The strength and heaviness of the leather so close to her skin was even obscurely comforting and reassuring, as if the belt were a talisman.

Chapter Five

The storm broke just as Cordelia alighted from the number 11 bus outside Somerset House. There was a jagged flash of lightning and, almost instantaneously, the thunder crashed like a barrage round her ears and she raced across the inner courtyard between the ranks of parked cars through a wall of water while the rain spouted around her ankles as if the paving stones were being raked with bullets. She pushed open the door and stood draining pools of water on the mat and laughing aloud with relief. One or two of the people present glanced up from their perusal of wills and smiled at her, while a motherly looking woman behind the counter tut-tutted her concern. Cordelia shook her jacket over the mat then hung it on the back of one of the chairs and tried ineffectually to dry her hair with her handkerchief before approaching the counter.

The motherly woman was helpful. Consulted by Cordelia on the correct procedure, she indicated the shelves of heavy, bound volumes in the middle of the hall and explained that the wills were indexed under the surname of the testator and the year in which the document was lodged with Somerset House. It was for Cordelia to trace the catalogue number and bring the volume to the desk. The original will would then be sent for and she could consult it for a fee of 20 pence.

Not knowing when George Bottley had died, Cordelia was in some perplexity where to begin her search. But she deduced that the will must have been made after the birth, or at least the conception, of Mark, since he had been left a fortune by his grandfather. But Mr. Bottley had also left money to his daughter and this part of his fortune had come on her death to her husband. The strong probability was that he had died before her, since otherwise he would surely have made a new will. Cordelia decided to begin her search with the year of Mark's birth, 1951.

Her deductions proved correct. George Albert Bottley of Stonegate Lodge, Harrogate, had died on 26th July 1951, exactly three months and one day after the birth of his grandson and only three weeks after making his will. Cordelia wondered whether his death had been sudden and unexpected or whether this was the will of a dying man. She saw that he had left an estate of nearly three quarters of a million pounds. How had he made this, she wondered? Surely not all from wool. She heaved the heavy book across to the counter, the clerk wrote the details on a white form and pointed out the way to the cashier's office. Within a surprisingly few minutes of paying what seemed to her a modest fee, Cordelia was seated under the light at one of the desks near the window with the will in her hands.

She hadn't liked what she had heard about George Bottley from Nanny Pilbeam and she didn't like him any better after reading his will. She had feared that the document might be long, complicated and difficult to understand; it was surprisingly short, simple and intelligible. Mr. Bottley directed that all his possessions should be sold, "since I wish to prevent the usual unseemly wrangling over bric-à-brac". He left modest sums to servants in his employ at the time of death but there was no mention, Cordelia noticed, of his gardener. He bequeathed half of the residue of his fortune to his daughter, absolutely, "now that she has demonstrated that she has at least one of the normal attributes of a woman." The remaining half he left to his beloved grandson Mark Callender on attaining his twenty-fifth birthday, "by which date, if he hasn't learned the value of money, he will at least be of an age to avoid exploitation." The income from the capital was left to six Bottley relations, some of them, apparently, only distant kinsmen. The will created a residual trust; as each beneficiary died his share would be distributed among the survivors. The testator was confident that this arrangement would promote in the beneficiaries a lively interest in each others' health and survival while encouraging them to achieve the distinction of longevity, no other distinction being within their reach. If Mark died before his twenty-fifth birthday the family trust would continue until all the beneficiaries were dead and the capital would then be distributed among a formidable list of charities chosen, as far as Cordelia could see, because they were well known and successful rather than because they represented any personal concern or sympathy on the part of the testator. It was as if he had asked his lawyers for a list of the more reliable charities, having no real interest in what happened to his fortune if his own issue were not alive to inherit it.

It was a strange will. Mr. Bottley had left nothing to his son-in-law yet had apparently been unworried by the possibility that his daughter, whom he knew not to be strong, might die and leave her fortune to her husband. In some respects it was a gambler's will and Cordelia wondered again how George Bottley had made his fortune. But, despite the cynical unkindness of its comments, the will was neither unfair nor ungenerous. Unlike some very rich men he hadn't attempted to control his great fortune from beyond the grave, obsessively determined that not one penny should ever get into unfavoured hands. His daughter and his grandson had both been left their fortunes absolutely. It was impossible to like Mr. Bottley but difficult not to respect him. And the implications of his will were very clear. No one stood to gain by Mark's death except a long list of highly respectable charities.

Cordelia made a note of the main clauses of the will, more because of Bernie's insistence on meticulous documentation than from any fear of forgetting them; slipped the receipt for 20p into the expenses page of her notebook; added the cost of her cheap day return ticket from Cambridge and her bus fare, and returned the will to the counter. The storm had been as short as it was violent. The hot sun was already drying the windows and the puddles lay bright on the rain-washed courtyard. Cordelia decided that she ought to charge Sir Ronald for half a day only and spend the rest of her time in London at the office. There might be post to collect. There might even be another case awaiting her.

But the decision was a mistake. The office seemed even more sordid than when she had left it and the air smelt sour in contrast to the rain-washed streets outside. There was a thick film of dust over the furniture and the bloodstain on the rug had deepened into a brick-brown which looked even more sinister than the original bright red. There was nothing in the letterbox but a final demand from the electricity board and a bill from the stationer. Bernie had paid dearly—or rather, had not paid—for the despised writing paper.

Cordelia wrote a cheque for the electricity bill, dusted the furniture, made one last and unsuccessful attempt to clean the rug. Then she locked the office and set off to walk to Trafalgar Square. She would seek consolation in the National Gallery.

She caught the eighteen-sixteen train from Liverpool Street and it was nearly eight o'clock before she arrived back at the cottage. She parked the Mini in its usual place in the shelter of the copse and made her way round the side of the cottage. She hesitated for a moment wondering whether to collect the gun from its hiding place, but decided that this could wait until later. She was hungry and the first priority was to get a meal. She had carefully locked the back door and had stuck a thin strip of Scotch tape across the window sill before leaving that morning. If there were any more secret visitors she wanted to be warned. But the tape was still intact. She felt in her shoulder bag for the key and, bending down, fitted it into the lock. She wasn't expecting trouble outside the cottage and the attack took her completely by surprise. There was the half-second of pre-knowledge before the blanket fell but that was too late. There was a cord around her neck pulling the mask of hot stifling wool taut against her mouth and nostrils. She gasped for breath and tasted the dry strong-smelling fibres on her tongue. Then a sharp pain exploded in her chest and she remembered nothing.

The movement of liberation was a miracle and a horror. The blanket was whipped off. She never saw her assailant. There was a second of sweet reviving air, a glimpse, so brief that it was barely comprehended, of blinding sky seen through greenness and then she felt herself falling, falling in helpless astonishment into cold darkness. The fall was a confusion of old nightmares, unbelievable seconds of childhood terrors recalled. Then her body hit the water. Ice-cold hands dragged her into a vortex of horror. Instinctively, she had closed her mouth at the moment of impact and she struggled to the surface through what seemed an eternity of cold encompassing blackness. She shook her head and, through her stinging eyes, she looked up. The black tunnel that stretched above her ended in a moon of blue light. Even as she looked, the well lid was dragged slowly back like the shutter of a camera. The moon became a half moon; then a crescent. At last there was nothing but eight thin slits of light.

Desperately she trod water, reaching tentatively for the bottom. There was no bottom. Frantically moving hands and feet, willing herself not to panic, she felt around the walls of the well for a possible foothold. There was none. The funnel of bricks, smooth, sweating with moisture, stretched around and above her like a circular tomb. As she gazed upwards they writhed, expanded, swayed and reeled like the belly of a monstrous snake.

And then she felt a saving anger. She wouldn't let herself drown, wouldn't die in this horrible place, alone and terrified. The well was deep but small, the diameter barely three feet. If she kept her head and took time, she could brace her legs and shoulders against the bricks and work her way upwards.

She hadn't bruised or stunned herself against the walls as she fell. Miraculously she was uninjured. The fall had been clean. She was alive and capable of thought. She had always been a survivor. She would survive.

She floated on her back, bracing her shoulders against the cold walls, spreading her arms and digging her elbows into the interstices of the bricks to get a better grip. Shuffling off her shoes, she planted both feet against the opposite wall. Just beneath the surface of the water, she could feel that one of the bricks was slightly unaligned. She curved her toes around it. It gave her a precarious but welcome foothold for the start of the climb. By means of it, she could lift her body out of the water and could relieve for a moment the strain on the muscles of her back and thighs.

Then slowly she began to climb, first shifting her feet, one after the other in tiny sliding steps, then humping up her body inch by painful inch. She kept her eyes fixed on the opposite curve of the wall, willing herself not to look down, nor up, counting progress by the width of each brick. Time passed. She couldn't see Bernie's watch, although its ticking seemed unnaturally loud, a regular obtrusive metronome to the thumping of her heart and the fierce gasping of her breath. The pain in her legs was intense and her shirt was sticking to her back with a warm, almost comforting effusion, which she knew must be blood. She willed herself not to think of the water beneath her or of the thin, but widening clefts of light above. If she were to survive, all her energy must be harnessed for the next painful inch.

Once, her legs slipped and she slithered back several yards before her feet, scrabbling ineffectually against the slimy walls, at last found a purchase. The fall had grazed her injured back and left her whimpering with self-pity and disappointment. She scourged her mind into courage and began climbing again. Once she was gripped by cramp and lay stretched as if on a rack until the agony passed and her fixed muscles could move. From time to time her feet found another small foothold and she was able to stretch her legs and rest. The temptation to stay in comparative safety and ease was almost irresistible and she had to will herself to start again on the slow torturous climb.

It seemed that she had been climbing for hours, moving in a parody of a difficult labour towards some desperate birth. Darkness was falling. The light from the well top was wider now but less strong. She told herself that the climb wasn't really difficult. It was only the darkness and loneliness which made it seem so. If this were a fabricated obstacle race, an exercise in the school gymnasium, surely she could have done it easily enough. She filled her mind with the comforting images of rib stools and vaulting horses, of the fifth form shouting their encouragement. Sister Perpetua was there. But why wasn't she looking at Cordelia? Why had she turned away? Cordelia called her and the figure turned slowly and smiled at her. But it wasn't Sister after all. It was Miss Leaming, the lean pale face sardonic under the white veil.

And now when she knew that, unaided, she could get no further, Cordelia saw salvation. A few feet above her was the bottom rung of a short wooden ladder fixed to the last few feet of the well. At first she thought that it was an illusion, a phantasm born of exhaustion and despair. She shut her eyes for a few minutes; her lips moved. Then she opened her eyes again. The ladder was still there, seen dimly but comfortingly solid in the fading light. She lifted impotent hands towards it knowing, even as she did so, that it was out of reach. It could save her life and she knew that she hadn't the strength to reach it.

It was then, without conscious thought or scheming, that she remembered the belt. Her hand dropped to her waist feeling for the heavy brass buckle. She undid it and drew the long snake of leather from her body. Carefully she threw the buckled end towards the bottom rung of the ladder. The first three times the metal struck the wood with a sharp crack but didn't fall over the rung; the fourth time it did. She pushed the other end of the belt gently upwards and the buckle dropped towards her until she could stretch out her hand and grasp it. She fastened it to the other end to form a strong loop. Then she pulled, at first very gently and then harder until most of her weight was on the strap. The relief was indescribable. She braced herself against the brickwork, gathering strength for the final triumphant effort. Then it happened. The rung, rotted at its joints, broke loose with a harsh tearing sound and spun past her into darkness, just missing her head. It seemed minutes rather than seconds before the distant splash reverberated round the wall.

She unbuckled the belt and tried again. The next rung was a foot higher and the throw more difficult. Even this small effort was exhausting in her present state and she made herself take time. Every unsuccessful throw made the next more difficult. She didn't count the number of attempts, but at last the buckle fell over the rung and dropped towards her. When it snaked within reach she found that she could only just buckle the strap. The next rung would be too high. If this one broke, it would be the end.

But the rung held. She had no clear memory of the last half hour of the climb but at last she reached the ladder and strapped herself firmly to the uprights. For the first time she was physically safe. As long as the ladder held she needn't fear falling. She let herself relax into brief unconsciousness. But then the wheels of the mind which had been spinning blissfully free, took hold again and she began to think. She knew that she had no hope of moving the heavy wooden cover unaided. She stretched out both hands and pushed against it but it didn't shift, and the high concave dome made it impossible for her to brace her shoulders against the wood. She would have to rely on outside help and that wouldn't come till daylight. It might not come even then, but she pushed the thought away. Sooner or later Miss Markland would come to the cottage. Sooner or later someone would come. She could hope to hold on, thus strapped, for several days. Even if she lost consciousness there was a chance that she would be rescued alive. Miss Markland knew that she was at the cottage; her things were still there. Miss Markland would come.

She gave thought to how she could attract attention. There was room to push something between the boards of wood if only she had something sufficiently stiff to push. The edge of the buckle was possible provided she strapped herself more tightly. But that must wait until the morning. There was nothing she could do now. She would relax and sleep and await rescue.

And then the final horror burst upon her. There would be no rescue. Someone would be coming to the well, coming on quiet and stealthy feet under the cover of darkness. But it would be her murderer. He had to return; it was part of his plan. The attack, which at the time had seemed so astonishingly, so brutally stupid, hadn't been stupid at all. It was intended to look like an accident. He would come back that night and remove the well cover again. Then, some time next day or within the next few days, Miss Markland would blunder through the garden and discover what had happened. No one would ever be able to prove that Cordelia's death wasn't an accident. She recalled the words of Sergeant Maskell: "It isn't what you suspect; it's what you can prove." But this time would there even be suspicion? Here was a young, impulsive, over-curious young woman living at the cottage without the owner's authority. She had obviously decided to explore the well. She had smashed the padlock, drawn back the lid with the coil of rope which the killer would leave ready to be found, and tempted by the ladder, had let herself down those few steps until the final rung broke beneath her. Her prints and no one else's would be found on the ladder, if they took the trouble to look. The cottage was utterly deserted; the chance that her murderer would be seen returning was remote. There was nothing she could do but wait until she heard his footsteps, his heavy breathing, and the lid was drawn slowly back to reveal his face.

After the first intensity of terror, Cordelia waited for death without hope and without further struggle. There was even a kind of peace in resignation. Strapped like a victim to the uprights of the ladder she drifted mercifully into brief oblivion and prayed that it might be so when her killer returned, that she might not be conscious at the moment of the final blow. She had no longer any interest in seeing her murderer's face. She wouldn't humiliate herself by pleading for her life, wouldn't beg for mercy from a man who had strung up Mark. She knew that there would be no mercy.

But she was conscious when the well lid began slowly to move. The light came in above her bowed head. The gap widened. And then she heard a voice, a woman's voice, low, urgent and sharp with terror.

"Cordelia!"

She looked up.

Kneeling at the rim of the well, her pale face immense and seeming to float disembodied in space like the phantasm of a nightmare, was Miss Markland. And the eyes which stared into Cordelia's face were as wild with terror as her own.

Ten minutes later Cordelia was lying slumped in the fireside chair. Her whole body ached and she was powerless to control her violent shivering. Her thin shirt was stuck to her wounded back and every shift of movement was pain. Miss Markland had put a light to the kindling and was now making coffee. Cordelia could hear her moving to and fro in the little kitchen and could smell the stove as it was turned high and, soon, the evocative aroma of coffee. These familiar sights and sounds would normally have been reassuring and comforting, but now she was desperate to be alone. The killer would still return. He had to return, and when he did, she wanted to be there to meet him. Miss Markland brought in the two mugs and pressed one into Cordelia's shivering hands. She stumped upstairs and came down with one of Mark's jumpers which she wound round the girl's neck. Her terror had left her, but she was as agitated as a young girl sharing her first half-shameful adventure. Her eyes were wild, her whole body trembled with excitement. She sat down directly in front of Cordelia and fixed her with her sharp inquisitive eyes.

"How did it happen? You must tell me."

Cordelia had not forgotten how to think.

"I don't know. I can't remember anything that happened before I hit the water. I must have decided to explore the well and lost my balance."

"But the well lid! The lid was in place!"

"I know. Someone must have replaced it."

"But why? Who would have come this way?"

"I don't know. But someone must have seen it. Someone must have dragged it back."

She said more gently:

"You saved my life. How did you notice what had happened?"

"I came to the cottage to see if you were still here. I came earlier today but there was no sign of you. There was a coil of rope—the one that you used, I expect—left in the path and I stumbled over it. Then I noticed that the well lid wasn't quite in place and that the padlock had been smashed."

"You saved my life," said Cordelia again, "but please go now. Please go. I'm all right, really I am."

"But you aren't fit to be left alone! And that man—the one who replaced the lid—he might return. I don't like to think of strangers snooping around the cottage and you here alone."

"I'm perfectly safe. Besides, I have a gun. I only want to be left in peace to rest. Please don't worry about me!"

Cordelia could detect the note of desperation, almost of hysteria, in her own voice.

But Miss Markland seemed not to hear. Suddenly she was on her knees in front of Cordelia and pouring out a spate of high, excited chatter. Without thought and without compassion, she was confiding to the girl her terrible story, a story of her son, the four-year-old child of herself and her lover, who had broken his way through the cottage hedge and fallen into the well to his death. Cordelia tried to shake herself free from the wild eyes. It was surely all a fantasy. The woman must be mad. And if it were true, it was horrible and unthinkable and she could not bear to hear it. Sometime later she would remember it, remember every word, and think of the child, of his last terror, his desperate cry for his mother, the cold suffocating water dragging him to his death. She would live his agony in nightmares as she would re-live her own. But not now. Through the spate of words, the self-accusations, the terror recalled, Cordelia recognized the note of liberation. What to her had been horror, to Miss Markland had been release. A life for a life. Suddenly Cordelia could bear it no longer. She said violently:

"I'm sorry! I'm sorry! You've saved my life and I'm grateful. But I can't bear to listen. I don't want you here. For God's sake go!"

All her life she would remember the woman's hurt face, her silent withdrawal. Cordelia didn't hear her go, didn't remember the soft closing of the door. All she knew was that she was alone. The shaking was over now although she still felt very cold. She went upstairs and pulled on her slacks then unwound Mark's jumper from her neck and put it on. It would cover the blood stains on her shirt and the warmth was immediately comforting. She was moving very quickly. She felt for the ammunition, took her torch and let herself out of the back door of the cottage. The gun was where she had left it, in the fold of the tree. She loaded it and felt its familiar shape and heaviness in her hand. Then she stood back among the bushes and waited.

It was too dark to see the dial of her wrist watch but Cordelia reckoned that she must have waited there immobile in the shadows for nearly half an hour before her ears caught the sound for which she was waiting. A car was approaching down the lane. Cordelia held her breath. The sound of the engine reached a brief crescendo and then faded away. The car had driven on without stopping. It was unusual for a car to pass down the lane after dark and she wondered who it could be.

Again she waited, moving deeper into the shelter of the elder bush so that she could rest her back against the bark. She had been clutching the gun so tightly that her right wrist ached and she moved the pistol to her other hand and rotated the wrist slowly, stretching the cramped fingers.

Again she waited. The slow minutes passed. The silence was broken only by the furtive scuffling of some small night prowler in the grass and the sudden wild hoot of an owl. And then once more she heard the sound of an engine. This time the noise was faint and it came no closer. Someone had stopped a car further up the road.

She took the gun in her right hand, cradling the muzzle with her left. Her heart was pounding so loudly that she felt its wild hammering must betray her. She imagined rather than heard the thin whine of the front gate but the sound of feet moving round the cottage was unmistakable and clear. And now he was in sight, a stocky, broad-shouldered figure, black against the light. He moved towards her and she could see her shoulder bag hanging from his left shoulder. The discovery disconcerted her. She had completely forgotten the bag. But now she had realized why he had seized it. He had wanted to search it for evidence, but it was important that, finally, it should be discovered with her body in the well.

He came forward gently on tip-toe, his long simian arms held stiffly away from his body like a caricature of a film cowboy ready for the draw. When he got to the rim of the well he waited and the moon struck the white of his eyes as he gazed slowly round. Then he bent down and felt in the grass for the coil of rope. Cordelia had lain it where Miss Markland had found it, but something about it, some slight difference perhaps in the way it was coiled, seemed to strike him. He rose uncertainly and stood for a moment with the rope dangling from his hand. Cordelia tried to control her breathing. It seemed impossible that he should not hear, smell or see her, that he should be so like a predator yet without the beast's instinct for the enemy in the dark. He moved forward. Now he was at the well. He bent and threaded one end of the rope through the iron hoop.

Cordelia moved with one step out of the darkness. She held

the gun firmly and straight as Bernie had shown her. This time the target was very close. She knew that she wouldn't fire but, in that moment, she knew too what it was that could make a man kill. She said loudly:

"Good evening, Mr. Lunn."

She never knew whether he saw the gun. But for one unforgettable second, as the clouded moon sailed into the open sky, she saw his face clearly; saw the hate, the despair, the agony and the rictus of terror. He gave one hoarse cry, threw down the shoulder bag and the rope and rushed through the garden in a blind panic. She gave chase, hardly knowing why, or what she hoped to achieve, determined only that he shouldn't get back to Garforth House before her. And still she didn't fire the gun.

But he had an advantage. As she threw herself through the gate she saw that he had parked the van some fifty yards up the road and left the engine running. She chased after him but could see that it was hopeless. Her only hope of catching up with him was to get the Mini. She tore down the lane feeling in her shoulder bag as she ran. The prayer book and her note book were both gone but her fingers found the car keys. She unlocked the Mini, threw herself in and reversed it violently onto the road. The rear lights of the van were about a hundred yards ahead of her. She didn't know what speed it could do, but doubted whether it could out-pace the Mini. She trod on the accelerator and gave pursuit. She turned left out of the lane on to the subsidiary road and now she could see the van still ahead. He was driving fast and was holding the distance. Now the road turned and for a few seconds he was out of sight. He must be getting very close now to the junction with the Cambridge road.

She heard the crash just before she herself reached the junction, an instantaneous explosion of sound which shook the hedges and made the little car tremble. Cordelia's hands tightened momentarily on the wheel and the Mini jerked to a stop. She ran forward round the corner and saw before her the gleaming, headlamp lit surface of the main Cambridge road. It was peopled with running shapes. The transporter, still upright, was an immense oblong mass blocking the sky line, a barricade slewed across the road. The van had crumpled under its front wheels like a child's toy. There was a smell of petrol, a woman's harsh scream, the squeal of braking tyres. Cordelia walked slowly up to the transporter. The driver was still in his seat, gazing rigidly ahead, his face a mask of dedicated concentration. People were shouting at him, stretching out their arms. He didn't move. Someone—a man in a heavy leather coat and goggles—said:

"It's shock. We'd better drag him clear."

Three figures moved between Cordelia and the driver. Shoulders heaved in unison. There was a grunt of effort. The driver was lifted out, rigid as a manikin, his knees bent, his clenched hands held out as if still grasping the immense wheel. The shoulders bent over him in secret conclave.

There were other figures standing round the crushed van. Cordelia joined the ring of anonymous faces. Cigarette ends glowed and faded like signals, casting a momentary glow on the shaking hands, the wide, horrified eyes. She asked:

"Is he dead?" The man in goggles replied laconically:

"What do you think?"

There was a girl's voice, tentative, breathless.

"Has anyone called the ambulance?"

"Yeah. Yeah. That chap in the Cortina's gone off to 'phone."

The group stood irresolute. The girl and the young man to whom she was clinging began to back away. Another car stopped. A tall figure was pushing his way through the crowd. Cordelia heard a high, authoritative voice.

"I'm a doctor. Has anyone called the ambulance?"

"Yes, sir."

The reply was deferential. They stood aside to let the expert through. He turned to Cordelia, perhaps because she was nearest.

"If you didn't witness the accident, young woman, you'd better get on your way. And stand back, the rest of you. There's nothing that you can do. And put out those cigarettes!"

Cordelia walked slowly back to the Mini, placing each foot carefully before the other like a convalescent trying her first painful steps. She drove carefully round the accident, bumping the Mini on the grass verge. There was the wail of approaching sirens. As she turned off the main road, her driving mirror glowed suddenly red and she heard a whoosh of sound followed by a low, concerted groan which was broken by a woman's high, single scream. There was a wall of flame across the road. The doctor's warning had been too late. The van was on fire. There was no hope now for Lunn; but then, there never had been.

Cordelia knew that she was driving erratically. Passing cars hooted at her and flashed their lights and one motorist slowed down and shouted angrily. She saw a gate and drew in off the road and switched off the engine. The silence was absolute. Her hands were moist and shaking. She wiped them on her handkerchief and laid them in her lap feeling that they were separate from the rest of her body. She was hardly aware of a car passing and then slowing to a halt. A face appeared at the window. The voice was slurred and nervous but horribly ingratiating. She could smell the drink on his breath.

"Anything wrong, Miss?"

"Nothing. I've just stopped for a rest."

"No point in resting alone—a pretty girl like you."

His hand was on the door handle. Cordelia felt in her shoulder bag and drew out the gun. She pushed it into his face.

"It's loaded. Go away at once or I'll shoot."

The menace in her voice struck cold even to her own ears. The pale, moist face disintegrated with surprise, the jaw fell. He backed away.

"Sorry, Miss, I'm sure. My mistake. No offence."

Cordelia waited until his car was out of sight. Then she turned on the engine. But she knew that she couldn't go on. She turned off the engine again. Waves of tiredness flowed over her, an irresistible tide, gentle as a blessing, which neither her exhausted mind nor body had the will to resist. Her head fell forward and Cordelia slept.

Chapter Six

Cordelia slept soundly but briefly. She didn't know what woke her, whether the blinding light of a passing car sweeping across her closed eyes or her own subconscious knowledge that rest must be rationed to a brief half hour, the minimum necessary to enable her to do what had to be done before she could give herself over to sleep. She eased her body upright, feeling the stab of pain in her strained muscles and the half-pleasurable itch of dried blood on her back. The night air was heavy and odorous with the heat and scents of the day; even the road winding ahead looked tacky in the glare of her headlights. But Cordelia's chilled and aching body was still grateful for the warmth of Mark's jersey. For the first time since she had pulled it over her head she saw that it was dark green. How odd that she hadn't noticed its colour before!

She drove the rest of the journey like a novice, sitting bolt upright, eyes rigidly ahead, hands and feet tense on the controls. And here at last were the gates of Garforth House. They loomed in her headlights far taller and more ornamental than she remembered them, and they were closed. She ran from the Mini praying that they wouldn't be locked. But the iron latch, although heavy, rose to her desperate hands. The gates swung soundlessly back.

There were no other cars in the drive and she parked the Mini some little way from the house. The windows were dark and the only light, gentle and inviting, shone through the open front door. Cordelia took the pistol in her hand and, without ringing, stepped into the hall. She was more exhausted in body than when she had first come to Garforth House, but tonight she saw it with a new intensity, her nerves sensitive to every detail. The hall was empty, the air expectant. It seemed as if the house had waited for her. The same smell met her of roses and lavender, but tonight she saw that the lavender came from a huge Chinese bowl set on a side table. She recalled the insistent ticking of a clock, but now she noticed for the first time the delicate carving of the clock case, the intricate scrolls and whirls on the face. She stood in the middle of the hall, swaying slightly, the pistol held lightly in her drooping right hand, and looked down. The carpet was a formal geometrical design in rich olive greens, pale blues and crimson, each pattern shaped like the shadow of a kneeling man. It seemed to draw her to her knees. Was it perhaps an eastern prayer mat?

She was aware of Miss Leaming coming quietly down the stairs towards her, her long red dressing-gown sweeping round her ankles. The pistol was taken suddenly but firmly from Cordelia's unresisting hand. She knew that it had gone because her hand felt suddenly lighter. It made no difference. She could never defend herself with it, never kill a man. She had learnt that about herself when Lunn had run from her in terror. Miss Leaming said:

"There is no one here you need defend yourself against, Miss Gray."

Cordelia said:

"I've come to report to Sir Ronald. Where is he?"

"Where he was the last time you came here, in his study."

As before, he was sitting at his desk. He had been dictating and the machine was at his right hand. When he saw Cordelia, he switched it off, then walked to the wall and pulled the plug from the socket. He walked back to the desk and they sat down opposite each other. He folded his hands in the pool of light from the desk lamp and looked up at Cordelia. She almost cried out with shock. His face reminded her of faces seen grotesquely reflected in grubby train windows at night—cavernous, the bones stripped of flesh, eyes set in fathomless sockets—faces resurrected from the dead.

When he spoke his voice was low, reminiscent.

"Half an hour ago I learned that Chris Lunn was dead. He was the best lab assistant I ever had. I took him out of an orphanage fifteen years ago. He never knew his parents. He was an ugly, difficult boy, already on probation. School had done nothing for him. But Lunn was one of the best natural scientists I've ever known. If he'd had the education, he'd have been as good as I am."

"Then why didn't you give him his chance, why didn't you educate him?"

"Because he was more useful to me as a lab assistant. I said that he could have been as good as I am. That isn't quite good enough. I can find plenty of scientists as good. I couldn't have found another lab assistant to equal Lunn. He had a marvellous hand with instruments."

He looked up at Cordelia, but without curiosity, apparently without interest.

"You've come to report, of course. It's very late, Miss Gray, and, as you see, I'm tired. Can't it wait until tomorrow?"

Cordelia thought that this was as close to an appeal as he could ever bring himself. She said:

"No, I'm tired too. But I want to finish the case tonight, now." He picked up an ebony paper-knife from the desk and, without looking at Cordelia, balanced it on his forefinger.

"Then tell me, why did my son kill himself? I take it that you do have news for me? You would hardly have burst in here at this hour without something to report."

"Your son didn't kill himself. He was murdered. He was murdered by someone he knew well, someone he didn't hesitate to let into the cottage, someone who came prepared. He was strangled or suffocated, then slung up on that hook by his own belt. Last of all, his murderer painted his lips, dressed him in a woman's underclothes and spread out pictures of nudes on the table in front of him. It was meant to look like accidental death during sexual experiment; such cases aren't so very uncommon."

There was half a minute of silence. Then he said with perfect calmness:

"And who was responsible, Miss Gray?"

"You were. You killed your son."

"For what reason?" He might have been an examiner, putting his inexorable questions.

"Because he discovered that your wife wasn't his mother, that the money left to her and to him by his grandfather had come by fraud. Because he had no intention of benefiting by it a moment longer, nor of accepting his legacy in four years' time. You were afraid that he might make this knowledge public. And what about the Wolvington Trust? If the truth came out, that would be the end of their promised grant. The future of your laboratory was at stake. You couldn't take the risk."

"And who undressed him again, typed out that suicide note, washed the lipstick from his face?"

"I think I know, but I shan't tell you. That's really what you employed me to discover, isn't it? That's what you couldn't bear not to know. But you killed Mark. You even prepared an alibi just in case it was needed. You got Lunn to ring you at college and announce himself as your son. He was the one person you could rely on absolutely. I don't suppose you told him the truth. He was only your lab assistant. He didn't require explanations, he did what you told him. And even if he did guess the truth, he was safe, wasn't he? You prepared an alibi which you dared not use, because you didn't know when Mark's body was first discovered. If someone had found him and faked that suicide before you had claimed to have spoken to him on the telephone, your alibi would have been broken, and a broken alibi is damning. So you made a chance to talk to Benskin and put matters right. You told him the truth; that it was Lunn who had rung you. You could rely on Lunn to back up your story. But it wouldn't really matter, would it, even if he did talk? No one would believe him."

"No, any more than they will believe you. You've been determined to earn your fee, Miss Gray. Your explanation is ingenious; there is even a certain plausibility about some of the details. But you know, and I know, that no police officer in the world would take it seriously. It's unfortunate for you that you couldn't question Lunn. But Lunn, as I said, is dead. He burnt to death in a road accident."

"I know, I saw. He tried to kill me tonight. Did you know that? And earlier, he tried to scare me into dropping the case. Was that because he had begun to suspect the truth?"

"If he did try to kill you, he exceeded his instructions. I merely asked him to keep an eye on you. I had contracted for your sole and whole-time services, if you remember; I wanted to be sure I was getting value. I am getting value of a kind. But you mustn't indulge your imagination outside this room. Neither the police nor the courts are sympathetic to slander nor to hysterical nonsense. And what proof have you? None. My wife was cremated. There is nothing alive or dead on this earth to prove that Mark was not her son."

Cordelia said:

"You visited Dr. Gladwin to satisfy yourself that he was too senile to give evidence against you. You needn't have worried. He never did suspect, did he? You chose him as your wife's doctor because he was old and incompetent. But I did have one small piece of evidence. Lunn was bringing it to you."

"Then you should have looked after it better. Nothing of Lunn except his bones has survived that crash."

"There are still the female clothes, the black pants and the bra. Someone might remember who bought them, particularly if that person was a man."

"Men do buy underclothes for their women. But if I were planning such a murder, I don't think buying the accessories would worry me. Would any harassed shop girl at the cash desk of a popular multiple store remember a particular purchase, a purchase paid for with cash, one of a number of innocuous items, all presented together at the busiest time of the day? The man might even have worn a simple disguise. I doubt whether she would even notice his face. Would you really expect her to remember, weeks afterwards, to identify one of thousands of customers and identify him with sufficient certainty to satisfy a jury? And if she did, what would it prove unless you have the clothes in question? Be sure of one thing, Miss Gray, if I needed to kill I should do it efficiently. I should not be found out. If the police ever learn how my son was found, as they well may do since, apparently, someone other than yourself knows it, they will only believe with greater certainty that he killed himself. Mark's death was necessary and, unlike most deaths, it served a purpose. Human beings have an irresistible urge towards self-sacrifice. They die for any reason or none at all, for meaningless abstractions like patriotism, justice, peace; for other men's ideals, for other men's power, for a few feet of earth. You, no doubt, would give your life to save a child or if you were convinced that the sacrifice would find a cure for cancer."

"I might. I like to think that I would. But I should want the decision to be mine, not yours."

"Of course. That would provide you with the necessary emotional satisfaction. But it wouldn't alter the fact of your dying nor the result of your death. And don't say that what I'm doing here isn't worth one single human life. Spare me that hypocrisy. You don't know and you're incapable of understanding the value of what I'm doing here. What difference will Mark's death make to you? You'd never heard of him until you came to Garforth House."

Cordelia said:

"It will make a difference to Gary Webber."

"Am I expected to lose everything I've worked for here because Gary Webber wants someone to play squash or discuss history with?"

Suddenly he looked Cordelia full in the face. He said sharply:

"What is the matter? Are you ill?"

"No I'm not ill. I knew that I must be right. I knew that what I had reasoned was true. But I can't believe it. I can't believe that a human being could be so evil."

"If you are capable of imagining it, then I'm capable of doing it. Haven't you yet discovered that about human beings, Miss Gray? It's the key to what you would call the wickedness of man."

Suddenly Cordelia could no longer bear this cynical antiphony. She cried out in passionate protest.

"But what is the use of making the world more beautiful if the people who live in it can't love one another?"

She had stung him at last into anger.

"Love! The most overused word in the language. Has it any meaning except the particular sentimental connotation which you choose to give it? What do you mean by love? That human beings must learn to live together with a decent concern for each other's welfare? The law enforces that. The greatest good of the greatest number. Beside that fundamental declaration of common sense all other philosophies are metaphysical abstractions. Or do you define love in the Christian sense, caritas? Read history, Miss Gray. See to what horrors, to what violence, hatred and repression the religion of love has led mankind. But perhaps you prefer a more feminine, more individual definition; love as a passionate commitment to another's personality. Intense personal commitment always ends in jealousy and enslavement. Love is more destructive than hate. If you must dedicate your life to something, dedicate it to an idea."

"I meant love, as a parent loves a child."

"The worse for them both, perhaps. But if he doesn't love, there is no power on earth which can stimulate or compel him to. And where there is no love, there can be none of the obligations of love."

"You could have let him live! The money wasn't important to him. He would have understood your needs and kept silent."

"Would he? How could he—or I—have explained his rejection of a great fortune in four years' time? People at the mercy of what they call their conscience are never safe. My son was a self-righteous prig. How could I put myself and my work in his hands?"

"You are in mine, Sir Ronald."

"You are mistaken. I am in no one's hands. Unfortunately for you that tape recorder is not working. We have no witnesses. You will repeat nothing that has been said in this room to anyone outside. If you do I shall have to ruin you. I shall make you unemployable, Miss Gray. And first of all I shall bankrupt that pathetic business of yours. From what Miss Leaming told me it shouldn't be difficult. Slander can be a highly expensive indulgence. Remember that if you are ever tempted to talk. Remember this too. You will harm yourself; you will harm Mark's memory; you will not harm me."

Cordelia never knew how long the tall figure in the red dressing-gown had been watching and listening in the shadow of the door. She never knew how much Miss Leaming had heard or at what moment she had stolen quietly away. But now she was aware of the red shadow moving soundlessly over the carpet, eyes on the figure behind the desk, the gun held closely against her breast. Cordelia watched in fascinated horror, not breathing. She knew exactly what was going to happen. It must have taken less than three seconds but they passed as slowly as minutes. Surely there had been time to cry out, time to warn, time to leap forward and wrench the gun from that steady hand? Surely there had been time for him to cry out? But he made no sound. He half rose, incredulous, and gazed at the muzzle in blind disbelief. Then he turned his head towards Cordelia as if in supplication. She would never forget that last look. It was beyond terror, beyond hope. It held nothing but the blank acceptance of defeat.

It was an execution, neat, unhurried, ritually precise. The bullet went in behind the right ear. The body leapt into the air, shoulders humped, softened before Cordelia's eyes as if the bones were melting into wax, and lay discarded at last over the desk. A thing; like Bernie; like her father.

Miss Leaming said:

"He killed my son."

"Your son?"

"Of course. Mark was my son. His son and mine. I thought you might have guessed."

She stood with the gun in her hand gazing with expressionless eyes through the open window to the lawn. There was no sound. Nothing moved. Miss Leaming said:

"He was right when he said that no one could touch him. There was no proof."

Cordelia cried out appalled:

"Then how could you kill him? How could you be so sure?"

Without releasing her hold on the pistol, Miss Leaming put her hand into the pocket of her dressing-gown. The hand moved over the desk top. A small gilt cylinder rolled over the polished wood towards Cordelia, then rocked into stillness. Miss Leaming said:

"The lipstick was mine. I found it a minute ago in the pocket of his dress suit. He hadn't worn that suit since he last dined in Hall on Feast night. He was always a magpie. He put small objects instinctively into his pocket."

Cordelia had never doubted Sir Ronald's guilt but now every nerve was desperate for reassurance.

"But it could have been planted there! Lunn could have put it there to incriminate him."

"Lunn didn't kill Mark. He was in bed with me at the time Mark died. He only left my side for five minutes and that was to make a telephone call shortly after eight o'clock."

"You were in love with Lunn!"

"Don't look at me like that! I only loved one man in my life and he's the one I've just killed. Talk about things you understand. Love had nothing to with what Lunn and I needed from each other."

There was a moment's silence. Then Cordelia said:

"Is there anyone in the house?"

"No. The servants are in London. No one is working late at the lab tonight."

And Lunn was dead. Miss Leaming said with weary resignation:

"Hadn't you better phone the police?"

"Do you want me to?"

"What does it matter?"

"Prison matters. Losing your freedom matters. And do you really want the truth to come out in open court? Do you want everyone to know how your son died and who killed him? Is that what Mark himself would want?"

"No. Mark never believed in punishment. Tell me what I have to do."

"We've got to work quickly and plan carefully. We have to trust each other and we have to be intelligent."

"We are intelligent. What must we do?"

Cordelia took out her handkerchief and dropping it over the gun, took the weapon from Miss Leaming and placed it on the desk. She grasped the woman's thin wrist and pushed her protesting hand against Sir Ronald's palm, pulling against the instinctive recoil, forcing the stiff but living fingers against the soft unresisting hand of the dead.

"There may be firing residue. I don't really know much about that, but the police may test for it. Now wash your hands and get me a pair of thin gloves. Quickly."

She went without a word. Left alone, Cordelia looked down at the dead scientist. He had fallen with his chin against the desk top and his arms swinging loosely at his sides, an awkward, uncomfortable-looking pose which gave him the appearance of peering malevolently over his desk. Cordelia could not look at his eyes, but she was conscious of feeling nothing, not hatred, or anger, or pity. Between her eyes and the sprawled figure swung an elongated shape, head hideously crooked, toes pathetically pointed. She walked over to the open window and looked out over the garden with the casual curiosity of a guest kept waiting in a strange room. The air was warm and very still. The scent of roses came in waves through the open window, alternately sickening sweet and then as elusive as a half-caught memory.

This curious hiatus of peace and timelessness must have lasted less than half a minute. Then Cordelia began to plan. She thought about the Clandon case. Memory pictured herself and Bernie, sitting astride a fallen log in Epping Forest and eating their picnic lunch. It brought back the yeasty smell of fresh rolls, butter and tangy cheese, the heavy fungoid smell of summer woods. He had rested the pistol on the bark between them and had mumbled at her through the bread and cheese. "How would you shoot yourself behind the right ear? Go on, Cordelia—show."

Cordelia had taken the pistol in her right hand, index finger lightly resting on the trigger, and with some difficulty had strained back her arm to place the muzzle of the gun against the base of the skull. "Like that?" "You wouldn't, you know. Not if you were used to a gun. That's the little mistake Mrs. Clandon made and it nearly hanged her. She shot her husband behind the right ear with his service revolver and then tried to fake a suicide. But she pressed the wrong finger on the trigger. If he'd really shot himself behind the right ear he'd have pressed the trigger with his thumb and held the revolver with his palm round the back of the butt. I remember that case well. It was the first murder I worked on with the Super—Inspector Dalgliesh, as he was then. Mrs. Clandon confessed in the end." "What happened to her, Bernie?" "Life. She'd probably have got away with manslaughter if she hadn't tried to fake a suicide. The jury didn't much like what they heard about Major Clandon's little habits."

But Miss Leaming couldn't get away with manslaughter; not unless she told the whole story of Mark's death.

She was back in the room now. She handed Cordelia a pair of thin cotton gloves. Cordelia said:

"I think you'd better wait outside. What you don't see you won't have the trouble of forgetting. What were you doing when you met me in the hall?"

"I was getting myself a nightcap, a whisky."

"Then you would have met me again coming out of the study as you took it up to your room. Get it now and leave the glass on the side table in the hall. That's the kind of detail the police are trained to notice."

Alone again, Cordelia took up the gun. It was astonishing how repulsive she found this inert weight of metal now. How odd that she should ever have seen it as a harmless toy! She rubbed it thoroughly with her handkerchief erasing Miss Leaming's prints. Then she handled it. It was her gun. They would expect to find some of her prints on the butt together with those of the dead man. She placed it again on the desk top and drew on the gloves. This was the more difficult part. She handled the pistol gingerly and took it over to the inert right hand. She pressed his thumb firmly against the trigger, then wound the cold, unresisting hand round the back of the butt. Then she released his fingers and let the gun fall. It struck the carpet with a dull thud. She peeled off the gloves and went out to Miss Leaming in the hall, closing the study door quietly behind her.

"Here, you'd better put these back where you found them. We mustn't leave them lying around for the police to find."

She was gone only a few seconds. When she returned, Cordelia said:

"Now we must act the rest just as it would have happened. You meet me as I come out of the room. I have been with Sir

Ronald about two minutes. You put down your glass of whisky on the hall table and walk with me to the front door. You say—what would you say?"

"Has he paid you?"

"No, I'm to come in the morning for my money. I'm sorry it wasn't a success. I've told Sir Ronald that I don't want to go on with the case."

"That's your concern, Miss Gray. It was a foolish business in the first place."

They were walking out of the front door now. Suddenly Miss Leaming turned to Cordelia and said urgently and in her normal voice:

"There's one thing you had better know. It was I who found Mark first and faked the suicide. He'd rung me earlier in the day and asked me to call. I couldn't get away until after nine because of Lunn. I didn't want him to be suspicious."

"But didn't it occur to you when you found Mark that there might be something odd about the death? The door was unlocked although the curtains were drawn. The lipstick was missing."

"I suspected nothing until tonight when I stood there in the shadows and heard you talking. We're all sexually sophisticated these days. I believed what I saw. It was all horror but I knew what I had to do. I worked quickly, terrified that someone would come. I cleaned his face with my hankerchief dampened with water from the kitchen sink. It seemed that the lipstick would never come off. I undressed him and pulled on his jeans which had been thrown over the back of a chair. I didn't wait to put on his shoes, that didn't seem important. Typing the note was the worst part. I knew that he would have his Blake with him somewhere in the cottage and that the passage I chose might be more convincing than an ordinary suicide note. The clattering of the typewriter keys sounded unnaturally loud in the quietness; I was terrified that someone would hear. He had been keeping a kind of journal. There wasn't time to read it but I burnt the typescript in the sitting-room grate. Last of all, I bundled up the clothes and the pictures and brought them back here to be burnt in the lab incinerator."

"You dropped one of the pictures in the garden. And you didn't quite succeed in cleaning the lipstick from his face."

"So that's how you guessed?"

Cordelia didn't reply immediately. Whatever happened she must keep Isabelle de Lasterie out of the case.

"I wasn't sure if it was you who had been there first but I thought it must have been. There were four things. You didn't want me to investigate Mark's death; you read English at Cambridge and could have known where to find that Blake quotation; you are an experienced typist and I didn't think that the note had been typed by an amateur despite the late attempt to make it look like Mark's work; when I was first at Garforth House and asked about the suicide note you spoke the whole of the Blake quotation; the typed version was ten words short. I first noticed that when I visited the police station and was shown the note. It pointed direct to you. That was the strongest evidence I had."

They had reached the car now and paused together. Cordelia said:

"We mustn't waste any more time before ringing the police. Someone may have heard the shot."

"It's not likely. We're some distance from the village. Do we hear it now?"

"Yes. We hear it now." There was a second's pause then Cordelia said:

"What was that? It sounded like a shot."

"It couldn't have been. It was probably a car back-firing."

Miss Leaming spoke like a bad actress, the words were stilted, unconvincing. But she spoke them; she would remember them.

"But there isn't a car passing. And it came from the house."

They glanced at each other, then ran back together through the open door into the hall. Miss Leaming paused for a moment and looked Cordelia in the face before she opened the study door. Cordelia came in behind her. Miss Leaming said:

"He's been shot! I'd better phone the police."

Cordelia said:

"You wouldn't say that! Don't ever think like that! You'd go up to the body first and then you'd say:

" 'He's shot himself. I'd better phone the police.' "

Miss Leaming looked unemotionally at her lover's body, then glanced round the room. Forgetting her role, she asked:

"What have you done in here? What about finger prints?"

"Never mind. I've looked after that. All you have to remember is that you didn't know I had a gun when I first came to Garforth House; you didn't know Sir Ronald took it from me. You haven't seen that gun until this moment. When I arrived tonight you showed me into the study and met me again when I came out two minutes later. We walked together to the car and spoke as we have just spoken. We heard the shot. We did what we have just done. Forget everything else that has happened. When they question you, don't embroider, don't invent, don't be afraid to say you can't remember. And now—ring the Cambridge police."

Three minutes later they were standing together at the open door waiting for the police to arrive. Miss Leaming said:

"We mustn't talk together once they're here. And, afterwards, we mustn't meet or show any particular interest in each other. They'll know that this can't be murder unless we two are in it together. And why should we conspire together when we've only met once before, when we don't even like each other?"

She was right, thought Cordelia. They didn't even like each other. She didn't really care if Elizabeth Leaming went to prison; she did care if Mark's mother went to prison. She cared, too, that the truth of his death should never be known. The strength of that determination struck her as irrational. It could make no difference to him now and he wasn't a boy who had cared over much what people thought of him. But Ronald Callender had desecrated his body after death; had planned to make him an object, at worse of contempt, at best of pity. She had set her face against Ronald Callender. She hadn't wanted him to die; wouldn't have been capable herself of pressing the trigger. But he was dead and she couldn't feel regret, nor could she be an instrument of retribution for his murderer. It was expedient, no more than that, that Miss Leaming shouldn't be punished. Gazing out into the summer night and waiting for the sound of the police cars, Cordelia accepted once and for all the enormity and the justification of what she had done and was still planning to do. She was never afterwards to feel the least tinge of regret or of remorse.

Miss Leaming said:

"There are things you probably want to ask me, things I suppose you've a right to know. We can meet in King's College Chapel after Evensong on the first Sunday after the inquest. I'll go through the screen into the chancel, you stay in the nave. It will seem natural enough for us to meet by chance there, that is if we are both still free."

Cordelia was interested to see that Miss Leaming was taking charge again. She said:

"We shall be. If we keep our heads this can't go wrong."

There was a moment's silence. Miss Leaming said:

"They're taking their time. Surely they should be here by now?"

"They won't be much longer."

Miss Leaming suddenly laughed and said with revealing bitterness:

"What is there to be frightened of? We shall be dealing only with men."

So they waited quietly together. They heard the approaching cars before the headlamps swept over the drive, illuminating every pebble, picking out the small plants at the edge of the beds, bathing the blue haze of the wisteria with light, dazzling the watchers' eyes. Then the lights were dimmed as the cars rocked gently to a stop in front of the house. Dark shapes emerged and came unhurriedly but resolutely forward. The hall was suddenly filled with large, calm men, some in plain clothes. Cordelia effaced herself against the wall and it was Miss Leaming who stepped forward, spoke to them in a low voice and led them into the study.

Two uniformed men were left in the hall. They stood talking together, taking no notice of Cordelia. Their colleagues were taking their time. They must have used the telephone in the study because more cars and men began to arrive. First the police surgeon, identified by his bag even if he hadn't been greeted with:

"Good evening Doc. In here please."

How often he must have heard that phrase! He glanced with brief curiosity at Cordelia as he trotted through the hall, a fat, dishevelled little man, his face crumpled and petulant as a child when forcibly woken from sleep. Next came a civilian photographer carrying his camera, tripod and box of equipment; a fingerprint expert; two other civilians whom Cordelia, instructed in procedure by Bernie, guessed were scenes-of-crime officers. So they were treating this as a suspicious death. And why not? It was suspicious.

The head of the household lay dead, but the house itself seemed to have come alive. The police talked, not in whispers, but in confident normal voices unsubdued by death. They were professionals doing their job, working easily to the prescribed routine. They had been initiated into the mysteries of violent death; its victims held no awe for them. They had seen too many bodies: bodies scraped off motorways; loaded piecemeal into ambulances; dragged by hook and net from the depths of rivers; dug putrefying from the clogging earth. Like doctors, they were kind and condescendingly gentle to the uninstructed, keeping inviolate their awful knowledge. This body, while it breathed, had been more important than others. It wasn't important now, but it could still make trouble for them. They would be that much more meticulous, that much more tactful. But it was still only a case.

Cordelia sat alone and waited. She was suddenly overcome with tiredness. She longed for nothing but to put down her head on the hall table and sleep. She was hardly aware of Miss Leaming passing through the hall on her way to the drawing room, of the tall officer talking to her as they passed. Neither took any notice of the small figure in its immense woollen jersey, sitting against the wall. Cordelia willed herself to stay awake. She knew what she had to say; it was all clear enough in her mind. If only they would come to question her and let her sleep.

It wasn't until the photographer and the print man had finished their work that one of the senior officers came out to her. She was never afterwards able to recall his face but she remembered his voice, a careful, unemphatic voice from which every tinge of emotion had been excluded. He held out the gun towards her. It was resting on his open palm, protected by a handkerchief from the contamination of his hand.

"Do you recognize this weapon, Miss Gray?"

Cordelia thought it odd that he should use the word weapon. Why not just say gun?

"I think so. I think it must be mine."

"You aren't sure?"

"It must be mine, unless Sir Ronald owned one of the same make. He took it from me when I first came here four days ago. He promised to let me have it back when I called tomorrow morning for my pay."

"So this is only the second time you've been in this house?"

"Yes."

"Have you ever met Sir Ronald Callender or Miss Leaming before?"

"No. Not until Sir Ronald sent for me to undertake this case."

He went away. Cordelia rested her head back against the wall and took short snatches of sleep. Another officer came. This time he had a uniformed man with him, taking notes. There were more questions. Cordelia told her prepared story. They wrote it down without comment and went away.

She must have dozed. She awoke to find a tall, uniformed officer standing over her. He said:

"Miss Leaming is making tea in the kitchen, Miss. Perhaps you would like to give her a hand. It's something to do, isn't it?"

Cordelia thought; they're going to take away the body. She said:

"I don't know where the kitchen is."

She saw his eyes flicker.

"Oh, don't you, Miss? You're a stranger here, are you? Well, it's this way."

The kitchen was at the back of the house. It smelt of spice, oil and tomato sauce, bringing back memories of meals in Italy with her father. Miss Leaming was taking down cups from a vast dresser. An electric kettle was already hissing steam. The police officer stayed. So they weren't to be left alone. Cordelia said:

"Can I help?" Miss Leaming did not look at her.

"There are some biscuits in that tin. You can put them out on a tray. The milk is in the fridge."

Cordelia moved like an automaton. The milk bottle was an icy column in her hands, the biscuit tin lid resisted her tired fingers and she broke a nail prising it off. She noticed the details of the kitchen—a wall calendar of St. Theresa of Avila, the saint's face unnaturally elongated and pale so that she looked like a hallowed Miss Leaming; a china donkey with two panniers of artificial flowers, its melancholy head crowned with a miniature straw hat; an immense blue bowl of brown eggs.

There were two trays. The police constable took the larger from Miss Leaming and led the way into the hall. Cordelia followed with the second tray, holding it high against her chest like a child, permitted as a privilege to help mother. Police officers gathered round. She took a cup herself and returned to her usual chair.

And now there was the sound of yet another car. A middle-aged woman came in with a uniformed chauffeur at her shoulder. Through the fog of her tiredness, Cordelia heard a high, didactic voice.

"My dear Eliza, this is appalling! You must come back to the Lodge tonight. No, I insist. Is the Chief Constable here?"

"No, Marjorie, but these officers have been very kind."

"Leave them the key. They'll lock up the house when they've finished. You can't possibly stay here alone tonight."

There were introductions, hurried consultations with the detectives in which the newcomer's voice was dominant. Miss Leaming went upstairs with her visitor and reappeared five minutes later with a small case, her coat over her arm. They went off together, escorted to the car by the chauffeur and one of the detectives. None of the little party glanced at Cordelia.

Five minutes later the Inspector came up to Cordelia, key in hand.

"We shall lock up the house tonight, Miss Gray. It's time you were getting home. Are you thinking of staying at the cottage?"

"Just for the next few days, if Major Markland will let me."

"You look very tired. One of my men will drive you in your own car. I should like a written statement from you tomorrow.

Can you come to the station as soon as possible after breakfast? You know where it is?"

"Yes, I know."

One of the police panda cars drove off first and the Mini followed. The police driver drove fast, lurching the little car around the corners. Cordelia's head lolled against the back of the seat and, from time to time, was thrown against the driver's arm. He was wearing shirt sleeves and she was vaguely conscious of the comfort of the warm flesh through the cotton. The car window was open and she was aware of hot night air rushing against her face, of the scudding clouds, of the first unbelievable colours of day staining the eastern sky. The route seemed strange to her and time itself disjointed; she wondered why the car had suddenly stopped and it took a minute for her to recognize the tall hedge bending over the lane like a menacing shadow, the ramshackle gate. She was home. The driver said:

"Is this the place, Miss?"

"Yes, this is it. But I usually leave the Mini further down the lane on the right. There's a copse there where you can drive it off the road."

"Right, Miss."

He got out of the car to consult the other driver. They moved on slowly for the last few yards of the journey. And now, at last, the police car had driven away and she was alone at the gate. It was an effort to push it open against the weight of the weeds and she lurched round the cottage to the back door like a drunken creature. It took some little time to fit the key into the lock, but that was the last problem. There was no longer a gun to hide; there was no longer need to check the tape sealing the windows. Lunn was dead and she was alive. Every night that she had slept at the cottage Cordelia had come home tired, but never before had she been as tired as this. She made her way upstairs as if sleepwalking and, too exhausted even to zip herself into her sleeping-bag, crept underneath it and knew nothing more.

And at last—it seemed to Cordelia after months, not days, of waiting—there was another inquest. It was as unhurried, as unostentatiously formal, as Bernie's had been, but there was a difference. Here, instead of a handful of pathetic casuals who had sneaked into the warmth of the back benches to hear Bernie's obsequies, were grave-faced colleagues and friends, muted voices, the whispered preliminaries of lawyers and police, an indefinable sense of occasion. Cordelia guessed that the grey-haired man escorting Miss Leaming must be her lawyer. She watched him at work, affable but not deferential to the senior police, quietly solicitous for his client, exuding a confidence that they were all engaged in a necessary if tedious formality, a ritual as unworrying as Sunday Matins.

Miss Leaming looked very pale. She was wearing the grey suit she had worn when Cordelia first met her but with a small black hat, black gloves and a black chiffon scarf knotted at her throat. The two women did not look at each other. Cordelia found a seat at the end of a bench and sat there, unrepresented and alone. One or two of the younger policemen smiled at her with a reassuring but pitying kindness.

Miss Leaming gave her evidence first in a low, composed voice. She affirmed instead of taking the oath, a decision which caused a brief spasm of distress to pass over her lawyer's face. But she gave him no further cause for concern. She testified that Sir Ronald had been depressed at his son's death and, she thought, had blamed himself for not knowing that something was worrying Mark. He had told her that he intended to call in a private detective, and it had been she who had originally interviewed Miss Gray and had brought her back to Garforth House. Miss Leaming said that she had opposed the suggestion; she had seen no useful purpose in it, and thought that this futile and fruitless enquiry would only remind Sir Ronald of the tragedy. She had not known that Miss Gray possessed a gun nor that Sir Ronald had taken it from her. She had not been present during the whole of their preliminary interview. Sir Ronald had escorted Miss Gray to view his son's room while she, Miss Leaming, had gone in search of a photograph of Mr. Callender for which Miss Gray had asked.

The coroner asked her gently about the night of Sir Ronald's death.

Miss Leaming said that Miss Gray had arrived to give her first report shortly after half past ten. She herself had been passing through the front hall when the girl appeared. Miss Leaming had pointed out that it was late, but Miss Gray had said that she had wanted to abandon the case and get back to town. She had showed Miss Gray into the study where Sir Ronald was working. They had been together, she thought, for less than two minutes. Miss Gray had then come out of the study and she had walked with her to her car; they had only talked briefly. Miss Gray said that Sir Ronald had asked her to call back in the morning for her pay. She had made no mention of a gun.

Sir Ronald had, only half an hour before that, received a telephone call from the police to say that his laboratory assistant, Christopher Lunn, had been killed in a road accident. She had not told Miss Gray the news about Lunn before her interview with Sir Ronald; it hadn't occurred to her to do so. The girl had gone almost immediately into the study to see Sir Ronald. Miss Leaming said that they were standing together at the car talking when they heard the shot. At first she had thought it was a car backfiring but then she had realized that it had come from the house. They had both rushed into the study and found Sir Ronald lying slumped over his desk. The gun had dropped from his hand to the floor.

No, Sir Ronald had never given her any idea that he contemplated suicide. She thought that he was very distressed about the death of Mr. Lunn but it was difficult to tell. Sir Ronald was not a man to show emotion. He had been working very hard recently and had not seemed himself since the death of his son. But Miss Leaming had never for a moment thought that Sir Ronald was a man who would put an end to his life.

She was followed by the police witnesses, deferential, professional, but managing to give an impression that none of this was new to them; they had seen it all before and would see it again.

They were followed by the doctors, including the pathologist, who testified in what the court obviously thought was unnecessary detail to the effect of firing a jacketed hollow-cavity bullet of ninety grains into the human brain. The coroner asked:

"You have heard the police evidence that there was the print of Sir Ronald Callender's thumb on the trigger of the gun and a palm mark smudged around the butt. What would you deduce from that?"

The pathologist looked slightly surprised at being asked to deduce anything but said that it was apparent that Sir Ronald had held the gun with his thumb on the trigger when pointing it against his head. The pathologist thought that it was probably the most comfortable way in which to hold the weapon, indeed the only comfortable way, having regard to the position of the wound of entry.

Lastly, Cordelia was called to the witness box and took the oath. She had given some thought to the propriety of this and had wondered whether to follow Miss Leaming's example. There were moments, usually on a sunny Easter morning, when she wished that she could with sincerity call herself a Christian; but for the rest of the year she knew herself to be what she was—incurably agnostic but prone to unpredictable relapses into faith. This seemed to her, however, a moment when religious scrupulosity was an indulgence which she couldn't afford. The lies she was about to tell would not be the more heinous because they were tinged with blasphemy.

The coroner let her tell her story without interruption. She sensed that the court was puzzled by her but not unsympathetic. For once, the carefully modulated middle-class accent, which in her six years at the convent she had unconsciously acquired, and which in other people often irritated her as much as her own voice had irritated her father, was proving an advantage. She wore her suit and had bought a black chiffon scarf to cover her head. She remembered that she must call the coroner "sir".

After she had briefly confirmed Miss Leaming's story of how she had been called to the case, the coroner said:

"And now, Miss Gray, will you explain to the court what happened on the night Sir Ronald Callender died?"

"I had decided, sir, that I didn't want to go on with the case.

I hadn't discovered anything useful and I didn't think there was anything to discover. I had been living in the cottage where Mark Callender had spent the last weeks of his life and I had come to think that what I was doing was wrong, that I was taking money for prying into his private life. I decided on impulse to tell Sir Ronald that I wanted to finish the case. I drove to Garforth House. I go there at about ten-thirty. I knew it was late but I was anxious to go back to London the next morning. I saw Miss Leaming as she was crossing the hall and she showed me straight into the study."

"Will you please describe to the court how you found Sir Ronald."

"He seemed to be tired and distracted. I tried to explain why I wanted to give up the case but I'm not sure that he heard me. He said I was to come back next morning for my money and I said that I only proposed to charge expenses, but that I would like to have my gun. He just waved a hand in dismissal and said, 'tomorrow morning, Miss Gray. Tomorrow morning.' "

"And then you left him?"

"Yes, sir. Miss Leaming accompanied me back to the car and I was just about to drive away when we heard the shot."

"You didn't see the gun in Sir Ronald's possession while you were in the study with him?"

"No, sir."

"He didn't talk to you about Mr. Lunn's death or give you any idea that he was contemplating suicide?"

"No, sir."

The coroner doodled on the pad before him. Without looking at Cordelia, he said:

"And now, Miss Gray, will you please explain to the court how Sir Ronald came to have your gun."

This was the difficult part, but Cordelia had rehearsed it. The Cambridge police had been very thorough. They had asked the same questions over and over again. She knew exactly how Sir Ronald had come to have the gun. She remembered a piece of Dalgliesh dogma, reported by Bernie, which had seemed to her at the time more appropriate advice for a criminal than a detective. "Never tell an unnecessary lie; the truth has great authority. The cleverest murderers have been caught, not because they told the one essential lie, but because they continued to lie about unimportant detail when the truth could have done them no harm."

She said:

"My partner, Mr. Pryde, owned the gun and was very proud of it. When he killed himself I knew that he meant me to have it. That was why he cut his wrists instead of shooting himself, which would have been quicker and easier."

The coroner looked up sharply.

"And were you there when he killed himself?"

"No, sir. But I found the body."

There was a murmur of sympathy from the court; she could feel their concern.

"Did you know that the gun wasn't licensed?"

"No, sir, but I think I suspected that it might not have been. I brought it with me on this case because I didn't want to leave it in the office and because I found it a comfort. I meant to check up on the licence as soon as I got back. I didn't expect ever to use the gun. I didn't really think of it as a lethal weapon. It's just that this was my first case and Bernie had left it to me and I felt happier having it with me."

"I see," said the coroner.

Cordelia thought that he probably did see and so did the court. They were having no difficulty in believing her because she was telling the somewhat improbable truth. Now that she was about to lie, they would go on believing her.

"And now will you please tell the court how Sir Ronald came to take the gun from you?"

"It was on my first visit to Garforth House when Sir Ronald was showing me his son's bedroom. He knew that I was the sole owner of the Agency, and he asked me if it wasn't a difficult and rather frightening job for a woman. I said that I wasn't frightened but that I had Bernie's gun. When he found that I had it with me in my bag he made me hand it over to him. He said that he didn't propose to engage someone who might be a danger to other people or herself. He said that he wouldn't take the responsibility. He took the gun and the ammunition."

"And what did he do with the gun?"

Cordelia had thought this one out carefully. Obviously he hadn't carried it downstairs in his hand or Miss Leaming would have seen it. She would have liked to have said that he put it into a drawer in Mark's room but she couldn't remember whether the bedside table had had any drawers. She said:

"He took it out of the room with him; he didn't tell me where. He was only away for a moment and then we went downstairs together."

"And you didn't set eyes on the gun again until you saw it on the floor close to Sir Ronald's hand when you and Miss Leaming found his body?"

"No, sir."

Cordelia was the last witness. The verdict was quickly given, one that the court obviously felt would have been agreeable to Sir Ronald's scrupulously exact and scientific brain. It was that the deceased had taken his own life but that there was no evidence as to the state of his mind. The coroner delivered at length the obligatory warning about the danger of guns. Guns, the court were informed, could kill people. He managed to convey that unlicensed guns were particularly prone to this danger. He pronounced no strictures on Cordelia personally although it was apparent that this restraint cost him an effort. He rose and the court rose with him.

After the coroner had left the bench the court broke up into little whispering groups. Miss Leaming was quickly surrounded. Cordelia saw her shaking hands, receiving condolences, listening with grave assenting face to the first tentative proposals for a memorial service. Cordelia wondered how she could ever have feared that Miss Leaming would be suspected. She herself stood a little apart, delinquent. She knew that the police would charge her with illegal possession of the gun. They could do no less. True, she would be lightly punished, if punished at all. But for the rest of her life she would be the girl whose carelessness and naïveté had lost England one of her foremost scientists.

As Hugo had said, all Cambridge suicides were brilliant. But about this one there could be little doubt. Sir Ronald's death would probably raise him to the status of genius.

Almost unnoticed, she came alone out of the courtroom on to Market Hill. Hugo must have been waiting; now he fell into step with her.

"How did it go? I must say death seems to follow you around, doesn't it?"

"It went all right. I seem to follow death."

"I suppose he did shoot himself?"

"Yes. He shot himself."

"And with your gun?"

"As you will know if you were in court. I didn't see you."

"I wasn't there, I had a tutorial, but the news did get around. I shouldn't let it worry you. Ronald Callender wasn't as important as some people in Cambridge may choose to believe."

"You know nothing about him. He was a human being and he's dead. That fact is always important."

"It isn't, you know, Cordelia. Death is the least important thing about us. Comfort yourself with Joseph Hall. 'Death borders upon our birth and our cradle stands in the grave.' And he did choose his own weapon, his own time. He'd had enough of himself. Plenty of people had had enough of him."

They walked together down St. Edward's Passage towards King's Parade. Cordelia wasn't sure where they were making for. Her need at present was just to walk, but she didn't find her companion disagreeable.

She asked:

"Where's Isabelle?"

"Isabelle is home in Lyons. Papa turned up unexpectedly yesterday and found that mademoiselle wasn't exactly earning her wages. Papa decided that dear Isabelle was getting less—or it may have been more—out of her Cambridge education than he had expected. I don't think you need worry about her. Isabelle is safe enough now. Even if the police decide that it's worthwhile going to France to question her—and why on earth should they?—it won't help them. Papa will surround her with a barrage of lawyers. He's not in a mood to stand any nonsense from Englishmen at present."

"And what about you? If anyone asks you how Mark died, you'll never tell them the truth?"

"What do you think? Sophie, Davie and I are safe enough. I'm reliable when it comes to essentials."

For a moment Cordelia wished that he were reliable in less essential matters. She asked:

"Are you sorry about Isabelle leaving?"

"I am rather. Beauty is intellectually confusing; it sabotages common sense. I could never quite accept that Isabelle was what she is: a generous, indolent, over-affectionate and stupid young woman. I thought that any woman as beautiful as she must have an instinct about life, access to some secret wisdom which is beyond cleverness. Every time she opened that delicious mouth I was expecting her to illumine life. I think I could have spent all my life just looking at her and waiting for the oracle. And all she could talk about was clothes."

"Poor Hugo."

"Never poor Hugo. I'm not unhappy. The secret of contentment is never to allow yourself to want anything which reason tells you you haven't a chance of getting."

Cordelia thought that he was young, well-off, clever, even if not clever enough, handsome; there wasn't much that he would have to forgo on that or any other criteria.

She heard him speaking:

"Why not stay in Cambridge for a week or so and let me show you the city? Sophie would let you have her spare room."

"No thank you, Hugo. I have to get back to town."

There was nothing in town for her, but with Hugo there would be nothing in Cambridge for her either. There was only one reason for staying in this city. She would remain at the cottage until Sunday and her meeting with Miss Leaming. After that, as far as she was concerned, the case of Mark Callender would be finished for good.

Sunday afternoon Evensong was over and the congregation, who had listened in respectful silence to the singing of responses, psalms and anthem by one of the finest choirs in the world, rose and joined with joyous abandon in the final hymn. Cordelia rose and sang with them. She had seated herself at the end of the row close to the richly carved screen. From here she could see into the chancel. The robes of the choristers gleamed scarlet and white; the candles flickered in patterned rows and high circles of golden light; two tall and slender candles stood each side of the softly illuminated Reubens above the high altar, seen dimly as a distant smudge of crimson, blue and gold. The blessing was pronounced, the final amen impeccably sung and the choir began to file decorously out of the chancel. The south door was opened and sunlight flooded into the chapel. The members of the college who had attended divine service strolled out after the Provost and Fellows in casual disarray, their regulation surplices dingy and limp over a cheerful incongruity of corduroy and tweed. The great organ snuffled and groaned like an animal gathering breath, before giving forth its magnificent voice in a Bach fugue. Cordelia sat quietly in her chair, listening and waiting. Now the congregation was moving down the main aisle—small groups in bright summer cottons whispering discreetly, serious young men in sober Sunday black, tourists clutching their illustrated guides and half-embarrassed by their obtrusive cameras, a group of nuns with calm and cheerful faces.

Miss Leaming was one of the last, a tall figure in a grey linen dress and white gloves, her head bare, a white cardigan slung carelessly around her shoulders against the chill of the chapel. She was obviously alone and unwatched and her careful pretence of surprise at recognizing Cordelia was probably an unnecessary precaution. They passed out of the chapel together.

The gravel path outside the doorway was thronged with people. A little party of Japanese, festooned with cameras and accessories, added their high staccato jabber to the muted Sunday afternoon chat. From here the silver stream of the Cam was invisible but the truncated bodies of punters glided against the far bank like puppets in a show, raising their arms above the pole and turning to thrust it backwards as if participating in some ritual dance. The great lawn lay unshadowed in the sun, a quintessence of greenness staining the scented air. A frail and elderly Don in gown and mortarboard was limping across the grass; the sleeves of his gown caught a stray breeze and billowed out so that he looked like a winged and monstrous crow struggling to rise. Miss Leaming said, as if Cordelia had asked for an explanation:

"He's a Fellow. The sacred turf is, therefore, uncontaminated by his feet."

They walked in silence by Gibbs Building. Cordelia wondered when Miss Leaming would speak. When she did, her first question was unexpected.

"Do you think you'll make a success of it?"

Sensing Cordelia's surprise, she added impatiently:

"The Detective Agency. Do you think you'll be able to cope?"

"I shall have to try. It's the only job I know."

She had no intention of justifying to Miss Leaming her affection and loyalty to Bernie; she would have had some difficulty in explaining it to herself.

"Your overheads are too high."

It was a pronouncement made with all the authority of a verdict.

"Do you mean the office and the Mini?" asked Cordelia.

"Yes. In your job I don't see how one person in the field can bring in sufficient income to cover expenses. You can't be sitting in the office taking orders and typing letters and be out solving cases at the same time. On the other hand, I don't suppose you can afford help."

"Not yet. I've been thinking that I might rent a telephone answering service. That will take care of the orders although, of course, clients much prefer to come to the office and discuss their case. If I can only make enough in expenses just to live, then any fees can cover the overheads."

"If there are any fees."

There seemed nothing to say to this and they walked on in silence for a few seconds. Then Miss Leaming said:

"There'll be the expenses from this case anyway. That at least should help towards your fine for illegal possession of the gun. I've put the matter in the hands of my solicitors. You should be getting a cheque fairly soon."

"I don't want to take any money for this case."

"I can understand that. As you pointed out to Ronald, it

falls under your fair deal clause. Strictly speaking you aren't entitled to any. All the same, I think it would look less suspicious if you took your expenses. Would thirty pounds strike you as reasonable?"

"Perfectly, thank you."

They had reached the corner of the lawn and had turned to walk towards King's Bridge. Miss Leaming said:

"I shall have to be grateful to you for the rest of my life. That for me is an unaccustomed humility and I'm not sure that I like it."

"Then don't feel it. I was thinking of Mark, not of you."

"I thought you might have acted in the service of justice or some such abstraction."

"I wasn't thinking about any abstraction. I was thinking about a person."

They had reached the bridge now and leaned over it side by side to look down into the bright water. The paths leading up to the bridge were, for a few minutes, empty of people. Miss Leaming said:

"Pregnancy isn't difficult to fake, you know. It only needs a loose corset and judicious stuffing. It's humiliating for the woman, of course, almost indecent if she happens to be barren. But it isn't difficult, particularly if she isn't closely watched. Evelyn wasn't. She had always been a shy, self-contained woman. People expected her to be excessively modest about her pregnancy. Garforth House wasn't filled with friends and relations swopping horror stories about the ante-natal clinic and patting her stomach. We had to get rid of that tedious fool Nanny Pilbeam, of course. Ronald regarded her departure as one of the subsidiary benefits of the pseudo pregnancy. He was tired of being spoken to as if he were still Ronnie Callender, the bright grammar school boy from Harrogate."

Cordelia said:

"Mrs. Goddard told me that Mark had a great look of his mother."

"She would. She was sentimental as well as stupid."

Cordelia did not speak. After a few moments silence Miss Leaming went on:

"I discovered that I was carrying Ronald's child at about the same time as a London specialist confirmed what the three of us already guessed, that Evelyn was most unlikely to conceive. I wanted to have the baby; Ronald desperately wanted a son; Evelyn's father was obsessional about his need for a grandson and was willing to part with half a million to prove it. It was all so easy. I resigned from my teaching job and went off to the safe anonymity of London and Evelyn told her father she was pregnant at last. Neither Ronald nor I had any conscience about defrauding George Bottley. He was an arrogant, brutal, self-satisfied fool who couldn't imagine how the world would continue without his issue to supervise it. He even subsidized his own deceit. The cheques for Evelyn began to arrive, each with a note imploring her to look after her health, to consult the best London doctors, to rest, to take a holiday in the sun. She had always loved Italy, and Italy became part of the plan. The three of us would meet in London every two months and fly together to Pisa. Ronald would rent a small villa outside Florence and, once there, I became Mrs. Callender and Evelyn became me. We had only daily servants and there was no need for them to look at our passports. They got used to our visits and so did the local doctor who was called in to supervise my health. The locals thought it flattering that the English lady should be so fond of Italy that she came back month after month, so close to her confinement."

Cordelia asked:

"But how could she do it, how could she bear to be there with you in the house, watching you with her husband, knowing that you were going to have his child?"

"She did it because she loved Ronald and couldn't bear to lose him. She hadn't been much success as a woman. If she lost her husband, what else was there for her? She couldn't have gone back to her father. Besides, we had a bribe for her. She was to have the child. If she refused, then Ronald would leave her and seek a divorce to marry me."

"I would rather have left him and gone off to scrub doorsteps."

"Not everyone has a talent for scrubbing doorsteps and not everyone has your capacity for moral indignation. Evelyn was religious. She was, therefore, practised in self-deception. She convinced herself that what we were doing was best for the child."

"And her father? Didn't he ever suspect?"

"He despised her for her piety. He always had. Psychologically he could hardly indulge that dislike and at the same time think her capable of deceit. Besides, he desperately needed that grandchild. It wouldn't have entered his mind that the child might not be hers. And he had a doctor's report. After our third visit to Italy we told Doctor Sartori that Mrs. Callender's father was concerned about her care. At our request he wrote a reassuring medical report on the progress of the pregnancy. We went to Florence together a fortnight before the baby was due and stayed there until Mark arrived. Luckily he was a day or two before time. We'd had the foresight to put back the expected date of delivery so that it genuinely looked as if Evelyn had been caught unexpectedly by a premature birth. Dr. Sartori did what was necessary with perfect competence and the three of us came home with the baby and a birth certificate in the right name."

Cordelia said:

"And nine months later Mrs. Callender was dead."

"He didn't kill her, if that's what you're thinking. He wasn't really the monster that you imagine, at least, not then. But in a sense we did both destroy her. She should have had a specialist, certainly a better doctor than that incompetent fool Gladwin. But the three of us were desperately afraid that an efficient doctor would know that she hadn't borne a child. She was as worried as we were. She insisted that no other doctor be consulted. She had grown to love the baby, you see. So she died and was cremated and we thought we were safe for ever."

"She left Mark a note before she died, nothing but a scribbled hieroglyphic in her prayer book. She left him her blood group."

"We knew that the blood groups were a danger. Ronald took blood from the three of us and made the necessary tests. But after she was dead even that worry ended."

There was a long silence. Cordelia could see a little group of tourists moving down the path towards the bridge. Miss Leaming said:

"The irony of it is that Ronald never really loved him. Mark's grandfather adored him; there was no difficulty there. He left half his fortune to Evelyn and it came automatically to her husband. Mark was to get the other half on his twenty-fifth birthday. But Ronald never cared for his son. He found that he couldn't love him, and I wasn't allowed to. I watched him grow up and go to school. But I wasn't allowed to love him. I used to knit him endless jerseys. It was almost an obsession. The patterns got more intricate and the wool thicker as he grew older. Poor Mark, he must have thought that I was mad, this strange, discontented women whom his father couldn't do without but wouldn't marry."

"There are one or two of the jerseys at the cottage. What would you like me to do with his things?"

"Take them away and give them to anyone who needs them. Unless you think I ought to unpick the wool and knit it up into something new? Would that be a suitable gesture, do you think, symbolic of wasted effort, pathos, futility?"

"I'll find a use for them. And his books?"

"Get rid of them too. I can't go again to the cottage. Get rid of everything if you will."

The little group of tourists was very close now but they seemed engrossed in their own chatter. Miss Leaming took an envelope out of her pocket and handed it to Cordelia.

"I've written out a brief confession. There's nothing in it about Mark, nothing about how he died or what you discovered. It's just a brief statement that I shot Ronald Callender immediately after you had left Garforth House and coerced you into supporting my story. You'd better put it somewhere safe. One day you may need it."

Cordelia saw that the envelope was addressed to herself. She didn't open it. She said:

"It's too late now. If you regret what we did, you should have spoken earlier. The case is closed now."

"I've no regrets. I'm glad that we acted as we did. But the case may not be over yet."

"But it is over! The inquest has given its verdict."

"Ronald had a number of very powerful friends. They have

influence and, periodically, they like to exercise it if only to prove that they still have it."

"But they can't get this case reopened! It practically takes an act of parliament to change a coroner's verdict."

"I don't say that they'll try to do that. But they may ask questions. They may have what they describe as a quiet word in the right ear. And the right ears are usually available. That's how they work. That's the sort of people they are."

Cordelia said suddenly:

"Have you a light?"

Without question or protest Miss Leaming opened her handbag and handed over an elegant silver tube. Cordelia didn't smoke and was unused to lighters. It took three clicks before the wick burst into flame. Then she leaned over the parapet of the bridge and set fire to the corner of the envelope.

The incandescent flame was invisible in the stronger light of the sun. All Cordelia could see was a narrow band of wavering purple light as the flame bit into the paper and the charred edges widened and grew. The pungent smell of burning was wafted away on the breeze. As soon as the flame tinged her fingers, Cordelia dropped the envelope, still burning, and watched it twist and turn as it floated down small and frail as a snowflake to be lost at last in the Cam. She said:

"Your lover shot himself. That is all that either of us need to remember now or ever."

They didn't speak again about Ronald Callender's death, but walked silently along the elm-lined path towards the Backs. At one point Miss Leaming glanced at Cordelia and said in a tone of angry petulance:

"You look surprisingly well!"

Cordelia supposed that this brief outburst was the resentment of the middle-aged at the resilience of the young which could so quickly recover from physical disaster. It had only taken one night of long and deep sleep to return her to the state which Bernie, with irritating coyness, used to describe as bright eyed and bushy tailed. Even without the benison of a hot bath the broken skin on her shoulders and back had healed cleanly. Physically, the events of the last fortnight had left her unscathed. She wasn't so sure about Miss Leaming. The sleek platinum hair was still swathed and shaped immaculately to the bones of the head; she still carried her clothes with cool distinction as if it were important to appear the competent and unharassed helpmate of a famous man. But the pale skin was now tinged with grey; her eyes were deeply shadowed, and the incipient lines at the side of the mouth and across the forehead had deepened so that the face, for the first time, looked old and strained.

They passed through King's Gate and turned to the right. Cordelia had found a place and had parked the Mini within a few yards of the gate; Miss Leaming's Rover was further down Queen's Road. She shook hands firmly but briefly with Cordelia and said goodbye as unemotionally as if they were Cambridge acquaintances, parting with unusual formality after an unexpected meeting at Evensong. She didn't smile. Cordelia watched the tall, angular figure striding down the path under the trees towards John's Gate. She didn't look back. Cordelia wondered when, if ever, they would see each other again. It was difficult to believe that they had met only on four occasions. They had nothing in common except their sex, although Cordelia had realized during the days following Ronald Callender's murder the strength of that female allegiance. As Miss Leaming herself had said, they didn't even like each other. Yet each held the other's safety in her hands. There were moments when their secret almost horrified Cordelia by its immensity. But these were few and would get fewer. Time would inevitably diminish its importance. Life would go on. Neither of them would ever forget completely while the brain cells still lived, but she could believe that a day might come when they would glimpse each other across a theatre or restaurant or be borne unprotestingly past on an underground escalator and would wonder whether what they both recalled in the shock of recognition had really once happened. Already, only four days after the inquest, Ronald Callender's murder was beginning to take its place in the landscape of the past.

There was no longer anything to keep her at the cottage. She spent an hour obsessionally cleaning and tidying rooms which no one would enter, probably for weeks. She watered the mug of cowslips on the sitting-room table. In another three days they would be dead and no one would notice, but she couldn't bear to throw out the still living flowers. She went out to the shed and contemplated the bottle of sour milk and the beef stew. Her first impulse was to take both and empty them down the lavatory. But they were part of the evidence. She wouldn't need that evidence again, but ought it to be completely destroyed? She recalled Bernie's reiterated admonition: "Never destroy the evidence." The Super had been full of cautionary tales to emphasize the importance of that maxim. In the end she decided to photograph the exhibits, setting them up on the kitchen table and paying great attention to exposure and light. It seemed a fruitless, somewhat ridiculous, exercise and she was glad when the job was done and the unsavoury contents of bottle and pan could be disposed of. Afterwards she carefully washed them both and left them in the kitchen.

Last of all she packed her bag and stowed her gear in the Mini together with Mark's jerseys and books. Folding the thick wool, she thought of Dr. Gladwin sitting in his back garden, his shrunken veins indifferent to the sun. He would find the jerseys useful, but she couldn't take them to him. That kind of gesture might have been accepted from Mark, but not from her.

She locked the door and left the key under a stone. She couldn't face Miss Markland again and had no wish to hand it back to any other member of the family. She would wait until she got to London, then send a brief note to Miss Markland thanking her for her kindness and explaining where the key could be found. She walked for the last time round the garden. She wasn't sure what impulse led her to the well but she came up to it with a shock of surprise. The soil around the rim had been cleared and dug and had been planted with a circle of pansies, daisies and small clumps of alyssum and lobelia, each plant looking well established in its hollow ring of watered earth. It was a bright oasis of colour among the encroaching weeds. The effect was pretty but ridiculous and disquietingly odd. Thus strangely celebrated, the well itself looked obscene, a wooden breast topped by a monstrous nipple. How could she have seen the well cover as a harmless and slightly elegant folly?

Cordelia was torn between pity and revulsion. This must be the work of Miss Markland. The well, which for years had been to her an object of horror, remorse and reluctant fascination, was now to be tended as a shrine. It was ludicrous and pitiable and Cordelia wished that she hadn't seen it. She was suddenly terrified of meeting Miss Markland, of seeing the incipient madness in her eyes. She almost ran out of the garden, pulled the gate shut against the weight of the weeds and drove finally away from the cottage without a backward glance. The case of Mark Callender was finished.

Chapter Seven

Next morning she went to the Kingly Street office promptly at nine o'clock. The unnaturally hot weather had broken at last and, when she opened the window, a keen breeze shifted the layers of dust on desk and filing cabinet. There was only one letter. This was in a long stiff envelope and was headed with the name and address of Ronald Callender's solicitors. It was very brief.

"Dear Madam, I enclose a cheque for £30.00 being expenses due to you in respect of the investigation which you carried out at the request of the late Sir Ronald Callender into the death of his son Mark Callender. If you agree this sum, I would be grateful if you would sign and return the attached receipt."

Well, as Miss Leaming had said, it would at least pay part of her fine. She had sufficient money to keep the Agency going for another month. If there were no further case by that time, there was always Miss Feakins and another temporary job. Cordelia thought of the Feakins Secretarial Agency without enthusiasm. Miss Feakins operated, and that was the appropriate word, from a small office as squalid as Cordelia's own, but which had had a desperate gaiety imposed upon it in the form of multi-coloured walls, paper flowers in a variety of urn-like containers, china ornaments and a poster. The poster had always fascinated Cordelia. A curvaceous blonde, clad in brief hot pants and laughing hysterically, was leap-frogging over her typewriter, a feat she managed to perform with a maximum of exposure while clutching a fistful of five pound notes in each hand. The caption read:
"Be a Girl Friday and join the fun people. All the best Crusoes are on our books."

Beneath this poster Miss Feakins, emaciated, indefatigably cheerful and tinsled like a christmas tree, interviewed a dispirited trail of the old, the ugly and the virtually unemployable. Her milch cows seldom escaped into permanent employment. Miss Feakins would warn against the unspecified dangers of accepting a permanent job much as Victorian mothers warned against sex. But Cordelia liked her. Miss Feakins would welcome her back, her defection to Bernie forgiven, and there would be another of those furtive telephone conversations with the fortunate Crusoe made with one bright eye on Cordelia, a brothel madam recommending her latest recruit to one of her fussier customers. "Most superior girl—well educated—you'll like her—and a worker!" The emphasis of amazed wonder on the last word was justified. Few of Miss Feakins' temporaries, beguiled by advertisements, seriously expected to have to work. There were other and more efficient agencies but only one Miss Feakins. Bound by pity and an eccentric loyalty, Cordelia had little hope of escaping that glittering eye. A series of temporary jobs with Miss Feakins' Crusoes might, indeed, be all that was left to her. Didn't a conviction for illegal possession of a weapon under Section I of the Firearms Act 1968 count as a criminal record, barring one for life from socially responsible and safe jobs in the civil service and local government?

She settled down at the typewriter, with the yellow telephone directory to hand, to finish sending out the circular letter to the last twenty solicitors on the list. The letter itself embarrassed and depressed her. It had been concocted by Bernie after a dozen preliminary drafts and, at the time, it hadn't seemed too unreasonable. But his death and the Callender case had altered everything. The pompous phrases about a comprehensive professional service, immediate attendance in any part of the country, discreet and experienced operators and moderate fees, struck her as ridiculously, even dangerously, pretentious. Wasn't there something about false representation in the Trades Description Act? But the promise of moderate fees and absolute discretion was valid enough. It was a pity, she thought drily, that she couldn't get a reference from Miss Leaming. Alibis arranged; inquests attended; murders efficiently concealed; perjury at our own special rates.

The raucous burr of the telephone startled her. The office was so quiet and still that she had taken it for granted that no one would call. She stared at the instrument for several seconds, wide-eyed and suddenly afraid, before stretching out her hand.

The voice was calm and assured, polite but in no way deferential. It uttered no threat, yet to Cordelia, every word was explicit with menace.

"Miss Cordelia Gray? This is New Scotland Yard. We wondered whether you would be back at your office yet. Could you please make it convenient to call here sometime later today? Chief Superintendent Dalgliesh would like to see you."

It was ten days later that Cordelia was called for the third time to New Scotland Yard. The bastion of concrete and glass off Victoria Street was, by now, fairly familiar to her although she still entered it with a sense of temporarily discarding part of her identity, like leaving shoes outside a mosque.

Superintendent Dalgliesh had imposed little of his own personality on his room. The books in the regulation bookcase were obviously textbooks on law, copies of regulations and Acts of Parliament, dictionaries and books of reference. The only picture was a large water colour of the old Norman Shaw building on the Embankment painted from the river, an agreeable study in greys and soft ochres lit by the bright golden wings of the R.A.F. Memorial. On this visit, as on previous occasions, there was a bowl of roses on his desk, garden roses with sturdy stems and thorns curved like strong beaks, not the etiolated scentless blooms of a West End florist.

Bernie had never described him; had only fathered on him his own obsessive, unheroic, rough-hewn philosophy. Cordelia, bored by his very name, had asked no questions. But the Superintendent she had pictured was very different from the tall, austere figure who had risen to shake her hand when she first came into this room and the dichotomy between her private imaginings and the reality had been disconcerning. Irrationally, she had felt a twinge of irritation against Bernie for so putting her at a disadvantage. He was old of course, over forty at least, but not as old as she had expected. He was dark, very tall and loose-limbed where she had expected him to be fair, thick set and stocky. He was serious and spoke to her as if she were a responsible adult, not avuncular and condescending. His face was sensitive without being weak and she liked his hands and his voice and the way she could see the structure of his bones under the skin. He sounded gentle and kind, which was cunning since she knew that he was dangerous and cruel, and she had to keep reminding herself of how he had treated Bernie. At some moments during the interrogation she had actually wondered whether he could be Adam Dalgliesh the poet.

They had never been alone together. On each of her visits a policewoman, introduced as Sergeant Mannering, had been present, seated at the side of the desk with her notebook. Cordelia felt that she knew Sergeant Mannering well having met her at school in the person of the head girl, Teresa Campion-Hook. The two girls could have been sisters. No acne had ever marked their shiningly clean skins; their fair hair curled at precisely the regulation length above their uniformed collars; their voices were calm, authoritarian, determinedly cheerful but never strident; they exuded an ineffable confidence in the justice and logic of the universe and the rightness of their own place in it. Sergeant Mannering had smiled briefly at Cordelia as she came in. The look was open, not overtly friendly since too generous a smile might prejudice the case, but not censorious either. It was a look which disposed Cordelia to imprudence; she disliked looking a fool before that competent gaze.

She had at least had time before her first visit to decide on tactics. There was little advantage and much danger in concealing facts which an intelligent man could easily discover for himself. She would disclose, if asked, that she had discussed Mark Callender with the Tillings and his tutor; that she had traced and interviewed Mrs. Goddard; that she had visited Dr. Gladwin. She decided to say nothing about the attempt on her life or about her visit to Somerset House. She knew which facts it would be vital to conceal: Ronald Callender's murder; the clue in the prayer book; the actual way in which Mark had died. She told herself firmly that she mustn't be drawn into discussing the case, mustn't talk about herself, her life, her present job, her ambitions. She remembered what Bernie had told her. "In this country, if people won't talk, there's nothing you can do to make them, more's the pity. Luckily for the police most people just can't keep their mouths shut. The intelligent ones are the worst. They just have to show how clever they are, and once you've got them discussing the case, even discussing it generally, then you've got them." Cordelia reminded herself of the advice she had given to Elizabeth Leaming: "Don't embroider, don't invent, don't be afraid to say you can't remember."

Dalgliesh was speaking:

"Have you thought of consulting a solicitor, Miss Gray?"

"I haven't got a solicitor."

"The Law Society can give you the names of some very reliable and helpful ones. I should think about it seriously if I were you."

"But I should have to pay him, shouldn't I? Why should I need a solicitor when I'm telling the truth?"

"It's when people start telling the truth that they most often feel the need of a solicitor."

"But I've always told the truth. Why should I lie?" The rhetorical question was a mistake. He answered it seriously as if she had really wanted to know.

"Well, it could be to protect yourself—which I don't think likely—or to protect someone else. The motive for that could be love, fear, or a sense of justice. I don't think you've known any of the people in this case long enough to care for them deeply so that rules out love, and I don't think you would be very easy to frighten. So we're left with justice. A very dangerous concept, Miss Gray."

She had been closely questioned before. The Cambridge police had been very thorough. But this was the first time she had been questioned by someone who knew; knew that she was lying; knew that Mark Callender hadn't killed himself; knew, she felt desperately, all there was to know. She had to force herself to an acceptance of reality. He couldn't possibly be sure. He hadn't any legal proof and he never would have. There was no one alive to tell him the truth except Elizabeth Leaming and herself. And she wasn't going to tell. Dalgliesh could beat against her will with his implacable logic, his curious kindness, his courtesy, his patience. But she wouldn't talk, and in England there was no way in which he could make her.

When she didn't reply, he said cheerfully:

"Well, let's see how far we've got. As a result of your enquiries you suspected that Mark Callender might have been murdered. You haven't admitted that to me but you made your suspicions plain when you visited Sergeant Maskell of the Cambridge police. You subsequently traced his mother's old nurse and learned from her something of his early life, of the Callender marriage, of Mrs. Callender's death. Following that visit you went to see Dr. Gladwin, the general practitioner who had looked after Mrs. Callender before she died. By a simple ruse you ascertained the blood group of Ronald Callender. There would only be point in that if you suspected that Mark wasn't the child of his parents' marriage. You then did what I would have done in your place, visited Somerset House to examine Mr. George Bottley's will. That was sensible. If you suspect murder, always consider who stands to gain by it."

So he had found out about Somerset House and the call to Dr. Venables. Well, it was to be expected. He had credited her with his own brand of intelligence. She had behaved as he would have behaved.

She still didn't speak. He said:

"You didn't tell me about your fall down the well. Miss Markland did."

"That was an accident. I don't remember anything about it, but I must have decided to explore the well and overbalanced. I was always rather intrigued by it."

"I don't think it was an accident, Miss Gray. You couldn't have pulled the lid free without a rope. Miss Markland tripped over a rope, but it was coiled neatly and half-hidden in the undergrowth. Would you have even troubled to detach it from the hook if you'd only been exploring?"

"I don't know. I can't remember anything that happened before I fell. My first memory is hitting the water. And I don't see what this has to do with Sir Ronald Callender's death."

"It might have a great deal to do with it. If someone tried to kill you, and I think that they did, that person could have come from Garforth House."

"Why?"

"Because the attempt on your life was probably connected with your investigation into Mark Callender's death. You had become a danger to someone. Killing is a serious business. The professionals don't like it unless it's absolutely essential and even the amateurs are less happy-go-lucky about murder than you might expect. You must have become a very dangerous woman to someone. Someone replaced that well lid, Miss Gray; you didn't fall through solid wood."

Cordelia still said nothing. There was a silence, then he spoke again:

"Miss Markland told me that after your rescue from the well she was reluctant to leave you alone. But you insisted that she should go. You told her that you weren't afraid to be alone in the cottage because you had a gun."

Cordelia was surprised how much this small betrayal hurt. Yet, how could she blame Miss Markland? The Superintendent would have known just how to handle her, probably persuaded her that frankness was in Cordelia's own interest. Well, she could at least betray in her turn. And this explanation, at least, would have the authority of truth.

"I wanted to get rid of her. She told me some dreadful story about her illegitimate child falling down the well to his death. I'd only just been rescued myself. I didn't want to hear it, I couldn't bear it just then. I told her a lie about the gun just to make her go. I didn't ask her to confide in me, it wasn't fair. It was only a way of asking for help and I hadn't any to give."

"And didn't you want to get rid of her for another reason? Didn't you know that your assailant would have to return that night; that the well cover would have to be dragged clear again if your death were to look like an accident?"

"If I'd really thought that I was in any danger I should have begged her to take me with her to Summertrees House. I wouldn't have waited alone in the cottage without my gun."

"No, Miss Gray, I believe that. You wouldn't have waited there alone in the cottage that night without your gun."

For the first time Cordelia was desperately afraid. This wasn't a game. It never had been, although at Cambridge the police interrogation had held some of the unreality of a formal contest in which the result was both foreseeable and unworrying since one of the opponents didn't even know he was playing. It was real enough now. If she were tricked, persuaded, coerced into telling him the truth, she would go to prison. She was an accessory after the fact. How many years did one get for helping to conceal murder? She had read somewhere that Holloway smelt. They would take away her clothes. She would be shut up in a claustrophobic cell. There was remission for good conduct but how could one be good in prison? Perhaps they would send her to an open prison. Open. It was a contradiction in terms. And how would she live afterwards? How would she get a job? What real personal freedom could there ever be for those whom society labelled delinquent?

She was terrified for Miss Leaming. Where was she now? She had never dared ask Dalgliesh, and Miss Leaming's name had hardly been mentioned. Was she even now in some other room of New Scotland Yard being similarly questioned? How reliable would she be under pressure? Were they planning to confront the two conspirators with each other? Would the door suddenly open and Miss Leaming be brought in, apologetic, remorseful, truculent? Wasn't that the usual ploy, to interview conspirators separately until the weaker broke down? And who would prove the weaker?

She heard the Superintendent's voice. She thought he sounded rather sorry for her.

"We have some confirmation that the pistol was in your possession that night. A motorist tells us that he saw a parked car on the road about three miles from Garforth House and when he stopped to enquire if he could help he was threatened by a young woman with a gun."

Cordelia remembered that moment, the sweetness and silence of the summer night suddenly overlaid by his hot, alcoholic breath.

"He must have been drinking. I suppose the police stopped him for a breath test later that night and now he's decided to come up with this story. I don't know what he expects to gain by it but it isn't true. I wasn't carrying a gun. Sir Ronald took the pistol from me on my first night at Garforth House."

"The Metropolitan Police stopped him just over the force border. I think he may persist in his story. He was very definite. Of course, he hasn't identified you yet but he was able to describe the car. His story is that he thought you were having trouble with it and stopped to help. You misunderstood his motives and threatened him with a gun."

"I understood his motives perfectly. But I didn't threaten him with a gun."

"What did you say, Miss Gray?"

"Leave me alone or I'll kill you."

"Without the gun, surely that was an empty threat?"

"It would always have been an empty threat. But it made him go."

"What exactly did happen?"

"I had a spanner in the front pocket of the car and when he shoved his face in at the window I grasped that and threatened him with it. But no one in his right senses could have mistaken a spanner for a gun!"

But he hadn't been in his right senses. The only person who had seen the gun in her possession that night was a motorist who hadn't been sober. This, she knew, was a small victory. She had resisted the momentary temptation to change her story. Bernie had been right. She recalled his advice; the Superintendent's advice; this time she could almost hear it spoken in his deep, slightly husky voice: "If you're tempted to crime, stick to your original statement. There's nothing that impresses the jury more than consistency. I've seen the most unlikely defence succeed simply because the accused stuck to his story. After all, it's only someone else's word against yours; with a competent counsel that's half-way to a reasonable doubt."

The Superintendent was speaking again. Cordelia wished that she could concentrate more clearly on what he was saying. She hadn't been sleeping very soundly for the past ten days—perhaps that had something to do with this perpetual tiredness.

"I think that Chris Lunn paid you a visit on the night he died. There's no other reason that I could discover why he should have been on that road. One of the witnesses to the accident said that he came out in the little van from that side road as if all the devils in hell were following him. Someone was following him—you, Miss Gray."

"We've had this conversation before. I was on my way to see Sir Ronald."

"At that hour? And in such a hurry?"

"I wanted to see him urgently to tell him that I'd decided to drop the case. I couldn't wait."

"But you did wait, didn't you? You went to sleep in the car on the side of the road. That's why it was nearly an hour after you'd been seen at the accident before you arrived at Garforth House."

"I had to stop. I was tired and I knew it wasn't safe to drive on."

"But you knew too, that it was safe to sleep. You knew that the person you had most to fear from was dead."

Cordelia didn't reply. A silence fell on the room but it seemed to her a companionable not an accusing silence. She wished that she wasn't so tired. Most of all, she wished that she had someone to talk to about Ronald Callender's murder. Bernie wouldn't have been any help here. To him the moral dilemma at the heart of the crime would have held no interest, no validity, would have seemed a wilful confusion of straightforward facts. She could imagine his coarse and facile comment on Eliza Leaming's relations with Lunn. But the Superintendent might have understood. She could imagine herself talking to him. She recalled Ronald Callender's words that love was as destructive as hate. Would Dalgliesh assent to that bleak philosophy? She wished that she could ask him. This, she recognized, was her real danger—not the temptation to confess but the longing to confide. Did he know how she felt? Was this too, part of his technique?

There was a knock at the door. A uniformed constable came in and handed a note to Dalgliesh. The room was very quiet while he read it. Cordelia made herself look at his face. It was grave and expressionless and he continued looking at the paper long after he must have assimilated its brief message.

She thought that he was making up his mind to something. After a minute he said:

"This concerns someone you know, Miss Gray. Elizabeth Leaming is dead. She was killed two days ago when the car she was driving went off the coast road south of Amalfi. This note is confirmation of identity."

Cordelia was swept with relief so immense that she felt physically sick. She clenched her fist and felt the sweat start on her brow. She began to shiver with cold. It never occurred to her that he might be lying. She knew him to be ruthless and clever but she had always taken it for granted that he wouldn't lie to her. She said in a whisper:

"May I go home now?"

"Yes. I don't think there's much point in your staying, do you?"

"She didn't kill Sir Ronald. He took the gun from me. He took the gun——"

Something seemed to have happened to her throat. The words wouldn't come out.

"That's what you've been telling me. I don't think you need trouble to say it again."

"When do I have to come back?"

"I don't think you need come back unless you decide that there's something you want to tell me. In that well-known phrase, you were asked to help the police. You have helped the police. Thank you."

She had won. She was free. She was safe, and with Miss Leaming dead, that safety depended only on herself. She needn't come back again to this horrible place. The relief, so unexpected and so unbelievable, was too great to be borne. Cordelia burst into dramatic and uncontrollable crying. She was aware of Sergeant Mannering's low exclamation of concern and of a folded white handkerchief handed to her by the Superintendent. She buried her face in the clean, laundry-smelling linen and blurted out her pent-up misery and anger. Strangely enough—and the oddness of it struck her even in the middle of her anguish—her misery was centred on Bernie. Lifting a face disfigured with tears and no longer caring what he thought of her, she blurted out a final, irrational protest:

"And after you'd sacked him, you never enquired how he got on. You didn't even come to the funeral!"

He had brought a chair over and had seated himself beside her. He handed her a glass of water. The glass was very cold but comforting and she was surprised to find how thirsty she was. She sipped the cold water and sat there hiccuping gently. The hiccups made her want to laugh hysterically but she controlled herself. After a few minutes he said gently:

"I'm sorry about your friend. I didn't realize that your partner was the Bernie Pryde who once worked with me. It's rather worse than that, actually. I'd forgotten all about him. If it's any consolation to you, this case might have ended rather differently if I hadn't."

"You sacked him. All he ever wanted was to be a detective and you wouldn't give him a chance."

"The Metropolitan Police hiring and firing regulations aren't quite as simple as that. But it's true that he might still have been a policeman if it hadn't been for me. But he wouldn't have been a detective."

"He wasn't that bad."

"Well, he was, you know. But I'm beginning to wonder if I didn't underrate him."

Cordelia turned to hand him back the glass and met his eyes. They smiled at each other. She wished that Bernie could have heard him.

Half an hour later Dalgliesh was seated opposite the Assistant Commissioner in the latter's office. The two men disliked each other but only one of them knew this and he was the one to whom it didn't matter. Dalgliesh made his report, concisely, logically, without referring to his notes. This was his invariable habit. The A.C. had always thought it unorthodox and conceited and he did so now. Dalgliesh ended:

"As you can imagine, sir, I'm not proposing to commit all that to paper. There's no real evidence and as Bernie Pryde used to tell us, hunch is a good servant but a poor master. God, how that man could churn out his horrible platitudes! He wasn't unintelligent, not totally without judgment, but everything, including ideas, came apart in his hands. He had a mind like a police notebook. Do you remember the Clandon case, homicide by shooting? It was in 1954 I think."

"Ought I to?"

"No. But it would have been helpful if I had."

"I don't really know what you're talking about, Adam. But if I understand you aright, you suspect that Ronald Callender killed his son. Ronald Callender is dead. You suspect that Chris Lunn tried to murder Cordelia Gray. Lunn is dead. You suggest that Elizabeth Leaming killed Ronald Callender. Elizabeth Leaming is dead."

"Yes, it's all conveniently tidy."

"I suggest we leave it that way. The Commissioner incidentally has had a telephone call from Dr. Hugh Tilling, the psychiatrist. He's outraged because his son and daughter have been questioned about Mark Callender's death. I'm prepared to explain his civil duties to Dr. Tilling, he's already well aware of his rights, if you really feel it necessary. But will anything be gained by seeing the two Tillings again?"

"I don't think so."

"Or by bothering the Sureté about that French girl who Miss Markland claims visited him at the cottage?"

"I think we can spare ourselves that embarrassment. There's only one person now alive who knows the truth of these crimes and she's proof against any interrogation we can use. I can comfort myself with the reason. With most suspects we have an invaluable ally lurking at the back of their minds to betray them. But whatever lies she's been telling, she's absolutely without guilt."

"Do you think that she's deluded herself that it's all true?"

"I don't think that young woman deludes herself about anything. I took to her, but I'm glad I shan't be encountering her again. I dislike being made to feel during a perfectly ordinary interrogation that I'm corrupting the young."

"So we can tell the Minister that his chum died by his own hand?"

"You can tell him that we are satisfied that no living finger pressed that trigger. But perhaps not. Even he might be capable of reasoning that one out. Tell him that he can safely accept the verdict of the inquest."

"It would have saved a great deal of public time if he'd accepted it in the first place."

The two men were silent for a moment. Then Dalgliesh said:

"Cordelia Gray was right. I ought to have enquired what happened to Bernie Pryde."

"You couldn't be expected to. That wasn't part of your duties."

"Of course not. But then one's more serious neglects seldom are part of one's duty. And I find it ironic and oddly satisfying that Pryde took his revenge. Whatever mischief that child was up to in Cambridge, she was working under his direction."

"You're becoming more philosophical, Adam."

"Only less obsessive, or perhaps merely older. It's good to be able to feel occasionally that there are some cases which are better left unsolved."

The Kingly Street building looked the same, smelt the same. It always would. But there was one difference. Outside the office a man was waiting, a middle-aged man in a tight blue suit, pig eyes sharp as flint among the fleshy folds of the face.

"Miss Gray? I'd nearly given you up. My name's Fielding. I saw your plate and just came up by chance, don't you know."

His eyes were avaricious, prurient.

"Well now, you're not quite what I expected, not the usual kind of Private Eye."

"Is there anything I can do for you, Mr. Fielding?"

He gazed furtively round the landing, seeming to find its sordidness reassuring.

"It's my lady friend. I've reason to suspect that she's getting a bit on the side. Well—a man likes to know where he stands. You get me?"

Cordelia fitted the key into the lock.

"I understand, Mr. Fielding. Won't you come in?"

The Black Tower

P. D. JAMES

CHARLES SCRIBNER'S SONS • NEW YORK

Copyright © 1975 P.D. James

Copyright under the Berne Convention

All rights reserved. No part of this book
may be reproduced in any form without the
permission of Charles Scribner's Sons.

1 3 5 7 9 11 13 15 17 19 C/C 20 18 16 14 12 10 8 6 4 2

Printed in the United States of America
Library of Congress Catalog Card Number 75-15120
ISBN 0-684-142635

Contents

Note

Lovers of Dorset will, I hope, forgive me for the liberties I have taken with the topography of their beautiful county and in particular for my temerity in erecting my twin follies of Toynton Grange and the black tower on the Purbeck coast. They will learn with relief that, although the scenery is borrowed, the characters are completely my own and bear no resemblance to any person living or dead.

1

Sentence of Life

It was to be the consultant physician's last visit and Dalgliesh suspected that neither of them regretted it, arrogance and patronage on one side and weakness, gratitude and dependence on the other being no foundation for a satisfactory adult relationship however transitory. He came into Dalgliesh's small hospital room preceded by Sister, attended by his acolytes, already dressed for the fashionable wedding which he was to grace as a guest later that morning. He could have been the bridegroom except that he sported a red rose instead of the customary carnation. Both he and the flower looked as if they had been brought and burnished to a peak of artificial perfection, gift wrapped in invisible foil, and immune to the chance winds, frosts and ungentle fingers which could mar more vulnerable perfections. As a final touch, he and the flower had both been lightly sprayed with an expensive scent, presumably an aftershave lotion. Dalgliesh could detect it above the hospital smell of cabbage and ether to which his nose had become so inured during the past weeks that it now hardly registered on the senses. The attendant medical students grouped themselves round the bed. With their long hair and short white coats they looked like a gaggle of slightly disreputable bridesmaids.

Dalgliesh was stripped by Sister's skilled impersonal hands for yet another examination. The stethoscope moved, a cold disc, over his chest and back. This last examination was a formality but the physician was, as always, thorough; nothing he did was perfunctory. If, on this occasion, his original diagnosis had been wrong his self-esteem was too secure for him to feel the need for more than a token excuse. He straightened up and said:

"We've had the most recent path. report and I think we can be certain now that we've got it right. The cytology was always obscure, of course, and the diagnosis was complicated by the pneumonia. But it isn't acute leukaemia, it isn't any type of leukaemia. What you're recovering from—happily—is an atypical mononucleosis. I congratulate you, Commander. You had us worried."

"I had you interested; you had me worried. When can I leave here?"

The great man laughed and smiled at his retinue, inviting them to share his indulgence at yet one more example of the ingratitude of convalescence. Dalgliesh said quickly:

"I expect you'll be wanting the bed."

"We always want more beds than we can get. But there's no great hurry. You've a long way to go yet. Still, we'll see. We'll see."

When they had left him he lay flat on his back and let his eyes range round the two cubic feet of anaesthetized space, as if seeing the room for the first time. The wash basin with its elbow-operated taps; the neat functional bedside table with its covered water jug; the two vinyl-covered visitors' chairs; the earphones curled above his head; the window curtains with their inoffensive flowered pattern, the lowest denominator of taste. They were the last objects he had expected to see in life. It had seemed a meagre, impersonal place in which to die. Like a hotel room, it was designed for transients. Whether its occupants left on their own feet or sheeted on a mortuary trolley, they left nothing behind them, not even the memory of their fear, suffering and hope.

The sentence of death had been communicated, as he suspected such sentences usually were, by grave looks, a certain false heartiness, whispered consultations, a superfluity of clinical tests, and, until he had insisted, a reluctance to pronounce a diagnosis or prognosis. The sentence of life, pronounced with less sophistry when the worst days of his illness were over, had certainly produced the greater outrage. It was, he had thought, uncommonly inconsiderate if not negligent of his doctors to reconcile him so thoroughly to death and then change their minds. It was embarrassing now to recall with what little regret he had let slip his pleasures and preoccupations, the imminence of loss revealing them for what they were, at best only a solace, at worst a trivial squandering of time and energy. Now he had to lay hold of them again and believe that they were important, at least to himself.

He doubted whether he would ever again believe them important to other people. No doubt, with returning strength, all that would look after itself. The physical life would re-assert itself given time. He would reconcile himself to living since there was no alternative and, this perverse fit of resentment and accidie conveniently put down to weakness, would come to believe that he had had a lucky escape. His colleagues, relieved of embarrassment, would congratulate him. Now that death had replaced sex as the great unmentionable it had acquired its own pudency; to die when you had not yet become a nuisance and before your friends could reasonably raise the ritual chant of "happy release" was in the worst of taste.

But, at present, he wasn't sure that he could reconcile himself to his job. Resigned as he had become to the role of spectator—and soon not even to be that—he felt ill-equipped to return to the noisy playground of the world and, if it had to be, was minded to find for himself a less violent corner of it. It wasn't something he had thought about deeply during his periods of consciousness; there hadn't been time. It was more a conviction than a decision. The time had come to change direction. Judges' Rules, rigor mortis, interrogation, the contemplation of decomposing flesh and smashed bone, the whole bloody business of manhunting, he was finished with it. There were other things to do with his time. He wasn't yet sure which things but he would find them. He had over two weeks of convalescence ahead, time to formulate decision, rationalize it, justify it to himself and, more difficult, find the words with which he would attempt to justify it to the Commissioner. It was a bad time to leave the Yard. They would see it as desertion. But then, it would always be a bad time.

He wasn't sure whether this disenchantment with his job was caused solely by his illness, the salutory reminder of inevitable death, or whether it was the symptom of a more fundamental malaise, that latitude in middle-life of alternate doldrums and uncertain winds when one realizes that hopes deferred are no longer realizable, that ports not visited will now never be seen, that this journey and others before it may have been a mistake, that one has no longer even confidence in charts and compass. More than his job now seemed to him trivial and unsatisfactory. Lying sleepless as so many patients must have done before him in that bleak impersonal room, watching the headlamps of passing cars sweep across the ceiling, listening to the secretive and muted noises of the hospital's nocturnal life, he took the dispiriting inventory of his life. His grief for his dead wife, so genuine, so heartbreaking at the time—how conveniently personal tragedy had excused him from further emotional involvement. His love affairs, like the one which at present spasmodically occupied a little of his time and somewhat more of his energy, had been detached, civilized, agreeable, undemanding. It was understood that his time was never completely his own but that his heart most certainly was. The women were liberated. They had interesting jobs, agreeable flats, they were adept at settling for what they could get. Certainly they were liberated from the messy, clogging, disruptive emotions which embroiled other female lives. What, he wondered, had those carefully spaced encounters, both participants groomed for pleasure like a couple of sleek cats, to do with love, with untidy bedrooms, unwashed dishes, babies' nappies, the warm, close, claustrophobic life of marriage and commitment. His bereavement, his job, his poetry, all had been used to justify self-sufficiency. His women had been more amenable to the claims of his poetry than of his dead wife. They had small regard for sentiment, but an exaggerated respect for art. And the worst of it—or perhaps the best—was that he couldn't now change even if he wanted and that none of it mattered. It was absolutely of no importance. In the last fifteen years he hadn't deliberately hurt a single human being. It struck him now that nothing more damning could be said about anyone.

Well, if none of that could be changed, his job could. But first there was one personal commitment to fulfil, one from which perversely he had been relieved that death would so conveniently excuse him. It wasn't going to excuse him now. Propping himself on his elbow he reached out and took Father Baddeley's letter from his locker drawer and read it carefully for the first time. The old man must be nearly eighty now; he hadn't been young when, thirty years ago, he had first come to the Norfolk village as curate to Dalgliesh's father, timid, ineffective, maddeningly inefficient, muddled in everything but the essentials, but never less than his uncompromising self. This was only the third letter which Dalgliesh had received from him. It was dated 11th September and was addressed from;

My dear Adam,

I know that you must be very busy but I would very much welcome a visit from you as there is a matter on which I would be glad of your professional advice. It isn't really urgent, except that my heart seems to be wearing out before the rest of me so that I ought not to rest too confidently on the thought of tomorrow. I am here every day, but perhaps a weekend would suit you best. I ought to tell you so that you will know what to expect, that I am Chaplain to Toynton Grange, a private home for the young disabled, and that I live here in Hope Cottage on the estate through the kindness of the Warden, Wilfred Anstey. Usually I eat my midday and evening meal at the Grange but this may not be agreeable to you and it would, of course, lessen our time together. So I shall take the opportunity of my next visit to Wareham to lay in a store of provisions. I have a small spare room in to which I can move so that there will be a room for you here.

Could you send me a card to let me know when you will arrive? I have no car but if you come by train William Deakin, who has a car hire service about five minutes from the station (the station staff will direct you), is very reliable and not expensive. The buses from Wareham are infrequent and don't come beyond Toynton Village. There is then a mile and a half to walk which is quite pleasant if the weather is good but which you may wish to avoid at the end of a long journey. If not, I have drawn a map on the back of this letter.

The map could be guaranteed to confuse anyone accustomed to depend on the orthodox publications of the National Survey rather than on early seventeenth-century charts. The wavy lines presumably represented the sea. Dalgliesh felt the omission of a spouting whale. The Toynton bus station was clearly marked, but the tremulous line thereafter meandered uncertainly past a diversity of fields, gates, pubs and copses of triangular, serrated firs, sometimes retreating upon itself as Father Baddeley realized that metaphorically he had lost his way. One tiny phallic symbol on the coast, and seemingly included as a landmark, since it was nowhere near the marked path, bore the legend "the black tower".

The map affected Dalgliesh much as a child's first drawing might affect an indulgent father. He wondered to what depth of weakness and apathy he must have sunk to reject its appeal. He fumbled in the drawer for a postcard and wrote briefly that he would arrive by car early in the afternoon of Monday 1st October. That should give him plenty of time to get out of hospital and return to his Queenhythe flat for the first few days of convalescence. He signed the card with his initials only, stamped it for first-class delivery and propped it against his water jug so that he shouldn't forget to ask one of the nurses to post it.

There was one other small obligation and one he felt less competent to handle. But it could wait. He must see or write to Cordelia Gray and thank her for her flowers. He didn't know how she discovered that he was ill except perhaps through police friends. Running Bernie Pryde's Detective Agency—if it hadn't by now collapsed as it should have done by all the laws of justice and economics—probably meant that she was in touch with one or two policemen. He believed too, that there had been a casual mention of his inconvenient illness in the London evening papers when they had commented on recent losses in the higher echelons of the Yard.

It had been a small, carefully arranged, personally picked bouquet, as individual as Cordelia herself, a charming contrast to his other offerings of hothouse roses, over-large chrysanthemums shaggy as dust mops, forced spring flowers and artificial-looking gladioli, pink plastic flowers smelling of anaesthetic rigid on their fibrous stems. She must have been recently in a country garden; he wondered where. He wondered too, illogically, whether she was getting enough to eat, but immediately put this ridiculous thought from him. There had, he remembered clearly, been silver discs of honesty, three sprigs of winter heather, four rosebuds, not the starved tight buds of winter but furls of orange and yellow, gentle as the first buds of summer, delicate sprigs of outdoor chrysanthemums, orange-red berries, one bright dahlia like a jewel in the centre, the whole bouquet surrounded by the grey furry leaves he remembered from his childhood as rabbits' ears. It had been a touching, very young gesture, one he knew that an older or more sophisticated woman would never have made. It had arrived with only a brief note to say that she had heard of his illness and had sent the flowers to wish him well again. He must see or write to her and thank her personally. The telephone call which one of the nurses had made on his behalf to the Agency was not enough.

But that, and other more fundamental decisions, could wait. First he must see Father Baddeley. The obligation was not merely pious or even filial. He discovered that, despite certain foreseen difficulties and embarrassments, he was looking forward to seeing the old priest again. He had no intention of letting Father Baddeley, however unwittingly, entice him back to his job. If this were really police work, which he doubted, then the Dorset Constabulary could take it over. And, if this pleasant early autumn sunshine continued unbroken, Dorset would be as agreeable a place as any in which to convalesce.

But the stark oblong of white, propped against his water jug, was oddly intrusive. He felt his eyes constantly drawn towards it as if it were a potent symbol, a written sentence of life. He was glad when the staff nurse came in to say that she was now going off duty, and took it away to post.

2

Death of a Priest

I

Eleven days later, still weak and with his hospital pallor but euphoric with the deceptive well-being of convalescence, Dalgliesh left his flat high above the Thames at Queenhythe just before the first light and drove south-west out of London. He had finally and reluctantly parted with his ancient Cooper Bristol two months before the onset of his illness and was now driving a Jensen Healey. He was glad that the car had been run in and that he was already almost reconciled to the change. To embark symbolically on a new life with a totally new car would have been irritatingly banal. He put his one case and a few picnic essentials including a corkscrew in the boot and, in the pocket, a copy of Hardy's poems, *The Return of the Native* and Newman and Pevsner's guide to the buildings of Dorset. This was to be a convalescent's holiday: familiar books; a brief visit to an old friend to provide an object for the journey; a route left to each day's whim and including country both familiar and new; even the salutary irritant of a personal problem to justify solitude and self-indulgent idleness. He was disconcerted when, taking his final look round the flat, he found his hand reaching for his scene-of-crime kit. He couldn't remember when last he had travelled without it, even on holiday. But now to leave it behind was the first confirmation of a decision which he would dutifully ponder from time to time during the next fortnight but which he knew in his heart was already made.

He reached Winchester in time for late breakfast at a hotel in the shadow of the Cathedral, then spent the next two hours rediscovering the city before finally driving into Dorset via Wimborne Minster. Now he sensed in himself a reluctance to reach journey's end. He meandered gently, almost aimlessly, north-west to Blandford Forum, bought there a bottle of wine, buttered rolls, cheese and fruit for his lunch and a couple of bottles of Amontillado for Father Baddeley, then wandered south-east through the Winterbourne villages through Wareham to Corfe Castle.

The magnificent stones, symbols of courage, cruelty and betrayal, stood sentinel at the one cleft in the ridge of the Purbeck Hills as they had for a thousand years. As he ate his solitary picnic, Dalgliesh found his eyes constantly drawn to those stark embattled slabs of mutilated ashlar silhouetted high against the gentle sky. As though reluctant to drive under their shadow and unwilling to end the solitude of this peaceful undemanding day he spent some time searching unsuccessfully for marsh gentians in the swampy scrubland before setting off on the last five miles of his journey.

Toynton Village; a thread of terraced cottages, their undulating grey stone roofs glittering in the afternoon sun; a not too picturesque pub at the village end; the glimpse of an uninteresting church tower. Now the road, bordered with a low stone wall, rose gently between sparse plantations of fir and he began to recognize the landmarks on Father Baddeley's map. Soon the road would branch, one narrow route turning westward to skirt the headland, the other leading through a barrier gate to Toynton Grange and the sea. And here, predictably, it was, a heavy iron gate set into a wall of flat, uncemented stones. The wall was up to three feet thick, the stones intricately and skilfully fitted together, bound with lichen and moss and crowned with waving grasses, and it formed a barrier as old and permanent as the headland from which it seemed to have grown. On each side of the gate was a notice painted on board. The one on the left was the newer; it read:

OF YOUR CHARITY PLEASE RESPECT OUR PRIVACY

The one on the right was more didactic, the lettering faded but more professional.

KEEP OUT
THIS LAND IS STRICTLY PRIVATE
DANGEROUS CLIFFS NO ACCESS TO BEACH
CARS AND CARAVANS PARKED HERE WILL BE MOVED

Under the notice was fixed a large postbox.

Dalgliesh thought that any motorist unmoved by this nicely judged mixture of appeal, warning and threats would hesitate before risking his car springs. The track deteriorated sharply beyond the gate and the contrast between the comparative smoothness of the approach road and the boulder edged and stony way ahead was an almost symbolic deterrent. The gate, too, although unlocked, had a heavy latch of intricate design, the manipulation of which gave an intruder ample time in which to repent of his rashness. In his still weakened state, Dalgliesh swung back the gate with some difficulty. When he had driven through and finally closed it behind him it was with a sense of having committed himself to an enterprise as yet imperfectly understood and probably unwise. The problem would probably be embarrassingly unrelated to any of his skills, something that only an unworldly old man—and he perhaps getting senile—could have imagined that a police officer could solve. But at least he had an immediate objective. He was moving, even if reluctantly, back into a world in which human beings had problems, worked, loved, hated, schemed for happiness, and since the job he had determined to relinquish would go on despite his defection, killed and were killed.

Before he turned again to the car his eye was caught by a small clump of unknown flowers. The pale pinkish white heads rose from a mossy pad on top of the wall and trembled delicately in the light breeze. Dalgliesh walked over and stood stock still, regarding in silence their unpretentious beauty. He smelt for the first time the clean half-illusory salt tang of the sea. The air moved warm and gentle against his skin. He was suddenly suffused with happiness and, as always in these rare transitory moments, intrigued by the purely physical nature of his joy. It moved along his veins, a gentle effervescence. Even to analyse its nature was to lose hold of it. But he recognized it for what it was, the first clear intimation since his illness that life could be good.

The car bumped gently over the rising track. When some two hundred yards further on he came to the summit of the rise he expected to see the English Channel spread blue and wrinkled before him to the far horizon and experienced all the remembered disappointment of childhood holidays when after so many false hopes, the eagerly awaited sea still wasn't in sight. Before him was a shallow rock-strewn valley, criss-crossed with rough paths, and to his right what was obviously Toynton Grange.

It was a powerfully built square stone house dating, he guessed, from the first half of the eighteenth century. But the owner had been unlucky in his architect. The house was an aberration, unworthy of the name of Georgian. It faced inland, north-east he estimated, thus offending against some personal and obscure canon of architectural taste which, to Dalgliesh, decreed that a house on the coast should face the sea. There were two rows of windows above the porch, the main ones with gigantic keystones, the row above unadorned and mean in size as if there had been difficulty in fitting them beneath the most remarkable feature of the house, a huge Ionic pediment topped by a statue, a clumsy and, at this distance, unidentifiable lump of stone. In the centre was one round window, a sinister cyclops eye glinting in the sun. The pediment debased the insignificant porch and gave a lowering and cumbersome appearance to the whole façade. Dalgliesh thought that the design would have been more successful if the façade had been balanced by extended bays, but either inspiration or money had run out and the house looked curiously unfinished. There was no sign of life behind the intimidating frontage. Perhaps the inmates—if that was the right word for them—lived at the back. And it was only just three-thirty, the dead part of the day as he remembered from hospital. Probably they were all resting.

He could see three cottages, a pair about a hundred yards from the Grange and a third standing alone higher on the foreland. He thought there was a fourth roof just visible to seaward, but couldn't be sure. It might be only an excrescence of rock. Not knowing which was Hope Cottage it seemed sensible to make first for the nearer pair. He had briefly turned off his car engine while deciding what next to do and now, for the first time, he heard the sea, that gentle continuous rhythmic grunt which is one of the most nostalgic and evocative of sounds. There was still no sign that his approach was observed; the headland was silent, birdless. He sensed something strange and almost sinister in its emptiness and loneliness which even the mellow afternoon sunlight couldn't dispel.

His arrival at the cottages produced no face at the window, no cassock-clad figure framed in the front porch. They were a pair of old, limestone single-storeyed buildings, whose heavy stone roofs, typical of Dorset, were patterned with bright cushions of emerald moss. Hope Cottage was on the right, Faith Cottage on the left, the names comparatively recently painted. The third more distant cottage was presumably Charity, but he doubted whether Father Baddeley had had any hand in this eponymous naming. He didn't need to read the name on the gate to know which cottage housed Father Baddeley. It was impossible to associate his remembered almost total uninterest in his surroundings with those chintzy curtains, that hanging basket of trailing ivy and fuchsia over the door of Faith Cottage or the two brightly painted yellow tubs still garish with summer flowers which had been artfully placed one each side of the porch. Two mushrooms, looking mass-produced in concrete, stood each side of the gate seeming so cosily suburban that Dalgliesh was surprised that they weren't crowned with squatting gnomes. Hope Cottage, in contrast, was starkly austere. There was a solid oak bench in front of the window serving as a seat in the sun, and a conglomeration of sticks and an old umbrella littered the front porch. The curtains, apparently of some heavy material in a dull red, were drawn across the windows.

No one answered to his knock. He had expected no one. Both cottages were obviously empty. There was a simple latch on the door and no lock. After a second's pause he lifted it and stepped into the gloom inside to be met with a smell, warm, bookish, a little musty, which immediately took him back thirty years. He drew back the curtains and light streamed into the cottage. And now his eyes recognized familiar objects: the round single-pedestal rosewood table, dull with dust, set in the middle of the room; the roll-top desk against one wall; the highbacked and winged armchair, so old now that the stuffing was pushing through the frayed cover and the dented seat was worn down to the wood. Surely it couldn't be the same chair? This stab of memory must be a nostalgic delusion. But there was another object, equally familiar, equally old. Behind the door hung Father Baddeley's black cloak with, above it, the battered and limp beret.

It was the sight of the cloak that first alerted Dalgliesh to the possibility that something was wrong. It was odd that his host wasn't here to greet him, but he could think of a number of explanations. His postcard might have gone astray, there might have been an urgent call to the Grange, Father Baddeley might have gone into Wareham to shop and missed the return bus. It was even possible that he had completely forgotten the expected arrival of his guest. But if he were out, why wasn't he wearing his cloak? It was impossible to think of him in summer or winter wearing any other garment.

It was then that Dalgliesh noticed what his eye must have already seen but disregarded, the little stack of service sheets on top of the bureau printed with a black cross. He took the top one over to the window as if hoping that a clearer light would show him mistaken. But there was, of course, no mistake. He read:

Michael Francis Baddeley, Priest
Born 29th October 1896 Died 21st September 1974
R.I.P. Buried at St. Michael & All Angels,
Toynton, Dorset
26th September 1974

He had been dead eleven days and buried five. But he would have known that Father Baddeley had died recently. How else could one account for that sense of his personality still lingering in the cottage, the feeling that he was so close that one strong call could bring his hand to the latch? Looking at the familiar faded cloak with its heavy clasp—had the old man really not changed it in thirty years?—he felt a pang of regret, of grief even, which surprised him by its intensity. An old man was dead. It must have been a natural death; they had buried him quickly enough. His death and burial had been unpublicized. But there had been something on his mind and he had died without confiding it. It was suddenly very important that he should be reassured that Father Baddeley had received his postcard, that he hadn't died believing that his call for help had gone unregarded.

The obvious place to look was in the early Victorian bureau which had belonged to Father Baddeley's mother. Father Baddeley, he remembered, had kept this locked. He had been the least secretive of men, but any priest had to have at least one drawer or desk private from the prying eyes of cleaning women or overcurious parishioners. Dalgliesh could remember Father Baddeley fumbling in the deep pockets of his cloak for the small antique key, secured by string to an old-fashioned clothes peg for easier handling and identification, which opened the lock. It was probably in one of the cloak pockets still.

He dug his hand into both pockets with a guilty feeling of raiding the dead. The key wasn't there. He went over to the bureau and tried the lid. It opened easily. Bending down he examined the lock, then fetched his torch from the car and looked again. The signs were unmistakable: the lock had been forced. It had been quite a neat job and one requiring little strength. The lock was decorative but unsubstantial, intended as a defence against the idly curious but not against determined assault. A chisel or knife, probably the blade of a penknife, had been forced between the desk and the lid and used to pry the lock apart. It had done surprisingly little damage, but the scratch marks and the broken lock itself told their story.

But not who had been responsible. It could have been Father Baddeley himself. If he had lost the key there would have been no chance of replacing it, and how in this remote spot would he have found a locksmith? A physical assault on the desk lid was an unlikely expedient for the man, Dalgliesh remembered; but it wasn't impossible. Or it might have been done after Father Baddeley's death. If the key couldn't be found, someone at Toynton Grange would have had to break open the lock. There might have been documents or papers which they needed; a health insurance card; names of friends to be notified; a will. He shook himself free from conjecture, irritated to find that he had actually considered putting on his gloves before looking further, and made a rapid examination of the contents of the desk drawers.

There was nothing of interest there. Father Baddeley's concern with the world had apparently been minimal. But one thing immediately recognizable caught his eye. It was a neatly stacked row of quarto-size child's exercise books bound in pale green. These, he knew, contained Father Baddeley's diary. So the same books were still being sold, the ubiquitous pale green exercise books, the back cover printed with arithmetical tables, as evocative of primary school as an ink-stained ruler or india rubber. Father Baddeley had always used these books for his diary, one book for each quarter of the year. Now, with the old black cloak hanging limply on the door, its musty ecclesiastical smell in his nose, Dalgliesh recalled the conversation as clearly as if he were still that ten-year-old boy and Father Baddeley, middle-aged then but already seeming ageless, sitting here at his desk.

"It's just an ordinary diary then, Father? It isn't about your spiritual life?"

"This is the spiritual life; the ordinary things one does from hour to hour."

Adam had asked with the egotism of the young.

"Only what you do? Aren't I in it?"

"No. Just what I do. Do you remember what time the Mothers' Union met this afternoon? It was your mother's drawing-room this week. The time was different, I think."

"It was 2.45 p.m. instead of 3.0 p.m., Father. The Archdeacon wanted to get away early. But do you have to be accurate?"

Father Baddeley had seemed to ponder this question, briefly but seriously as if it were new to him and unexpectedly interesting.

"Oh, yes, I think so. I think so. Otherwise it would lose its point."

The young Dalgliesh, to whom the point was already lost beyond ken, had wandered away to pursue his own more interesting and immediate concerns. The spiritual life. It was a phrase he had often heard on the lips of his father's more ultra mundane parishioners although never on the Canon's own. He had occasionally tried to visualize this mysterious other existence. Was it lived at the same time as the ordinary regulated life of getting up, meal times, school, holidays; or was it an existence on some other plane to which he and the uninitiated had no access but into which Father Baddeley could retreat at will? Either way it had surely little to do with this careful recording of daily trivia.

He picked up the last book and looked through it. Father Baddeley's system had not been changed. It was all here, two days to the page, neatly ruled off. The times at which he had daily said morning prayer and evensong; where he had walked and how long it had taken; the monthly trip by bus into Dorchester; the weekly trip to Wareham; his hours spent helping at Toynton Grange; odd treats baldly recorded; the methodical account of how he had disposed of every hour of his working day year after unremarkable year, documented with the meticulousness of a book-keeper. "But this is the spiritual life; the ordinary things that one does from day to day." Surely it couldn't be as simple as that?

But where was the current diary, the book for the third quarter of 1974? It had been Father Baddeley's habit to keep old copies of his diary covering the last three years. There should have been fifteen books here; there were only fourteen. The diary stopped at the end of June 1974. Dalgliesh found himself searching almost feverishly through the desk drawers. The diary wasn't there. But he did find something. Pushed beneath three receipted bills for coal, paraffin and electricity was a sheet of cheap rather thin paper with Toynton Grange printed inexpertly and lopsidedly at the top. Underneath someone had typed:

"Why don't you get out of the cottage you silly old hypocrite and let someone have it who would really be some use here? Don't think we don't know what you and Grace Willison get up to when you're supposed to be hearing her confession. Don't you wish you could really do it? And what about that choir boy? Don't think we don't know."

Dalgliesh's first reaction was to be more irritated by the note's silliness than angered by its malice. It was a childish piece of gratuitous spite but without even the dubious merit of verisimilitude. Poor old seventy-seven-year-old Father Baddeley, accused simultaneously of fornication, sodomy and impotence! Could any reasonable man have taken this puerile nonsense seriously enough even to be hurt by it? Dalgliesh had seen plenty of poison pen letters in his professional life. This was a comparatively mild effort; he could almost suppose that the writer's heart hadn't been in it. "Don't you wish you could really do it?" Most poison pen writers could find a more graphic description of that implied activity. And the belated reference to the choir boy, no name, no date. That hadn't been dredged from any real knowledge. Could Father Baddeley really have been concerned enough to have sent for a professional detective and one he hadn't seen for nearly thirty years just to advise on or investigate this petty nastiness? Perhaps. This might not be the only letter. If the trouble were endemic at Toynton Grange, then it was more serious. A poison pen at work in a closed community could cause real trouble and distress, occasionally he or she could literally be a killer. If Father Baddeley suspected that others had received similar letters he might well have looked around for professional help. Or, and this was more interesting, had someone intended Dalgliesh to believe precisely that? Had the note been deliberately planted for him to find? It was odd, surely, that no one had discovered and destroyed it after Father Baddeley's death. Someone from Toynton Grange must have looked through his papers. This was hardly a note one would leave for others to read.

He folded it away in his wallet and began to wander around the cottage. Father Baddeley's bedroom was much as he had expected. A mean window with a dingy cretonne curtain, a single bed still made-up with sheets and blankets but with the counterpane pulled taut over the single lumpy pillow; books lining two walls; a small bedside table with a shoddy lamp; a Bible; a cumbersome and gaudily decorated china ashtray bearing an advertisement for beer. Father Baddeley's pipe still rested in its bowl and beside it Dalgliesh saw a half-used booklet of cardboard matches, the kind given away in restaurants and bars. This bore an advertisement for Ye Olde Tudor Barn near Wareham. One single used match was in the ashtray; it had been shredded down to the burnt-out tip. Dalgliesh smiled. So this small personal habit, too, had survived over thirty years. He could recall Father Baddeley's small squirrel-like fingers delicately shredding the sliver of thin cardboard as if attempting to beat some previous personal record. Dalgliesh picked up the match and smiled; six segments. Father Baddeley had excelled himself.

He wandered into the kitchen. It was small, ill-equipped, neat but not very clean. The small gas stove of old-fashioned design looked as if it would soon qualify for a folk museum. The sink under the window was of stone fitted on one side with a scarred and discoloured wooden draining board smelling of stale fat and sour soap. The faded cretonne curtains faintly patterned with overblown roses and daffodils unseasonably intertwined were pulled back to show an inland view of the far Purbeck hills. Clouds tenuous as smoke puffs were drifting and dissolving in the limitless blue sky and the sheep lay like white slugs on their distant pasture.

He explored the pantry. Here at least was evidence that he was expected. Father Baddeley had indeed bought extra food and the tins were a dispiriting reminder of what for him had constituted an adequate diet. Pathetically, he had obviously provided for two, one of whom he confidently expected to have a larger appetite. There was one large tin and one small of many of the staple provisions: baked beans, tuna fish, Irish stew, spaghetti, rice pudding.

Dalgliesh went back to the sitting-room. He was aware of weariness, that the journey had tired him more than he had expected. He saw by the heavy oak clock over the fireplace still ticking solidly on, that it was still not four o'clock, but his body protested that this had already been a long hard day. He craved tea. There had been a caddy of tea in the pantry but no milk. He wondered whether the gas was still on.

It was then that he heard the footfall at the door, the clank of the latch. There was a woman's figure framed against the afternoon light. He heard a gravelly deep but very feminine voice with a trace, no more, of an Irish accent.

"For God's sake! A human being and a male at that. What are you doing here?"

She came into the room leaving the door open behind her and he saw her clearly. She was about thirty-five, he guessed, sturdy, long-legged, her mane of yellow hair, visibly darker at the roots, worn in a long sweep to her shoulders. Her eyes were full-lidded and narrow in the square face, her mouth wide. She was wearing brown ill-fitting slacks with a strap under the foot, dirty, grass-stained white plimsoles and a sleeveless white cotton top, low-necked, which showed a brown and mottled triangle of sunburn. She wore no brassiere and the full, heavy breasts swung loose under the thin cotton. Three wooden bangles clanked on her left forearm. The total impression was of a raffish but not unattractive sexuality, so strong that, although she wore no scent, she brought into the room her own female and individual smell.

He said: "My name's Adam Dalgliesh. I came here intending to visit Father Baddeley. It seems that it won't now be possible."

"Well, that's one way of putting it. You're exactly eleven days late. Eleven days too late to see him and five days too late to bury him. Who are you, a chum? We didn't know that he had any. But then, there were quite a number of things we didn't know about our Reverend Michael. He was a secretive little man. He certainly kept you hidden."

"We hadn't met except briefly since I was a boy and I only wrote to tell him I was coming the day before he died."

"Adam. I like that. They call a lot of kids that nowadays. It's getting trendy again. But you must have found it a bit of a drag when you were at school. Still, it suits you. I can't think why. You aren't exactly of the earth, earthy are you? I know about you now. You've come to collect the books."

"Have I?"

"The ones Michael left you in his will. To Adam Dalgliesh, only son of the late Canon Alexander Dalgliesh, all my books to keep or dispose of as he sees fit. I remember it exactly because I thought the names were so unusual. You haven't lost much time, have you?

I'm surprised that the solicitors have even got round to writing to you. Bob Loder isn't usually that efficient. But I shouldn't get too excited if I were you. They never looked particularly valuable to me. A lot of dry old theological tomes. By the way, you weren't expecting to be left any of his money were you? If so, I've got news for you."

"I didn't know that Father Baddeley had any money."

"Nor did we. That was another of his little secrets. He left £19,000. Not a great fortune, but useful. He left it all to Wilfred for the benefit of Toynton Grange, and it came just in time from all I hear. Grace Willison is the only other legatee. She got that old bureau. At least she will get it when Wilfred bothers to have it moved."

She had settled down in the fireside chair, her hair thrown back against the headrest, both legs splayed wide. Dalgliesh pulled out one of the wheel-backed chairs and sat facing her.

"Did you know Father Baddeley well?"

"We all know each other well here, that's half our trouble. Are you thinking of staying here?"

"In the district perhaps for a day or two. But it doesn't seem possible now to stay here . . ."

"I don't see why not if you want to. The place is empty, at least until Wilfred finds another victim—tenant, I should say. I shouldn't think that he'd object. Besides you'll have to sort out the books won't you? Wilfred will want them out of the way before the next incumbent moves in."

"Wilfred Anstey owns the cottage then?"

"He owns Toynton Grange and all the cottages except Julius Court's. He's further out on the headland, the only one with a sea view. Wilfred owns all the rest of the property and he owns us."

She looked at him appraisingly.

"You haven't any useful skills, have you? I mean you're not a physiotherapist or a male nurse or a doctor, or even an accountant? Not that you look like one. Anyway, if you are I'd advise you to keep away before Wilfred decides that you're too useful to let go."

"I don't think that he'd find my particular skills of much use."

"Then I should stay on if it suits you. But I'd better put you in the picture. You might then change your mind."

Dalgliesh said:

"Start with yourself. You haven't told me who you are."

"Good God, nor have I! Sorry. I'm Maggie Hewson. My husband is resident medical officer at the Grange. At least, he lives with me in a cottage provided by Wilfred and appropriately named Charity Cottage, but he spends most of his time at Toynton Grange. With only five patients left you'd wonder what he finds to amuse him. Or would you? What do you suppose he finds to amuse him, Adam Dalgliesh?"

"Did your husband attend Father Baddeley?"

"Call him Michael, we all did except Grace Willison. Yes, Eric looked after him when he was alive and signed the death certificate when he died. He couldn't have done that six months ago, but now that they've graciously restored him to the Medical Register he can actually put his name to a piece of paper to say that you're properly and legally dead. God, what a bloody privilege."

She laughed, and fumbling in the pocket of her slacks produced a packet of cigarettes and lit one. She handed the packet to Dalgliesh. He shook his head. She shrugged her shoulders and blew a puff of smoke towards him.

Dalgliesh asked:

"What did Father Baddeley die of?"

"His heart stopped beating. No, I'm not being facetious. He was old, his heart was tired and on 21st September it stopped. Acute myocardic infarction complicated by mild diabetes, if you want the medical jargon."

"Was he alone?"

"I imagine so. He died at night, at least he was last seen alive by Grace Willison at 7.45 p.m. when he heard her confession. I suppose he died of boredom. No, I can see I shouldn't have said that. Bad taste, Maggie. She says he seemed as usual, a bit tired of course, but then he'd only been discharged from hospital that morning. I came in at nine o'clock the next day to see if he wanted anything from Wareham—I was taking the eleven o'clock bus; Wilfred doesn't allow private cars—and there he lay, dead."

"In bed?"

"No, in that chair where you're sitting now, slumped back with his mouth open and his eyes closed. He was wearing his cassock and a purple ribbon thing round his neck. All quite seemly. But very, very dead."

"So it was you who first found the body?"

"Unless Millicent from next door came pussy-footing in earlier, didn't like the look of him and tiptoed home again. She's Wilfred's widowed sister in case you're interested. Actually, it's rather odd that she didn't come in, knowing that he was ill and alone."

"It must have been a shock for you."

"Not really. I was a nurse before I married. I've seen more dead bodies than I can remember. And he was very old. It's the young ones—the kids particularly—who get you down. God, am I glad to be finished with all that messy business."

"Are you? You don't work at Toynton Grange then?"

She got up and moved over to the fireplace before replying. She blew a cloud of smoke against the looking glass over the mantelpiece then moved her face close to the glass as if studying her reflection.

"No, not when I can avoid it. And by God, do I try to avoid it. You may as well know. I am the delinquent member of the community, the non-co-operator, the drop-out, the heretic. I sow not, neither do I reap. I am impervious to the charms of dear Wilfred. I close my ears to the cries of the afflicted. I do not bend the knee at the shrine."

She turned towards him with a look half challenging, half speculative. Dalgliesh thought that the outburst had been less than spontaneous, the protest had been made before. It sounded like a ritual justification and he suspected that someone had helped her with the script. He said:

"Tell me about Wilfred Anstey."

"Didn't Michael warn you? No, I suppose he wouldn't. Well, it's an odd story but I'll try to make it short. Wilfred's great grandfather built Toynton Grange. His grandfather left it in trust jointly to Wilfred and his sister Millicent. Wilfred bought her out when he started the Home. Eight years ago Wilfred developed multiple sclerosis. It progressed very swiftly; within three months he was chairbound. Then he went on a pilgrimage to Lourdes and got himself cured. Apparently he made a bargain with God. You cure me and I'll devote Toynton Grange and all my money to serving the disabled. God obliged, and now Wilfred's busy fulfilling his part of the bargain. I suppose he's afraid to back out of the agreement in case the disease returns. I don't know that I blame him.

I'd probably feel the same myself. We're all superstitious at heart, particularly about disease."

"And is he tempted to back out?"

"Oh, I don't think so. This place gives him a sensation of power. Surrounded by grateful patients, regarded as a half-superstitious object of veneration by the women, Dot Moxon—the matron so-called—fussing round him like an old hen. Wilfred's happy enough."

Dalgliesh asked:

"When exactly did the miracle happen?"

"He claims, when they dipped him in the well. As he tells it, he experienced an initial shock of intense cold followed immediately by a tingling warmth which suffused his whole body, and a feeling of great happiness and peace. That's exactly what I get after my third whisky. If Wilfred can produce it in himself by bathing in ice cold germ-laden water, then all I can say is, he's bloody lucky. When he got back to the hospice he stood on his legs for the first time in six months. Three weeks later he was skipping around like a young ram. He never bothered to return to St. Saviour's hospital in London where he was treated, so that they could record the miraculous cure on his medical record. It would have been rather a joke if he had."

She paused as if about to say something further and then merely added:

"Touching, isn't it?"

"It's interesting. How does he find the money to fulfil his part of the bargain?"

"The patients pay according to means and some of them are sent here under contractual arrangements by local authorities. And then, of course, he's used his own capital. But things are getting pretty desperate, or so he claims. Father Baddeley's legacy came just in time. And, of course, Wilfred gets the staff on the cheap. He doesn't exactly pay Eric the rate for the job. Philby, the odd job man, is an ex-convict and probably otherwise unemployable; and the matron, Dot Moxon, wouldn't exactly find it easy to get another job after that cruelty investigation at her last hospital. She must be grateful to Wilfred for taking her on. But then, we're all terribly, terribly grateful to dear Wilfred."

Dalgliesh said:

"I suppose I'd better go up to the Grange and introduce myself. You say there are only five patients left?"

"You're not supposed to refer to them as patients, although I don't know what else Wilfred thinks you can call them. Inmates sounds too much like a prison although, God knows, its appropriate enough. But there are only five left. He's not admitting from the waiting list until he's made up his mind about the Home's future. The Ridgewell Trust's angling for it and Wilfred's considering handing the whole place over to them, lock, stock and gratis. Actually, there were six patients a fortnight or so ago, but that was before Victor Holroyd threw himself over Toynton Head and smashed himself on the rocks."

"You mean he killed himself?"

"Well, he was in his wheelchair ten feet from the cliff-edge and either he slipped the brakes and let himself be carried over or Dennis Lerner, the male nurse with him, pushed him. As Dennis hasn't the guts to kill a chicken let alone a man the general feeling is that Victor did it himself. But as that notion is distressing to dear Wilfred's feelings we're all busy pretending that it was an accident. I miss Victor, I liked him. He was about the only person here I could talk to. But the rest hated him. And now, of course, they've all got bad consciences wondering if they may have misjudged him. There's nothing like dying for putting people at a disadvantage. I mean, when a chap keeps on saying that life isn't worth living you take it that he's just stating the obvious. When he backs it up with action you begin to wonder if there wasn't more to him than you thought."

Dalgliesh was spared the need to reply by the sound of a car on the headland. Maggie, whose ears were apparently as keen as his own, sprang from her chair and ran outside. A large black saloon was approaching the junction of the paths.

"Julius," Maggie called back to him in brief explanation and began a boisterous semaphoring.

The car stopped and then turned towards Hope Cottage. Dalgliesh saw that it was a black Mercedes. As soon as it slowed down Maggie ran like an importunate schoolgirl beside it, pouring her explanation through the open window. The car stopped and Julius Court swung himself lightly out.

He was a tall, loose-limbed young man dressed in slacks and a green sweater patched army fashion on the shoulders and elbows. His light brown hair, cut short, was shaped to his head like a pale glinting helmet. It was an authoritative, confident face but with a trace of self-indulgence in the perceptible pouches under the wary eyes and the slight petulance of the small mouth set in a heavy chin. In middle age he would be heavy, even gross. But now he gave an immediate impression of slightly arrogant good looks, enhanced rather than spoilt by the white triangular scar like a colophon above his right eyebrow.

He held out his hand and said:

"Sorry you missed the funeral."

He made it sound as if Dalgliesh had missed a train. Maggie wailed:

"But darling, you don't understand! He hasn't come for the funeral. Mr. Dalgliesh didn't even know that the old man had snuffed out."

Court looked at Dalgliesh with slightly more interest.

"Oh, I'm sorry. Perhaps you'd better come up to the Grange. Wilfred Anstey will be able to tell you more about Father Baddeley than I. I was at my London flat when the old man died so I can't even provide interesting death bed revelations. Hop in both of you. I've got some books in the back for Henry Carwardine from the London Library. I may as well deliver them now."

Maggie Hewson seemed to feel that she had been remiss in not effecting a proper introduction; she said belatedly:

"Julius Court. Adam Dalgliesh. I don't suppose you've come across each other in London. Julius used to be a diplomat, or is it diplomatist?"

As they got into the car Court said easily:

"Neither is appropriate at the comparatively lowly level I reached in the service. And London is a large place. But don't worry, Maggie, like the clever lady in the TV panel game, I think I can guess what Mr. Dalgliesh does for a living."

He held open the car door with elaborate courtesy. The Mercedes moved slowly towards Toynton Grange.

II

Georgie Allan looked up from the high narrow bed in the sick bay. His mouth began to work grotesquely. The muscles of his throat stood out hard and taut. He tried to raise his head from the pillow.

"I'll be all right for the Lourdes pilgrimage won't I? You don't think I'll be left behind?"

The words came out in a hoarse, discordant wail. Helen Rainer lifted up the edge of the mattress, tucked the sheet neatly back into place in the orthodox hospital approved style and said briskly:

"Of course you won't be left behind. You'll be the most important patient on the pilgrimage. Now stop fretting, that's a good boy, and try to rest before your tea."

She smiled at him, the impersonal, professionally reassuring smile of the trained nurse. Then lifted her eyebrow at Eric Hewson. Together they went over to the window. She said quietly:

"How long can we go on coping with him?"

Hewson replied:

"Another month or two. It would upset him terribly to have to leave now. Wilfred too. In a few months' time both of them will be readier to accept the inevitable. Besides, he's set his heart on this Lourdes trip. Next time we go I doubt whether he will be alive. He certainly won't be here."

"But he's really a hospital case now. We aren't registered as a nursing home. We're only a home for the young chronic sick and disabled. Our contract is with the local authorities not the National Health Service. We don't pretend to offer a full medical nursing service. We aren't even supposed to. It's time Wilfred either gave up or made up his mind what he's trying to do here."

"I know." He did know, they both did. This wasn't a new problem. Why, he wondered, had so much of their conversation become a boring repetition of the obvious, dominated by Helen's high didactic voice.

Together they looked down at the small paved patio, bordered by the two new single-storey wings which contained the bedrooms and dayrooms, where the little group of remaining patients had gathered for the last sit in the sun before tea. The four wheelchairs were carefully placed a little apart and faced away from the house. The two watchers could see only the back of the patients' heads. Unmoving, they sat looking fixedly toward the headland. Grace Willison, her grey untidy hair ruffled by the light breeze; Jennie

Pegram, her neck sunk into her shoulders, her aureole of yellow hair streaming over the back of her wheelchair as if bleaching in the sun; Ursula Hollis's small round poll on its thin neck, high and motionless as a decapitated head on a pole; Henry Carwardine's dark head on its twisted neck, slumped sideways like a broken puppet. But then, they were all puppets. Dr. Hewson had a momentary and insane picture of himself rushing on to the patio and setting the four heads nodding and wagging, pulling invisible strings at the back of the necks so that the air was filled with their loud, discordant cries.

"What's the matter with them?" he asked suddenly. "Something's wrong about this place."

"More than usual?"

"Yes. Haven't you noticed?"

"Perhaps they're missing Michael. God knows why. He did little enough. If Wilfred's determined to carry on here he can find a better use for Hope Cottage now. As a matter of fact, I thought about suggesting that he let me live there. It would be easier for us."

The thought appalled him. So that was what she had been planning. The familiar depression fell on him, physical as a lead weight. Two positive, discontented women, both wanting something that he couldn't give. He tried to keep the panic from his voice.

"It wouldn't do. You're needed here. And I couldn't come to you at Hope Cottage, not with Millicent next door."

"She hears nothing once she's switched on the TV. We know that. And there's a back door if you do have to make a quick get-a-way. It's better than nothing."

"But Maggie would suspect."

"She suspects now. And she's got to know some time."

"We'll talk about it later. It's a bad time to worry Wilfred just now. We've all been on edge since Victor died."

Victor's death. He wondered what perverse masochism had made him mention Victor. It reminded him of those early days as a medical student when he would uncover a suppurating wound with relief because the sight of blood, inflamed tissue and pus was so less frightening than the imagination of what lay beneath the smooth gauze. Well, he had got used to blood. He had got used to death. In time he might even get used to being a doctor.

They moved together into the small clinical room at the front of the building. He went to the basin and began methodically sluicing his hands and forearms as if his brief examination of young Georgie had been a messy surgical procedure requiring a thorough cleansing. Behind his back he could hear the clink of instruments. Helen was unnecessarily tidying the surgical cupboard yet once more. With a sinking heart he realized that they were going to have to talk. But not yet. Not yet. And he knew what she would say. He had heard it all before, the old insistent arguments spoken in that confident school prefect's voice. "You're wasted here. You're a doctor, not a dispensing chemist. You've got to break free, free of Maggie and Wilfred. You can't put loyalty to Wilfred before your vocation." His vocation! That was the word his mother had always used. It made him want to break into hysterical laughter.

He switched on the tap to full and the water came gushing out, swirling round the basin, filling his ears like the sound of the incoming tide. What had it been like for Victor, that hurtle into oblivion? Had the clumsy wheelchair, heavy with its own momentum, sailed into space like one of those ridiculous flying contraptions in a James Bond film, the little manikin secure among his gadgets, ready to pull the lever and sport wings? Or had it twisted and tumbled through the air, bouncing off the rock face, with Victor coffined in canvas and metal, flailing impotent arms, adding his screams to the cry of the gulls? Had his heavy body broken free of the strap in mid-air, or had the canvas held until that final annihilating crash against the flat iron rocks, the first sucking wave of the relentless unthinking sea? And what had been in his mind? Exaltation or despair, terror or a blessed nothingness? Had the clean air and the sea wiped it all away, the pain, the bitterness, the malice?

It was only after his death that the full extent of Victor's malice had been known, in the codicil to his will. He had taken trouble to let the other patients know that he had money, that he paid the full fee at Toynton Grange, modest though that was, and wasn't, as were all the others except Henry Carwardine, dependent upon the benevolence of a local authority. He had never told them the source of his wealth—he had, after all, been a schoolmaster and they were hardly well paid—and they still didn't know. He might have told Maggie of course. There were a number of things he might have told Maggie. But on this she had been unaccountably silent.

Eric Hewson didn't believe that Maggie had taken an interest in Victor simply because of the money. They had, after all, had something in common. They had both made no secret that they hated Toynton Grange, that they were there of necessity not of choice, that they despised their companions. Probably Maggie found Victor's rebarbative malice to her liking. They had certainly spent a great deal of time together. Wilfred had seemed almost to welcome it, almost as if he thought Maggie was at last finding her proper place at Toynton. She had taken her turn at wheeling Victor in his heavy chair to his favourite spot. He had found some kind of peace in sight of the sea. Maggie and he had spent hours together, out of sight of the house, high on the edge of the cliff. But it hadn't worried him. He knew, none better, that Maggie could never love a man who couldn't satisfy her physically. He welcomed the friendship. At least it gave her something to occupy her time, kept her quiet.

He couldn't remember exactly when she had begun to become excited about the money. Victor must have said something. Maggie had changed almost overnight. She had become animated, almost gay. There had been a kind of feverish and suppressed excitement about her. And then Victor had suddenly demanded that he be driven to London for an examination at St. Saviour's Hospital and to consult his solicitor. It was then that Maggie had hinted to him about the will. He had caught something of her excitement. He wondered now what either of them had hoped for. Had she seen the money as a release merely from Toynton Grange, or also from him? Either way, surely, it would have brought salvation for them both. And the idea wasn't absurd. It was known that Victor had no relatives except a sister in New Zealand to whom he never wrote. No, he thought, reaching for the towel and beginning to dry his hands, it hadn't been an absurd dream; less absurd than the reality.

He thought of that drive back from London; the warm, enclosed world of the Mercedes; Julius silent, his hands resting lightly on the wheel; the road a silver reel punctuated with stars slipping endlessly under the bonnet; road signs leaping out of darkness to pattern the blue-black sky; small petrified animals, fur erect, briefly glorified in the headlamps; the road verges drained pale gold in their glare. Victor had sat with Maggie in the back, wrapped in his plaid cloak and smiling, always smiling. And the air had been heavy with secrets, shared and unshared.

Victor had indeed altered his will. He had added a codicil to the bequest which left the whole of his fortune to his sister, a final testimony of petty malice. To Grace Willison, a bar of toilet soap; to Henry Carwardine, a mouthwash; to Ursula Hollis, body deodorant; to Jennie Pegram, a toothpick.

Eric reflected that Maggie had taken it very well. Really very well indeed; if you could call that wild, ringing, uncontrolled laughter taking it well. He recalled her now, reeling about their small stone sitting-room, helpless with hysteria, throwing back her head and baying out her laughter so that it echoed harshly back from the walls, like a menagerie, and rang out over the headland so that he was afraid they would hear it as far as Toynton Grange.

Helen was standing by the window. She said, her voice sharp: "There's a car outside Hope Cottage."

He walked over to her. Together they looked out. Slowly their eyes met. She took his hand, and her voice was suddenly gentle, the voice he had heard when they had first made love.

"You've got nothing to worry about, darling. You know that, don't you? Nothing to worry about at all."

III

Ursula Hollis closed her library book, shut her eyes against the afternoon sun and entered into her private daydream. To do so now in the brief fifteen minutes before teatime was an indulgence, and quick as always to feel guilt at so ill-disciplined a pleasure, she was at first afraid that the magic wouldn't work. Usually, she made herself wait until she was in bed at night, wait even until Grace Willison's rasping breath, heard through the unsubstantial partition, had gentled into sleep before she allowed herself to think of Steve and the flat in Bell Street. The ritual had become an effort of will. She would lie there hardly daring to breathe because the images, however clearly conjured up, were so sensitive, so easily dispelled. But now it was happening beautifully. She concentrated, seeing the amorphous shapes and the changing patterns of colour focus into a picture, clearly as a developing negative, tuning in her ears to the sounds of home.

She saw the brick wall of the nineteenth-century house opposite with the morning sun lighting its dull façade so that each brick was individually distinct, multi-coloured, a pattern of light. The pokey two-roomed flat above Mr. Polanski's delicatessen, the street outside, the crowded heterogeneous life of that square mile of London between Edgware Road and Marylebone Station had absorbed and enchanted her. She was back there now, walking again with Steve through Church Street market on Saturday morning, the happiest day of the week. She saw the local women in their flowered overalls and carpet slippers, heavy wedding rings sunk into their bulbous toil-scarred fingers, their eyes bright in amorphous faces, as they sat gossiping beside their prams of second-hand clothes; the young people, joyfully garbed, squatting on the kerbstone behind their stalls of bric-à-brac; the tourists cheerfully impulsive or cautious and discerning by turns, conferring over their dollars or displaying their bizarre treasures. The street smelt of fruit, flowers and spice, of sweating bodies, cheap wine and old books. She saw the black women with their jutting buttocks and high barbaric staccato chatter, heard their sudden deep-throated laughter, as they crowded round the stall of huge unripe bananas and mangoes as large as footballs. In her dreams she moved on, her fingers gently entwined with Steve's like a ghost passing unseen down familiar paths.

The eighteen months of her marriage had been a time of intense but precarious happiness, precarious because she could never feel that it was rooted in reality. It was like becoming another person. Before, she had taught herself contentment and had called it happiness. After, she realized that there was a world of experience, of sensation, of thought even, for which nothing in those first twenty years of life in the Middlesbrough suburb, or the two and a half years in the Y.W.C.A. hostel in London, had prepared her. Only one thing marred it, the fear which she could never quite suppress that it was all happening to the wrong person, that she was an imposture of joy.

She couldn't imagine what it was about her that had so capriciously caught Steve's fancy that first time when he had called at the enquiry desk in the Council offices to ask about his rates. Was it the one feature which she had always thought of as close to a deformity; the fact that she had one blue and one brown eye? Certainly it was an oddity which had intrigued and amused him, had given her, she realized, an added value in his eyes. He had changed her appearance, making her grow her hair shoulder length, bringing home for her long gaudy skirts in Indian cotton found in the street markets or the shops in the back streets of Edgware Road. Sometimes, catching a glimpse of herself in a shop window, so marvellously altered, she would wonder again which strange predilection had led him to choose her, what possibilities undetected by others, unknown to herself, he had seen in her. Some quality in her had caught his eccentric fancy as did the odd items of bric-à-brac on the Bell Street stalls. Some object, unregarded by the passers-by, would catch his eye and he would turn it to the light this way and that in the palm of his hand, suddenly enchanted. She would make a tentative protest.

"But darling, isn't it rather hideous?"

"Oh, no, it's amusing. I like it. And Mogg will love it. Let's buy it for Mogg."

Mogg, his greatest and, she sometimes thought, his only friend, had been christened Morgan Evans but preferred to use his nickname, regarding it as more appropriate to a poet of the people's struggle. It was not that Mogg struggled greatly himself; indeed Ursula had never met anyone who drank and ate so resolutely at other people's expense. He chanted his confused battle cries to anarchy and hatred in local pubs where his hairy and sad-eyed followers listened in silence or spasmodically banged the table with their beer mugs amid grunts of approval. But Mogg's prose style had been more comprehensible. She had read his letter only once before returning it to the pocket in Steve's jeans, but she could recall every word. Sometimes she wondered whether he had intended her to find it, whether it was fortuitous that he had forgotten to clear out the pockets of his jeans on the one evening when she always took their dirty clothes to the washeteria. It was three weeks after the hospital had given her a firm diagnosis.

"I would say I told you so except that this is my week for abjuring platitudes. I prophesized disaster, but not total disaster. My poor bloody Steve! But isn't it possible for you to get a divorce? She must have had some symptoms before you married. You can—or could—get a divorce for V.D. existing at the time of marriage and what's a dose of clap compared with this? It astounds me, the irresponsibility of the so-called establishment about marriage. They bleat about its sanctity, about protecting it as a staple foundation of society, and then let people acquire a wife with less physical check-up than they would give to a second-hand car. Anyway, you do realize that you must break free don't you? It will be the end of you if you don't. And don't take refuge in the cowardice of compassion. Can you really see yourself wheeling her invalid chair and wiping her bottom? Yes, I know some men do it. But you never did get much of a kick out of masochism did you? Besides, the husbands who can do that know something about loving, and even you, my darling Steve, wouldn't presume to claim that. By the way, isn't she an R.C.? As you married in a Registry Office I doubt whether she considers herself properly married at all. That could be a way out for you. Anyway, see you in the Paviours Arms, Wednesday 8.0 p.m. I will celebrate your misfortune with a new poem and a pint of bitter."

She hadn't really expected him to wheel her chair. She hadn't wanted him to perform the simplest, least intimate physical service for her. She had learnt very early in their marriage that any illness, even transitory colds and sickness, disgusted and frightened him. But she had hoped that the disease would spread very slowly, that she could continue to manage on her own at least for a few precious years. She had schemed how it might be possible. She would get up early so that he needn't be offended by her slowness and ungainliness. She could move the furniture just a few inches, he probably wouldn't even notice, to provide unobtrusive supports so that she needn't take too quickly to sticks and callipers. Perhaps they could find an easier flat, one on the ground floor. If she could have a front door ramp she could get out in the daytime to do her shopping. And there would still be the nights together. Surely nothing could change those?

But it had quickly become evident that the disease, moving inexorably along her nerves like a predator, was spreading at its own pace, not hers. The plans she had made, lying stiffly beside him, distanced in the large double bed, willing that no spasm of muscle should disturb him, had become increasingly unrealistic. Watching her pathetic efforts, he had tried to be considerate and kind. He hadn't reproached her except by his withdrawal, hadn't condemned her growing weakness except by demonstrating his own lack of strength. In her nightmares she drowned; thrashing and choking in a limitless sea, she clutched at a floating bough and felt it sink, sponge soft and rotten, beneath her hands. She sensed morbidly that she was acquiring the propitiatory, simperingly pathetic air of the disabled. It was hard to be natural with him, harder still to talk. She remembered how he used to lie full length on the sofa watching her while she read or sewed, the creature of his selection and creation, draped and celebrated with the eccentric clothes which he had chosen for her. Now he was afraid for their eyes to meet.

She remembered how he had broken the news to her that he had spoken to the medical social worker at the hospital and that there might be a vacancy soon at Toynton Grange.

"It's by the sea darling. You've always liked the sea. Quite a small community too, not one of those huge impersonal institutions. The chap who runs it is very highly regarded and it's basically a religious foundation. Anstey isn't a Catholic himself but they do go regularly to Lourdes. That will please you; I mean that you've always been interested in religion. It's one of the subjects that we haven't really seen eye to eye about. I probably wasn't as understanding about your needs as I ought to have been."

He could afford now to be indulgent of that particular foible. He had forgotten that he had taught her to do without God. Her religion had been one of those possessions that, casually, neither understanding them nor valuing them, he had taken from her. They hadn't really been important to her, those consoling substitutes for sex, for love. She couldn't pretend that she had relinquished them with much of a struggle, those comforting illusions taught in St. Matthew's Primary School, assimilated behind the draped terylene curtains of her aunt's front sitting-room in Alma Terrace, Middlesbrough, with its holy pictures, its photograph of Pope John, its framed papal blessing of her aunt and uncle's wedding. All were part of that orphaned, uneventful, not unhappy childhood which was as remote now as a distant, once-visited alien shore. She couldn't return because she no longer knew the way.

In the end she had welcomed the thought of Toynton Grange as a refuge. She had pictured herself with a group of patients sitting in their chairs in the sun and looking at the sea; the sea, constantly changing but eternal, comforting and yet frightening, speaking to her in its ceaseless rhythm that nothing really mattered, that human misery was of small account, that everything passed in time. And it wasn't, after all, to be a permanent arrangement. Steve, with the help of the local authority social services department, planned to move into a new and more suitable flat; this was only to be a temporary separation.

But it had lasted now for eight months; eight months in which she had become increasingly disabled, increasingly unhappy. She had tried to conceal it since unhappiness at Toynton Grange was a sin against the Holy Ghost, a sin against Wilfred. And for most of the time she thought that she had succeeded. She had little in common with the other patients. Grace Willison, dull, middle aged, pious. Eighteen-year-old George Allan with his boisterous vulgarity; it had been a relief when he became too ill to leave his bed. Henry Carwardine, remote, sarcastic, treating her as if she were a junior clerk. Jennie Pegram, for ever fussing with her hair and smiling her stupid secret smile. And Victor Holroyd, the terrifying Victor, who had hated her as much as he hated everyone at Toynton Grange. Victor who saw no virtue in concealing unhappiness, who frequently proclaimed that if people were dedicated to the practice of charity they might as well have someone to be charitable about.

She had always taken it for granted that it was Victor who had typed the poison pen letter. It was a letter as traumatic in its way as the one she had found from Mogg. She felt for it now, deep in a side pocket in her skirt. It was still there, the cheap paper limp with much handling. But she didn't need to read it. She knew it now by heart, even the first paragraph. She had read that once, and then had turned the paper over at the top so that the words were hidden. Even to think about them burnt her cheek. How could he—it must be a man surely?—know how she and Steve had made love together, that they had done those particular acts and in that way? How could anyone know? Had she, perhaps, cried out in her sleep, moaning her need and her longing? But, if so, only Grace Willison could possibly have heard from the adjoining bedroom, and how could she have understood?

She remembered reading somewhere that obscene letters were usually written by women, particularly by spinsters. Perhaps it hadn't been Victor Holroyd after all. Grace Willison, dull, repressed, religious Grace. But how could she have guessed what Ursula had never admitted to herself?

"You must have known you were ill when you married him. What about those tremors, the weakness in your legs, the clumsiness in the mornings? You knew you were ill, didn't you? You cheated him. No wonder he seldom writes, that he never visits. He's not living alone, you know. You didn't really expect him to stay faithful, did you?"

And there the letter broke off. Somehow she felt that the writer hadn't really come to the end, that some more dramatic and revelationary finish was intended. But perhaps he or she had been interrupted; someone might have come into the office unexpectedly. The note had been typed on Toynton Grange paper, cheap and absorbent and with the old Remington typewriter. Nearly all the patients and staff occasionally typed. She thought she could remember seeing most of them use the Remington at one time or another. Of course, it was really Grace's machine; it was recognized as primarily hers; she used it to type the stencils for the quarterly newsletter. Often she worked alone in the office when the rest of the patients considered that they had finished the working day. And there would be no difficulty in ensuring that it reached the right recipient.

Slipping it into a library book was the surest way of all. They all knew what the others were reading, how could they help it? Books were laid down on tables, on chairs, were easily accessible to anyone. All the staff and patients must have known that she was reading the latest Iris Murdoch. And, oddly enough, the poison letter had been placed at exactly the page which she had reached.

At first she had taken it for granted that this was just a new example of Victor's power to hurt and humiliate. It was only since his death that she had felt these doubts, had glanced surreptitiously at the faces of her fellow inmates, had wondered and feared. But surely this was nonsense? She was tormenting herself unnecessarily. It must have been Victor and, if it were Victor, then there would be no more letters. But how could even he have known about her and Steve; except that Victor did mysteriously know things. She remembered the scene when she and Grace Willison had been sitting with him here in the patients' patio. Grace lifting her face to the sun and wearing that silly, gentle smile had begun to talk of her happiness, about the next Lourdes pilgrimage. Victor had broken in roughly:

"You're cheerful because you're euphoric. It's a feature of your disease, D.S. patients always have this unreasonable happiness and hope. Read the textbooks. It's a recognized symptom. It's certainly no virtue on your part and it's bloody irritating for the rest of us."

She recalled Grace's voice already tremulous with hurt.

"I wasn't claiming happiness as a virtue. But even if it's only a symptom, I can still give thanks for it; it's a kind of grace."

"As long as you don't expect the rest of us to join in, give thanks by all means. Thank God for the privilege of being no bloody use to yourself or anyone else. And while you're about it, thank Him for some of the other blessings of His creation; the millions toiling to get a living out of barren soil swept by flood, burnt by drought; for pot-bellied children; for tortured prisoners; for the whole doomed, bloody, pointless mess."

Grace Willison had protested quietly through the first smart of her tears:

"But Victor, how can you talk like that? Suffering isn't the whole of life; you can't really believe that God doesn't care. You come with us to Lourdes."

"Of course I do. It's the one chance to get out of this boring crack-brained penitentiary. I like movement, I like travel, I like the sight of the sun shining on the Pyrenees, I enjoy the colour. I even get some kind of satisfaction from the blatant commercialism of it all, from the sight of thousands of my fellow beings who are more deluded than I."

"But that's blasphemy!"

"Is it? Well, I enjoy that too."

Grace persisted: "If only you would talk to Father Baddeley, Victor. I'm sure that he would help you. Or perhaps to Wilfred. Why not talk to Wilfred?"

He had burst into raucous laughter, jeering but strangely and frighteningly shot through with genuine amusement.

"Talk to Wilfred! My God, I could tell you something about our saintly Wilfred that would give you a laugh, and one day, if he irritates me enough, I probably shall. Talk to Wilfred!"

She thought she could still hear the distant echo of that laughter. "I could tell you something about Wilfred." Only he hadn't told them, and now he never would. She thought about Victor's death. What impulse had led him on that particular afternoon to make his final gesture against fate? It must have been an impulse: Wednesday wasn't his normal day for an outing and Dennis hadn't wanted to take him. She remembered clearly the scene in the patio. Victor, importunate, insistent, exerting every effort of will to get what he wanted. Dennis flushed, sulky, a recalcitrant child, finally giving way but with a poor grace. And so, they had left together for that final walk, and she had never seen Victor again. What was he thinking of when he released those brakes and hurled himself and the chair towards annihilation? Surely it must have been the impulse of a moment. No one could choose to die with such spectacular horror while there were gentler means available. And surely there were gentler means; sometimes she found herself thinking about them, about those two most recent deaths, Victor's and Father Baddeley's. Father Baddeley, gentle, ineffectual, had passed away as if he had never been; his name now was hardly mentioned. It was Victor who seemed to be still among them. It was Victor's bitter uneasy spirit which hung over Toynton Grange. Sometimes, particularly at dusk, she dared not turn her face towards an adjacent wheelchair in case she should see, not the expected occupant, but Victor's heavy figure shrouded in his heavy plaid cloak, his dark sardonic face with its fixed smile like a rictus. Suddenly, despite the warmth of the afternoon sun, Ursula shivered. Releasing the brakes on her chair she turned and wheeled herself towards the house.

IV

The front door of Toynton Grange was open and Julius Court led the way into a high square hall, oak panelled and with a chequered black and white marble floor. The house struck very warm. It was like passing through an invisible curtain of hot air. The hall smelt oddly; not with the usual institutional smell of bodies, food and furniture polish overlaid with antiseptic, but sweeter and strangely exotic as if someone had been burning incense. The hall was as dimly lit as a church. An impression reinforced by the two front windows of Pre-Raphaelite stained glass one on each side of the main door. To the left was the expulsion from Eden, to the right the sacrifice of Isaac. Dalgliesh wondered what aberrant fancy had conceived that effeminate angel with his curdle of yellow hair under the plumed helmet or the sword embellished with glutinous lozenges in ruby, bright blue and orange with which he was ineffectively barring the two delinquents from an apple orchard Eden. Adam and Eve, their pink limbs tactfully if improbably entwined with laurel, wore expressions respectively of spurious spirituality and petulant remorse. On the right the same angel swooped like a metamorphosized batman over Isaac's bound body, watched from the thicket by an excessively woolly ram whose face, understandably, bore an expression of the liveliest apprehension.

There were three chairs in the hall, bastard contraptions in painted wood covered with vinyl, themselves deformities, one with an unusually high seat, two very low. A folded wheelchair rested against the far wall and a wooden rail was screwed waist high into the panelling. To the right an open door gave a glimpse of what could be a business room or cloakroom. Dalgleish could see the fold of a plaid cloak hanging on the wall, a pegboard of keys and the edge of a heavy desk. A carved hall table bearing a brass tray of letters and surmounted by a huge fire bell stood to the left of the door.

Julius led the way through a rear door and into a central vestibule from which rose a heavily carved staircase, its banister half cut away to accommodate the metal cage of a large modern lift. They came to a third door. Julius threw it dramatically open and announced:

"A visitor for the dead. Adam Dalgliesh."

The three of them passed into the room together. Dalgliesh, flanked by his two sponsors, had the unfamiliar sensation of being under escort. After the dimness of the front hall and the central vestibule the dining-room was so bright that he blinked. The tall mullioned windows gave little natural light but the room was harshly lit by two tubes of fluorescent lighting incongruously suspended from the moulded ceiling. Images seemed to fuse together and then parted and he saw clearly the inhabitants of Toynton Grange grouped like a tableau round the oak refectory table at tea.

His arrival seemed to have struck them momentarily into silent surprise. Four of them were in wheelchairs, one a man. The two remaining women were obviously staff; one was dressed as a matron except for the customary status symbol of a cap. Without it, she looked curiously incomplete. The other, a fair-haired younger woman, was wearing black slacks and a white smock but succeeded, despite this unorthodox uniform, in giving an immediate impression of slightly intimidating competence. The three able-bodied men all wore dark brown monk's habits. After a second's pause, a figure at the head of the table rose and came with ceremonial slowness towards them with hands held out.

"Welcome to Toynton Grange, Adam Dalgliesh. My name is Wilfred Anstey."

Dalgliesh's first thought was that he looked like a bit-player acting with practised conviction the part of an ascetic bishop. The brown monk's habit suited him so well that it was impossible to imagine him in any other garb. He was tall and very thin, the wrists from which the full woollen sleeves fell away were brown and brittle as autumn sticks. His hair was grey but strong and shaved very short revealing the boyish curve of the skull. Beneath it the thin long face was mottled brown as if the summer tan were fading unevenly; two shining white patches on the left temple had the appearance of diseased skin. It was difficult to guess his age; fifty perhaps. The gentle questioning eyes with their suggestion of other people's suffering meekly borne were young eyes, the blue irises very clear, the whites opaque as milk. He smiled, a singularly sweet lopsided smile spoilt by the display of uneven and discoloured teeth. Dalgliesh wondered why it was that philanthropists so often had a reluctance to visit their dentist.

Dalgliesh held out his hand and felt it imprisoned between Anstey's two palms. It took an effort of will not to flinch from this clammy encounter of moist flesh. He said:

"I had hoped to pay a few days' visit to Father Baddeley. I'm an old friend. I didn't know until I arrived that he was dead."

"Dead and cremated. His ashes were buried last Wednesday in the churchyard of St. Michael's Toynton. We knew that he would wish them to lie in consecrated ground. We didn't announce his death in the papers because we didn't know that he had friends."

"Except us here." It was one of the women patients who added the gentle but firm correction. She was older than the other patients, grey haired and angular as a Dutch doll propped in her chair. She looked at Dalgliesh steadily with kind and interested eyes.

Wilfred Anstey said:

"Of course. Except us here. Grace was, I think, closer to Michael than anyone else and was with him on the night he died."

Dalgliesh said:

"He died alone, Mrs. Hewson tells me."

"Unhappily yes. But so at the last do we all. You'll join us for tea I hope. Julius, you too, and Maggie of course. And did you say that you hoped to stay with Michael? Then you must, of course, spend the night here."

He turned to the matron.

"Victor's room, I think, Dot. Perhaps, after tea, you would prepare it for our guest."

Dalgliesh said:

"That's very kind of you, but I don't want to be a nuisance. Would there be any objection if, after tonight, I spent a few days in the cottage? Mrs. Hewson tells me that Father Baddeley left me his library. It would be helpful if I could sort and pack the books while I'm here."

Was it his imagination that the suggestion wasn't entirely welcome? But Anstey hesitated only for a second before saying:

"Of course, if that is what you prefer. But first let me introduce you to the family."

Dalgliesh followed Anstey in a formal charade of greetings. A succession of hands, dry, cold, moist, reluctant or firm clasped his. Grace Willison, the middle-aged spinster; a study in grey; skin, hair, dress, stockings, all of them slightly dingy so that she looked like an old-fashioned, stiffly jointed doll neglected too long in a dusty cupboard. Ursula Hollis; a tall, spotty-faced girl dressed in a long skirt of Indian cotton who gave him a tentative smile and brief, reluctant handshake. Her left hand lay limply in her lap as if wearied by the weight of the thick wedding ring. He was aware of something odd about her face but had moved on before he realized that she had one blue eye, one brown. Jennie Pegram; the youngest patient but probably older than she looked with a pale, sharp face and mild lemur-like eyes. She was so short necked that she seemed hunched into her wheelchair. Corn gold hair, parted in the middle, hung like a crimped curtain around the dwarfish body. She cringed deprecatingly at his touch, gave him a sickly smile and whispered "hullo" on a gasp of intaken breath. Henry Carwardine; a handsome, authoritative face but cut with deep lines of strain; a high beaky nose and long mouth. The disease had wrenched his head to one side so that he looked like a supercilious bird of prey. He took no notice of Dalgliesh's proffered hand but said a brief "how do you do" with an uninterest amounting almost to discourtesy. Dorothy Moxon, the matron; sombre, stout and gloomy eyed under the dark fringe. Helen Rainer; large, slightly protruding green eyes under lids as thin as grape skins and a shapely figure which even the loose-fitting smock couldn't wholly disguise. She would, he thought, be attractive were it not for the discontented droop of the slightly marsupial cheeks. She shook hands firmly with Dalgliesh and gave him a minatory glance as if welcoming a new patient from whom she expected trouble. Dr. Eric Hewson; a fair, good-looking man with a boyish vulnerable face, mud-brown eyes fringed with remarkably long lashes. Dennis Lerner; a lean, rather weak face, eyes blinking nervously behind the steel-rimmed spectacles, a moist handshake. Anstey added, almost as if he thought Lerner needed a word of explanation, that Dennis was the male nurse.

"The two remaining members of our family, Albert Philby, our handyman, and my sister Millicent Hammitt you will meet later I hope. But I mustn't, of course, forget Jeoffrey." As if catching his name, a cat, who had been slumbering on a window seat, uncurled himself, dropped ponderously to the floor and stalked towards them, tail erect. Anstey explained:

"He is named after Christopher Smart's cat. I expect you remember the poem.

'For I will consider my cat Jeoffrey.
For he is the servant of the living God, duly
  and daily serving him,
For he counteracts the powers of darkness by his
  electric skin and glaring eyes,
For he counteracts the Devil, who is death, by
  brisking about the life.'"

Dalgliesh said that he knew the poem. He could have added that if Anstey had destined his cat for this hieratic role, then he had been unlucky in his choice of the litter. Jeoffrey was a barrel-shaped tabby with a tail like a fox's brush who looked as if his life were dedicated less to the service of his creator than to the gratification of feline lusts. He gave Anstey a disagreeable look compounded of long suffering and disgust and leapt with lightness and precision on to Carwardine's lap where he was ill-received. Gratified at Carwardine's obvious reluctance to acquire him, he settled down with much purring and foot padding and permitted his eyes to close.

Julius Court and Maggie Hewson had settled themselves at the far end of the long table. Suddenly Julius called out:

"Be careful what you say to Mr. Dalgliesh, it may be taken down and given in evidence. He chooses to travel incognito but actually he's Commander Adam Dalgliesh of New Scotland Yard. His job is catching murderers."

Henry Carwardine's cup began an agitated rattle in its saucer. He tried ineffectively to steady it with his left hand. No one looked at him. Jennie Pegram gave an apprehensive gasp, then looked complacently round the table as if she had done something clever. Helen Rainer said sharply:

"How do you know?"

"I live in the world, my darlings, and occasionally read the newspapers. There was a notorious case last year which gained the Commander some public notice."

He turned to Dalgliesh:

"Henry will be drinking wine with me after dinner tonight and listening to some music. You may care to join us. You could perhaps wheel him over. Wilfred will excuse you, I know."

The invitation hardly seemed courteous, excluding as it did all but two of the company and peremptorily claiming the new arrival with no more than a token acknowledgement to his host. But no one seemed to mind. Perhaps it was usual for the two men to drink together when Court was at his cottage. After all, there was no reason why the patients should be compelled to share each other's friends, or those friends obliged to issue a general invitation. Besides, Dalgliesh was obviously invited to provide an escort. He said a brief thank you and sat down at the table between Ursula Hollis and Henry Carwardine.

It was a plain, boarding-school tea. There was no cloth. The scarred oak table reamed with scorch marks held two large brown teapots wielded by Dorothy Moxon, two plates of thickly cut brown bread, thinly spread with what Dalgliesh suspected was margarine, a jar of honey and one of marmite, a dish of rock buns, home made and pebbled with an excrescence of bullet black currants. There was also a bowl of apples. They looked like windfalls.

Everyone was drinking from brown earthenware mugs. Helen Rainer went over to a cupboard set under the window and brought over three similar mugs and matching plates for the visitors.

It was an odd tea party. Carwardine ignored the guest except to push the plate of bread and butter towards him, and Dalgliesh at first made little headway with Ursula Hollis. Her pale intense face was turned perpetually towards him, the two discordant eyes searched his. He felt uncomfortably that she was making some demand on him, desperately hoping to evoke a response of interest, of affection even, which he could neither recognize nor was competent to give. But, by happy chance, he mentioned London. Her face brightened, she asked him if he knew Marylebone, the Bell Street market? He found himself involved in a lively, almost obsessive discussion about London's street markets. She became animated, almost pretty and, strangely, it seemed to give her some comfort.

Suddenly Jennie Pegram leaned forward across the table and said with a moue of simulated distaste:

"A funny job catching murderers and getting them hanged. I don't see how you fancy it."

"We don't fancy it, and nowadays they don't get hanged."

"Well, shut up for life then. I think that's worse. And I bet some of those you caught when you were younger got hanged."

He detected the anticipatory, almost lascivious gleam in her eyes. It wasn't new to him. He said quietly:

"Five of them. It's interesting that those are the ones people always want to hear about."

Anstey smiled his gentle smile and spoke as one determined to be fair.

"It isn't only a question of punishment though, Jennie, is it? There is the theory of deterrence; the need to mark public abhorrence of violent crime; the hope of reforming and rehabilitating the criminal; and, of course, the importance of trying to ensure that he doesn't do it again."

He reminded Dalgliesh of a school master he had much disliked who was given to initiating frank discussion as a matter of duty but always with the patronizing air of permitting a limited expression of unorthodox opinion provided the class came back within the allotted time to a proper conviction of the rightness of his own views. But now Dalgliesh was neither compelled nor disposed to co-operate. He broke into Jennie's simple, "Well, they can't do it again if they're hanged, can they?" by saying:

"It's an interesting and important subject, I know. But forgive me if I don't personally find it fascinating. I'm on holiday—actually I'm convalescing—and I'm trying to forget about work."

"You've been ill?" Carwardine, with the deliberate care of a child uncertain of its powers, reached across and helped himself to honey.

"I hope your call here isn't, even subconsciously, on your own behalf. You aren't looking for a future vacancy? You haven't a progressive incurable disease?"

Anstey said:

"We all suffer from a progressive incurable disease. We call it life."

Carwardine gave a tight self-congratulatory smile, as if he had scored a point in some private game. Dalgliesh, who was beginning to feel himself part of a mad hatter's tea party, wasn't sure whether the remark was spuriously profound or merely silly. What he was sure was that Anstey had made it before. There was a short, embarrassed silence, then Anstey said:

"Michael didn't let us know he was expecting you." He made it sound like a gentle reproof.

"He may not have received my postcard. It should have arrived on the morning of his death. I couldn't find it in his bureau."

Anstey was peeling an apple, the yellow rind curved over his thin fingers. His eyes were intent on his task. He said:

"He was brought home by the ambulance service. It wasn't convenient that morning for me to fetch him. I understand that the ambulance stopped at the postbox to collect any letters, probably at Michael's request. He later handed a letter to me and one to my sister, so he should have received your card. I certainly found no postcard when I looked in the bureau for his will and for any other written instructions he may have left. That was early on the morning after his death. I may, of course, have missed it."

Dalgliesh said easily:

"In which case it would still be there. I expect Father Baddeley threw it away. It's a pity you had to break into the bureau."

"Break into?" Anstey's voice expressed nothing but a polite, unworried query.

"The lock has been forced."

"Indeed. I imagine that Michael must have lost the key and was forced to that extremity. Forgive the pun. I found the bureau open when I looked for his papers. I'm afraid I didn't think to examine the lock. Is it important?"

"Miss Willison may think so. I understood that the bureau is now hers."

"A broken lock does, of course, reduce its value. But you will find that we place little store on material possessions at Toynton Grange."

He smiled again, dismissing a frivolity, and turned to Dorothy Moxon. Miss Willison was concentrating on her plate. She didn't look up. Dalgliesh said:

"It's probably foolish of me, but I wish I could be sure that Father Baddeley knew that I hoped to visit him. I thought he might have slipped my postcard into his diary. But the last volume isn't in his desk."

This time Anstey looked up. The blue eyes met the dark brown, innocent, polite, unworried.

"Yes, I noticed that. He gave up keeping a diary at the end of June apparently. The surprise is that he kept one, not that he gave up the habit. In the end one grows impatient of the egotism which records trivia as if it had a permanent value."

"It's unusual surely after so many years to stop in mid-year."

"He had just returned from hospital after a grave illness and can't have been in much doubt about the prognosis. Knowing that death could not be far off, he may have decided to destroy the diaries."

"Beginning with the last volume?"

"To destroy a diary must be like destroying memory. One would begin with the years one could best endure to lose. Old memories are tenacious. He made a start by burning the last volume."

Grace Willison again spoke her gentle but firm correction:

"Not by burning, Wilfred. Father Baddeley used his electric fire when he got home from hospital. The grate is filled with a jam pot of dried grasses."

Dalgliesh pictured the sitting-room of Hope Cottage. She was, of course, right. He recalled the old-fashioned grey stone jar, the crumpled bunch of dried leaves and grasses filling the narrow fireplace and thrusting their dusty and soot laden stalks between the bars. They probably hadn't been disturbed for the best part of a year.

The animated chatter at the other end of the table died into speculative silence as it does when people suddenly suspect that something interesting is being said which they ought to hear.

Maggie Hewson had seated herself so close to Julius Court that Dalgliesh was surprised that he had room to drink his tea and had been overtly flirting with him during the meal, whether for her husband's discomfiture or Court's gratification it was difficult to say. Eric Hewson, when he glanced towards them, had the shame-faced look of an embarrassed schoolboy. Court, perfectly at his ease, had distributed his attention among all the women present, with the exception of Grace. Now Maggie looked from face to face and said sharply:

"What's the matter? What did she say?"

No one replied. It was Julius who broke the moment of sudden and inexplicable tension:

"I forgot to tell you. You're doubly privileged in your visitor. The Commander doesn't confine his talents to catching murderers, he publishes verse. He's Adam Dalgliesh, the poet."

This announcement was met with a confused congratulatory murmur during which Dalgliesh fastened on Jennie's comment of "how nice" as the most irritatingly inept. Wilfred smiled encouragingly and said:

"Of course. We are certainly privileged. And Adam Dalgliesh comes at an opportune time. We are due to hold our monthly family social evening on Thursday. May we hope that our guest will recite some of his poems for our pleasure?"

There were a number of answers to that question but, in the present disadvantaged company, none of them seemed either kind or possible.

Dalgliesh said:

"I'm sorry but I don't travel with copies of my own books."

Anstey smiled,

"That will present no problem. Henry has your last two volumes. I am sure he will lend them."

Without looking up from his plate, Carwardine said quietly:

"Given the lack of privacy in this place, I've no doubt you could provide a verbal catalogue of my whole library. But, since you've shown a complete lack of interest in Dalgliesh's work until now, I have no intention of lending my books so that you can blackmail a guest into performing for you like a captive monkey!"

Wilfred flushed slightly and bent his head over his plate.

There was nothing further to be said. After a second's silence, the talk flowed on, innocuous, commonplace. Neither Father Baddeley nor his diary were mentioned again.

V

Anstey was obviously unworried by Dalgliesh's expressed wish after tea to talk to Miss Willison in private. Probably the request struck him as no more than the pious protocol of courtesy and respect. He said that Grace had the task of feeding the hens and collecting the eggs before dusk. Perhaps Adam could help her?

The two larger wheels of the chair were fitted with a second interior wheel in chrome which could be used by the occupant to drive the chair forward. Miss Willison grasped it and began to make slow progress down the asphalt path jerking her frail body like a marionette. Dalgliesh saw that her left hand was deformed and had little power so that the chair tended to swivel, and progress was erratic. He moved to her left and, while walking beside her, he laid his hand unobtrusively on the back of the chair and gently helped it forward. He hoped that he was doing the acceptable thing. Miss Willison might resent his tact as much as she did the implied pity. He thought that she sensed his embarrassment and had resolved not to add to it even by smiling her thanks.

As they walked together he was intensely aware of her, noting the details of her physical presence as keenly as if she were a young and desirable woman and he on the verge of love. He watched the sharp bones of her shoulders jerking rhythmically under the thin grey cotton of her dress; the purple tributaries of the veins standing like cords on her almost transparent left hand, so small and fragile in contrast to its fellow. This, too, looked deformed in its compensating strength and hugeness as she gripped the wheel as powerfully as a man. Her legs, clad in wrinkled woollen stockings, were thin as sticks; her sandalled feet, too large surely for such inadequate supports, were clamped to the footrest of her chair as if glued to the metal. Her grey hair flecked with dandruff had been combed upward in a single heavy plait fixed to the crown of her head with a plastic white comb, not particularly clean. The back of her neck looked dingy either with fading suntan or inadequate washing. Looking down he could see the lines on her forehead contracting into deeper furrows with the effort of moving the chair, the eyes blinking spasmodically behind the thin framed spectacles.

The hen house was a large ramshackle cage bounded by sagging wire and creosoted posts. It had obviously been designed for the disabled. There was a double entry so that Miss Willison could let herself in and fasten the door behind her before opening the second door into the main cage, and the smooth asphalt path, just wide enough for a wheelchair, ran along each side and in front of the nesting boxes. Inside the first door a rough wooden shelf had been nailed waist high to one of the supports. This held a bowl of prepared meal, a plastic can of water and a wooden spoon riveted to a long handle, obviously for the collection of eggs. Miss Willison took them in her lap with some difficulty and reached forward to open the inner door. The hens, who had unaccountably bunched themselves in the far corner of the cage like the nervous virgins, lifted their beady spiteful faces and instantly came squawking and swooping towards her as if determined on a feathered hecatomb. Miss Willison recoiled slightly and began casting handfuls of meal before them with the air of a neophyte propitiating the furies. The hens began an agitated pecking and gulping. Scraping her hand against the rim of the bowl Miss Willison said:

"I wish I could get more fond of them, or they of me. Both sides might get more out of this activity. I thought that animals developed a fondness for the hand that feeds them but it doesn't seem to apply to hens. I don't see why it should really. We exploit them so thoroughly, first take their eggs and when they're past laying wring their necks and consign them to the pot."

"I hope you don't have to do the wringing."

"Oh, no, Albert Philby has that unpleasant job; not that I think he finds it altogether unpleasant. But I eat my share of the boiled fowl."

Dalgliesh said:

"I feel rather the same. I was brought up in a Norfolk vicarage and my mother always had hens. She was fond of them and they seemed fond of her but my father and I thought they were a nuisance. But we liked the fresh eggs."

"Do you know, I'm ashamed to tell you that I can't really tell the difference between these eggs and the ones from the supermarket. Wilfred prefers us not to eat any food which hasn't been naturally produced. He abhors factory farming and, of course, he's right. He would really prefer Toynton Grange to be vegetarian, but that would make the catering even more difficult than it is now. Julius did some sums and proved to him that these eggs cost us two and a half times more than the shop ones, not counting of course for my labour. It was rather discouraging."

Dalgliesh asked:

"Does Julius Court do the book-keeping here then?"

"Oh, no! Not the real accounts, the ones included in the annual report. Wilfred has a professional accountant for those. But Julius is clever with finance and I know Wilfred looks to him for advice. It's usually rather disheartening advice, I'm afraid; we run on a shoe-string really. Father Baddeley's legacy was a real blessing. And Julius has been very kind. Last year the van which we hired to drive us back from the port after our return from Lourdes had an accident. We were all very shaken. The wheelchairs were in the back and two of them got broken. The telephone message that reached here was rather alarmist; it wasn't as bad as Wilfred thought. But Julius drove straight to the hospital where we had been taken for a check-up, hired another van, and took care of everything. And then he bought the specially adapted bus which we have now so that we're completely independent. Dennis and Wilfred between them can drive us all the way to Lourdes. Julius never comes with us, of course, but he's always here to arrange a welcome home party for us when we return after the pilgrimage."

This disinterested kindness was unlike the impression that, even after a short acquaintanceship, Dalgliesh had formed of Court. Intrigued he asked carefully:

"Forgive me if I sound crude but what does Julius Court get out of it, this interest in Toynton?"

"Do you know, I've sometimes asked myself that. But it seems an ungracious question when it's so apparent what Toynton Grange gets out of him. He comes back from London like a breath of the outside world. He cheers us all. But I know that you want to talk about your friend. Shall we just collect the eggs and then find somewhere quiet?"

Your friend. The quiet phrase quietly spoken, rebuked him. They filled up the water containers and collected the eggs together, Miss Willison scooping them up in her wooden spoon with the expertise born of long practice. They found only eight. The whole procedure, which an able-bodied person could have completed in ten minutes, had been tedious, time-consuming and not particularly productive. Dalgliesh, who saw no merit in work for the sake of work, wondered what his companion really thought about a job which had obviously been designed in defiance of economics to give her the illusion of being useful.

They made their way back to the little courtyard behind the house. Only Henry Carwardine was sitting there, a book on his lap but his eyes staring towards the invisible sea. Miss Willison gave him a quick worried glance and seemed about to speak. But she said nothing until they had settled themselves some thirty yards from the silent figure; Dalgliesh at the end of one of the wooden benches and she at his side. Then she said:

"I can never get used to being so close to the sea and yet not being able to look at it. One can hear it so plainly sometimes as we can now. We're almost surrounded by it, we can sometimes smell it and listen to it, but we might be a hundred miles away."

She spoke wistfully but without resentment. They sat for a moment in silence. Dalgliesh could indeed hear the sea clearly now, the long withdrawing rasp of the shingled tide borne to him on the onshore breeze. To the inmates of Toynton Grange that ceaseless murmur must evoke the tantalizingly close but unobtainable freedom of wide blue horizons, scudding clouds, white wings falling and swooping through the moving air. He could understand how the need to see it might grow into an obsession. He said deliberately:

"Mr. Holroyd managed to get himself wheeled to where he could watch the sea."

It had been important to see her reaction and he realized at once that to her the remark had been worse than tactless. She was deeply shaken and distressed. The frail left hand, curved in her lap, began an agitated shaking. Her right hand tightened on the arm of the chair. Her face crimsoned in an unlovely wave, and then became very pale. For a moment he almost wished that he hadn't spoken. But the regret was transitory. It was returning despite himself, he thought with sardonic humour, this professional itch to seek out the facts. They were seldom discovered without some cost, however irrelevant or important they finally proved to be, and it wasn't usually he who paid. He heard her speaking so quietly that he had to bend his head to catch the words.

"Victor had a special need to get away by himself. We understood that."

"But it must have been very difficult to push a light wheelchair like this over the rough turf and up to the edge of the cliff."

"He had a chair which belonged to him, like this type but larger and stronger. And it wasn't necessary to push him up the steep part of the headland. There's an inland path which leads, I understand, to a narrow sunken lane. You can get to the cliff edge that way. Even so it was hard on Dennis Lerner. It took him half an hour hard pushing each way. But you wanted to talk about Father Baddeley."

"If it won't distress you too much. It seems that you were the last person to see him alive. He must have died very soon after you left the cottage since he was still wearing his stole when Mrs. Hewson found his body next morning. Normally he would surely have taken it off very soon after hearing a confession."

There was a silence as if she were making up her mind to something. Then she said:

"He did take it off, as usual, immediately after he'd given me absolution. He folded it up and placed it over the arm of his chair."

This, too, was a sensation which in the long dog days in hospital he had thought never to experience again, the frisson of excitement along the blood at the first realization that something important had been said, that although the quarry wasn't yet in sight nor his spore detectable, yet he was there. He tried to reject this unwelcome surge of tension but it was as elemental and involuntary as the touch of fear. He said:

"But that means that Father Baddeley put on his stole again after you had left. Why should he do that?"

Or someone else had put it on for him. But that thought was best unspoken and its implications must wait.

She said quietly:

"I assume that he had another penitent; that is the obvious explanation."

"He wouldn't wear it to say his evening Office?"

Dalgliesh tried to remember his father's practice in these matters on the very rare occasions when the rector did not say his Office in church; but memory provided only the unhelpful boyhood picture of them both holed up in a hut in the Cairngorms during a blizzard, himself watching, half bored, half fascinated, the patterns of the swirling snow against the windows, his father in leggings, anorak and woollen cap quietly reading from his small black prayer book. He certainly hadn't worn a stole then.

Miss Willison said:

"Oh no! He would wear it only when administering a sacrament. Besides, he had said evensong. He was just finishing when I arrived and I joined him in a last collect."

"But if someone followed you, then you weren't the last person to see him alive. Did you point that out to anyone when you were told of his death?"

"Should I have done? I don't think so. If the person himself—or herself—didn't choose to speak it wasn't for me to invite conjecture. Of course, if anyone but you had realized the significance of the stole it wouldn't have been possible to avoid speculation. But no one did, or if they did, they said nothing. We gossip too much at Toynton, Mr. Dalgliesh. It's inevitable perhaps, but it isn't—well—healthy morally. If someone other than I went to confession that night, it's nobody's business but theirs and Father Baddeley's."

Dalgliesh said:

"But Father Baddeley was still wearing his stole next morning. That suggests that he might have died while his visitor was actually with him. If that happened surely the first reaction, however private the occasion, would be to summon medical help?"

"The visitor might have had no doubts that Father Baddeley had died and was beyond that kind of help. If so there might be a temptation to leave him there sitting peaceably in his chair and slip away. I don't think Father Baddeley would call that a sin, and I don't think you could call it a crime. It might seem callous but would it necessarily be so? It could argue an indifference to form and decorum perhaps, but that isn't quite the same thing, is it?"

It would argue, too, thought Dalgliesh, that the visitor had been a doctor or a nurse. Was that what Miss Willison was hinting? The first reaction of a lay person would surely be to seek help, or at least confirmation that death had actually occurred. Unless, of course, he knew for the best or worst of reasons that Baddeley was dead. But that sinister possibility seemed not to have occurred to Miss Willison. Why, indeed, should it? Father Baddeley was old, he was sick, he was expected to die and he had died. Why should anyone suspect the natural and the inevitable? He said something about determining the time of death and heard her gentle, inexorable reply.

"I expect that in your job the actual time of death is always important and so you get used to concentrating on that fact. But in real life does it matter? What matters is whether one dies in a state of grace."

Dalgliesh had a momentary and impious picture of his detective sergeant punctiliously attempting to determine and record this essential information about a victim in an official crime report and reflected that Miss Willison's nice distinction between police work and real life was a salutory reminder of how other people saw his job. He looked forward to telling the Commissioner about it. And then he remembered that this wasn't the kind of casual professional gossip which they would exchange in that final slightly formal and inevitably disappointing interview which would mark the end of his police career.

Ruefully, he recognized in Miss Willison the type of unusually honest witness whom he had always found difficult. Paradoxically, this old-fashioned rectitude, this sensitivity of conscience, were more difficult to cope with than the prevarications, evasions, or flamboyant lying which were part of a normal interrogation. He would have liked to have asked her who at Toynton Grange was likely to have visited Father Baddeley for the purpose of confession, but recognized that the question would only prejudice confidence between them and that, in any case, he wouldn't get a reply. But it must have been one of the able bodied. No one else could have come and gone in secret, unless, of course, he or she had an accomplice. He was inclined to dismiss the accomplice. A wheelchair and its occupant, whether pushed from

Toynton Grange or brought by car, must surely have been seen at some stage of the journey.

Hoping that he wasn't sounding too much like a detective in the middle of an interrogation he asked:

"So when you left him he was—what?"

"Just sitting there quietly in the fireside chair. I wouldn't let him get up. Wilfred had driven me down to the cottage in the small van. He said that he would visit his sister at Faith Cottage while I was with Father Baddeley and be outside again in half an hour unless I knocked on the wall first."

"So you can hear sounds between the two cottages? I ask because it struck me that if Father Baddeley had felt ill after you'd left, he might have knocked on the wall for Mrs. Hammitt."

"She says that he didn't knock, but she might not have heard if she had the television on very loudly. The cottages are very well built, but you can hear sounds through that interior wall, particularly if voices are raised."

"You mean that you could hear Mr. Anstey talking to his sister?"

Miss Willison seemed to regret that she had gone so far, and she said quickly:

"Well, just now and then. I remember that I had to make an effort of will to prevent it disturbing me. I wished that they would keep their voices lower, and then felt ashamed of myself for being so easily distracted. It was good of Wilfred to drive me to the cottage. Normally, of course, Father Baddeley would come up to the house to see me and we would use what is called the quiet room next to the business room just inside the front door. But Father Baddeley had only been discharged from hospital that morning and it wasn't right that he should leave the cottage. I could have postponed my visit until he was stronger but he wrote to me from hospital to say that he hoped I would come and precisely at what time. He knew how much it meant to me."

"Was he fit to be alone? It seems not."

"Eric and Dot—that's Sister Moxon—wanted him to come here and be looked after at least for the first night, but he insisted on going straight back home. Then Wilfred suggested that someone should sleep in his spare room in case he wanted help in the night. He wouldn't agree to that either. He really was adamant that he should be left alone that night; he had great authority in his quiet way. Afterwards I think Wilfred blamed himself for not having been more firm. But what could he do? He couldn't bring Father Baddeley here by force."

But it would have been simpler for all concerned if Father Baddeley had agreed to spend at least his first night out of hospital at Toynton Grange. It was surely untypically inconsiderate of him to resist the suggestion so strenuously. Was he expecting another visitor? Was there someone he wanted to see, urgently and in private, someone to whom, like Miss Willison, he had written to give a precisely timed appointment? If so, whatever the reason for the visit, that person must have come on his own feet. He asked Miss Willison if Wilfred and Father Baddeley had spoken together before she had left the cottage.

"No. After I'd been with Father Baddeley about thirty minutes he knocked on the wall with the poker and, soon afterwards, Wilfred honked on the horn. I manoeuvred my chair to the front door just as Wilfred arrived to open it. Father Baddeley was still in his chair. Wilfred called out goodnight to him, but I don't think he answered. Wilfred seemed in rather a hurry to get home. Millicent came out to help push my chair into the back of the van."

So neither Wilfred nor his sister had spoken to Michael before driving away that evening, neither had seen him closely. Glancing down at Miss Willison's strong right hand Dalgliesh toyed momentarily with the possibility that Michael was already dead. But that notion, apart from its psychological unlikelihood, was of course, nonsense. She couldn't have relied on Wilfred not coming into the cottage. Come to think of it, it was odd that he hadn't done so. Michael had only returned from hospital that morning. Surely it would have been natural to come in and enquire how he was feeling, to spend at least a few minutes in his company. It was interesting that Wilfred Anstey had made so quick a getaway, that no one had admitted visiting Father Baddeley after seven forty-five.

He asked:

"What lighting was there in the cottage when you were with Father Baddeley?" If the question surprised her, she didn't show it.

"Only the small table lamp on the bureau top behind his chair. I was surprised that he could see to say Evensong, but the prayers, of course, would be familiar to him."

"And the lamp was off next morning?"

"Oh yes, Maggie said that she found the cottage in darkness."

Dalgliesh said:

"I find it rather strange that no one looked in later that night to enquire how Father Baddeley was or help him get to bed."

She said quickly:

"Eric Hewson thought that Millicent was going to look in last thing and she had somehow got the impression that Eric and Helen—Nurse Rainer, you know—had agreed to do so. They all blamed themselves very much the next day. But, as Eric told us, medically it could have made no difference. Father Baddeley died quite peaceably soon after I left."

They sat in silence for a minute. Dalgliesh wondered whether this was the right time to ask her about the poison pen letter. Remembering her distress over Victor Holroyd, he was reluctant to embarrass her further. But it was important to know. Looking sideways at the thin face with its look of resolute tranquillity, he said:

"I looked in Father Baddeley's writing bureau very soon after I arrived, just in case there was a note or unposted letter for me. I found a rather unpleasant poison pen letter under some old receipts. I wondered whether he had spoken to anyone about it, whether anyone else at Toynton Grange had received one."

She was even more distressed by the question than he had feared. For a moment she could not speak. He stared straight ahead until he heard her voice. But, when at last she answered, she had herself well in hand.

"I had one, about four days before Victor died. It was . . . it was obscene. I tore it into small fragments and flushed it down the lavatory."

Dalgliesh said with robust cheerfulness:

"Much the best thing to do with it. But, as a policeman, I'm always sorry when the evidence is destroyed."

"Evidence?"

"Well, sending poison pen letters can be an offence; more important, it can cause a great deal of unhappiness. It's probably best always to tell the police and let them find out who's responsible."

"The police! Oh, no! We couldn't do that. It isn't the kind of problem the police can help with."

"We aren't as insensitive as people sometimes imagine. It isn't inevitable that the culprit would be prosecuted. But it is important to put a stop to this kind of nuisance, and the police have the best facilities. They can send the letter to the forensic science laboratory for examination by a skilled document examiner."

"But they would need to have the document. I couldn't have shown the letter to anyone."

So it had been as bad as that. Dalgliesh asked:

"Would you mind telling me what kind of letter it was? Was it handwritten, typed, on what kind of paper?"

"The letter was typed on Toynton Grange paper, in double spacing, on our old Imperial. Most of us here have learned typewriting. It's one of the ways in which we try to be self-supporting. There was nothing wrong with the punctuation or spelling. There were no other clues that I could see. I don't know who typed it, but I think the writer must have been sexually experienced."

So, even in the middle of her distress, she had applied her mind to the problem. He said:

"There are only a limited number of people with access to that machine. The problem wouldn't have been too difficult for the police."

Her gentle voice was stubborn.

"We had the police here over Victor's death. They were very kind, very considerate. But it was terribly upsetting. It was horrible for Wilfred—for all of us. I don't think we could have stood it again. I'm sure that Wilfred couldn't. However tactful the police are, they have to keep on asking questions until they've solved the case, surely? It's no use calling them in and expecting them to put people's sensitivities before their job."

This was undeniably true and Dalgliesh had little to argue against it. He asked her what, if anything, she had done apart from flushing away the offending letter.

"I told Dorothy Moxon about it. That seemed the most sensible thing to do. I couldn't have spoken about it to a man. Dorothy told me that I shouldn't have destroyed it, that no one could do anything without the evidence. But she agreed that we ought to say nothing at present. Wilfred was particularly worried about money at the time and she didn't want him to have anything else on his mind. She knew how much it would distress him. Besides, I think she had an idea who might have been responsible. If she were right, then we shan't be getting any more letters."

So Dorothy Moxon had believed, or had pretended to believe, that Victor Holroyd was responsible. And if the writer now had the sense and self-control to stop, it was a comfortable theory which, in the absence of the evidence, no one could disprove.

He asked whether anyone else had received a letter. As far as she knew, no one had. Dorothy Moxon hadn't been consulted by anyone else. The suggestion seemed to distress her. Dalgliesh realized that she had seen the note as a single piece of gratuitous spite directed against herself. The thought that Father Baddeley had also received one, was distressing her almost as much as the original letter. Knowing only too well from his experience the kind of letter it must have been, he said gently:

"I shouldn't worry too much about Father Baddeley's letter. I don't think it would have distressed him. It was very mild really, just a spiteful little note suggesting that he wasn't of much help to Toynton Grange and that the cottage could be more usefully occupied by someone else. He had too much humility and sense to be bothered by that kind of nonsense. I imagine that he only kept the letter because he wanted to consult me in case he wasn't the only victim. Sensible people put these things down the WC. But we can't always be sensible. Anyway, if you do receive another letter, will you promise to show it to me?"

She shook her head gently but didn't speak. But Dalgliesh saw that she was happier. She put out her withered left hand and placed it momentarily over his, giving it a slight press. The sensation was unpleasant, her hand was dry and cold, the bones felt loose in the skin. But the gesture was both humbling and dignified.

It was getting cold and dark in the courtyard; Henry Carwardine had already gone in. It was time for her to move inside. He thought quickly and then said:

"It isn't important, and please don't think that I take my job with me wherever I go. But if during the next few days you can recall how Father Baddeley spent the last week or so before he went into hospital, it would be helpful to me. Don't ask anyone else about this. Just let me know what he did from your own memory of him, the times he came to Toynton Grange, where else he may have spent his hours. I should like to have a picture in my mind of his last ten days."

She said:

"I know that he went into Wareham on the Wednesday before he was taken ill, he said to do some shopping and to see someone on business. I remember that because he explained on the Tuesday that he wouldn't be visiting the Grange as usual next morning."

So that, thought Dalgliesh, was when he had bought his store of provisions, confident that his letter wouldn't go unanswered. But then he had been right to be confident.

They sat for a minute not speaking. He wondered what she had thought of so odd a request. She hadn't seemed surprised. Perhaps she saw it as perfectly natural, this wish to build up a picture of a friend's last days on earth. But suddenly he had a spasm of apprehension and caution. Ought he perhaps to stress that his request was absolutely private? Surely not. He had told her not to ask anyone else. To make more of it would only arouse suspicion. And what danger could there be? What had he to go on? A broken bureau lock, a missing diary, a stole replaced as if for confession. There was no real evidence here. With an effort of will he reasoned away this inexplicable spasm of apprehension, strong as a premonition. It was too disagreeable a reminder of those long nights in hospital when he had struggled in restless half-consciousness against irrational terrors and half-understood fears. And this was equally irrational, equally to be resisted by sense and reason, the ridiculous conviction that a simple, almost casual and not very hopeful request had sounded so clearly a sentence of death.

3

A Stranger for the Night

I

Before dinner Anstey suggested that Dennis Lerner should show Dalgliesh round the house. He apologized for not escorting the guest himself, but he had an urgent letter to write. The post was delivered and collected shortly before nine o'clock each morning from the box on the boundary gate. If Adam had letters to send he had only to leave them on the hall table, and Albert Philby would take them to the box with the Toynton Grange letters. Dalgliesh thanked him. There was one urgent letter he needed to write, to Bill Moriarty at the Yard, but he proposed to post that himself later in the day at Wareham. He had certainly no intention of leaving it exposed to the curiosity or speculation of Anstey and his staff.

The suggestion for a tour of the Grange had the force of a command. Helen Rainer was helping the patients wash before dinner and Dot Moxon had disappeared with Anstey, so that he was taken round only by Lerner accompanied by Julius Court. Dalgliesh wished the tour were over, or better still, that it could have been avoided without giving hurt. He recalled with discomfort a visit he had paid as a boy with his father to a geriatric hospital on Christmas Day; the courtesy with which the patients accepted yet one more invasion of their privacy, the public display of pain and deformity, the pathetic eagerness with which the staff demonstrated their small triumphs. Now, as then, he found himself morbidly sensitive to the least trace of revulsion in his voice and thought that he detected what was more offensive, a note of patronizing heartiness. Dennis Lerner didn't appear to notice it and Julius walked jauntily with them looking round with lively curiosity as if the place were new to him. Dalgliesh wondered whether he had come to keep an eye on Lerner or on Dalgliesh himself.

As they passed from room to room, Lerner lost his first diffidence and became confident, almost voluble. There was something endearing about his naïve pride in what Anstey was trying to do. Anstey had certainly laid out his money with some imagination. The Grange itself, with its large, high rooms and cold marble floors, its oppressively panelled dark oak walls and mullioned windows, was a depressingly unsuitable house for disabled patients. Apart from the dining-room and the rear drawing-room, which had become a TV and communal sitting-room, Anstey had used the house mainly to accommodate himself and his staff and had built on to the rear a one-storey stone extension to provide ten individual patients' bedrooms on the ground floor and a clinical room and additional bedrooms on the floor above. This extension had been joined to the old stables which ran at right angles to it providing a sheltered patio for the patients' wheelchairs. The stables themselves had been adapted to provide garages, a workshop and a patients' activity room for woodwork and modelling. Here, too, the handcream and bath powder which the Home sold to help with finances were made and packed at a workbench behind a transparent plastic screen erected, presumably, to indicate respect for the principle of scientific cleanliness. Dalgliesh could see, hanging on the screen, the white shadows of protective overalls.

Lerner said:

"Victor Holroyd was a chemistry teacher and he gave us the prescription for the handcream and powder. The cream is really only lanolin, almond oil and glycerine but it's very effective and people seem to like it. We do very well with it. And this corner of the workroom is given over to modelling."

Dalgliesh had almost exhausted his repertoire of appreciative comments. But now he was genuinely impressed. In the middle of the workbench and mounted on a low wooden base was a clay head of Wilfred Anstey. The neck, elongated and sinewy, rose tortoise-like from the folds of the hood. The head was thrust forward and held a little to the right. It was almost a parody, and yet it had an extraordinary power. How, Dalgliesh wondered, had the sculptor managed to convey the sweetness and the obstinacy of that individual smile, to model compassion and yet reduce it to self-delusion, to show humility garbed in a monk's habit and yet convey an overriding impression of the puissance of evil. The plastic wrapped lumps and rolls of clay which lay, disorderly, on the workbench only emphasized the force and technical achievement of this one finished work.

Lerner said:

"Henry did the head. Something's gone a little wrong with the mouth, I think. Wilfred doesn't seem to mind it but no one else thinks that it does him justice."

Julius put his head on one side and pursed his lips in a parody of critical assessment.

"Oh, I wouldn't say that. I wouldn't say that. What do you think of it, Dalgliesh?"

"I think it's remarkable. Did Carwardine do much modelling before he came here?"

It was Dennis Lerner who answered:

"I don't think he did any. He was a senior civil servant before his illness. He modelled this about a couple of months ago without Wilfred giving him a sitting. It's quite good for a first effort, isn't it?"

Julius said:

"The question which interests me is did he do it intentionally, in which case he's a great deal too talented to waste himself here, or were his fingers merely obeying his subconscious? If so, it raises interesting speculations about the origin of creativity and even more interesting ones about Henry's subconscious."

"I think it just came out like that," said Dennis Lerner simply. He looked at it with puzzled respect, clearly seeing nothing in it either for wonder or explanation.

Lastly, they went into one of the small rooms at the end of the extension. It had been arranged as an office and was furnished with two wooden ink-stained desks which looked as if they were rejects from a government office. At one Grace Willison was typing names and addresses on a perforated sheet of sticky labels. Dalgliesh saw with some surprise that Carwardine was typing what looked like a private letter at the other desk. Both the typewriters were very old. Henry was using an Imperial; Grace a Remington. Dalgliesh stood over her and glanced at the list of names and addresses. He saw that the newsletter was widely distributed. Apart from local rectories, and other homes for the chronic sick, it went to addresses in London and even to two in the United States and one near Marseilles. Flustered at his interest, Grace jerked her elbow clumsily and the bound list of names and addresses from which she was working fell to the floor. But Dalgliesh had seen enough; the unaligned small e, the smudged o, the faint almost indecipherable capital w. There was no doubt that this was the machine on which Father Baddeley's note had been typed. He picked up the book and handed it to Miss Willison. Without looking at him, she shook her head and said:

"Thank you, but I don't really need to look at it. I can type all the sixty-eight names by heart. I've done it for so long you see. I can imagine what the people are like just from their names and the names they give to their houses. But I've always been good at remembering names and addresses. It was very useful to me when I worked for a charity to help discharged prisoners and there were so many lists to type. This is quite short, of course. May I add your name so that you get our quarterly magazine? It's only ten pence. I'm afraid with postage so expensive we have to charge more than we'd like."

Henry Carwardine looked up and spoke:

"I believe this quarter we have a poem by Jennie Pegram which begins:

> Autumn is my favourite time,
> I love its glowing tints.'

It's worth ten pence to you Dalgliesh, I should have thought, to discover how she tackles that little problem of rhyming."

Grace Willison smiled happily.

"It's only an amateur production I know, but it does keep the League of Friends in touch with what is going on here, our personal friends too, of course."

Henry said:

"Not mine. They know I've lost the use of my limbs but I've no wish to suggest that I've lost the use of my mind. At best the newsletter reaches the literary level of a parish magazine; at worst, which is three issues out of four, it's embarrassingly puerile."

Grace Willison flushed and her lip trembled. Dalgliesh said quickly:

"Please add my name. Would it be easier if I paid for a year now?"

"How kind! Perhaps six months would be safer. If Wilfred does decide to transfer the Grange to the Ridgewell Trust they may have different plans for the newsletter. I'm afraid the future is very uncertain for all of us at present. Would you write your address here? Queenhythe. That's by the river, isn't it? How pleasant for you. You won't be wanting any of the handcream or bath powder, I suppose, although we do send the powder to one or two gentlemen customers. But this is really Dennis's department. He sees to the distribution and does most of the packing himself. I'm afraid our hands are too shaky to be much use. But I'm sure he could spare you some of the bath powder."

Dalgliesh was saved from the need to reply to this wistful enquiry by the booming of a gong. Julius said:

"The warning gong. One more boom and dinner will be on the table. I shall return home and see what my indispensable Mrs. Reynolds has left for me. By the way, have you warned the Commander that dinner at Toynton Grange is eaten Trappist fashion in silence? We don't want him to break the rule with inconvenient questions about Michael's will or what possible reason a patient in this abode of love could have for hurling himself over the cliff."

He disappeared at some speed as if afraid that any tendency to linger would expose him to the risk of an invitation to dine.

Grace Willison was obviously relieved to see him go but she smiled bravely at Dalgliesh.

"We do have a rule that no one talks during the evening meal. I hope that it won't inconvenience you. We take it in turns to read from any work we choose. Tonight it's Wilfred's turn so we shall have one of Donne's sermons. They're very fine of course—Father Baddeley enjoyed them, I know—but I do find them rather difficult. And I don't really think that they go well with boiled mutton."

II

Henry Carwardine wheeled his chair to the lift, drew back the steel grill with difficulty, clanged the gate closed and pressed the button to the floor above. He had insisted on having a room in the main building, firmly rejecting the unsubstantial, meanly proportioned cells in the annex, and Wilfred, despite what Henry thought were obsessive, almost paranoid fears that he might be trapped in a fire, had reluctantly agreed. Henry had confirmed his committal to Toynton Grange by moving one or two chosen pieces of furniture from his Westminster flat and virtually all his books. The room was large, high ceilinged and pleasantly proportioned, its two windows giving a wide view south-west across the headland. Next door was a lavatory and shower which he shared only with any patient being nursed in the sickroom. He knew, without the least qualm of guilt, that he had the most comfortable quarters in the house. Increasingly he was retreating into this tidy and private world, closing the heavy carved door against involvement, bribing Philby to bring up occasional meals on a tray, to buy for him in Dorchester special cheeses, wines, pâté and fruit to augment the institutional meals which the staff of the Grange took it in turns to cook. Wilfred had apparently thought it prudent not to comment on this minor insubordination, this trespass against the law of togetherness.

He wondered what had provoked him to that spatter of malice against harmless, pathetic Grace Willison. It wasn't the first time since Holroyd's death that he had caught himself speaking with Holroyd's voice. The phenomenon interested him. It set him thinking again about that other life, the one he had so prematurely and resolutely renounced. He had noticed it when chairing committees, how the members played their individual roles, almost as if these had been allocated in advance. The hawk; the dove; the compromiser; the magisterial elder statesman; the unpredictable maverick. How swiftly, if one were absent, a colleague modified his views, subtly adapted even his voice and manner to fill the gap. And so, apparently, he had assumed the mantle of Holroyd. The thought was ironic and not unsatisfying. Why not? Who else at Toynton Grange better fitted that rebarbative, non-conforming role?

He had been one of the youngest Under Secretaries of State ever appointed. He was confidently spoken of as the future head of a Department. That was how he saw himself. And then the disease, touching nerves and muscles at first with tentative fingers, had struck at the roots of confidence, at all the carefully laid plans. Dictating sessions with his personal assistant had become mutual embarrassments to be dreaded and deferred. Every telephone conversation was an ordeal; that first insistent, anxiety pitched ring was enough to set his hand trembling. Meetings which he had always enjoyed and chaired with a quiet if abrasive competence had become unpredictable contests between mind and unruly body. He had become unsure where he had been most confident.

He wasn't alone in misfortune. He had seen others, some of them in his own Department, being helped from their grotesquely graceless invalid cars into their wheelchairs, accepting a lower grade and easier work, moving to a division which could afford to carry a passenger. The Department would have balanced expediency and the public interest with proper consideration and compassion. They would have kept him on long after his usefulness justified it. He could have died, as he had watched others die, in official harness, harness lightened and adjusted to his frail shoulders, but nevertheless harness. He accepted that there was a kind of courage in that. But it wasn't his kind.

It had been a joint meeting with another Department, chaired by himself, that had finally decided him. He still couldn't think of the shambles without shame and horror. He saw himself again, feet impotently padding, his stick beating a tattoo on the floor as he strove to take one step towards his chair, the mucus spluttering out with his welcoming words to shower over his neighbour's papers. The ring of eyes around the table, animals' eyes, watchful, predatory, embarrassed, not daring to meet his. Except for one boy, a young good-looking Principal from the Treasury. He had looked fixedly at the Chairman, not with pity but with an almost clinical interest, noting for future reference one more manifestation of human behaviour under stress. The words had come out at last, of course. Somehow he had got through the meeting. But for him, it had been the end.

He had heard of Toynton Grange as one did hear of such places, through a colleague whose wife received the Home's quarterly newsletter and contributed to its funds. It had seemed to offer an answer. He was a bachelor without family. He couldn't hope indefinitely to look after himself, nor on a disability pension could he buy a permanent nurse. And he had to get out of London. If he couldn't succeed, then he would opt out completely, retire to oblivion, away from the embarrassed pity of colleagues, from noise and foul air, from the hazards and inconveniences of a world aggressively organized for the healthy and able bodied. He would write the book on decision-making in Government planned for his retirement, catch up on his Greek, re-read the whole of

Hardy. If he couldn't cultivate his own garden, at least he could avert fastidious eyes from the lack of cultivation in everyone else's.

And for the first six months it had seemed to work. There were disadvantages which, strangely, he hadn't expected or considered; the unenterprising, predictable meals; the pressures of discordant personalities; the delay in getting books and wine delivered; the lack of good talk; the self-absorption of the sick, their preoccupation with symptoms and bodily functions; the awful childishness and spurious joviality of institutional life. But it had been just supportable and he had been reluctant to admit failure since all alternatives seemed worse. And then Peter had arrived.

He had come to Toynton Grange just over a year ago. He was a polio victim, the seventeen-year-old only child of a haulage contractor's widow from the industrial Midlands who had made three preparatory visits of officious and ill-informed inspection before calculating whether she could afford to accept the vacancy. Henry suspected that, panicked by the loneliness and debased status of the early months of widowhood, she was already looking for a second husband and was beginning to realize that a seventeen-year-old chairbound son was an obstacle to be carefully weighed by likely candidates against her late husband's money, her own ageing and desperate sexuality. Listening to her spate of obstetric and marital intimacies, Henry had realized once again that the disabled were treated as a different breed. They posed no threat, sexual or otherwise, offered no competition. As companions they had the advantage of animals; literally anything could be spoken in front of them without embarrassment.

So Dolores Bonnington had expressed herself satisfied and Peter had arrived. The boy had made little impression on him at first. It was only gradually that he had come to appreciate his qualities of mind. Peter had been nursed at home with the help of district nurses and had been driven, when his health permitted, to the local comprehensive school. There he had been unlucky. No one, least of all his mother, had discovered his intelligence. Henry Carwardine doubted whether she was capable of recognizing it. He was less ready to acquit the school. Even with the problem of understaffing and over-large classes, the inevitable logistic difficulties of a huge city comprehensive, someone on the staff of that over-equipped and ill-disciplined menagerie, he thought with anger, ought to have been able to recognize a scholar. It was Henry who conceived the idea that they might provide for Peter the education he had lost; that he might in time enter a university and become self-supporting.

To Henry's surprise, preparing Peter for his 'O' levels had provided the common concern, the sense of unity and community at Toynton Grange which none of Wilfred's experiments had achieved. Even Victor Holroyd helped.

"It seems that the boy isn't a fool. He's almost totally uneducated, of course. The staff, poor sods, were probably too busy teaching race relations, sexual technique and other contemporary additions to the syllabus and preventing the barbarians from pulling the school down around their ears to have time for someone with a mind."

"He ought to have maths and one science, Victor, at least at 'O' level. If you could help . . ."

"Without a lab?"

"There's the clinical room, you could fix something up there. He wouldn't be taking a science as a main subject at 'A' level?"

"Of course not. I realize my disciplines are included merely to provide an illusion of academic balance. But the boy ought to be taught to think scientifically. I know the suppliers of course. I could probably fix something up."

"I shall pay, of course."

"Certainly. I could afford it myself but I'm a great believer in people paying for their own gratifications."

"And Jennie and Ursula might be interested."

Henry had been amazed to find himself making the suggestion. Affection—he had not yet come to use the word love—had made him kind.

"God forbid! I'm not setting up a kindergarten. But I'll take on the boy for maths and general science."

Holroyd had given three sessions a week each of a carefully measured hour. But there had been no doubt about the quality of his teaching.

Father Baddeley had been pressed into service to teach Latin. Henry himself took English literature and history and undertook the general direction of the course. He discovered that Grace Willison spoke French better than anyone else at Toynton Grange and after some initial reluctance, she agreed to take French conversation twice a week. Wilfred had watched the preparations indulgently, taking no active part but raising no objections. Everyone was suddenly busy and happy.

Peter himself was accepting rather than dedicated. But he proved incredibly hardworking, gently amused perhaps by their common enthusiasm but capable of the sustained concentration which is the mark of a scholar. They found it almost impossible to overwork him. He was grateful, biddable, but detached. Sometimes Henry, looking at the calm girlish face, had the frightening feeling that the teachers were all seventeen-year-old children and the boy alone burdened with the sad cynicism of maturity.

Henry knew that he would never forget that moment when, at last, and joyfully, he had acknowledged love. It had been a warm day in early spring; was it really only six months ago? They had been sitting together where he sat now in the early afternoon sunshine, books on their laps ready to begin the two-thirty history lesson. Peter had been wearing a short-sleeve shirt, and he had rolled up his own sleeves to feel the first warmth of the sun prickling the hairs of his forearm. They had been sitting in silence as he was sitting now. And then, without turning to look at him, Peter had lain the length of his soft inner forearm against Henry's and, deliberately, as if every movement were part of a ritual, an affirmation, had twined their fingers together so that their palms too were joined flesh against flesh. Henry's nerves and blood remembered that moment and would do until he died. The shock of ecstasy, the sudden realization of joy, a spring of sheer unalloyed happiness which for all its surging excitement was yet paradoxically rooted in fulfilment and peace. It seemed in that moment as if everything which had happened in life, his job, his illness, coming to Toynton Grange, had led inevitably to this place, this love. Everyything—success, failure, pain, frustration—had led to it and was justified by it. Never had he been so aware of another's body; the beat of the pulse in the thin wrist; the labyrinth of blue veins lying against his, blood flowing in concert with his blood; the delicate unbelievably soft flesh of the forearm; the bones of the childish fingers confidently resting between his own. Besides the intimacy of this first touch all previous adventures of the flesh had been counterfeit. And so they had sat silently, for unmeasured unfathomable time, before turning to look, at first gravely and then smilingly, into each other's eyes.

He wondered now how he could have so underestimated Wilfred. Happily secure in the confidence of love acknowledged and returned, he had treated Wilfred's innuendos and expostulations—when they pierced his consciousness—with pitying contempt, seeing them as no more real or threatening than the bleatings of a timid, ineffectual schoolmaster obsessively warning his boys against unnatural vice.

"It's good of you to give up so much time to Peter, but we ought to remember that we are one family at Toynton Grange. Other people would like a share of your interest. It isn't perhaps kind or wise to show too marked a preference for one person. I think that Ursula and Jennie and even poor Georgie sometimes feel neglected."

Henry had hardly heard; had certainly not bothered to reply.

"Henry, Dot tells me that you've taken to locking your door when giving Peter his lesson. I would prefer that you didn't. It is one of our rules that doors are never locked. If either of you needed medical help suddenly, it could be very dangerous."

Henry had continued to lock his door keeping the key always with him. He and Peter might have been the only two people at Toynton Grange. Lying in bed at night he began to plan and to dream, at first tentatively and then with the euphoria of hope. He had given up too early and too easily. There was still some future before him. The boy's mother hardly visited him, seldom wrote. Why shouldn't the two of them leave Toynton Grange and live together? He had his pension and some capital. He could buy a small house, at Oxford or Cambridge perhaps, and get it adapted for their two wheelchairs. When Peter was at university he would need a home. He made calculations, wrote to his bank manager, schemed how it might be organized so that the plan in its ultimate reasonableness and beauty could be presented to Peter. He knew that there were dangers. He would get worse; with luck Peter might even slightly improve. He must never let himself be a burden to the boy. Father Baddeley had only once spoken to him directly of Peter. He had brought over to Toynton Grange a book from which Henry had planned to set a passage of précis. On leaving he had said gently, as always not baulking the truth.

"Your disease is progressive, Peter's isn't. One day he's going to have to manage without you. Remember that, my son." Well, he would remember.

In early August Mrs. Bonnington arranged for Peter to spend a fortnight with her at home. She called it taking him for a holiday. Henry had said:

"Don't write. I never expect anything good from a letter. I shall see you again in two weeks."

But Peter hadn't come back. The evening before he was due to return Wilfred had announced the news at dinner, eyes carefully avoiding Henry's.

"You'll be glad for Peter's sake to hear that Mrs. Bonnington has found a place for him nearer his home and that he won't be returning to us. She hopes to marry again fairly soon and she and her husband want to visit Peter more frequently and have him home for occasional weekends. The new home will make arrangements for Peter's education to continue. You have all worked so hard with him. I know you'll be glad to hear that it won't be wasted."

It had been very cleverly planned; he had to give Wilfred that credit. There must have been discreet telephone calls and letters to the mother, negotiations with the new home. Peter must have been on the waiting list for weeks, possibly months. Henry could imagine the phrases.

"Unhealthy interests; unnatural affection; driving the boy too hard; mental and psychological pressure."

Hardly anyone at Toynton Grange had spoken to him about the transfer. They had avoided the contamination of his misery. Grace Willison had said, shrinking from his angry eyes:

"We shall all miss him, but his own mother . . . It's natural that she should want him close to her."

"Of course. By all means let us defer to the sacred rights of motherhood."

Within a week they had apparently forgotten Peter and returned to their old pursuits as easily as children discarding new and unwanted Christmas toys. Holroyd had disconnected his apparatus and packed it away.

"Let it be a lesson to you, my dear Henry. Put not your trust in pretty boys. We can hardly expect that he was dragged to the new home by force."

"He may have been."

"Oh, come now! The boy is practically of age. He has the use of brain and speech. He can hold a pen. We have to face it that our company here was less fascinating than we had deluded ourselves. Peter is amenable. He made no objections when he was dumped here and I've no doubt he made none when he was dragged away."

Henry, on impulse, had grasped Father Baddeley's arm as he passed and asked him:

"Did you collude in this triumph for morality and mother-love?"

Father Baddeley had briefly shaken his head, a gesture so slight that it was hardly discernible. He had seemed about to speak and then, with one pressure on Henry's shoulder, had moved on, for once at a loss, offering no comfort. But Henry had felt a spurt of anger and resentment against Michael as he hadn't against anyone else at Toynton Grange. Michael who had the use of his legs and voice, who wasn't reduced by anger into a jibbering, slobbering buffoon. Michael who could surely have prevented this monstrous thing if he hadn't been inhibited by timidity, by his fear and disgust of the flesh. Michael who had no place at Toynton Grange if not to affirm love.

There had been no letter. Henry had been reduced to bribing Philby to collect the post. His paranoia had reached the stage when he believed that Wilfred might be intercepting letters. He didn't write himself. Whether or not to do so was a preoccupation which took most of his waking hours. But, less than six weeks later, Mrs. Bonnington had written to Wilfred to say that Peter was dead of pneumonia. It could, Henry knew, have happened anywhere at any time. It didn't necessarily mean that the medical and nursing care at the new home had been less good than at Toynton Grange. Peter had always been peculiarly at risk. But in his heart Henry knew that he could have kept Peter safe. In scheming his transfer from Toynton Grange Wilfred had killed him.

And Peter's murderer went about his business, smiled his indulgent lop-sided smile, ceremoniously drew the folds of his cloak around him to preserve him from the contamination of human emotion, surveyed complacently the flawed objects of his beneficence. Was it his imagination, Henry wondered, that Wilfred had become afraid of him? Now they seldom spoke. Naturally solitary, Henry had become morose since Peter's death. Except for meal times he spent most of his days in his room, looking out over the desolate headland, neither reading nor working, possessed by a profound ennui. He knew that he hated rather than felt hatred. Love, joy, anger, grief even, were emotions too powerful for his diminished personality. He could entertain only their pale shadows. But hatred was like a latent fever dormant in the blood; sometimes it could flare into terrifying delirium. It was during one such a mood that Holroyd had whispered to him, had wheeled his chair across the patio and manoeuvred it close to Henry. Holroyd's mouth, pink and precise as a girl's, a neat, suppurating wound in the heavy blue jaw, puckered to discharge its venom. Holroyd's breath sour in his nostrils.

"I have learnt something of interest about our dear Wilfred. I shall share it with you in time but you must forgive me if I savour it alone for a little longer. There will be a right moment for disclosure. One strives always for the maximum dramatic effect." Hatred and boredom had reduced them to this, thought Henry, two schoolboy buddies whispering secrets together, planning their petty stratagems of vengeance and betrayal.

He looked out of the tall, curved window westward over the rising headland. The darkness was falling. Somewhere out there the restless tide was scouring the rocks, rocks washed clean for ever of Holroyd's blood. Not even a twist of torn cloth remained for the barnacles to fasten on. Holroyd's dead hands like floating weeds moving sluggishly in the tide, sand-filled eyes turned upwards to the swooping gulls. What was that poem of Walt Whitman which Holroyd had read at dinner on the night before he died:

"Approach strong deliveress,
When it is so, when thou hast taken them I joyously
    sing the dead,
Lost in the loving floating ocean of thee,
Laved in the flood of thy bliss O death.

The night in silence under many a star,
The ocean shore and the husky whispering wave whose
    voices I know,
And the soul turning to thee O vast and well-veiled death,
And the body gratefully nestling close to thee."

Why that poem, in its sentimental resignation, at once so alien to Holroyd's embattled spirit, and yet so prophetically apposite?

Was he telling them, even subconsciously, that he knew what must happen, that he embraced and welcomed it? Peter and Holroyd. Holroyd and Baddeley. And now this policeman friend of Baddeley's had arrived out of his past. Why, and for what? He might learn something when they drank together after dinner with Julius. And so, of course, might Dalgliesh. "There is no art to find the mind's construction in the face." But Duncan was wrong. There was a great deal of art and one in which a Commander of the Metropolitan Police would be better practised than most. Well, if that was what he had come for, he could make a beginning after dinner. Tonight he, Henry, would dine in his room. Philby when summoned would bring up his tray and plonk it unceremoniously and grudgingly in front of him. It wasn't possible to buy civility from Philby but it was possible, he thought with grim exultation, to buy almost anything else.

III

"My body is my prison; and I would be so obedient to the Law, as not to break prison; I would not hasten my death by starving or macerating this body. But if this prison be burnt down by continual fevers, or blown down with continual vapours, would any man be so in love with the ground upon which that prison stood, as to desire rather to stay there than to go home?"

It wasn't so much, thought Dalgliesh, that the Donne didn't go with the stewed mutton, as that the mutton didn't go with the home-brewed wine. Neither was in itself unpalatable. The mutton, cooked with onions, potatoes and carrots, and flavoured with herbs, was unexpectedly good if a little greasy. The elderberry wine was a nostalgic reminder of duty visits paid with his father to house-bound and hospitable parishioners. Together they tasted lethal. He reached for the water carafe.

Opposite him sat Millicent Hammitt, her square slab of a face softened by the candlelight, her absence during the afternoon explained by the pungent scent of lacquer which was wafted to him from the stiff, corrugated waves of greying hair. Everyone was present except the Hewsons, dining presumably in their own cottage, and Henry Carwardine. At the far end of the table, Albert Philby sat a little apart, a monkish Caliban in a brown habit, half crouching over his food. He ate noisily, tearing his bread into crusts and wiping them vigorously around his plate. All the patients were being helped to eat. Dalgliesh, despising his squeamishness, tried to shut his ears to the muted slobbering, the staccato rattle of spoon against plate, the sudden retching, unobtrusively controlled.

"If thou didst depart from that Table in peace, thou canst depart from this world in peace. And the peace of that Table is to come to it in pace desiderii, with a contended minde. . . ."

Wilfred stood at a reading desk at the head of the table, flanked by two candles in metal holders. Jeoffrey, distended with food, lay ceremoniously curved at his feet. Wilfred had a good voice and knew how to use it. An actor manqué? Or an actor who had found his stage and played on, happily oblivious of the dwindling audience, of the creeping paralysis of his dream? A neurotic driven by obsession? Or a man at peace with himself, secure at the still centre of his being?

Suddenly the four table candles flared and hissed. Dalgliesh's ears caught the faint squeak of wheels, the gentle thud of metal against wood. The door was slowly swinging open. Wilfred's voice faltered, and then broke off. A spoon rasped violently against a plate. Out of the shadows came a wheelchair, its occupant, head bent, swaddled in a thick plaid cloak. Miss Willison gave a sad little moan and scratched the sign of the cross on her grey dress. There was a gasp from Ursula Hollis. No one spoke. Suddenly Jennie Pegram screamed, thin and insistent as a tin whistle. The sound was so unreal that Dot Moxon jerked her head round as if uncertain where the sound was coming from. The scream subsided into a giggle. The girl clamped her hand against her mouth. Then she said:

"I thought it was Victor! That's Victor's cloak."

No one else moved or spoke. Glancing along the table, Dalgliesh let his eyes rest speculatively on Dennis Lerner. His face was a mask of terror which slowly disintegrated into relief, the features seeming to droop and crumble, amorphous as a smudged painting. Carwardine wheeled his chair to the table. He had some difficulty in getting out his words. A globule of mucus gleamed like a yellow jewel in the candle light and dribbled from his chin. At last he said in his high distorted voice:

"I thought I might join you for coffee. It seemed discourteous to absent myself on our guest's first night."

Dot Moxon's voice was sharp:

"Did you have to wear that cloak?"

He turned to her:

"It was hanging in the business room and I felt cold. And we hold so much in common. Need we exclude the dead?"

Wilfred said:

"Shall we remember the Rule?"

They turned their faces to him like obedient children. He waited until they had again begun to eat. The hands which gripped the sides of the reading desk were steady, the beautiful voice perfectly controlled.

"That so riding at Anchor, and in that calme, whether God enlarge thy voyage, by enlarging thy life, or put thee into the harbour by the breath, by the breathlesnesse of Death, either way, East or West, thou maist depart in peace. . . ."

IV

It was after eight-thirty before Dalgliesh set out to wheel Henry Carwardine to Julius Court's cottage. The task wasn't easy for a man in the first stages of convalescence. Carwardine, despite his leanness, was surprisingly heavy and the stony path wound uphill. Dalgliesh hadn't liked to suggest using his car since to be hoisted through the narrow door might be more painful and humiliating for his companion than the customary wheelchair. Anstey had been passing through the hall as they left. He had held open the door and helped guide the wheelchair down the ramp, but had made no attempt to assist, nor did he offer the use of the patients' bus. Dalgliesh wondered whether it was his imagination that detected a note of disapproval of the enterprise in Anstey's final goodnight.

Neither man spoke for the first part of the journey. Carwardine rested a heavy torch between his knees and tried to steady its beam on the path. The circle of light, reeling and spinning before them with every lurch of the chair, illumined with dazzling clarity a secret circular night world of greenness, movement and scurrying life. Dalgliesh, a little light-headed with tiredness, felt disassociated from his physical surroundings. The two thick rubber handgrips, slippery to the touch, were loose and twisted irritatingly beneath his hands, seeming to have no relation to the rest of the chair. The path ahead was real only because its stones and crevices jarred the wheels. The night was still and very warm for autumn, the air heavy with the smell of grass and the memory of summer flowers. Low clouds had obscured the stars and they moved forwards in almost total darkness towards the strengthening murmur of the sea and the four oblongs of light which marked Toynton Cottage. When they were close enough for the largest oblong to reveal itself as the rear door of the cottage, Dalgliesh said on impulse:

"I found a rather disagreeable poison pen letter in Father Baddeley's bureau. Obviously someone at Toynton Grange didn't like him. I wondered whether this was personal spite or whether anyone else had received one."

Carwardine bent his head upwards. Dalgliesh saw his face intriguingly foreshortened, his sharp nose a spur of bone, the jaw hanging loose as a marionette's below the shapeless void of mouth. He said:

"I had one about ten months ago, placed inside my library book, I haven't had one since, and I don't know of anyone else who has. It's not the kind of thing people talk about, but I think the news would have got around if the trouble had been endemic. Mine was, I suppose, the usual muck. It suggested what methods of somewhat acrobatic sexual self-gratification might be open to me supposing I still had the physical agility to perform them. It took the desire to do so for granted."

"It was obscene, then, rather than merely offensive?"

"Obscene in the sense of calculated to disgust rather than to deprave or corrupt, yes."

"Have you any idea who was responsible?"

"It was typed on Toynton Grange paper and on an old Remington machine used chiefly by Grace Willison to send out the quarterly newsletter. She seemed the most likely candidate. It wasn't Ursula Hollis; she didn't arrive until two months later. And aren't these things usually sent by respectable middle-aged spinsters?"

"In this case I doubt it."

"Oh, well—I defer to your greater experience of obscenity."

"Did you tell anyone?"

"Only Julius. He counselled against telling anyone else and suggested I tear the note up and flush it down the WC. As that advice coincided with my own inclination, I took it. As I said, I haven't had another. I imagine that the sport loses its thrill if the victim shows absolutely no sign of concern."

"Could it have been Holroyd?"

"It didn't really seem his style. Victor was offensive but not, I should have thought, in that particular way. His weapon was the voice, not the pen. Personally I didn't mind him as much as some of the others did. He hit out rather like an unhappy child. There was more personal bitterness than active malice. Admittedly, he added a somewhat childish codicil to his will the week before he died; Philby and Julius's housekeeper, Mrs. Reynolds, witnessed it. But that was probably because he'd made up his mind to die and wanted to relieve us all of any obligation to remember him with kindness."

"So you think he killed himself?"

"Of course. And so does everyone else. How else could it have happened? It seems the most likely hypothesis. It was either suicide or murder."

It was the first time anyone at Toynton Grange had used that portentous word. Spoken in Carwardine's pedantic, rather high voice it sounded as incongruous as blasphemy on the lips of a nun.

Dalgliesh said:

"Or the chair brakes could have been defective."

"Given the circumstances, I count that as murder."

There was silence for a moment. The chair lurched over a small boulder and the torch light swung upwards in a wide arc, a miniature and frail searchlight. Carwardine steadied it and then said:

"Philby oiled and checked the chair brakes at eight-fifty on the night before Holroyd died. I was in the workroom messing about with my modelling clay at the time. I saw him. He left the workroom shortly afterwards and I stayed on until about ten o'clock."

"Did you tell the police that?"

"Since they asked me, yes. They enquired with heavy tact where exactly I had spent the evening and whether I had touched Holroyd's chair after Philby had left. Since I would hardly have admitted the fact if I had, the question was naïve. They questioned Philby, although not in my presence, and I've no doubt that he confirmed my story. I have an ambivalent attitude towards the police; I confine myself strictly to answering their questions, but on the premise that they are, in general, entitled to the truth."

They had arrived. Light streamed from the rear door of the cottage and Julius Court, a dark silhouette, emerged to meet them. He took the wheelchair from Dalgliesh and pushed it along the short stone passage leading into the sitting-room. On the way Dalgliesh just had time to glimpse through an open door the pine-covered walls, red tiled floor and gleaming chrome of Julius's kitchen, a kitchen too like his own where a woman, overpaid and underworked to assuage her employer's guilt for hiring her at all, cooked the occasional meal to gratify one person's over-fastidious taste.

The sitting-room occupied the whole of the front ground floor of what had obviously originally been two cottages. A fire of driftwood crackled on the open hearth but both the long windows were open to the night. The stone walls vibrated with the thudding of the sea. It was disconcerting to feel so close to the cliff edge and yet not know precisely how close. As if reading his thoughts, Julius said:

"We're just six yards from the forty-foot drop to the rocks. There's a stone patio and low wall outside; we might sit there later if it's warm enough. What will you drink, spirits or wine? I know Henry's preference is for claret."

"Claret please."

Dalgliesh didn't repent of his choice when he saw the labels on the three bottles which were standing, two already uncorked, on the low table near the hearth. He was surprised that wine of such quality should be produced for two casual guests. While Julius busied himself with the glasses, Dalgliesh wandered about the room. It contained enviable objects, if one were in a mood to prize personal possessions. His eyes lit on a splendid Sunderland lustreware jug commemorating Trafalgar, three early Staffordshire figures on the stone mantelpiece, a couple of agreeable seascapes on the longest wall. Above the door leading to the cliff edge was a ship's figure-head finely and ornately carved in oak; two cherubs supported a galleon topped with a shield and swathed with heavy seaman's knots. Seeing his interest, Julius called out:

"It was made about 1660 by Grinling Gibbons, reputedly for

Jacob Court, a smuggler in these parts. As far as I can discover, he was absolutely no ancestor of mine, worse luck. It's probably the oldest merchant ship figure-head known to exist. Greenwich think they have one earlier, but I'd give mine the benefit of a couple of years."

Set on a pedestal at the far end of the room and faintly gleaming as if luminous was the marble bust of a winged child holding in his chubby hand a posy of rosebuds and lilies of the valley. The marble was the colour of pale coffee except over the lids of the closed eyes which were tinged with a faint pink. The unveined hands held the flowers with the upright, unselfconscious grip of a child; the boy's lips were slightly parted in a half-smile, tranquil and secretive. Dalgliesh stretched out a finger and gently stroked the cheek; he could imagine it warm to his touch. Julius came over to him carrying two glasses.

"You like my marble? It's a memorial piece, of course, seventeenth or very early eighteenth century and derived from Bernini. Henry, I suspect, would like it better if it were Bernini."

Henry called out:

"I wouldn't like it better. I did say I'd be prepared to pay more for it."

Dalgliesh and Court moved back to the fireplace and settled down for what was obviously intended to be a night of serious drinking. Dalgliesh found his eyes straying around the room. There was no bravura, no conscious striving after originality or effect. And yet, trouble had been taken; every object was in the right place. They had, he thought, been bought because Julius liked them; they weren't part of a careful scheme of capital appreciation, nor acquired out of an obsessive need to add to his collection. Yet Dalgliesh doubted whether any had been casually discovered or cheaply bought. The furniture too, betrayed wealth. The leather sofa and the two winged and back buttoned leather chairs were perhaps too opulent for the proportions and basic simplicity of the room, but Julius had obviously chosen them for comfort. Dalgliesh reproached himself for the streak of puritanism which compared the room unfavourably with the snug, unindulgent, shabbiness of Father Baddeley's sitting-room.

Carwardine, sitting in his wheelchair and staring into the fire above the rim of his glass asked suddenly:

"Did Baddeley warn you about the more bizarre manifestations of Wilfred's philanthropy, or was your visit here unpremeditated?"

It was a question Dalgliesh had been expecting. He sensed that both men were more than casually interested in his reply.

"Father Baddeley wrote to say that he would be glad to see me. I decided to come on impulse. I've had a spell in hospital and it seemed a good idea to spend a few days of my convalescence with him."

Carwardine said:

"I can think of more suitable places than Hope Cottage for convalescence, if the inside is anything like the exterior. Had you known Baddeley long?"

"Since boyhood; he was my father's curate. But we last met, and only briefly, when I was at university."

"And having been content to know nothing of each other for a decade or so, you're naturally distressed to find him so inconveniently dead."

Unprovoked, Dalgliesh replied equably:

"More than I would have expected. We seldom wrote except to exchange cards at Christmas but he was a man more often in my thoughts, I suppose, than some people I saw almost daily. I don't know why I never bothered to get in touch. One makes the excuse of busyness. But, from what I remember of him, I can't quite see how he fitted in here."

Julius laughed:

"He didn't. He was recruited when Wilfred was going through a more orthodox phase, I suppose to give Toynton Grange a certain religious respectability. But in recent months I sensed a coolness between them, didn't you, Henry? Father Baddeley was probably no longer sure whether Wilfred wanted a priest or a guru. Wilfred picks up any scraps of philosophy, metaphysics and orthodox religion which take his fancy to make his Technicolor dreamcoat. As a result, as you'll probably discover if you stay long enough, this place suffers from the lack of a coherent ethos. There's nothing more fatal to success. Take my London club, dedicated simply to the enjoyment of good food and wine and the exclusion of bores and pederasts. It's unstated of course, but we all know where we stand. The aims are simple and comprehensible and, therefore, realizable. Here the poor dears don't know whether they're in a nursing home, a commune, a hotel, a monastery or a particularly dotty lunatic asylum. They even have meditation sessions from time to time. I'm afraid Wilfred may be getting a touch of the Zens."

Carwardine broke in:

"He's muddled, but which of us isn't? Basically he's kind and well meaning, and at least he's spent his own personal fortune at Toynton Grange. In this age of noisy and self-indulgent commitment when the first principle of private or public protest is that it mustn't relate to anything for which the protestor can be held in the least responsible or involve him in the slightest personal sacrifice that, at least, is in his favour."

"You like him?" asked Dalgliesh.

Henry Carwardine answered with surprising roughness.

"As he's saved me from the ultimate fate of incarceration in a long-stay hospital and gives me a private room at a price I can afford, I'm naturally bound to find him delightful."

There was a short, embarrassed silence. Sensing it, Carwardine added:

"The food is the worst thing about Toynton, but that can be remedied, even if I do occasionally feel like a greedy schoolboy feasting alone in my room. And listening to my fellow inmates read their favourite bleeding chunks from popular theology and the less enterprising anthologies of English verse is a small price to pay for silence at dinner."

Dalgliesh said:

"Staffing must be a difficulty. According to Mrs. Hewson, Anstey chiefly relies on an ex-convict and an otherwise unemployable matron."

Julius Court reached out for the claret and refilled the three glasses. He said:

"Dear Maggie, discreet as always. It's true that Philby, the handyman, has some kind of record. He's not exactly an advertisement for the place, but someone has to sluice the foul linen, slaughter the chickens, clean the lavatories and do the other jobs which Wilfred's sensitive soul cringes at. Besides, he's passionately devoted to Dot Moxon, and I've no doubt that helps to keep her happy. Since Maggie has let slip so much, you may as well know the truth about Dot. Perhaps you remember something of the case—she was that notorious staff nurse at Nettingfield Geriatric Hospital. Four years ago she struck a patient. It was only a light blow but the old woman fell, knocked her head against a bedside locker and nearly died. Reading between the lines at the subsequent enquiry report, she was a selfish, demanding, foul-mouthed virago who would have tempted a saint. Her family would have nothing to do with her—didn't even visit—until they discovered that there was a great deal of agreeable publicity to be made out of righteous indignation. Perfectly proper too, no doubt. Patients, however disagreeable, are sacrosanct and it's in all our ultimate interests to uphold that admirable precept. The incident sparked off a spate of complaints about the hospital. There was a full-dress enquiry covering the administration, medical services, food, nursing care, the lot. Not surprisingly, they found plenty to enquire into. Two male nurses were subsequently dismissed and Dot left of her own accord. The enquiry, while deploring her loss of control, exonerated her from any suspicion of deliberate cruelty. But the damage was done; no other hospital wanted her. Apart from the suspicion that she wasn't exactly reliable under stress, they blamed her for provoking an enquiry which did no one any good and lost two men their jobs. Afterwards, Wilfred tried to get in touch with her; he thought from the accounts of the enquiry that she'd been hard done by. He took some time to trace her, but succeeded in the end and invited her here as a kind of matron. Actually, like the rest of the staff, she does anything that's needed from nursing to cooking. His motives weren't entirely beneficent. It's never easy to find nursing staff for a remote specialized place like this, apart from the unorthodoxy of Wilfred's methods. If he lost Dorothy Moxon he wouldn't easily find a replacement."

Dalgliesh said:

"I remember the case but not her face. It's the young blonde girl—Jennie Pegram, isn't it?—who looks familiar."

Carwardine smiled; indulgent, a little contemptuous.

"I thought you might ask about her. Wilfred ought to find a way of using her for fund raising, she'd love it. I don't know anyone who's better at assuming that expression of wistful, uncomprehending, long-suffering fortitude. She'd make a fortune for the place properly exploited."

Julius laughed:

"Henry, as you have gathered, doesn't like her. If she looks familiar, you may have seen her on television about eighteen months ago. It was the month for the media to lacerate the British conscience on behalf of the young chronic sick, and the producer sent out his underlings to scavenge for a suitable victim. They came up with Jennie. She had been nursed for twelve years, and very well nursed, in a geriatric unit, partly, I gather, because they couldn't find a more suitable place for her, partly because she rather liked being the petted favourite of the patients and visitors, and partly because the hospital had group physiotherapy and occupational therapy facilities of which our Jennie took advantage. But the programme, as you can imagine, made the most of her situation—"Unfortunate twenty-five-year-old girl incarcerated among the old and dying; shut away from the community; helpless; hopeless.' All the most senile patients were carefully grouped round her for the benefit of the camera with Jennie in the middle doing her stuff magnificently. Shrill accusations against the inhumanity of the Department of Health, the regional hospital board, the hospital managers. Next day, predictably, there was a public outburst of indignation which lasted, I imagine, until the next protest programme. The compassionate British public demanded that a more suitable place be found for Jennie. Wilfred wrote offering a vacancy here, Jennie accepted, and fourteen months ago she arrived. No one quite knows what she makes of us. I should give a lot to look into what passes for Jennie's mind."

Dalgliesh was surprised that Julius had such an intimate knowledge of the patients at Toynton Grange, but he asked no more questions. He dropped unobtrusively out of the chatter and sat drinking his wine, half listening to the desultory voices of his companions. It was the quiet, undemanding talk of men who had acquaintances and interests in common, who knew just enough about each other and cared just sufficiently to create an illusion of companionship. He had no particular wish to share it. The wine deserved silence. He realized that this was the first fine wine he had drunk since his illness. It was reassuring that yet another of life's pleasures still held its power to solace. It took him a minute to realize that Julius was talking to him directly.

"I'm sorry about the proposed poetry reading. But I'm not altogether displeased. It illustrates one thing that you'll realize about Toynton. They exploit. They don't mean to, but they can't help it. They say that they want to be treated as ordinary people, and then make demands no ordinary person would dream of making, and naturally one can't refuse. Now, perhaps, you won't think too harshly of those of us who seem less than enthusiastic about Toynton."

"Us?"

"The little group of normals, physically normal anyway, in thrall to the place."

"Are you?"

"Oh, yes! I get away to London or abroad so that the spell never really has a chance to take hold. But think of Millicent, stuck in that cottage because Wilfred lets her have it rent free. All she wants is to get back to the bridge tables and cream cakes of Cheltenham Spa. So why doesn't she? And Maggie. Maggie would say that all she wanted was a bit of life. Well, that's what we all want, a bit of life. Wilfred tried to get her interested in bird watching. I remember her reply. 'If I have to watch another bloody seagull shitting on Toynton Head I'll run screaming into the sea.' Dear Maggie. I rather take to Maggie when she's sober. And Eric? Well, he could break away if he had the courage. Looking after five patients and medically supervising the production of hand lotion and bath powder is hardly an honourable job for a registered medical practitioner, even one with an unfortunate predilection for little girls. And then there's Helen Rainer. But I rather fancy that our enigmatic Helen's reason for staying is more elemental and understandable. But they're all a prey of boredom. And now I'm boring you. Would you like to hear some music? We usually listen to records when Henry's here."

The claret, unaccompanied by speech or music, would have contented Dalgliesh. But he could see that Henry was as anxious to hear a record as Julius probably was to demonstrate the superiority of his stereo equipment. Invited to choose Dalgliesh asked for Vivaldi. While the record was playing he strolled out into the night. Julius followed him and they stood in silence at the low barricade of stone at the cliff edge. The sea lay before them, faintly luminous, ghostly under a scatter of high, unemphatic stars. He thought that the tide was on the ebb but it still sounded very close, thudding against the rocky beach in great chords of sound, a base accompaniment to the high, sweet counterpoint of the distant violins. Dalgliesh thought that he could feel the spume light on his forehead, but when he put up his hand he found it was only a trick of the freshening breeze.

So there must have been two poison pen writers, only one genuinely committed to his or her obscene trade. It was obvious from Grace Willison's distress and Carwardine's laconic disgust that they had received a very different type of letter from the one found at Hope Cottage. It was too great a coincidence that two poison pens should be operating at the same time in so small a community. The assumption was that Father Baddeley's note had been planted in the bureau after his death, with small attempt at concealment, for Dalgliesh to find. If this were so, then it must have been put there by someone who knew about at least one of the other letters; had been told that it was typed on a Toynton Grange machine and on Toynton Grange paper, but who hadn't actually seen it. Grace Willison's letter had been typed on the Imperial machine and she had confided only in Dot Moxon. Carwardine's, like Father Baddeley's, had been typed on the Remington, and he had told Julius Court. The inference was obvious. But how could a man as intelligent as Court expect such a childish ruse to deceive a professional detective, or even an enthusiastic amateur? But then, had it been intended to? Dalgliesh had signed his postcard to Father Baddeley only with his initials. If it had been found by someone with a guilty secret as he searched feverishly through the bureau it would have told him nothing except that Father Baddeley was expecting a visitor on the afternoon of 1st October, a visitor who was probably as innocuous as a fellow clergyman or an old parishioner. But, just in case Father Baddeley had confided that something was on his mind, it might have seemed worthwhile to concoct and plant a false clue. Almost certainly, it had been placed in the bureau shortly before his arrival. If Anstey were telling the truth about looking through Father Baddeley's papers on the morning after his death, it was impossible that he should have missed the poison pen note or failed to remove it.

But even if all this were an elaborate and over-sophisticated edifice of conjecture, and Father Baddeley had indeed received the poison pen note, Dalgliesh now felt certain that it wasn't the reason for his summons. Father Baddeley would have felt perfectly competent both to discover the sender and to deal with him. He was unworldly but not naïve. Unlike Dalgliesh, he had probably seldom become involved professionally with the more spectacular sins but that didn't mean they were outside his comprehension or, for that matter, his compassion. It was arguable, anyway, that those were the sins which did least damage. Of the more corrosive, petty, mean-minded delinquencies in all their sad but limited variety he, like any other parish priest, would have had his fill. He had his answer ready, compassionate but inexorable, offered, Dalgliesh remembered wryly with all the gentle arrogance of absolute certainty. No, when Father Baddeley wrote he wanted professional advice he meant just that; advice which he could only get from a police officer on a matter which he felt unable to deal with himself. And that was unlikely to include the detection of a spiteful but not particularly vicious poison pen writer operating in a small community of which every member must have been known intimately to him.

The prospect of trying to discover the truth filled Dalgliesh with a profound depression. He was at Toynton Grange merely as a private visitor. He had no standing, no facilities, no equipment even. The task of sorting Father Baddeley's books could be stretched to cover a week, perhaps longer. After that, what excuse would he have to remain? And he had discovered nothing which would justify bringing in the local police. What did these vague suspicions, this sense of foreboding amount to? An old man, dying of heart disease, suffering his final and expected attack peacefully in his fireside chair, reaching perhaps in his last conscious moment for the familiar feel of his stole, lifting it over his head for the last time for reasons, probably only half understood, of comfort, of reassurance, of symbolism, of the simple affirmation of his priesthood or his faith. One could think of a dozen explanations, all simple, all more plausible than the secret visit of a murderous mock penitent. The missing diary; who could ever prove that Father Baddeley hadn't himself destroyed it before his admission to hospital? The forced bureau lock; nothing but the diary was missing and, as far as he knew, nothing valuable had been stolen. In the absence of other evidence, how could he possibly justify an official enquiry into a mislaid key and a broken lock?

But Father Baddeley had sent for him. There had been something on his mind. If Dalgliesh, without too great involvement, inconvenience or embarrassment, could discover in the next week or ten days what it had been, then he would do so. He owed that at least to the old man. But there it would end. Tomorrow he would pay a duty visit to the police and to Father Baddeley's solicitor. If anything came to light, then the police could deal with it. He was finished with police work, professional or amateur, and it would take more than the death of one old priest to change that decision.

V

When they got back to Toynton Grange shortly after midnight Henry Carwardine said roughly:

"They'll be relying on you to help me to bed, I'm afraid. Dennis Lerner usually wheels me to Toynton Cottage and calls for me at midnight, but since you're here . . . As Julius said, we're great exploiters at Toynton Grange. And I'd better shower. Dennis is off duty tomorrow morning and I can't stomach Philby. My room is on the first floor. We take the lift."

Henry knew that he sounded ungracious but that, he guessed, would be more acceptable to his silent companion than humility or self-pity. It struck him that Dalgliesh looked as if he could have done with help himself. Perhaps the man had been more sick than they realized. Dalgliesh said calmly:

"Another half bottle and I suspect we would both have needed help. But I'll do my best. Put down my clumsiness to inexperience and the claret."

But he was surprisingly gentle and competent, getting Henry out of his clothes, supporting him to the lavatory, and finally, wheeling him under the shower. He spent a little time examining the hoist and equipment and then used them intelligently. When he didn't know what was needed, he asked. Apart from these brief and necessary exchanges, neither spoke. Henry thought that he had seldom been put to bed with such imaginative gentleness. But, catching a glimpse in the bathroom mirror of his companion's drawn preoccupied face, of the dark secretive eyes cavernous with fatigue, he wished suddenly that he hadn't asked for help, that he had tumbled unshowered and fully dressed on to his bed, free from the humiliating touch of these competent hands. He sensed that, behind the disciplined calm, every contact with his naked body was a disagreeable duty. And for Henry himself, illogically and surprisingly, the touch of Dalgliesh's cool hands was like the touch of fear. He wanted to cry out:

"What are you doing here? Go away; don't interfere; leave us in peace." The urge was so strong that he could almost believe that he had spoken the words aloud. And when, at last, he was comfortably bedded by his temporary nurse and Dalgliesh said an abrupt goodbye and immediately left him without another word, he knew that it was because he couldn't bear to hear even the most perfunctory and least gracious word of thanks.

4

The Dreadful Shore

I

He awoke sluggishly soon before seven to disagreeably familiar noises; intrusive plumbing, the clang of apparatus, the squeal of chair wheels, sudden hurrying footsteps, determinedly cheerful exhortatory voices. Telling himself that the bathrooms would be needed for the patients, he shut his eyes resolutely on the bleak, impersonal room and willed himself to sleep again. When he woke an hour later after a fitful doze the annexe was silent. Someone—he dimly remembered a brown cloaked figure—had placed a mug of tea on his bedside table. It was cold, the greyish surface mottled with milk. He dragged on his dressing gown and went in search of the bathroom.

Breakfast at Toynton Grange was, as he had expected, laid out in the communal dining-room. But, at eight-thirty, he was either too early or too late for the majority of the inmates. Only Ursula Hollis was breakfasting when he arrived. She gave him a shy good morning, then returned her eyes to the library book precariously propped against a jar of honey. Dalgliesh saw that the breakfast was simple, but adequate. There was a bowl of stewed apples; home-made muesli consisting mostly of porridge oats, bran and shredded apple; brown bread and margarine, and a row of boiled eggs each in its eggcup and individually named. The two remaining were cold. Presumably they were all cooked together earlier in the morning, and those who wanted their egg warm took the trouble to be on time. Dalgliesh helped himself to the egg pencilled with his name. It was glutinous at the top and very hard at the bottom, a result which he felt must have taken some perverse culinary skill to achieve.

After breakfast he went in search of Anstey to thank him for his overnight hospitality and to ask if there was anything he wanted in Wareham. He had decided that some of the afternoon had better be given over to shopping if he were to make himself comfortable in Michael's cottage. A short search of the seemingly deserted house found Anstey with Dorothy Moxon in the business room. They were seated together at the table with an open ledger before them. As he knocked and entered they looked up simultaneously with something of the air of guilty conspirators. It seemed to take a couple of seconds before they realized who he was. Anstey's smile, when it came, was as sweet as ever but his eyes were preoccupied and his enquiries over his guest's comforts were perfunctory. Dalgliesh sensed that he wouldn't be sorry to see him go. Anstey might see himself in the role of a welcoming medieval abbot, always ready with the bread and ale, but what he really craved were the gratifications of hospitality without the inconvenience of a guest. He said there was nothing he wanted in Wareham and then asked Dalgliesh how long he expected to be in the cottage. There was absolutely no hurry, of course. Their guest wasn't to feel himself at all in the way. When Dalgliesh replied that he would stay only until Father Baddeley's books were sorted and packed, it was difficult for him to conceal his relief. He offered to send Philby to Hope Cottage with some packing cases. Dorothy Moxon said nothing. She continued to stare fixedly at Dalgliesh as if determined not to betray her irritation at his presence and her desire to get back to the ledger by so much as a flicker of her sombre eyes.

It was comforting to be back in Hope Cottage, to smell again the familiar faintly ecclesiastical smell and to look forward to a long exploratory walk along the cliff before setting out for Wareham. But he had scarcely had time to unpack his case and change into stout walking shoes when he heard the patients' bus stopping outside and, going to the window, saw Philby unloading the first of the promised packing cases. Swinging it on to his shoulder, he marched up the short path, kicked open the door, bringing with him into the room a powerful smell of stale sweat, and dropped the case at Dalgliesh's feet with a brusque:

"There's a couple more in the back."

It was an obvious invitation to help unload them, and Dalgliesh took the hint. It was the first time he had seen the handyman in the full light, and the sight wasn't agreeable. He had, in fact, seldom encountered a man whose physical appearance so repelled him. Philby was only a little over five feet tall and stockily built with short plump arms and legs as pale and shapeless as peeled tree trunks. His head was round and his skin, despite his outdoor life, was pink and glossy and very smooth as if blown-up with air. His eyes would have been remarkable in a more attractive face. They were slightly slanted and the irises were large and blue-black in colour. His black hair was scanty and combed straight back over the domed skull to end in an untidy and greasy fringe. He was wearing sandals, the right one fastened with string; a pair of dirty white shorts, so brief that they were almost indecent; and a grey vest, stained with sweat. Over this he wore, loosely open and held together only by a cord at the waist, his brown monk's habit. Without this incongruous garb he would have looked merely dirty and disreputable. With it he looked positively sinister.

As he made no attempt to go once the cases were unloaded, Dalgliesh deduced that he expected a tip. The proffered coins were slipped into the pocket of the habit with sly expertise but with no thanks. Dalgliesh was interested to learn that, despite the expensive experiment with home-produced eggs, not all the economic laws were defunct in this unworldly abode of brotherly love. Philby gave the three boxes a vicious valedictory kick as if to earn his tip by demonstrating that they were sound. As they disappointingly remained intact, he gave them a final look of sour displeasure and then departed. Dalgliesh wondered where Anstey had recruited this particular member of the staff. To his prejudiced eye the man looked like a category 'A' rapist on licence, but perhaps that was going a little too far even for Wilfred Anstey.

His second attempt to set out was frustrated by a second visitor, this time Helen Rainer who had cycled the short distance from Toynton Grange with her bicycle basket piled high with the linen from his bed. She explained that Wilfred was concerned in case the sheets at Hope Cottage were inadequately aired. It surprised Dalgliesh that she hadn't taken the opportunity to come with Philby in the bus. But perhaps, understandably, she found his proximity distasteful. She came in quietly but briskly and without too obviously making Dalgliesh feel he was a nuisance, unmistakably conveyed the impression that this wasn't a social visit, that she hadn't come to chat, and that there were more important duties awaiting her. They made the bed together, Nurse Rainer flicking the sheets into place and neatly mitring each corner with such brisk expertise that Dalgliesh, a second or two behind her, felt himself slow and incompetent. At first they worked in silence. He doubted whether this was the time to ask, however tactfully, how the misunderstanding had arisen over the neglected visit to Father Baddeley on the last night of his life. His stay in hospital must have intimidated him. It took an effort of will to say:

"I'm probably being over-sensitive, but I wish that someone had been with Father Baddeley when he died, or at least had looked in on him later that night to see that all was well."

She could with justice, he thought, reply to this implied criticism by pointing out that it came inappropriately from someone who had shown no concern for the old man for nearly thirty years. But she said without rancour, almost eagerly:

"Yes, that was bad. It couldn't have made any difference medically, but the misunderstanding shouldn't have happened, one of us ought to have looked in. Do you want this third blanket? If not, I'll take it back to Toynton Grange, it's one of ours."

"Two will be enough. What exactly happened?"

"To Father Baddeley? He died of acute myocarditis."

"I mean, how did the misunderstanding arise?"

"I served him a cold lunch of chicken and salad when he arrived back from hospital and then settled him for his afternoon rest. He was ready for it. Dot took him his afternoon tea and helped him to wash. She got him into his pyjamas and he insisted on wearing his cassock on top. I cooked scrambled eggs for him in the kitchen here shortly after six-thirty. He was absolutely insistent that he wanted to spend the rest of the evening undisturbed, except, of course, for Grace Willison's visit, but I told him that someone would come in about ten and he seemed perfectly happy with that. He said that he'd rap on the wall with the poker if he were in any distress. Then I went next door to ask Millicent to listen for him and she offered to look in on him last thing. At least, that's what I understood. Apparently she thought that Eric or I would come. As I said, it shouldn't have happened. I blame myself. It wasn't Eric's fault. As his nurse, I should have ensured that he was seen again professionally before he went to bed."

Dalgliesh asked:

"This insistence on being alone; did you get the impression that he was expecting a visitor?"

"What visitor could he be expecting, other than poor Grace? I think he'd had enough of people while he was in hospital and just wanted some peace."

"And you were all here at Toynton Grange that night?"

"All except Henry who hadn't got back from London. Where else could we be?"

"Who unpacked his case for him?"

"I did. He was admitted to hospital as an emergency and had very few things with him, only those which we found by his bed and packed."

"His Bible, prayer book and his diary?"

She looked up at him briefly, her face expressionless, before bending again to tuck in a blanket.

"Yes."

"What did you do with them?"

"I left them on the small table beside his chair. He may have moved them later."

So the diary had been with Father Baddeley in hospital. That meant that the record would have been up to date. And if Anstey were not lying about its being missing next morning, then it had been removed some time within those twelve hours.

He wondered how he could phrase his next question without arousing her suspicions. Keeping his voice light, he said:

"You may have neglected him in life but you looked after him very thoroughly after he died. First cremation and then burial. Wasn't that a little over-conscientious?"

To his surprise she burst out as if he had invited her to share a justified indignation:

"Of course it was! It was ridiculous! But that was Millicent's fault. She told Wilfred that Michael had frequently expressed his strong wish to be cremated. I can't think when or why. Although they were neighbours, she and Michael didn't exactly live in each other's pockets. But that's what she said. Wilfred was equally sure that Michael would want an orthodox Christian burial, so the poor man got both. It meant a lot of extra trouble and expense and Dr. McKeith from Wareham had to sign a medical certificate as well as Eric. All that fuss just because Wilfred had a bad conscience."

"Did he? About what?"

"Oh, nothing. I just got the impression that he felt that Michael had been a bit neglected one way and another, the usual self-indulgent compunction of the bereaved. Is this pillow going to be adequate? It feels very lumpy to me, and you look as if you could do with a good night's rest. Don't forget to come up to the Grange if there's anything you need. The milk is delivered to the boundary gate. I've ordered a pint for you each day. If that's too much, we can always use it. Now, have you everything you need?"

With a sensation of being under firm discipline Dalgliesh said meekly that he had. Nurse Rainer's briskness, her confidence, her concentration on the job in hand, even her reassuring smile of farewell, all relegated him to the status of a patient. As she wheeled her bicycle down the path and remounted, he felt that he had been visited by the district nurse. But he felt an increased respect for her. She hadn't appeared to resent his questions, and she had certainly been remarkably forthcoming. He wondered why.

II

It was a warm misty morning under a sky of low cloud. As he left the valley and began to trudge up the cliff path a reluctant rain began to fall in slow heavy drops. The sea was a milky blue, sluggish and opaque, its slopping waves pitted with rain and awash with shifting patterns of floating foam. There was a smell of autumn as if someone far off, undetected even by a wisp of smoke, was burning leaves. The narrow path rose higher skirting the cliff edge, now close enough to give him a brief vertiginous illusion of danger, now twisting inland between a tatter of bronzed bracken crumpled with the wind, and low tangles of bramble bushes, their red and black berries tight and meagre compared with the luscious fruit of inland hedgerows. The headland was dissected by low broken walls of stone and studded with small limestone rocks. Some, half buried, protruded tipsily from the soil like the relics of a disorderly graveyard.

Dalgliesh walked warily. It was his first country walk since his illness. The demands of his job meant that walking had always been a rare and special pleasure. Now he moved with something of the uncertainty of those first tentative steps of convalescence, muscles and senses rediscovering remembered pleasures, not with keen delight but with the gentle acceptance of familiarity. The brief metallic warble and churling note of stonechats, busy among the brambles; a solitary black-headed gull motionless as a ship's figurehead on a promontory of rock; clumps of rock samphire, their umbels stained with purple; yellow dandelions, pinpoints of brightness on the faded autumnal grass.

After nearly ten minutes of walking the cliff path began to slope gently downhill and was eventually dissected by a narrow lane running inland from the cliff edge. About six yards from the sea it broadened into a gently sloping plateau of bright green turf and moss. Dalgliesh stopped suddenly as if stung by memory. This then, must be the place where Victor Holroyd had chosen to sit, the spot from which he had plunged to his death. For a moment he wished that it hadn't lain so inconveniently in his path. The thought of violent death broke disagreeably into his euphoria. But he could understand the attraction of the spot. The lane was secluded and sheltered from the wind, there was a sense of privacy and peace; a precarious peace for a man captive in a wheelchair and with only the power of its brakes holding the balance between life and death. But that may have been part of the attraction. Perhaps only here, poised above the sea on this secluded patch of bright moss, could Holroyd, frustrated and chairbound, gain an illusion of freedom, of being in control of his destiny. He might always have intended to make here his final bid for release, insisting month after month on being wheeled to the same spot, biding his time so that no one at Toynton Grange suspected his real purpose. Instinctively, Dalgliesh studied the ground. Over three weeks had passed since Holroyd's death but he thought he could still detect the faint indentation of the soft turf where the wheels had rested and, less plainly, marks where the short grass had been matted with the scuffle of policemen's feet.

He walked to the cliff edge and looked down. The view, spectacular and frightening, made him catch his breath. The cliffs had changed and here the limestone had given place to an almost vertical wall of blackish clay larded with calcareous stone. Almost a hundred and fifty feet below, the cliff tumbled into a broad fissured causeway of boulders, slabs and amorphous chunks of blue-black rock which littered the foreshore as if hurled in wild disorder by a giant hand. The tide was out and the oblique line of foam moved sluggishly among the furthest rocks. As he looked down on this chaotic and awe-inspiring waste of rock and sea and tried to picture what the fall must have done to Holroyd, the sun moved fitfully from behind the clouds and a band of sunlight moved across the headland lying warm as a hand on the back of his neck, gilding the bracken, marbling the strewn rocks at the cliff edge. But it left the foreshore in shadow, sinister and unfriendly. For a moment Dalgliesh believed that he was looking down on a cursed and dreadful shore on which the sun could never shine.

Dalgliesh had been making for the black tower marked on Father Baddeley's map, less from a curiosity to see it than from the need to set an object for his walk. Still musing on Victor Holroyd's death, he came upon the tower almost unexpectedly. It was a squat intimidating folly, circular for about two-thirds of its height but topped with an octagonal cupola like a pepperpot pierced with eight glazed slit windows, compass points of reflected light which gave it something of the look of a lighthouse. The tower intrigued him and he moved round it touching the black walls. He saw that it had been built of limestone blocks but faced with the black shale as if capriciously decorated with pellets of polished jet. In places the shale had flaked away giving the tower a mottled appearance; black nacreous scales littered the base of the walls and gleamed among the grasses. To the north, and sheltered from the sea, was a tangle of plants as if someone had once tried to plant a small garden. Now nothing remained but a dishevelled clump of Michaelmas daisies, patches of self-seeded antirrhinums, marigolds and nasturtiums, and a single etiolated rose with two white, starved buds, its stem bent double against the stone as if resigned to the first frost.

To the east was an ornate stone porch above an iron-bound oak door. Dalgliesh lifted the heavy handle and twisted it with difficulty. But the door was locked. Looking up he saw that there was a rough stone plaque set in the wall of the porch with a carved inscription:

IN THIS TOWER DIED WILFRED MANCROFT ANSTEY
27th OCTOBER 1887 AGED 69 YEARS
CONCEPTIO CULPA   NASCI PENA   LABOR VITA   NECESSI MORI
ADAM OF ST. VICTOR AD 1129

A strange epitaph for a Victorian landed gentleman and a bizarre place in which to die. The present owner of Toynton Grange had perhaps inherited a degree of eccentricity. CONCEPTIO

CULPA: the theology of original sin had been discarded by modern man with other inconvenient dogma; even in 1887 it must have been on the way out. NASCI PENA: anaesthesia had mercifully done something to vitiate that dogmatic assertion. LABOR VITA: not if twentieth-century technological man could help it. NECESSI MORI: ah, there was still the rub. Death. One could ignore it, fear it, even welcome it, but never defeat it. It remained as obtrusive but more durable than these commemorative stones. Death: the same yesterday, today and for ever. Had Wilfred Mancroft Anstey himself chosen and taken comfort from this stark memento mori?

He continued walking along the cliff edge, skirting a small pebbled bay. About twenty yards ahead was a rough path to the beach, steep and probably treacherous in wet weather but obviously partly the result of a felicitous natural arrangement of the rock face and partly the work of man. Immediately beneath him, however, the cliff fell away in an almost vertical face of limestone. He saw with surprise that even at this early hour there were two roped climbers on the rock. The upper and bareheaded figure was instantly recognizable as Julius Court. When the second looked up Dalgliesh glimpsed the face under the red climbing helmet and saw that his companion was Dennis Lerner.

They were climbing slowly but competently, so competently that he felt no temptation to move back in case the unexpected sight of a spectator should break their concentration. They had obviously done this climb before; the route, the techniques were familiar to them. Now they were on the last pitch. Watching Court's smooth unhurrying movements, the splayed limbs leech-like on the rock face, he found himself reliving some of the climbs of his boyhood and making the ascent with them, mentally documenting each stage. Traverse right about fifteen feet with peg protection; step up with difficulty; then on to a small pinnacle block; gain the next ledge by a mantelshelf; climb the groove with the aid of two pegs and one sling to the horizontal crack; follow the groove again to a small ledge in the corner; finally climb with the aid of two pegs to the top.

Ten minutes later Dalgliesh strolled slowly round to where Julius was heaving his shoulders over the edge of the cliff. He drew himself up and stood, slightly panting, beside Dalgliesh. Without speaking he banged a peg into a crack of the rock beside one of the larger boulders, clipped a sling through the peg and into his waistline and started hauling in the rope. There was a cheerful shout from the rock face. Julius settled himself back against the boulder, rope around his waist, shouted "Climb when you're ready," and began inching the rope through careful hands. Less than fifteen minutes later, Dennis Lerner stood beside him and began coiling the rope. Blinking rapidly Dennis took off his steel-rimmed spectacles, rubbed away what could have been spray or rain drops from his face and twisted the ends behind his ears with shaking fingers. Julius looked at his watch:

"One hour twelve minutes, our best so far."

He turned to Dalgliesh.

"There aren't many climbs on this part of the coast because of the shale, so we try to improve our time. Do you climb? I could lend you some gear."

"I haven't done much since I left school and judging from what I've just seen, I'm not in your class."

He didn't bother to explain that he was still too convalescent to climb safely. Once he might have found it necessary to justify his reluctance, but it had been some years now since he bothered how other people judged his physical courage. Julius said:

"Wilfred used to climb with me but about three months ago we discovered that someone had deliberately frayed one of his ropes. We were about to tackle this particular climb, incidentally. He refused to try to discover who was responsible. Someone at the Grange expressing a personal grievance, I suppose. Wilfred must expect these occasional contretemps. It's an occupational hazard for playing God. He was never in real danger. I always insist on checking equipment before we start. But it unnerved him, perhaps gave him the excuse he was looking for to give up climbing. He was never much good. Now I depend on Dennis when he has a day off, as today."

Lerner turned and smiled directly at Dalgliesh. The smile transformed his face, releasing it from strain. He looked suddenly boyish, confiding:

"I'm just as terrified as Wilfred most of the time but I'm learning. It's fascinating; I'm getting to love it. There's a mild climb about half a mile back, guillemot ledge. Julius started me off there. It's really quite gentle. We could tackle that if you'd like to try."

His naïve eagerness to communicate and share his pleasure was endearing.

Dalgliesh said:

"I hardly think I shall be long enough at Toynton to make it worthwhile."

He intercepted their quick glance at each other, an almost imperceptible meeting of eyes in what? Relief? Warning? Satisfaction?

The three men stood silently while Dennis finished coiling the rope. Then Julius nodded towards the black tower.

"Ugly, isn't it? Wilfred's great grandfather built it shortly after he rebuilt the Grange. It replaced—the Grange I mean—a small Elizabethan manor house which originally stood on the site and was destroyed by fire in 1843. A pity. It must have been more agreeable than the present house. Great grandfather had no eye for form. Neither the house nor the folly have quite come off have they?"

Dalgliesh asked:

"How did he die here, by design?"

"You could say that. He was one of those unamiable and obstinate eccentrics which the Victorian age seemed to breed. He invented his own religion, based I understand on the book of Revelation. In the early autumn of 1887 he walled himself up inside the tower and starved himself to death. According to the somewhat confused testament he left, he was waiting for the second coming. I hope it arrived for him."

"And no one stopped him?"

"They didn't know he was here. The old man was crazy but cunning. He made his secret preparations here, stones and mortar and so on, and then pretended to set off to winter in Naples. It was over three months before they found him. Long before that, he'd torn his fingers to the bone trying to claw himself out. But he'd done his brick and mortar work too well, poor devil."

"How horrible!"

"Yes. In the old days before Wilfred closed the headland, the locals tended to avoid the place, and so to be honest do I. Father Baddeley used to come here occasionally. According to Grace Willison, he said some prayers for great grandfather's soul, sprinkled holy water around and that decontaminated the tower as far as he was concerned. Wilfred uses it for meditation, or so he says. Personally I think it's to get away from the Grange. The sinister family association doesn't seem to worry him. But then, it doesn't really touch him personally. He was adopted. But I expect Millicent Hammitt has told you all about that."

"Not yet. I've hardly spoken to her."

"She will, she will."

Dennis Lerner said surprisingly:

"I like the black tower, particularly in summer when the headland is peaceful and golden and the sun glints on the black stone. It's a symbol really, isn't it? It looks magical, unreal, a folly built to amuse a child. And underneath there's horror, pain, madness and death. I said that to Father Baddeley once."

"And what did he reply?" asked Julius.

"He said, 'Oh, no my son. Underneath there's the love of God.'"

Julius said roughly:

"I don't need a phallic symbol erected by a Victorian eccentric to remind me of the skull under the skin. Like any reasonable man I prepare my own defences."

Dalgliesh asked:

"What are they?"

The quiet question, even in his own ears, sounded stark as a command. Julius smiled:

"Money and the solace it can buy. Leisure, friends, beauty, travel. And when they fail, as your friend Father Baddeley would have reminded me, they inevitably will, and Dennis's four horses of the apocalypse take over, three bullets in a Luger." He looked up once more at the tower.

"In the meantime, I can do without reminders. My half Irish blood makes me superstitious. Let's get down to the beach."

They slid and clambered cautiously down the cliff path. At the foot of the cliff Dennis Lerner's brown monk's habit lay neatly folded, topped by a rock. He corded it round himself, exchanged his climbing boots for sandals taken from the pocket of the cloak and, thus metamorphosed and with his climbing helmet tucked under his arm, joined his companions as they trudged through the shingle.

All three seemed weary and no one spoke until the cliffs changed and they passed under the shadow of the black shale. The shore was even more remarkable seen close-to, a wide shining platform of boulder-strewn clay, fractured and crevassed as if by an earthquake, a bleak uncompromising shore. The pools were blue-black pits festooned with slimy seaweed; surely no northern sea bred such an exotic green? Even the ubiquitous litter of the shore—tarred splinters of wood, cartons in which the foam bubbled like brown scum, bottles, ends of tarred rope, the fragile bleached bones of a sea bird—looked like the sinister debris of catastrophe, the sad sludge of a dead world.

As if by common consent they moved closer together and picked their way cautiously over the viscous rocks towards the sea until the tide was washing the flatter stones and Dennis Lerner had to hitch up his cloak. Suddenly Julius paused and turned towards the rock face. Dalgliesh turned with him, but Dennis still looked steadfastly out to sea.

"The tide was coming in fast. It must have reached to about here. I got down to the beach by the path we used. It took some minutes of hard running but it was the nearer, really the only way. I didn't see either him or the chair as I plunged and scrambled through the shingle. When I reached the black cliff I had to force myself to look at him. At first I could see nothing unusual, only the sea boiling between the rocks. Then I caught sight of one of the wheels of his chair. It was lying in the centre of a flat rock, the sun gleaming on the chrome and the metal spokes. It looked so decorative, so precisely placed, it couldn't surely have landed there by chance. I suppose that it bounced off with the shock of impact and finally rolled on to the stone. I remember that I picked it up and hurled it towards the shore, laughing aloud. Shock, I suppose. The sound echoed back from the rock face."

Lerner, without turning, said in a stifled voice:

"I remember. I heard you. I thought it was Victor laughing; it sounded like Victor."

Dalgliesh asked:

"You saw the accident, then?"

"From a distance of about fifty yards. I'd got back to the cottage from London after lunch and decided to have a swim. It was an exceptionally warm day for September. I was just coming over the headland when I saw the chair lurch forward. There was nothing I, or anyone, could do. Dennis was lying on the grass about ten yards from Holroyd. He scrambled to his feet and ran after the chair hooting like a banshee. Then he ran backwards and forwards along the cliff edge, flailing his arms like a great brown demented crow."

Lerner said through tight lips:

"I know that I didn't behave with much courage."

"It wasn't exactly an occasion for courage, dear boy. No one could expect you to hurl yourself over the cliff after him, although, for a second, I thought you were going to."

He turned to Dalgliesh.

"I left Dennis lying prone on the grass in what I suppose was a state of shock, paused long enough to yell at him to get help from Toynton Grange, and made for the cliff path. It took Dennis about ten minutes to pull himself together and get moving. It might have been more sensible if I'd paid more attention to him and then got him down here with me to help with the corpse. I nearly lost it."

Dalgliesh said:

"The chair must have come over the cliff with considerable speed if he landed as far out as here."

"Yes, odd isn't it? I was looking for him further inshore. Then I saw a tangle of metal about twenty feet to the right already being washed by the tide. And lastly I saw Holroyd. He looked like a great stranded fish rolling in the tide. His face was pale and bloated, even when he was alive poor devil; something to do with the steroids Eric was giving him. Now he looked grotesque. He must have parted from the chair before impact; anyway he was some distance from the wreckage. He was wearing only slacks and a cotton shirt when he died, and now the shirt had been torn away by the rocks and the sea so that all I could see was this great white torso turning and rising as the tide washed over him. He had gashed open his head and cut the neck artery. He must have bled copiously, and the sea had done the rest. By the time I reached him the foam was still stained pink, pretty as a bubble bath. He looked bloodless, as if he had been in the sea for months. A bloodless corpse, half naked, wallowing in the tide."

A bloodless corpse. A bloodless murder.

The phrase fell unbidden into Dalgliesh's mind. He asked, making his voice unemphatic, hardly interested:

"How did you manage to get hold of him?"

"It wasn't easy. As I've said, the tide was coming in fast. I managed to get my bathing towel under his belt and tried to haul him on to one of the higher rocks, an undignified, clumsy business for both of us. He was considerably heavier than I and his waterlogged trousers added to the weight. I was afraid they would come off. I suppose it wouldn't have mattered if they had, but it seemed important at the time to preserve some dignity for him. I took advantage of each onrush of wave to heave him further to shore and managed to get him on to this rock here, as far as I can remember. I was soaking myself and shivering despite the heat. I remember thinking it odd that the sun didn't seem to have the power to dry my clothes."

Dalgliesh had glanced at Lerner's profile during this recital. A pulse in the thin sun-reddened neck was beating like a pump. He said coolly:

"We must hope that Holroyd's death was less distressing for him than it obviously was for you."

Julius Court laughed:

"You must remember that not everyone has your professional predilection for these entertainments. When I'd got him this far I just hung on grimly like a fisherman to his catch until the party from Toynton Grange arrived with a stretcher. They came stumbling along the beach, the quicker way, strung out, falling over the stones, overladen like a disorganized picnic party."

"What about the wheelchair?"

"I only remembered it when we got back to Toynton. It was a write-off, of course. We all knew that. But I thought that the police might want to examine it to see if the brakes were defective. Rather clever of me wasn't it? The idea didn't seem to occur to anyone else. But when a party from the Grange came back to look they could only find the two wheels and the main part of the body. The two side pieces with the ratchet hand-brakes were missing. The police searched more thoroughly next morning but with no better luck."

Dalgliesh would have liked to have asked who it was from Toynton Grange who had done the searching. But he was determined not to betray real curiosity. He told himself that he had none. Violent death was no longer his concern and, officially, this violent death never would be. But it was odd that the two vital pieces of the wheelchair hadn't been found. And this rocky shore, with its deep crevices, its pools, its numerous hiding places would have been an ideal place in which to conceal them. But the local police would have thought of that. It was, he supposed, one of the questions he would tactfully have to ask them. Father Baddeley had written to ask for his help the day before Holroyd had died, but that didn't mean that the two events were totally unconnected. He asked:

"Was Father Baddeley very distressed about Holroyd's death? I imagine so."

"Very much, when he knew. But that wasn't until a week later. We'd had the inquest by then and Holroyd had been buried. I thought Grace Willison would have told you. Michael and Victor between them gave us quite a day. When Dennis arrived back at the Grange with his news, the rescue party set out without saying anything to the patients. It was understandable but unfortunate. When we all staggered through the front door about forty minutes later, with what remained of Holroyd half slipping off the stretcher, Grace Willison was wheeling herself through the hall. Just to add to the excitement, she collapsed with shock. Anyway, Wilfred thought that Michael might start earning his money, and sent Eric off to Hope Cottage. Eric found Father Baddeley in the throes of his heart attack. So yet another ambulance was summoned—we thought it might finish Michael off if he had to share his journey to the hospital with what remained of Victor—and the old man went off in happy ignorance. The ward sister broke the news about Victor as soon as the doctors thought he was well enough to take it. According to her, he took it quietly, but was obviously upset. He wrote to Wilfred I believe; a letter of condolence. Father Baddeley had the professional knack of taking other people's death in his stride, and he and Holroyd weren't exactly close. It was the idea of suicide which upset his professional susceptibilities, I imagine."

Suddenly Lerner said in a low voice:

"I feel guilty because I feel responsible."

Dalgliesh said:

"Either you pushed Holroyd over the cliff or you didn't. If you didn't, guilt is an indulgence."

"And if I did?"

"Then it's a dangerous indulgence."

Julius laughed:

"Victor committed suicide. You know it, I know it, so does everyone who knew Victor. If you're going to start fantasizing about his death, it's lucky for you that I decided to swim that afternoon and came over the brow of the hill when I did."

The three of them, as if by common consent, began squelching their way along the shingled shore. Looking at Lerner's pale face, the twitch of muscle at the corner of the slack mouth, the perpetually anxious blinking eyes, Dalgliesh felt they'd had enough of Holroyd. He began to ask about the rock. Lerner turned to him eagerly.

"It's fascinating isn't it? I love the variety of this coast. You get the same shale further to the west at Kimmeridge; there it's known as Kimmeridge coal. It's bituminous you know, you can actually burn it. We did try at Toynton Grange; Wilfred liked the idea that we might be self-supporting even for heating. But the stuff smelt so offensive that we had to give it up. It practically stank us out. I believe people have tried to exploit it from the middle of the eighteenth century but no one's managed yet to deodorize it. The blackstone looks a bit dull and uninteresting now, but if it's polished with beeswax it comes up like jet. Well, you saw the effect on the black tower. People used to make ornaments of it as far back as Roman times. I've got a book on the geology of this coast if you're interested and I could show you my collection of fossils. Wilfred thinks that I ought not to take them now that the cliffs are so denuded, so I've given up collecting. But I've got quite an interesting collection. And I've got what I think is part of an Iron Age shale armlet."

Julius Court was grating through the shingle a few feet ahead. He turned and shouted back at them:

"Don't bore him with your enthusiasm for old rocks, Dennis. Remember what he said. He won't be long enough at Toynton to make it worthwhile."

He smiled at Dalgliesh. He made it sound like a challenge.

III

Before setting out for Wareham, Dalgliesh wrote to Bill Moriarty at the Yard. He gave such brief information as he had about the staff and patients at Toynton Grange and asked whether anything was officially known. He thought that he could imagine Bill's reaction to the letter, just as he could predict the style of his reply. Moriarty was a first-class detective but, except mercifully in official reports, he affected a facetious, spuriously jovial style when talking or writing about his cases as if nervously anxious to decontaminate violence with humour, or to demonstrate his professional sang-froid in the face of death. But if Moriarty's style was suspect, his information was invariably detailed and accurate. What was more, it would come quickly.

Dalgliesh, when stopping in Toynton village to post his letter, had taken the precaution of telephoning the police before calling in at divisional headquarters. His arrival was, therefore, expected and provided for. The Divisional Superintendent, called away unexpectedly to a meeting with his Chief Constable, had left apologies and instructions for the entertainment of the visitor. His final words to Detective Inspector Daniel, deputed to do the honours, had been:

"I'm sorry to miss the Commander. I met him last year when he lectured at Bramshill. At least he tempers the arrogance of the Met. with good manners and a plausible show of humility. It's refreshing to meet someone from the smoke who doesn't treat provincial forces as if we recruit by lurking outside the hill caves with lumps of raw meat on a pole. He may be the Commissioner's blue-eyed boy but he's a good copper."

"Doesn't he write verse, Sir?"

"I shouldn't try to ingratiate yourself by mentioning that. I invent crossword puzzles for a hobby, which probably requires much the same level of intellectual skill, but I don't expect people to compliment me on it. I got his last book from the library. *Invisible Scars.* Do you suppose, given the fact that he's a copper, that the title is ironic?"

"I couldn't say, Sir, not having read the book."

"I only understood one poem in three but I may have been flattering myself. I suppose he didn't say why we're being honoured."

"No, Sir, but as he's staying at Toynton Grange he may be interested in the Holroyd case."

"I can't see why; but you'd better arrange for Sergeant Varney to be available."

"I've asked Varney to join us for lunch, Sir. The usual pub, I thought."

"Why not? Let the Commander see how the poor live."

And so Dalgliesh found himself, after the usual polite preliminaries, invited to lunch at the Duke's Arms. It was an unprepossessing pub, not visible from the High Street, but approached down a dark alleyway between a corn merchant and one of those general stores common in country towns where every possible garden implement and an assortment of tin buckets, hip baths, brooms, twine, aluminium tea pots and dogs' leads swing from the ceiling above a pervading smell of paraffin and turpentine. Inspector Daniel and Sergeant Varney were greeted with uneffusive but evident satisfaction by the burly, shirt-sleeved landlord who was obviously a publican who could afford to welcome the local police to his bar without the fear of giving it a bad name. The saloon bar was crowded, smoky and loud with the burr of Dorset voices. Daniel led the way down a narrow passage smelling strongly of beer and faintly of urine and out into an unexpected and sun-filled cobbled yard. There was a cherry tree in the centre, its trunk encircled by a wooden bench, and half a dozen sturdy tables and slatted wooden chairs set out on the paved stones which surrounded the cobbles. The yard was deserted. The regulars probably spent too much of their working lives in the open air to see it as a desirable alternative to the camaraderie of the snug, smoke-filled bar, while tourists who might have valued it were unlikely to penetrate to the Duke's Arms.

Without being summoned the publican brought out two pints of beer, a plate of cheese-filled rolls, a jar of home-made chutney and a large bowl of tomatoes. Dalgliesh said he would have the same. The beer proved excellent, the cheese was English Cheddar, the bread had obviously been baked locally and was not the gutless pap of some mass-production oven. The butter was unsalted and the tomatoes tasted of the sun. They ate together in companionable silence.

Inspector Daniel was a stolid six-footer, with a jutting comb of strong undisciplined grey hair and a ruddy sun-tanned face. He looked close to retirement age. His black eyes were restless, perpetually moving from face to face with an amused, indulgent, somewhat self-satisfied expression as if he felt himself personally responsible for the conduct of the world and was, on the whole, satisfied that he wasn't making too bad a job of it. The contrast between these glittering unquiet eyes and his unhurried movements and even more deliberate countryman's voice was disconcerting.

Sergeant Varney was two inches shorter with a round, bland, boyish face on which experience had so far, left no trace. He looked very young, the prototype of that officer whose boyish good looks provoke the perennial middle-aged complaint that the policemen get younger each year. His manner to his superiors was easy, respectful, but neither sycophantic nor deferential. Dalgliesh suspected that he enjoyed an immense self-confidence which he was at some pains to conceal. When he talked about his investigation of Holroyd's death, Dalgliesh could understand why. Here was an intelligent and highly competent young officer who knew exactly where he was going and how he proposed to get there.

Dalgliesh carefully understated his business.

"I was ill at the time Father Baddeley wrote and he was dead when I arrived. I don't suppose he wanted to consult me about anything important, but I have something of a conscience about having let him down. It seemed sensible to have a word with you and see whether anything was happening at Toynton Grange which might have worried him. I must say it seems to me highly unlikely. I've been told about Victor Holroyd's death, of course, but that happened the day after Father Baddeley wrote to me. I did wonder, though, whether there was anything leading up to Holroyd's death which might have worried him."

Sergeant Varney said:

"There was no evidence that Holroyd's death concerned anyone but himself. As I expect you know, the verdict at the inquest was accidental death. Dr. Maskell sat with a jury and if you ask me he was relieved at the verdict. Mr. Anstey is greatly respected in the district even if they do keep themselves very much to themselves at Toynton Grange, and no one wanted to add to his distress. But in my opinion, Sir, it was a clear case of suicide. It looks as if Holroyd acted pretty much on impulse. It wasn't his usual day to be wheeled to the cliff top and he seemed to make up his mind to it suddenly. We had the evidence of Miss Grace Willison and Mrs. Ursula Hollis, who were sitting with Holroyd on the patients' patio, that he called Dennis Lerner over to him and more or less nagged him into wheeling him out. Lerner testified that he was in a particularly difficult mood on the journey and when they got to their usual place on the cliff he became so offensive that Lerner took his book and lay some little distance from the chair. That is where Mr. Julius Court saw him when he breasted the hill in time to see the chair jerk forward and hurtle down the slope and over the cliff. When I examined the ground next morning I could see by the broken flowers and pressed grass exactly where Lerner had been lying and his library book, *The Geology of the Dorset Coast*, was still on the grass where he'd dropped it. It looks to me, Sir, as if Holroyd deliberately taunted him into moving some distance away so that he wouldn't be able to get to him in time once he'd slipped the brakes."

"Did Lerner explain in court exactly what it was that Holroyd said to him?"

"He wasn't specific, Sir, but he more or less admitted to me that Holroyd taunted him with being a homosexual, not pulling his weight at Toynton Grange, looking for an easy life, and being an ungentle and incompetent nurse."

"I would hardly describe that as unspecific. How much truth is there in any of it?"

"That's difficult to say, Sir. He may be all of those things including the first; which doesn't mean to say that he'd welcome Holroyd telling him so."

Inspector Daniel broke in:

"He's not an ungentle nurse and that's for certain. My sister Ella is a staff nurse at the Meadowlands Nursing Home outside Swanage. Old Mrs. Lerner—over eighty she is now—is a patient there. Her son visits regularly and isn't above lending a hand when they're busy. It's odd that he doesn't take a post there, but perhaps it's no bad thing to keep your professional and private life separate. Anyway, they may not have a vacancy for a male nurse. And no doubt he feels some loyalty to Wilfred Anstey. But Ella thinks very highly of Dennis Lerner. A good son, is how she describes him. And it must take the best part of his salary to keep Mum at Meadowlands. Like all the really good places, it's not cheap. No, I'd say that Holroyd was a pretty impossible chap. The Grange will be a good deal happier without him."

Dalgliesh said:

"It's an uncertain way of committing suicide, I should have thought. What surprises me is that he managed to move that chair."

Sergeant Varney took a long drink of his beer.

"It surprised me too, Sir. We weren't able to get the chair intact so I couldn't experiment with it. But Holroyd was a heavy chap, about half a stone heavier than I am, I estimate, and I experimented with one of the older chairs at Toynton Grange as close as possible to the model of his. Provided it were on fairly firm ground and the slope was more than one in three, I could get it moving with a sharp jerk. Julius Court testified that he saw Holroyd's body jerk although he couldn't say from that distance whether the chair was being thrust forward or whether it was a spontaneous reaction on Holroyd's part to the shock of finding himself moving. And one has to remember, Sir, that other methods of killing himself weren't readily to hand. He was almost entirely helpless. Drugs would have been the easiest way, but those are kept locked in the clinical room on the upper floor; he hadn't a hope of getting to anything really dangerous without help. He might have tried hanging himself with a towel in the bathroom but there are no locks on the bathroom or lavatory doors. That, of course, is a precaution against patients collapsing and being too ill to summon assistance, but it does mean that there's a lack of privacy about the place."

"What about a possible defect of the chair?"

"I thought about that, Sir, and it was, of course, brought out at the inquest. But we only recovered the seat of the chair and one of the wheels. The two side pieces with the hand-brakes and the cross-bar with the ratchets have never been found."

"Exactly the parts of the chair where any defects of the brakes, whether natural or deliberately produced, might have been apparent."

"If we could have found the pieces in time, Sir, and the sea hadn't done too much damage. But we never found them. The body had broken free of the chair in mid-air or on impact and Court naturally concentrated on retrieving the body. It was being tumbled by the surf, the trousers were waterlogged and it was too heavy for him to shift far. But he got his bathing towel into Holroyd's belt and managed to hold on until help, in the persons of Mr. Anstey, Dr. Hewson, Sister Moxon and the handyman Albert Philby arrived with a stretcher. Together they managed to get the body on to it and struggled back along the beach to Toynton Grange. It was only then that they rang us. It occurred to Mr. Court as soon as they reached the Grange that the chair ought to be retrieved for examination and he sent Philby back to look for it. Sister Moxon volunteered to go with him. The tide had gone out about twenty yards by then and they found the main part of the chair, that is the seat and the back, and one of the wheels."

"I'm surprised that Dorothy Moxon went to search, I would have expected her to stay with the patients."

"So should I, Sir. But Anstey refused to leave Toynton Grange and Dr. Hewson apparently thought that his place was with the body. Nurse Rainer was off duty for the afternoon, and there was no one else to send unless you count Mrs. Millicent Hammitt, and I don't think anyone thought of counting Mrs. Hammitt. It did seem important that two pairs of eyes should be looking for the chair before the light faded."

"And what about Julius Court?"

"Mr. Court and Mr. Lerner thought they ought to be at Toynton Grange to meet us when we arrived, Sir."

"A very proper thought. And by the time you did arrive no doubt it was too dark to make an effective search."

"Yes, Sir, it was seven fourteen when we got to Toynton Grange. Apart from taking statements and arranging for the body to be removed to the mortuary, there was very little we could do until the morning. I don't know whether you've seen that shore at low tide, Sir. It looks like a great sheet of black treacle toffee which some prodigious giant has amused himself by smashing-up with a gigantic hammer. We searched pretty thoroughly over a wide area but if the metal pieces are lodged in the crevasses between any of those rocks it would take a metal detector to find them—and we'd be lucky then—and lifting tackle to retrieve them. It's most likely, I think, that they've been dragged down under the shingle. There's a great deal of turbulence there at high tide."

Dalgliesh said:

"Was there any reason to suppose that Holroyd had suddenly become suicidal, I mean—why choose that particular moment?"

"I asked about that, Sir. A week earlier, that is on the 5th September, Mr. Court with Doctor and Mrs. Hewson had taken him in Court's car up to London to see his solicitors and a consultant at St. Saviour's Hospital. That's Dr. Hewson's own training hospital. I gather that Holroyd wasn't given much hope that anything more could be done for him. Dr. Hewson said that the news didn't seem to depress him unduly. He hadn't expected anything else. Dr. Hewson more or less told me that Holroyd had insisted on the consultation just for the trip to London. He was a restless man and liked an excuse to get away from Toynton Grange occasionally. Mr. Court was travelling up anyway and offered the use of his car. That matron, Mrs. Moxon, and Mr. Anstey were both adamant that Holroyd hadn't come back particularly depressed; but then they've got something of a vested interest in discrediting the suicide theory. The patients told me a rather different story. They noticed a change in Holroyd after his return. They didn't describe him as depressed, but he certainly wasn't any easier to live with. They described him as excited. Miss Willison used the word elated. She said that he seemed to be making up his mind to something. I don't think that she has much doubt that Holroyd killed himself. When I questioned her she was obviously shocked by the idea and distressed on Mr. Anstey's account. She didn't want to believe it. But I think that she did."

"What about Holroyd's visit to his solicitor? Did he learn anything there to distress him I wonder."

"It's an old family firm, Holroyd and Martinson in Bedford Row. Holroyd's elder brother is now the senior partner. I did ring him to ask but I didn't get far. According to him, the visit was almost entirely social and Victor was no more depressed than usual. They were never close but Mr. Martin Holroyd did visit his brother occasionally at Toynton Grange, particularly when he wanted to talk to Mr. Anstey about his affairs."

"You mean that Holroyd and Martinson are Anstey's solicitors?"

"They've acted for the family for over 150 years I understand. It's a very old connection. That's how Victor Holroyd came to hear about the Grange. He was Anstey's first patient."

"What about Holroyd's wheelchair? Could anyone at Toynton Grange have sabotaged that, either on the day Holroyd died or on the evening before?"

"Philby could, of course. He had the best opportunity. But a number of people could have done it. Holroyd's rather heavy chair, the one which was used for these outings, was kept in the workroom at the end of the passage in the southern extension. I don't know whether you know it, Sir, but it's perfectly accessible even to wheelchairs. Basically it's Philby's workshop. He has the usual standard equipment and tools for carpentry and some metal work there. But the patients can use it too and are, in fact, encouraged either to help him or to indulge in their own hobbies. Holroyd used to do some fairly simple carpentry before he got too ill and Mr. Carwardine occasionally models in clay. The women patients don't usually use it but there'd be nothing surprising to seeing one of the men there."

Dalgliesh said:

"Carwardine told me that he was in the workroom when Philby oiled and checked the brakes at eight forty-five."

"That's rather more than he told me. He gave me the impression that he hadn't really seen what Philby was up to. Philby was a bit coy about whether he could actually remember testing the brakes. I wasn't surprised. It was pretty obvious that they all wanted it to look like an accident if that could be done without provoking the coroner into too many strictures about carelessness. I had a bit of luck, however, when I questioned them about the actual morning of Holroyd's death. After breakfast Philby went back to the workroom shortly after eight forty-five. He was there for just an hour and when he left he locked the place up. He was glueing some repairs and didn't want them disturbed. I got the impression that Philby thinks of the workroom as his domain and doesn't exactly welcome the patients being allowed to use it. Anyway, he pocketed the key and didn't unlock the room until Lerner came fussing to ask for the key shortly before four o'clock so that he could get Holroyd's wheelchair. Assuming that Philby was telling the truth, the only people at Toynton Grange without alibis for the time when the workroom was unlocked and unoccupied early on the morning of 12th September are Mr. Anstey, Holroyd himself, Mr. Carwardine, Sister Moxon and Mrs. Hewson. Mr. Court was in London and didn't arrive back at his cottage until just before Lerner and Holroyd set out. Lerner is clear too. He was busy with the patients at all the relevant times."

That was all very well, thought Dalgliesh, but it proved very little. The workroom had been unlocked the previous evening after Carwardine and Philby had left and, presumably, also during the night. He said:

"You were very thorough, Sergeant. Did you manage to discover all this without alarming them too much?"

"I think so, Sir. I don't think they thought for a moment that anyone else could have been responsible. They took it that I was checking-up on what opportunity Holroyd had to muck about with the chair himself. And if it were deliberately damaged, then my bet is he did it. He was a malicious man, from what I hear. It probably amused him to think that, when the chair was recovered from the sea and the damage discovered, then everyone at Toynton Grange would be under suspicion. That's the kind of final thought that would give him quite a kick."

Dalgliesh said:

"I just can't believe that both brakes failed simultaneously and accidentally. I've seen those wheelchairs at the Grange. The brakes system is very simple but it's effective and safe. And it's almost as difficult to imagine that there was deliberate sabotage. How could the murderer possibly rely on the brakes failing at that particular moment? Lerner or Holroyd might easily have tested them before starting out. The defect might be discovered when the chair was braked on the cliff top or even on the journey. Besides, no one apparently knew that Holroyd was going to insist on an outing that afternoon. What did exactly happen on the cliff top, by the way? Who braked the chair?"

"According to Lerner, Holroyd did. Lerner admits that he never looked at the brakes. All he can say is that he noticed nothing wrong with the chair. The brakes weren't used until they reached their usual stopping place."

For a moment there was silence. They had finished eating and Inspector Daniel felt in the pocket of his tweed jacket and produced his pipe. As he stroked its bowl with his thumb before filling it, he said quietly:

"Nothing was worrying you about the old gentleman's death was it, Sir?"

"He was medically diagnosed as a dying man and somewhat inconveniently for me he died. I worry that I didn't visit him in time to hear what was on his mind; but that's a private worry. Speaking as a policeman, I should rather like to know who saw him last before he died. Officially, it was Grace Willison, but I've a feeling he had a later visitor than she; another patient. When he was found dead next morning he was wearing his stole. His diary is missing, and someone broke into his bureau. As I haven't seen Father Baddely for over twenty years it's probably unreasonable of me to be so sure that it wasn't he."

Sergeant Varney turned to his Inspector.

"What would be the theological position, Sir, if someone confessed to a priest, got absolution and then killed him to make sure that he kept his mouth shut. Would the confession take as it were?"

The young face was prenaturally grave, it was impossible to tell whether the enquiry had been serious, whether this was a private joke directed against the Inspector, or made with some more subtle motive. Daniel took his pipe from his mouth:

"God, you young men are an ignorant lot of heathens! When I was a kid in Sunday School I put pennies in the collection plate for black bambinos not half as ignorant as your lot. Take it from me lad, it would do you no good theologically or otherwise."

He turned to Dalgliesh.

"Wearing his stole, was he? Now that's interesting."

"I thought so."

"And yet, is it so unnatural? He was alone and may have known that he was dying. Maybe he just felt more comfortable with the feel of it round his neck. Wouldn't you say that, Sir?"

"I don't know what he'd do, or what he'd feel. I've been content not to know for the past twenty years."

"And the forced bureau. Maybe he'd decided to make a start with destroying his papers and couldn't remember where he'd put the key."

"It's perfectly possible."

"And he was cremated?"

"Cremated, on the insistence of Mrs. Hammitt, and his ashes buried with the appropriate rite of the Church of England."

Inspector Daniel said nothing more. There was, Dalgliesh thought bitterly as they rose to go, nothing else to say.

IV

Father Baddeley's solicitors, the firm of Loder and Wainwright, occupied a simple but harmonious house of red brick facing directly on to South Street and typical, Dalgliesh thought, of the more agreeable houses which were built after the old town was virtually destroyed by fire in 1762. The door was propped open by a brass doorstop shaped like a miniature canon, its dazzling muzzle pointing intimidatingly towards the street. Apart from this bellicose symbol the house and its furnishings were reassuringly welcoming, producing an atmosphere of solid affluence, tradition and professional rectitude. The white painted hall was hung with prints of eighteenth-century Dorchester and smelt of furniture polish. To the left, an open door led to a large waiting-room with an immense circular table on a carved pedestal, half a dozen carved mahogany chairs heavy enough to accommodate a robust farmer in upright discomfort, and an oil painting of an unnamed Victorian gentleman, presumably the founder of the firm, bewhiskered and beribboned and displaying the seal of his watch chain between a delicate thumb and finger as if anxious that the painter should not overlook it. It was a house in which any of Hardy's more prosperous characters would have felt themselves at home, could with confidence have discussed the effects of the abolition of the corn laws or the perfidy of the French privateers. Opposite the waiting-room was a partitioned office occupied by a young girl, dressed up to the waist in black boots and a long skirt like a Victorian governess and above the waist like a pregnant milkmaid. She was laboriously typing at a speed which could have explained Maggie Hewson's strictures about the firm's dilatoriness. In response to Dalgliesh's enquiry she glanced up at him through a curtain of lank hair and said that Mr. Robert was out at present but was expected back in ten minutes. Taking his time over lunch, thought Dalgliesh, and resigned himself to a half-hour wait.

Loder returned some twenty minutes later. Dalgliesh heard him galumphing happily into the reception office; there was the murmur of voices and a second later he appeared in the waiting-room and invited his visitor into his office at the rear of the house. Neither the room—poky, stuffy and untidy—nor its owner were quite what Dalgliesh had expected. Neither suited the house. Bob Loder was a swarthy, heavily built, square-faced man with a blotched skin and unhealthy pallor and small, discouraged eyes. His sleek hair was uniformly dark—too dark to be entirely natural—except for a thin line of silver at the brow and sides. His moustache was dapper and trim above lips so red and moist that they looked about to ooze blood. Noting the lines at the corner of the eyes and the sagging muscles of the neck Dalgliesh suspected that he was neither as young nor as vigorous as he was at pains to suggest.

He greeted Dalgliesh with a heartiness and bonhomie which

seemed as unsuited to his personality as it was to the occasion. His manner recalled to Dalgliesh something of the desperate heartiness of ex-officers of his acquaintance who hadn't adjusted themselves to civilian life, or perhaps of a car salesman with little confidence that the chassis and engine will hang together long enough to complete the sale.

Dalgliesh briefly explained the ostensible reason for his visit.

"I didn't know that Father Baddeley was dead until I arrived at Toynton and the first I heard about his bequest to me was from Mrs. Hewson. That isn't important. You probably haven't had a chance to write yet. But Mr. Anstey wants the cottage cleared for the new occupant and I thought that I'd better check with you before removing the books."

Loder put his head outside the door and yelled for the file. It was produced in a surprisingly quick time. After a perfunctory examination he said:

"That's OK. Perfectly. Sorry about no letter. It wasn't so much the lack of time as no address, don't you know. The dear old chap didn't think of that. Name familiar, of course. Ought I to know you?"

"I don't think so. Perhaps Father Baddeley mentioned my name when he visited you. I believe he did call in a day or so before the start of his last illness."

"That's right, on Wednesday the eleventh p.m. That was only the second time we'd met, come to think of it. He first consulted me about three years ago, soon after he arrived at Toynton Grange. That was to make his will. He didn't have much but, then, he hadn't been spending much and it had accumulated into quite a nice little sum."

"How did he hear of you?"

"He didn't. The dear old chap wanted to make his will, knew that he'd need a solicitor and just took the bus into Wareham, and walked into the first solicitors' office he came to. I happened to be here at the time so I got him. I drew up the will there and then since that was what he wanted and two of the staff here signed it. I'll say this for the old dear, he was the easiest client I've ever had."

"I wondered whether his visit on the eleventh was to consult you about anything that was worrying him. From his last letter to me I rather gathered that he had something on his mind. If there's anything I ought to do . . ."

He let his voice trail away in a long interrogation.

Loder said cheerfully:

"The dear old chap came in some perturbation of spirit. He was thinking of changing his will but hadn't quite made up his mind. He seemed to have got the idea that I could somehow put the money into limbo for him while he came to a decision. I said: "My dear Sir, if you die tonight the money goes to Wilfred Anstey and Toynton Grange. If you don't want that to happen, then you'll have to make up your mind what you do want and I'll draw up a new will. But the money exists. It won't just disappear. And if you don't cancel the old will or change it, then it stands."

"Did he strike you as sensible?"

"Oh, yes, muddled perhaps but more in his imagination than his comprehension if you get me. As soon as I pointed out the facts he understood them. Well, he always had understood them. It's just that he wished for a moment that the problem wasn't there. Don't we all know the feeling?"

"And a day later he went into hospital, and less than a fortnight later the problem was solved for him."

"Yes, poor old dear. I suppose he would have said that providence decided it for him. Providence certainly made its views known in no uncertain way."

"Did he give you any idea what was on his mind? I don't want to pry into professional confidences, but I did get a strong impression that he wanted to consult me about something. If he had a commission for me I'd like to try to carry it out. And I suppose I have the policeman's curiosity to find out what he wanted, to clear up unfinished business."

"A policeman?"

Was the flicker of surprise and polite interest in those tired eyes a little too obvious to be natural?

Loder said:

"Did he invite you as a friend or in a professional capacity?"

"Probably a bit of both."

"Well, I don't see what you can do about it now. Even if he'd told me his intentions about the will and I knew whom he wanted to benefit it's too late to do anything about it now."

Dalgliesh wondered whether Loder seriously thought that he had been hoping for the money himself and was enquiring into a possible way of upsetting Father Baddeley's will.

He said:

"I know that. I doubt whether it was anything to do with his will. It's odd, though, that he never wrote to tell me about my legacy, and he left the main beneficiary in the same ignorance apparently." It was entirely a shot in the dark but it found its mark. Loder spoke carefully, a trifle too carefully.

"Did he? I'd rather thought that that particular embarrassment was part of the old chap's dilemma, the reluctance to disappoint when he'd promised."

He hesitated, seeming to think that he had said either too much or too little and added:

"But Wilfred Anstey could confirm that."

He paused again as if disconcerted by some subtle implication in his words and, obviously irritated at the devious paths into which the conversation was leading him, said more strongly:

"I mean if Wilfred Anstey says he didn't know that he was the principal legatee then he didn't know and I'm wrong. Are you staying long in Dorset?"

"Rather less than a week, I imagine. Just long enough to sort out and pack the books."

"Oh, yes, the books, of course; perhaps that's what Father Baddeley meant to consult you about. He may have thought that a library of theological tomes would be more of a liability than an acceptable bequest."

"It's possible." The conversation seemed to have died. There was a brief, somewhat embarrassed pause before Dalgliesh said, rising from his chair:

"So there was nothing else worrying him as far as you know except this problem of the disposal of his money? He didn't consult you about anything else?"

"No, nothing. If he had, it might have been something I wouldn't have felt able to tell you without breaking a professional confidence. But, as he didn't, I don't see why you shouldn't know that. And what would he have to consult me over, poor old gentleman? No wife, no children, no relatives, as far as I know, no family troubles, no car, a blameless life. What would he need a solicitor for except to draw up his will?"

It was a little late to talk about professional confidence, thought Dalgliesh. There was really no need for Loder to have confided that Father Baddeley had been thinking of changing his will.

Given the fact that he hadn't in fact done so that was the kind of information which a prudent solicitor would feel was best left undisclosed. As Loder walked with him to the door, Dalgliesh said casually:

"Father Baddeley's will probably gave nothing but satisfaction. One can hardly say as much of Victor Holroyd's."

The dull eyes were suddenly sharp, almost conspiratorial. Loder said:

"So you've heard about that, have you?"

"Yes. But I'm surprised that you have."

"Oh, news gets around, don't you know, in a country district. As a matter of fact I have friends at Toynton. The Hewsons. Well, Maggie really. We met at the Conservative dance here last winter. It's a pretty dull life stuck there on the cliff for a lively girl."

"Yes. It must be."

"She's quite a lass is our Maggie. She told me about Holroyd's will. I gather that he went up to London to see his brother and it was rather taken for granted that he wanted to discuss his will. But it looks as if big brother didn't much like what Victor proposed and suggested that he thought again. In the event, Holroyd drew up the codicil himself. It wouldn't exactly present any problem for him. All that family have been brought up in the law and Holroyd started reading for the Bar himself before he decided to switch to schoolteaching."

"I understand that Holroyd and Martinson act for the Anstey family."

"That's right, and have for four generations. It's a pity grandfather Anstey didn't consult them before drawing up his will. That case was quite a lesson in the unwisdom of trying to act as your own lawyer. Well, good afternoon, Commander. I'm sorry I couldn't be of more help."

As he looked back when turning out of South Street, Dalgliesh could see Loder still watching after him, the brass canon shining like a toy at his feet. There were a number of things about the solicitor which he found interesting. Not the least was how Loder had learned his rank.

But there was one other task before he turned his mind to his shopping. He called at the early nineteenth-century hospital, Christmas Close. But here he was unlucky. The hospital knew nothing of Father Baddeley; they admitted only chronic cases.

If his friend had suffered a heart attack he would almost certainly have been admitted to the acute ward of a district general hospital despite his age. The courteous porter suggested that he should try either Poole General Hospital, Blandford or the Victoria Hospital at Wimborne, and helpfully directed him to the nearest public telephone.

He tried Poole Hospital first as being the nearest. And here he was luckier than he could have hoped. The clerk who answered the telephone was efficient. Given the date of Father Baddeley's discharge he was able to confirm that the Reverend Baddeley had been a patient and to put Dalgliesh through to the right ward. The staff nurse answered. Yes, she remembered Father Baddeley. No, they hadn't heard that he had died. She spoke the conventional words of regret and was able to make them sound sincere. Then she fetched Nurse Breagan to the telephone. Nurse Breagan usually offered to post patients' letters. Perhaps she could help Commander Dalgliesh.

His rank, he knew, had something to do with their helpfulness, but not all. They were kindly women who were disposed to take trouble, even with a stranger. He explained his dilemma to Nurse Breagan.

"So you see, I didn't know that my friend had died until I arrived yesterday at Toynton Grange. He promised to return the papers we were working on to me, but they're not among his things, I wondered whether he posted them back to me from hospital, either to my London address or to the Yard."

"Well now, Commander, the Father wasn't a great one for writing. Reading, yes; but not writing. But I did post two letters for him. They were both local as far as I can remember. I have to look at the addresses, you see, so that I post them in the right box. The date? Well, I couldn't remember that. But he did hand them to me together."

"Would those be the two letters he wrote to Toynton, one to Mr. Anstey and one to Miss Willison?"

"Come to think of it, Commander, I do seem to remember those names. But I couldn't be sure, you understand."

"It's very clever of you to remember so much. And you're quite sure you only posted those two?"

"Oh, quite sure. Mind you, one of the other nurses might have posted a letter for him, but I couldn't find out for you without difficulty. Some of them have changed wards. But I don't think so. It's usually me that takes the letters. And he wasn't one for writing. That's how I remember the two letters he did send."

It could mean something or nothing. But the information had been worth the trouble. If Father Baddeley had made an appointment for the night of his return home, he must have done so either by telephoning from the hospital once he was well enough, or by letter. And only Toynton Grange itself, the Hewsons and Julius Court were on the telephone. But it might have been more convenient for him to write. The letter to Grace Willison would have been the one arranging her appointment for confession. The one to Anstey might have been the letter of condolence on Holroyd's death to which she had referred. But, on the other hand, it might not.

Before ringing off he asked whether Father Baddeley had made any telephone calls from the hospital.

"Well, he made one, that I do know. That was when he was up and about. He went down to make it from the outpatients' waiting-hall and he asked me if there'd be a London directory there. That's how I remember."

"At what time was this?"

"The morning. Just before I went off duty at twelve."

So Father Baddeley had needed to make a London call, to a number he had to look up. And he had made it, not during the evening, but in office hours. There was one obvious enquiry Dalgliesh could make. But not yet. He told himself that as yet he had learned nothing which could justify even his unofficial involvement. And even if he had, where would all the suspicions, all the clues, ultimately lead? Only to a few fistfuls of ground bones in Toynton churchyard.

V

It wasn't until after an early dinner at an inn near Corfe Castle that Dalgliesh drove back to Hope Cottage and settled down to begin sorting Father Baddeley's books. But first there were small but necessary domestic chores to tackle. He replaced the dim bulb in the table lamp with a higher wattage; cleaned and adjusted the pilot light on the gas boiler over the sink; cleared a space in the food cupboard for his provisions and wine; and discovered in the outside shed by the aid of his torch a pile of driftwood for kindling, and a tin bath. There was no bathroom at Hope Cottage. Father Baddeley had probably taken his baths at Toynton Grange. But Dalgliesh had every intention of stripping and sluicing himself in the kitchen. Austerity was a small price to pay to avoid the bathroom at Toynton with its hospital smell of strong disinfectant, its intrusive reminders of sickness and deformity. He put a match to the dried grasses in the grate and watched them flare instantaneously into black needles in one sweet-smelling flame. Then he lit a small experimental fire and found to his relief that the chimney was clear. With a wood fire, a good light, books, food and a stock of wine he saw no reason to wish himself elsewhere.

He estimated that there were between two hundred and three hundred books on the sitting-room shelves and three times as many in the second bedroom; indeed the books had so taken over the room that it was almost impossible to get to the bed. The books presented very few surprises. Many of the theological tomes might be of interest to one of the London theological libraries; some, he thought, his aunt might be glad to give a home to; some were destined for his own shelves. There was H. B. Swete's *Greek Old Testament* in three volumes, Thomas à Kempis's *Imitation of Christ*; William Law's *Serious Call*; a leather-bound *Life and Letters of Eminent 19th Century Divines* in two volumes; a first edition of Newman's *Parochial and Plain Sermons*. But there was also a representative collection of the major English novelists and poets and, since Father Baddeley had indulged himself by buying an occasional novel, there was a small but interesting collection of first editions.

At a quarter to ten he heard approaching footsteps and the squeak of wheels, there was a peremptory knock on the door, and Millicent Hammitt entered bringing with her an agreeable smell of fresh coffee and wheeling after her a laden trolley. There was a sturdy blue banded jug of coffee, a similar jug of hot milk, a bowl of brown sugar, two blue banded mugs, and a plate of digestive biscuits.

Dalgliesh felt that he could hardly object when Mrs. Hammitt cast an appreciative glance at the wood fire, poured out two mugs of coffee and made it obvious that she was in no hurry to go.

Dalgliesh had been briefly introduced to her before dinner the previous evening, but there had been time for only half a minute's conversation before Wilfred had taken his stance at the reading desk and the ordained silence fell. She had taken the opportunity to discover, by the expedient of a blunt interrogation with no attempt at finesse, that Dalgliesh was holidaying alone because he was a widower and that his wife had died in childbirth with her baby. Her response to this had been, "Very tragic. And unusual, surely, for these days?" spoken with an accusatory glance across the table and in a tone which suggested that someone had been inexcusably careless.

She was wearing carpet slippers and a thick tweed skirt, incongruously topped by an openwork jumper in pink wool, liberally festooned with pearls. Dalgliesh suspected that her cottage was a similar unhappy compromise between utility and fussiness, but had no inclination to find out. To his relief she made no attempt to help with the books but sat squatting on the edge of the chair, coffee mug cradled in her lap, her legs planted firmly apart to reveal twin balloons of milky white and varicosed thigh above the bite of the stockings. Dalgliesh continued with his job, coffee mug on the floor at his side. He shook each volume gently before allocating it to its pile in case some message should drop out. If it did, Mrs. Hammitt's presence would be embarrassing. But he knew that the precaution was merely his professional habit of leaving nothing to chance. This wouldn't be Father Baddeley's way.

Meanwhile Mrs. Hammitt sipped her coffee and talked, encouraged in her volubility and occasional indiscretion by the belief which Dalgliesh had noticed before that a man who is physically working only hears half what is said to him.

"No need to ask you if you had a comfortable night. Those beds of Wilfred's are notorious. A certain amount of hardness is supposed to be good for disabled patients but I like a mattress I can sink into. I'm surprised that Julius didn't invite you to sleep at his cottage, but he never does have visitors. Doesn't want to put Mrs. Reynolds out I suppose. She's the village constable's widow from Toynton Village and she does for Julius whenever he's here. Grossly overpaid, of course. Well, he can afford it. And you'll be sleeping here tonight, I understand. I saw Helen Rainer coming in with the bed linen. I suppose it won't worry you, sleeping in Michael's bed. No, of course it wouldn't, being a policeman. You aren't sensitive or superstitious about things like that. Quite right too; our death is but a sleep and a forgetting. Or do I mean life? Wordsworth anyway. I used to be very fond of poetry when I was a girl but I can't get along with these modern poets. Still, I should have quite looked forward to your reading."

Her tone suggested that it would have been a solitary and eccentric pleasure. But Dalgliesh had momentarily stopped listening to her. He had found a first edition of *Diary of a Nobody* with an inscription written in a boyish hand, on the title page.

> To Father Baddeley for his Birthday with love from Adam. I bought this from Mr. Snelling in Norwich and he let me have it cheap because of the red stain on page twenty. But I've tested it and it isn't blood.

Dalgliesh smiled. So he'd tested it, had he, the arrogant little blighter. What mysterious concoction of acids and crystals from the remembered chemistry set had resulted in that confident scientific pronouncement? The inscription reduced the value of the book rather more than had the stain, but he didn't think that Father Baddeley had thought so. He placed it on the pile reserved for his own shelves and again let Mrs. Hammitt's voice pierce his consciousness.

"And if a poet can't take the trouble to make himself intelligible to the educated reader, then the educated reader had better leave him alone, that's what I always say."

"I'm sure you do, Mrs. Hammitt."

"Call me Millicent, won't you? We're supposed to be one happy family here. If I have to put up with Dennis Lerner and Maggie Hewson and even that appalling Albert Philby calling me by my Christian name—not that I give him much opportunity, I assure you—I don't see why you shouldn't. And I shall try to call you Adam but I don't think it's going to come easily. You aren't a Christian name person."

Dalgliesh carefully dusted the volumes of Maskell's *Monumenta Ritualica Ecclesiae Anglicanae* and said that, from what he had heard, Victor Holroyd hadn't done much towards promoting the concept of all one happy family.

"Oh, you've heard about Victor then? Maggie gossiping, I suppose. He really was an extremely difficult man, inconsiderate in life and in death. I managed to get on with him fairly well. I think he respected me. He was a very clever man and full of useful information. But no one at the Grange could stand him. Even Wilfred more or less gave up in the end and left him alone. Maggie Hewson was the exception. Odd woman; she always has to be different. Do you know, I believe she thought Victor had willed his money to her. Of course we all knew that he had money. He took good care to let us know that he wasn't one of those patients paid for by the local authority. And I suppose she thought that if she played her cards right some of it might come to her. She more or less hinted it to me once. Well, she was half drunk at the time. Poor Eric! I give that marriage another year at the most. Some men might find her physically attractive, I suppose, if you like that dyed blonde, blowzy, over-sexed type. Of course, her affair, if you can call it an affair, with Victor was just indecent. Sex is for the healthy. I know that the disabled are supposed to have feelings like the rest of us but you'd think that they'd put that sort of thing behind them when they get to the wheelchair stage. That book looks interesting. The binding's good anyway. You might get a shilling or two for that."

Placing a first edition of *Tracts for the Times* out of reach of Millicent's nudging foot and among the books selected for himself, Dalgliesh recognized with transitory self-disgust that, however much he deplored Mrs. Hammitt's uninhibited expression, the sentiment wasn't far from his own thoughts. What, he wondered, must it be like to feel desire, love, lust even, and be imprisoned in an unresponsive body? Or worse, a body only too responsive to some of its urges, but uncoordinated, ugly, grotesque. To be sensitive to beauty, but to live always with deformity. He thought that he could begin to understand Victor Holroyd's bitterness. He asked:

"What happened in the end to Holroyd's money?"

"It all went to his sister in New Zealand, all sixty-five thousand of it. Very right too. Money ought to be kept in the family. But I daresay Maggie had her hopes. Probably Victor more or less promised her. It's the sort of thing he would do. He could be very spiteful at times. But at least he left his fortune where it ought to go. I should be very displeased indeed if I thought that Wilfred had bequeathed Toynton Grange to anyone but me."

"But would you want it?"

"Oh, the patients would have to go, of course. I can't see myself running Toynton Grange as it is now. I respect what Wilfred's trying to do, but he has a particular need to do it. I expect you've heard about his visit to Lourdes and the miracle. Well, that's all right by me. But I haven't had a miracle, thank God, and I've no intention of putting myself in the way of one. Besides, I've done quite enough for the chronic sick already. Half the house was left to me by father and I sold out to Wilfred so that he could start the Home. We had a proper valuation made at the time, naturally, but it wasn't very high. At that time large country houses were a drag on the market. Now, of course, it's worth a fortune. It's a beautiful house isn't it?"

"It's certainly interesting architecturally."

"Exactly. Regency houses of character are fetching fantastic prices. Not that I'm set on selling. After all, it was our childhood home and I have an affection for it. But I should probably get rid of the land. As a matter of fact, Victor Holroyd knew someone locally who would be interested in buying, someone who wants to set up another holiday caravan camp."

Dalgliesh said involuntarily:

"What a horrible thought!"

Mrs. Hammitt was unabashed. She said complacently:

"Not at all. A very selfish attitude on your part, if I may say so. The poor need holidays just like the rich. Julius wouldn't like it, but I'm under no obligation to consider Julius. He'd sell his cottage and get out I suppose. He owns that acre and a half of the headland, but I can't see him driving through a caravan park every time he comes here from London. Besides, they'd more or less have to pass his windows to get down to the beach. That's the only spot with a beach at high tide. I can see them, can't you; knobbly-kneed fathers in natty little shorts carrying the picnic bag, mum following with a blaring transistor, squealing kids, yelling babies. No, I can't see Julius staying here."

"Does everyone here know that you stand to inherit Toynton Grange?"

"Of course; it's no secret. Who else should get it? As a matter of fact, the whole estate should belong to me by right. Perhaps you didn't know that Wilfred isn't really an Anstey, that he was adopted?"

Dalgliesh said cautiously that he thought someone had mentioned as much.

"Then you may as well know the whole of it. It's quite interesting if you're concerned with the law."

Mrs. Hammitt refilled her mug and wriggled back into her chair as if settling herself for a complicated dissertation.

"My father was particularly anxious for a son. Some men are like that, daughters don't really count with them. And I can quite see that I was a disappointment. If a man really wants a son, the only thing that reconciles him to a daughter is her beauty. And that I've never had. Luckily, it didn't seem to worry my husband. We suited very well."

As the only possible answer to this announcement was a vague, congratulatory murmur, Dalgliesh made the appropriate sound.

"Thank you," said Mrs. Hammitt, as if acknowledging a compliment. She went happily on:

"Anyway, when the doctors told father that my mother couldn't bear another child, he decided to adopt a son. I believe he got Wilfred from a children's home, but I was only six at the time and I don't think I was ever told how and where they found him. Illegitimate, of course. People minded more about that kind of thing in 1920 and you could take your pick of unwanted babies. I remember how excited I was at the time to have a brother. I was a lonely child and with more than my share of natural affection. At the time, I didn't see Wilfred as a rival. I was very fond of Wilfred when we were young. I still am. People forget that sometimes."

Dalgliesh asked what happened.

"It was my grandfather's will. The old man distrusted lawyers, even Holroyd and Martinson who were the family solicitors, and he drew up his own will. He left a life interest in the estate to my parents and the whole property in equal shares to his grandchildren. The question was, did he intend to include Wilfred? In the end we had to go to law about it. The case made quite a stir at the time and raised the whole question of the rights of adopted children. Perhaps you remember the case?"

Dalgliesh did have a vague memory of it. He asked:

"When was your grandfather's will made, I mean in relation to your brother's adoption?"

"That was the vital part of the evidence. Wilfred was legally adopted on 3rd May 1921, and grandfather signed his will exactly ten days later on 13th May. It was witnessed by two servants, but they were dead by the time the case was fought. The will was perfectly clear and in order, except that he didn't put in the names.

But Wilfred's lawyers could prove that grandfather knew about the adoption and was happy about it. And the will did say children, in the plural."

"But he might have had it in mind that your mother would die first and your father remarry."

"How clever of you! I can see that you've a lawyer's devious mind. That's exactly what my counsel argued. But it was no good. Wilfred won. But you can understand my feelings over the Grange. If grandfather had only signed that will before 3rd May things would be very different, I can tell you."

"But you did get half the value of the estate?"

"That didn't last long I'm afraid. My dear husband got through money very quickly. It wasn't women, I'm glad to say. It was horses. They're just as expensive and even more unpredictable but a less humiliating rival for a wife. And, unlike another woman, you can at least be glad when they win. Wilfred always said that Herbert became senile when he retired from the army, but I didn't complain. I rather preferred him that way. But he did get through the money."

Suddenly she glanced round the room, leaned forward and gave Dalgliesh a sly conspiratorial glance.

"I'll tell you something that no one at Toynton Grange knows, except Wilfred. If he does sell out I shall get half the sale price. Not just half the extra profit, fifty per cent of what he gets. I've got an undertaking from Wilfred, properly signed and witnessed by Victor. Actually it was Victor's suggestion. He thought it would stand up in law. And it isn't kept where Wilfred can get his hands on it. It's with Robert Loder, a solicitor in Wareham. I suppose Wilfred was so confident that he'd never need to sell, that he didn't care what he signed or perhaps he was arming himself against temptation. I don't think for one minute that he will sell. He cares too much about the place for that. But if he should change his mind, then I shall do very nicely."

Dalgliesh said, greatly daring:

"When I arrived, Mrs. Hewson said something about the Ridgewell Trust. Hasn't Mr. Anstey got it in mind to transfer the Home?"

Mrs. Hammitt took the suggestion more calmly than he had expected. She retorted robustly:

"Nonsense! I know Wilfred talks about it from time to time,

but he'd never just hand over Toynton Grange. Why should he? Money's tight, of course, but money always is tight. He'll just have to put up the fees or get the local authorities to pay more for the patients they send. There's no reason why he should subsidize the local authorities. And if he still can't make the place pay, then he'd do better to sell out, miracle or no miracle."

Dalgliesh suggested that, in all the circumstances, it was surprising that Anstey hadn't become a Roman Catholic. Millicent seized on the thought with vehemence.

"It was quite a spiritual struggle for him at the time." Her voice deepened and throbbed with the echo of cosmic forces linked in mortal struggle. "But I was glad that he decided to remain in our church. Our father"—her voice boomed out in such a sudden access of hortatory fervour that Dalgliesh, startled, half expected that she was about to launch into the Lord's prayer—"would have been so very distressed. He was a great churchman, Commander Dalgliesh. Evangelical of course. No, I was glad that Wilfred didn't go over."

She spoke as if Wilfred, faced with the Jordan river, had neither liked the look of the water nor had confidence in his boat.

Dalgliesh had already asked Julius Court about Anstey's religious allegiance and had received a different and, he suspected, a more accurate explanation. He recalled their conversation on the patio before they had rejoined Henry; Julius's amused voice: "Father O'Malley who was supposed to be instructing Wilfred, made it plain that his church would in future proclaim on a number of matters that Wilfred had seen as coming within his personal jurisdiction. It occurred to dear Wilfred that he was on the point of joining a very large organization and one which thought that, as a convert, he was receiving rather than bestowing benefit. In the end, after what I have no doubt was a gratifying struggle, he decided to remain in a more accommodating fold."

"Despite the miracle?" Dalgliesh had asked.

"Despite the miracle. Father O'Malley is a rationalist. He admits the existence of miracles but prefers the evidence to be submitted to the proper authorities for thorough examination. After a seemly delay the Church in her wisdom will then pronounce. To go about proclaiming that one has been the recipient of special grace smacks to him of presumption. Worse, I suspect he thinks it in poor taste. He's a fastidious man, is Father O'Malley. He and Wilfred don't really get on. I'm afraid that Father O'Malley has lost his church a convert."

"But the pilgrimages to Lourdes still go on?" Dalgliesh had asked.

"Oh, yes. Twice a year regularly. I don't go. I used to when I first came here but it isn't, in the contemporary idiom, exactly my scene. But I usually make it my business to provide a slap-up tea to welcome them all back."

Dalgliesh, his mind recalled to the present, was aware that his back was beginning to ache. He straightened up just as the clock on the mantelshelf struck the three-quarters. A charred log tumbled from the grate shooting up a final cascade of sparks. Mrs. Hammitt took it as a signal that it was time to go. Dalgliesh insisted first on washing up the coffee mugs and she followed him into the little kitchen.

"It has been a pleasant hour, Commander, but I doubt whether we shall repeat it. I'm not one of those neighbours who keep dropping in. Thank God I can stand my own company. Unlike poor Maggie, I have resources. And I'll say one thing for Michael Baddeley, he did keep himself to himself."

"Nurse Rainer tells me that you persuaded him of the advantages of cremation."

"Did she say that? Well, I daresay she's right. I may have mentioned it to Michael. I strongly disapprove of wasting good ground to bury putrifying bodies. As far as I remember, the old man didn't care what happened to him as long as he ended up in consecrated earth with the proper words said over him. Very sensible. My view entirely. And Wilfred certainly didn't object to the cremation. He and Dot Moxon agreed with me absolutely. Helen protested over the extra trouble, but what she didn't like was having to get a second doctor's signature. Thought it cast some kind of aspersion on dear Eric's clinical judgement, I suppose."

"But surely no one was suggesting that Dr. Hewson's diagnosis was wrong?"

"Of course not! Michael died of a heart attack, and even Eric was competent to recognize that, I should hope. No, don't bother to see me home, I've got my torch. And if there's anything you need at any time, just knock on the wall."

"But would you hear? You didn't hear Father Baddeley."

"Naturally not, since he didn't knock. And after about nine-thirty I wasn't really listening for him. You see, I thought someone had already visited to settle him for the night."

The darkness outside was cool and restless, a black mist, sweet-tasting and smelling of the sea, not the mere absence of light but a positive, mysterious force. Dalgliesh manoeuvred the trolley over the doorstep. Walking beside Millicent down the short path, and steadying the trolley with one hand, he asked with careful uninterest:

"Did you hear someone, then?"

"Saw, not heard. Or so I thought. I was thinking of making myself a hot drink and I wondered whether Michael would like one. But when I opened my front door to call in and ask, I thought I saw a figure in a cloak disappearing into the darkness. As Michael's light was off—I could see that the cottage was completely dark—naturally I didn't disturb him. I know now that I was mistaken. Either that or I'm going potty. It wouldn't be difficult in this place. Apparently no one did visit him and now they've all got a bad conscience about it. I can see how I was deceived. It was a night like this. Just a slight breeze but the darkness seeming to move and form itself into shapes. And I heard nothing, not even a footfall. Just a glimpse of a bent head, hooded and a cloak swirling into the darkness."

"And this was at about nine-thirty?"

"Or a little later. Perhaps it was about the time he died. A fanciful person could frighten herself imagining that she'd seen his ghost. That was what Jennie Pegram actually suggested when I told them at Toynton Grange. Ridiculous girl!"

They had almost reached the door of Faith Cottage. She hesitated and then said as if on impulse, and, he thought, with some embarrassment:

"They tell me that you're worried about the broken lock of Michael's bureau. Well, it was all right the night before he came back from hospital. I found I'd run out of envelopes and I had an urgent letter to write. I thought that he wouldn't mind if I took a look in the bureau. It was locked then."

Dalgliesh said:

"And broken when your brother looked for the will shortly after the body was found."

"So he says, Commander. So he says."

"But you have no proof that he broke it?"

"I've no proof that anyone did. The cottage was full of people running in and out. Wilfred, the Hewsons, Helen, Dot, Philby, even Julius when he arrived from London; the place was like a wake. All I know is that the bureau was locked at nine o'clock on the night before Michael died. And I've no doubt that Wilfred was keen to get his eyes on that will and see if Michael really had left Toynton Grange all he possessed. And I do know that Michael didn't break the lock himself."

"How, Mrs. Hammitt?"

"Because I found the key, just after lunch on the day he died. In the place where, presumably, he always kept it—that old tea tin on the second shelf of the food cupboard. I didn't think he'd mind my having any little bits of food he'd left. I slipped it into my pocket in case it got lost when Dot cleared the cottage. After all, that old bureau desk is quite valuable and the lock ought to be repaired. As a matter of fact, if Michael hadn't left it to Grace in his will, I would have moved it into here and looked after it properly."

"So you still have the key?"

"Of course. No one has ever bothered about it but you. But, as you seem so interested you may as well take it."

She dug her hand into the pocket of her skirt and he felt the cold metal pressed into his palm. She had opened the door of her cottage now and had reached for the light switch. In the sudden glare he blinked, and then saw it clearly, a small silver key, delicate as filigree, but tied now with thin string to a red plastic clothes peg, the red so bright that, for a dazzled second, it looked as if his palm were stained with blood.

5
Act of Malice

I

When he looked back on his first weekend in Dorset, Dalgliesh saw it as a series of pictures, so different from the later images of violence and death that he could almost believe that his life at Toynton Head had been lived on two levels and at different periods of time. These early and gentle pictures, unlike the later harsh black and white stills from some crude horror film, were suffused with colour and feeling and smell. He saw himself plunging through the sea-washed shingle of Chesil Bank, his ears loud with bird cries and the grating thunder of the tide to where Portland reared its dark rocks against the sky; climbing the great earthworks of Maiden Castle and standing, a solitary windblown figure, where four thousand years of human history were encompassed in numinous contours of moulded earth; eating a late tea in Judge Jeffrey's lodgings in Dorchester as the mellow autumn afternoon faded into dusk; driving through the night between a falling tangle of golden bracken and high untrimmed hedgerows to where the stone-walled pub waited with lighted windows on some remote village green.

And then, late at night when there could be small risk of a visitor from Toynton Grange disturbing him, he would drive back to Hope Cottage to the familiar and welcoming smell of books and a wood fire. Somewhat to his surprise, Millicent Hammitt was faithful to her promise not to disturb him after that first visit. He soon guessed why; she was a television addict. As he sat drinking his wine and sorting Father Baddeley's books, he could hear through the chimney breast the faint and not disagreeable sounds of her nightly entertainment; the sudden access of a half familiar advertising jingle; the antiphonal mutter of voices; the bark of gun shots; feminine screams; the blaring fanfare to the late night film.

He had a sense of living in a limbo between the old life and the new, excused by convalescence from the responsibility of immediate decision, from any exertion which he found disagreeable. And he found the thought of Toynton Grange and its inmates disagreeable. He had taken what action he could. Now he was waiting on events. Once, looking at Father Baddeley's empty and shabby chair, he was reminded irreverently of the fabled excuse of the distinguished atheist philosopher, ushered after death to his astonishment into the presence of God.

"But Lord, you didn't provide sufficient evidence."

If Father Baddeley wanted him to act he would have to provide more tangible clues than a missing diary and a broken lock.

He was expecting no letters except Bill Moriarty's reply since he had left instructions that none were to be forwarded. And he intended to collect Bill's letter himself from the postbox. But it arrived on the Monday, at least a day earlier than he had thought possible. He had spent the morning in the cottage and hadn't walked to the postbox until after his lunch at two-thirty when he had taken back his milk bottles for collection.

The postbox contained the one letter, a plain envelope with a W.C. postmark; the address was typed but his rank omitted. Moriarty had been careful. But as he slipped his thumb under the flap, Dalgliesh wondered if he himself had been careful enough. There was no obvious sign that the letter had been opened; the flap was intact. But the glue was suspiciously weak, and the flap slid open a little too easily under the pressure of his thumb. And the postbox was otherwise empty. Someone, probably Philby, must already have collected the Toynton Grange post. It was odd that he hadn't delivered this letter at Hope Cottage. Perhaps he should have used a poste restante in Toynton village or Wareham. The thought that he had been careless irritated him. The truth is, he thought, that I don't know what, if anything, I'm investigating, and I only spasmodically care. I haven't the stomach to do the job properly or the will and courage to leave it alone. He was in the mood to find Bill's prose style more than usually irritating.

"Nice to see your elegant handwriting again. There's general relief here that the reports of your impending decease were exaggerated. We're keeping the wreath contributions for a celebration party. But what are you doing anyway gum-shoeing in Dorset among such a questionable group of weirdies? If you pine for work there's plenty here. However, here's the gen.

Two of your little lot have records. You know, apparently, something about Philby. Two convictions for GBH in 1967 and 1969, four for theft in 1970 and a miscellany of earlier misdemeanours. The only extraordinary thing about Philby's criminal history is the leniency with which judges have sentenced him. Looking at his CRO I'm not altogether surprised. They probably felt that it was unjust to punish too harshly a man who was following the only career for which physiognomy and talents had fitted him. I did manage to have a word with 'the open door' about him. They admit his faults, but say that he is capable, given affection, of a ferocious loyalty. Watch out that he doesn't take a fancy to you.

Millicent Hammitt was convicted twice for shoplifting by the Cheltenham Magistrates in 1966 and 1968. In the first case there was the usual defence of menopausal difficulties, and she was fined. She was lucky to escape so easily the second time. But that was a couple of months after her husband, a retired army major, had died and the court were sympathetic. They were probably influenced too, by Wilfred Anstey's assurances that she was coming to live with him at Toynton Grange and would be under his eye. There's been no trouble since so I assume that Anstey's surveillance has been effective, the local shopkeepers more accommodating, or Mrs. Hammitt more skilful in lifting the goods.

That's all the official gen. The rest of them are clean, at least as far as the CRO is concerned. But if you're looking for an interesting villain—and I hardly suppose that Adam Dalgliesh is wasting his talents on Albert Philby—then may I recommend Julius Court? I got a line on him from a man I know who works at the FCO. Court is a bright grammar school boy from Southsea who entered the foreign service after university equipped with all the usual elegant appurtenances but rather short on cash. He was at the Paris Embassy in 1970 when he gave evidence in the notorious murder trial when Alain Michonnet was accused of murdering Poitaud the racing driver. You may remember the case. There was a fair amount of publicity in the English press. It was pretty clear cut, and the French police were salivating happily at the thought of nailing Michonnet. He's the son of Theo d'Estier Michonnet who owns a chemical manufacturing plant near Marseilles and they've had their eyes on père and fils for quite a time. But Court gave his chum an alibi. The odd thing was that they weren't really chums—Michonnet is aggressively heterosexual as the media make only too boringly plain—and the horrid word blackmail was hissed round the Embassy. No one believed Court's story; but no one could shake it. My informant thinks that Court's motive was nothing more sinister than a desire to amuse himself and to get his superiors twisting their knickers. If that was his motive he certainly succeeded. Eight months later his godfather conveniently died leaving him £30,000 and he chucked the service. He's said to have been rather clever with his investments. Anyway, that's all water under the bridge. Nothing is known to his discredit as they say, except, perhaps, a tendency to be a little too accommodating to his friends. But I give you the story for what it's worth."

Dalgliesh folded the letter and stuffed it into his jacket pocket. He wondered how much, if any, of either story was known at Toynton Grange. Julius Court was unlikely to worry. His past was his own affair; he was independent of Wilfred's suffocating hold. But Millicent Hammitt had a double weight of gratitude. Who else except Wilfred knew, he wondered, about those two discreditable and pathetic incidents? How much would she care if the story became generally known at Toynton Grange? He wished again that he had used a poste restante.

A car was approaching. He looked up. The Mercedes, driven very fast, was coming down the coast road. Julius stepped on the brakes and the car rocked to a stop, its front bumper inches from the gate. He wrenched himself out and began tugging at the gate, calling out to Dalgliesh.

"The black tower's on fire! I saw the smoke from the coast road. Have you a rake at Hope Cottage?"

Dalgliesh put his shoulder to the gate.

"I don't think so. There's no garden. But I found a yard broom—a besom—in the shed."

"Better than nothing. D'you mind coming? It may take the two of us."

Dalgliesh slipped quickly into the car. They left the gate open. Julius drove to Hope Cottage with little regard for the car springs or his passenger's comfort. He opened the boot while Dalgliesh ran to the yard shed. There among the paraphernalia of past occupants was the remembered besom, two empty sacks, and, surprisingly, an old shepherd's crook. He threw them into the capacious boot. Julius had already turned the car and the engine was running. Dalgliesh got in beside him and the Mercedes leapt forward.

As they swung on to the coast road Dalgliesh asked:

"Is anyone there do you know? Anstey?"

"Could be. That's the worry. He's the only one who goes there now. And I can't see otherwise how the fire started. We can get closest to the tower this way, but it means foot slogging it over the headland. I didn't try when I first spotted the smoke. It's no use without something to tackle the fire."

His voice was tight, the knuckles on the wheel shone white. In the driving mirror Dalgliesh saw that the irises of his eyes were large and bright. The triangular scar above the right eye, normally almost invisible, had deepened and darkened. Above it he could see the insistent beat of the temple pulse. He glanced at the speedometer; they were doing over a hundred but the Mercedes, beautifully handled, held the narrow road easily. Suddenly the road twisted and rose and they caught a glimpse of the tower. The broken panes in the slitted windows below the cupola were belching puff-balls of greyish smoke like miniature canon fire. They tumbled merrily over the headland until the wind shook them into shredded dusters of cloud. The effect was absurd and picturesque, as innocuous as a child's entertainment. And then the road dipped and the tower was lost to view.

The coast road, wide enough only for a single car, was bounded to the seaward by a drystone wall. Julius was sure of his way. He had swung the car to the left even before Dalgliesh noticed the narrow gap, gateless but still bounded by two rotting posts. The car bumped to a standstill in a deep hollow to the right of the entry. Dalgliesh seized the crook and sacks and Julius the broom. Thus ridiculously lumbered, they began running across the headland.

Julius had been right; this was the quickest way. But they had to do it on foot. Even had he been willing to drive over this rough, rock-strewn ground it wouldn't have been possible. The headland was crossed with fragmented stone walls, low enough to leap over and with plenty of gaps, but none wide enough for a vehicle. The ground was deceptive. At one minute the tower seemed almost to recede, separated from them by interminable barriers of tumbling stone. Then it was upon them.

The smoke, acrid as a damp bonfire, was rolling strongly from the half-open door. Dalgliesh kicked it wide and leapt to one side as the gusts billowed out. There was an immediate roar and the tongue of flame fanged out at him. With the crook he began raking out the burning debris, some still identifiable—long dried grass and hay, rope ends, what looked like the remains of an old chair—the years of accumulated rubbish since the headland had been public land and the black tower, unlocked, used as a shepherd's shelter or a night lodging for tramps. As he raked out the burning, malodorous clumps he could hear Julius behind him frantically beating them out. Little fires started and crawled like red tongues among the grasses.

As soon as the doorway was clear Julius rushed in stamping down the smouldering remnants of grass and hay with the two sacks. Dalgliesh could see his smoke-shrouded figure coughing and reeling. He dragged him unceremoniously out and said:

"Keep back until I've cleared it. I don't want the two of you on my hands."

"But he's there! I know he is. He must be. Oh, God! The bloody fool!"

The last smouldering clump of grass was out now. Julius, pushing Dalgliesh aside, ran up the stone stairway which circled the walls. Dalgliesh followed. A wooden door to a middle chamber was ajar. Here there was no window, but in the smoke-filled darkness they could see the huddled sack-like figure against the far wall. He had drawn the hood of the monk's cloak over his head and had swathed himself into its folds like a human derelict wrapped against the cold. Julius's feverish hands got lost in its folds. Dalgliesh could hear him cursing. It took seconds before Anstey's arms were freed and, together, they dragged him to the door and, with difficulty, supported and manoeuvred the inert body between them down the narrow stairs and into the fresh-smelling air.

They laid him prone on the grass. Dalgliesh had dropped to his knees, ready to turn him and start artificial respiration. Then Anstey slowly stretched out both arms and lay in an attitude both theatrical and vaguely blasphemous. Dalgliesh, relieved that he wouldn't now have to fasten his mouth over Anstey's, got to his feet. Anstey drew up his knees and began to cough convulsively in hoarse whooping gasps. He turned his face to one side, his cheek resting on the headland. The moist mouth coughing out saliva and bile, seemed to be sucking at the grass as if avid for nourishment. Dalgliesh and Court knelt and raised him between them. He said weakly:

"I'm all right. I'm all right."

Dalgliesh asked:

"We've got the car on the coast road. Can you walk?"

"Yes. I'm all right, I tell you. I'm all right."

"There's no hurry. Better rest for a few minutes before we start."

They lowered him against one of the large boulders and he sat there a little apart from them, still coughing spasmodically, and looking out to sea. Julius paced the cliff edge, restlessly as if fretting at the delay. The stench of the fire was blown gently from the blackened headland like the last waves of a fading pestilence.

After five minutes Dalgliesh called:

"Shall we start now?"

Together and without speaking, they raised Anstey and supported him between them across the headland and to the car.

II

No one spoke on the drive back to Toynton Grange. As usual, the front of the house seemed deserted, the tessellated hall was empty, unnaturally silent. But Dorothy Moxon's sharp ears must have heard the car, perhaps from the clinical room at the front of the house. Almost immediately she appeared at the top of the stairs.

"What is it? What happened?"

Julius waited until she had come swiftly down, then said quietly:

"It's all right. Wilfred managed to set fire to the black tower with himself inside. He isn't hurt, just shocked. And the smoke hasn't done his lungs any good."

She glanced accusingly from Dalgliesh to Julius as if it were their fault, then put both her arms round Anstey in a gesture fiercely maternal and protective and began to urge him gently up the stairs, muttering encouragement and remonstration into his ear in a soft grumbling monotone which, to Dalgliesh, sounded like an endearment. Anstey, he noticed, seemed less capable of supporting himself now than he had been on the headland and they made slow progress. But when Julius came forward to help, a glance from Dorothy Moxon made him draw back. With difficulty she got Anstey into his small white-painted bedroom at the back of the house and helped him on to the narrow bed. Dalgliesh made a swift mental inventory. The room was much as he had expected. One small table and chair set under the window giving a view of the patients' rear courtyard; a well-stocked bookcase; one rug; a crucifix over the bed; a bedside table with a simple lamp and a carafe of water. But the thick mattress bounced gently as Wilfred rolled on to it. The towel hanging beside the wash basin looked luxuriantly soft. The bedside rug, plain in design, was no strip of worn, discarded carpet. The hooded dressing gown in white towelling hanging behind the door had a look of simplicity, almost austerity; but Dalgliesh did not doubt that it was agreeably soft to the skin. This might be a cell, but it lacked none of the essential comforts.

Wilfred opened his eyes and fixed his blue gaze on Dorothy Moxon. It was interesting, Dalgliesh thought, how he managed to combine humility with authority in one look. He held out a suppliant hand.

"I want to talk to Julius and Adam, Dot dear. Just for a moment. Will you?"

She opened her mouth, clamped it shut again, and stomped out without a word, closing the door firmly behind her. Wilfred closed his eyes again and appeared mentally to withdraw himself from the scene. Julius looked down at his hands. His right palm was red and swollen and a blister had already formed over the bowl of the thumb. He said with a note of surprise:

"Funny! My hand's burnt. I never felt it at the time. Now it's beginning to hurt like hell."

Dalgliesh said:

"You should get Miss Moxon to dress it. And it might be as well to let Hewson have a look at it."

Julius took a folded handkerchief from his pocket, soaked it in cold water at the wash basin and wrapped it inexpertly round his hand.

He said:

"It can wait."

The realization that he was in pain appeared to have soured his temper. He stood over Wilfred and said crossly:

"Now that a definite attack has been made on your life and damn nearly succeeded, I suppose you'll act sensibly for once and send for the police."

Wilfred did not open his eyes, he said weakly:

"I have a policeman here."

Dalgliesh said:

"It isn't for me. I can't undertake an official investigation for you. Court is right, this is a matter for the local police."

Wilfred shook his head.

"There's nothing to tell them. I went to the black tower because there were things I needed to think over in peace. It's the only place where I can be absolutely alone. I was smoking; you know how you all complain about my smelly old pipe. I remember knocking it out against the wall as I went up. It must have been still alight. All that dried grass and straw would have gone up at once."

Julius said grimly:

"It did. And the outside door? I suppose you forgot to lock it after you, despite all the fuss you make about never leaving the black tower open. You're a careless lot at Toynton Grange aren't you? Lerner forgets to check the wheelchair brakes and Holroyd goes over the cliff. You knock out your pipe above a floor strewn with highly combustible dry straw, leave the door open to provide a draught, and bloody nearly immolate yourself."

Anstey said:

"That's how I prefer to believe it happened."

Dalgliesh said quickly:

"Presumably there's a second key to the tower. Where is it kept?"

Wilfred opened his eyes and stared into space as if patiently dissociating himself from this dual interrogation.

"Hanging on a nail on the keyboard in the business room. It was Michael's key, the one I brought back here after his death."

"And everyone knows where it's hung?"

"I imagine so. All the keys are kept there and the one to the tower is distinctive."

"How many people at Toynton Grange knew that you planned to be in the tower this afternoon?"

"All of them. I told them my plans after prayers. I always do. People have to know where to find me in an emergency. Everyone was there except Maggie and Millicent. But what you're suggesting is ridiculous."

"Is it?" asked Dalgliesh.

Before he could move, Julius, who was nearer the door, had slipped out. They waited in silence. It was another two minutes before he returned. He said with grim satisfaction:

"The business room is empty and the key isn't there. That means whoever took it hasn't yet had a chance to put it back. Incidentally, I called in on Dot on my way back. She's lurking in her surgical hell sterilizing enough equipment for a major operation. It's like confronting a harpy through a hiss of steam. Anyway, she claims with bad grace that she was in the business room continually from 2 p.m. until about five minutes before we got back. She can't remember whether the tower key was on the keyboard. She didn't notice it. I'm afraid I've made her suspicious, Wilfred, but it seemed important to establish some facts."

Dalgliesh thought that the facts could have been established without direct questioning. But it was too late now to initiate more discreet enquiries and in any case he had neither the heart nor stomach to undertake them. Certainly, he had no wish to pit the claims of orthodox detection against Julius's enthusiastic amateurism. But he asked:

"Did Miss Moxon say whether anyone had come into the business room while she was there? They may have made an attempt to replace the key."

"According to her, the place was—untypically—like a railway station. Henry wheeled himself in shortly after two, and then went out again. No explanation. Millicent dropped in about half an hour ago looking, so she said, for you, Wilfred. Dennis arrived a few minutes later to look up an unspecified telephone number. Maggie arrived just before we did. Again, no explanation. She didn't stay, but she did ask Dot whether she'd seen Eric. The only safe deduction from all this is that Henry couldn't have been on the headland at the material time. But then, we know he wasn't.

Whoever started that fire had the use of a pair of very sound legs."

His own, or someone else's, thought Dalgliesh.

He spoke again directly to the quiet figure on the bed.

"Did you see anyone when you were in the tower, either before or after the fire started?"

Wilfred paused before replying.

"I think so."

Seeing Julius's face, he went on quickly:

"I'm sure I did, but only very briefly. When the fire started I was sitting at the southern window, the one overlooking the sea. I smelt smoke and went down into the middle chamber. I opened the door to the base of the tower and saw the hay smouldering and a sudden tongue of flame. I could have got out then, but I panicked. I'm terrified of fire. It isn't a rational fear. It goes well beyond that. I suppose you'd call it a phobia. Anyway, I scrambled ignominiously back into the top room and began running from window to window looking hopelessly for help. It was then I saw—unless it was an hallucination—a figure in a brown habit slipping between that clump of boulders to the south-west."

Julius said:

"From which he could escape unrecognized by you either to the road or down the cliffs to the beach. That's if he were agile enough for the cliff path. What sort of figure, a man or a woman?"

"Just a figure. I only had a glimpse. I shouted but the wind was against me and he obviously didn't hear. I never thought of it being a woman."

"Well, think now. The hood was up, I suppose?"

"Yes. Yes it was."

"And on a warm afternoon! Think it out for yourself, Wilfred. Incidentally, there are three brown habits hanging in the business room. I felt in the pockets for the key. That's why I noticed. Three habits. How many have you altogether?"

"Eight of the lightweight summer ones. They're always kept hanging in the business room. Mine has rather different buttons, but otherwise we have them in common. We're not really particular which one we take."

"You're wearing yours; presumably Dennis and Philby are wearing theirs. That means two are missing."

"Eric may be wearing one, he does occasionally. And Helen sometimes slips into one if the day is chilly. I seem to remember that one is in the sewing room being mended. And I think one was missing just before Michael died, but I can't be sure. It may have turned up again. We don't really keep a check on them."

Julius said:

"So it's practically impossible to know whether one is missing. I suppose what we ought to be doing, Dalgliesh, is to check up on them now. If she hasn't had a chance to replace the key, presumably she's still got the habit."

Dalgliesh said:

"We've no proof that it was a woman. And why hang on to the habit? It could be discarded anywhere in Toynton Grange without suspicion."

Anstey propped himself up and said with sudden strength:

"No, Julius, I forbid it! I won't have people questioned and cross-examined. It was an accident."

Julius, who seemed to be relishing his role of chief inquisitor, said:

"All right. It was an accident. You forgot to lock the door. You knocked out your pipe before it was dead and started the fire smouldering. The figure you saw was just someone from Toynton Grange taking an innocent stroll on the headland, somewhat overclad for the time of year and so immersed in the beauty of nature that he, or she, neither heard your shout, smelt the fire nor noticed the smoke. What happened then?"

"You mean, after I saw the figure? Nothing. I realized of course that I couldn't get out of the windows and I climbed down again into the middle room. I opened the door to the bottom of the tower. The last thing I remember was a great billow of choking smoke and a sheet of flame. The smoke was suffocating me. The flames seemed to be searing my eyes. I hadn't even time to shut the door again before I was overcome. I suppose I should have kept both doors shut and sat tight. But it isn't easy to make sensible decisions in a state of panic."

Dalgliesh asked:

"How many people here knew that you are abnormally afraid of fire?"

"Most of them suspect, I should think. They may not know just how obsessive and personal a fear it is, but they do know that fire worries me. I insist on all the patients sleeping on the ground floor. I've always worried about the sick room, and I was reluctant to let Henry have an upper room. But someone has to sleep in the main part of the house, and we must have the sick room close to the clinical room and the nurses' bedrooms in case there's an emergency at night. It's sensible and prudent to fear fire in a place like this. But prudence has nothing to do with the terror I feel at the sight of smoke and flame."

He put one hand up to his eyes and they saw that he had begun to tremble. Julius looked down at the shaking figure with almost clinical interest.

Dalgliesh said:

"I'll get Miss Moxon."

He had hardly turned to the door when Anstey shot out a protesting hand. They saw that the trembling had stopped. He said, looking at Julius:

"You do believe that the work I'm doing here is worthwhile?"

Dalgliesh wondered if only he had noticed a fraction of a second's pause before Julius replied evenly:

"Of course."

"You're not just saying that to comfort me, you believe it?"

"I wouldn't say it otherwise."

"Of course not, forgive me. And you agree that the work is more important than the man?"

"That's more difficult. I could argue that the work is the man."

"Not here. This place is established now. It could go on without me if it had to."

"Of course it could, if it's adequately endowed, and if the local authorities continue to send contractual patients. But it won't have to go on without you if you act sensibly instead of like the reluctant hero of a third-rate TV drama. It doesn't suit you, Wilfred."

"I'm trying to be sensible and I'm not being brave. I haven't much physical courage you know. It's the virtue I most regret. You two have it—no, don't argue. I know, and I envy you for it. But I don't really need courage for this situation. You see, I can't believe that someone is really trying to kill me." He turned to Dalgliesh.

"You explain, Adam. You must see what I'm getting at."

Dalgliesh said carefully:

"It could be argued that neither of the two attempts were serious. The frayed climbing rope? It's hardly a very certain method, and most people here must know that you wouldn't start a climb without checking your equipment and that you certainly wouldn't climb alone. This afternoon's little charade? You would probably have been safe enough if you'd closed both the doors and stayed in the top room; uncomfortably hot probably, but in no real danger. The fire would have burnt itself out in time. It was opening the middle door and gasping in a lungful of smoke which nearly did for you."

Julius said:

"But suppose the grass had burnt fiercely and the flames had caught the wooden floor of the first storey? The whole of the middle of the tower would have gone up in a matter of seconds; the fire must have reached the top room. If it had, nothing could have saved you." He turned to Dalgliesh:

"Isn't that true?"

"Probably. That's why you ought to tell the police. A practical joker who takes risks like that has to be taken seriously. And the next time there mightn't be someone handy to rescue you."

"I don't think there will be a next time. I think I know who's responsible. I'm not really quite as foolish as I seem. I'll take care, I promise. I have a feeling that the person responsible won't be here with us much longer."

Julius said:

"You're not immortal, Wilfred."

"I know that, too, and I could be wrong. So I think it's time I spoke to the Ridgewell Trust. The Colonel is overseas, visiting his homes in India, but he's due back on the 18th. The trustees would like my answer by the end of October. It's a question of tying-up capital for future developments. I wouldn't hand over to them without a majority agreement from the family. I propose to hold a family council. But, if someone is really trying to frighten me into breaking my vow, then I'll see that my work here is made indestructible, whether I'm alive or dead."

Julius said:

"If you hand the whole property over to the Ridgewell Trust, it isn't going to please Millicent."

Wilfred's face set into a mask of obstinacy. Dalgliesh was interested to see how the features changed. The gentle eyes became stern and glazed as if unwilling to see, the mouth set into an uncompromising line. And yet the whole expression was one of petulant weakness.

"Millicent sold out to me perfectly willingly and at a fair valuation. She can't reasonably complain. If I'm driven out of here, the work goes on. What happens to me isn't important."

He smiled at Julius.

"You aren't a believer, I know, so I'll find another authority for you. How about Shakespeare? 'Be absolute for death, and life and death shall thereby be the sweeter.'"

Julius Court's eyes briefly met Dalgliesh's over Wilfred's head. The message simultaneously passed was simultaneously understood. Julius had some difficulty in controlling his mouth. At last he said dryly:

"Dalgliesh is supposed to be convalescent. He's already practically passed out with the exertion of saving you. I may look healthy enough but I need my strength for the pursuit of my own personal pleasures. So if you are determined to hand over to the Ridgewell Trust by the end of the month, try being absolute for life, at least for the next three weeks, there's a good chap."

III

When they were outside the room Dalgliesh asked:

"Do you believe he's in real danger?"

"I don't know. It was probably a closer thing this afternoon than someone intended." He added with affectionate scorn:

"Silly old pseud! Absolute for death! I thought we were about to move on to *Hamlet* and be reminded that the readiness is all. One thing is certain though, isn't it? He isn't putting on a show of courage. Either he doesn't believe that someone at Toynton Grange has it in for him, or he thinks he knows his enemy and is confident that he can deal with him, or her. Or, of course, he started the fire himself. Wait until I've had this hand bandaged and then come in for a drink. You look as if you need it."

But there were things Dalgliesh had to do. He left Julius, volubly apprehensive, to the mercies of Dorothy Moxon and walked back to Hope Cottage to collect his torch. He was thirsty, but there was no time for anything but cold water from the kitchen tap. He had left the cottage windows open but the little sitting-room, insulated by thick stone walls, was as warm and stuffy as on the day he had arrived. As he closed the door, Father Baddeley's cassock swung against it and he caught again the musty, faintly ecclesiastical smell. The crochet chair back and arm covers were sleekly in place uncrumpled by Father Baddeley's head and hands. Something of his personality still lingered here, although already Dalgliesh felt its presence less strongly. But there was no communication. If he wanted Father Baddeley's counsel he would have to seek it in paths familiar but unaccustomed and to which he no longer felt that he had any right of way.

He was ridiculously tired. The cool, rather harsh-tasting water only brought him to a clearer realization of just how tired. The thought of the narrow bed upstairs, of throwing himself down upon its hardness, was almost irresistible. It was ridiculous that so comparatively little exertion could so exhaust him. And it seemed to have become insufferably hot. He drew a hand over his brow and felt the sweat, clammy and cold on his fingers. Obviously he had a temperature. He had, after all, been warned by the hospital that the fever might recur. He felt a surge of anger against his doctors, against Wilfred Anstey, against himself.

It would be easy now to pack his things and get back to the London flat. It would be cool and unencumbered there high above the Thames at Queenhythe. People would leave him alone supposing him to be still in Dorset. Or he could leave a note for Anstey and drive away now; the whole of the West Country was open to him. There were a hundred better places for convalescence than this claustrophobic, self-regarding community dedicated to love and self-fulfilment through suffering, where people sent each other poison pen letters, played at childish and malicious pranks or got tired of waiting for death and hurled themselves into annihilation. And there was nothing to keep him at Toynton; he told himself so with stubborn insistence, resting his head against the coolness of the small square of glass over the sink which had obviously served Father Baddeley as a shaving mirror. It was probably some freak aftermath of illness that made him at once so indecisive and so stubbornly reluctant to leave. For someone who had made up his mind never to go back to detection, he was giving a good imitation of a man committed to his job.

He saw no one as he left the cottage and began the long trudge up the cliff. It was still a bright day on the headland with that sudden almost momentary intensification of light which comes before the setting of the autumn sun. The cushions of moss on the fragmented walls were an intense green, dazzling the eye. Each individual flower was bright as a gem, its image shimmering in the gently moving air. The tower, when at last he came up to it, glistened like ebony and seemed to shiver in the sun. He felt that if he touched it it would reel and dissolve. Its long shadow lay like a monitory finger across the headland.

Taking advantage of the light, since the torch would be more use inside the tower, he began his search. The burnt straw and blackened debris lay in untidy heaps close to the porch, but the light breeze, never absent from this peak of the headland, had already begun to shift the humps and had strewn odd strands almost to the edge of the cliff. He began by scrutinizing the ground close to the walls, then moved out in widening circles. He found nothing until he reached the clump of boulders about fifty yards to the south-west. They were a curious formation, less a natural outcrop of the headland than an artifact, as if the builder of the tower had transported to the site double the weight of stone needed and had amused himself by arranging the surplus in the form of a miniature mountain range. The stones formed a long semi-circle about forty yards long, the peaks, from six to eight feet high, linked by smaller, more rounded uplands. There was adequate cover here for a man to escape undetected either to the cliff path or by way of the rapidly falling ground to the north-west to within a couple of hundred yards of the road.

It was here, behind one of the larger boulders, that Dalgliesh found what he had expected to find, a lightweight brown monk's habit. It was tightly rolled into a bolster and wedged into the crevice between two smaller stones. There was nothing else to be seen, no discernible footprints in the firm dry turf, no tin smelling of paraffin. Somewhere he expected to find a tin. Although the straw and dry grass in the base of the tower would have burned quickly enough once a fire was well established, he doubted whether a thrown match could have been relied upon to start a blaze.

He tucked the habit under his arm. If this were a murder hunt the forensic scientists would examine it for traces of fibre, for dust, for paraffin, for any biological or chemical link with someone at Toynton Grange. But it wasn't a murder hunt; it wasn't even an official investigation. And even if fibres were identified on the habit which matched those from a shirt, a pair of slacks, a jacket, a dress even, of someone at Toynton Grange, what did that prove? Apparently any of the helpers had a right to array themselves in Wilfred's curious idea of a working uniform. The fact that the habit had been abandoned, and at that point, suggested that the wearer had chosen to escape down the cliff rather than by way of the road; otherwise why not continue to rely on its camouflage? Unless, of course, the wearer were a woman and one who didn't normally thus array herself. In that case, to be seen by chance on the headland shortly after the fire would be damning. But no one, man or woman, would choose to wear it on the cliff path. It was the quicker but the more difficult route and the habit would be a dangerously entangling garment. Certainly it would bear telltale traces of sandy earth or green stains from the seaweed-covered rocks on that difficult scramble to the beach. But perhaps that was what he was meant to believe. Had the habit, like Father Baddeley's letter, been planted for him to discover, so neatly, so precisely placed exactly where he might have expected to find it? Why abandon it at all? Thus rolled, it was hardly an impossible burden to manage on that slippery path to the shore.

The door of the tower was still ajar. Inside the smell of the fire still lingered but half pleasantly now in the first cool of the early evening, an evocative autumnal smell of burnt grass. The lower part of the rope banister had burnt away and hung from the iron rings in scorched and tattered fragments.

He switched on his torch and began systematically to search among the blackened threads of burnt straw. He found it within minutes, a battered, soot-covered and lidless tin which could once have held cocoa. He smelt it. It could have been his imagination that a trace of paraffin still lingered.

He made his way up the stone steps carefully hugging the fire-blackened wall. He found nothing in the middle chamber and was glad to climb out of this dark, windowless and claustrophobic cell into the upper room. The contrast with the chamber below was immediate and striking. The little room was filled with light. It was only six feet wide and the domed and ribbed ceiling gave it a charming, feminine and slightly formal air. Four of the eight compass point windows were without their glass and the air streamed in, cool and scented with the sea. Because the room was so small the height of the tower was accentuated. Dalgliesh had the sensation of being suspended in a decorative pepper pot between sky and sea. The quiet was absolute, a positive peace. He could hear nothing but the ticking of his watch and the ceaseless anodyne surge of the sea. Why, he wondered, hadn't that self-tormented Victorian Wilfred Anstey signalled his distress from one of these windows? Perhaps, by the time his will to endure had been broken by the tortures of hunger and thirst, the old man had been too weak to mount the stairs. Certainly nothing of his final terror and despair had penetrated to this miniature light-filled eyrie. Looking out of the southern window Dalgliesh could see the crinkled sea layered in azure and purple with one red triangle of sail stationary on the horizon. The other windows gave a panoramic view of the whole sunlit headland; Toynton Grange and its clutter of cottages could be identified only by the chimney of the house itself since they lay in the valley. Dalgliesh noticed too that the square of mossy turf, where Holroyd's wheelchair had rested before that final convulsive heave towards destruction, and the narrow sunken lane were also invisible. Whatever had happened on that fateful afternoon, no one could have seen it from the black tower.

The room was simply furnished. There was a wooden table and a chair set against the seaward window, a small oak cupboard, a rush mat on the floor, a slatted old-fashioned easy chair with cushions set in the middle of the room; a wooden cross nailed to the wall. He saw that the door of the cupboard was ajar and the key in the lock. Inside he found a small and unedifying collection of paperback pornography. Even allowing for the natural tendency—to which Dalgliesh admitted himself not immune—to be disdainful of the sexual tastes of others, this was not the pornography that he would have chosen. It was a paltry and pathetic little library of flagellation, titillation and salacity, incapable, he thought, of stimulating any emotion beyond ennui and vague disgust. True it contained *Lady Chatterley's Lover*—a novel which Dalgliesh considered overrated as literature and not qualifying as pornography—but the rest was hardly respectable by any standard. Even after a gap of over twenty years, it was difficult to believe that the gentle, aesthetic and fastidious Father Baddeley had developed a taste for this pathetic trivia. And if he had, why leave the cupboard unlocked or the key where Wilfred could find it? The obvious conclusion was that the books were Anstey's and that he had only just had time to unlock the cupboard before he smelt the fire. In the subsequent panic he had forgotten to lock away the evidence of his secret indulgence. He would probably return in some haste and confusion as soon as he was fit enough and got the opportunity. And, if this were true, it proved one thing: Anstey could not have started the fire.

Leaving the cupboard door ajar precisely as he had found it, Dalgliesh then carefully searched the floor. The rough mat of what looked like plaited hemp was torn in places and overlaid with dust. From the drag on its surface and the lie of the torn and minute filaments of fibre he deduced that Anstey had moved the table from the eastern to the southern window. He found too, what looked like traces of two different kinds of tobacco ash, but they were too small to be collected without his magnifying glass and tweezers. But, a little to the right of the eastern window and resting between the interstices of the mat, he found something which could be identified easily with the naked eye. It was a single used yellow match identical with those in the booklet by Father Baddeley's bed, and it had been peeled down in five separate pieces to its blackened head.

IV

The front door of Toynton Grange was, as usual, open. Dalgliesh walked swiftly and silently up the main staircase to Wilfred's room. As he approached he could hear talking, Dot Moxon's expostulatory and belligerent voice dominating the broken murmur of male voices. Dalgliesh went in without knocking. Three pairs of eyes regarded him with wariness and, he thought, with some resentment. Wilfred was still lying propped up in his bed. Dennis Lerner quickly turned away to look fixedly out of the window, but not before Dalgliesh had seen that his face was blotched as if he had been crying. Dot was sitting by the side of the bed, stolid and immovable as a mother watching a sick child. Dennis muttered, as if Dalgliesh had asked for an explanation:

"Wilfred has told me what happened. It's unbelievable."

Wilfred spoke with a mulish obstinacy which only emphasized his satisfaction at not being believed.

"It happened, and it was an accident."

Dennis was beginning "How could . . ." when Dalgliesh interrupted by laying the rolled habit on the foot of the bed. He said:

"I found this among the boulders by the black tower. If you hand it over to the police it may tell them something."

"I'm not going to the police and I forbid anyone here—anyone—to go on my behalf."

Dalgliesh said calmly:

"Don't worry; I've no intention of wasting their time. Given your determination to keep them out of it, they'd probably suspect that you lit the fire yourself. Did you?"

Wilfred cut swiftly into Dennis's gasp of incredulity and Dot's outraged protest.

"No, Dot, it's perfectly reasonable that Adam Dalgliesh should think as he does. He has been professionally trained in suspicion and scepticism. As it happens, I didn't attempt to burn myself to death. One family suicide in the black tower is enough. But I think I know who did light the fire and I shall deal with that person in my own time and in my own way. In the meantime nothing is to be said to the family, nothing. Thank God I can be sure of one thing, none of them can have had a hand in this. Now that I'm assured of that I shall know what to do. And now if you would all be kind enough to leave . . ."

Dalgliesh didn't wait to see if the others proposed to obey. He contented himself with one final word from the door.

"If you're thinking of private vengeance, then forget it. If you can't, or daren't, act within the law, then don't act at all."

Anstey smiled his sweet infuriating smile.

"Vengeance, Commander? Vengeance? That word has no place in our philosophy at Toynton Grange."

Dalgliesh saw and heard no one as he passed again through the main hall. The house might have been an empty shell. After a second's thought he walked briskly over the headland to Charity Cottage. The headland was deserted except for a solitary figure making its way down the slope from the cliff; Julius carrying what looked like a bottle in either hand. He held them aloft in a half pugilistic, half celebratory gesture. Dalgliesh lifted his hand in a brief salute and, turning, made his way up the stone path to the Hewsons' cottage.

The door was open and at first he heard no sign of life. He

knocked, and getting no reply, stepped inside. Charity Cottage, standing on its own, was larger than the other two and the stone sitting-room, bathed now in sunshine from its two windows, was agreeably proportioned. But it looked dirty and unkempt, reflecting in its untidiness Maggie's dissatisfied and restless nature. His first impression was that she had proclaimed her intention that their stay would be brief by not bothering to unpack. The few items of furniture looked as if they still stood where the whim of the removal men had first deposited them. A grubby sofa faced the large television screen which dominated the room. Eric's meagre medical library was stacked flat on the shelves of the bookcase, which held also a miscellany of crockery, ornaments, records and crushed shoes. A standard lamp of repellent design was without its shade. Two pictures were propped with their faces against the wall, their cords hanging knotted and broken. There was a square table set in the middle of the room bearing what looked like the remains of a late lunch; a torn packet of water biscuits spilling crumbs; a lump of cheese on a chipped plate; butter oozing from its greasy wrapping; a topless bottle of tomato ketchup with the sauce congealed round the lip. Two bloated flies buzzed their intricate convolutions above the debris.

From the kitchen came the rush of water and the roar of a gas boiler. Eric and Maggie were washing up. Suddenly the boiler was turned off and he heard Maggie's voice:

"You're so bloody weak! You let them all use you. If you are poking that supercilious bitch—and don't think I care a damn either way—it's only because you can't say no to her. You don't really want her any more than you want me."

Eric's reply was a low mutter. There was a crash of crockery. Then Maggie's voice rose again:

"For Christ's sake, you can't hide away here for ever! That trip to St. Saviour's, it wasn't as bad as you feared. No one said anything."

This time Eric's reply was perfectly intelligible:

"They didn't need to. Anyway, who did we see? Just the consultant in physical medicine and that medical records officer. She knew all right and she let me see it. That's how it'd be in general practice, if I ever got a job. They'd never let me forget it. The practice delinquent. Every female patient under sixteen tactfully diverted to one of the partners, just in case. At least Wilfred treats me like a human being. I can make a contribution. I can do my job."

Maggie almost yelled at him:

"What kind of a job, for God's sake?" And then both their voices were lost in the roar from the boiler and the rush of water. Then it stopped and Dalgliesh heard Maggie's voice again, high, emphatic.

"All right! All right! All right! I've said I won't tell, and I won't. But if you keep on nagging about it, I may change my mind."

Eric's reply was lost but it sounded like a long expostulatory murmur. Then Maggie spoke again:

"Well, what if I did? He wasn't a fool, you know. He could tell that something was up. And where's the harm? He's dead, isn't he? Dead. Dead. Dead."

Dalgliesh suddenly realized that he was standing stock still, straining his ears to hear as if this were an official case, his case, and every surreptitiously stolen word was a vital clue. Irritated, he almost shook himself into action. He had taken a few steps back to the doorway and had raised his fist to knock again and more loudly when Maggie, carrying a small tin tray, emerged from the kitchen with Eric at her back. She recovered quickly from her surprise and gave a shout of almost genuine laughter.

"Oh God, don't say Wilfred has called in the Yard itself to grill me. The poor little man has got himself into a tizzy. What are you going to do, darling, warn me that anything I say will be taken down and may be given in evidence?"

The door darkened and Julius came in. He must, thought Dalgliesh, have run down the headland to arrive so quickly. Why the hurry, he wondered. Breathing heavily, Julius swung two bottles of whisky on to the table.

"A peace offering."

"So I should think!" Maggie had become flirtatious. Her eyes brightened under the heavy lids and she slewed them from Dalgliesh to Julius as if uncertain where to bestow her favours. She spoke to Dalgliesh:

"Julius has been accusing me of attempting to roast Wilfred alive in the black tower. I know: I realize that it isn't funny. But Julius is, when he's trying to be pompous. And honestly, it's a nonsense. If I wanted to get my own back on St. Wilfred I could do it without pussyfooting about the black tower in drag, couldn't I darling?"

She checked her laughter and her glance at Julius was at once minatory and conspiratorial. It provoked no response. Julius said quickly:

"I didn't accuse you. I simply enquired with the utmost tact where you'd been since one o'clock."

"On the beach, darling. I do go there occasionally. I know I can't prove it, but neither can you prove that I wasn't there."

"That's rather a coincidence isn't it, your happening to walk on the beach?"

"No more a coincidence than your happening to drive along the coast road."

"And you didn't see anyone?"

"I told you darling, not a soul. Was I expected to? And now, Adam, it's your turn. Are you going to charm the truth out of me in the best Metropolitan tradition?"

"Not I. This is Court's case. That's one of the first principles of detection, never interfere with another man's conduct of his case."

Julius said:

"Besides, Maggie dear, the Commander isn't interested in our paltry concerns. Strange as it may seem, he just doesn't care. He can't even pretend an interest in whether Dennis hurled Victor over the cliff and I'm covering up for him. Humiliating, isn't it?"

Maggie's laugh was uneasy. She glanced at her husband like an inexperienced hostess who fears that the party is getting out of control.

"Don't be silly, Julius. We know that you aren't covering up. Why should you? What would there be in it for you?"

"How well you know me, Maggie! Nothing. But then, I might have done it out of sheer good nature." He looked at Dalgliesh with a sly smile and added:

"I believe in being accommodating to my friends."

Eric said suddenly and with surprising authority:

"What was it you wanted, Mr. Dalgliesh?"

"Just information. When I arrived at the cottage I found a booklet of matches by Father Baddeley's bed advertising the Olde Tudor Barn near Wareham. I thought I might try it for dinner tonight. Did he go there often, do you know?"

Maggie laughed:

"God, no! Never I should think. It's hardly Michael's scene. I gave him the matches. He liked trifles like that. But the Barn's not bad. Bob Loder took me there for lunch on my birthday and they did us quite well."

Julius said:

"I'll describe it. Ambience: a chain of coloured fairy lights strung round an otherwise genuine and agreeable seventeenth-century barn. First course: tinned tomato soup with a slice of tomato to add verisimilitude and colour contrast; frozen prawns in bottled sauce on a bed of limp lettuce; half a melon—ripe if you're lucky; or the chef's own home-made pâté fresh from the local supermarket. The rest of the menu you may imagine. It's usually a variety of steak served with frozen vegetables and what they describe as french fried. If you must drink, stick to the red. I don't know whether the owner makes it or merely sticks the labels on the bottles but at least it's wine of a kind. The white is cat's pee."

Maggie laughed indulgently.

"Oh, don't be such a snob darling, it's not as bad as that. Bob and I had quite a decent meal. And, whoever bottled the wine, it had the right effect as far as I was concerned."

Dalgliesh said:

"But it may have deteriorated. You know how it is. The chef leaves and a restaurant changes almost overnight."

Julius laughed:

"That's the advantage of the Olde Barn Menu. The chef can and does change fortnightly but the tinned soup is guaranteed to taste the same."

Maggie said:

"It won't have changed since my birthday. That was only the 11th September. I'm Virgo, darlings. Appropriate, isn't it?"

Julius said:

"There are one or two decent places within driving distance. I can let you have a few names."

He did so and Dalgliesh dutifully noted them at the back of his diary. But as he walked back to Hope Cottage his mind had already registered more important information.

So Maggie was on lunching terms with Bob Loder; the obliging Loder, equally ready to alter Father Baddeley's will—or to dissuade him from altering it?— and to help Millicent cheat her brother out of half his capital from the sale of Toynton Grange. But that little ploy, had, of course, been Holroyd's idea. Had Holroyd and Loder cooked it up between them? Maggie had told them about her luncheon date with sly satisfaction. If her husband neglected her on her birthday she wasn't without consolation. But what of Loder? Was his interest no more than a readiness to avail himself of a complaisant and dissatisfied woman, or had he a more sinister motive for keeping in touch with what happened at Toynton Grange? And the shredded match? Dalgliesh hadn't yet compared it with the stubs in the booklet still by Father Baddeley's bed, but he had no doubt that one of the stubs would match. He couldn't question Maggie further without rousing suspicion, but he didn't need to. She couldn't have given the booklet of matches to Father Baddeley before the afternoon of 11th September, the day before Holroyd's death. And on the afternoon of the eleventh, Father Baddeley had visited his solicitor. He couldn't, then, have received the booklet of matches until that evening at the earliest. And that meant that he must have been in the black tower on either the following morning or afternoon. It would be useful when opportunity offered, to have a word with Miss Willison and ask whether Father Baddeley had been at the Grange on the Wednesday morning. According to the entries in his diary it had certainly been his invariable routine to visit the Grange every morning. And that meant that he had almost certainly been in the black tower on the afternoon of the twelfth, and, possibly, sitting at the eastern window. Those drag marks on the fibre matting had looked very recent. But even from that window, he couldn't have seen Holroyd's chair go over the cliff; couldn't even have watched the distant figures of Lerner and Holroyd making their way along the sunken lane to that patch of green turf. And, even if he could, what would his evidence be worth, an old man sitting alone, reading and probably dozing in the afternoon sun? It was surely ludicrous to search here for a motive for murder. But suppose Father Baddeley had known beyond doubt that he had neither dozed nor read? Then it wasn't a question of what he had seen, but of what he had singularly failed to see.

6

A Bloodless Murder

I

The next afternoon, on the last day of her life, Grace Willison sat in the courtyard in the afternoon sun. Its rays were still warm on her face but now they touched her parched skin with a gentler valedictory warmth. From time to time a cloud moved across the face of the sun and she found herself shivering with the first intimation of winter. The air smelt keener, the afternoons were darkening fast. There wouldn't be many more days warm enough for her to sit outside. Even today she was the only patient in the courtyard and she was grateful for the warmth of the rug across her knees.

She found herself thinking about Commander Dalgliesh. She wished that he had come more often to Toynton Grange. He was still at Hope Cottage apparently. Yesterday he had helped Julius rescue Wilfred from the fire in the black tower. Wilfred had bravely made light of his ordeal as one would expect. It had only been a small fire caused entirely by his own carelessness; he had never been in real danger. But, all the same, she thought, it was fortunate that the Commander had been at hand to help.

Would he leave Toynton, she wondered, without coming to say goodbye to her? She hoped not. She had liked him so much in their brief time together. How pleasant it would be if he could be sitting here with her now, talking about Father Baddeley. No one at Toynton Grange now ever mentioned his name. But, of course, the Commander couldn't be expected to give up his time.

The thought was entirely without bitterness or resentment. There really wasn't anything to interest him at Toynton Grange. And it wasn't as if she could issue a personal invitation. She allowed herself for one minute to indulge in regret for the retirement which she had hoped for and planned. Her small pension from the Society, a little cottage, sun filled and bright with chintz and geraniums; her dear mother's possessions, the ones she had sold before she came to Toynton; the rose-patterned tea service; the rosewood writing table; the series of water colours of English cathedrals; how lovely to be able to invite anyone she liked to her own home to take tea with her. Not a communal institutional tea at a bleak refectory table, but proper afternoon tea. Her table; her tea service; her food; her guest.

She became aware of the weight of the book on her lap. It was a paperback edition of Trollope's *Last Chronicle of Barset*. It had lain there all the afternoon. Why, she wondered, was she so strangely reluctant to read it? And then she remembered. This had been the book she was re-reading on that dreadful afternoon when Victor's body had been brought home. She hadn't opened it since. But that was ridiculous. She must put the thought out of her mind. It was stupid, no, it was wrong, to spoil a book she so loved—its leisurely world of cathedral intrigue, its sanity, its delicate moral sensibility—by contaminating it with images of violence, hatred and blood.

She curved her deformed left hand around the book and parted the pages with her right. There was a book mark between the last pages she had read, a single pink antirrhinum pressed between a sheet of tissue. And then she remembered. It was a flower from the small posy Father Baddeley had brought her on the afternoon of Victor's death. Normally he never picked wild flowers except for her. They hadn't lasted long, less than a day. But this single flower she had pressed at once between the leaves of her book. She gazed at it, motionless.

A shadow fell across the page. A voice said:

"Anything wrong?"

She looked up and smiled.

"Nothing. It's just that I've remembered something. Isn't it extraordinary how the mind rejects anything which it associates with horror or great distress? Commander Dalgliesh asked me if I knew what Father Baddeley did on the few days before he went into hospital. And, of course, I do know. I know what he did on the Wednesday afternoon. I don't suppose it's the least important, but it would be nice to tell him. I know that everyone here is terribly busy but do you think that . . . ?"

"Don't worry. I'll find time to drop in at Hope Cottage. It's time he showed his face here if he proposes to stay on much longer. And now, don't you think it would be wise for you to come in? It's getting chilly."

Miss Willison smiled her thanks. She would have preferred to have stayed out a little longer. But she didn't like to insist. It was meant kindly. She closed her book again and her murderer grasped the chair with strong hands and wheeled her in to her death.

II

Ursula Hollis always asked her nurses to leave her curtains undrawn and tonight in the faint haze of light from her luminous bedside clock, she could still just discern the oblong frame which separated darkness outside from the darkness within. It was nearly midnight. The night was starless and very still. She lay in blackness so thick that it was almost a weight on her chest, a dense curtain descending to stifle breath. Outside, the headland was asleep, except, she supposed, for the small animals of the night scurrying among the rigid grasses. Inside Toynton Grange she could still hear distant sounds; brisk footsteps passing down a passage; the quiet closing of a door; the squeak of unoiled wheels as someone moved a hoist or a wheelchair; the mouselike scrabbling sounds from next door as Grace Willison moved restlessly in her bed; a sudden blare of music, instantly muted, as someone opened and shut the sitting-room door. Her bedside clock snatched at the seconds and ticked them into oblivion. She lay rigid, the warm tears flowing in a constant stream over her face to seep, suddenly cold and sticky, into her pillow. Under the pillow was Steve's letter. From time to time she folded her right arm painfully across her chest and insinuated her fingers under the pillow to feel the envelope's knife sharp edge.

Mogg had moved into the flat; they were living together. Steve had written the news almost casually as if it were merely a temporary and mutually convenient arrangement for sharing the rent and the chores. Mogg was doing the cooking; Mogg had redecorated the sitting-room and put up more shelves; Mogg had found him a clerical job with his publishers which might lead to a permanent and better post. Mogg's new book of poems were due out in the spring. There was only a perfunctory enquiry after

Ursula's health. He hadn't even made the usual vague and insincere promises to visit. He had written no word about her return home, the planned new flat, his negotiations with the local authority. There was no need. She never would return. They both knew it. Mogg knew it.

She hadn't received the letter until teatime. Albert Philby had been unaccountably late in fetching the post and it was after four o'clock before it was placed in her hand. She was grateful that she had been alone in the sitting-room, that Grace Willison hadn't yet come in from the courtyard to get ready for tea. There had been no one to watch her face as she read it, no one to make tactful enquiries, or, more tactfully, to refrain. And anger and shock had carried her through until now. She had held on to anger, feeding it with memory and imagination, willing herself to eat her usual two slices of bread, to drink her tea, to contribute her sentences of platitude and small talk to the party. Only now, when Grace Willison's heavy breathing had settled into a gentle snoring, when there was no longer a risk that Helen or Dot might pay a last visit, when Toynton Grange was finally wrapping itself in silence for the night, could she give way to desolation and loss and indulge in what she knew was self-pity. And the tears, when once they started, would not stop. The grief once indulged was unassuageable. She had no control over her crying. It no longer even distressed her; it had nothing to do with grief or longing. It was a physical manifestation, involuntary as a hiccup, but silent and almost consoling; an interminable stream.

She knew what she had to do. She listened through the rhythm of her tears. There was no sound from next door except Grace Willison's snoring which was now regular. She put out her hand and switched on the light. The bulb had the lowest wattage which Wilfred could buy but the brightness was still blinding. She imagined it, a dazzling oblong of light shining out to signal her intention to all the world. She knew that there was no one to see it, but in imagination the headland was suddenly full of running feet and loud with calling voices. She had stopped crying now but her swollen eyes saw the room as if it were a half-developed photograph, an image of bleared and distorted shapes, shifting and dissolving and seen through a stinging curtain pierced with needles of light.

She waited. Nothing happened. There was still no sound from

next door but Grace's harsh and regular breathing. The next step was easy; she had done it twice before. She dropped both her pillows on the floor and, manoeuvring her body to the edge of the bed, let herself drop gently on top of their soft cushion. Even with the pillows to break her weight it seemed that the room shook. Again she waited. But there were no quick footsteps hurrying down the passage. She raised herself upwards on the pillows against the bed and began propelling herself towards its foot. It was an easy matter to stretch out her hand and withdraw the cord from her dressing gown. Then she began her painful progress towards the door.

Her legs were powerless; what strength she had was in her arms. Her dead feet lay white and flabby as fish on the cold floor, the toes splayed like obscene excrescences vainly scrabbling for a grip. The linoleum was unpolished but smooth and she slid along with surprising speed. She remembered with what joy she had discovered that she could do this; that, ridiculous and humiliating as the trick might be, she could actually move around her room without the use of her chair.

But now she was going farther afield. It was lucky that the modern insubstantial doors of the annexe rooms were opened by depressing a handle and not turning a knob. She made the dressing gown cord into a loop and, at the second attempt, managed to throw it over the handle. She tugged and the door quietly opened. Discarding one of the pillows, she edged her way into the silent passage. Her heart was thudding with such power it must surely betray her. Again she slipped the cord over the handle and, manoeuvring herself a few feet down the passage, heard the door click shut.

One single light-bulb, heavily shaded, was always kept burning at the far end of the corridor and she could see without difficulty where the short staircase led to the upper floor. This was her objective. Reaching it proved astonishingly easy. The linoleum in the passage, although never polished, seemed smoother than that in her room; or perhaps she had gained the knack of progress. She slid forward with almost exhilarating ease.

But the staircase was more difficult. She was relying on pulling herself up by the banister, step by step. But it was necessary to take the pillow with her. She would need it on the floor above. And the pillow seemed to have swollen into a gigantic, soft, white encumbrance. The stairs were narrow and it was difficult to prop it safely. Twice it tumbled down and she had to slide after it to retrieve it. But after four steps had been painfully negotiated she worked out the best method of progress. She tied one end of the dressing gown cord around her waist and the other tightly round the middle of the pillow. She wished she had put on the dressing gown. It would have hampered her progress, but she was already shivering.

And so, step by step, gasping and sweating despite the cold, she pulled herself up, grasping the banisters with both hands. The stairs creaked alarmingly. She expected any minute to hear the faint summons of a bedside bell and hear from the distance Dot or Helen's hurrying footsteps.

She had no idea how long it took to reach the top of the stairs. But at last she was sitting crouched and shivering on the final step, grasping the banisters with both hands so convulsively that the wood shook, and peering down at the hall below. It was then that the cloaked figure appeared. There were no warning footsteps, no cough, no sound of human breath. One second the passage was empty. In the next a brown cloaked figure—head bent, hood drawn well over the face—had moved silently and swiftly beneath her, and disappeared down the passage. She waited terrified, hardly daring to breathe, huddling herself as far as possible out of view. It would come back. She knew that it would come back. Like the dreadful figure of death which she had seen in old books, carved on monumental tombs, it would pause beneath her and throw back the concealing hood to reveal the grinning skull, the eyeless sockets, would poke at her through the banister its fleshless fingers. Her heart, beating in icy terror against the rib cage, seemed to have grown too large for her body. Surely its frantic thudding must betray her! It seemed an eternity, but she realized that it could only have been less than a minute before the figure reappeared and passed, beneath her terrified eyes, silently and swiftly into the main house.

Ursula realized then that she wasn't going to kill herself. It had only been Dot, or Helen, or Wilfred. Who else could it have been? But the shock of that silent figure, passing like a shadow, had restored in her the will to live. If she had really wanted to die, what was she doing here crouched in cold discomfort at the top of the stairs? She had her dressing gown cord. Even now she could tie it round her neck and let herself slip unresisting down the stairs. But she wouldn't. The very thought of that last fall, the strangling cord biting into her neck, made her moan in agonized protest. No, she had never meant to kill herself. No one, not even Steve, was worth an eternity of damnation. Steve might not believe in Hell, but what did Steve really know about anything that mattered? But she had to complete her journey now. She had to get hold of that bottle of aspirin which she knew must be somewhere in the clinical room. She wouldn't use it, but she would keep it always within reach. She would know that, if life became intolerable, the means to end it was at hand. And perhaps, if she just took a handful, and left the bottle by the bed they would realize at last that she was unhappy. That was all she intended; all she had ever intended. They would send for Steve. They would take some notice of her misery. Perhaps they might even force Steve to take her back to London. Having come so far at such cost, she had to get to the clinical room.

The door presented no problem. But when she had sidled through, she realized that this was the end. She couldn't switch on the light. The low bulb in the corridor gave a faint diffused glow but, even with the door of the clinical room ajar, it was inadequate to show her the position of the light. And if she were to succeed in switching it on with the dressing gown cord, she had to know accurately at what spot to aim. She stretched out her hand and felt along the wall. Nothing. She held the cord in a loop and flung it softly and repeatedly where she thought the switch might be. But it fell away uselessly. She began to cry again, defeated, desperately cold, suddenly realizing that she had the whole painful journey to do again in reverse, and that dragging herself back into bed would be the most difficult and painful of all.

And then, suddenly, a hand stretched out of the darkness and the light was switched on. Ursula gave a little scream of fright. She looked up. Framed in the doorway, wearing a brown habit open down the front and with the hood flung back was Helen Rainer. The two women, petrified, stared at each other speechlessly. And Ursula saw that the eyes bent on hers were as full of terror as her own.

III

Grace Willison's body jerked into wakefulness and immediately began to tremble uncontrollably as if a strong hand were shaking her into full consciousness. She listened in the darkness, raising her head with difficulty from the pillow; but she could hear nothing. Whatever noise, real or imagined, had woken her was now stilled. She switched on her bedside lamp; nearly midnight. She reached for her book. It was a pity that the paperback Trollope was so heavy. It meant that it had to be propped up on the coverlet and since, once stretched into her conventional attitude for sleep she couldn't easily bend her knees, the effort of slightly raising her head and peering down at the small print was tiring both to her eyes and to the muscles of her neck. The discomfort sometimes made her wonder whether reading in bed was the pleasant indulgence she had always believed it to be since those childhood days when her father's parsimony over the electricity bill and her mother's anxiety about eye strain and eight hours good sleep each night, had denied her a bedside lamp.

Her left leg was jerking uncontrollably and she watched, detached and interested the erratic jump of the coverlet as if an animal were loose among the bed clothes. To wake suddenly like this once she had first fallen asleep was always a bad sign. She was in for a restless night. She dreaded sleeplessness and for a moment was tempted to pray that she might be spared it just for tonight. But she had finished her prayers and it seemed pointless to pray again for a mercy which experience had taught her she wasn't going to receive. Pleading to God for something which he had already made it perfectly plain he wasn't disposed to give you was to behave like a peevish, importunate child. She watched her limb's antics with interest, vaguely comforted by the sensation which was now almost self-induced of being detached from her unruly body.

She lay down her book and decided instead to think about the pilgrimage to Lourdes in fourteen days' time. She pictured the happy bustle of departure—she had a new coat saved for the occasion—the drive across France with the party gay as a picnic; the first glimpse of the mists swirling around the foothills of the Pyrenees; the snowcapped peaks; Lourdes itself with its concentrated business, its air of being always *en fête*. The Toynton

Grange party, except for the two Roman Catholics, Ursula Hollis and Georgie Allan, were not part of an official English pilgrimage, did not take Mass, grouped themselves with becoming humility at the back of the crowd when the bishops in their crimson robes made their slow way round Rosary Square, the golden monstrance held high before them. But how inspiring, how colourful, how splendid it all was! The candles weaving their patterns of light, the colours, the singing, the sense of belonging again to the outside world but a world in which sickness was honoured, no longer regarded as an alienation, a deformity of the spirit as well as the body. Only thirteen more days now. She wondered what her father, implacably Protestant, would have said about this keenly awaited pleasure. But she had consulted Father Baddeley about the propriety of going on pilgrimage and his advice had been very clear. "My dear child, you enjoy the change and the journey, and why not? And surely no one could believe themselves harmed by a visit to Lourdes. By all means help Wilfred to celebrate his bargain with the Almighty."

She thought about Father Baddeley. It was still difficult to accept that she wouldn't ever again be talking with him in the patients' courtyard or praying with him in the quiet room. Dead; an inert, neutral, unattractive word. Short, uncompromising, a lump of a word. The same word, come to think of it, for a plant, an animal or a man. That was an interesting thought. One would have expected a distinctive, more impressive or momentous word for the death of a man. But why? He was only part of the same creation, sharing its universal life, dependent on the same air. Dead. She had hoped to be able to feel that Father Baddeley was close to her; but it hadn't happened, it just wasn't true. They are all gone into the world of light. Well, gone away; not interested any more in the living.

She ought to put out her light; electricity was expensive; if she didn't intend to read it was her duty to lie in the darkness. Lighten our darkness; her mother had always liked that collect; and by Thy great mercy defend us from all the perils and dangers of this night. Only there was no peril here, only sleeplessness and pain; the familiar pain to be tolerated, almost welcomed as an old acquaintance because she knew that she could cope with the worst it could do; and this new frightening pain which, sometime soon, she would have to worry someone about.

The curtain trembled in the breeze. She heard a sudden click, unnaturally loud, so that for a second her heart thudded. There was a rasp of metal on wood. Maggie hadn't checked the window fastening before bedding her down for the night. It was too late now. Her chair was at the side of the bed but she couldn't get into it without help. But all would be well unless it were a stormy night. And she was perfectly safe, no one would climb in. There was nothing at Toynton Grange to steal. And beyond that fluttering curtain of white, nothing; nothing but a black void, dark cliffs stretching to the unsleeping sea.

The curtain billowed, bursting into a white sail, a curve of light. She exclaimed at the beauty of it. Cool air streamed across her face. She turned her eyes to the door and smiled a welcome. She began to say:

"The window—would you be good enough . . . ?"

But she didn't finish. There were three seconds only left to her of earthly time. She saw the cloaked figure, hood well down obscuring the face, moving swiftly towards her on silent feet like an apparition, familiar but horribly different, ministering hands that held death, blackness bearing down on her. Unresisting, since that was her nature and how could she resist, she did not die ungently, feeling at the last through the thin veil of plastic only the strong, warm, oddly comforting lineaments of a human hand. Then the hand reached out and delicately, without touching the wooden stand, switched off the bedside lamp. Two seconds later the light was switched on again, and, as if by afterthought, the cloaked figure stretched out a hand for the Trollope, gently rustled the pages, found the pressed flower between the fold of tissue, and crumpled them both with strong fingers. Then the hand reached out for the lamp again and the light went out for the last time.

IV

At last they were back in Ursula's room. Helen Rainer closed the door with quiet firmness and leaned back momentarily against it as if exhausted. Then she went quickly over to the window and swept the curtains across in two swift gestures. Her heavy breathing filled the little room. It had been a difficult journey. Helen had left her in the clinical room briefly while she positioned Ursula's wheelchair at the foot of the stairs. Once they reached it all would be well. Even if they were seen together in the ground-floor corridor it would be assumed that Ursula had rung her night bell and was being helped to the bathroom. The stairs were the problem and the descent, with Helen half-supporting, half-carrying her, had been exhausting and noisy, five long minutes of laboured breathing, creaking banisters, hissed instructions, of Ursula's half-stifled moans of pain. It seemed now like a miracle that no one had appeared in the hall. It would have been quicker and easier to have moved into the main part of the Grange and used the lift, but the clanging metal grill and the noisy engine would have woken half the house.

But at last they were safely back and Helen, white faced but calm, pulled herself together and moved away from the door and began with professional competence to put Ursula to bed. Neither spoke until the task was completed and Ursula lay in rigid half-fearful silence.

Helen bent her face close to Ursula's, unpleasantly close. In the glare of the bedside lamp she could see the features magnified, coarsened, pores like miniature craters, two unplucked hairs standing like bristles at the corner of the mouth. Her breath smelt slightly sour. Odd, thought Ursula, that she hadn't noticed it before. The green eyes seemed to grow and protrude as she hissed her instructions, her dreadful warning.

"When the next patient goes, he'll have to start admitting from the waiting list or give in. He can't run this place on less than six patients. I've taken a look at the books when he's left them about in the business room and I know. He'll either sell out completely or hand over to the Ridgewell Trust. If you want to get out of here there are better ways than killing yourself. Help me to ensure that he sells out, and get back to London."

"But how?"

Ursula found herself whispering back like a conspirator.

"He'll hold what he calls a family council. He always does when there's something important affecting all the household to decide. We all give our views. Then we go away to meditate in silence for one hour. Then we all vote. Don't let anyone persuade you to vote for the Ridgewell Trust. That way you'll be trapped here for life. It's hard enough for local authorities to find a place for the young chronic sick. Once they know you're being looked after, they'll never transfer you."

"But if the Grange does close down, will they really send me home?"

"They'll have to, back to London anyway. That's still your permanent address. You're the responsibility of your own local authority, not of Dorset. And once back, at least you'll see him. He could visit you, take you out, you could go home for weekend leaves. Besides, the disease isn't really advanced yet. I don't see why you shouldn't manage together in one of those flats for disabled couples. After all he is married to you. He's got responsibilities, duties."

Ursula tried to explain:

"I don't mind about responsibilities and duties. I want him to love me."

Helen had laughed, a coarse, uncomfortable sound.

"Love. Is that all? Isn't that what we all want? Well he can't stay in love with someone he never sees, can he? It doesn't work like that with men. You've got to get back to him."

"And you won't tell?"

"Not if you promise."

"To vote your way?"

"And to keep your mouth shut about trying to kill yourself, about everything that's happened here tonight. If anyone mentions hearing a noise in the night, you rang for me and I was taking you to the lavatory. If Wilfred discovers the truth he'll send you to a mental hospital. You wouldn't want that, would you?"

No, she wouldn't want that. Helen was right. She had to get home. How simple it all was. She felt suddenly filled with gratitude, and struggled to hold out her arms towards Helen. But Helen had moved away. Firm hands were tucking in the bed clothes, rocking the mattress. The sheets were drawn taut. She felt imprisoned, but secure, a baby swaddled for the night. Helen stretched out her hand to the light. In the darkness a white blur moved towards the door. Ursula heard the soft click of the latch.

Lying there alone exhausted but strangely comforted she remembered that she hadn't told Helen about the cloaked figure. But it could be of no importance. It was probably Helen herself answering Grace's bell. Was that what Helen had meant when she warned, say nothing about anything that happened here tonight? Surely not. But she would say nothing. How could she speak without betraying that she had been crouching there on the stairs. And everything was going to be all right. She could sleep now. How lucky that Helen had gone to the clinical room to get a couple of aspirin for a headache and had found her! The house was blessedly unnaturally quiet. There was something strange, something different, about the silence. And then, smiling into the darkness she remembered. It was Grace. No sound, no rasp of snoring breath came through the thin partition to disturb her. Tonight even Grace Willison was sleeping in peace.

V

Usually Julius Court fell asleep within minutes of turning out his bedside light. But tonight he turned in restless wakefulness, mind and nerves fidgety, his legs as cold and heavy as if it were winter. He rubbed them together, considering whether to dig out his electric blanket. But the bother of re-making the bed discouraged him. Alcohol seemed a better and quicker remedy both for sleeplessness and the cold.

He walked over to the window and looked out over the headland. The waning moon was obscured by scudding clouds; the darkness inland pierced only by a single oblong of yellow light. But as he watched, blackness was drawn like a shutter over the far window. Instantaneously the oblong became a square; then that, too, was extinguished. Toynton Grange lay, a faintly discerned shape etched in darkness on the silent headland. Curious, he looked at his watch. The time was eighteen minutes past midnight.

VI

Dalgliesh awoke at first light, to the cold, quiet morning, and dragging on his dressing gown, went downstairs to make tea. He wondered if Millicent was still at the Grange. Her television had been silent all the previous evening and now, although she was neither an early nor a noisy riser, Hope Cottage was wrapped in the slightly clandestine and unmistakable calm of complete isolation. He lit the lamp in the sitting-room, carried his cup to the table, and spread out his map. Today he would explore the north-east of the county aiming to arrive at Sherborne for lunch. But first it would be courteous to call at Toynton Grange and enquire after Wilfred. He felt no real concern; it was difficult to think of yesterday's charade without irritation. But it might be worth making one more attempt to persuade Wilfred to call in the police, or at least to take the attack on himself more seriously. And it was time that he paid some rent for the use of Hope Cottage. Toynton Grange could hardly be so prosperous that a tactful contribution wouldn't be welcome. Neither chore need keep him at the Grange for longer than ten minutes.

There was a knock on the door and Julius came in. He was fully dressed and, even at this early hour, gave his usual impression of slightly elegant informality. He said, calmly, and as if the news were hardly worth the trouble of telling.

"I'm glad you're up. I'm on my way to Toynton Grange. Wilfred has just rung. Apparently Grace Willison has died in her sleep and Eric is in a tizzy about the death certificate. I don't know what Wilfred thinks I can do about it. Restoring Eric to the medical register seems to have restored him also to the customary arrogance of his profession. Grace Willison wasn't due, in his opinion, to die for at least another eighteen months, possibly two years. That being so he's at a loss to put a name to this insubordination. As usual, they're all extracting the maximum drama from the situation. I shouldn't miss it if I were you."

Dalgliesh glanced towards the adjacent cottage without speaking. Julius said cheerfully:

"Oh, you needn't worry about disturbing Millicent; I'm afraid she's there already. Apparently her television broke down last night so she went up to Toynton Grange to see a late programme and decided, for some unaccountable reason, to stay the night. Probably saw an opportunity of saving her own bed linen and bath water."

Dalgliesh said:

"You go on, I'll follow you later."

He drank his tea without haste and spent three minutes shaving. He wondered why he had been so reluctant to accompany Julius, why, if he had to go to Toynton Grange, he preferred to walk there on his own. He wondered, too, why he felt so keen a regret. He had no wish to involve himself in the controversy at Toynton. He had no particular curiosity about Grace Willison's death. He was aware of feeling nothing except an inexplicable unease amounting almost to grief for a woman he had barely known and a vague distaste that the start of a beautiful day should have been spoilt by the intimations of decay. And there was something else; a sense of guilt. It seemed to him both unreasonable and unfair. By dying she seemed to have allied herself with Father Baddeley. There were two accusing ghosts, not one. This was to be a double failure. It was by an effort of will that he set out for Toynton Grange.

He could be in no doubt which room was Grace Willison's, he could hear the raised voices even as he entered the annexe. When he opened the door he saw that Wilfred, Eric, Millicent, Dot and Julius were grouped around the bed with the desultory, uneasy air of strangers meeting fortuitously at the scene of an accident with which they would much prefer not to become involved but which they hardly like to leave.

Dorothy Moxon stood at the end of the bed, her heavy hands, red as hams, clasped to the rail. She was wearing her matron's cap. The effect, so far from providing a touch of professional reassurance, was grotesque. The high frilled pie crust of muslin looked like a morbid and bizarre celebration of death. Millicent was still in her dressing gown, an enveloping plaid in heavy wool frogged like a ceremonial uniform which must once have belonged to her husband. In contrast, her slippers were insubstantial fripperies in pink fur. Wilfred and Eric were wearing their brown habits. They glanced briefly at the door when he entered, then immediately turned their attention back to the bed. Julius was saying:

"There was a light in one of the annexe rooms shortly after midnight. Isn't that when you say she died, Eric?"

"It could have been about then. I'm only going by the cooling of the body and the beginning of rigor mortis. I'm not an expert in these things."

"How odd! I thought that death was the one thing you were expert at."

Wilfred said quietly:

"The light was from Ursula's room. She rang shortly after midnight to be taken to the lavatory. Helen looked after her, but she didn't go into Grace. There was no need. She didn't ring. No one saw her after Dot put her to bed. She made no complaint then."

Julius turned again to Eric Hewson:

"You haven't any option, have you? If you can't say what she died of, you can't write a certificate. Anyway, I should play for safety if I were you. After all, you've only recently been permitted to sign a death certificate. Better not take any chances of getting it wrong."

Eric Hewson said:

"You keep out of it, Julius, I don't need your advice. I don't know why Wilfred rang you."

But he spoke without conviction, like an insecure and frightened child, his eyes flicking to the door as if hoping for the arrival of an ally. Julius was unabashed:

"It seems to me that you need any advice that's going. What's worrying you anyway? Do you suspect foul play? What a ridiculous phrase that is, come to think of it, so delightfully British, compounded of the public school ethos and the boxing ring."

Eric exerted himself to make a show of authority.

"Don't be ridiculous! Obviously it's a natural death. The difficulty is that I'm puzzled why it should have happened now. I know D.S. patients can go off quickly like that, but in her case I didn't expect it. And Dot says that she seemed just as usual when she put her to bed at ten o'clock. I'm wondering whether there was some other organic disease present which I missed."

Julius went on happily:

"The police do not suspect foul play. Well, you've got a representative of them here if you want professional advice. Ask the Commander if he suspects foul play."

They turned and looked at Dalgliesh as if fully aware of his presence for the first time. The window latch was rattling with irritating insistence. He went across to the window and glanced out. The ground close to the stone wall had been dug for a width of about four feet as if someone had intended to plant a border. The sandy earth was smooth and undisturbed. But of course it was! If a secret visitor had wanted to get into Grace's room unseen, why climb in at the window when the door of Toynton Grange was never locked?

He fastened the catch and, moving back to the bed, looked down at the body. The dead face looked not exactly peaceful, but slightly disapproving, the mouth a little open, the front teeth, more rabbity than in life, pressing against the lower lip. The eyelids had contracted showing a glimpse of the irises of the eye so that she seemed to be peering at her own two hands disposed so neatly over the taut coverlet. The strong right hand, blotched with the brown stigmata of age, was curved over the withered left as if instinctively protecting it from his pitying gaze. She was shrouded for her last sleep in an old-fashioned white nightdress of creased cotton with a child's bow in narrow blue ribbon tied incongruously under her chin. The long sleeves were gathered into frilled wrists. There was a fine darn about two inches from her elbow. His eyes fixed obsessively on it. Who today, he wondered, would take such trouble? Certainly her diseased tormented hands couldn't have woven that intricate pattern of repair. Why should he find that darn more pathetic, more heart shaking, than the concentrated calm of the dead face?

He was aware that the company had stopped arguing, that they were looking at him in a half-wary silence. He picked up the two books on Miss Willison's bedside table, her prayer book and a paperback copy of *The Last Chronicle of Barset*. There was a book mark in the prayer book. She had, he saw, been reading the collect and gospel for the day. The place was marked by one of those sentimental cards favoured by the pious, a coloured picture of a haloed St. Francis surrounded by birds and apparently preaching to a motley and incongruous congregation of animals remote from their habitat and drawn with finicky precision. He wondered, irrelevantly, why there was no book-mark in the Trollope. She was not a woman to turn down the pages, and surely of the two volumes this was the one in which she would more easily lose her place. The omission vaguely worried him.

"Is there a next of kin?" he asked, and Anstey answered:

"No. She told me that her parents were only children. They were both over forty when she was born and they died within months of each other about fifteen years ago. She had an older brother but he was killed in the war in North Africa. El Alamein, I believe."

"What about her estate?"

"Oh, nothing, nothing at all. After her parents' death she worked for several years for Open Door, the discharged prisoners charity, and had a small disability pension from them, a pittance merely. That, of course, dies with her. Her fees here were paid by the local authority."

Julius Court said with sudden interest:

"The Open Door. Did she know Philby before you took him on?"

Anstey looked as if he found this irrelevant question in poor taste.

"She may have done; she certainly never said so. It was Grace who suggested that The Open Door might find us a handyman, that this was a way in which Toynton Grange could help the work of the charity. We have been very glad of Albert Philby. He's one of the family. I haven't repented my decision to take him on."

Millicent broke in:

"And you got him cheap, of course. Besides it was Philby or no one wasn't it? You didn't have much luck with the labour exchange when the applicants found that you were offering £5 a week and all found. I sometimes wonder why Philby stays."

Discussion of this point was prevented by the entrance of Philby himself. He must have been told of Miss Willison's death for he showed no surprise to find her room full of people and gave no explanation of his presence. Instead he stationed himself beside the door like an embarrassing and unpredictable guard dog. The company behaved as if they had decided that it would be prudent not to notice him. Wilfred turned to Eric Hewson:

"Can't you reach a diagnosis, without a post-mortem? I hate the idea of her being cut up, the indignity, the impersonality. She was so sensitive about her body, so modest in a way we don't understand nowadays. An autopsy is the last thing she herself would have wanted."

Julius said coarsely:

"Well, it's the last thing she's going to get, isn't it?"

Dot Moxon spoke for the first time. She swung round on him in sudden anger, her heavy face blotched, hands clenched.

"How dare you! What has it to do with you? You didn't care about her dead or alive, her or any of the patients. You only use this place for your own purpose."

"Use?" The grey eyes flickered and then widened; Dalgliesh could almost see the irises growing. Julius stared at Dot with incredulous anger.

"Yes, use! Exploit, if you like. It gives you a kick, doesn't it, to come visiting Toynton Grange when London begins to bore you, patronizing Wilfred, pretending to advise him, handing out treats to the inmates like Father Christmas? It makes you feel good, reinforces your ego to contrast your health with their deformity. But you take damned good care not to put yourself out. The kindness doesn't really cost you anything. No one but Henry gets invited to your cottage. But then Henry was quite important in his time wasn't he? He and you have things to gossip about. You're the only one here with a view of the sea, but we don't find you inviting us to wheel the chairs on to your patio. No bloody fear! That's one thing you could have done for Grace, take her to your place occasionally, let her sit quietly and look at the sea. She wasn't stupid, you know. You might even have enjoyed her conversation. But that would have spoilt the appearance of your elegant patio wouldn't it, an ugly middle-aged woman in a wheelchair? And now she's dead you come here pretending to advise Eric. Well, for God's sake, cut it out!"

Julius laughed uneasily. He seemed to have himself in hand but his voice was high and brittle.

"I don't know what I've done to deserve that outburst. I didn't realize that by buying a cottage from Wilfred I'd made myself responsible for Grace Willison or for anyone else at Toynton Grange for that matter. I've no doubt it's a shock for you, Dot, losing another patient so soon after Victor, but why take it out on me? We all know that you're in love with Wilfred and I've no doubt that's pretty unrewarding for you, but it's hardly my fault. I may be a little ambivalent in my sexual tastes but I'm not competing for him, I assure you."

Suddenly she blundered up to him and threw back her arm to slap his face in a gesture at once theatrical and absurd. But before she could strike, Julius had caught her wrist. Dalgliesh was surprised at the quickness and effectiveness of his reaction. The taut hand, white and trembling with effort, held hers high in a muscled vice so that they looked like two ill-matched contestants locked in a tableau of conflict. Suddenly he laughed and dropped her hand. He lowered his hand more slowly, his eyes still on her face, and began massaging and twisting his wrist. Then he laughed again, a dangerous sound, and said softly:

"Careful! Careful! I'm not a helpless geriatric patient, you know."

She gave a gasp and, bursting into tears, blundered sobbing from the room, an ungainly and pathetic but not a ridiculous figure. Philby slipped out after her. His departure caused as little interest as his arrival. Wilfred said softly:

"You shouldn't have said that, Julius, any of it."

"I know. It was unforgivable. I'm sorry. I'll tell Dot so when we are feeling calmer."

The brevity, the absence of self-justification and the apparent sincerity of the apology silenced them. Dalgliesh said quietly:

"I imagine that Miss Willison would have found this quarrelling over her body a great deal more shocking than anything that could happen to her on the mortuary slab."

His words recalled Wilfred to the matter in hand; he turned to Eric Hewson:

"But we didn't have all this trouble with Michael, you gave a certificate without difficulty then."

Dalgliesh could detect the first trace of peevishness in his voice.

Eric explained:

"I knew why Michael had died, I had seen him only that morning. It was only a matter of time for Michael after that last heart attack. He was a dying man."

"As we all are," said Wilfred. "As we all are."

The pious platitudes seemed to irritate his sister. She spoke for the first time.

"Don't be ridiculous, Wilfred. I'm certainly not dying and you would be very disconcerted to be told that you were. And as for Grace, she always looked to me a great deal sicker than anyone here seemed to understand. Now perhaps you will realize that it isn't always the ones who make the most fuss who need the most attention."

She turned to Dalgliesh:

"What exactly will happen if Eric doesn't give a certificate? Does it mean that we'll have the police here again?"

"A policeman will probably come, yes; just an ordinary policeman. He'll be the coroner's officer and he will take charge of the body."

"And then?"

"The coroner will arrange for a post-mortem. According to the result he will either issue a certificate for the registrar or he'll conduct an inquest."

Wilfred said:

"It's all so horrible, so unnecessary."

"It's the law and Dr. Hewson knows that it is the law."

"But what do you mean, it's the law? Grace died of D.S., we all know that. What if there was some other disease present? Eric can't treat her or do anything to help her now. What law are you talking about?"

Dalgliesh patiently explained:

"The doctor who attends a dead person during his last illness is required to sign and deliver to the registrar a certificate in a prescribed form stating the cause of death to the best of his knowledge and belief. At the same time he is required to deliver to a qualified informant, and that could be the occupant of the house where the death occurred, a notice to the effect that he has signed such a certificate. There is no statutory duty on a doctor to report any death to the coroner, but it's usual to do so where there is any doubt. When the doctor reports a death to a coroner he's not relieved of his duty to issue a certificate of the cause of death but there is provision for him to state on the form that he has reported the death so that the registrar will know that he must defer registration until he hears from the coroner. Under Section 3 of the Coroners Act 1887 a coroner has a duty to make enquiries whenever he is informed that there is lying within his jurisdiction the body of a person who there is reason to believe may have died a violent or unnatural death or a sudden death, the cause of which is unknown, or who has died in prison or in any place or circumstances which under another Act require an inquest to be held. That, since you have enquired—and in somewhat tedious detail—is the law. Grace Willison has died suddenly and in Dr. Hewson's opinion the cause is at present unknown. His best course is to report the death to the coroner. It will mean a post-mortem, but not necessarily an inquest."

"But I hate the thought of her lying mangled on an autopsy slab." Wilfred was beginning to sound like an obstinate child. Dalgliesh said coolly:

"Mangled isn't exactly the word. A post-mortem is an organized and perfectly tidy procedure. And now if you will excuse me I'll get back to my breakfast."

Suddenly Wilfred made an almost physical effort to pull himself together. He straightened up, and crossed his hands into the wide sleeves of his habit and stood for a moment in silent meditation.

Eric Hewson looked at him, puzzled, then glanced from Dalgliesh to Julius as if seeking guidance. Then Wilfred spoke:

"Eric, you had better ring the coroner's officer now. Normally Dot would lay out the body but that had better wait until we get instructions. After you have telephoned, please let everyone know that I want to talk to all the family immediately after breakfast. Helen and Dennis are with them at present. Millicent, perhaps you could find Dot and see that she is all right. And now I should like to speak to you Julius, and to Adam Dalgliesh."

He stood for a moment, eyes closed, at the foot of Grace's bed. Dalgliesh wondered whether he were praying. Then he led the way out. As they followed, Julius whispered with hardly a movement of his lips:

"Unpleasantly reminiscent of those summonses to the headmaster's study. We should have fortified ourselves with breakfast."

In the business room Wilfred wasted no time.

"Grace's death means that I have to make my decision sooner than I'd hoped. We can't carry on with only four patients. On the other hand, I can hardly start admitting from the waiting list if the Grange isn't going to continue. I shall hold a family council on the afternoon Grace is buried. I think it would be right to wait until then. If there are no complications, that should be in less than a week's time. I should like you both to take part and help us to our decision."

Julius said quickly:

"That's impossible, Wilfred. I've absolutely no interest; interest, I mean in the legal or insurance sense. It just isn't my business."

"You live here. I've always thought of you as one of the family."

"Sweet of you, and I'm honoured. But it isn't true. I'm not one of the family and I have absolutely no right to vote on a decision that can't really affect me one way or the other. If you decide to sell out, and I wouldn't blame you, I probably shall too. I don't fancy living on Toynton Head once it's a caravan site. But it won't matter to me. I'll get a good price from some bright young executive from the Midlands who won't give a damn about peace and quiet but who will build a natty cocktail bar in the sitting-room and run up a flagpole on the patio. I shall probably look for my next cottage in the Dordogne after careful enquiries about any bargains which the owner may have made with God or the devil. Sorry, but it's a definite no."

"And you, Adam?"

"I've even less right to an opinion than Court. This place is home to the patients. Why on earth should their future be decided, at least in part, by the vote of a casual visitor?"

"Because I greatly trust your judgement."

"There's no reason why you should. In this matter, better trust your accountant."

Julius asked:

"Are you inviting Millicent to the family council?"

"Of course. She may not have always given me the support I hoped for from her, but she is one of the family."

"And Maggie Hewson?"

Wilfred said curtly:

"No."

"She's not going to like that. And isn't it a little hurtful to Eric?"

Wilfred said magisterially:

"As you have just made it plain that you don't consider yourself in any way concerned, why not leave me to decide what's hurtful to Eric. And now, if you will both excuse me, I shall join the family for breakfast."

VII

As they left Wilfred's room, Julius said roughly and as if on impulse:

"Come up to the cottage and have breakfast. Have a drink anyway. Or if it's too early for alcohol, have coffee. Anyway, please come. I've started the day in a mood of self-disgust and I'm bad company for myself."

It was too close to an appeal to be easily disregarded. Dalgliesh said:

"If you can give me about five minutes. There's someone I want to see. I'll meet you in the hall."

He remembered from his first conducted tour of the Grange which was Jennie Pegram's room. There might, he thought, be a better time for this encounter but he couldn't wait for it. He knocked and heard the note of surprise in her answering "come in". She was sitting in her wheelchair in front of her dressing table, her yellow hair flowing over her shoulders. Taking the poison pen letter from his wallet he walked up behind her and laid it in front of her. In the mirror their eyes met.

"Did you type that?"

She let her glance travel over it without picking it up. Her eyes flickered; a red stain began to travel like a wave over her neck. He heard the hiss of in-drawn breath, but her voice was calm.

"Why should I?"

"I can suggest reasons. But did you?"

"Of course not! I've never seen it before."

She glanced at it again dismissively, contemptuously.

"It's . . . it's stupid, childish."

"Yes, a poor effort. Done in a hurry, I imagine. I thought you might take rather a poor view of it. Not quite as exciting or imaginative as the others."

"What others?"

"Come now, let's start with the one to Grace Willison. That did you credit. An imaginative effort, cleverly composed to spoil her pleasure in the only real friend she had made here, and nasty enough to ensure that she would be ashamed to show it to anyone. Except, of course, to a policeman. Even Miss Willison didn't mind showing it to a policeman. Where obscenity is concerned, we enjoy an almost medical dispensation."

"She wouldn't dare! And I don't know what you're talking about."

"Wouldn't she? It's a pity you can't ask her. You know that she's dead?"

"That's nothing to do with me."

"Luckily for you, I don't think it is. She wasn't the suicidal type. I wonder if you were as lucky—or unlucky—with your other victims, with Victor Holroyd for example."

There was no mistaking her terror now. The thin hands were twisting the handle of her hairbrush in a desperate pantomime.

"That wasn't my fault! I never wrote to Victor! I never wrote to anyone."

"You aren't as clever as you think are you. You forget about fingerprints. Perhaps you didn't realize that forensic laboratories can detect them on writing paper. And then there's the timing. All the letters have been received since you arrived at Toynton

Grange. The first was received before Ursula Hollis was admitted and I think we can rule out Henry Carwardine. I know that they've stopped since Mr. Holroyd's death. Was that because you realized just how far you'd gone? Or did you hope that Mr. Holroyd would be held responsible? But the police will know that those letters weren't written by a man. And then there's the saliva test. All except fifteen per cent of the population excrete their blood group in their saliva. It's a pity you didn't know that before you licked the envelope flaps."

"The envelopes . . . but they weren't . . ."

She gasped at Dalgliesh. Her eyes widened with terror. The flush receded leaving her very pale.

"No, there weren't any envelopes. The notes were folded and placed in the victim's library book. But no one knows that except the recipients and you."

She said, not looking at him:

"What are you going to do?"

"I don't know yet."

And he didn't know. He felt a mixture, strange to him, of embarrassment, anger and some shame. It had been so easy to trick her, so easy and so contemptible. He saw himself as clearly as if he were an onlooker, healthy and able, sitting magisterially in judgement on her weakness, delivering the customary admonition from the bench, deferring sentence. The picture was distasteful. She had caused Grace Willison pain. But at least she could claim some psychological excuse. How much of his own anger and disgust had its roots in guilt? What had he done to make Grace Willison's last days happier? Yet something would have to be done about her. She was unlikely at present to make more mischief at Toynton Grange, but what of the future? And Henry Carwardine presumably had a right to know. So, one could argue, had Wilfred and the Ridgewell Trustees if they took over. Some people, too, would argue that she needed help. They would produce the orthodox contemporary solution, referral to a psychiatrist. He just didn't know. It wasn't a remedy in which he had much confidence. It would gratify her vanity, perhaps, and minister to her urge for self-importance to be taken seriously. But if the victims had resolved to keep silent, if only to protect Wilfred from worry, what right had he to deride their motive or break their confidence? He had been used in his job to working to rules. Even when he had taken an unorthodox decision, which wasn't seldom, the moral issues—if one could use that word and he never had—had been clear and unambiguous. His illness must have sapped his will and judgement as well as his physical strength for this paltry problem to defeat him. Ought he to leave a sealed note for Anstey or his successor to open in case of further trouble? Really it was ridiculous to be driven to such a weak and histrionic expedient. For God's sake, why couldn't he make a straight decision? He wished that Father Baddeley were alive, knowing on whose frail shoulders he could safely have lain this particular burden.

He said:

"I shall leave it to you to tell the victims, all of them, that you were responsible and that it won't happen again. You had better see that it doesn't. I leave it to your ingenuity to think out an excuse. I know that you must miss all the fuss and attention you had at your last hospital. But why compensate by making other people unhappy?"

"They hate me."

"Of course they don't. You hate yourself. Did you write these notes to anyone else except Miss Willison and Mr. Carwardine?"

She looked up at him slyly from under her eyelids.

"No. Only those two."

It was probably a lie, he thought wearily. Ursula Hollis had probably had a letter. Would it do more harm or less if he asked her?

He heard Jennie Pegram's voice, stronger now, more confident. She lifted her left hand and began stroking her hair, drawing the strands across her face. She said:

"No one here cares about me. They all despise me. They never wanted me to come here. I didn't want it either. You could help me but you don't really care. You don't even want to listen."

"Get Dr. Hewson to refer you to a psychiatrist and confide in him. He's paid to listen to neurotics talking about themselves. I'm not."

He regretted the unkindness as soon as the door was closed. He knew what had prompted it; the sudden remembrance of Grace Willison's shrunken, ugly body in its cheap nightdress. It was well, he thought, in a mood of self-disgust, that he was giving up his job if pity and anger could so destroy his detachment. Or was it Toynton Grange? This place, he thought, is getting on my nerves.

As he walked quickly down the passage the door next to Grace Willison's room opened and he saw Ursula Hollis. She beckoned him in, swivelling her wheelchair to clear the doorway.

"They've told us to wait in our rooms. Grace is dead."

"Yes, I know."

"What is it? What happened?"

"No one really knows yet. Dr. Hewson is arranging for a post-mortem."

"She didn't kill herself—or anything."

"I'm sure not. It looked as if she died quietly in her sleep."

"You mean like Father Baddeley?"

"Yes, just like Father Baddeley."

They paused, staring at each other. Dalgliesh asked:

"You didn't hear anything last night?"

"Oh, no! Nothing! I slept very well, that is, after Helen had been in to me."

"Would you have heard if she called out or if anyone went in to her?"

"Oh yes, if I wasn't asleep. Sometimes she kept me awake with her snoring. But I didn't hear her call out, and she went to sleep before I did. My light was out before twelve-thirty and I thought then how quiet she was."

He moved towards the door and then paused, feeling that she was reluctant to see him go. He asked:

"Is anything worrying you?"

"Oh, no! Nothing. It was just the uncertainty about Grace, not knowing, everyone being so mysterious. But if they're going to do a post-mortem . . . I mean the post-mortem will tell us how she died."

"Yes," he said without conviction, as if reassuring himself as well as her, "the post-mortem will tell us."

VIII

Julius was waiting alone in the front hall and they left the Grange together walking through the bright morning air, abstracted, a little apart, their eyes fixed on the path. Neither spoke. As if yoked by an invisible cord, they paced, carefully distanced, towards the sea. Dalgliesh was glad of his companion's silence. He was thinking about Grace Willison, trying to understand and analyse the root of his concern and unrest, emotions which seemed to him illogical to the point of perversity. There had been no visible marks on the body; no lividity; no petechiae on face or forehead; no sign of disturbance in her room; nothing unusual except an unlatched window. She had lain there stiffening in the quietus of natural death. Why then this irrational suspicion? He was a professional policeman, not a clairvoyant. He worked by evidence not by intuition. How many post-mortems were carried out in a year? Over 170,000 wasn't it? 170,000 deaths which required at least some preliminary investigation. Most of them could provide an obvious motive, at least for one person. Only the pathetic derelicts of society had nothing to leave, however meagre, however uncoveted to sophisticated eyes. Every death benefited someone, enfranchised someone, lifted a burden from someone's shoulders, whether of responsibility, the pain of vicarious suffering or the tyranny of love. Every death was a suspicious death if one looked only at motive, just as every death, at the last, was a natural death. Old Dr. Blessington, one of the first and greatest of the forensic pathologists, had taught him that. It had, he remembered, been Blessington's last post-mortem, the young Detective Constable Dalgliesh's first. The hands of both had been shaking, but for very different reasons, although the old man had been as steady as a surgeon once the first incision was made. The body of a forty-two-year-old, red-haired prostitute was on the slab. The post-mortem assistant had with two strokes of his gloved hand wiped from her face the blood, the dirt, the pancake of paint and matted powder, leaving it pale, vulnerable, anonymous. His strong living hand, not death, had erased from it all personality. Old Blessington had demonstrated the cunning of his craft:

"You see, lad, the first blow, warded off by her hand, slipped down the neck and throat towards the right shoulder. A lot of blood, a lot of mess, but no great harm done. With the second, directed upwards and across, he severed the trachea. She died of shock, blood loss and asphyxia, probably in that order from the look of the thymus. When we get them on the slab, lad, there's no such thing as unnatural death."

Natural or unnatural, he was through with it now. It was irritating that with a will so strong, his mind apparently needed this constant reassurance, that it was so obstinately reluctant to leave the problems alone. What possible justification, anyway, had he for going to the local police with a complaint that death was becoming a little too common at Toynton? An old priest dying of heart disease, without enemies, without possessions, except a modest fortune unexceptionally willed for charitable purposes to the man who had befriended him, a notable philanthropist whose character and reputation were beyond reproach. And Victor Holroyd? What could the police do about that death other than they had already most competently done. The facts had been investigated, the inquest jury had pronounced their finding. Holroyd had been buried, Father Baddeley cremated. All that remained was a coffin of broken bones and decaying flesh and a fistful of grey, gritty dust in Toynton churchyard; two more secrets added to the store of secrets buried in that consecrated earth. All of them were beyond human solving now.

And now this third death, the one for which everyone at Toynton Grange had probably been superstitiously waiting, in thrall to the theurgy that death comes in threes. They could all relax now. He could relax. The coroner would order a post-mortem, and Dalgliesh had little doubt of the result. If Michael and Grace Willison had both been murdered, their killer was too clever to leave signs. And why should he? With a frail, sick, disease-ridden woman, it would have been only too easy, as simple and quick as a firm hand placed over nose and mouth. And there would be nothing to justify his interference. He couldn't say: I, Adam Dalgliesh, have had one of my famous hunches—I disagree with the coroner, with the pathologist, with the local police, with all the facts. I demand in the light of this new death that Father Baddeley's incinerated bones be resurrected and forced to yield up their secret.

They had reached Toynton Cottage. Dalgliesh followed Julius round to the seaward porch which led directly from the stone patio into the sitting-room. Julius had left the door unlocked. He pushed it open and stood a little aside so that Dalgliesh could go in first. Then they both stood stock still, stricken into immobility. Someone had been there before them. The marble bust of the smiling child had been smashed to pieces.

Still without speaking they moved together warily over the carpet. The head, hacked into anonymity lay among a holocaust of marble fragments. The dark grey carpet was bejewelled with gleaming grits of stone. Broad ribbons of light from the windows and open door lay across the room and, in their rays, the jagged slivers twinkled like a myriad of infinitesimal stars. It looked as if the destruction had at first been systematic. Both ears had been cleanly severed, and lay together, obscene objects oozing invisible blood, while the bouquet of flowers, so delicately carved that the lilies of the valley had seemed to tremble with life, lay a little distance from the hand as if tossed lightly aside. A miniature dagger of marble had lodged upright in the sofa, a microcosm of violence.

The room was very still; its ordered comfort, the measured ticking of the carriage clock on the mantelshelf, the insistent thudding of the sea, all heightened the sense of outrage, the crudity of destruction and hate.

Julius dropped to his knees and picked up a shapeless lump which had once been the child's head. After a second he let it drop from his loosened grasp. It rolled clumsily, obliquely, across the floor and came to rest against the foot of the sofa. Still without speaking, he reached over and picked up the posy of flowers cradling it gently in his hands. Dalgliesh saw that his body was shaking; he was very pale and his forehead, bent over the carving, glistened with sweat. He looked like a man in shock.

Dalgliesh went over to the side table which held a decanter and poured out a generous measure of whisky. Silently he handed the glass to Julius. The man's silence and the dreadful shaking worried him. Anything, he thought, violence, a storm of rage, a spate of obscenity would be better than this unnatural silence. But when Julius did speak his voice was perfectly steady. He shook his head at the offered glass.

"No, thank you. I don't need a drink. I want to know what I'm feeling, know it here in my belly not just in my head. I don't want my anger dulled, and by God, I don't need it stimulated! Think of it, Dalgliesh. He died three hundred years ago, this gentle boy. The marble must have been carved very shortly afterwards. It was of absolutely no practical use to anyone for three hundred years except to give comfort and pleasure and remind us that we are dust. Three hundred years. Three hundred years of war, revolution, violence, greed. But it survived. It survived until this year of grace. Drink that whisky yourself, Dalgliesh. Raise the glass and toast the age of the despoiler. He didn't know that this was here, unless he peers and pries when I am away. Anything of mine would have served. He could have destroyed anything. But when he saw this, he couldn't resist it. Nothing else could have given him quite such an exaltation of destruction. This isn't just hatred of me you know. Who ever did it, hated this too. Because it gave pleasure, was made with an intention, not just a lump of clay thrown against a wall, paint stamped into a canvas, a piece of stone smoothed into innocuous curves. It had gravity and integrity. It grew out of privilege and tradition, and contributed to it. God, I should have known better than to bring it here among these barbarians!"

Dalgliesh knelt beside him. He picked up two portions of a smashed forearm and fitted them together like a puzzle. He said:

"We know probably to within a few minutes when it was done. We know that it needed strength and that he—or she—probably used a hammer. There ought to be marks on that. And he couldn't have walked here and back in the time. Either he escaped down your path here to the shore, or he came by van and then went on to collect the post. It shouldn't be difficult to find out who is responsible."

"My God, Dalgliesh, you have a policeman's soul haven't you? Is that thought supposed to comfort me?"

"It would me; but then, as you say, it's probably a matter of soul."

"I'm not calling in the police if that's what you're suggesting. I don't need the local fuzz to tell me who did this. I know, and so do you, don't you?"

"No. I could give you a short list of suspects in order of probability, but that's not the same thing."

"Spare yourself the trouble. I know and I'll deal with him in my own way."

"And give him the added satisfaction of seeing you brought up on a charge of assault or G.B.H. I suppose."

"I wouldn't get much sympathy from you would I, or from the local bench? Vengeance is mine saith Her Majesty's Commission of the Peace. Naughty, destructive boy, underprivileged lad! Five pounds fine and put him on probation. Oh! don't worry! I shan't do anything rash. I'll take my time, but I'll deal with it. You can keep your local pals out of it. They weren't exactly a flaming success when they investigated Holroyd's death were they? They can keep their clumsy fingers out of my mess."

Getting to his feet he added with sulky obstinacy, almost as an after-thought.

"Besides, I don't want any more fuss here at present, not just after Grace Willison's death. Wilfred's got enough on his plate. I'll clear this mess away and tell Henry that I have taken the marble back to London. No one else from the Grange comes here, thank God, so I shall be spared the usual insincere condolences."

Dalgliesh said:

"I find it interesting, this concern for Wilfred's peace of mind."

"I thought you might. In your book I am a selfish bastard. You've got an identikit to selfish bastards, and I don't precisely fit. Ergo, find a reason. There has to be a first cause."

"There's always a cause."

"Well, what is it? Am I somehow in Wilfred's pay? Am I fiddling the books? Has he some hold over me? Is there, perhaps some truth in Moxon's suspicions? Or perhaps I'm Wilfred's illegitimate son."

"Even a legitimate son might reasonably feel that it was worth causing Wilfred some distress to discover who did this. Aren't you being too scrupulous? Wilfred must know that someone at Toynton Grange, probably one of his disciples, nearly killed him, intentionally or otherwise. My guess is that he'd take the loss of your marble fairly philosophically."

"He doesn't have to take it. He's not going to know. I can't explain to you what I don't understand myself. But I am committed to Wilfred. He is so vulnerable and pathetic. And it is all so hopeless! If you must know, he reminds me in some way of my parents. They had a small general store in Southsea. Then when I was about fourteen, a large chain store opened next door. That was the end for them. They tried everything; they wouldn't give in. Extended credit when they weren't getting their money anyway; special offers when their profit margins were practically nil; hours spent after closing time rearranging the window; balloons given free to the local kids. It didn't matter, you see. It was all utterly pointless and futile. They couldn't succeed. I thought

I could have borne their failure. What I couldn't bear was their hope."

Dalgliesh thought that, in part, he did see. He knew what Julius was saying. Here am I, young, rich, healthy. I know how to be happy. I could be happy, if only the world were really as I want it to be. If only other people wouldn't persist in being sick, deformed, in pain, helpless, defeated, deluded. Or if only I could be just that bit more selfish so that I didn't care. If only there weren't the black tower. He heard Julius speaking:

"Don't worry about me. Remember I am bereaved. Don't they say that the bereaved always have to work through their grief? The appropriate treatment is a detached sympathy and plenty of good plain nourishment. We'd better get some breakfast."

Dalgliesh said quietly:

"If you're not going to ring the police, then we might as well clear up this mess."

"I'll get a dustbin. I can't bear the noise of the vacuum cleaner."

He disappeared into his immaculate, fashionably over-equipped kitchen, and came back with a dustpan and two brushes. In an odd companionship they knelt together to their task. But the brushes were too soft to dislodge the slivers of marble, and in the end they had to pick them up laboriously one by one.

IX

The forensic pathologist was a locum tenens senior registrar, and if he had expected this three-week stint of duty in the agreeable West Country to be less arduous than his London job, he was disappointed. When the telephone rang for the tenth time that morning he peeled off his gloves, tried not to think about the fifteen naked cadavers still waiting on their refrigerated shelves and lifted the receiver philosophically. The confident masculine voice, except for its pleasant country burr, could have been the voice of any Metropolitan police officer, and the words, too, he had heard before.

"That you Doc? We've got a body in a field three miles north of Blandford which we don't like the look of. Could you come to the scene?"

The summons seldom differed. They always had a body they

didn't like the look of, in a ditch, a field, a gutter, in the tangled steel of a smashed car. He took up his message pad and asked the usual questions, heard the expected replies. He said to the mortuary assistant:

"OK Bert, you can sew her up now. She's no twelve-guinea special. Tell the Coroner's officer that he can issue the disposal order. I'm off to a scene. Get the next two ready for me, will you?"

He glanced for the last time at the emaciated body on the table. There had been nothing difficult about Grace Miriam Willison, spinster, aged 57. No external signs of violence, no internal evidence to justify sending the viscera for analysis. He had muttered to his assistant with some bitterness that if the local GPs were going to look to an over-stretched forensic pathology service to settle their differential diagnoses the service might as well pack up. But her doctor's hunch had been right. There was something he'd missed, the advanced neoplasm in the upper stomach. And much good that knowledge now would do him or her. That, or the D.S. or the heart condition had killed her. He wasn't God and he'd taken his choice. Or maybe she'd just decided that she had had enough and turned her face to the wall. In her state it was the mystery of continuing life not the fact of death that needed explaining. He was beginning to think that most patients died when they decided that it was their time to die. But you couldn't put that on a certificate.

He scribbled a final note on Grace Willison's record, called out a final instruction to his assistant, then pushed his way through the swing doors towards another death, another body, towards, he thought, with something like relief, his proper job.

7

Mist on the Headland

I

The church of St. Michael's at Toynton was an uninteresting Victorian reconstruction of an earlier building, the churchyard a triangular patch of swathed grass between the west wall, the road and a row of rather dull cottages. Victor Holroyd's grave, pointed out by Julius, was an oblong mound crudely patched with squares of weedy turf. Beside it, a simple wooden cross marked the spot where Father Baddeley's ashes had been buried. Grace Willison was to lie next to him. Everyone at Toynton Grange was at the funeral except Helen Rainer who had been left to nurse Georgie Allan, and Maggie Hewson whose absence, unremarked, was apparently taken for granted. But Dalgliesh, when he arrived alone, had been surprised to see Julius's Mercedes parked opposite the lych gate beside the Toynton Grange bus.

The churchyard was encumbered and the path between the headstones narrow and overgrown so that it took some time to manoeuvre the three wheelchairs round the open grave.

The local vicar was taking a belated holiday and his substitute, who apparently knew nothing of Toynton Grange, was obviously surprised to see four of the mourners garbed in brown monk's habits. He asked if they were Anglican Franciscans, an enquiry which provoked a fit of nervous giggling from Jennie Pegram. Anstey's answer, unheard by Dalgliesh, apparently failed to reassure and the priest, puzzled and disapproving, took the service with carefully controlled speed as if anxious to free the churchyard as soon as possible from the risk of contamination by the imposters. The little party sang, at Wilfred's suggestion, Grace's favourite hymn "Ye Holy Angels Bright". It was, thought Dalgliesh, a hymn peculiarly unsuited for amateur unaccompanied singing and their uncertain and discordant voices rose reed thin in the crisp autumnal air.

There were no flowers. Their absence, the rich smell of newly turned earth, the mellow autumn sunlight, the ubiquitous scent of burning wood, even the sense of unseen but inquisitive eyes peering morbidly from behind the hedges, brought back with stabbing pain the memory of another funeral.

He had been a fourteen-year-old schoolboy, at home for his half term. His parents were in Italy and Father Baddeley was in charge of the parish. A local farmer's son, a shy, gentle, over-conscientious eighteen-year-old, home for the weekend from his first term at university, had taken his father's gun and shot dead both parents, his fifteen-year-old sister and, finally, himself. They were a devoted family, he a loving son. For the young Dalgliesh, who was beginning to imagine himself in love with the girl, it had been a horror eclipsing all subsequent horrors. The tragedy, unexplained, appalling, had at first stunned the village. But grief had quickly given way to a wave of superstitious anger, terror and repulsion. It was unthinkable that the boy should be buried in consecrated ground and Father Baddeley's gentle but inexorable insistence that all the family should lie together in one grave had made him temporarily an outcast. The funeral, boycotted by the village, had been held on such a day as this. The family had no close relatives. Only Father Baddeley, the sexton and Adam Dalgliesh had been there. The fourteen-year-old boy, rigid with uncomprehended grief, had concentrated on the responses willing himself to divorce the unbearably poignant words from their sense, to see them merely as black unmeaning symbols on the prayer book page, and to speak them with firmness, even with nonchalance, across the open grave. Now, when this unknown priest raised his hand to speak the final blessing over Grace Willison's body, Dalgliesh saw instead the frail upright figure of Father Baddeley, the wind ruffling his hair. As the first sods fell on the coffin and he turned away he felt like a traitor. The memory of one occasion on which Father Baddeley had not relied on him in vain only reinforced his present nagging sense of failure.

It was probably this which made him reply tartly to Wilfred when he walked up to him and said:

"We are going back for luncheon now. We shall start the family council at half past two and the second session at about four. Are you quite sure you won't help us?"

Dalgliesh opened the door of his car.

"Can you give me one reason why it would be right that I should?" Wilfred turned away; for once he looked almost disconcerted. Dalgliesh heard Julius's low laugh.

"Silly old dear! Does he really think that we don't know that he wouldn't be holding a family council if he weren't confident that the decision would go his way. What are your plans for the day?"

Dalgliesh said that they were still uncertain. In fact he had decided to exercise away his self-disgust by walking along the cliff path as far as Weymouth and back. But he wasn't anxious to invite Julius's company.

He stopped at a nearby pub for a luncheon of cheese and beer, drove quickly back to Hope Cottage, changed into slacks and windcheater and set off eastwards along the cliff path. It was very different from that first early morning walk the day after his arrival when all his newly awakened senses had been alive to sound and colour and smell. Now he strode strongly forward, deep in thought, eyes on the path, hardly aware even of the laboured, sibilant breath of the sea. He would soon have to make a decision about his job; but that could wait for another couple of weeks. There were more immediate if less onerous decisions. How much longer should he stay at Toynton? He had little excuse to linger. The books had been sorted, the boxes were almost ready for cording. And he was making no progress with the problem which had kept him in Hope Cottage. There was small hope now of solving the mystery of Father Baddeley's summons. It was as if, living in Father Baddeley's cottage, sleeping in his bed, Dalgliesh had absorbed something of his personality. He could almost believe that he smelt the presence of evil. It was an alien faculty which he half resented and almost wholly distrusted. And yet it was increasingly strong. He was sure now that Father Baddeley had been murdered. And yet, when as a policeman he looked hard at the evidence, the case dissolved like smoke in his hand.

Perhaps because he was deep in unproductive thought the mist took him by surprise. It rode in from the sea, a sudden physical invasion of white obliterating clamminess. At one moment he was striding in the mellow afternoon sunlight with the breeze prickling the hairs on his neck and arms. The next, sun, colour and smell were blotted out and he stood stock still pushing at the mist as if it were an alien force. It hung on his hair, caught at this throat and swirled in grotesque patterns over the headland. He watched it, a writhing transparent veil passing over and through the brambles and bracken, magnifying and altering form, obscuring the path. With the mist came a sudden silence. He was only aware that the headland had been alive with birds now that their cries were mute. The silence was uncanny. In contrast, the sound of the sea swelled and became all pervasive, disorganized, menacing, seeming to advance on him from all sides. It was like a chained animal, now moaning in sullen captivity, now breaking free to hurl itself with roars of impotent rage against the high shingles.

He turned back towards Toynton, uncertain of how far he had walked. The return journey was going to be difficult. He had no sense of direction except for the thread of trodden earth under his feet. But he thought that the danger would be slight if he went slowly. The path was barely visible but for most of the route it was fringed with brambles, a welcome if prickly barrier when, momentarily disorientated, he lost his way. Once the mist lifted slightly and he strode forward more confidently. But it was a mistake. Only just in time he realized that he was teetering on the edge of a wide crevice splitting the path and that what he had thought was a rising bank of moving mist was foam dying on the cliff face fifty feet below.

The black tower reared out of the mist so suddenly that his first realization of its presence was to scrape his palms—instinctively flung forward—against its cold infrangible scales. Then, suddenly, the mist rose and thinned and he saw the top of the tower. The base was still shrouded in swirls of white clamminess but the octagonal cupola with its three visible slits seemed to float gently from behind the last sinuous threads of mist to hang motionless in space, dramatic, menacingly solid, and yet unsubstantial as a dream. It moved with the mist, a fugitive vision, now descending so low that he could almost believe it within his reach, now rising, numinous and unobtainable, high over the thudding sea. It could surely have no contact with the cold stones on which his palms rested or the firm earth beneath his feet. To steady his balance he rested his head against the tower and felt reality hard and sharp against his forehead. Here at least was a landmark.

From here he thought he could remember the main twists and turns of the path.

It was then that he heard it; the spine-chilling scrape, unmistakable, of bone ends clawing against the stone. It came from inside the tower. Reason asserted itself over superstition so quickly that his mind hardly had time to recognize its terror. Only the painful thudding of his heart against the rib cage, the sudden ice in the blood, told him that for one second he had crossed the border into the unknowable world. For one second, perhaps less, childish nightmares long suppressed rose to confront him. And then the terror passed. He listened more carefully, and then explored. The sound was quickly identified. To the seaward side of the tower and hidden in the corner between the porch and the round wall was a sturdy bramble. The wind had snapped one of the branches and two sharp unleashed ends were scraping against the stone. Through some trick of acoustics the sound, distorted, seemed to come from within the tower. From such coincidences, he thought, smiling grimly, were ghosts and legends born.

Less than twenty minutes later he stood above the valley and looked down on Toynton Grange. The mist was thinning now and he could just discern the Grange itself—a substantial, dark shadow marked by blurs of lights from the windows. His watch showed that it was eight minutes past three. So they would all be closeted now in solitary meditation waiting for the four o'clock summons to announce their final votes. He wondered how, in fact, they were passing their time. But the result was hardly in doubt. Like Julius he thought it unlikely that Wilfred would have called a council unless he were sure of getting his way. And that, presumably, would mean handing over to the Ridgewell Trust. Dalgliesh assessed how the votes might go. Wilfred would no doubt have received an undertaking that all jobs would be safe. Given that assurance Dot Moxon, Eric Hewson and Dennis Lerner would probably vote for the take-over. Poor Georgie Allan would have little choice. The views of the other patients were less certain but he had the feeling that Carwardine would be content enough to stay, particularly with the increased comfort and professional skill which the Trust would bring. Millicent, of course, would want to sell out and she would have had an ally in Maggie Hewson, if Maggie had been allowed to participate.

Looking down on the valley he saw the twin squares of light

from the windows of Charity Cottage where, excluded, Maggie waited alone for the return of Eric. There was a stronger and brighter haze from the edge of the cliff. Julius, when at home, was extravagant with electricity.

The lights, although temporarily obscured as the mist shifted and re-formed, were a useful beacon. He found himself almost running down the slope of the headland. And then, curiously, the light in the Hewson cottage windows went off and on again three times, deliberate as a signal.

He had such a strong impression of an individual call for help that he had to remind himself of reality. She couldn't know that he, or anyone, was on the headland. It could only be by chance if the signal were seen by anyone at Toynton Grange, preoccupied as they were with meditation and decision. Besides, most of the patients' rooms were at the back of the house. It had probably been no more than a fortuitous flickering of the lights; she had been uncertain, perhaps, whether to watch television in the dark.

But the twin smudges of yellow light, now shining more strongly as the mist thinned, drew him towards the Hewson cottage. It was only about three hundred yards out of his way. She was there alone. He might as well look in, even at the risk of becoming involved in an alcoholic recital of grievances and resentment.

The front door was unlocked. When no voice responded to his knock he pushed it open and went in. The sitting-room, dirty, untidy, with its grubby air of temporary occupation, was empty. All three bars of the portable electric fire were glowing red and the room struck very warm. The television screen was a blank. The single unshaded light-bulb in the middle of the ceiling shone down garishly on the square table, the opened and almost empty bottle of whisky, the upturned glass, the sheet of writing paper with its scrawl of black biro, at first relatively firm, then erratic as an insect trail across the white surface. The telephone had been moved from its usual place on the top of the bookcase and stood now, cord taut, on the table, the receiver hanging loosely over the edge.

He didn't wait to read the message. The door into the back hall was ajar and he pushed it open. He knew with the sick and certain premonition of disaster, what he would find. The hall was very narrow and the door swung against her legs. The body twisted so that the flushed face slowly turned and looked down at him with what seemed a deprecating, half melancholy, half rueful surprise at finding herself at such a disadvantage. The light in the hall, from a single bulb, was garish, and she hung elongated like a bizarre and gaudily painted doll strung up for sale. The scarlet tight-fitting slacks, the white satin overblouse, the painted toe and finger nails and the matching gash of mouth looked horrible but unreal. One thrust of a knife and the sawdust would surely spill out from the stuffed veins to pyramid at his feet.

The climber's rope, a smooth twist of red and fawn, gay as a bell rope, was made to take the weight of a man. It hadn't failed Maggie. She had used it simply. The rope had been doubled and the two ends passed through the loop to form a noose, before being fastened, clumsily but effectively, to the top banister. The surplus yards lay tangled on the upper landing.

A high kitchen stool fitted with two steps had fallen on its side obstructing the hallway as if she had kicked it from under her. Dalgliesh placed it beneath the body and, resting her knees on its cushioned plastic, mounted the steps and slipped the noose over her head. The whole weight of her inert body sagged against him. He let it slip through his arms to the floor and half carried it into the sitting-room. Laying her on the mat in front of the fireplace he forced his mouth over hers and began artificial respiration.

Her mouth was fumed with whisky. He could taste her lipstick, a sickly ointment on his tongue. His shirt, wet with sweat, stuck to her blouse, gumming together his thudding chest and her soft, still warm but silent body. He pumped his breath into her, fighting an atavistic repugnance. It was too like raping the dead. He felt the absence of her heart beat as keenly as an ache in his chest.

He was aware that the door had opened only by the sudden chill of flowing air. A pair of feet stood beside the body. He heard Julius's voice.

"Oh, my God! Is she dead? What happened?"

The note of terror surprised Dalgliesh. He glanced up for one second into Court's stricken face. It hung over him like a disembodied mask, the features bleached and distorted with fear. The man was fighting for control. His whole body was shaking. Dalgliesh, intent on the desperate rhythm of resuscitation, jerked out his commands in a series of harsh disjointed phrases.

"Get Hewson. Hurry."

Julius's voice was a high, monotonous mutter.

"I can't! Don't ask me. I'm no good at that sort of thing. He doesn't even like me. We've never been close. You go. I'd rather stay here with her than face Eric."

"Then ring him. Then the police. Wrap the receiver in your handkerchief. May be prints."

"But they won't answer! They never do when they are meditating."

"Then for God's sake fetch him!"

"But her face! It's covered with blood!"

"Lipstick. Smudged. Phone Hewson."

Julius stood unmoving. Then he said:

"I'll try. They will have finished meditating by now. It's just four. They may answer."

He turned to the telephone. From the corner of his eye Dalgliesh glimpsed the lifted receiver shaking in his hands, and the flash of white handkerchief which Julius had wrapped around the instrument as awkwardly as if trying to bandage a self-inflicted wound. After two long minutes the telephone was answered. He couldn't guess by whom. Nor did he afterwards remember what Julius had said.

"I've told them. They're coming."

"Now the police."

"What shall I tell them?"

"The facts. They'll know what to do."

"But oughtn't we to wait? Suppose she comes round?"

Dalgliesh straightened himself up. He knew that for the last five minutes he had been working on a dead body. He said:

"I don't think she's going to come round."

Immediately he bent again to his task, his mouth clamped over hers, feeling with his right palm for the first pulse of life in the silent heart. The pendant light-bulb swung gently in the movement of air from the open door so that a shadow moved like a drawn curtain over the dead face. He was aware of the contrast between the inert flesh, the cool unresponsive lips bruised by his own, and her look of flushed intentness, a woman preoccupied in the act of love. The crimson stigmata of the rope was like a double-corded bracelet clasping the heavy throat. Remnants of cold mist stole in the door to twine themselves round the dust-encrusted legs of table and chairs. The mist stung his nostrils like an anaesthetic; his mouth tasted sour with the whisky-tainted breath.

Suddenly there was a rush of feet; the room was full of people and voices. Eric Hewson was edging him aside to kneel beside his wife; behind him Helen Rainer flicked open a medical bag. She handed him a stethoscope. He tore open his wife's blouse. Delicately, unemotionally, she lifted Maggie's left breast so that he could listen to the heart. He pulled off the stethoscope and threw it aside holding out his hand. This time, still without speaking, she handed him a syringe.

"What are you going to do?" It was Julius Court's hysterical voice.

Hewson looked up at Dalgliesh. His face was deathly white. The irises of his eyes were huge. He said:

"It's only digitalis."

His voice, very low, was a plea for reassurance, for hope. But it sounded, too, like a plea for permission, a small abdication of responsibility. Dalgliesh nodded. If the stuff were digitalis it might work. And surely the man wouldn't be fool enough to inject anything lethal? To stop him now might be to kill her. Would it have been better to carry on with the artificial respiration? Probably not; in any case that was a decision for a doctor. And a doctor was here. But in his heart Dalgliesh knew that the argument was academic. She was as beyond harm as she was beyond help.

Helen Rainer now had a torch in her hand and was shining it on Maggie's breast. The pores of the skin between the pendulous breasts looked huge, miniature craters clogged with powder and sweat. Hewson's hand began to shake. Suddenly she said:

"Here, let me do it."

He handed over the syringe. Dalgliesh heard Julius Court's incredulous "Oh, no! No!" and then watched the needle go in as cleanly and surely as a *coup de grâce*.

The slim hands didn't tremble as she withdrew the syringe, held a pad of cotton wool over the puncture mark and, without speaking, handed the syringe to Dalgliesh.

Suddenly Julius Court stumbled out of the room. He came back almost immediately holding a glass. Before anyone could stop him he had grasped the whisky bottle by the top of its neck and had poured out the last half inch. Jerking one of the chairs out from the table he sat down and slumped forward, his arms half circling the bottle.

Wilfred said:

"But Julius . . . nothing should be touched until the police arrive!"

Julius took out his handkerchief and wiped it over his face.

"I needed that. And what the hell! I haven't interfered with her prints. And she's had a rope round her neck, or haven't you noticed? What d'you think she died of—alcoholism?"

The rest of them stood in a tableau round the body. Hewson still knelt at his wife's side; Helen cradled her head. Wilfred and Dennis stood one on each side, the folds of their habits hanging motionless in the still air. They looked, thought Dalgliesh, like a motley collection of actors posing for a contemporary diptych, their eyes fixed with wary anticipation on the bright body of the martyred saint.

Five minutes later Hewson stood up. He said dully:

"No response. Move her to the sofa. We can't leave her there on the floor."

Julius Court rose from his chair and he and Dalgliesh together lifted the sagging body and placed it on the sofa. It was too short, and the scarlet-tipped feet, looking at once grotesque and pathetically vulnerable, stuck out stiffly over the end. Dalgliesh heard the company sigh gently, as if they had satisfied some obscure need to make the body comfortable. Julius looked round, apparently at a loss, searching for something with which to cover the corpse. It was Dennis Lerner who, surprisingly, produced a large white handkerchief, shook it free of its folds and placed it with ritual precision over Maggie's face. They all looked at it intently as if watching for the linen to stir with the first tentative breath.

Wilfred said:

"I find it a strange tradition that we cover the faces of the dead. Is it because we feel that they are at a disadvantage, exposed defenceless to our critical gaze? Or is it because we fear them? I think the latter."

Ignoring him, Eric Hewson turned to Dalgliesh.

"Where . . .?"

"Out there in the hall."

Hewson went to the door and stood silently surveying the

dangling rope, the bright chrome and yellow kitchen stool. He turned towards the circle of watchful, compassionate faces.

"How did she get the rope?"

"It may be mine." Wilfred's voice sounded interested, confident. He turned to Dalgliesh.

"It's newer looking than Julius's rope. I bought it shortly after the old one was found frayed. I keep it on a hook in the business room. You may have noticed it. It was certainly hanging there when we left for Grace's funeral this morning. You remember, Dot?"

Dorothy Moxon moved forward from her shadowed refuge against the far wall. She spoke for the first time. They looked round as if surprised to find her in the company. Her voice sounded unnatural, high, truculent, uncertain.

"Yes, I noticed. I mean, I'm sure I would have noticed if it hadn't been there. Yes, I remember. The rope was there."

"And when you got back from the funeral?" asked Dalgliesh.

"I went alone into the business room to hang up my cloak. I don't think it was there then. I'm almost sure not."

"Didn't that worry you?" asked Julius.

"No, why should it? I'm not sure that I consciously noticed that the rope was missing at the time. It's only now, looking back, that I am fairly confident that it wasn't there. Its absence wouldn't have particularly concerned me even had I registered it. I should have assumed that Albert had borrowed it for some purpose. He couldn't have done so, of course. He came with us to the funeral, and got into the bus before me."

Lerner said suddenly:

"The police have been telephoned?"

"Of course," said Julius, "I rang them."

"What were you doing here?" Dorothy Moxon's didactic question sounded like an accusation, but Julius who seemed to have taken control of himself, answered calmly enough:

"She switched the light off and on three times before she died. I happened to see it through the mist from my bathroom window. I didn't come at once. I didn't think it was important or that she was really in trouble. Then I felt uneasy and decided to walk over. Dalgliesh was already here."

Dalgliesh said:

"I saw the signal from the headland. Like Julius, I didn't feel more than slightly uneasy, but it seemed right to look in."

Lerner had moved over to the table. He said:

"She's left a note."

Dalgliesh said sharply:

"Don't touch it!"

Lerner withdrew his hand as if it had been stung. They moved round the table. The note was written in black biro on the top sheet of a quarto-size pad of white writing paper. They read silently:

> "Dear Eric, I've told you often
> enough that I couldn't stick it out
> in this lousy hole any longer. You
> thought it was just talk. You've been
> so busy fussing over your precious
> patients I could die of boredom and you
> wouldn't notice. Sorry if I've mucked
> up your little plans. I don't kid
> myself you'll miss me. You can have her
> now and by God you're welcome to each
> other. We had some good times. Remember
> them. Try to miss me. Better dead. Sorry
> Wilfred. The black tower."

The first eight lines were plainly and strongly written, the last five were an almost illegible scrawl.

"Her handwriting?" asked Anstey.

Eric Hewson replied in a voice so low that they could barely hear him.

"Oh, yes. Her handwriting."

Julius turned to Eric and said with sudden energy:

"Look, its perfectly plain how it happened. Maggie never intended to kill herself. She wouldn't. She's not the type. For God's sake, why should she? She's young enough, healthy, if she didn't like it here she could walk out. She's an SRN. She's not unemployable. This was all meant to frighten you. She tried to telephone Toynton Grange and get you over here—just in time, of course. When no one replied, she signalled with the lights. But by that time she was too drunk to know exactly what she was doing and the whole thing became horribly real. Take that note, does it read like a suicide note?"

"It does to me," said Anstey. "And I suspect it will to the coroner."

"Well, it doesn't to me. It could just as well be the note of a woman planning to go away."

Helen Rainer said calmly:

"Only she wasn't. She wouldn't be leaving Toynton wearing just a shirt and slacks. And where is her case? No woman plans to leave home without taking her make-up and nightwear."

There was a capacious black shoulder bag beside a leg of the table. Julius picked it up and began rummaging in it. He said:

"There's nothing here. No nightdress or toilet bag."

He continued his inspection. Then he glanced suddenly from Eric to Dalgliesh. An extraordinary succession of emotions crossed his face; surprise, embarrassment, interest. He closed the bag and placed it on the table.

"Wilfred's right. Nothing should be touched until the police arrive."

They stood in silence. Then Anstey said:

"The police will want to know where we all were this afternoon, no doubt. Even in an obvious case of suicide these questions have to be asked. She must have died when we were nearly at the end of our meditation hour. That means, of course, that none of us has an alibi. Given the circumstances it is perhaps fortunate that Maggie chose to leave a suicide note."

Helen Rainer said calmly:

"Eric and I were together in my room for the whole of the hour."

Wilfred stared at her, disconcerted. For the first time since he had entered the cottage he seemed at a loss. He said:

"But we were holding a family council! The rules are that we meditate in silence and alone."

"We didn't meditate and we weren't precisely silent. But we were alone—alone together." She stared past him, defiant, almost triumphant, into the eyes of Eric Hewson. He gazed at her appalled.

Dennis Lerner, as if to dissociate himself from controversy, had moved over to stand by Dot Moxon by the door. Now he said quietly:

"I think I can hear cars. It must be the police."

The mist had muffled the sound of their approach. Even as Lerner spoke Dalgliesh heard the dual slam of car doors. Eric's first reaction was to kneel by the sofa, shielding Maggie's body from the door. Then he scrambled clumsily to his feet as if afraid to be discovered in a compromising position. Dot, without looking round, moved her solid body away from the door.

The little room was suddenly as overcrowded as a bus shelter on a wet night, smelling of mist and damp raincoats. But there was no confusion. The new arrivals moved solidly and calmly in, bringing with them their equipment, moving as purposefully as encumbered members of an orchestra taking their appointed places. The group from Toynton Grange fell back and regarded them warily. No one spoke. Then Inspector Daniel's slow voice broke the silence.

"Well, now, and who found the poor lady?"

"I did," said Dalgliesh. "Court arrived about twelve minutes later."

"Then I'll just have Mr. Dalgliesh, Mr. Court and Dr. Hewson. That'll do to start with."

Wilfred said:

"I should prefer to stay, if you please."

"Well, Sir, I daresay. Mr. Anstey isn't it? But we can't always have what we'd prefer. Now if you'll all go back to the Grange, Detective Constable Burroughs will accompany you and anything that's on your minds you can say to him. I'll be with you later."

Without a further word, Wilfred led the way.

Inspector Daniel looked at Dalgliesh:

"Well, Sir, seemingly for you there's no convalescence from death at Toynton Head."

II

When he had handed over the syringe and given his account of the finding of the body Dalgliesh didn't wait to watch the investigation. He had no wish to give the impression that he was keeping a critical eye on Inspector Daniel's handling of the case; he disliked the role of spectator, and he felt uncomfortably that he was getting in their way. None of the men present were getting in each other's. They moved confidently in the cramped space, each a specialist, yet giving the impression of a team. The photographer manoeuvred his portable lights into the narrow hall; the plain-clothes fingerprint expert, his case open to display the neatly arranged tools of his craft, settled down at the table, brush poised, to begin his methodical dusting of the whisky bottle; the police surgeon knelt, absorbed and judicial, beside the body and plucked at Maggie's mottled skin as if hoping to stimulate it into life. Inspector Daniel leaned over him and they conferred together. They looked, thought Dalgliesh, like two poulterers expertly assessing the qualities of a dead chicken. He was interested that Daniel had brought the police surgeon and not a forensic pathologist. But why not? A Home Office pathologist, given the huge areas which most of them had to cover, could seldom arrive promptly on the scene. And the initial medical examination here presented no obvious problems. There was no sense in committing more resources than were needed for the job. He wondered whether Daniel would have come himself if it hadn't been for the presence at Toynton Grange of a Metropolitan Police Commander.

Dalgliesh formally asked Daniel's permission to return to Hope Cottage. Eric Hewson had already left. Daniel had asked him only a few necessary brief and gentle questions before suggesting that he should join the others at Toynton Grange. Dalgliesh sensed the relief at his departure. Even these imperturbable experts moved more freely released from the inhibiting restraints of public grief. Now the Inspector exerted himself to do more than nod a curt dismissal. He said:

"Thank you, Sir. I'll call in for a word with you before I leave if I may," and bent again to his contemplation of the body.

Whatever Dalgliesh had expected to find at Toynton Head it wasn't this; the old familiar routine commemoration of unnatural death. For a moment he saw it with Julius Court's eyes, an esoteric necromantic rite, carried out by its drab practitioners in silence or between grunts and muttered words as brief as incantations, a secret ministration to the dead. Certainly Julius seemed engrossed by the procedure. He made no move to leave but stood to one side of the door and, without taking his fascinated eyes from Inspector Daniel, held it open for Dalgliesh. Daniel didn't suggest that he, too, might now leave but Dalgliesh thought it unlikely that this was because the Inspector had forgotten his presence.

It was nearly three hours later before Inspector Daniel's car drove up to Hope Cottage. The Inspector was alone; Sergeant Varney and the others, he explained, had already left. He came in bringing with him remnants of mist like ectoplasm and a rush of cold damp air. His hair was jewelled with moisture and his long ruddy face glowed as if he had come in from a walk in the sun. At Dalgliesh's invitation he took off his trench coat and settled himself in the wheelbacked chair in front of the wood fire. His black lively eyes roamed over the cottage, taking in the scruffed rug, the meagre grate, the shabbiness of the wallpaper. He said:

"So this is where the old gentleman lived."

"And died. You'll take whisky? Or there's coffee if you prefer it."

"Whisky, thank you, Mr. Dalgliesh. Mr. Anstey didn't exactly make him comfortable, did he? But I daresay all the money goes on the patients, and very rightly no doubt."

Some went on Anstey himself, thought Dalgliesh, remembering the sybaritic cell which was Wilfred's bedroom. He said:

"It's better than it looks. My packing cases don't exactly add to the cosiness. But I doubt whether Father Baddeley noticed the shabbiness or if he did, that he cared."

"Well, it's warm enough anyway. This sea mist seems to seep into your bones. It's clearer inland, though, once you get beyond Toynton village. That's why we made good time."

He sipped his whisky gratefully. After a minute's silence he said:

"This business tonight, Mr. Dalgliesh. It looks straightforward enough. Her prints and Court's on the whisky bottle, and hers and Hewson's on the telephone. There's no hope of getting any dabs from the electric light switch, of course, and those on the biro don't amount to anything. We found a couple of samples of her handwriting. The document chappies at the lab can take a look at them but it's clear enough to me—and Dr. Hewson incidentally—that she wrote that suicide note. It's a strong distinctive scrawl for a woman."

"Except for the last three lines."

"The reference to the black tower? She was pretty far gone when she added that. Incidentally, Mr. Anstey takes it as an admission that it was she who started the fire which nearly killed him. And that wasn't the first attempt according to him. You've heard, no doubt, about the frayed climbing rope? He gave me a full account of the incident in the black tower including your finding the brown habit."

"Did he? He was anxious enough at the time to keep it from

the police. So now it's to be laid very neatly at Maggie Hewson's door."

"It always surprises me—although it shouldn't by now—how violent death unlooses tongues. He says that she was the one he suspected from the start; that she made no secret of her hatred of Toynton Grange or her resentment of him in particular."

Dalgliesh said:

"Nor did she. I would be surprised if a woman who expressed her feelings with such uninhibited relish should feel the need for any other release. The fire; the frayed climbing rope; they strike me as being either part of a deliberate stratagem or the manifestations of frustrated hatred. Maggie Hewson was nothing if not candid about her dislike of Anstey."

"Mr. Anstey sees the fire as part of a deliberate stratagem. According to him she was trying to frighten him into selling out. She was desperate to get her husband away from Toynton Grange."

"Then she'd misjudged her man. My guess is that Anstey isn't selling out. By tomorrow he'll have made up his mind to pass Toynton Grange to the Ridgewell Trust."

"He's making up his mind now, Mr. Dalgliesh. Apparently Mrs. Hewson's death interrupted their final decision. He was anxious for me to interview all the inmates as quickly as possible so that they could get down to it. Not that it took much time, to get the basic facts, anyway. No one was seen leaving Toynton Grange after the party arrived back after the funeral. Apart from Dr. Hewson and Nurse Rainer, who admit to having spent the meditation hour together in her room, all the others claim that they were alone. The patients' quarters, as you no doubt know, are at the back. Anyone, anyone not disabled that is, could have left the house. But there's no evidence that anyone did."

Dalgliesh said:

"And even if someone did, this mist would have been an effective shield. Anyone could have walked about the headland unseen. Were you convinced, by the way, that Maggie Hewson did start the fire?"

"I'm not investigating arson or attempted murder, Mr. Dalgliesh. Mr. Anstey told me what he did in confidence and said that he wanted the whole subject dropped. She could have done it, but there is no real evidence. He could have done it himself."

"I doubt that. But I did wonder if Henry Carwardine might have had a hand in it. He couldn't have started the fire himself, of course, but he might have paid an accomplice. I don't think he likes Anstey. But that's hardly a motive. He doesn't have to stay at Toynton Grange. But he's highly intelligent and, I should have thought, fastidious. It's difficult to imagine him embroiling himself with such childish mischief."

"Ah, but he isn't using his intelligence is he, Mr. Dalgliesh? That's his trouble. He gave up too easily and too early, that one. And who can know the truth about motive? Sometimes I think not even the villain himself. I daresay it isn't easy for a man like that, living in such a restricted community, dependent always on others, having always to be grateful to Mr. Anstey. Well, no doubt he is grateful to Mr. Anstey; they all are. But gratitude can be the very devil sometimes, particularly if you have to be grateful for services you'd rather be without."

"You're probably right. I know little of Carwardine's feelings, or of anyone else's at Toynton Grange. I've taken very good care not to know. Did the proximity of violent death induce any of the others to reveal their little secrets?"

"Mrs. Hollis had a contribution. I don't know what she thought it proved, or why she thought it worth telling for that matter. But she may have wanted her little moment of importance. That blonde patient was the same—Miss Pegram isn't it? Kept hinting that she knew Dr. Hewson and Nurse Rainer were lovers. No real evidence, of course, just spite and self-importance. I may have my ideas about those two, but I'd want more evidence than I heard tonight before I started thinking about conspiracy to murder. Mrs. Hollis's story wasn't even particularly relevant to Maggie Hewson's death. She said that the night Grace Willison died she glimpsed Mrs. Hewson passing along the dormitory corridor wearing a brown habit and with the hood drawn over her face. Apparently Mrs. Hollis is in the habit of slipping out of bed at night and propelling herself round the room on her pillow. She says that its a form of exercise, that she's trying to be more mobile and independent. Anyway on the night in question, she managed to get her door ajar—no doubt the idea of taking a skid down the passage—and saw this cloaked figure. She thought afterwards that it must have been Maggie Hewson. Anyone with proper business—any of the staff—would have worn the hood down."

"If they were about their proper business. When exactly was this?"

"A little after midnight she says. She closed the door again and got back into bed with some difficulty. She heard and saw nothing more."

Dalgliesh said consideringly:

"I'm surprised from the little I've seen of her that she could manage to get back to bed unaided. Getting out is one thing, pulling herself back would be a great deal more difficult. Hardly worth the exercise, I should have thought."

There was a short silence. Then Inspector Daniel asked, his black eyes full on Dalgliesh's face:

"Why did Dr. Hewson refer that death to the coroner, Sir? If he had doubts about his medical diagnosis, why not ask the hospital pathologist, or one of his local chums to open her up for him?"

"Because I forced his hand and gave him no choice. He couldn't refuse to refer it without looking suspicious. And I don't think he has any local chums. He's not on those terms with his medical colleagues. How did you hear about it?"

"From Hewson. After hearing the girl's story I had another word with him. But Miss Willison's death was apparently straightforward."

"Oh, yes. Just like this suicide. Just like Father Baddeley's death. All apparently straightforward. She died of cancer of the stomach. But this business tonight. Did you find out anything about the rope?"

"I forgot to mention that, Mr. Dalgliesh. It's the rope which has clinched it. Nurse Rainer saw Mrs. Hewson taking it from the business room at about half past eleven this morning. Nurse Rainer had been left behind to look after that bed-bound patient—Georgie Allan isn't it?—but everyone else was at Miss Willison's funeral. She was writing up the patient's medical record and needed a fresh sheet. All the stationery is kept in a filing cabinet in the business room. It's expensive and Mr. Anstey doesn't like to issue it wholesale. He's afraid that people will use it as scribbling pads. When she reached the hall Nurse Rainer saw Mrs. Hewson slipping out of the business room with the rope over her arm."

"What explanation did Maggie give?"

"According to Nurse Rainer all she said was: 'Don't worry, I'm not going to fray it. Quite the reverse. You'll get it back practically as good as new, if not from me.'"

Dalgliesh said:

"Helen Rainer wasn't in any particular hurry to provide that information when we first found the body. But, assuming she isn't lying, it certainly completes your case."

"I don't think she is lying, Mr. Dalgliesh. But I did look at the boy's medical record. Nurse Rainer began a fresh sheet this afternoon. And there seems little doubt that the rope was hanging in the business room when Mr. Anstey and Sister Moxon left for the funeral. Who else could have taken it? They were all at the funeral except Nurse Rainer, that very sick boy and Mrs. Hammitt."

Dalgliesh said:

"I'd forgotten about Mrs. Hammitt. I noticed that almost everyone from Toynton Grange was at the cemetery. It didn't occur to me that she wasn't."

"She says she disapproves of funerals. People ought to be cremated in what she calls decent privacy. She says that she spent the morning cleaning her gas stove. For what it's worth, the stove has certainly been cleaned."

"And this evening?"

"Meditating at Toynton Grange with the others. They were all supposed to be separate and alone. Mr. Anstey placed the small interviewing room at her disposal. According to Mrs. Hammitt, she never left it until her brother rang the bell to summon them together just before four o'clock. Mr. Court telephoned shortly afterwards. She died sometime during the meditation hour, no doubt about that. And the police surgeon reckons nearer four than three."

Was Millicent strong enough, Dalgliesh wondered, to have strung up Maggie's heavy body? Probably, with the help of the kitchen stool. And the strangling itself would have been easy enough once Maggie was drunk. A silent movement behind her chair, the noose dropped by gloved hands over the drooping head, the sudden upward jerk as the rope bit into the flesh. Any one of them could have done it, could have crept out unnoticed into the concealing mist towards the smudge of light marking the Hewson cottage. Helen Rainer was the slightest; but Helen was a nurse, skilful in lifting heavy bodies. And Helen Rainer might not have been alone. He heard Daniel speaking:

"We'll get that stuff in the syringe analysed and we had better ask the lab to take a look at the whisky. But those two little jobs shouldn't hold up the inquest. Mr. Anstey is anxious to get that over as soon as possible so that it doesn't interfere with the pilgrimage to Lourdes on the twenty-third. None of them seems worried about the funeral. That can wait until they get back. I don't see why they shouldn't get away, if the lab can do the analysis quickly. And we know that the whisky's all right; Court still seems healthy enough. I was wondering, Mr. Dalgliesh, just why he took that swig. Incidentally, he'd given her the whisky; half a dozen bottles for her birthday on 11th September. A generous gentleman."

Dalgliesh said:

"I thought he might have been feeding her whisky. But I don't think Court took that drink to save the forensic boys trouble. He needed it."

Daniel gazed consideringly into his half-empty glass:

"Court's been pressing his theory that she never intended killing herself, that the whole set-up was play-acting, a desperate plea for attention. She might well have chosen that moment. They were all at the Grange making an important decision which affected her future, and yet she'd been excluded. He could be right; the jury may buy it. But it won't provide much consolation for the husband."

Hewson, thought Dalgliesh, might be looking elsewhere for consolation. He said:

"It seems out of character. I can see her making some dramatic *démarche* if only to relieve the monotony. What I can't see is her wanting to stay on at Toynton as a failed suicide, attracting the slightly pitying contempt that people feel for someone who can't even succeed in killing herself. My problem is that I find a genuine suicide attempt even less in character."

Daniel said:

"Maybe she didn't expect to have to stay at Toynton. Maybe that was the idea, to convince her husband that she'd kill herself unless he found another job. I can't see many men taking that risk. But she did kill herself, Mr. Dalgliesh, whether she intended to or not. This case rests on two bits of evidence: Nurse Rainer's story about the rope, and the suicide note. If Rainer convinces the jury, and the document examiner confirms that Mrs. Hewson wrote that note, then I'll be taking no bets on the verdict. In character or not, you can't get away from the evidence."

But there was other evidence, thought Dalgliesh, less strong but not uninteresting. He said:

"She looked as if she were going somewhere, or perhaps expecting a visitor. She'd recently had a bath, her pores were clogged with powder. Her face was made up and she'd painted her nails. And she wasn't dressed for a solitary evening at home."

"So her husband said. I thought myself that it looked as if she'd dolled herself up. That could support the theory of a faked suicide attempt. If you're planning to be the centre of attraction you may as well dress for the show. There's no evidence that she did have a visitor, although it's true enough that no one would have seen him in the mist. I doubt whether he could have found his way once he'd left the road. And if she was planning to leave Toynton, then someone would have had to fetch her. The Hewsons have no car, Mr. Anstey doesn't allow private transport; there's no bus today; and we've checked the car hire firms."

"You've wasted no time."

"A matter of a few telephone calls, Mr. Dalgliesh. I like to get these details out of the way while they're in my mind."

"I can't see Maggie sitting quietly at home while the rest of them settled her future. She was friendly with a solicitor in Wareham, Robert Loder. I suppose he wasn't calling for her?"

Daniel shifted his heavy weight forward and threw another plank of driftwood on the fire. The fire was burning sluggishly as if the chimney were blocked with mist. He said:

"The local boy friend. You aren't the only one to suggest that, Mr. Dalgliesh. I thought it as well to ring the gentleman's home and have a word. Mr. Loder's in Poole General Hospital having his piles operated on. He was admitted yesterday and they gave him a week's notice. A nasty painful complaint. Hardly a comfortable time, you might say, to plan to run away with another man's wife."

Dalgliesh asked:

"What about the one person at Toynton who did have his own car? Court?"

"It was an idea I had put to him, Mr. Dalgliesh. I got a definite reply if not a very gentlemanlike one. What it amounted to was that he'd do a great deal for dear Maggie but that self-preservation was the first law of nature and it just happens that his tastes don't run in that direction. Not that he was against the idea that she planned to leave Toynton. As a matter of fact, he suggested it, although I don't know how he thought it tied up with his previous view that Mrs. Hewson faked a suicide attempt. Both theories can't be true."

Dalgliesh asked:

"What was it that he found in her bag, a contraceptive?"

"Ah, you noticed that, did you? Yes, her Dutch cap. She wasn't on the pill seemingly. Court tried to be tactful about it, but as I told him, you can't be tactful about violent death. That's the one social catastrophe that the etiquette books can't help with. It's the strongest indication that she might have been planning to leave, that and her passport. They were both in the bag. You could say she was equipped for any eventuality."

Dalgliesh said:

"She was equipped with the two items which she couldn't replace by a brief visit to the nearest chemist. I suppose you could argue that it's reasonable to keep the passport in her handbag. But the other?"

"Who's to know how long it was there. And women do keep things in odd places. No point in getting fanciful. And there's no reason to suppose that the two of them were set for a flit, she and Hewson. If you ask me he's as tied to Anstey and the Grange as any of the patients, poor devil. You know his story, I suppose?"

"Not really. I told you. I've taken good care not to become involved."

"I had a sergeant like him once. The women couldn't leave him alone. It's that vulnerable, lost small boy look they have, I suppose. Name of Purkiss. Poor devil. He couldn't cope with the women and he couldn't cope without them. It did for his career. He runs a garage now, somewhere near Market Harborough, they tell me. And it's worse for Hewson. He doesn't even like his job. Forced into it, I gather, by one of those strong-minded mothers, a widow, determined to make her ewe lamb into a doctor. Appropriate enough, I suppose. It's the modern equivalent of the priesthood isn't it? He told me that the training wasn't so bad. He's got a phenomenal memory and can learn almost any facts. It's the responsibility he can't take. Well, there's not much of that at Toynton Grange. The patients are incurable and there's not much that they or anyone else expect him to do about it. Mr. Anstey wrote to him and took him on, I gather, after he'd had his name removed from the Register by the GMC. He'd been having an affair with a patient, a girl of sixteen. There was a suggestion that it had started a year or so earlier, but he was lucky. The girl stuck to her story. He couldn't write prescriptions for dangerous drugs at Toynton Grange or sign death certificates, of course. Not until they restored his name to the Register six months ago. But they couldn't take away his medical knowledge and I've no doubt that Mr. Anstey found him useful."

"And cheap."

"Well, there's that, of course. And now he doesn't want to leave. I suppose he might have killed his wife to stop her nagging him to go, but personally I don't believe it and neither will a jury. He's the sort of man who gets a woman to do his dirty work."

"Helen Rainer?"

"That'd be daft, wouldn't it, Mr. Dalgliesh? And where's the evidence?"

Dalgliesh wondered briefly whether to tell Daniel about the conversation between Maggie and her husband which he had overheard after the fire. But he put the thought from him. Hewson would either deny it or be able to explain it. There were probably a dozen petty secrets in a place like Toynton Grange. Daniel would feel bound to question him, of course. But he would see it as an irritating duty forced on him by an over suspicious and officious intruder from the Met. determined to twist plain facts into a tangle of complicated conjecture. And what possible difference could it make? Daniel was right. If Helen stuck to her story about seeing Maggie collect the rope; if the document examiner confirmed that Maggie had written the suicide note; then the case was closed. He knew now what the inquest verdict would be, just as he had known that the post-mortem on Grace Willison would reveal nothing suspicious. Once again he saw himself, as if in a nightmare, watching impotently as the bizarre charabanc of facts and conjecture hurtled on its predestined course. He couldn't stop it because he had forgotten how. His illness seemed to have sapped his intelligence as well as his will.

The spar of driftwood, charred now into a blackened spear, jewelled with sparks, slowly toppled and died. Dalgliesh was aware that the room was very cold and that he was hungry. Perhaps because of the occluding mist smudging the twilight hour between day and night, the evening seemed to have lasted for ever. He wondered whether he ought to offer Daniel a meal. Presumably the man could eat an omelette. But even the effort of cooking seemed beyond him.

Suddenly the problem solved itself. Daniel got slowly to his feet and reached for his coat. He said:

"Thank you for the whisky, Mr. Dalgliesh. And now I'd best be on my way. I'll see you at the inquest, of course. It'll mean your staying on here. But we'll get on with the case as quickly as we can."

They shook hands. Dalgliesh almost winced at the grip. At the doorway Daniel paused, tugging on his coat.

"I saw Dr. Hewson alone in that small interviewing room which they tell me Father Baddeley used to use. And if you ask me, he'd have been better off with a priest. No difficulty in getting him to talk. Trouble was to stop him. And then he began crying and it all came out. How could he go on living without her? He'd never stopped loving her, longing for her. Funny, the more they're feeling, the less sincere they sound. But you'll have noticed that, of course. And then he looked up at me, his face blubbered with tears and said,

'She didn't lie for me because she cared. It was only a game to her. She never pretended to love me. It was just that she thought the GMC committee were a set of pompous old bores who despised her and she wasn't going to give them the satisfaction of seeing me go to prison. And so she lied.'

"Do you know, Mr. Dalgliesh, it was only then that I realized that he wasn't speaking about his wife. He wasn't even thinking of her. Or of Nurse Rainer for that matter. Poor devil! Ah, well, it's an odd job we have, you and I."

He shook hands again as if he had already forgotten that last crushing grip, and with a final keen-eyed survey of the sitting-room as if to reassure himself that everything was still in place, slipped out into the mist.

III

In the business room Dot Moxon stood with Anstey at the window and looked out of the curtain of misty darkness. She said bitterly:

"The Trust won't want either of us, you realize that? They may name the home after you, but they won't let you stay on as Warden, and they'll get rid of me."

He laid his hand on her shoulder. She wondered how she could ever have longed for that touch or been comforted by it. He said with the controlled patience of a parent comforting a wilfully obtuse child:

"They've given me an undertaking. No one's job will be lost. And everyone will get a rise. From now on you'll all be paid National Health Service rates. And they have a contributory pension scheme, that's a big advantage. I've never been able to provide that."

"And what about Albert Philby? You're not telling me that they've promised to keep Albert on, an established, respectable national charity like the Ridgewell Trust."

"Philby does present a problem. But he'll be dealt with sympathetically."

"Dealt with sympathetically! We all know what that means. That's what they said to me in my last job, before they forced me out! And this is his home! He trusts us. We've taught him to trust us! And we have a responsibility for him."

"Not any longer, Dot."

"So we betray Albert and exchange what you've tried to build up here for Health Service rates of pay and a pension scheme! And my position? Oh, they won't sack me, I know that. But it won't be the same. They'll make Helen matron. She knows that too. Why else did she vote for the take-over?"

He said quietly:

"Because she knew that Maggie was dead." Dot laughed bitterly: "It's worked out very nicely for her hasn't it? For both of them."

He said:

"Dot dear, you and I have to accept that we cannot always choose the way in which we are called to serve."

She wondered how she had never noticed it before, that irritating note of unctuous reproof in his voice. She turned abruptly away. The hand, thus rejected, slipped heavily from her shoulders. She remembered suddenly what he reminded her of: the sugar Father Christmas on her first Christmas tree, so desirable, so passionately desired. And you bit into nothingness; a trace of sweetness on the tongue and then an empty cavity grained with white sand.

IV

Ursula Hollis and Jennie Pegram sat together in Jennie's room, the two wheelchairs side by side in front of the dressing table. Ursula was leaning across and brushing Jennie's hair. She wasn't sure how she came to be here, so oddly employed. Jennie had never asked her before. But tonight, waiting for Helen to put them to bed, Helen, who had never before been so late, it was comforting not to be alone with her thoughts, comforting even to watch the corn gold hair rise with each brush stroke, to fall slowly, a delicate shining mist, over the hunched shoulders. The two women found themselves whispering, cosily, like conspiring schoolgirls. Ursula said:

"What do you think will happen now?"

"To Toynton Grange? The Trust will take over and Wilfred will go, I expect. I don't mind. At least there'll be more patients. It's boring here now with so few of us. And Wilfred told me that they plan to build a sun-lounge out on the cliff. I'll like that. And we're bound to get more treats, trips and so on. We haven't had many recently. As a matter of fact, I was thinking of leaving. They keep writing from my old hospital wanting me back."

Ursula knew that they hadn't written. But it didn't matter. She contributed her own morsel of fantasy.

"So was I. Steve is keen for me to move nearer London so that he can visit. Just until he's found us a more suitable flat of course."

"Well, the Ridgewell Trust have a home in London haven't they? You could be transferred there."

How strange that Helen hadn't told her that! Ursula whispered:

"It's odd that Helen voted for the take-over. I thought she wanted Wilfred to sell out."

"Probably she did until she knew that Maggie was dead. Now that she's got rid of Maggie, I suppose she feels she may as well stay on. I mean the field's clear now, isn't it?"

Got rid of Maggie. But surely no one had got rid of Maggie but Maggie herself? And Helen couldn't have known that Maggie was going to die. Only six days ago she had been urging Ursula to vote for the sell out. She couldn't have known then. Even at the preliminary family council, before they all parted for their meditation hour, she had made it plain where her interests lay. And then during that meditation hour, she had changed her mind. No, Helen couldn't have known that Maggie was going to die. Ursula found the thought comforting. Everything was going to be all right. She had told Inspector Daniel about the hooded figure she had seen on the night of Grace's death, not the whole truth, of course, but enough to lift a weight of nagging and irrational worry from her mind. He hadn't thought it important. She had sensed that from the way he had listened, his few brief questions. And he was right, of course. It wasn't important. She wondered now how she could ever have lain awake fretted by inexplicable anxieties, haunted by images of evil and death, cloaked and hooded, stalking the silent corridors. And it must have been Maggie. With the news of Maggie's death she had suddenly become sure of it. It was difficult to know why, except that the figure had looked at once theatrical and surreptitious, so much a stranger, wearing the monk's robe with none of the slovenly familiarity of the Toynton Grange staff. But she had told the Inspector about it. There was no need to worry any more. Everything was going to be all right. Toynton Grange wouldn't close down after all. But it didn't matter. She would get a transfer to the London home, perhaps on exchange. Someone there was sure to want to come to the seaside. She heard Jennie's high childish voice.

"I'll let you into a secret about Maggie if you swear not to tell. Swear."

"I swear."

"She wrote poison pen letters. She sent one to me."

Ursula's heart seemed to lurch. She said quickly:

"How do you know?"

"Because mine was typed on Grace Willison's typewriter and I actually saw Maggie typing it the evening before. The office door was ajar. She didn't know that I was watching."

"What did she say?"

"It was all about a man who is in love with me. One of the television producers actually. He wanted to divorce his wife and take me away with him. It made a great deal of fuss and jealousy at the hospital at the time. That's partly why I had to leave. As a matter of fact I could still go to him if I chose."

"But how did Maggie know?"

"She was a nurse, wasn't she? I think she knew one of the staff nurses at my old hospital. Maggie was clever at finding out things. I think she knew something about Victor Holroyd, too, but she didn't say what. I'm glad that she's dead. And if you had one of the letters, then you won't have any more now. Maggie's dead and the letters will stop. Brush a little harder and to the right Ursula. That's lovely, lovely. We ought to be friends, you and me. When the new patients start arriving we must stick together. That's if I decide to stay, of course."

Brush poised in mid-air, Ursula saw in the mirror the reflection of Jennie's sly, self-satisfied smile.

V

Shortly after ten o'clock, his supper eaten, Dalgliesh walked out into the night. The mist had lifted as mysteriously as it had appeared and the cool air, smelling of rain-washed grass, moved gently against his hot face. Standing in the absolute silence he could just hear the sibilant whisper of the sea.

A torch light, erratic as a will-o'-the-wisp, was weaving towards him from the direction of the Grange. Out of the darkness a bulky shadow emerged and took form. Millicent Hammitt had returned home. At the door of Faith Cottage she paused and called out to him.

"Goodnight, Commander. Your friends have left, then?"

Her voice was high, almost belligerent.

"The inspector has gone, yes."

"You may have noticed that I didn't join the rush to participate in Maggie's ill-considered charade. I have no taste for these excitements. Eric has decided to sleep tonight at Toynton Grange. Much the best thing for him, no doubt. But, as I understand that the police have taken away the body, he needn't pretend to over-sensitivity. Incidentally, we've voted for the Ridgewell Trust take-over. What with one thing and another, quite an eventful evening."

She turned to open the door. Then she paused and called out again. "They tell me that her nails were painted red."

"Yes, Mrs. Hammitt."

"Her toe nails, too."

He didn't reply. She said with sudden anger.

"Extraordinary woman!"

He heard the door close. A second later her light shone through the curtains. He went inside. Almost too weary to climb the stairs to bed, he stretched himself in Father Baddeley's chair staring into the dead fire. As he watched, the white ash shifted gently, a blackened spar of driftwood glowed momentarily into life, and he heard for the first time that night the familiar and comforting moan of the wind in the chimney. And then there followed another familiar sound. Faintly through the wall came a merry syncopated jingle. Millicent Hammitt had turned on the television.

8

The Black Tower

I

Next day Dalgliesh walked up to the Grange to explain to Wilfred that he must now stay on at Hope Cottage until after the inquest, and to pay his token rent. He found Wilfred alone in the business room. Surprisingly, there was no sign of Dot Moxon. Wilfred was studying a map of France spread out on the desk. A bundle of passports in a rubber band weighed down one corner. He seemed hardly to hear what his guest said. He replied "The inquest. Yes, of course," as if it were a forgotten luncheon engagement, then bent again over the map. He made no mention of Maggie's death and Dalgliesh's formal condolences were coldly received as if they were in poor taste. It was as if by divesting himself of Toynton Grange, he had detached himself from further responsibility, even from concern. Now nothing remained but his twin obsessions, his miracle and the pilgrimage to Lourdes.

Inspector Daniel and the forensic laboratory worked quickly. The inquest was held exactly one week after Maggie's death, a week in which the inhabitants of Toynton Grange seemed as resolutely determined to keep out of Dalgliesh's way as he was to avoid them. No one, not even Julius, showed any inclination to chat over Maggie's death. It was as if they saw him now merely as a police officer, an unwelcome intruder of uncertain allegiance, a potential spy. He drove away from Toynton Head early every morning and returned late each night to darkness and silence. Neither the police activities nor the life at Toynton Grange touched him. He continued his daily, compulsive exploration of Dorset like a prisoner on licence and looked forward to the inquest as the final day of release.

It came at last. None of the patients from Toynton Grange

attended except Henry Carwardine, surprisingly since he was not required to give evidence. As the company stood in whispering reverential groups outside the courthouse in the usual disorganized hiatus which follows attendance at the more sombre public rituals, he wheeled his chair with vigorous thrusts of the arms to where Dalgliesh stood. He looked and sounded euphoric.

"I realize that these ceremonial tidying up of legal loose ends aren't exactly a novelty to you as they are to me. But this one wasn't without interest, I thought. Less fascinating technically and forensically than Holroyd's, but with more human interest."

"You sound like a connoisseur of inquests."

"If we go on like this at Toynton Grange I soon shall be. Helen Rainer was the star turn today, I thought. That extraordinary suit and hat in which she chose to appear were, I take it, the dress uniform of a state registered nurse. A very wise choice. Hair up; the merest trace of make-up; a general air of dedicated professionalism. 'Mrs. Hewson may have believed that there was a relationship between me and her husband. She had too much free time to brood. Naturally Dr. Hewson and I have to work closely together. I have a high opinion of his kindness and competence but there has never been anything improper between us. Dr. Hewson was devoted to his wife.' Nothing improper! I never believed that people actually used that expression."

Dalgliesh said:

"At inquests they do. Did the jury believe her, do you suppose?"

"Oh, I think so, don't you? Difficult to imagine our lady with the lamp garbed as she was this afternoon in grey samite—gabardine anyway—mystic, wonderful, romping between the sheets. She was wise I think to admit that she and Hewson had spent the meditation hour together in her room. But that, as she explained, was because both had already come to their decision and couldn't afford to waste sixty minutes mulling it over when they had so much to discuss professionally together."

"They had to choose between their alibi for what it was worth, and the risk to reputation. On the whole they chose wisely."

Henry swung round his wheelchair with aggressive exuberance.

"It rather foxed the honest jurymen of Dorset, though. You could see the way their minds were working. If they aren't lovers why were they closeted together? But if they were together, then

Hewson couldn't have killed his wife. But unless they were lovers he wouldn't have had a motive for murdering his wife. But if he had such a motive, why admit that they were together? Obviously to give him an alibi. But he wouldn't need an alibi if he hadn't the usual motive. And if he had such a motive, then he and the girl would have been together. Very puzzling."

Mildly amused, Dalgliesh asked:

"What did you think about Hewson's performance?"

"He did well too. Not quite the professional competence and detachment of yourself, my dear Commander, but quiet, sincere, some natural grief bravely under control. Sensible of him to admit that Maggie desperately wanted him to leave Toynton Grange but that he felt an obligation to Wilfred, 'who took me on when I wasn't finding it easy to get a job'. No mention, of course, of being struck off the Medical Register and no one tactless enough to bring it up."

Dalgliesh said:

"And no one tactless enough to suggest that he and Helen may have been lying about their relationship."

"What else do you expect? What people know and what they can legally prove—or care to state in a court of law—are two very different things. Besides, we must at all costs protect dear Wilfred from the contamination of truth. No, I thought it went very well. Suicide while the balance of her mind, etc., etc. Poor Maggie! Stigmatized as a selfish, pleasure-seeking slut addicted to the bottle, out of sympathy with her husband's dedication to his noble profession and not even competent to make a comfortable home for him. Court's suggestion that it might have been an accidental death, play-acting which got out of hand, received no credence from the jury, did it? They took the view that a woman who drank the best part of a bottle of whisky, borrowed a rope and wrote a farewell letter was carrying play-acting a little far and did Maggie the compliment of believing that she intended what she did. I thought that the forensic scientist was extraordinarily definite in his opinion, given the basically subjective nature of document examination. There seems no doubt that Maggie did write the suicide note."

"The first four lines of it, which were all he felt competent to pronounce on. What did you think of the verdict?"

"Oh, I agree with Julius. She was planning to be cut down just in time amidst general hullabaloo. But with the best part of a bottle of whisky inside her she wasn't even competent to stage-manage her own resurrection. Incidentally, Julius gave me a graphic description of the drama in Charity Cottage, including Helen's impressive debut in the role of Lady Macbeth;

'Give me the syringe. The sleeping and the dead,
Are but as pictures; 'tis the eye of childhood
That fears a painted devil.'"

There was no expression on Dalgliesh's face or in his voice. He said:

"How entertaining for you both. It's a pity Court wasn't as detached at the time. He might have made himself useful instead of behaving like a hysterical queer."

Henry smiled, gratified to have provoked the response he wanted. He said:

"So you don't like him? Neither, I suspect, did your friend in holy orders."

Dalgliesh spoke on impulse:

"I know that this is nothing to do with me, but isn't it time that you got away from Toynton Grange?"

"Got away? To where do you suggest?"

"There must be other places."

"The world is full of places. But what do you suppose I could do, or be, or hope for in any of them? As a matter of fact, I did once plan to leave. It was a particularly foolish dream. No, I shall stay on at the Grange. The Ridgewell Trust have the professionalism and experience which Anstey lacks. I could do worse. Besides, Wilfred himself is to stay; and I still have a debt to pay Wilfred. In the meantime, this formality over, we can all relax and set off tomorrow to Lourdes in peace. You ought to come with us, Dalgliesh. You've hung around here so long that I suspect you rather enjoy our company. Besides, I don't think your convalescence has really done you a great deal of good. Why not come to Lourdes and see what the odour of incense and a change of scene can do for you?"

The Toynton Grange bus, driven by Philby, had drawn level with them now and the back ramp was being lowered. Dalgliesh watched in silence as Eric and Helen detached themselves from Wilfred, laid their hands simultaneously on the handle bars and wheeled Henry briskly into the bus. The ramp was raised, Wilfred took his seat in the front beside Philby, and the Toynton Grange bus disappeared from view.

Colonel Ridgewell and the trustees arrived after lunch. Dalgliesh watched as the car drew up and the sombre-suited party disappeared into the house. Later they emerged and walked with Wilfred over the headland towards the sea. Dalgliesh was a little surprised to see that Eric and Helen were with them but not Dorothy Moxon. He could see the Colonel's grey hair lifting in the breeze as he paused to swing his walking stick in wide explanatory sweeps or stood suddenly still conferring with the little group who quickly closed round him. No doubt, thought Dalgliesh, they would want to inspect the cottages. Well, Hope Cottage was ready for them. The book shelves were empty and dusted, the packing cases corded and labelled for the carrier, his suitcase packed except for the few things he needed on this his last night. But he had no wish to get involved in introductions or to stand making small talk.

When the party finally turned back and made their way towards Charity Cottage, he got into his car and drove off, with no clear direction in mind, no particular aim, no intention except to keep driving long into the night.

II

The next morning was airless and sultry, inducing headache, the sky a tent of stained calico ponderous with unspilt rain. The pilgrimage party was due to set out at nine o'clock and at half past eight Millicent Hammitt barged in, without a preliminary knock, to say goodbye. She was wearing a blue-grey tweed suit badly seated, with a short double-breasted jacket; a blouse in a harsher and discordant blue adorned with a garish brooch at the neck; brogues; and a grey felt hat pulled down to cover the ears. She dumped a bulging airline bag and her shoulder bag at her feet, drew on a pair of fawn cotton gloves and held out her hand. Dalgliesh put down his coffee cup. His right hand was grasped in a crushing grip.

"Goodbye then, Commander. Odd, but I've never really got used to using your Christian name. You'll be gone, I understand, by the time we return?"

"I plan to drive back to London later this morning."

"I hope you've enjoyed your stay. At least it has been eventful. One suicide, one natural death and the end of Toynton Grange as an independent institution. You can't have been bored."

"And one attempted murder."

"Wilfred in the burning tower? It sounds like the title of an *avant-garde* play. I've always had my doubts about that particular excitement. If you ask me, Wilfred set it up himself to justify handing over his responsibilities. No doubt that explanation occurred to you."

"Several explanations occurred to me but none of them made much sense."

"Little at Toynton Grange ever does. Well, the old order changeth yielding place to new and God fulfils Himself in many ways. We must hope that He will."

Dalgliesh asked if Millicent had any plans.

"I shall stay on in the cottage. Wilfred's agreement with the Trust stipulates that I may live there for life, and I assure you, I've every intention of dying at my own convenience. It won't be the same, of course, knowing that the place belongs to strangers."

Dalgliesh asked:

"How does your brother feel about the hand-over?"

"Relieved. Well, it's what he schemed for isn't it? He doesn't know what he's let himself in for, of course. Incidentally, he hasn't given this cottage to the Trust. This will continue to belong to him and he plans to move in after the place has been converted into something more civilized and comfortable. He's also offered to help at Toynton Grange in any capacity in which the Trust feel he can be of use. If he imagines that they'll let him stay on as warden he's in for a shock. They've got their own plans for the Grange and I doubt whether they include Wilfred, even if they have agreed to pander to his vanity by naming the home after him. I suppose Wilfred imagines that everyone will defer to him as their benefactor and the original owner. I can assure you they won't. Now that the deed of gift—or whatever it is—is signed and the Trust are the legal owners, Wilfred counts for as little as Philby, less probably. It's his own fault. He should have sold out completely."

"Wouldn't that have broken faith?"

"Superstitious nonsense! If Wilfred wanted to dress up in monk's garb and behave like a medieval abbot he should have applied for entry to a monastery. An Anglican one would have been perfectly respectable. The twice yearly pilgrimage will go on, of course. That's one of Wilfred's stipulations. It's a pity you aren't coming with us Commander. We stay at an agreeable little pension, really quite cheap and the food is excellent; and Lourdes is a cheerful little place. Quite an atmosphere. I don't say I wouldn't have preferred Wilfred to have had his miracle in Cannes, but it might have been worse. He could have got cured at Blackpool."

She paused at the door to turn and say:

"I expect the bus will stop here so that the others can take leave of you." She made it sound as if they would be conferring a privilege. Dalgliesh said that he would walk up with her and say goodbye at Toynton Grange. He had discovered one of Henry Carwardine's books on Father Baddeley's shelf and wanted to return it. There was also his bed linen to take back and some left-over tins of food which Toynton Grange could probably use.

"I'll take the tins later. Just leave them here. And you can return the linen any time. The Grange is never locked. Philby will be back later anyway. He only drives us to the port and sees us on the boat and then comes back to caretake and feed Jeoffrey and, of course, the hens. They're rather missing Grace's help with the hens although no one thought that she did anything very useful when she was alive. And it's not only the hens. They can't lay their hands on her list of the Friends. Actually, Wilfred wanted Dennis to stay at home this time. He's got one of his migraines and looks like death. But no one can make Dennis miss a pilgrimage."

Dalgliesh walked up to the Grange with her. The bus was drawn up outside the front door and the patients were already loaded. The pathetically depleted party had a bizarre air of slightly spurious joviality. Dalgliesh's first impression from their varied garb was that they proposed to pursue quite different and unrelated activities. Henry Carwardine, in a belted tweed coat and deerstalker hat, looked like an Edwardian gentleman on his way to the grouse moors. Philby, incongruously formal in a dark suit with high collar and black tie, was an undertaker's man loading a hearse. Ursula Hollis had dressed like a Pakistani immigrant in full fig whose only concession to the English climate was an ill-cut jacket in mock fur. Jennie Pegram, wearing a long blue headscarf, had apparently made an attempt to impersonate Saint Bernadette. Helen Rainer, dressed as she had been at the inquest, was a prison matron in charge of a group of unpredictable delinquents. She had already taken her seat at the head of Georgie Allan's stretcher. The boy's eyes were feverishly bright and Dalgliesh could hear his high frenetic chatter. He was wearing a blue and white striped woollen scarf and clutching an immense teddy bear, its neck adorned with pale blue ribbon and what, to Dalgliesh's astounded eyes, looked like a pilgrimage medal. The party could have been an oddly assorted party of team supporters on their way to a football match, but one, Dalgliesh thought, that hardly expected the home side to win.

Wilfred was gently fussing over the remainder of the luggage. He, Eric Hewson and Dennis Lerner were wearing their monk's habits. Dennis looked desperately ill, his face was taut with pain and his eyes half closed as if even the dull morning light were intolerable. Dalgliesh heard Eric whisper to him:

"For God's sake, Dennis, give up and stay at home! With two wheelchairs less we can perfectly well manage."

Lerner's high voice held a tinge of hysteria.

"I'll be all right. You know it never lasts more than twenty-four hours. For God's sake leave me alone!"

At last the medical paraphernalia, decently shrouded, was loaded, the ramp was raised, the rear door finally slammed and they were off. Dalgliesh waved in response to the frantically signalling hands and watched as the brightly painted bus lurched slowly over the headland looking, as it receded, as vulnerable and insubstantial as a child's toy. He was surprised, and a little saddened, that he could feel such pity and regret for people with whom he had taken such care not to become involved. He remained watching until the bus bumped slowly up the slope of the valley and finally tipped over the headland out of sight.

Now the headland was deserted, Toynton Grange and its cottages stood unlit and unpeopled under the heavy sky. It had grown darker in the last half hour. There would be a storm before midday. Already his head ached with the premonition of thunder. The headland lay in the sinister anticipatory calm of a chosen battlefield. He could just hear the thudding of the sea, less a noise than a vibration on the dense air like the sullen menace of distant guns.

Restless and perversely reluctant to leave now that he was at last free to go, he walked up to the gate to collect his paper and any letters. The bus had obviously stopped for the Toynton Grange post and there was nothing in the box but the day's copy of *The Times*, an official-looking buff envelope for Julius Court and a square white one addressed to Father Baddeley. Tucking the newspaper under his arm he split open the stout linen-backed envelope and began to walk back, reading on his way. The letter was written in a firm, strong masculine hand; the printed address was a Midlands deanery. The writer was sorry not to have replied earlier to Father Baddeley's letter but it had been posted on to him in Italy, where he had taken a locum post for the summer. At the end of the conventional enquiries, the methodical recording of family and diocesan concerns, the perfunctory and predictable comments on public affairs, came the answer to the mystery of Father Baddeley's summons:

"I went at once to visit your young friend, Peter Bonnington, but he had, of course, been dead for some months. I am so very sorry. In the circumstances there seemed little point in enquiring whether he had been happy at the new home or had really wanted to move from Dorset. I hope that his friend at Toynton Grange managed to visit before he died. On your other problem, I don't think I can offer much guidance. Our experience in the diocese where, as you know, we are particularly interested in young offenders, is that providing residential care for ex-prisoners whether in a home or in the kind of self-supporting hostel you envisage requires a great deal more capital than you have available. You could probably buy a small house even at today's prices, but at least two experienced staff would be needed initially and you would have to support the venture until it became established. But there are a number of existing hostels and organizations who would very much welcome your help. There certainly couldn't be a better use for your money, if you have decided, as you obviously have, that it ought not now to go to Toynton Grange. I think that you were wise to call in your policeman friend. I'm sure that he will be best able to advise you."

Dalgliesh almost laughed aloud. Here was an ironical, and fitting end to failure. So that was how it had begun! There had been nothing sinister behind Father Baddeley's letter, no suspected crime, no conspiracy, no hidden homicide. He had simply wanted, poor, innocent, unworldly old man, some professional advice on how to buy, equip, staff and endow a hostel for young ex-offenders for the sum of £19,000. Given the present state of the property market and the level of inflation, what he had needed was a financial genius. But he had written to a policeman, probably the only one he knew. He had written to an expert in violent death. And why not? To Father Baddeley all policemen were fundamentally alike, experienced in crime and familiar with criminals, dedicated to prevention as well as detection. And I, thought Dalgliesh bitterly, have done neither. Father Baddeley had wanted professional advice, not advice on how to deal with evil. There he had his own infallible guidelines; there he was at home. For some reason, almost certainly connected with the transfer of that young, unknown patient, Peter Bonnington, he had become disenchanted with Toynton Grange. He had wanted advice on how else to use his money. How typical of my arrogance, thought Dalgliesh, to suppose that he wanted me for anything more.

He stuffed the letter into his jacket pocket and strolled on, letting his eyes glance over the folded newspaper. An advertisement stood out as clearly as if it had been marked, familiar words leaping to the eye.

> "Toynton Grange. All our friends will wish to know that from the day of our return from the October Pilgrimage we shall be part of the larger family of the Ridgewell Trust. Please continue to remember us in your prayers at this time of change. As our list of friends has unfortunately been mislaid will all those who wish to keep in touch please write to me urgently.
>
> Wilfred Anstey, Warden."

Of course! The list of Toynton Grange Friends, unaccountably mislaid since Grace Willison's death, those sixty-eight names which Grace had known by heart. He stood stock still under the menacing sky and read the notice again. Excitement gripped him, as violently physical as a twist of the stomach, a surge of the blood. He knew with immediate, with heart-lifting certainty that here at last was the end of the tangled skein. Pull gently on this one fact and the thread would begin, miraculously, to run free.

If Grace Willison had been murdered, as he obstinately believed, post-mortem result notwithstanding, it had been because of something she knew. But it must have been vital information, knowledge which she alone possessed. One did not kill merely to silence intriguing but evidentially useless suspicions about where Father Baddeley had been on the afternoon of Holroyd's death. He had been in the black tower. Dalgliesh knew it and could prove it; Grace Willison might have known it too. But the shredded match and Grace's testimony taken together could prove nothing. With Father Baddeley dead, the worst anyone could do would be to point out that it was strange that the old priest hadn't mentioned seeing Julius Court walking over the headland. And Dalgliesh could imagine Julius's contemptuous, sardonic smile. A sick, tired old man, sitting with his book at the eastern window. Who could say now that he hadn't slept the hours away before making his way back to Toynton Grange across the headland while, on the beach unseen below, the rescue party toiled with their burden? With Father Baddeley dead, his testimony silenced, no police force in the world would re-open the case on that second-hand evidence. The worst harm Grace could have done to herself might have been to betray that Dalgliesh wasn't just convalescing at Toynton, that he too was suspicious. That betrayal might just have tipped the scales for her from life to death. Then she might have become too dangerous to let live. Not because she knew that Father Baddeley had been in the black tower on the afternoon of the 12th September, but because she possessed more specific, more valuable information. There was only one distribution list of the Friends of Toynton Grange and she could type it by heart. Julius had been present when she made that claim. The list could be torn up, burnt, utterly destroyed. But there was only one way in which those sixty-eight names could be erased from one frail woman's consciousness.

Dalgliesh quickened his pace. He found himself almost running down the headland. His headache seemed surprisingly to have lifted despite the lowering sky, the dense, storm-laden air. Change the metaphor, still trite but well proved. In this job it wasn't the last piece of jigsaw, the easiest of all, that was important. No, it was the neglected, uninteresting small segment which, slotted into place, suddenly made sense of so many other discarded pieces. Delusive colours, amorphous and ambiguous shapes came together as now to reveal the first recognizable outline of the finished picture.

And now, that piece in place, it was time to move the others speculatively over the board. For the present, forget proof, forget autopsy reports and the formal legal certainty of inquest verdicts; forget pride, the fear of ridicule, the reluctance to become involved. Get back to the first principle applied by any divisional detective constable when he smelt villainy on his patch. *Cui bono?* Who was living above his means? Who was in possession of more money than could reasonably be explained? There were two such people at Toynton Grange, and they were linked by Holroyd's death. Julius Court and Dennis Lerner. Julius who had said that his answer to the black tower was money and the solace it could buy; beauty, leisure, friends, travel. How could a legacy of £30,000, however cleverly invested, enable him to live as he lived now? Julius, who helped Wilfred with the accounts and knew better than anyone how precarious were the finances of Toynton Grange. Julius who never went to Lourdes because it wasn't his scene, but who took care to be at his cottage to give a welcome home party for the pilgrims. Julius who had been so untypically helpful when the pilgrimage bus had had an accident, driving immediately to the scene, taking charge, buying a new and specially adapted bus so that the pilgrimages could be independent. Julius, who had provided the evidence to clear Dennis Lerner from any suspicion of Holroyd's murder.

Dot had accused Julius of using Toynton Grange. Dalgliesh recalled the scene at Grace's death bed; Dot's outburst, the man's first incredulous look, the quick reactive spite. But what if he were using the place for a more specific purpose than to gratify the insidious pleasure of patronage and easy generosity. Using Toynton Grange. Using the pilgrimage. Scheming to preserve them both because both were essential to him.

And what of Dennis Lerner? Dennis, who stayed on at Toynton Grange being paid less than the normal wages and who could yet support his mother in an expensive nursing home. Dennis who resolutely overcame his fear so that he could go climbing with Julius. What better opportunity to meet and talk in absolute privacy without exciting suspicion? And how convenient that Wilfred had been frightened by the frayed rope into giving up rock climbing. Dennis, who could never bear to miss a pilgrimage even when as today, he could hardly stand with migraine. Dennis who was in charge of distributing the handcream and bath powder, who did most of the packing himself.

And it explained Father Baddeley's death. Dalgliesh had never been able to believe that his friend had been killed to prevent him disclosing that he hadn't glimpsed Julius walking over the headland on the afternoon of Holroyd's death. In the absence of clear proof that the old man hadn't, even momentarily, slumbered at his window, an allegation that Julius had lied, based on that evidence, would have been embarrassing perhaps but hardly dangerous. But what if Holroyd's death had been part of a larger and more sinister conspiracy? Then it might well have seemed necessary to snuff out—and how simply!—an obstinate, intelligent and ever-present watcher who could have been silenced in no other way once he smelt out the presence of evil. Father Baddeley had been taken to hospital before he learnt of Holroyd's death. But when he did learn, the significance of what he had so singularly failed to see must have struck him. He would have taken some action. And he had taken action. He had made a telephone call to London, to a number he had needed to look up. He had made an appointment with his murderer.

Dalgliesh walked quickly on, past Hope Cottage and, almost without conscious decision, to Toynton Grange. The heavy front door opened to his touch. He smelt again the slightly intimidating spicy smell, masking more sinister, less agreeable odours. It was so dark that he had at once to switch on the light. The hall blazed like an empty film set. The black and white chequered floor was dazzling to the eyes, a gigantic chess board, waiting for the pieces to move into place.

He paced through the empty rooms switching on the lights as he went. Room after room burst into brilliance. He found himself touching tables and chairs as he passed as if the wood were a talisman, looking intently around with the wary eye of a traveller returning unwelcomed to a deserted home. And his mind continued to shuffle the pieces of jigsaw. The attack on Anstey, the final and most dangerous attempt in the black tower. Anstey himself assumed that it was a final attempt to frighten him into selling out. But suppose it had had another purpose, not to close Toynton Grange but to make its future secure? And there was no other way, given Anstey's dwindling resources, than to pass it over to an organization financially sound and already well established. And Anstey hadn't sold out. Satisfied by the last, the most dangerous attack on him, that it couldn't have been the work of a patient and that his dream was still intact, he had given his inheritance away. Toynton Grange would go on. The pilgrimages would continue. Was that what someone—someone who knew only too well how financially precarious the home was—had always schemed for and intended?

Holroyd's visit to London. It was obvious that he had learnt something on that visit, had somehow acquired knowledge which had sent him back to Toynton Grange restless and elated. Was it also knowledge which had made him too dangerous to live? Dalgliesh had assumed that he had been told something by his solicitor, something perhaps about his own financial concerns or those of the Anstey family. But the visit to the solicitor hadn't been the main purpose of the trip. Holroyd and the Hewsons had also been to St. Saviour's hospital, the hospital where Anstey had been treated. And there, in addition to seeing the consultant in physical medicine with Holroyd, they had visited the medical records department. Hadn't Maggie said when she and Dalgliesh first met? "He never went back to St. Saviour's hospital so that they could record the miraculous cure on his medical record. It would have been rather a joke if he had." Suppose Holroyd had gained some knowledge in London but gained it, not directly, but through a confidence from Maggie Hewson given, perhaps, during one of their lonely periods together on the cliff edge. He remembered Maggie Hewson's words:

"I've said I won't tell. But if you keep on nagging about it I may change my mind." And then: "What if I did? He wasn't a fool you know. He could tell that something was up. And he's dead, dead, dead!" Father Baddeley was dead. But so was Holroyd. And so was Maggie. Was there any reason why Maggie had to die, and at that particular time?

But this was to go too fast. It was still all conjecture, all speculation. True, it was the only theory which fitted all the facts. But that wasn't evidence. He had still no proof that any of the deaths at Toynton Head had been murder. One fact was certain. If Maggie had been killed, then somehow she had been persuaded unwittingly to connive in her own death.

He became aware of a faint bubbling sound and detected the

pungent smell of grease and hot soap from the direction of the kitchen. The kitchen itself stank like a Victorian workhouse laundry. A pail of teacloths was simmering on the old-fashioned gas stove. In the bustle of departure Dot Moxon must have forgotten to turn off the gas. The grey linen was billowing above the dark evil-smelling scum, the gas plate was splattered with sponges of dried foam. He turned off the gas and the teacloths subsided into their murky bath. With the extinguishing plop of the flame the silence was suddenly intensified; it was as if he had turned off the last evidence of human life.

He moved on into the activity room. The work tops were shrouded with dust sheets. He could see the outline of the row of polythene bottles and the tins of bath powder waiting to be sieved and packed. Henry Carwardine's bust of Anstey still stood on its wooden plinth. It had been covered by a white plastic bag tied at the throat with what looked like one of Carwardine's old ties. The effect was peculiarly sinister; the nebulous features under the transparent shroud, the empty eye sockets, the sharp nose pointing the thin plastic made it as potent an image as a severed head.

In the office at the end of the annexe Grace Willison's desk still stood squarely under the north window, the typewriter under its grey cover. He pulled open the desk drawers. They were as he expected, immaculately tidy and ordered, banks of writing paper with Toynton Grange heading; envelopes carefully graded by size; typewriter ribbons; pencils; erasers; carbon paper still in its box; the sheets of perforated sticky labels on which she had typed the names and addresses of the Friends. Only the bound list of names was missing, the list of sixty-eight addresses; one of them in Marseilles. And here typed in that book and imprinted on Miss Willison's mind had been the vital link in the chain of greed and death.

The heroin had travelled far before it was finally packed at the bottom of a tin of bath powder in Toynton Grange. Dalgliesh could picture each stage of that journey as clearly as if he had travelled it himself. The fields of opium poppies on the high Anatolian plateau, the bulging pods oozing their milky sap. The secret rendering down of the raw opium into base morphine even before it left the hills. The long journey by mule train, rail, road or air towards Marseilles, one of the main distribution ports of the world. The refinement into pure heroin in one of a dozen clandestine laboratories. And then, the arranged rendezvous among the crowds at Lourdes, perhaps at Mass, the package slipped quickly into the waiting hand. He remembered wheeling Henry Carwardine across the headland on his first evening at Toynton, the thick rubber handgrips twisting beneath his hand. How simple to wrench one off, to insert a small plastic bag into the hollow strut, its drawstring taped to the metal. The whole operation would take less than a minute. And there would be plenty of opportunity. Philby didn't go on the pilgrimages. It would be Dennis Lerner who would have charge of the wheelchairs. What safer way for a drug smuggler to pass through customs than as the member of a recognized and respected pilgrimage. And the subsequent arrangements had been equally foolproof. The suppliers would need to know in advance the date of each pilgrimage, just as the customers and distributors would need to be told when the next consignment would come in. How more easily than by means of an innocuous newsletter from a respectable charity, a newsletter despatched so conscientiously and so innocently each quarter by Grace Willison.

And Julius's testimony in a French court, the alibi for a murderer. Had that been, not a reluctant yielding to blackmail, not a payment for services rendered, but payment in advance for services to come? Or had Julius, as Bill Moriarty's informant suggested, given Michonnet his alibi with no other motive than a perverse pleasure in thwarting the French police, gratuitously obliging a powerful family and causing his superiors the maximum of embarrassment? Possibly. He might neither have expected nor wanted any other reward. But if one were offered? If it were tactfully made known to him that a certain commodity could be supplied in strictly limited quantities if he could find a way to smuggle it into England? Would he later have been able to resist the temptation of Toynton Grange and its six-monthly pilgrimage?

And it was so easy, so simple, so foolproof. And so incredibly profitable. What was illegal heroin fetching now? Something like £4,000 an ounce. Julius had no need to deal in bulk or complicate his distribution arrangements beyond the one or two trusted agents to make himself secure for life. Ten ounces brought in each time would buy all the leisure and beauty that any man could desire. And with the Ridgewell Trust take-over the future was secure. Dennis Lerner would keep his job. The pilgrimages would continue. There would be other homes open to his exploitation, other pilgrimages. And Lerner was completely in his power. Even if the newsletter was discontinued and the home no longer needed to pack and sell its handcream and powder, the heroin would still come in. The arrangements for notification and distribution were a minor matter of logistics compared with the fundamental problem of getting the drug safely, reliably and regularly through the port.

There was as yet no proof. But with luck, and if he were right, there would be in three days' time. He could telephone the local police now and safely leave it to them to contact the central drug control branch. Better still, he could telephone Inspector Daniel and arrange to call in to see him on his way back to London. Secrecy was essential. There must be no risk of suspicion. It would take only one telephone call to Lourdes to cancel this consignment and leave him again with nothing but a hotchpotch of half-formulated suspicions, coincidences, unsubstantiated allegations.

The nearest telephone, he remembered, was in the dining-room. It had an external line, and he saw that this had been switched through to the exchange. But when he lifted the receiver, the line was dead. He felt the usual momentary irritation that an instrument, taken for granted, should be reduced to a ridiculous and useless lump of plastic and metal, and reflected that a house with a dead telephone seemed always so much more isolated than one with no telephone at all. It was interesting, perhaps even significant, that the line was silent. But it didn't matter. He would get on his way and hope to find Inspector Daniel at police headquarters. At this stage when his theory was still little more than conjecture he was reluctant to talk to anyone else. He replaced the receiver. A voice from the doorway said:

"Having difficulty, Commander?"

Julius Court must have stepped through the house as delicately as a cat. He stood now, one shoulder resting lightly against the door post, both hands deep in his jacket pockets. The assumption of ease was deceptive. His body, poised on the balls of his feet as if to spring, was rigid with tension. The face above the high rolled collar of his sweater was as skeletal and defined as a carving, the muscles taut under the flushed skin. His eyes unblinking, unnaturally bright, were fixed on Dalgliesh with the speculative intentness of a gambler watching the spinning balls.

Dalgliesh said calmly:

"It's out of order apparently. It doesn't matter. My housekeeper will expect me when she sees me."

"Do you usually roam about other people's houses to make your private calls? The main telephone is in the business room. Didn't you know?"

"I doubt whether I should have been any luckier."

They looked at each other, silent in the greater silence. Across the length of the room Dalgliesh could recognize and follow the process of his adversary's thought as plainly as if it were registering visibly on a graph, the black needle tracing the pattern of decision. There was no struggle. It was the simple weighing of probabilities.

When Julius at last drew his hand slowly out of his pocket it was almost with relief that Dalgliesh saw the muzzle of the Luger. The die was cast. Now there was no going back, no more pretence, no more uncertainty.

Julius said quietly:

"Don't move, I'm an excellent shot. Sit down at the table. Hands on the top. Now, tell me how you found me out. I'm assuming that you have found me out. If not, then I've miscalculated. You will die and I shall be put to a great deal of trouble and inconvenience and we'll both be aggrieved to know that it wasn't after all necessary."

With his left hand Dalgliesh took Father Baddeley's letter from his jacket pocket and slid it across the table.

"This will interest you. It came this morning addressed to Father Baddeley."

The grey eyes did not move from his.

"Sorry. I'm sure it's fascinating but I have my mind on other matters. You read it to me."

"It explains why he wanted to see me. You needn't have worried to concoct the poison pen letter or destroy his diary. His problem had nothing to do with you. Why kill him anyway? He was in the tower when Holroyd died; he knew perfectly well that he hadn't slept, that you hadn't come over the headland. But was that knowledge dangerous enough to snuff him out?"

"It was, in Baddeley's hands. The old man had a deep-rooted

instinct for what he would describe as evil. That meant he had a deep-rooted suspicion of me, particularly of what he saw as my influence over Dennis. We were playing out our private comedy on a level which I don't think the procedures of the Metropolitan Police would recognize. It could only have one end. He telephoned me at my London flat from the hospital three days before he was discharged and asked me to come to see him on 26th September after nine o'clock. I went prepared. I drove down from London and left the Mercedes in that hollow behind the stone wall off the coast road. I took one of the habits from the business room while they were all at dinner. Then I walked to Hope Cottage. If anyone had seen me, then I should have had to change my plan. But no one did. He was sitting alone by the dying fire waiting for me. I think he knew about two minutes after I entered that I would kill him. There wasn't even a flicker of surprise when I pressed the plastic against his face. Plastic, you note. It wouldn't leave any telltale threads in the nostrils or windpipe. Not that Hewson would have noticed, poor fool. Baddeley's diary was on the table and I took it away with me just in case he'd made any incriminating entries. Just as well. He had, I discovered, a tedious habit of recording precisely where he'd been and when. But I didn't break into the bureau. I didn't need to. You can put that little peccadillo down to Wilfred. He must have been frantic to get his eyes on the old man's will. Incidently, I never found your postcard and I suspect Wilfred looked no further once he'd found the will. Probably the old man tore it up. He disliked keeping trifles. Afterwards I went back and slept in some discomfort in the car. Next morning I rejoined the London road and arrived here when all the excitement was over. I saw in the diary that he had invited an A.D. to stay and that the visitor was expected on the first of October. It struck me as a bit odd. The old man didn't have visitors. So I planted the poison pen letter the evening before, just in case Baddeley had confided that something was on his mind. I must say, it was a bit disconcerting to discover that the mysterious A.D. was you, my dear Commander. Had I known, I might have tried for a little more subtlety."

"And the stole? He was wearing his stole."

"I should have removed it, but one can't remember everything. You see, he didn't believe I was protecting Dennis to save Wilfred grief or out of kindness to Dennis. He knew me too well. When he accused me of corrupting Dennis, of using Toynton for some purpose of my own, I said that I would tell him the truth, that I wanted to make my confession. He must have known in his heart that this was death, that I was only amusing myself. But he couldn't take the risk. If he refused to take me seriously, then all his life would have been a lie. He hesitated for just two seconds, then he put the stole round his neck."

"Didn't he even give you the gratification of a flicker of fear?"

"Oh, no! Why should he? We were alike in one thing. Neither of us feared death. I don't know where Baddeley thought he was going as he just had time to make that last archaic sign of his allegiance, but wherever it was he apparently saw nothing to fear. Neither do I. I know just as certainly as he did what will follow my death. Annihilation. It would be unreasonable to fear that. I'm not so unreasonable. Once you have lost the fear of death—absolutely lost it—then all other fears are meaningless. Nothing can touch you. All that is necessary is to keep the means of death to hand. Then one is invulnerable. I apologize for the fact that, in my case, it has to be a gun. I do realize that at the moment I look melodramatic, ridiculous. But I can't fancy killing myself any other way. Drowning? That onrush of suffocating water? Drugs? Some interfering fool might drag me back. Besides, I do fear that shadow land between life and death. A knife? Messy and uncertain. There are three bullets here, Dalgliesh. One for you, and two, in case they should be needed, for me."

"If you trade in death as you do, it's as well no doubt to come to terms with it."

"Everyone who takes hard drugs wants to die. You know that as well as I do. There is no other way they can do it with so little inconvenience and so much profit to others, and with such pleasure to themselves, at least initially."

"And Lerner? I suppose you paid his mother's nursing home fees. What are they, about £200 a month? You got him cheap. Even so, he must have known what he was bringing in."

"Will be bringing in, three days from now. Will go on bringing in. I told him that it was cannabis, a perfectly harmless drug; one which an over-sensitive government have chosen to make illegal but which my London friends happen to fancy and are prepared to pay highly for. He chooses to believe me. He knows the truth, but he won't admit to himself that he knows. That's reasonable, sensible, a necessary self-deception. It's how we all manage to go on living. You must know that your job is a dirty job, crooks catching crooks, and that you waste your intelligence by doing it. But it wouldn't exactly add to your peace of mind to admit the fact. And if you ever chuck it, you won't give that as your reason. Are you going to chuck it, by the way? Somehow I've gained the impression that you might be."

"That shows some discernment. I did have it in mind. But not now."

The decision to go on, arrived at when and why Dalgliesh didn't know, seemed to him as irrational as the decision to give up. It wasn't a victory. A kind of defeat even. But there would be time enough, if he lived, to analyse the vicissitudes of that personal conflict. Like Father Baddeley, a man lived and died as he had to. He heard Julius's amused voice.

"A pity. But as this seems likely to be your last job, why not tell me how you found me out."

"Is there time? I don't relish spending my last five minutes in a recital of professional incompetence. It won't give me any satisfaction and I don't see why I should gratify your curiosity."

"No. But it's more in your interests than mine. Oughtn't you to be playing for time? Besides, if it's fascinating enough I might relax my guard, might give you a chance to pounce or fling a chair at me or whatever they train you to do in this kind of situation. Or somebody may come, or I may even change my mind."

"Will you?"

"No."

"Then gratify my curiosity. I can guess about Grace Willison. You killed her in the same way you killed Father Baddeley once you decided that I was getting dangerously suspicious, because she could type by heart the list of Friends, the list which included your distributors. But Maggie Hewson, why did she have to die?"

"Because of something she knew. Haven't you guessed that? I've over-estimated you. She knew that Wilfred's miracle was a delusion. I drove the Hewsons and Victor to London for his appointment at St. Saviour's hospital. Eric and Maggie went to the medical records department to have a look at Wilfred's folder. I suppose they wanted to gratify a natural professional curiosity while they were there. They discovered that he'd never had disseminated sclerosis, that his latest tests had shown that it was a wrong diagnosis. All he'd suffered from was hysterical paralysis. But I must be shocking you, my dear Commander. You're a pseudo-scientist, aren't you? It must be hard for you to accept that medical technology can err."

"No. I believe in the possibility of a wrong diagnosis."

"Wilfred, apparently, doesn't share your healthy scepticism. He never returned to the hospital for his next check-up, so no one bothered to write to him about their little mistake. Why should they? But it was knowledge that the two Hewsons couldn't keep to themselves. They told me, and subsequently Maggie must have told Holroyd. He probably guessed on the drive back to Toynton that something was up. I tried to bribe her with whisky to keep the knowledge to herself—she actually believed in my solicitude for dear Wilfred—and it worked until Wilfred excluded her from the decision on the future of the home. She was furious. She told me that she planned to burst into the last session at the end of the meditation and publicly proclaim the truth. I couldn't risk that. It was the one fact, the only fact, that could have made him sell out. It would have stopped the hand-over to the Ridgewell Trust. Toynton Grange and the pilgrimage had to go on.

"She wasn't really looking forward to the fracas that would follow breaking the news and it was easy enough to persuade her to leave the party at Toynton Grange to indulge their various reactions to her news and escape up to town with me immediately afterwards. I suggested that she should leave a deliberately ambiguous note, one which could be read as a threat of suicide. Then she could return to Toynton if and when she felt like it and see how Eric was reacting as a presumptive widower. It was the kind of histrionic gesture which appealed to dear Maggie. It got her out of an awkward situation here, provided the maximum of worry and inconvenience to Wilfred and Eric, and provided her with a free holiday in my London flat and the prospect of plenty of excitement if and when she chose to return. She even volunteered to fetch the rope herself. We sat there drinking together until she was too fuddled to suspect me but still sober enough to write the note. The last scrawled lines, the reference to the black tower, were, of course, added by me."

"So that was why she was bathed and dressed."

"Of course. Tarted up to make an effective entrance at Toynton Grange, and also I flatter myself, to impress me. I was gratified that I ranked clean underclothes and painted toe nails. I don't know what precisely she thought I had in mind for us when we reached London. Dear Maggie was never quite in touch with reality. To pack her contraceptive was perhaps more optimistic than discreet. But she may have had her plans. The dear girl was certainly delirious at the thought of leaving Toynton. She died happy I assure you."

"And, before leaving the cottage, you gave the signal with the light."

"I had to have some excuse for turning up and finding the body. It seemed prudent to add verisimilitude. Someone might have looked out of a window and been able to confirm my story. I didn't bargain for it being you. Finding you here busily doing your boy scout turn gave me a bad moment. And you were remarkably obstinate about not leaving the body."

It must have been almost as bad a moment, thought Dalgliesh, as finding Wilfred so nearly choked to death. There had been nothing faked about Julius's terror either then or after Maggie's death. He asked:

"And was Holroyd pushed over the cliff for the same reason, to stop him talking?"

Julius laughed:

"Now this will amuse you; a delicious irony. I didn't even know that Maggie had confided in Holroyd until I challenged her with it after his death. And Dennis never knew. Holroyd began taunting Dennis as he usually did. Dennis was more or less inured to it and merely moved with his book a little way apart. Then Holroyd began on a more sinister line of torment. He began shouting at Dennis. He wondered what Wilfred would say when he learned that his precious pilgrimages were a fraud, that Toynton Grange itself was founded on a lie. He told Dennis to make the most of the next pilgrimage; it would certainly be the last. Dennis panicked; he thought that Holroyd had discovered about the drug smuggling. He didn't pause to ask himself how in the hell Holroyd could have found out. He told me afterwards that he couldn't even remember scrambling to his feet, releasing the brakes and hurling the chair forward. But he did, of course. There was no one else to do it. It couldn't have landed where it did if it hadn't gone over the cliff with considerable force. I was on the beach beneath them when Holroyd came over. One of the irritating things about that murder was that I've never received any sympathy for the traumatic experience of having Holroyd smashed to death only twenty yards from me. I hope you will give it to me now."

Dalgliesh reflected that the murder must have been doubly convenient for Julius. It removed Holroyd and his dangerous knowledge; it put Dennis Lerner finally in his power. He said:

"And you disposed of the two side pieces of the wheelchair while Lerner was fetching help."

"About fifty yards away, down a deep cleft between two rocks. It seemed, at the time, a sensible way of complicating the case. Without the brakes no one could be sure that it wasn't an accident. On reflection I should have left well alone and let it be assumed that Holroyd killed himself. Essentially he did. That's what I've persuaded Dennis."

Dalgliesh asked:

"What are you going to do now?"

"Put a bullet in your head, conceal your body in your own car and get rid of both together. It's a trite method of murder I know, but I understand that it works."

Dalgliesh laughed. He was surprised that the sound could be so spontaneous.

"You propose to drive about sixty miles, I take it, in an easily identifiable car with the murdered body of a Commander of the Metropolitan Police in the boot—his own boot incidentally. A number of men of my acquaintance in the maximum security wings of Parkhurst and Durham would admire your nerve even while not exactly relishing the prospect of welcoming you to their company. They're a quarrelsome, uncivilized bunch. I don't think you're going to have a lot in common."

"I shall be at risk. But you'll be dead."

"Of course. So in effect will you from the moment the bullet enters my body, unless you count a life sentence as living. Even if you try to fake finger prints on the trigger, they'll know that I was murdered. I'm not the type to kill myself or to drive my car into remote woods and quarries to put a bullet in my brain. And the forensic evidence will give the lab a field day."

"If they find your body. How long before they even begin looking? Three weeks?"

"They'll be looking hard. If you can think of a suitable spot to dump me and the car, so can they. Don't assume that the police can't read an ordnance survey. And how do you propose to get back here? By picking up a train at Bournemouth or Winchester? By hitch-hiking, hiring a bicycle, walking through the night? You can hardly travel on to London by train, and pretend that you joined the train at Wareham. It's a small station and you're known there. Going or returning, you'll be remembered."

Julius said consideringly:

"You're right, of course. Then it means the cliffs. They must fish you out of the sea."

"With a bullet in my head? Or are you expecting me to walk over the cliff edge to suit your convenience? You could try physical force, of course, but then you'll have to come dangerously close, close enough for a fight. We're fairly evenly matched. I take it you don't intend to be dragged over with me? Once they find my body and that bullet, then you're finished. The trail begins here remember. I was last seen alive when the Toynton Grange bus left, and there's no one here but we two."

It was then that, simultaneously, they heard the distant slam of the front door. The sound, sharp as a gunshot, was followed by the thud of footsteps, heavy and firm, crossing the front hall.

III

Julius said quickly:

"Call out, and I kill you both. Stand to the left of the door."

The footsteps were crossing the central hall now unnaturally loud in the eerie silence. Both men held their breath. Philby stood in the doorway.

He saw the gun immediately. His eyes widened and then blinked rapidly. He looked from one man to the other. When he spoke he sounded hoarse, apologetic. He spoke directly to Dalgliesh like a child explaining a misdemeanour:

"Wilfred sent me back early. Dot thought she'd left the gas on."

His eyes turned again to Julius. This time the terror was unmistakable. He said "Oh, no!" Almost instantaneously, Julius fired. The crack of the revolver, although expected, was still shattering, still unbelievable. Philby's body stiffened, rocked, then fell backward like an axed tree with a crash which shook the room. The bullet had gone in precisely between the eyes. Dalgliesh knew that this was where Julius had intended it to go; that he had used this necessary killing to demonstrate that he knew how to use his gun. This had been target practice. He said calmly, his gun now turned on Dalgliesh again:

"Go over to him."

Dalgliesh bent by the dead man. The eyes still seemed to hold their last look of wild surprise. The wound was a neat grumous slit in the low heavy forehead, so unremarkable that it could have been used for a forensic ballistics demonstration of the effect of discharge at six feet. There were no powder marks, as yet little blood, only the soiling of the skin by the spin of the bullet. It was a precise, almost decorative stigma giving no clue to the destructive tumult within.

Julius said:

"That settles the score for my smashed marble. Is there an exit wound?"

Gently Dalgliesh turned the heavy head.

"No. You must have hit a bone."

"That's what I intended. Two bullets left. But this is a bonus, Commander. You were wrong about my being the last person to see you alive. I shall drive away to establish my alibi and, in the eyes of the police, the last person to see you alive will have been Philby, a criminal with a propensity to violence. Two bodies in the sea with bullet wounds. A pistol, licensed, I may say, stolen from my bedside drawer. Let the police concoct a theory to explain that. It shouldn't be difficult. Is there any blood?"

"Not yet. There will be. But not much."

"I'll remember that. It will be easy enough to wipe it from this linoleum. Get that plastic hood from Carwardine's bust of Wilfred and tie it over his head. Use his own tie. And hurry. I shall be just six paces behind you. And if I get impatient I might feel it worthwhile doing my own work."

Hooded with white plastic, his wound a third eye, Philby was transformed into an inert guy, its bulging body grotesquely stuffed into a dapper undersized suit, its tie askew under the clownish features. Julius said:

"Now get one of the lighter wheelchairs."

He motioned Dalgliesh once again towards the workroom and followed, always a careful six feet behind. Three folded chairs were standing against the wall. Dalgliesh prized one open and wheeled it in beside the body. There would be finger prints to find here. But what did they prove? This might even be the chair in which he had wheeled Grace Willison.

"Now get him into it."

As Dalgliesh hesitated he said, allowing his voice a trace of controlled impatience:

"I don't want to have to manage two bodies alone. But I can if I need to. There's a hoist in the bathroom. If you can't lift him unaided, then get it. But I thought they taught policemen useful little knacks like this."

Dalgliesh managed without the hoist. But it wasn't easy. The wheel brakes slid on the linoleum and it took more than two minutes before the heavy, unresponsive body slumped back against the canvas. Dalgliesh had succeeded in gaining some time but at a cost; he had lost strength. He knew that he would stay alive just as long as his mind with its store of dreadfully appropriate experience, and his physical strength could be used by Julius. It would be inconvenient for Julius to have to carry two bodies to the cliff edge, but it could be done. Toynton Grange had facilities for moving inert bodies. At present Dalgliesh was less of an encumbrance alive than dead, but the margin was dangerously narrow; there was no sense in reducing it further. The optimum moment for action would come, and it would come for both of them. Both of them were waiting for it, Dalgliesh to attack, Julius to shoot. Both knew the cost of a mistake in recognizing that moment. Two bullets left and he had to ensure that neither of them ended in his body. And as long as Julius kept his distance and held the gun he was inviolable. Somehow Dalgliesh had to draw him close enough for physical contact. Somehow he had to divert that concentration if only for a fraction of a second.

Julius said:

"And now we'll take a walk together to Toynton Cottage."

He still kept his careful distance behind as Dalgliesh wheeled the chair with its grotesque burden down the ramp of the front door and across the headland. The sky was a grey suffocating blanket pressing down on them. The close air was harsh and metallic on the tongue and smelt as strong as rotting seaweed. In the half-light the pebbles on the path glittered like semi-precious stones. Half way across the headland Dalgliesh heard a high querulous wail and, looking back, saw that Jeoffrey was following them, tail erect. The cat padded behind Julius for another fifty yards and then, as unpredictably as he had appeared, turned tail and made off for home. Julius, his unblinking eyes on Dalgliesh's back, seemed to notice neither his arrival nor his departure. They walked on in silence. Philby's head had fallen back, his neck collared by the canvas of the chair. His cyclops wound, gummed to the plastic, stared into Dalgliesh's face in what seemed mute reproach. The path was dry. Looking down Dalgliesh saw that the wheels made only an imperceptible thread on the patches of dry turf and the dusty, gritty path. And behind him he could hear Julius's shoes scuffing the marks into oblivion. There would be no useful evidence left here.

And now they stood on the stone patio. It seemed to shake under their feet with the thunder of the waves as if earth and sea anticipated the coming storm. But the tide was ebbing. No curtain of spray rose between them and the cliff edge. Dalgliesh knew that it was the moment of great danger. He made himself laugh aloud, and wondered whether the sound rang as false to Julius's ears as it did to his own.

"Why so amused?"

"It's easy to see that your killing is normally done at a distance, a commercial transaction merely. You propose to hurl us into the sea at your own back door, a broad enough hint for even the stupidest detective constable. And they won't be putting stupid officers on this crime. Your cleaning woman is expected this morning isn't she? And this is one part of the coast with a beach, even at high tide. I thought you wanted to delay discovery of the bodies."

"She won't come out here. She never does."

"How do you know what she does when you aren't here? She may shake the dusters over the cliff. It may even be her habit to paddle. But have it your own way. I'm merely pointing out that your only hope of success—and I don't rate it high—is to delay discovery of our bodies. No one will start looking for Philby until the pilgrimage returns in three days' time. If you get rid of my car it will be even longer before they start looking for me. That gives you opportunity to dispose of this consignment of heroin before the hunt is up, assuming you still intend to let Lerner bring it in. But don't let me interfere."

Julius's hand on the gun did not waver. As if considering a proposition for a picnic site, he said:

"You're right, of course. You ought to go into deep water and further along the coast. The best place is the black tower. The sea will be still washing the cliffs there. We've got to get him to the tower."

"How? He must weigh over twelve stone. I can't push him unaided up the cliff edge. You'll hardly be much help if you walk behind with a gun in my back. And what about wheel marks?"

"The rain will finish those. And we shan't go up the headland. We'll drive along the coast road and approach the tower over the cliff as we did when we rescued Anstey. Once the couple of you are in the boot of the car I'll watch for Mrs. Reynolds through my glasses. She cycles in from Toynton village, and she's always exactly on time. We ought to plan to meet her just outside the boundary gate. I'll stop and let her know that I shan't be back for dinner. That pleasant minute of ordinary conversation should impress the coroner if they ever get your bodies to an inquest. And eventually, the tedious business over, I'll drive off to Dorchester for an early luncheon."

"With the wheelchair and the plastic hood in the boot?"

"With the chair and the hood locked in the boot. I shall establish an alibi for the whole of today and return to Toynton Grange this evening. And I shan't forget to wash the plastic hood before replacing it, dust the chair to remove your prints and examine the floor for blood-stains. And, of course, retrieve the cartridge case. Were you hoping I would overlook that? Don't worry, Commander. I do realize that, by then, I'll be planning without your valuable assistance, but thanks to you, I shall have a day or two to work out the details. One of two sophistications attract me. I'm wondering if I could make use of the smashed marble. Couldn't that be worked in to provide the motive for Philby's murderous attack on you?"

"I should keep it simple."

"Perhaps you're right. My first two murders were models of simplicity and none the worse for it. Now get him into the boot of the Mercedes. It's parked at the back. But first through into the scullery. You'll find two sheets in the washing machine. Take the one from the top. I don't want fibres and shoe dust in the car."

"Won't Mrs. Reynolds notice that one is missing?"

"She washes and irons tomorrow. A woman of strict routine. By this evening I shall have replaced it. Don't waste time."

Julius's mind must be registering every second, thought Dalgliesh, yet his voice betrayed no anxiety. Not once did he glance at his watch, or even at the clock on the kitchen wall. He kept his eyes and the muzzle of the Luger on his victim. Somehow that concentration had to be broken. And the time was running out.

The Mercedes was parked outside the stone garage. Under Julius's direction Dalgliesh raised the unlocked lid of the boot and spread the creased sheet over the floor. It was an easy matter to tumble Philby's body from the wheelchair. Dalgliesh folded the chair and placed it on top of the body. Julius said:

"Now get in beside him."

Could this be the best opportunity, the last opportunity even, to act; here outside Julius's own cottage with the murdered man in his car and the evidence plain? But plain to whom? Dalgliesh knew that if he sprang on Julius now he would gain nothing but a second's release from frustration and anger before the bullet hit him. Two bodies instead of one would be driven to the black tower and tumbled into deep water. In his mind's eye he could see Julius poised in solitary triumph on the edge of the cliff, the gun curving through the air like a falling bird to cleave the tumbling waves, beneath which two bodies were being torn and tugged by the ebbing tide. The plan would go ahead. A little more tedious, taking longer since there would be two bodies to wheel unaided across the headland. But who was there to prevent it? Certainly not Mrs. Reynolds even now cycling along the road from Toynton village. And if she suspected, if she even mentioned casually when she dismounted to greet Julius on the road that she had heard what sounded like a shot? Then there were still two bullets left in the gun. And he was no longer sure that Julius was sane.

But there was at least something he could do at this moment, something he had planned to do. But it wasn't going to be easy. He had hoped that, for a couple of seconds at least, the raised lid of the boot would have partly screened him from Julius's view. But Julius was standing immediately behind the car; Dalgliesh was in full view. But there was one advantage. The grey eyes never flickered, dared not flicker from his face. If he were quick and cunning, if he were lucky, he might bring it off. He placed his hands as if casually on his hips. He could feel the slight weight of his thin leather wallet in his back trouser pocket lying curved against his buttock. Julius said with dangerous quietness:

"I said get in on top of him. I'm not risking driving with you any closer."

Dalgliesh's right thumb and forefinger twisted at the pocket button. Thank God the button hole was reasonably loose. He said:

"Then you'd better drive fast unless you want to have a corpse dead of suffocation to explain."

"A night or two in the sea and your lungs will be too water-logged for that kind of diagnosis."

The button was undone now. He insinuated his right fore-finger and thumb gently into the top of the pocket and grasped the wallet. Everything now depended on its sliding out easily, on his being able to drop it unseen behind the wheel of the car. He said:

"They won't, you know. The PM will show perfectly clearly that I was dead before I hit the water."

"And so you will be, with a bullet in your body. Given that, I doubt whether they'll look for signs of suffocation. But thank you for the warning. I'll drive fast. Now get in."

Dalgliesh shrugged his shoulders and bent with sudden energy to get into the boot as if momentarily relinquishing hope. He rested his left hand on the bumper. Here, at least, there would be a palm mark which would be difficult to explain. But then he remembered. He had rested his palm on the bumper when loading the shepherd's crook, the sacks and the besom into the boot. It was only a small discouragement but it depressed him. He let his right hand dangle and the leather slipped from his finger and thumb to fall under the right wheel. No dangerously quiet word of command followed. Julius neither spoke nor moved, and he was still alive. With luck he would stay alive now until they reached the black tower. He smiled at the irony that his heart should now rejoice at a gift which a short month ago he had so grudgingly welcomed.

The boot lid slammed down. He was cramped in total black-ness, total silence. He felt a second of claustrophobic panic, the irresistible urge to stretch his curled body and batter his clenched hands against the metal. The car did not move. Julius would be free now to check his timing. Philby's body lay heavily against him. He could smell the dead man as if he still breathed, an amalgam of grease, mothballs and sweat, the air of the boot was hot with his presence. He felt a moment of guilt that Philby was dead; he alive. Could he have saved him by calling out a warning? It could only have resulted, he knew, in both their deaths. Philby would have come on; must have come on. And even if he had turned and run, Julius would have followed and disposed of him. But now the feel of the cold moist flesh pressing against him, the hairs on the limp wrist sharp as bristles, pricked him like a reproach. The car rocked gently and began to move.

He had no means of knowing if Julius had seen the wallet and removed it; he thought it unlikely. But would Mrs. Reynolds find it? It was lying in her path. She would almost certainly dismount from her bicycle outside the garage. If she did find it, then he guessed she would have no rest until it was returned. He thought of his own Mrs. Mack, a Metropolitan police constable's widow who cleaned and occasionally cooked for him; of her almost obsessive honesty, her meticulous concern for her employer's belongings, the perpetual explanatory notes about missing laundry, the increased cost of shopping, a mislaid cuff link. No, Mrs. Reynolds wouldn't rest with the wallet in her possession. He had cashed a cheque on his last visit to Dorchester; the three ten pound notes, the bundle of credit cards, his police warrant, all would particularly worry her. She would probably waste some time going to Hope Cottage. Not finding him there, what then? His guess was that she would ring the local police, terrified that he might discover his loss before she had reported it. And the police? If he were lucky they would see the incongruity of a wallet dropped so conveniently in her path. Suspicious or not, they would be courteous enough to get in touch with him at once. They might find it worthwhile ringing Toynton Grange since the cottage was not on the telephone. They would discover that the telephone was inexplicably out of order. It was at least an even chance that they would think it worthwhile sending a patrol car, and if one were reasonably close it could come quickly. Logically, one action must follow another. And he had one piece of luck. Mrs. Reynolds, he remembered, was the village constable's widow. At least she wouldn't be afraid of using the telephone, would know whom to ring. His life depended on her seeing the wallet. A few square inches of brown leather on the paved courtyard. And the light was darkening under the storm-laden sky.

Julius was driving very fast even over the bumpy ground of the headland. The car stopped. Now he would be opening the boundary gate. Another few seconds of driving and the car stopped again. Now he must have met Mrs. Reynolds and was exchanging that half-minute of conversation. Now they were off again, this time with smooth road under their wheels.

There was something else he could do. He moved his hand under his cheek and bit into his left thumb. The blood tasted warm and sweet. He smeared it across the roof of the boot and, scuffling aside the sheet, pressed his thumb into the carpet. Group AB rhesus negative. It was a rare enough group. And with any luck Julius would miss these minute telltale smears. He hoped the police searcher would be more perspicacious.

He began to feel stifled, his head thudded. He told himself that there was plenty of air, that this pressure on his chest was no more than psychological trauma. And then the car rocked gently and he knew that Julius was driving off the road and into the hollow behind the stone wall which divided the headland from the road. It was a convenient stopping place. Even if another car passed, and this was unlikely, the Mercedes wouldn't be visible. They had arrived. The final part of the journey was about to begin.

There were only about one hundred and fifty yards of rock-strewn and lumpy turf to where the black tower stood squat and malignant under the menacing sky. Dalgliesh knew that Julius would prefer to make a single journey. He would want to get as quickly as possible out of all sight of the road. He would want the business over so that he could get on his way. More important, he needed to make no physical contact with either victim. Their clothes would yield nothing when their bloated bodies were finally fished from the sea; but Julius would know how difficult to eradicate, without telltale cleaning, would be the infinitesimally small traces of hair, fibre or blood on his own clothes. So far he was absolutely clean. It would be one of his strongest cards. Dalgliesh would be allowed to live at least until they reached the shelter of the tower. He felt confident enough of this to take his time in getting Philby's body strapped into the chair. Afterwards he leaned for a moment over the handlebars breathing heavily, simulating more exhaustion than he felt. Somehow, despite the hard pushing ahead, he must conserve his strength. Julius slammed down the boot lid and said:

"Get a move on. The storm is almost on us."

But he didn't shift his fixed gaze to glance at the sky, nor had he need. They could almost smell the rain in the freshening breeze.

Although the wheels of the chair were well oiled the going was hard. Dalgliesh's hands slid on the rubber handgrips. Philby's body, strapped like a recalcitrant child, jerked and rolled as the wheels struck stones or clumps of grass. Dalgliesh felt the sweat rolling into his eyes. It gave him the opportunity he needed to get rid of his jacket. When it came to the last physical struggle the man least encumbered would have an advantage. He stopped pushing and stood gasping. The feet behind him stopped too.

It might happen now. There was nothing he could do if it did. He comforted himself with the thought that he would know nothing. One press of Julius's finger on the trigger and his busy fearful mind would be stilled. He remembered Julius's words. "I know what will happen to me when I die; annihilation. It would be unreasonable to fear that." If only it were that simple! But Julius did not press. The dangerously quiet voice behind him said:

"Well?"

"I'm hot. May I take off my jacket?"

"Why not? Drape it over Philby's knees. I'll chuck it in the sea after you. It would be torn off your body by the tide anyway."

Dalgliesh slid his arms from his jacket and placed it folded over Philby's knees. Without looking round he said:

"You'd be unwise to shoot me in the back. Philby was killed instantly. It has to look as if he shot me first but only to wound, before I wrenched the gun from him and finished him off. No fight with only one gun could reasonably result in two instantaneous killings, and one in the small of the back."

"I know. Unlike you, I may be inexperienced in the cruder manifestations of violence but I'm not a fool and I do understand about firearms. Get on."

They moved forward, carefully distanced, Dalgliesh pushing his macabre passenger and hearing behind him the soft rustle of the following feet. He found himself thinking about Peter Bonnington. It was because an unknown boy, now dead, had been moved from Toynton Grange that he, Adam Dalgliesh, was now walking across Toynton Head with a gun at his back. Father Baddeley would have discerned a pattern. But then Father Baddeley had believed that there was a great underlying pattern. Given that assurance, all human perplexities were no more than exercises in spiritual geometry. Suddenly Julius began speaking. Dalgliesh could almost imagine that he felt the need to entertain his victim on this last tedious walk, that he was making some attempt at justification.

"I can't be poor again. I need money as I need oxygen. Not just enough; more than enough. Much more. Poverty kills. I don't fear death but I fear that particular slow and corrosive process of dying. You didn't believe me, did you—that story about my parents?"

"Not altogether. Was I expected to?"

"Yet that at least was true. I could take you to pubs in Westminster—Christ, you probably know them—and bring you face to face with what I fear; the pathetic elderly queens managing on their pensions. Or not managing. And they, poor sods, haven't even been used to having money. I have. I'm not ashamed of my nature. But if I'm to live at all, I have to be rich. Did you really expect me to let one sick old fool and a dying woman stand in my way?"

Dalgliesh didn't reply. Instead he asked:

"I suppose you came this way when you set fire to the tower."

"Of course. I did as we've done now, drove to the hollow and came on foot. I knew when Wilfred, a creature of habit, was likely to be in the tower and I watched him walk over the headland through my binoculars. If it wasn't that day, it would be another. There was no difficulty in helping myself to the key and a habit. I saw to that a day in advance. Anyone who knows Toynton Grange can move about it undetected. Even if I were seen, I don't have to explain my presence there. As Wilfred says, I'm one of the family. That's why killing Grace Willison was so easy. I was home and in bed soon after midnight and with no worse affects than cold legs and a little difficulty in getting to sleep. By the way, I ought to say, in case you harbour any doubts, that Wilfred knows nothing of the smuggling. If I were about to die and you to live instead of the other way round you could look forward to the pleasure of breaking the news. Both pieces of news. His miracle a delusion and his abode of love a staging post for death. I should give a great deal to see his face."

They were within feet now of the black tower. Without overtly changing direction Dalgliesh steered the wheelchair as close as he dared to the porch. The wind was gently rising in short moaning crescendos. But then, there would always be a breeze on this wind-scoured promontory of grass and rock. Suddenly he stopped. He held the chair with his left hand and half turned towards Julius, carefully balancing his weight. It was now. It had to be now.

Julius said sharply:

"Well, what is it?"

Time stopped. A second was stilled into infinity. In that brief, timeless lacuna, Dalgliesh's mind was drained free of tension and fear. It was as if he were detached from the past and the future, aware simultaneously of himself, of his adversary, of the sound, scent and colour of sky, cliff and sea. The pent up anger at Father Baddeley's death, the frustration and indecision of the last few weeks, the controlled suspense of the past hour; all were calmed in this moment before their final release. He spoke, his voice, high and cracked, simulating terror. But, even to his own ears, the terror sounded horribly real.

"The tower! There's someone inside!"

It came again as he had prayed it would, the bone ends, piercing the torn flesh, scrabbling frantically against unyielding stone. He sensed rather then heard the sharp hiss of Julius's intake of breath. Then time moved on, and in that second, Dalgliesh sprang.

As they fell, Julius's body beneath him, Dalgliesh felt the hammer blow on his right shoulder, the sudden numbness, the sticky warmth, soothing as a balm, flowing into his shirt. The shot echoed back from the black tower, and the headland came alive. A cloud of gulls rose screaming from the rock face. Sky and cliff were a tumult of wildly beating wings. And then as if the laden clouds had waited for this signal, the sky was ripped open with the sound of tearing canvas, and the rain fell.

They fought like famished animals clawing at their prey, without skill, eyes stung and blinded by rain, locked in a rigor of hate.

Dalgliesh, even with the weight of Julius's body beneath him, felt his strength ebbing. It had to be now, now while he was on top. And he still had the use of his good left shoulder. He twisted Julius's wrist into the clammy earth and pressed with all his strength on the beat of the pulse. He could feel Julius's breath like a hot blast on his face. They lay cheek to cheek in a horrible parody of exhausted love. And still the gun did not drop from those rigid fingers. Slowly, in painful spasms, Julius bent his right arm towards Dalgliesh's head. And then the gun went off. Dalgliesh felt the bullet pass over his hair to spend itself harmlessly in the sheeting rain.

And now they were rolling towards the cliff edge. Dalgliesh, weakening, felt himself clutching Julius as if for support. The rain was a stinging lance on his eyeballs. His nose was pressed suffocatingly into the sodden earth. Humus. A comforting and familiar last smell. His fingers clawed impotently at the turf as he rolled. It came apart in moist clumps in his hands. And suddenly Julius was kneeling over him, hands at his throat, forcing his head back over the cliff edge. The sky, the sea and the sheeting rain were one turbulent whiteness, one immense roaring in his ears. Julius's streaming face was out of his reach, the rigid arms pressing down the cruel encircling hands. He had to bring that face closer. Deliberately he slackened his muscles and loosened his already weakening hold on Julius's shoulders. It worked. Julius relaxed his grasp and instinctively bent his head forward to look into Dalgliesh's face. Then he screamed as Dalgliesh's thumbs gouged into his eyes. Their bodies fell apart. And Dalgliesh was on his feet and scrambling up the headland to fling himself behind the wheelchair.

He crouched behind it, heaving against the sagging canvas for support, watching Julius advance, hair streaming, eyes wild, the strong arms stretching forward, eager for that final clutch. Behind him the tower streamed black blood. The rain slashed like hail against the boulders, sending up a fine mist to mingle with his hoarse breath. Its painful rhythm tore at his chest and filled his ears like the death throes of some great animal. Suddenly he released the brakes and with his last strength hurled the chair forward. He saw his murderer's astonished and desperate eyes. For one second he thought that Julius would fling himself against the chair. But at the last moment he leapt aside, and the chair and its dreadful burden sailed over the cliff.

"Explain that when they fish it out!" Dalgliesh never knew

whether he spoke to himself or shouted the words aloud. And then Julius was on him.

This was the end. He wasn't fighting now, only letting himself be rolled downwards towards death. He could hope for nothing except to carry Julius over with him. Hoarse, discordant cries were hurting his ears. The crowd were shouting for Julius. All the world was shouting. The headland was full of voices, of shapes. Suddenly the weight on his chest lifted. He was free. He heard Julius whisper "Oh, no!" Dalgliesh heard the sad despairing protest as clearly as if the voice had been his own. It wasn't the last horrified cry of a desperate man. The words were quiet, rueful, almost amused. Then the air was darkened by a shape, black as a great bird, passing spread-eagled over his head in what seemed slow motion. Earth and sky turned slowly together. A solitary seagull screamed. The earth thudded. A white ring of amorphous blobs was bending over him. But the ground was soft, irresistibly soft. He let his consciousness bleed away into it.

IV

The surgical registrar came out of Dalgliesh's room to where a group of large men were obstructing the corridor. He said:

"He'll be OK for questioning in about half an hour or so. We've extracted the bullet. I've handed it over to your chap. We've put up a drip but don't let that worry you. He's lost a fair amount of blood but there's no real damage. There's no harm now in your going in."

Daniel asked:

"Is he conscious?"

"Barely. Your chap in there says he's been quoting King Lear. Something about Cordelia anyway. And he's fretting because he hasn't said thank you for the flowers."

Daniel said:

"He won't be needing flowers this time, thank God. He can thank Mrs. Reynolds's sharp eyes and common sense for that. And the storm helped. But it was a close thing. Court would have carried him over the cliff if we hadn't come up on them before he noticed us. Well, we may as well go in if you think it's OK."

A uniformed constable appeared, helmet under his arm.

"Well?"

"The Chief Constable's on his way, Sir. And they've pulled out Philby's body half strapped to a wheelchair."

"And Court's?"

"Not yet, Sir. They reckon he'll be washed in further down the coast."

Dalgliesh opened his eyes. His bed was ringed with black and white figures advancing and receding in a ritual dance. Nurses' caps floated like disembodied wings above the smudged faces as if uncertain where to settle. Then the picture cleared and he saw the circle of half familiar faces. Sister was here, of course. And the consultant had got back early from his wedding. He wasn't wearing his rose any more. The faces broke simultaneously into wary smiles. He made himself smile back. So it wasn't acute leukaemia; it wasn't any kind of leukaemia. He was going to get better. And once they'd removed this heavy contraption which for some reason they'd fixed to his right arm he could get out of here and back to his job. Wrong diagnosis or not, it was nice of them, he thought sleepily, looking up into the ring of smiling eyes, to look so pleased that he wasn't going to die after all.

MP3L